THE ARC OF INTERSECTION

A novel by Chris DuBose

Well, I could have loved you better
Didn't mean to be unkind
You know that was the last thing on my mind

from *The Last Thing On My Mind* by Tom Paxton

The Arc of Intersection

To
Jan, who knew this story before I wrote it

And to
All the young men who shared the same hope as mine

Casteline Boys Basketball
2008-09

12	Andreas Pinson	6'4"	12
14	Geoff Willis (CAPT)	6'2"	12
15	Mark Payne	6'4"	12
20	James Rush	6'1"	11
21	Pete Semineau	6'0"	11
22	Andrew Monaghan	6'3"	12
23	Jason Grutchfield	6'0"	12
25	Archie Stedham	6'0"	11
30	Jonas Boynton	6'2"	12
31	Bobbie Pitaro	5'10"	12
32	Dan Owings	5'11"	11
34	Nick Mavrikos	6'4"	11
41	Alex White	5'9"	12

James

The afternoon before the first day of practice, Sunday afternoon, James Rush spent almost two hours shooting on the hoop in his driveway. The glass backboard that had been pristinely pellucid when he took his first shots as a sixth grader had become cloudy. The weather was getting cold: at first James wore light gloves as he shot, partly to keep his hands warm, and partly to try to develop his feel for the ball. His dad had told him when he was in middle school that shooting and dribbling with gloves on would increase the feel when he took the gloves off. The cotton gloves he wore were both thin and crusted, and tight on his hands.

"Hey, man, what's with the gloves?" Pete asked, as he slithered from the driver's seat of his A6, at about 4:00, when James had already been shooting for over an hour. Pete would also be trying out for the varsity on Monday, making the jump from JV. James was a returning varsity player hoping for a starting position.

"Oh, you know, it's to create a better feel. I don't know. All I know is I can outshoot you with gloves on. Your shot."

"Whoa, whoa, let me get warmed up. I'll play you in a minute."

James fed Pete for a few silent minutes as he warmed up. Pete's shot was a sound one, good mechanics. He had strong legs that took the pressure off his upper body. Pete had the makings of a good player, but he had taken no interest in improving his game or conditioning in the past year. For that matter, James admitted, James hadn't exactly pursued athletic excellence with much commitment as they prepared for their junior year.

"Hey, you run this weekend? Are you getting close to the six-minute mile?"

Swishing another jumper, Pete replied, "I ran a little yesterday, even though it was fuckin freezing. I'll be ready tomorrow. Maybe we won't have time to run the mile."

"Oh no, we'll run the mile. Probably at 2:45, so it doesn't conflict with practice. He's got to let the football guys run." James had run the mile in 5:54 a week ago, a disappointing time, fourteen seconds slower than he had run his sophomore year.

4

Pete shrugged. "Yeah, you're right. I think I'll come in under 6. I've been doing some lifting in gym class. I think my legs are stronger. I'm getting more lift on my jump shot."

"Yeah, it looks good. Think you've warmed up enough? I'm tired of preparing you just to lose." With that challenge, Pete started a game of HORSE, probably the fiftieth of their friendship. There had been times when Pete had dominated the games and times when James was the consistent winner. Overall, they each considered themselves the long-time champion. Pete hit three in a row, but James had no trouble matching those mid-range jumpers, and when Pete missed a bank shot, James went to work with his shots off a dribble and his own assortment of bank shots. It took less than ten minutes to claim a victory, when Pete picked up the E, ending the game.

"Run it back?" asked Pete, and the two eased into a second, then a third, then a fourth game. Even with the cloth gloves on, James could feel the flow of the shot, being sure his center of gravity was equally dispersed over both his feet, as Coach LaMott had shown him five years ago. As he caught the ball from Pete, he felt: left/right/shoot. Meet the ball with the left foot, square up with the right, leave the ground and release the ball. Left/right/shoot. It felt good.

After four games, James, feeling warmer, took off his gloves and one of his sweatshirts, starting to regain a comfort that he hadn't felt for a few weeks. In the fading light they had to rely on the spotlight that shed an arc of luminescence over half the court and the backboard.

"Let's play Beat the Pro," he suggested. Pete nodded, becoming rebounder while James began the shooting game in which a made-shot counted one point for the shooter, missed-shot counted two points for the opponent.

Shot. Good. Shot. Good. Shot. Good. After his release, James followed the arc of the ball, making sure it didn't come out flat, which would mean his release was horizontal rather than vertical. Shoot up, not out, Coach LaMott had always said. The ball-flight was good. A nice arc, something like the arcs Mr. Tilson, their Geometry teacher, drew on the board with his oversized wooden compass. James moved out, close to the 3-point line distance, though it wasn't marked on his driveway. James had heard Coach LaMott say too many times that there was an overemphasis on shooting the 3, and that good shot form came from taking and making the fifteen footer.

"8 – 12," called Pete, keeping score for James. James had to get hot. Shot. Made. Shot. Made. Shot. Made. As he continued to catch and shoot, he started to try for more elevation, more legs in his shot, to keep his arm fresh. More legs: less pressure on the arm.

5

"18 – 16," Pete called out. James needed to make three more shots, before he missed three. Easy. Shot. Swish. Shot. Rattle and in. Shot. Miss. Shot. Miss. He knew: 20 – 20. It came down to this shot. He extended his hands in front of his chest. As Pete's pass bounced into the hands, he let the ball slide into his right hand, his wrist back, ready to launch. James's left hand slid to the side of the ball. He trained his eyes on the rim, though the light from the spotlight was faint. Weight already on the left foot, he brought his right foot underneath his right shoulder, sprang into the air, raised the ball to release point (top of the forehead), and let it go. This one would be the game-winner (or -loser). He didn't even follow the flight of the ball. He knew it was in.

Pete's turn to play, as the dark and cold gathered around them. James became the feeder as Pete caught and shot. He had an early 12 – 4 lead, but Pete wore down as he needed to make shots. He finally lost, 17 – 22. Not bad. James knew Pete hadn't been working on his shooting at all recently, focusing on other elements of high school development.

"Hey, I gotta go. Good times. See ya tomorrow. 5:00." It was as if there were no school day to intervene between this evening and their first practice. And no 6-minute mile.

"Yeah, 5 it is. Gonna be fun."

"Later," and Pete hopped into his silver Audi, clicking on the seat-warmer before he shut the door. He pressed in the lighter, then laughed as James's eyes widened.

James continued to shoot, luxuriating in the feel of the ball on his hands. In the cold he had to lick the tips of the fingers continually on his right hand to achieve the natural contact between ball and skin, since no sweat could be produced in the night, November air. There had been only one slight snowstorm so far this year, but there was more to come next week, so said the weather reporters.

When he walked into the house, bouncing the ball on the tile of the foyer as he took off his inner sweatshirt, his mother asked, "Are you going to shower before supper?" He felt instantly warm as soon as he entered the moist house.

"Nah." His hands felt gritted with the dried saliva and dirt embedded into the fingertips of the right hand. He strode to the bathroom to wash his hands, and with a little soap and the warmth of the house, he felt comfortable, though his dry hands rubbed roughly on his jeans.

In the family room, his father looked up from the West Coast football game on TV. "You ready for tomorrow?"

"Oh yeah. Gonna be a good season." James knew that his father was emotionally invested in his success, like most fathers. His father hadn't played basketball in high school; he had been a kid that worked after school as soon as he could, and he had made it clear to James that sports were a fulfilling way to spend the after-school hours, but if he didn't play sports, work would also be a productive outlet. James remembered when he was entering high school, as a freshman, his father had told him, "As long as you're playing a sport, you'll get a free pass from me about working and doing yard work during the season. In the off-season, I'll expect you to do your share around the yard and the pool. And when you're sixteen, you can start earning your spending money down at the shop." James understood. His dad had grown up in Melrose, a working class city, and neither he nor his parents had gone to college. He had made a good living as a small shop owner, making commercial signage, and James worked in the shop from time to time. This fall he had swept floors, delivered work requests, and even operated a simple machine once a week at the shop. In Mr. Rush's mind, basketball would be the ticket to admission at a college, maybe providing some financial aid, but, more importantly, gaining the notice of a college coach, who could provide a shortcut through admissions.

Mr. Rush looked at James. "Have you been working hard?"

"Yeah, I was just out there for a couple hours!"

Mr. Rush looked steadily at James. "Oh, I see you today. But have you been putting in the time over the past month? Are you keeping your eye on the prize?"

James found his father's triteness a little amusing, but he knew better than to smirk. His father was serious. "As much as I can. Junior year is a tough year, Dad. I got some serious homework."

Mr. Rush turned back to the football game. "I just know that some kids keep pushing themselves, and some kids don't. I've seen too many good ball players turn out to be knuckleheads, just because they don't keep pushing themselves. Too many cars. Too many girls. Too many Saturday nights."

James agreed with his father. And he wasn't sure which side of the road he was on. Too many girls? Well, that was a joke. Too many Saturday nights? Well, there was no doubt, he was responding to the lure of Saturday nights. But his father didn't ask him to stay at home on Saturday nights either. Too many cars? James was still four months from gaining his license, and he doubted that his parents had the means or the desire to provide him with his own car.

"Well? Are you falling into bad habits?" his father continued. James was surprised to hear his father pursuing this line of inquiry. He didn't remember his father ever having the need to find out what was going on in his life away from home. And, naturally, James had no impulse to tell his father what was actually going on in his life. He felt there was an assumed contract between child and parent: I'll do what I need to do to make the transition from child to adult, and you keep your distance, complimenting me on any progress I make, and rendering the punishments when I publicly fail to make the right decisions. James and his father (and mother) had enjoyed a smooth relationship thus far through his adolescent years, but James knew that there would come a day when some part of his growing life would suddenly appear before his parents' eyes and they would be shocked out of their innocence. But for now, all was good.

"Dad, you know that there's lots of things I could be doing, lots of things I see. I know how to make smart decisions." James tried to be as honest as he could in speaking of his life to his father, while still remaining as vague as possible. He had learned not to reveal much of anything, unless asked directly.

At the kitchen table, James sat between his mother and his little sister Rachel, who was an eighth grader. He had put his Patriots hat on, celebrating their victory over the Jets. With the bill of the hat lowered, he could practice eating with his eyes closed, feeling the weight of the noodles on his fork, reaching for his glass of milk by sensing where he had put it down. He had read that he was using a kinesthetic awareness, when his eyes were closed. He spilled some corn at times, with his affectation of blindness, but he felt the gain was worth it. He always checked under the table when he was done, to clean up any mess he had created. The kitchen floor was easy to pick up, and he would naturally spill some food anyway, so a little more was no big deal. Of course, he would not want his parents to detect his habit, so he kept his head low, adjusting his hat down over his eyes, peeking as he set it all up, so that, if he looked, all he could see was his plate and not even his glass of milk.

But Rachel cried out, "Mom, James is doing that blind thing again!" and James could feel a burn in his chest at her betrayal. Once, months ago, she had seen him trying to work on his calculator for math with his eyes closed. The idea had evolved naturally and easily out of his facility on the keyboard where he could fluently operate with his eyes closed. That day, as he sat at his desk trying to compute simple operations, nothing to do with his homework, just adding and dividing, Rachel had appeared in his doorway.

"What are you doing?"

James turned to her, his eyes flashing open. "Just some math problems."

"Why don't you have a math book at your desk?"

"I'm just finishing up a problem that I didn't get a chance to finish in school. I remember the numbers."

"Oh yeah? . . . And why were your eyes closed?"

Without a moment's hesitation, James replied, "I know the keyboard so well, I don't need to look. I'm trying to memorize the board better, so I'm closing my eyes sometimes. No big deal. I text on my cell all the time without looking. It's a necessity when you're texting while you're paying attention in class. You better get the system down if you want to survive in high school. I bet you can't text or use the calculator with your eyes closed."

"I wouldn't want to, idiot."

And that was that. James didn't know Rachel had said anything to his parents, but now she was bringing it out in the open again.

"James, are you eating with your eyes closed?" his mother asked him.

"Why would I be doing that? Rachel's crazy," James said.

Mr. Rush broke in, "It does seem a little crazy, what Rachel's claiming. Why would anyone do that?"

James agreed. "I can't think of any possible reason to do anything so stupid."

And the matter was put to rest. But James knew that Rachel knew. Someday he'd have to fill her in on the benefits of handicapping oneself.

Looking around his plate, James saw that he had not spilled more than a few corn kernels and no pot roast. He was getting better.

A half hour after supper was over, James got a call from the team captain, Geoff Willis, asking him to come to school at 7 the next morning. The team was going to meet in the gym to represent to each other a commitment to the season. James got a chill in his backbone hearing from the captain.

"Should we change and shoot around, or just meet?"

Geoff said, "No, it's just to meet and show support for each other. Some of the younger guys haven't run the mile yet, and I want to get us off to a good start, set some groundrules.

"Speaking of ground rules, were you at the Graysons' on Saturday night?"

James couldn't help but be honest with the captain. "Yeah, I was there." His brief comment met with silence, suggesting to James that he needed to explain himself a little. "A couple of us were over there for a couple of hours. It was mellow for a while, then it got a little out of control. That's when we left."

"Mmmm. Yeah. I guess some pictures were taken at the party, some of the guys, and then they made it onto the internet. It's that kind of thing that I'm trying to avoid this year. I kind of think that we have two types of guys on the team: the partiers and the straight guys. I'm hoping you can join me on the quiet guys' side."

James was thrilled to hear Geoff's advocacy. "Oh, yeah. Now that we're into the season, that stuff is gone. I'm right beside you." James made this claim sincerely.

"That's good to hear. I'll see you at 7:00 in the gym. Thanks."

"Thanks for calling, bye." James put the phone down and stared into the kitchen down the hallway, where the shadow of his father moved back and forth, putting dishes away after washing and rinsing them. Out his door, he could see the light from Rachel's room slant across the dark hall carpet, a soft glow. He thought about the previous night, an unremarkable evening for James, actually, though it had not been devoid of excitement.

At about 9:00 Pete had picked him up, with Tommy Kilkenney, a hockey player, riding shotgun. They had made it slowly over to Cheryl Grayson's house, past slumbering streets, oversized houses, and frosted windows. Cheryl was a junior who had recently gotten her license. Since that time she had become one of the more sedulous social girls, cruising unfailingly in her BMW, accompanied by her crew. She had had one slightly successful party at the end of October, but it really turned out to be a bust when the seniors all left after an hour, heading to another house where there was more beer and less control. Cheryl's house was actually set up nicely for a party: it was on a very quiet street and there was a lot of space between houses. Parking was the big problem for parties in Casteline because a multitude of cars tipped the police off to the house party, and, upon their approach, the responding officers would write down license plates before they made their presence known. The rise of cell phones had allowed the kids to be more prepared because there was always someone out in front of the house, coming in or leaving, or just finding a quiet place to talk, and as soon as the police slid down the street, a call was made and the beer and smoke disappeared behind counters and inside closets and cabinets.

James and Pete had smoked a little in the car on the way to Grayson's, enjoying the extended ease of a long weekend. They still had another day off before school began again, they didn't have any homework, and some of the older kids were in town for Thanksgiving weekend.

As they got near the party, they could see cars lining both sides of the street, some of them squeezed slantwise between others, some on the edge of the lawns of houses down the street from Grayson's. James knew the party wouldn't last long, under these conditions, but he was looking forward to seeing the crowd, all his friends.

"Looks like a good one," Pete hooted as he slammed his door shut. He had parked next to a tree, where no one else had wanted to park, and James had to slide across the seat to get out on Pete's side of the car.

The three juniors glided down the street and across the frosty lawn to the Graysons' front door. On the way they saw groups of their friends, huddling at the edge of the woods that framed the Graysons' lawn. James could see the glow of a lit ember, at the center of each little group. He could feel the shivers of his lightly clad friends, as they murmured and giggled.

Inside, the front hallway was lined with people, more people than James was used to seeing at a party. It seemed that most of the juniors and seniors were there, and, of course, the college freshmen had made this party their official meet-and-greet evening. James tossed his $10.00 into the bowl on the kitchen counter and headed right to the refrigerator for a Bud Light. The kitchen table was occupied by the Quarters players, trying to flick their coins into cups of beer, only too willing to pay the penalty for missing. James looked past them into the family room, noting six or eight friends, mostly girls. The music from that room competed with the frenzy of the noise of teenagers trying to talk over the din of other teenagers talking.

James turned to go downstairs when a soft hand pulled his left shoulder.

"Oh, hi, Meredith. Whew. Hell of a party, isn't it?"

"Oh yeah. I'm having trouble hearing myself think. 'D'you just get here?"

"Yeah. Fashionably late, you know? How ya doin?" One week before, at a party at Bob Hackett's, James and Meredith had hooked up in an upstairs bedroom; lying together on the narrow single bed, they had spent the time talking about Meredith's parents' likely divorce. Of course, their friends had noticed their paired absence, making their inevitable, vicarious assumptions.

11

Meredith looked at him frankly. "Not bad. I'm not really into this, ya know? It's kinda crazy."

James knew exactly what she was saying. In fact, James had little desire to be there too, but there he was, invading the refrigerator, clapping the shoulders of guys he knew next to nothing about. He laughed to himself, marveling at his weak resolve. He had always told himself that he would be strong enough to avoid the parties, but time and opportunity had proven him wrong.

"I don't feel that good, James. Do you think we could go outside for a minute?"

James looked at Meredith, noting the sad lines drooping from the sides of her mouth. "You don't look that good either. I mean, you look great, but you look like you don't feel all that good." Ushering Meredith out the slider to the deck behind the house, he steered her to the railing that rimmed the deck. Meredith leaned back onto the railing, took a deep breath, and looked skyward, trying to see the stars in the clear sky. The lights from the kitchen extruded on the darkness of the deck, muting the starlight completely.

"I don't know, I hate being here, but I hate being home more," Meredith said, looking down.

James nodded his head, looking over Meredith's shoulder to the far reaches of the Graysons' lot, noticing a fallen tree at the edge of the property. He wondered if it had fallen recently, or if it was just too far away for the Graysons to notice.

"I know exactly what you're saying. I feel like a chicken shit being here, but I love my friends more." James put his hand on Meredith's shoulder, moved closer to her, her warmth a slight protection against the cold.

"Did your friends say anything about last weekend?" Meredith asked.

James deliberated. "Yeah, they were pretty psyched that we were upstairs for a while. You know them."

"Yeah, I do. I know what they think. I just hope you don't think like them. You don't seem to be like them. You seem a little more – like you've got your head squarely on your shoulders."

James, at that moment, rested his head on Meredith's shoulder, silently giggling at resting his head on her shoulder, after her last observation, but desiring the closeness that she offered. With his eyes closed, he could hear the liveliness of the party, shouts from the garage, hoots from the kitchen. It was like his impression of a college party, the coeds in bright colors floating in a flamboyant way across the rooms, the young men hunkering near each other for support. As Meredith spoke to him, he tried to listen to her, but he was drawn to the greater impression of the gathering, discerning the beat of the party emerging from the bass in the basement, the tinkling piano notes of bottle necks clinking each other in celebration, the guitar riffs floating from the family room, where the dance was down, a discordant harmony that resembled an abstract narrative, a story of immature maturation, his story.

"Do you even believe her?" Meredith asked, and James had to refocus.

"Uh, I'm sorry, Mer, I was off in space. Believe who?"

Meredith pulled away from James, as best she could with his head on her shoulder and her hips pinned against the railing. James still languished on her shoulder. "My mother. She thinks I should go out for the musical. She thinks it'll be good on my transcript."

"Yeah, too many parents with too many plans for their children. They just have to let us find our own way. My dad is that way too, expecting me to play sports, even though he says there's no pressure." James felt guilty speaking of his father in this way, because he respected the way his father restrained his deep-seated desire for James to be a hotshot. He didn't want to sell his father out. "I mean he's really reasonable and everything, but I can tell that he really gets off when I make the big play or contribute to a big win. He can't help it."

Meredith made a noise in her throat, a *hmmph*. "I don't think I could call my mother 'reasonable.' She has a plan, and she works on me every day to make it happen. It's pretty scary."

James could hear the sound behind him shift, as a mass of people came up the stairs from the basement to flood the kitchen and living room. He could hear Cheryl Grayson's voice, at a high pitch, screaming, "Not in the living room. My parents will kill me." He wondered what was transpiring in the living room. He would venture to say that it was people ashing their cigarettes across the window sills, trying to flick outdoors, but meeting window screens. He felt sorry for Cheryl.

"Let's go for a walk, OK?" said Meredith.

James sighed to himself; Meredith felt the sigh on her shoulder. And with that, she moved him away from her.

She said, "No, let's go inside. I feel better. Thanks." He looked her in the eye to see what she was thinking, and she looked at him cleanly, without judgment.

13

"I just don't want to go too far. Sorry." James gritted his teeth, unsatisfied with his explanation and his feeling. A walk in a back yard was not going far.

In the kitchen the faces had changed, but the game was the same. The sound of the quarters ringing off the oaken table was overwhelmed now by the insistence of the cheers and the depth of the groans. James and Meredith separated easily and adroitly, appearing to all bystanders to be two people heading in different directions, though James sensed that Meredith would keep a close watch on him. He sidled into the living room, which had re-filled with a crowd, like water filling a tub. Despite Cheryl's plea, cigarettes and joints were burning down in cupped hands and over half-filled plastic cups. Pete stood with two other boys from the junior class, watching the BC game on the television, watching Mark Herzlich, the strong-side linebacker, fake a blitz, as BC tried to hold on to their lead over Maryland.

The living room led to a study, where just a few quiet couples began their amorous interplay. If all went well, James knew that a back staircase led upstairs to one of five bedrooms, the script that James and Meredith had followed the previous Saturday night. This night James vowed to stay downstairs – unless, of course . . .

But that was just idle dreaming.

Two family rooms decorated the Graysons' house, one on the first floor and one in the basement. James cruised through the upstairs family room, saying hi to Jonas Boynton, a senior on the team. Jonas broke away from his group to address James.

"Hey, you all set for Monday?"

"Oh yeah. You better be ready for me. Think you can shut me down?" James was experienced at the woofing that lay at the base of the relationships on the team, especially between members of different grades.

"Don't worry. I've got you covered. You'll be lucky to even catch the ball. I know your moves," Jonas huffed.

James and Jonas were similar players, each of whom could shoot the ball, each of whom could put the ball on the floor. They knew that they were competing for playing time, and that knowledge made them a little uncomfortable with each other. James, a year younger, stepped carefully in Jonas's radius, not wanting to piss the senior off. James knew that the attitude of individual players and, more importantly, the relationships among the team members were prime variables in the team's chance for success.

"I'll try to flash a few new moves on you Monday. I'm sure you've got some new ones yourself," James finished, letting Jonas know that he respected the senior.

The stairs to the downstairs family room were paneled with a rich cherry two-by-six tongue-in-groove, clear-stained. This subterranean family room was a man's little fantasy world, Mr. Grayson's tribute to manly pursuits. The heptagonal poker table, custom-made, of course, sat in one corner; three long, leather couches made a deep U, facing an oversized flat-screen TV tuned endlessly to sports events. Down here, the football players sported, and their efforts left a malodorous wake: crushed and tipped beer cans and empty bottles of tequila, the contents still filtering through partly filled plastic cups. The football season was officially finished, and the young men who had spent three months laboring on the practice field together wanted one celebratory evening to commemorate their achievement. The thin carpeting squished a wet tribute.

No girls graced the downstairs family room. James strode toward Mark Payne, a sizable teammate who had finished his career as a linebacker for the Panthers with eleven tackles on Thanksgiving. Mark was teetering unevenly, his eyes half closed.

"Marky. What's up, man?"

"Hey, Rushie. What's goin on?"

"Nothin, man. Just lookin for some fun. You got any fun goin on down here?"

"Are you shittin me? These guys are the best. There's no one else on the planet that I'd rather spend my night with than these guys."

James knew that football at Casteline – and everywhere else, for that matter, if the football program was viable – generated a brotherhood. He envied these guys for feeling so loyal and responsible to each other. "You guys played awesome Thursday. Tough finish, but you played your hearts out."

Mark swayed. "Yeah, it was kick in the groin to lose that game. But we gave it every fuckin ounce."

At that moment, shouts rang out upstairs and on the stairs: "Five-oh. Five-oh."

With police approaching the house, a full-scale escape would commence in the next few seconds.

James leapt toward the stairs, but, seeing that they were filled with fleeing (and wide) football players, James looked elsewhere for his escape route. Thinking there must be an egress from this lower level somewhere, he darted through a door into the boiler room, squinting his eyes to make out the outline of a door frame. Running to the door, he

15

wrenched it open, and fled up the bulkhead stairs into the back yard, joining a river of Casteline students and graduates in their flight to the back woods behind the Graysons' house. He ran across the dark, smooth lawn, into the safety of the trees, and kept running. He was glad he hadn't had more than a couple beers, because the lower branches of the trees, empty of leaves, kept surprising him as he tried to put distance between himself and the house. At one point his left shoulder smashed into the sharp end of a branch, pointed at him, unseen, knocking him off-stride. A few seconds later, the knob from another branch knocked his hat off. Bending to retrieve it, he kept running. He knew there were other evacuees near him, but he seemed aware only of his own path. After about three minutes of sporadic progress, James stopped and huddled over an empty spot in the woods, listening. He could hear voices, but he couldn't see any lights from the house any more. He felt safe.

An hour later, at about 11:00 James emerged from the woods about four houses down from the Graysons' house. He turned away from the house where the party had taken place, not daring to pass in front of it for fear the police were still present. He called Pete's phone, but got no answer. It looked like a long walk home, unless someone familiar drove by. He estimated a one hour walk to his house.

And that's what it took him to get home. He eased himself in the door quietly, hoping his parents were sleeping. His mother came downstairs, when she heard his shoes on the kitchen floor. She was wearing her flannel pajamas, and she was barefoot.

"How you doing, dear? Have a good time?"

"Yeah. It was OK." James pulled the cover off the cake with sour cream frosting, as he turned on the burner underneath the tea kettle. "You're up late. Everything OK?"

"Oh, just worrying about you. You know. I'm glad you're home," she said and gave him a hug. He hugged her back, glad again that he hadn't drunk much beer or spilled it on his clothes. "G'night, honey. See you tomorrow."

"G'night, Mum."

As the hot water heated, James shed his coat, tossing it on the stairs leading to the bedrooms, thinking about the party. He knew that there were probably a few, probably more than a few, of his friends that were talking to their parents right now, after their parents had been called from the Graysons'. At those houses, alerted by the call from the police, the parents were wondering whether their sons and daughters were beginning to waste their lives. James was glad his parents didn't have to face these uncertainties, but he also knew that he himself was not exempt from those same uncertainties.

The filled teacup felt warm in his hands. He sliced the cake and sat down to eat, thankful for his mother's loving trust, fearing the day when the line of that trust crossed the truth of his life.

Trust yourself,
Trust yourself to do the things that only you know best.
Trust yourself,
Trust yourself to do what's right and not be second-guessed.
Don't trust me to show you beauty
When beauty may only turn to rust.
If you need somebody you can trust, trust yourself.

Trust yourself,
Trust yourself to know the way that will prove true in the end.
Trust yourself,
Trust yourself to find the path where there is no if and when.
Don't trust me to show you the truth
When the truth may only be ashes and dust.
If you want somebody you can trust, trust yourself.

Well, you're on your own, you always were,
In a land of wolves and thieves.
Don't put your hope in ungodly man
Or be a slave to what somebody else believes.

Trust yourself
And you won't be disappointed when vain people let you down.
Trust yourself
And look not for answers where no answers can be found.
Don't trust me to show you love
When my love may be only lust.
If you want somebody you can trust, trust yourself

Trust Yourself by Bob Dylan

Ben

As usual, at 5:30 on Monday, November 29th, Ben LaMott, Casteline's boys' basketball coach, woke up and stretched his arms and torso as he sat on the side of the bed. He bent his neck side to side, trying to stretch the muscles leading from his shoulders and upper back, extending into his neck. Once he felt a little looser, he stood and crept quietly to the bathroom, keeping quiet so Willa could sleep undisturbed. She would wake up at the second alarm, to make sure that Scott and Mary responded to their own alarms.

In the shower Ben thought about the first minutes of practice, the words he would use to set a tone for the season, trying to picture all the boys, in their new sneakers and bright jerseys. He planned to tell them about the team from the late-eighties that had no reigning stars but that had gone on to the state semi-finals, their success the product of their cohesion and unselfishness. It had been one of Ben's favorite teams.

Ben also made a mental note to track down Archie Stedham, a boy who had introduced himself to Ben one week ago, having just moved to Casteline from Granby, a small, rural town in the western part of the state. Ben was intrigued by the new player, his expectations running well ahead of the probability of his making a great contribution. But that was what sports meant to Ben: the chance to dream and then try to make those dreams become real. So while Ben stood in the shower, rinsing the soap off his belly and back, he took the liberty of seeing Archie as an impact player, with great ball handling skills and, while he was at it, a form-perfect jump shot.

Archie had returned the information sheet and the permission slip on Wednesday; he had also brought in a physical exam form, filled out, just two days after he had received them. Ben nodded to himself, as he turned off the water: this young man took his responsibilities seriously. He was ahead of half the team in turning in forms. Ben, jaded from recent disappointing seasons, felt that the effect of a Casteline upbringing softened his players as they matured. Fairly or not, accurately or not, he was glad that Archie had stepped into his classroom, promising a fresh approach to the game.

An hour later, Ben put his arms around Willa in the kitchen. She had succeeded in dispatching both Mary and Scott from their beds, and he could hear them upstairs. He said, "See you tonight. We'll be done about 7:15. I should be home by 8."

"Uh huh. I'll see you around 8:30. Have a great practice." She returned his embrace and found his mouth with hers.

Ben felt Willa's wish for him. She supported the burden of his coaching efforts gracefully, but she also reminded him regularly that he needed to keep grounded in his expectations. There were times when she wondered if he was becoming excessively desirous of his own success, though he always asserted that it was all about the players. Ben wrapped his lips around Willa's, searching for her passion, as he pressed against her. When she pulled back just slightly, he reached down and rubbed the softness of her hip through her bathrobe.

"See you tonight. I love you."

Second period, after taking attendance, Ben looked over the class silently. They quickly came to order, curious about Ben's silence.

"Does anyone listen to Holden?"

Of course, Ben's question, as intellectually based and fincly phrased as it was, met with no flicker of a response. Ben stood, his eyes moving from retreating faces to concealed faces. No one wanted to be the first to give Mr. LaMott what he wanted. If a student made an effort to meet the teacher's challenge, he lost his foothold in the culture – especially just a few hours removed from a brief vacation.

"All right, I'll rephrase the question. Pam, does Holden act nicely toward Stradlater, his roommate?"

Pam, alert and poised, sat up a little straighter. "Yeah, he does."

Ben knew that she was just trying to push the focus off herself with her non-committal answer.

"OK. Let's turn to page 53 and look at what Holden says to Stradlater, when he flies in the door on his way to the date.

"By the way, who is his date with?"

"Anyone significant?"

"Is Jane Gallagher someone Holden knows?"

Class lurched on slowly, in this stunted way: Ben providing the direction, the first half of the answer, and the page references in the book for character assessment. After almost twenty-six years, Ben had accepted the fact that his students were rarely going to provide the energy in his classroom. He felt that other teachers' classes held much more excitement for the students. He heard the students talking about debates that took place in Bryan Taft's classroom (Bryan was his long-time friend, his irreplaceable JV coach) and vocabulary game shows that

Rich Grove designed for in-class study. Ben admitted to himself, quite often, that he was not an innovator, nor was he an inspiration. He could only hope that he provided a good role model for those who chose to observe his attention to detail and his preparation for each of his classes.

As the discussion meandered without substance concerning Holden Caulfield's attitude toward his classmates, Ben reached out once again, trying to make a connection to his students. "I know that you won't have a response right away, but I want you to think whether you agree with this statement that I'm going to make. Here's the statement: 'I think that there are winners and losers in school.' "

A flicker of recognition flashed across some of the faces in front of Ben. He let this idea settle in to their thoughts. "Just decide, each of you, whether you agree with that concept: Here it is once again: There are winners and losers in this school – and in every other school, for that matter, if we want to generalize."

A few furrowed brows gave the impression that some students were contemplating Ben's question. Ben let another twenty seconds pass, though it felt to him like five minutes.

"Brittany, can you give us your thoughts about my question?"

Brittany, slender but usually animated, gathered her thoughts for a short lapse of time. "I think many of us *think* that there are winners and losers. I mean, we see our own set of friends as the right group and other groups as just not as good, in a way."

Ben welcomed her honesty and, even more, her attempt to respond to him. "But aside from our own set of friends, do you think that there is a group of people in the school that most of the students regard as the privileged ones, and that they get certain latitude from the administration and the students both?"

Brittany accepted Ben's challenge again. "Yeah, I do. The jocks, the cheerleaders, the funny guys. You know. They sit in a certain place in the cafeteria and they walk more confidently. They're louder. They walk in bigger crowds."

Ben was pleased with Brittany's observations. "You see? Brittany senses that there is a class system at work here at Casteline, and I agree with her.

"I have to tell you a story, about when I was a kid, a seventh grader." Ben began a story that he had repeated almost every year he had taught, a self-revelatory story about his own insecurities as a seventh grader. "In seventh grade, I was a pimply, glasses, smart kid who wanted to be a successful athlete, but I wasn't making it at the time. Three other guys in my division – we had divisions, which meant levels, and spent the whole day together, start of the day to the finish, except

21

for homeroom – and these three guys and I made up this bogus organization: The Big Four. Let's see, the other guys' names were Donnie Mason, Paul Brown, and something Wilson, I think. I think the Big Four lasted about two weeks, but at the time, it provided us with a very important social standing." Ben wasn't sure whether his irony was clear, but he proceeded.

"One day another class member, Peter Caruso, asked us if we would make it the Big Five. It was a novel concept, one that we said we would consider. Peter was much like us, scrawny, somewhat smart, nothing special – just like us.

"In seventh grade we – I attended Needham High School and it was a huge school system. We shared two buildings for junior high, spreading over into the third floor of a grade school that was two blocks away. In the middle of every day, we took a long walk from the grade school to the main building, for a shop class and then lunch. So every day we took a walk from building to building, crossing the street and walking down the sidewalk.

"The day Peter asked us if we would include him in our little society, we were walking on the sidewalk. We said we would let him know the next day." Ben's face felt a little warm as he recounted his story, some thirty-five years old now, but still, for some reason, a story in which his classes usually found value. The faces of these class members were trained on Ben's, as they heard his naming of their own uncertainties.

"The next day, we decided that we didn't want this intruder in our little group, even though our group meant nothing more than a name. We never did anything as a group, and we were even ashamed to speak of our group to anyone outside our group, but we still, for some reason, needed that little boundary around us.

"So the next day, we – I don't remember if I did it or another member of the Big Four did it – took Peter's books and tossed them in a water puddle at the curb of the street, to let him know of our decision."

Ben saw many heads recoil at his confession. He saw Paul, the class's most ardent slacker, stare at him with fascination, as Paul came to the realization that Ben had once been twelve years old and afraid to grow up, though he had hidden that fear behind a cruel bravado. Paul rarely noted Ben's clumsy attempts to reach his students. On the second day of school in September, Paul had sidled up to Ben, as the class relaxed in the minute after class, and asked, surreptitiously, "Hey, man, are you cool?" Ben, not knowing how to respond, had replied, "You'll know in a few months, Paul." Paul now knew: Ben was not cool.

"I'm not proud of that decision or of that act on my part. I only tell you about it so that you can understand that I once wondered if I would ever make an impression on this world. Just like Holden Caulfield. And just like you."

As class continued, Ben felt some warmth in the room, a warmth bred from his admission of his own weakness. At one point Paul turned to a classmate across the room, telling him, "I bet you don't even know that you sound wicked smart when you talk in class."

The accused laughed. "I'm not smart. If I was smart, would I be in this class?"

For another twenty minutes, the class spoke to each other, responding to observations and suggestions with some interest and a little insight. As the class wound down, Ben wrapped up with, "Class, I want to thank you for this class. It's not common for a class to really talk about things that matter to them. Obviously, the subject of social status and the way people gain or lose control over others struck a chord with you, and you got involved in a real and personal way. As a teacher, I can't ask for anything more.

"Tonight, please write two pages in your notebook, making an argument that Holden is either fair to other people or not fair."

"Is this an essay?" asked Chris Whelan. The students needed clarification, partly because Ben was always so explicit.

Ben approached the blackboard. He wrote, "Subject: Holden Caulfield's attitude toward his peers. Length: two pages. Requirement: three specific things Holden says or does that show his attitude (include page numbers for these specifics)." Ben thought for a second, as his class wrote down his directions. "FCA: Present tense."

"Don't forget to write in the present tense. Before you finish your essay, look back over it to make sure you're writing in the present tense."

"Are we gonna hand this in?" asked Joanna from the right side of the room.

"No, I don't think so. I'll check it for credit, but I won't give it a grade. But we will read four responses to the class as a whole."

The bell rang at that moment, completing Ben's attempts to improve the assignment and his class's understanding of that assignment. His freshmen gathered their books, notebooks, and jackets and noisily left the room with great relief. They met the first of the juniors that unwillingly sidled through the door, filling his classroom to capacity for their American Literature class. Ben picked up his copy of *The Catcher in the Rye* and took it to his desk at the side of the room where he retrieved a copy of *The Death of a Salesman*, the next book under study in American Lit. He gathered his notes that were scrawled on three notecards placed at the end of Act One Scene Four.

"Any good meals over the Thanksgiving weekend?" he offered as a greeting to his class , and, after some indifferent discussion of the weekend on their part, proceeded to fashion a discussion of Biff Loman's life as a young man, intent on becoming a hero, but devoid of the morals that would make it so.

In his free period after lunch Ben had called a meeting with his captain Geoff Willis, just to go over the roster and see whether Geoff had any insights into situations involving the players trying out for the team, situations that Ben should be made aware of. Ben thought highly of Geoff, knowing that he was not a really talented player nor was he particularly athletic. But Geoff had earned the respect of his peers, being elected sole captain of the 2008-09 team. As a junior, Geoff had started some of the games, when there had been an injury. He had rarely scored double figures, but he took care of the ball, rebounded very well, and set a good tone for the team. He would be a good person to serve as the liaison between Ben and the players, because he had the players' trust, though Ben felt he also would tell the truth to Ben.

They met in the back of the library, at a small table. Ben had asked Geoff to bring any questions he had, so that Ben would be able to answer them. Geoff stood a solid 6'2", probably weighed a little under 190 pounds; he was strong.

"Hey, Coach. Big day, huh?"

"Yeah. I'm excited. You feel good?"

"Oh yeah. It's finally here. Senior year. I can't believe it. It seems like just a few days ago I was playing on the JV, scrapping for playing time." Geoff had worked his way up, from his days as a freshman barely getting on the floor, to an occasional start on the JV team, to a solid replacement player on the varsity as a junior, and now, as a senior, the captain and, potentially, the leading rebounder on the team.

"I love your story, Geoff. You show all the guys that you don't have to be the best shooter, or the fastest player on the court, or the most highly skilled, to be a valuable player. I'm really happy for you. You deserve being captain, and I know you'll be a great one."

"Thanks, Coach. It's quite an honor to be captain. I have to say, I don't understand why Andrew didn't get elected captain instead of me, or with me."

Ben nodded. "That's a great question. I think the guys know Andrew's got the talent; he's gonna lead us in many ways statistically. He's our best player, no doubt – no offense, Geoff."

Geoff laughed easily. "I know what you're saying."

Ben continued. "But the guys recognize that you've done the dirty work, working with weights, getting in the absolute best shape. It's really an honor to be captain, when Andrew is also a senior. You should be really proud."

Geoff looked down. "Yeah, I know. I am proud. You're right." He stopped. "I've got just a couple questions. Do we have scrimmages lined up? You didn't put those on the schedule."

"Yeah, we have the usual ones. We've got Wayland on Saturday of the first week, Newton South on Tuesday of the second week, and West Roxbury on the second Thursday. That gives us three, against strong competition. Those dates sound OK?" Ben had pulled out his pocket calendar to assure himself of the dates, but he knew them. "First two are away and the West Roxbury is at home. I've got to make sure the managers are ready for that one.

"By the way, do you know if Nancy and Bridget will be able to manage this year? They were great last year. They've spoken to me a couple times, but they still aren't sure."

"Bridget is definite. I just talked to her today. She doesn't know about Nancy. But she said she can get Janet Hsu if Nancy can't do it."

"Good, I hate to go into a season with inexperienced managers. They need to take the stats accurately for us. And they make practice a little more fun, because they're always smiling and happy."

Geoff agreed. "I love the managers. They're awesome. Food on the bus? Signs in the hallways? They're great."

"Did you have something else?"

Geoff nodded. "Uh, yeah, Coach. I just wanted to talk to you about the team attitude. I'm pretty psyched about most of the guys, but there are a few that could go the wrong way. I wanted to ask you if there is anything I can do about that – if you have any suggestions to how we can be sure not to lose them."

Ben was happy to hear Geoff bring up the subject of attitude. "You're right. I can think of a few guys, myself, that I don't have all my trust in. I hope I'm wrong, but I know in the past that some players will just drift away from the team rules and go their own way. Did you have anyone in particular in mind?" Ben knew that Geoff would be hesitant to mention specific names, but it would be a good sign if he would do so.

After a slight hesitation, Geoff offered, "Well, I think the only senior we have to worry about is Bobbie. He's not sure he's going to get big minutes, so he's been slacking ever since last season. He's just afraid to work hard if he's not going to get anything out of it."

Ben knew what Geoff was talking about. "I've seen it in a lot of marginal players over the years. They don't want to look as if they're working hard, because if they work hard, and they still don't get playing time, it's as if they're not very good. So they just go through the motions to cushion the blow of limited playing time. To be honest, the attitude of Bobbie and a couple of guys like him are one of the keys to the team's overall attitude. They can either bring us up or bring us down."

"I agree, Coach. I'm talking to Bobbie, but I'm not sure he's listening. He's onto the college search, visiting schools. It's like he's left high school behind."

"Yeah, that's right, but it's also a natural thing. We have to let him handle his situation in his own way. I'll talk to him the first week, once I have a sense of his role, to try to bring him in.

"Any others?"

"Yeah, the juniors aren't the most disciplined bunch I've ever seen. You got Pete Semineau, Dan Owings, and even James Rush. I'm not hearing much good stuff about them around the school."

"Yeah, me too," said Ben. "Pete's always been a little on the wild side, but James worries me a little. I'm not even sure Pete will make the team, but we're counting on James. If he goes south, we've got a little problem." Ben felt a little funny talking about the players in this way with Geoff, but he felt Geoff would not abuse his position to reveal Ben's predispositions about his players. Ben enjoyed being honest with Geoff.

"Yeah, I don't know about James. He's a really good kid, but he's being influenced."

Unfortunately, Ben had heard the same statement about thirty players over his years at Casteline; he knew that "being influenced" was another word for "growing up," and kids just grew up all the time. There was no stopping them. Ben tried to reassure Geoff. "I think we can keep a good hold on James. You do your part. Keep talking to him. He respects you. If you can get to him on the court, telling him how much he's helping the team, he'll buy into the off-court stuff. And use Jason too. As the point guard, Jason has a real handle on moving the ball and setting up the offense. He has to learn the habits and work ethic of the other guys on the floor with him. I'll talk to Jason, and we can use him a little to try to keep the lines of communication open with those juniors.

"I know that juniors always look immature to the seniors. Nothing you can do. You guys are ready for the next step: college. And you also know that you have no more chances after this year. This is your year. The juniors don't have that same sense of urgency. They're still feeling their way along."

"Mmmm. Yeah. I'll keep talking to them. I've been trying to get to all the guys in the late part of the fall, to get them focused. I think we've got a chance to be really good."

Ben agreed. "Me too. Now, there's one more thing I'm going to ask you to do. You're the captain. The way you approach drills and sprints is the way the team will approach drills and sprints. Last year you were a leader, and as a result, you were elected captain. I think you deserved it, without question.

"You've done a great job setting up summer league, ordering practice jerseys, setting up the bowling night for Friday. Now I want you to realize what being a captain means. It's not just a title or a job. It's the spine of the team. If you show respect to the refs, the team will. If you touch every line on sprints, the team will. If you come to the middle of the court first when I call you, the team will follow you right away. I don't think you realize what an influence you have over the rest of the players, but they look at you for direction. Can you accept that role? It's not easy. There will be times when you'll disagree with something I've decided. You might be sitting down at a crucial time in the game. But you'll have to accept it as the best thing for the team at the time. Do you see what I'm saying?"

Geoff looked directly at Ben with his deep-set eyes. "Coach, being captain of this team is something I've always wanted to be. I never dreamed it would actually happen. I've worked hard for this chance. I won't let myself down. This means too much to me. It's not as if I think I'm going to lead the team in scoring or anything. But I do want to lead the team in leadership, if you can measure that."

"I think I'll be able to measure it. Hearing you say that makes me feel good about our season." With that, Ben told Geoff he could leave, and Ben also walked out of the library, his step quickened by the sincerity of Geoff's strength. Ben knew that Geoff's resolve was more important than the skills that he taught or the strength that the players were developing.

As Ben turned toward the teachers' room, his plan book in hand, one class more to teach for the day, he remembered that he wanted to make contact with Archie Stedham, the new junior. Ben turned toward the main office, to track down his schedule. He looked in the alphabetized set of schedules, but Archie's hadn't been filed yet.

In Guidance Ben asked Millie, the secretary, "Do you have a schedule on file for a new student, Archie Stedham?"

Millie set aside her transcript work to walk Ben to the schedules to be filed, and there it was. Archie was in Milo Lansing's Spanish class at the time, and he'd be free in about five minutes.

"Thanks, Millie. I appreciate the help."

Ben strolled toward the World Language wing, on the second floor above the math rooms. Milo taught a Spanish 3 class that Ben knew met with a lot of stubborn resistance. Not everyone at Casteline was excited about foreign language.

When the class let out, Ben spied Archie, gathering his book and bag at his desk at the side of the room. He stood near the door as Archie quietly headed out. "Hey, Archie, you all set for today?"

Archie, clad in jeans and a flannel overshirt, smiled immediately. "Oh, hi, Coach. Yeah, I am. Hey, do we just hang around until 5:00, or do we go home? If I take the bus, I'll have a hard time getting back to school."

Ben's forehead creased in uncertainty. "I really don't know, Archie. I think most of the guys go home, but a lot of them have their licenses, so they go home, grab a snack, and head back around 4:30. You probably don't know anyone yet, so I'd say just stay here, do your homework in the library, head down to the gym around 4:30, and I'll see you there and then."

Ben turned suddenly to Archie. "Hey, I forgot, have I told you about the six-minute mile?"

Archie replied, "No, but I've heard rumors about it. When do we run it?"

"Most of the guys have already run it. But there's a small crew running on the outdoor track this afternoon at 3:00. You want to join them?"

"Yeah, that sounds great. Might be a little cold, though."

Ben agreed. "Yeah, it's supposed to be mid-forties, but dry. You got a sweatshirt?"

"Yeah. I'll see you at the track at 3," Archie said with assurance.

"You looking forward to practice?" Ben asked, continuing the conversation.

"Of course. At the end of last season, I started an unofficial count of days before the next season's first practice, and now I'm down to zero. I'll be there early."

"Good. See you there. Actually, I'll see you on the track after school." Ben placed his hand on Archie's left shoulder, patting it proprietarily. He found that he often did this patting on the shoulder, trying, he supposed, to establish some relationship between the players and himself. He felt a little like a father in making this gesture, and being fatherly felt good to him.

When Ben and Archie separated, there were about three and a half hours until the first practice.

At almost quarter of four, after running three more players, including Archie Stedham, through the mile, Ben entered Fidelity Nursing and Convalescent Home, to visit his mother. Ben had arranged his mother's entry into the nursing home in 2007, a little more than a year ago, and his mother had been living there since that admission. She was still fiercely proud, but increasingly confused, as the months illogically passed. Ben took the stairs up to the room she shared with her roommate Yolanda.

"Hi, Mom. How're you doing?"

Margot LaMott looked at her son as though he were a member of a rival outpost.

"Who dat?" she croaked, in her mock-surprised style. The room was a little dark, the sun nowhere to be found behind the gray November clouds. Margot sat in her wheelchair, facing her bed, a handful of papers and envelopes strewn across in front of her.

"Are you sorting your papers?" Ben asked in a tone that he hoped was not patronizing. She spent several hours each day trying to arrange the envelopes and letters that were housed in her bedside table. She would come upon a system, stacking papers as neatly as she could into piles, then loop a large green rubber band around the pile. Ben gently sat on the bed so as not to disturb the piles. "Want some help?"

Margot looked pleadingly at him. "Yes, I'd love some help. It seems that I never get the job done, and then tomorrow there's more mail, and I'm even further behind."

As Ben pulled greeting cards, advertisements, newspaper clippings, and store coupons together in an apparently orderly fashion, he looked at his mother.

"Do you want to go for a walk before supper?" Ben asked, adding, "I have a few minutes before I have to get back for practice."

"Oh, do we have time?" With her right hand Margot patted the quilt that hung on the footboard of the bed, a quilt she had made twenty years ago, still bright with its yellow sun.

"Let's go for a little ride."

After storing the packets of paper neatly in her bedside table, Ben bent down to unlock the brakes on his mother's wheelchair. As they rolled out the door of her room, he asked, "Do you have to go to the bathroom?"

"No, I'll be fine for a little while."

Turning right out the door, Ben shepherded his mother past the nurses' station, nodding to the caretakers who gathered there, relaxing at the end of the drowsy afternoon. Hearing his mother talking, but unable to decipher her words, Ben moved next to the chair as he pushed it, leaning over to place his head near his mother's. In this position he could hear her, though he had a hard time looking up as he steered the chair.

"Do you know that there were monkeys hanging from the trees outside my window this afternoon?"

Ben had heard this assessment from his mother before, and had tried to dissuade her from believing in her hallucinations, but they persisted.

"Huh. Were there a lot?"

"They hung from cobwebs that hung from the trees. They were swinging like pendulums. The trees were swaying with the weight of them."

"Woah. That must have been quite a scene. Did it last for long?" Ben had taken the attitude of drawing his mother out when she talked of the things that she thought she saw. He tried to hide any disbelief that inevitably crept into his voice.

"Well, I can only see it in certain light. I think as the light begins to fade in the afternoon, they come out for a short time. They disappeared pretty quickly, just as quickly as they had arrived. But they were dancing brightly for a few minutes." Margot stared straight ahead. She didn't want to see Ben's eyes, for fear that his incredulity would be plain.

"Does it seem that they're always there? Or do they just suddenly appear?"

Margot paused, trying to detect condescension in her son's voice. Finding none, she continued her analysis. "I think they're always there. I just can't see them except in certain light conditions. They sway and sway, their paths seeming to intersect sometimes." Margot was becoming animated, now that she felt she had a supportive audience. "I almost see them changing branches, or vines, or webs, or whatever it is they cling to. It's almost as if they are swinging on swings on a school playground. I can see a few of them swinging way up in the air, up and down, and then up the other side of the arc."

Ben let his mother continue until she had exhausted her conception. He thought about his mother's visions, wondering where they came from, assuming that they emerged from her weakening vision. He knew that she had little to occupy her day, just the personal needs that demanded attention: having to get to the bathroom, consuming her meals, getting into and out of her wheelchair. He reasoned, logically, he thought, that, since there wasn't really a narrative to her life anymore, the things she thought she saw were as logical (or illogical) as the things that actually happened to her.

After a minute of thinking about his mother, Ben could feel his mind drift back to the narrative of his own life: the upcoming basketball season, another season in his persistent quest for a perfect season. He thought of James Rush, a boy he saw as critical to this season's success, a junior who had made great contributions to the varsity as a sophomore. He also thought of Archie Stedham, who added a variable that Ben wanted quantified as soon as possible, another derivative that would affect this season's outcome. He loved to weigh the ingredients of each team, eager to mix them together, anticipating the finished product. In less than an hour he would start practice, at 5:00 on the newly sealed gymnasium floor, starting with some leisurely laps, stretching, then full court layups, first the right hand, then the left, then the crossovers .

Looking at his watch, Ben said, "Let's head back. I gotta hustle." His mother nodded compliantly.

Turning his mother's chair toward her room, he thought of their conversation about the monkeys. In a way their dialogue was like those monkeys: two differing views of reality, passing across each other like monkeys swinging from cobwebs. Every so often Ben's ideas and Margot's were consistent with each other, but usually they were two arcs in the sky, two shooting stars, with no point of intersection. Hence, the skepticism on his part, and the reluctance to share her perspective on his mother's. Ben shook his head slightly, overcome by the distance between them. He sighed.

As they headed back to Margot's room, with more urgency and direction than they had felt leaving it, they passed a handsome man seated in a wheelchair in front of his room. Displayed on the chair rail outside his door were brightly painted animals, wooden figures that he apparently had carved himself at some productive time in his past. Margot stared hungrily at the figures, reaching upward to them from her chair. Ben stopped to let her admire.

"Do you want one?" asked the man kindly. "Any one you want. Just say the word."

31

Margot's hands moved cautiously toward a yellow duck with a red beak. "I'd love this one. Are you sure?" she asked wonderingly.

The man smiled. "That one was made for you. Keep it. Spread the word."

Margot clutched the duck to her flat chest as Ben started pushing the chair back to her room.

Oh, leaves were falling
They're just like embers
In colors red and gold they set us on fire
Burning just like moonbeams in our eyes

Someone said they saw me
They said I was swinging the world by the tail
Bouncing over the white clouds
That I was killing the blues
Just killing the blues

Well, I am guilty of something
That I hope you never do
'Cause nothing is sadder
Than losing yourself in love

Someone said they saw me
They said I was swinging the world by the tail
Bouncing over the white clouds
Just killing the blues
Just killing the blues

Oh, when you asked me
Just to leave you
And set out on my own to find what I needed
You asked me to find what I already had

Someone said they saw me
They said I was swinging the world by the tail
Bouncing over the white clouds
I was killing the blues
Just killing the blues

Killing the Blues by Chris Smither

James

Last period of the day James sat in computer design class, working on his project, an advertising campaign for a product he had conceived: a sneaker that gave its wearer great resiliency and bounce. He knew the idea was derivative; in thinking of it, he felt as if he were six or seven years old, dreaming of flying. But Mrs. Antonellis encouraged her students to use their imaginations, and James thought of the fecund minds of Bill Gates and Steven Jobs, knowing that they had become successful by generating ideas that had never been considered before. So James dreamed of rising high over the rim, not exactly a novel concept, but certainly a foreign feeling for James.

Earlier in the day Mr. Tilson had shown James's Geometry class how to draw the perpendicular bisector of a line. He demonstrated the method on the board, using his old-fashioned, foot-long wooden compass, with yellow chalk inserted into the hollow tube of one leg. From the right endpoint he drew a long arc above the line; then, keeping the legs of the compass spread the same span, he drew a complementary arc below the line. James Rush followed Tilson halfway to the intersection.

Maintaining the angle of the compass, Mr. Tilson then moved the contact point to the left endpoint. He drew two more arcs, each of which crossed the first arcs, creating two specific points.

"Now, if I draw a straight line connecting the intersecting points of the pairs of arcs, that line will of necessity cross the original line. The line we have drawn is the perpendicular bisector to that line." Mr. Tilson looked at his demonstration as if the class members should applaud. James had managed to stay alert through the first portion of the lesson, mainly because he found the archaic large wooden compass an artifact that belonged more in a museum than in a contemporary classroom. James's focus was an accomplishment far beyond Rick's: he was clicking away on his calculator, playing a video game under cover of determining an urgent mathematical solution. Mr. Tilson knew that many of his students amused themselves during class, but he didn't seem to mind. Test and quiz scores were the basis of Mr. Tilson's grades, and James's class did pretty well on the quizzes, not quite as well on the tests. James kept his scores in the Bs and Cs, studying when he needed to.

The Arc of Intersection

James liked the idea of being able to envision a construct that added to his awareness of a geometric figure. He was actually intrigued by the problems and solutions that Mr. Tilson offered the class. Tilson seemed to be an interesting guy; he tried hard to make geometry not boring – even though there was nothing he could really do to avoid it. But James considered Mr. T. cool: he coached the cross country team and the lacrosse team. He was probably sixty or something, but he didn't act like it.

When Mr. Tilson was done with his explanation, he erased his work and asked for a volunteer to come up to the board and make the same drawing. Susan Fryer raised her hand, as she always did, and rose from her seat. Closing his eyes, James heard her flipflops slapping the floor as she moved to the front board. James kept his eyes closed (his frayed BC capbill covered his eyes from Mr. Tilson's gaze) and listened to hear if he could tell what she was doing.

Turning his attention to the more honest focus of his consciousness, James thought he could make out Adrienne's voice from her desk up front. He could picture her ponytail hanging down over her lavender shirt, lots of different hair colors blending into a varied blond. He liked the way her shoulders were set wide and the way she sat up straight, like an athlete. She could run like a mustang. He'd seen her on the track accelerating past other girls who fruitlessly tried to maintain her pace, in her lacrosse workouts. Adrienne ran fast – and she didn't even look like she was straining. Though he had laid his head on Meredith's shoulder at Grayson's party, it was Adrienne's that he coveted.

James didn't hear any explanation coming from Susan up at the board. He wondered if she was done. No word from Mr. Tilson. James thought he could hear the scratching of chalk on the board, but he wasn't sure. He wanted to peek at Susan, but he didn't want to cheat. He liked to try to learn without watching. It was a little game he played with himself, to entertain himself during school.

"Is she doing it correctly?" intoned Mr. Tilson.

James pictured Susan at the board, her white pullover shirt extending softly down her back, covering the upper portion of a pair of designer jeans, the stitching etched boldly. He determined that Susan had successfully drawn one arc, but she then was unsure about her next step. James knew Mr. T's m.o.: he would not assist Susan, and he had already erased his own template, so she couldn't follow his model.

James wanted to open his eyes, but then he would be done with his inner reverie, and those were the best moments of school, the moments when he filtered out all the detritus of the school day, playing with the sounds that came through, imagining the people whose voices he heard, thinking about them growing, having known most of them when they were little kids climbing on the monkey bars with him, wearing Red Sox T-shirts and dirty name-brand sneakers.

A petite, delicate voice came from the front right of the room. James could almost hear the comment. " . . . she draws the second . . . . . without . . ."

"That's right, Felicity. She changed the span of the compass. That's why she can't find two points that will lead to a bisector, when connected. Good thinking, Felicity. Would you like to do it on the board yourself?"

James couldn't hear Felicity's response, but he knew that she would not want to get up out of her seat in front of the class. One time she had tried to lead a discussion in History and Politics, and she had been unable to raise her eyes from the paper that lay in front of her from which she had been reading.

"Adrienne, can you give it a try?" Mr. Tilson asked.

James was now torn. He didn't want to look up, but he couldn't bear the thought of missing Adrienne walking up to the board. He could picture her grace, the easy flow of her body as she stood up, not even using her arms to push off the desk, all the strength and balance of her legs raising her like a flag up a morning flagpole, then her simple, light gait covering the seven steps to the blackboard. He could hear her whispery ballet slippers softly scuffing the linoleum floor as she floated forward. And he could, at the same time, hear Susan Fryer, her flipflops less strident this time, as she returned to her seat, just a little worn down from only one short trip to the blackboard.

Adrienne easily performed the exercise. James tried to predict the moment she would turn around, when her face would be turned toward his, though her eyes would never make contact with anyone's. But the beauty was that, at the same time, she didn't avoid eye contact either. She just made herself present in all her completeness.

After waiting three more seconds, James opened his eyes, expecting to see Adrienne three steps away from her seat. He was dismayed to see that she was already turning to sit down, her right arm swinging around as she pivoted on her left slipper. He saw her, once again, with her back to him, her ponytail trailing resplendently over her shirt, which wasn't lavender. It was yellow, and he could just make out the shadow of a bra-strap underneath it. When she sat down, she disappeared from James's view, two classmates set in his row, between Adrienne and James, interrupting his view.

Two minutes later, as the discussion of perpendicular bisectors lost its small head of steam, James was jostled by a sock thrown by Pete, a relic from his gym bag, an attempt to get James's attention.

"Yeah?" he answered.

"Time you headin down to practice?" Pete whispered.

"Probably about 4:30. You goin at 3:00 to run the mile?"

"He didn't say anything specific to me, so I'm just going at 4:45. I know I'll have to run at 5, but what the hell."

When the bell rang, James got up slowly, as Pete waited for him. James walked up the aisle. "Hey, Adrienne, you goin out for b-ball?"

Adrienne looked up, surprised. "To be honest, I'm still not sure. I'm pretty sure I'm not, but it's not 100%. I'll know at 3:00, when practice starts." She giggled. "I guess I'm not very decisive."

James rushed to assure her. "No, you're being very decisive. Very decisive in your vacillation."

They both laughed. That was a good thing.

"See you around," James bleated.

And she was gone, her stride as reassuring as a child's trust.

The rest of the day plodded. James attended his classes methodically, rarely retreating into himself, until he reached Mrs. Antonellis's computer design class, where he could contemplate the plan for the sneakers that provided a jump. As he considered his design, he reviewed a videotape he had downloaded, a collection of NBA players soaring well above the rim, from outlying places on the court, to make a series of outlandish dunks. The thought of flight brought James back to a video clip he had seen of Dr. J, Julius Erving, who had attacked the basket from the right side, in a playoff game, met a defensive presence, circled behind the backboard to avoid the defender, and come up on the other side of the rim, from behind the board, to score the basket off the glass – this extemporaneous alteration accomplished entirely after he had left his feet. In James's mind, Dr. J.'s dunk was the epitome of flying with a basketball. James tried to incorporate this vision into his graphics, searching for the video on-line, but he didn't have the necessary focus on this day, the first day of practice, so he pretty much doodled through the period and then the school day was over.

After school James grabbed Pete as he was jumping into his car.

"Hey, no stupid stuff today. We're starting practice in a couple hours. You want to be on top of your game."

James hopped into the passenger seat.

"Not to worry, my man. I'm going cold turkey starting today. You'll see. I'm going to rip through the mile and beat your ass down the floor all night long." Pete looked at James with an expression of hope.

James nodded. "That's the attitude. You're an important cog in the wheel. I don't think LaMott has a clue how good you are. You gotta show him right from the opening whistle."

Pulling out of the parking lot, Pate gunned the Audi just out of habit, but he slowed more quickly than usual. On both the straightaways and turns to his house, he kept the speedometer below fifty-five the entire way, an act of great restraint prompted more by his regard for the sanctity of the day than by the two speeding tickets that lay in his glove compartment.

Inside the house, Pete and James feasted on lemonade and pop-tarts, not the diet of champions, but an answer to the sense of emptiness that the house gave them. With Pete's sister still fifteen minutes from home, they had the place to themselves. That meant either Madden Football or NBA LIVE on the Xbox. They decided on NBA LIVE, where they pummeled each other with fast breaks, dunks, and electronic woofing. James couldn't defeat Pete on his home court.

At 4:15 they left for practice, James with no bag because he had already left it in his gym locker. Pete stuffed sneakers, shorts, shirt, socks, and deodorant into his bag, ready for a long night's practice. After a short drive, punctuated by the deep boom of the bass on Pete's iPod track routed through the Audi's speakers, they arrived in the parking lot, hopping out of the car. Ten minutes later, they were shooting on the side floor as the girls ended their practice with sprints. James and Pete joined James's old friend Dan and three others at the side hoop on the girls' side of the gym, shooting, rebounding, making impressive behind-the-back bounce passes to each other, trying to show each other how comfortable they all were.

At 5:00 Coach LaMott called the team together, as the girls retreated to their locker room for a post-practice wrapup. "Welcome, men. This is a moment we've all been waiting for for a long time. I think I've had as much anticipation of this day as you have. I want to offer a challenge to you, because I think you can be a great team. Here is the challenge: be better tomorrow than you are today.

"Now, how can we accomplish that? How can you be better tomorrow? How do you know you'll be better?' Mr. LaMott waited for a response.

Finally, Bobbie Pitaro, a senior guard, suggested, "If we work really hard, we'll always be getting better. Then it will happen naturally."

Coach LaMott didn't seem completely satisfied. "But *when* do you have to work hard, in order to be better tomorrow? That's my point."

James knew. "Coach, we have to work hard today, if we want to be better tomorrow. I see what you mean," he said.

"Yes, that's what I mean. Thank you, James.

"I had a team about twenty years ago, a team that you guys remind me of."

James could feel Pete trying to get his attention, to note the coach's usual ploy of comparing this team to one of his past ones, trying to sound inspirational. James knew that Pete had a hard time with comparisons. But James was interested in hearing the coach out.

"This team, I think it was the '85-'86 team, was coming off a 10 – 13 season, nothing great, a little like last year's team. We started a little slow, maybe 3 and 3, and then we got it going and ended up 18 – 5. It was a fantastic growth on the part of everyone on the team. Our best player got a lot better, dominating games and becoming league MVP. Our sixth man became one of our most important people, coming into the game and hitting shots right away. That was just about the time of the change to 3 pointers, but I don't think it had happened yet. The guys at the end of the bench – they improved the most, I'd say. They gave us a real solid look in practice and at some point during the season, every player helped us win a game. There was one tournament game, when one of our tri-captains, Mike Murphy, who had scored only about 15 points all year, came in and hit three jumpers in the first half to help us break away, in a game down in Chatham on the Cape.

"Here's my point: that was a great team because every player contributed to its success. Even the managers were awesome. The fans were awesome. The coaches – well, some people thought they were awesome, but I'm not one to judge that.

"Today is November 29th. Today we're not a very good team. In fact, I don't even know if we're a team today. I'll know more in a couple of hours. I'm hoping that, by the time we hit December, and then January, then February, and, hopefully March, we'll become a great team. And that will happen only if we forget about ourselves and give that energy and attention to the team.

"Now let's go. Geoff, in front, to lead the stretching. Then three slow laps followed by two full sprinting laps."

39

The season was underway. James's heart was lifted, hearing the coach's words. He was attendant to the coach's message, just as Geoff had urged them to be at the 7:00 a.m. meeting in this gym that morning. Stretching his legs with a hurdler's stretch, one leg straight, arms reaching to that ankle, attempting to touch his head to his knee, James could feel the tightness in his body, especially in his back, that burden of expectation. In his back he could feel his father, wanting him to be special. He could feel Geoff Willis, willing the team to be cohesive. He could feel Steve Ramos, now a junior at Union College, coming back to visit the team over Christmas break, expecting to see talent covering the court, bringing his efforts to fruition. Tightness. James stretched into that tightness, dissipating it slightly, but only slightly. He knew that that tightness, that anxiety, was indispensable. He could call on that tightness when he needed strength. But if he couldn't fashion that tightness into looseness when he needed to, he would never fulfill his ambitions for himself. He liked to think of his career as an ascending line, a little like one side of Mr. Tilson's parabolas.

After stretching and jog/sprinting, the team settled into its practice routine, starting with 11-man drill, one of the players' favorites. James moved through the drill with ease, comfortably catching the ball from his spot at the foul-line extended, pushing the ball to the opposite foul line with his weak hand (as Mr. LaMott liked), coming to a solid and squeaky jump-stop, and bouncing a pass to Jason Grutchfield on the left wing. After his layup, James took a spot at the foul-line, to try to stop the next fast break coming toward his basket.

Following 11-man, the boys paired up for cross-court jumpers off the bounce-pass. James paired with Jonas Boynton, the senior he had woofed with at Grayson's party. James liked to find a good shooter for this drill because the drill ended when one pair of shooters reached 11, and James liked to be the winner – Coach LaMott noticed the winners of each drill, he was sure. James and Jonas reached 10 when someone from the other half of the court hit 11.

"OK, guys, wing run the left sideline now, going to 11 again," Coach LaMott shouted, after blowing his whistle. The jog began again, this time down the left side. James tried to sprint at least five of the steps down the sideline, just to work on his conditioning, but in doing so, he ran into Pete, who was running with Dan.

"Hey, we're moving through. Look out," James said, his breath coming in little bursts now, attempting to push through his increasing fatigue.

"Go ahead, get ahead. I'm gonna take my time and hit all my shots," Pete replied, as James and Jonas moved through. It took about nine trips across the floor back and forth, James's legs becoming increasingly tired, before Jonas hit #11. "Eleven," James shouted, just as someone from the other half said the same.

"OK, guys, let's get into full court dribble drill," Coach LaMott said, maintaining the continuous movement through his endless supply of drills. James knew that, in this first week, Coach liked to keep the boys moving constantly, building their stamina, giving him time to see who could stay at the pace of the drills, and who fell behind.

James got under a basket, and, hearing Geoff Willis call for two more balls at his end of the court, James grabbed two that were sitting against the wall, and bounced them down to Geoff.

The whistle blew and Coach started counting. When the team made ten consecutive layups off one particular dribble crossover move, they started working on another one.

"One . . . two, three . . . Four . . . oh, zero . . .One." If they missed a shot, they started again.

The Arc of Intersection

Said I'm willin' and I'm able
I'm ready 2 place my cards on the table
I've been holdin' back this feelin'
4 far 2 long
Now that I'm willin', it's a fact
It's truly mighty strong
Like a child lost in the wilderness
'Till I reach my destination, I won't rest

Cuz I'm willin'
And I'm able
I'm ready 2 place my cards on the table

There's some kings in my deck and a queen or 2
So u know there ain't nothin',
Nothin' that I wouldn't do
It 'twas a long time coming,
But now that it's here
All the non-believers better fear me

Cuz I'm willin'
And I'm able
I got good and plenty cards
2 place on the table

Been holdin' back this feeling 4 far 2 long
Now that I'm willing
This feelin'
It's truly mighty strong

I'm willing
And able
My vision is all clear, I'm feelin' kinda stable
U know I am, u know I am
Ready 2 whisper
Ready 2 shout
Ready 2 scream
From the highest mountain top

Lord, I'm willing and able
I wanna dance and sing, somebody watch me do my thing

from *Willin' and Able* by Prince

Ben

Just a minute into the full court dribble drill, Ben started to get a sense of the players' conditioning level. Geoff Willis, of course, was leading everyone in speed and endurance. He was like a missile, moving effortlessly down the court with the ball – and he was a 6'2" rebounder, not a perimeter player. Geoff was taking his captaincy seriously. Ben couldn't help but sneak looks at his new player, Archie Stedham, the junior who had moved from Granby. Archie ran gracefully and handled the ball even more gracefully, though he never seemed to reach a full sprint when he ran. His head was up, but his vision was not as complete as Ben would have liked. Archie's left hand was well developed, and his footwork at the point of the crossover was exemplary. Ben smiled to himself, pleased to have gained some talent.

When the team reached ten consecutive makes, Ben would let them know of the next crossover dribble that they would need to utilize: straight-cross, through the legs, behind the back, spin dribble. They had a hard time reaching ten, because a few players who would have a hard time making the team consistently missed their layups, because of a lack of smoothness and difficulty in making shots when they were tired. Finally, they hit their last shot, reaching #10.

"OK. Let's move to the left wing for the outlet pass. Straight in with the left hand, now, speed dribble, high dribble, no more than four dribbles." Ben waited for the boys, their heads hanging now, to get into lines, waited for two balls to be positioned underneath each basket, in the hands of the rebounders, and blew his whistle to start the drill again, this time working on moves off the left hand.

After the left handed moves and a quick set of foul shots, Ben blew the whistle for the six-minute mile. He didn't like to line the guys up and make them run around the gym, but it was a tradition that he had established more than twenty years ago, and it set a tone around which he could build his conditioning program ("program" was a little formal a word; it was more like running some sprints). In the eighties, everyone had been able to get the mile done in the preseason. Even the football players would run it on the Monday before Thanksgiving, which was a light day for them. Some of them even used to join the pre-season basketball players when they would run the mile on the track in early

November. But, as the years had gone by, the number of boys that entered the season in shape had become less absolute. Of course, there were always the football linemen, strong but not necessarily fleet of foot, for whom the timed mile was a problem. But some of the perimeter players, for whom speed was essential in basketball, were approaching the season in less than 6-minute-mile-shape now, evidence of something that they were doing that was not salubrious to their health. The timed mile was as black-and-white as the old Chuck Taylor Cons that Ben used to wear as a player at Needham in the early 70s. The mile had not become any longer in the past twenty years, nor had the watch become any less accurate. Each year, now, a few candidates had to undergo two or three trials before they could get it done.

This year there were five players who had to run the mile during practice: White, Pinson, Semineau, Payne, and Carnechie. Payne and Carnechie were football players who hadn't had an opportunity to get the mile completed, but the other three should have gotten this taken care of by this time. Ben knew that the indoor mile was a little shorter than the outdoor mile (he measured sixteen laps to a mile, but as the players circled the gym, their teammates, stationed at the corners of the gym floor, inevitably moved in to make their circuit a little less arduous), and he figured that some of the boys just chose to take the easier route indoors.

"OK, guys, let's line up at half court, right here, under the banner. You've got sixteen laps to complete a mile. If you run twenty-second laps, you'll be done in 5:40, so something like 22 seconds will get it done. I've got the game clock going, so you can see how you're doing. At three minutes, you should have eight laps done. Ready?" Ben motioned to Janet to start the clock as he blew his whistle, and the five boys sprinted the sideline from the halfcourt toward the corner of the gym, where two teammates stood as markers to be skirted. There were eighteen boys trying out, all juniors and seniors, no hotshot sophomores this year, as James Rush had been the previous year. The competition would be close for the last few spots, as usual. Ben liked to keep thirteen players, but just about every year he kept fourteen because he didn't want to end the career for a boy who had spent five or six years preparing for this team.

As the players ran past him on their third lap, Ben glanced at the clock: 4:54 . . . 4:52 . . . 4:48. The last two would probably not make it today.

After school three boys had completed the mile on the track, bringing the group that had finished the mile to thirteen. Archie

Stedham had had little difficulty, floating in at 5:40, clearly the leader of the three. The others were in under 5:55, a good time.

At the halfway mark, two players, Carnechie and White were under three minutes. Payne was at 3:03, close enough to close the gap, and Semineau was right on his tail, at 3:05; Pinson was above 3:10, effectively precluding his completion of the mile. Pinson's stats were puzzling to Ben. He had the skills to make the team and to help the team succeed, but his disregard for his preparation for the season indicated a malaise that seemed to consume him. It was always a see-saw for Ben, whether to give greater weight to attitude or skills in his assessment of a player's potential contribution to the team. In the end he gave them equal weight, and at times kept a player who had not completed the mile, making him run each week once or twice until he got it done.

As the clock neared 30 seconds, counting down, the players in the corners of the gym and in the middle started shouting encouragement to their teammates. "Let's go, Payno!" "You're closing in, Rob." Semineau had picked up, closing the gap between himself and Alex White, who was slowing. Ben loved to see what his players had in their final sprints. Some boys could increase their speed significantly when it came down to crunch time, and some were incapable of turning their legs over any faster. Ben couldn't tell whether it was a physical or a mental variable, but he felt that the same variable would affect their ability to sprint the floor when they were tired.

On the last lap Payne and Carnechie came in easily, at about 5:51. White and Semineau started sprinting with one lap to go, and sixteen seconds on the clock. It was a good race. On the far straightaway Semineau pulled up on White, only to see White pull away from him, but they both turned the next-to-last corner at 5:55. Ben counted down the final seconds, "Five . . . four . . ." as they beat their legs on the last turn. As the buzzer sounded, both Semineau and White crossed the line, leaving Pinson a full lap away, a project for another day. It was good to get the mile done for four more players. Ben assumed that Pinson would progress daily on his conditioning, and that it would not be a factor for long.

Ben walked to each of the boys who had run, as they crumbled to the floor, exhausted. The look on Pete Semineau's face told Ben that demanding the mile was worth it, because Pete's mouth was spread open with the need for oxygen, but also with a grin of satisfaction. "It's nice to get it done, isn't it?" Ben offered. Pete nodded, gasping heavily, but raising his head to acknowledge the coach. "Congratulations."

As Ben addressed each of the boys, he took their limp hands and squeezed out a handshake, happy for them. Then he moved to Andreas Pinson, the lone failure in today's run. "Don't worry, Andre, 6:12 today. It was 6:22 last week. You've made progress."

Andreas nodded confidently. Ben knew that this time was no setback for Andreas. He was a big guy, probably weighed over two hundred pounds. A six-minute mile did not and would not come easily to Andreas. But he would get it done.

"OK, a little breather for the milers. The rest of you, three-man reverse weave. Milers join us when you're feeling up to it. We're passing and moving away from the ball. Returning varsity players first, to demonstrate. We add one for a made basket, subtract one for a turnover or a missed layup."

Three returning players, Andrew Monaghan, Jason Grutchfield, and James Rush ran up the court, passing and moving away, with the off-wing moving toward the ball. Smooth. Effortless. Four passes and a layup. "That's all it takes. Remember, pass and move away. It's not the regular system. At first, guys up from JV, take it slow, to get it down."

Once the drill began, the boys, in their turn, moved up the court, making sharp passes in most cases, showing their hands as they moved to the ball, maintaining a symmetry that was aesthetically balanced, though Ben didn't care to notice it. He was trained on the players' shoulders, seeing whether they were slumping, an indication of fatigue, or wide and square, an indication that they were still pushing themselves. He also noted the angle of their cuts: sharp lines toward the ball, or lazy curvatures. A sharp cut was effective, enabling the receiver to meet the ball. A rounded cut would be ineffective in a game, when a strong defensive player would step into the passing lane and take away the pass.

Ben kept the pace of practice at near-full-tilt for about an hour and a half. Twice he slowed it down to shoot foul shots, but just ten at a time per player, and then it was back to full-court work. With half an hour to go, Ben outlined a simple fast break offense, against no defense for demonstration purposes. This was always the moment when he showed his hand to the players, when he called for five players to come out to demonstrate the drill, knowing that he was showing the players what he considered to be his first team. "Let's have Jason, James, Jonas, Andrew, and Geoff out here. Three Js, another J-sound, and Andrew." He always tried to soften the blow of naming a first team with a little lame humor The five came out humbly, happy for the coach's endorsement, but unwilling to look back at their teammates that had been left behind.

Outlining a break pattern with proper spacing and good angles at the backboard for layups, Ben ran them through four up-and-downs, and then called on five more to run the same pattern. The next five ran the break almost as explosively, Ben was pleased to note. Ben kept bringing the first team back onto the floor to run through the fast break, alternating a second and third team in, giving all the players at least four long sets of trips up and down the floor. The cohesion dropped off noticeably as the second-tier players ran the lanes, but Ben didn't comment on their lack of grace; rather, he shouted, "Let's keep up the pace, guys. I want these shots going up at game speed. Push yourselves." Ben would rather the players gain in conditioning than in shooting percentage this first day.

The last twenty minutes of practice entailed these two teams running the break against each other, with a fifteen second shot clock ensuring that the pace would be constant. Ben worked all the candidates for the team into the drill, and, as he did so, the fluency broke down quickly. The fast break games were played to a four-minute clock, at the completion of which a different collection of players took the court, to run the same fifteen-second breaks for four minutes.

At the end, he called the team to the baseline. "OK, guys, we're going to run 10 in a minute. Let's get all the perimeter players on the line."

He could hear the anxious groans from his players. Most of them hated the cold-truth of 10 in a minute: a sprint to the other end of the court and back, five times. 10 in a minute. Ben strolled stiffly to the clock console, placing 1:00 on the clock face.

"Everybody ready? Touch all the lines." Ben moved toward the group that was set to run, to give them a little more preparation time. "Men, listen for a minute. I know most of you will complete this sprint within a minute, and some of you won't. But I want to tell you what I think is important about this drill.

"You need to touch the line every time you turn. Try to touch with just your lead foot. Try to make a quick push-off, sending you back to the center of the court. The faster you can change direction, the better you can be on defense. And the reason to run to the line and touch it is the fact that when you try to take a charge on the baseline or the sideline, you can't give the ball handler a little alley to push the ball through. We'll be a good defensive team if we can get to the line quickly and not take shortcuts. Running these lines will prepare you to set your feet on the sideline defensively.

"So let's get to the line in every case. If someone is not getting to the line, I'm going to call him out, and he'll run again. Let's go."

Ben walked back to the clock console, whistle in his mouth, the old shoelace he used as a cord hanging from around his neck, suspended from the whistle. Blowing his whistle, he started the clock.

The boys raced the first sprint, Bobbie Pitaro and Alexander White in the lead, Dan Owings and Pete Semineau at the back of the pack. Ben shouted, "Let's go, knees high. James, chase down Alex. Don't let him get away from you. Archie, let's go after it. You can do it."

Most of the players looked exhausted, but they still pushed the pace, glancing at the clock to measure their progress. When there were twelve seconds left, time for one more down-and-back, only three of the twelve players were on pace, but most of the boys broke into a complete sprint. When the buzzer sounded, only two boys had not crossed the finish line. "Pete and Paul, come again with a 6 in 36, but let's have the big guys run first."

Only one of the big guys, Mark Payne, came in slower than a minute, and when Pete Semineau, Paul Ramsey, and Mark Payne had all completed their shorter extra sprint, Ben called the players in to the center circle.

"Great first practice. We're a long way from being a great team, but there are a lot of good signs here. We shot well, we are in pretty good shape, well ahead of many teams I've had. Congratulations for being prepared for our season, men. You should feel proud of yourselves.

"Today, we have finished our first practice. I'll make my decisions on who's making the team and who won't at the end of Thursday. We have a scrimmage against Wayland on Saturday. So we have to put some half-court offense in over these next three days, while I'm making decisions about who makes the team.

The loud breathing of the team around Ben diminished as the players' heart rate slowed. Some of the boys dragged the toes of their sneakers across the painted flooring in the center of the gym, too spent to stand still. Most of them looked down. Only Geoff Willis, the team's captain, and Andrew Monaghan, likely to be the team's leading scorer, looked up at the coach.

"This practice serves as our benchmark. Let's assume that today's work will strengthen our legs and lungs for tomorrow's workout, so we can run a little faster tomorrow, so that we can pass a little more sharply tomorrow.

"Geoff, do you have anything for us?" Ben asked his captain.

"Coach, I just want to say something in the locker room after practice. Nothing right now."

"OK, then we're all set. Guys, let's get your hands in here. At the end of each practice, at the end of a timeout in a game, after a game, we call 'Tight,' for two reasons. First, we want to tell each other – and anyone else who's listening – that we're a *tight* bunch of guys, that we will hang together for the season and nothing can split us up. But secondly, in our defensive drills, you'll see that when the player you're guarding picks up his dribble, we want to call "tight" to let our teammates know that they no longer have to provide help defense, and that they can go to full denial on their men. If we can get five turnovers by forcing our opponent to make a bad pass after picking up his dribble, those extra possessions may be the difference in the game.

"So on three . . .. One, Two, Three, 'Tight.'"

A few minutes later, Ben met Bryan Taft, his JV coach, in the coach's tiny locker room. Bryan's team had practiced in the small gym at 5:00 also. Bryan was dressed in black sweats, his sneakers a pair of Nike mid-ankle cuts. The cinder blocks of the room were bare gray; lockers huddled together on two walls. There were no other decorations. The football coaches had left a muddy floor that the custodians had tried to clean, but not much else. "How'd it go?" Ben asked Bryan.

"We got a good team, I'm not kidding – you know, the usual weakness with the left hand, and no one's shooting all that well, but you can't believe the way they run the floor. It's unbelievable. I mean, as freshmen they were good last year, what, nine and seven? This is a good squad."

"Anyone that would help me? What about Kenney? How about Willis's younger brother? Any great shooters?"

Bryan thought quickly. "Not really. I mean, I'll keep an eye on them. If anyone starts dominating, I'll let you know."

As the two coaches discussed the personnel, they changed from their coaching sweats to their teaching clothes, ready to go home. The small room was empty except for these two. The freshman team had already practiced in the small gym prior to Bryan's practice with his junior varsity candidates.

"Hey, would you mind giving me a ride home?" asked Bryan. "My car is getting worked on, down at Turner's, and I got a ride to school from Tracy."

Ben was surprised. "Sorry, I didn't know that. Of course, no problem. Is your car going to be ready tonight, now?"

"Probably not. It's a transmission thing. Might take a few days. He's looking it over today. He didn't call during the day, but maybe there's a call on my cell now. I'll check."

The two coaches slammed their lockers shut, put on their lined coats, and shoved the outside door open, entering the chill night air of late November. Ben yanked on a pair of leather-palmed woolen gloves. The warmth of the gym and locker room rapidly dissipated in the starry chill. There was no snow on the ground, but the ground sparkled with a frost in the exterior lights of the school. They walked through their vapor to the parking lot in front of the building, Ben with a canvas book bag slung over his shoulder, Bryan with no bag.

"No work tonight?" asked Ben.

"Nah, I finished it after school," Bryan replied. "I'm in a good place with my correcting. No big assignments coming in until the end of the week, too. I'm prepared for the season."

"I wish I could have your discipline. I'm always swamped."

As they turned out of the parking lot, Bryan asked Ben, "Would you mind taking me to Willow's? I'll just grab a bite there."

"No problem." Ben knew that Bryan was divorced, but he had never visited Bryan in his new apartment, which he had moved into in August. Bryan lived hand-to-mouth, spreading his paycheck out to last two weeks, but no longer. He dressed very nicely, fashionably, in a homespun way. Lots of cotton fibers. His pants were never pressed, but never dirty. Ben pictured Bryan on an elevator in his apartment, a basket of clothes in one hand, an iPod in the other, late at night, heading down to the basement laundry. This was all conjecture, of course, because Ben didn't even know if Bryan lived in an apartment complex or in a subdivided house.

"Is your apartment in a complex, or in a part of a house?" Ben asked.

"It's in a complex. Not very big, just a studio, in fact. It's all I need," Bryan answered. "It's not the greatest, but I'm not there all the time either."

Willow's, where they were heading, was a tavern just over the town line, in Natick, with more than one big-screen TV for sports viewing. Ben had watched some NCAA games there with Willa over the years. The patrons and the bartenders seemed to know each other very well. It was just a few miles from the school. "How you gonna get home after you eat?" asked Ben.

"Ah, someone'll give me a ride home. I got lots of friends," Bryan said summarily. It seemed he didn't want Ben to worry about him at all.

In the parking lot, Ben eased his car into a slot and said, "I'll come in for a quick one. Just one. We can plan for the week a little."

They slammed the doors of the Corolla, walking carefully over the slippery surface of the parking lot, well lit by two high-intensity, crime-preventing floodlights. Inside, the air was warm as flannel, steaming up Bryan's glasses. They slid their butts over two stools at the bar.

"Sam's."

"Corona."

The bartender pulled on the knob for the Sam's while reaching into the floor refrigerator for the Corona. "You done with your first practice?" he asked Bryan.

"Yeah, it was a good day. Smooth."

"How the team gonna be?"

"Pretty good. First game is with Natick, your home town. Look out," Bryan replied, swallowing the foam and top one-third of his beer. On TV Maryland was paired with Michigan in an early season ACC-Big Ten matchup. Bryan turned to the game, eased himself forward onto the bar with his elbows, and assumed a comfortable and familiar posture. Ben settled himself too, though with less familiarity.

The bar seemed old: the wood of the bar was dark, marred with imperfections of bottles being banged, comestibles being delivered, and rings being knocked against the forgiving wood. Behind the bartenders, transparent and amber bottles stood against a mirror that reflected the darkness behind them. Above the bar next to the TV was a clock, in blue neon: 7:40. Ben knew he needed to call Willa if he was planning on staying for anything more than one beer. But he was staying only for one, so he didn't pull out his cell.

As Maryland's 2-guard attacked Michigan's zone trap, Bryan checked his own cell phone, looking for a message from the mechanic who was working on his car. Hunched over the bar, he checked a series of messages, replying to none of them, deleting more than one only partway into the message. As he sipped his Corona silently, Ben, in the mirror, saw an athletically trim, young woman sit down at one of the tall tables. She wore a maroon sweater with a bright orange scarf wrapped artfully around her neck. She looked at the basketball game on TV. Bryan finished his beer and ordered another by pushing his glass to the inside rim of the bar. The bartender came back with another beer quickly.

51

Ben and Bryan talked cursorily about the team, about the conditioning of Ben's players. "Archie Stedham, the new kid, looked pretty good. He's gonna help. He can handle," Ben assured Bryan. "He'll make us deeper."

"That's great. You can never have too many guards. How big is he, 5'11"?"

"I'd say that's right. He gets off the ground a little. Might be a good rebounder because of his jumping ability. He seems like a well-focused kid. I like him."

"Now, don't start believing in something that isn't there," Bryan warned, knowing Ben's tendency to see great value in players who were not always blessed with commensurate talent.

"I know. I know. I'm not saying he's a stud. He's just a good kid who will contribute."

Just then, Ben saw a long-fingered hand slide on Bryan's right shoulder, the shoulder away from Ben. Ben looked behind Bryan to see the orange scarf of the girl who had been sitting behind them alone at the circular table. Bryan turned away from Ben to acknowledge the girl. "Ben, I'd like you to meet Lisa. Lisa, this is my friend Ben. We coach together."

Lisa leaned between Bryan and Ben. "Nice to meet you. I've heard about you from Bry. Have a good first day?"

Ben looked at Bryan to see who she was talking to.

"She's talking to you, big guy. How'd it go?"

Ben looked back at the woman. "It was fun to be back in the gym. We had a great first day." As he talked, he looked more carefully at the young lady. She had a chin that jutted forward boldly and a mouth that glistened promisingly. Her eyes were dark and clear. Turning back to his beer so he didn't appear to be staring, Ben took a short sip.

Bryan filled the awkward silence. "We both had practice at the same time, so I didn't get to see his guys. He's got a wagon. Championship season. Think you might come to a few games?"

Lisa smiled at Bryan, punching him lightly in the shoulder of the heavy fleece that he still wore, in spite of the comforting heat of the bar. "I'll make a game if I have the time. I'm a busy girl, you know. Hey, are you in a hurry? Why don't you take your coat off and enjoy the comforts of this place?" she asked Bryan. She reached around him with both arms to unzip the jacket.

When the girl took Bryan's jacket to an empty chair at her table, Ben knew it was time to leave. Draining most of the remainder of his beer, he turned to Bryan. " I gotta shove off. I wish I could stay for more, but I have a date."

Bryan let out a low moan. "Woah. I don't want to get in the way of a date. You sure you're goin home?" Ben and Bryan moved to the girl's table and Bryan slid into a chair next to Lisa. "Tell Willa hello for me. See ya tomorrow."

Ben turned to Lisa. "Nice to meet you. Maybe I'll see you at a game some time."

Lisa smiled brightly. "I don't live nearby, but you never know. It's great to meet you. I'll try to keep this guy on the straight and narrow."

"I can see it's a full time occupation. But someone's gotta do it," Ben parried.

"Oh, yeah. You get some fringe benefits, but it's a lot of work," Lisa said as Ben eased toward the exit door. He reached over the table, reaching for Lisa's hand. She gave him a firm handshake, fingers wiry and palm coarse. She looked directly at him. "Bye."

Out the door Ben felt his hand tingling – from what, he wasn't sure. He also felt his face crinkling in the cold air outside, after the warmth of Willow's. In a way he could see the attraction of a place like that: a couple cold beers, sports on TV, an attractive, athletic-looking girl at the next table. Though he had felt sympathy for Bryan when he had lost his marriage, he felt a sense of renewal for him in the radiant warmth of the tavern and the sure hand of the woman.

In twenty-five minutes, Ben opened the door of his home, entering the kitchen, lit dimly by the light over the stove. He pushed his keys into the front pocket of his pants, crossed the empty kitchen, hung his coat up in the hall closet, storing his hat on the shelf above the hanging coats, and called to his family. "Hey, how's everybody doing?"

In the living room, Willa sat at the corner of the couch, the phone in her left hand. She raised her right hand to quiet Ben as she listened intently to the person on the line. She concentrated on the words of the speaker, her brow furrowed. Ben didn't think she was hearing good news, but he knew she'd fill him in.

"Hey, kids, how was your day?" Ben shouted as he turned toward the stairs. Mary called from her room, "Great, Dad." She was polite.

"Scott, how'd it go?" Ben called. There was no answer. Ben looked over his shoulder at Willa, but she was huddled again, her shoulder turned to him, as she listened on the phone, occasionally inserting a short comment. Ben jumped up the stairs, then turned to

Scott's room, only to find it empty and dark. At 8:30 at night that was unusual. He turned into Mary's room. "Where's Scott?" he asked her.

"I don't know. He was home earlier; then he left. I think Mom might be on the phone with him." She was hunched over her homework, sitting on her bed, a pen in her left hand, a book spread open in front of her, a well-doodled notebook open on the bed next to the book. On the bed was a patterned plate holding a remnant of a grilled cheese sandwich. Her cell phone was close by her left knee on the bed.

"I'll go down to see what's up. You got a lot of homework?" asked Ben.

"Yeah, I got slammed. First day after Thanksgiving break. All you teachers are the same. 'Only four weeks to Christmas. We have to accelerate the pace a little.' They all think we don't have a life or something.

"Did you assign a lot of stuff today?"

Ben thought. "No, not really. I'm old enough to know that we can let a few things slide and no one gets hurt. I've cut out a few things here and there, and it makes the students happier and it makes me happier. Everyone's a winner." Ben leaned over Mary, collecting her long hair in his right hand and then kissing the collected hair. "Love you, honey. I'll be back up."

When he came down the stairs, Willa was just hanging up the phone. She looked wiped out. "That was Perry Street's father. Scott was supposed to be over at Perry's house to do some project, and then the two of them went out of the house, God knows where. I mean they don't have a license, they can't drive anywhere, but they were gone for more than an hour, in the dark.

"They're back now, but they don't have any explanation for what they were doing. I talked to Mr. Street and to Scott, and I got nowhere. I'm going to go get him now and we can have a little talk."

"Sweetheart, I'll go. You're tired. I haven't seen Scott all day, and we'll have a chance to talk on the way home. Can you remind me what street the Streets live on?"

"It's over near Bryant Park. At the park, take a left on Endover. He's the fifth house on the right. I don't know the number. I'll look it up in the phone book."

"Is he expecting one of us?"

"He sure is. He knows he has some questions to answer. I mean what do you think they were doing? Smoking pot? Cigarettes?"

"I don't know. We'll see." He looked at Willa. Her hair was hanging in front of her face as she looked at Ben. She still wore the navy sweater and pants that she had worn to work at Spingold's, the engineering office where she worked four days a week. She was well invested in the company and sometimes worked till seven in the evening. "When did you get home? How was work today?"

"Hectic. I rushed out of there at six-thirty, to get home to get supper for Mary and Scott, but when I got home, Mary had already made herself a grilled cheese and Scott had gotten a ride to Perry's. I just can't keep track of them anymore." She looked at him pleadingly, hoping for an answer that he could not provide. "I don't know if I should cut back more on my hours. Spingold's treats me well, and I love the work, but I can't stand not being there for Scott and Mary. They shouldn't have to make their own supper." Her disappointment resounded.

Ben agreed silently. He didn't know how to respond. "Well, tomorrow, I've got early practice, so I'll be home at 6:00 for sure. I'll make hamburg casserole for all of us." He hoped that his offer could provide a little relief for Willa.

She smiled wanly. "That's a nice offer, but I'll make a pot roast tonight and you can just put it in the oven when you get home with five potatoes." She shook her head. "I don't know. It all gets so crazy at Christmas time. I don't have any of my shopping done yet, we've got parties to go to, and the kids are starting to have very full weekends too. It's as if we're flying off into space, all in a different direction. I want us to be getting closer as a family, and we're getting farther apart." Willa's remarks made Ben think of the flying swings of an amusement park ride, the seats angling centrifugally into the perimeter surrounding the ride, hell-bent to fly away into space. But it was just their family she was talking about, not some metaphoric image.

Ben reached down to embrace Willa, but she remained curled up inside herself, unable to return his warmth. She kept her head, full of uncertainty, down.

"I'll get going. Fifth house on the right after taking a left at the park. Need anything at the store?"

"Actually, yes. I made out a small list of things for the store, but I never got a chance to go. It's tacked to the bulletin board. Can you stop at Shaw's and pick up just a few things?"

"Sure." Ben stood up, heading to the closet to put on his coat and hat again. "Do you have a Shaw's card nearby? I've never had one, and I know that we can get better prices with one of those cards." Putting his coat on, he waited as Willa stood and walked to the bottom step where she left her pocketbook. Inside the card-holder, she found the Shaw's card and carried it over to Ben. He went to take her in his arms, but she was already pulling away. He brushed her hair with his hand softly as he turned toward the door.

"I'll warm up your supper. I'll get it ready for 9:00. Don't take any detours. It's number 14," she said over her shoulder.

Ben nodded, turning out the door into the cold air again, the frost glistening off the body of Willa's Subaru. As he slid his hand into his woolen glove, he could still feel Willa's slack hair as it had whispered past his hand. The stars shone brightly, and the half-moon sat behind the skeletal trees behind his house.

Just a boy on a street corner as the evening fades
Empty book under his elbow so familiar it's strange
Just these tired fingers hell bent on letting go
So high from the singing as I make my way home

It's the story of the story
It's the still place behind my words
It's the look on his face that makes me think he heard
All these vanishing points I've learned

They said it'd be easy to find
Simple as a dot and two lines
If I held my straight edge I'd be fine
Failed to mention limits of the naked eye

It's the story of the story
It's the still place behind my words
It's the look on his face that makes me think he heard
All these vanishing points I've learned

Moving through this dark country
Thinking how would I know?
If the one that disappeared
Could've been standing so close?

It's the story of the story
It's the still place behind my words
It's the look on his face that makes me think he heard
All these vanishing points I've learned

Vanishing Points by Meg Hutchinson

James

Easing into his chair at his computer desk in his bedroom, James felt the familiar tightness in his thighs from the first day of practice. No matter how much he prepared for the workout, his body was never completely prepared. Two hours of non-stop activity was just more than he was accustomed to.

He looked at the inbox of his e-mail, seeing just three messages, two of which he could delete immediately: a promise of adding inches to his length and an announcement of improved home mortgage rates. Neither offer piqued his interest, though both were relevant to future long-range plans. The third message blinked at him, a message from Geoff Willis, the captain. The subject read: team unity.

Opening his message, James found that Geoff wanted the team to meet early at school again tomorrow, not in the gym this time, but in the cafeteria, to get coffee and hot chocolate, a team-building exercise. James loved the idea of team unity, but he didn't really see how drinking hot liquids with his teammates instilled team unity. He called Pete.

"Hey, 'sup?"

"Hey, man. How you doin?" Pete replied.

"Good. Muscles are a little tight, but I'm doing fine. Nice job, today, bro. You picked 'em up and put 'em down. Nice run."

"I gutted it out in the mile. Next to last fuckin time I run that thing. I did not want to have to do it again."

"You get a message from Geoff?"

"I didn't check messages yet. I'm just chillin. Watching Michigan. What's he sayin?"

"He wants us to come in early again tomorrow, meet in the caf. Have some coffee and doughnuts." James emitted a humph of displeasure.

Pete hesitated as he considered the idea. "Well, I got nothing against doughnuts and coffee. What time's he sayin?"

"7:00."

"Well, let's say I pick you up at 7. We'll get there at 7:15 or 7:20, time enough to appear in the caf, but not ungodly early. OK?"

"Ehh, OK. I'm not much for this team unity shit, but at least it gets us to school on time. See you at 7."

James hung up, and then held the phone in his hand for a minute, contemplating a call to Adrienne. As he thought about it, he looked at the picture of last year's team, a team that was a disappointment to himself and nearly everyone in the photo, finishing 9 and 11, losing their last two games to wind up missing the post-season by a game. He remembered clearly the final game, down two with less than a minute on the clock, the ball in his hands, against Wellesley. He had a clear lane to the basket, took the ball strong, got bumped, no call, and missed the shot. When the game was over, Coach LaMott, extending his arm around James's left shoulder, had said, "James, that was a good shot. You took the right shot. Next year that shot will go in, and we'll win the game. Don't be disappointed."

James had been disappointed that night and for the succeeding nine months, until this day. He had wanted to play in the state tournament, ever since he was nine, when he attended one regular season game and then three post-season games of the Panthers, watching Peter Kaplan and Pat McCarthy lead the team to two thrilling wins over Chatham and Avon. The stands were nearly full at these first two games, and then at the sectional semi-final game against Sacred Heart, at Braintree, the stands were completely full, probably over a thousand people watching, including James. Ever since that game James had wanted to play in a post-season game. Today had been Step One in getting to that point. Last year he and the team had fallen one basket short in their attempt.

He opened his history book to Chapter Nine, the Reconstruction Era. Beginning to read the double-columned first page of the chapter, he wondered whether Adrienne had gone out for basketball. He hadn't seen her in the gym as he came in for his practice, but he hadn't thought to look for her either, since he was thinking about his own practice. He felt his cell phone in the pocket of his jeans, the image of Adrienne sitting erect in her seat in Geometry class, regally, filling his mind. James fished the phone out of his pocket, scrolling down to her number, though he knew it without assistance. He poised the thumb over the call button, ready to give it a try, and pressed.

"Hello?" opened an unfamiliar voice, probably Adrienne's younger sister.

"Hello, is Adrienne there?" James asked simply.

"Yeah, just a minute." James could hear the phone dropped onto a table and the girl shout, "Aide!" James wondered why he hadn't called Adrienne's cell. What a stupid move – letting the whole family in on his call. But then he remembered he did not know Adrienne's cell number.

After close to a minute, Adrienne picked up the phone. "Hello?"

"Hi, Adrienne, this is James. How ya doing?"

"Not bad," she said, unprepared for his call.

"Hey, did you go out for basketball? I didn't see you in the gym, but I might have just missed you."

"Yeah, I did. I just couldn't stay away. It was a blast. I really missed it last year."

"How'd you do? Did you blow them away?"

"Well, let's just say there's a little rust. I ran up and down the floor fine, but I didn't distinguish myself as a ball handler. But, you know, it was great."

"Yeah, I agree. It's not just being the star, it's about being part of something good," Pete offered, not really believing himself. He didn't know whether Adrienne was able to set her ego aside in a way that he couldn't.

"Oh, yeah. I'm gonna have a blast out there. I don't even know if I'll play much, but I know I'll improve."

A short silence followed this last statement, as James wondered how to steer the conversation away from basketball to . . . what? What on earth was he doing? He didn't have a thing to say to Adrienne, though, in fact, he had hours of things to say to Adrienne, things like, did you know that I think about you when I wake up in the morning? did you know that I know where your locker is? did you know that I have pushed your number on my cell about a hundred times and this is the first time I've ever not negated the call? did you know that my dad thinks I'm not making much of myself?

Adrienne filled the silence. "How'd you do? You feel in shape?"

James nodded. "Yeah, sort of. I got a long way to go, but today is the first step." He wanted to tell her about a series of jumpers he had rained down on Alex White, but he didn't want to sound like a meathead. "I hit a few shots, a little better than last year, when I was just trying to make the team." James fingered the magnetized game schedule that was attached to his computer tower. Looking at the schedule, he reminded himself of the first game vs. Natick, a team that usually had a stronger player base than Casteline. "Do you have any scrimmages coming up?" he asked Adrienne. He knew that there would be a scrimmage on Saturday for the boys.

"I don't really know. I didn't get all the pre-season literature. But I think I heard the girls talking about something next Saturday."

James nodded, knowing that his gesture went unnoticed across the span of space, but not knowing how to continue the conversation. He'd like to tell Adrienne that these phone conversations were a first step toward a relationship he would love to foster. But he also knew that tonight was a little early to offer such prophecies. He had little experience in drawing close to a girl that he dreamed about.

Adrienne surprised him with her next comment. "Hey, you're kinda quiet, aren't you?"

James wanted to nod again, and indeed he did, but he knew he needed to make some noise. "Yeah, I really don't have a lot to say. I like to stay behind the scenes a little bit. Sorry, because it makes things a little awkward, I know.

"I'll get used to it. I'll get warmed up. After a few weeks, you'll have to shut me up," he said, knowing that his reference to a few weeks was presumptuous on his part, but he felt he had to take the chance.

Adrienne called him on his presumption. "Oh, we're going to be talking for a few weeks?" Her voice was tinted with mockery.

"Well, you never know. I'll have to check in with you on math homework from time to time. And then we have to check on our progress on the basketball teams, too." James leaned back in his computer chair, searching in his head for another source of chitchat. "Then, maybe we'll need to talk about weekend plans or something." He was taking a chance now. His eyes had been closed for the entire conversation, since he had glanced at his game schedule. In this comfortable state, he could picture her with baggy sweats on, her hair propped up on her head in a stylish mess. He could see her long fingers playing with the computer mouse as she kept up with her internet connection even while she talked with him.

"Oh, I don't know about weekend plans. I'm kind of a home body. Weekends are not a big social thing for me. I'm usually off playing lacrosse somewhere." She let this pronouncement sit, untended.

James knew she had provided an opening for him. "Well, I don't know if you think going to a movie is a big social thing, but maybe we could do that some time."

"Sounds like a plan. I'm the quiet type, too, if you hadn't noticed. And we can both be quiet at a movie. That sounds like a perfect place for us." She laughed lightly, and he joined her. She made things sound so easy.

"Well, I gotta go," James said, wanting to let this idea of a movie-date linger in both their minds.

"Me too. Thanks for calling. See you tomorrow."

"Bye."
"Bye."

The next few days were busy. As the teachers at Casteline approached the Christmas break, they always loaded the work on, knowing that there were only three weeks left in the second term when they returned from New Year's. James spent his time in study hall completing his Spanish homework and reading *Gatsby*. He was supposed to take notes, but he found himself with an empty notebook at the completion of his reading assignments. However, he loved the concept of Jay Gatsby emerging from the person of James Gatz, the idea that something new can be born out of something old, a metamorphosis. He hadn't finished the book yet, to see what came of Gatsby's self-creation, but James loved Gatsby's initiative. He would like to have that same boldness.

Practices went very well. James was shooting well, and he felt in pretty good shape, until Coach LaMott called him aside on Thursday. The team was shooting free throws, ten apiece, spread out at all six baskets.

"James, how you feeling?" Coach LaMott asked.

"Pretty good, Coach. I'm improving my wind every day. I haven't felt the sprints as much this year. I think I'm in better shape." James stretched his neck as he talked to Coach LaMott. They were now about the same height, about 6'1", though James was very slender. As James talked about his improved conditioning, he remembered clearly the difficulty he had had this year completing the mile in an impressive time. He wondered whether he was just forgetting how hard he had run in sprints last year.

"Well, just make sure you're working your hardest every minute you're in the gym. We've got less than two weeks before our first game. And we've got a lot of details to cover between now and then." Coach seemed to want to say more, but he didn't. He just pulled his black plastic whistle back and forth across in front of his Panthers sweatshirt, swinging it like a pendulum along the shoestring that he used as a lanyard.

The coach turned away from James then, heading to another basket to talk to Dan Owings and Robert Carnechie. James wondered what their conversation had been about. He didn't think he was working at less than full-speed, but he got the idea that the coach doubted him in some way. He turned to Pete, shrugged his shoulders and tilted his head to the right side. "Guess he thinks I'm doggin it a little," he said to Pete's questioning gaze.

Fifteen minutes later, when the team started scrimmaging, James made his greatest effort to be the first one down the floor in both directions. He caught more than one pass ahead of the pack for an easy layin, off Jason's lead pass. And he sprinted as hard as he could to avoid the defensive imbalance that was disastrous. For at least four minutes he was the fastest man on the floor. The scrimmage was scored to eleven points, and as his team, the first team, approached the end of the game, he felt further invigorated, competing for the win. In Coach LaMott's practices, the losers ran.

James's team won the first scrimmage, 11 – 7. Coach LaMott changed up the teams, putting James with three second teamers and Paul Ramsey, a player who would probably not make the team. James hit a shot, but the other team made a 3 (which counted for 2) and a steal and layin, to take a 3 – 1 lead. James tried to move without the ball, but Jonas and Geoff switched out onto him as he came around screens, so he was unable to get the ball. When Bobbie missed a shot, the other team went down for a layup, and James made it to halfcourt before turning around.

By the time the second scrimmage was done, James's legs were starting to feel hollow. He lost 11 – 4, meaning he and his teammates had to run 7 down-and-backs for the score margin.

After foul shots, James went out again for another scrimmage, this time with more first-team players. He and Jonas Boynton teamed up for a solid pick-and-roll, and James fed off to Mark Payne for an easy hoop. James tried for a half-court steal on the way back downcourt, but missed it. The other team scored.

At 10 – 9, James fed Jason for an open jumper, but he missed. The other team gathered the rebound, outletted, sending Alex White in for an easy shot. Alex stopped at the 3 point line, taking a jumpshot in transition, and made it, sending James's team to another defeat, 11 – 10. James felt a wave of disgust move across his shoulders. He shouldn't be losing to the second teamers. He was better than that. How the hell did Alex White, who couldn't hit five out of ten foul shots, pull up to hit a game-winner in a scrimmage?

James ran – actually, he jogged, because he was pissed – his one down-and-back, along with his teammates. He kept his head down, not daring to look at his fellow runners. None of them liked to run, and these sprints were just reminders of their weakness.

Coach called everyone together. "Just a few more quick scrimmages. I'm trying to see who will push himself to win. If you find yourself running after these games to eleven, then put more into it when you play. The ball is in your hands. Who are the winners here?"

James knew the coach was trying to cultivate the habit of winning, but he seemed to miss the point that, when someone won, then someone lost. Why did he want half his team to feel like losers?

Fourth scrimmage (these were just five- or seven-minute games, the time depending on the accuracy of the shooting), James joined two starters, playing against two starters on the other team. James's matchup was Archie Stedham, the new kid who had moved in. James had paid attention to Archie in these four days. Archie had a good handle, and he seemed to be able to get past people to make some plays. James made a note to himself to shut Archie down.

On the second defensive play, James got picked off without the ball, giving Archie a back-door layup. "Hey, Willis, let me know, will you?" James shouted, as they headed down the floor on offense.

"I called 'back-screen,' you just didn't get around it," Geoff shouted back.

The next time Archie set up at the 3 point line. James hadn't seen Archie shoot threes very accurately in drills, so he didn't put good pressure on Archie.

Archie shot and turned to the backcourt before the ball had approached the rim. James was fuming. No newcomer should show such arrogance, James felt.

At the other end of the court, James came off the screen pretty clean, caught the ball and shot in one motion. But Pete came from the weakside to block his shot, leading to a fastbreak the other way.

Back and forth. James scored a lefty putback; Archie beat a double-team to feed Andrew Monaghan for an easy, uncontested twelve footer.

The game ended 11 – 8, James's team losing, meaning three more down-and-backs for James. He trotted his way through them.

Coach LaMott noticed the lack of energy. Raising his arms toward the ceiling lights, he bellowed, "Let's take those sprints again. And this time, let's run. There's no room in this gym for half-effort. If you can't run, you shouldn't be here," he spat, his lips in an angry line, straight as the edge of the backboard. He didn't look at any one particular player, but James could feel Coach's eyes on him as he started running hard. Two and a half sprints to go. This was Thursday. There were still five or six practices before the first game, and the season was already starting to get old.

Coming out of the locker room, Pete hustled to get to his car. He seemed excited about something. James had to hurry to catch up to him.

"Hey, man, what's the hurry? You got a date?"

Pete did not slow down. "No, but I want to hustle home to catch UFC. I love that show."

James did not share Pete's love for licensed assault that was named the Ultimate Fighting Championship, but, needing a ride home, he continued chasing Pete. "Well, shit, do you have time to drop me off at home, or do I need to call my mom?"

Pete distractedly waved his arm in an inclusive fashion as he opened the door to the Audi.

Inside, James let out a long sigh. "Well, that was a bitch of a practice. What's with LaMott? He had the rag on today."

Pete looked bemusedly at James. "He did? I thought he was just being his usual prick. I didn't notice anything different." He backed the car out of his parking space and slid the gear into drive. The Audi accelerated smoothly toward the exit of the parking lot.

"But he was on my case, all day long. It's like he has it out for me. It's like he's happy when I fuck up."

"Dude, like when I blocked you from behind? That was fuckin awesome. You didn't fuck up. I just made a sick play." Pete's face beamed in the oncoming headlights.

James sat silently. If he stepped back from his self-pity, he could recognize Pete's play. But he wanted to sit in his misery. He had been anticipating this season, the season of gaining control of his game and of the team for too long. He hadn't factored any criticism from Coach LaMott into his vision of the season. Didn't Coach LaMott know how much he wanted from this season? How could Coach undercut him so mercilessly?

Pete noted James's silence. "You OK?"

James didn't know what to say. He was pissed, but he didn't want to be a whiner. "Eh, I'll get over it. Just a bad day, I guess." But that's not how he felt. He felt the coach had shifted his allegiance to some of the other guys, Archie Stedham especially. James shook his head in the darkness of Pete's Audi. What a comedown it would be if a new kid from the boonies of the state beat him out of a starting position.

Pete sang softly to the beatbox tune on his iPod/radio. He was satisfied: he had made the team, and he knew he didn't figure dearly into Coach's plans. But for James it was different. Coach had told him he was counting on him; then he ripped him in practice. James couldn't figure it out. Either the coach was with him or he was against him, and it seemed the latter had been ratified today.

As James got out at his house, Pete crooned, "Everybody's workin for the weekend," a refrain from an old 80s tune that he liked. It was Pete's reminder that the week could fade quickly in the haze of the weekend, if they chose.

James thought that Pete had sworn off the indulgences that sustained him. "Dude, didn't you turn your back on the weed?"

"Oh, that was at the beginning of the week. We're getting close to the weekend, and I've been on the straight and narrow all week long. Time to let loose!" Pete grinned fully at James.

James tilted his head toward his shoulder to let Pete know he wasn't in total agreement with his approach to the weekend, now that they were engaged in the basketball season. He'd have to figure it out for himself.

Supper was quiet. Mr. Rush asked James how the team was proceeding, as usual. James said, "We've got some good depth this year. I think we'll be able to substitute a lot, and not get hurt. I don't think anyone's gonna have to go more than twenty-five minutes."

"But how're you doing? Shooting it OK?"

"Pretty good. Not my best yet, but it's getting there. We've still got a long ways to go. Andrew is playing at the top of his game already, and we have to catch up to him."

"Well, don't let any opportunities slip by. If you can beat someone, beat them. Coach wants a guy out there that isn't afraid to take the big shots. If you can step it up, you'll guarantee your spot on the team.

"And you've gotta play the D. If you can shut someone down, Coach will love you. I know what he likes. I've been going to the games for ten years now, when you were still playing cops and robbers. He wants someone that loves to compete. And you've just got to challenge your opponent every day, every minute." Mr. Rush raised his fork in the air as if it were a symphony director's stick, pointing it at James.

James could feel that point pushing at his heart.

"Arthur, can you let up just a little?" James's mother said. "I mean, it's just a game. If James is doing his best, that's all anyone can ask for." Mrs. Rush pushed her eyebrows down over her eyes with concern for her boy.

"Louise, we can't baby him his whole life. He's got to start stepping up and taking charge."

James had heard his parents on these two parallel tracks before. His mother wanted things to work out comfortably; his father wanted things to work out victoriously.

"But, Arthur, he's just sixteen years old. We don't want to blot out the love of the sport. Honey, do you still love the game as much as always?"

That was a good question. At the moment, he certainly did not. In fact, at this moment, he could see the season as a long tunnel filled with anguish and potential disappointment. But he couldn't tell his parents his feelings. "Yeah, Mom, I do. But I know it's not always a smooth ride."

James was smart enough to resent the fact that when he was pushed to express himself, he always resorted to the platitudes that he had heard his whole life: "smooth ride" . . . "push yourself to the limit" . . . "it's not always easy." He wished he could give his mother a more truthful and original answer, but he didn't have the vocabulary (or the knowledge of his feelings) to be as truthful as he could be.

In his room after supper, James pulled his books out of his bookbag. He had a quiz in Chemistry second period the next day for which he half-heartedly studied for more than a half hour. After realizing that none of his exploration of the principles of valence were sinking in, he closed his book and lay down on his bed. His iTunes played soft Kanye as he closed his eyes. After ten minutes of aimless mind-rest, he stood up and approached the picture of last year's team that sat on a shelf over his desk. He looked at himself in the photo, standing as assertively as he could, a smile of satisfaction on his face. He looked also at Coach LaMott, standing at the same end of the team, his eyes seeming to shine, his chin thrust forward, evidence of the passion that burned in him for this team. James wondered if he would be burning with that same passion at the end of the season.

The Arc of Intersection

No matter which way the wind blows
It's always cold when you're alone
Ain't no candle in the window
You've got to find your own way home
The rain ain't gonna hurt you
It's come to wash away your blues
It's all up to you

No one said it would be easy
But it don't have to be this hard
If you're lookin' for a reason
Just stand right where you are
Now there ain't no one out to get you
They've got to walk in their own shoes

It's all up to you
No one else can get you through
Right or wrong, win or lose
It's all up to you

You can stand out on that highway
Look as far as you can see
But when you get to that horizon
There's always someplace else to be
But don't you stop to look behind you
'Cause you've got some travelin' left to do
It's all up to you

It's All Up To You by Steve Earl

Ben

On Friday after practice the teams went bowling – Freshman team, JVs, and Varsity, all together. Thirteen boys had made the varsity team. Ben had cut two players (Robert Carnechie one of them, a good football player who had surprised Ben with the limits of his coordination) and told Paul Ramsey that he would make the team, but that he was at the #14 spot (at the moment). Paul, a junior, decided he would spend his winter in the batting cage in Natick (he had been all-Commonwealth League as a sophomore second-baseman). Ben arranged this social get-together to try to bring the three teams together in some sort of unity. He knew the freshmen were excited about the possibility of playing alongside a varsity player; he just had to be sure that the varsity players didn't act dismissive with the young guys.

A total of 33 players and managers and coaches were at Kent's Bowl at 7:15 in Dedham, by which time Ben had set up eight teams. He sat out to allow an even number of players to play on each team. As the boys began their first string, Ben kept an eye on his varsity players, to ensure that they graciously teamed with the younger players. He also thought about the first week of practice.

Monaghan, Rush, and Willis had clearly stood out from their peers, being in good shape, playing hard, and playing effectively. These three were clearly ahead of the rest. He had played Rush with some weaker players, to see if James could raise the level of their play, but he wasn't assertive enough yet to accomplish that sort of transcendence. However, James had more range and accuracy on his shot this year than last, and he seemed to be headed in a positive direction. Ben always feared the decline of players under his tutelage: as they grew up, they could – and did – find ways to amuse themselves that did not include basketball. It was a sad fact of adolescence: as the months went by, it became increasingly difficult for a young boy to stay focused on whatever he had decided mattered.

Ben knew that it was his job to persuade his players to remain excited about an activity that would provide them great satisfaction, valuable integration of skills with others', and a way to learn how to deal with adversity. For Ben, sports had been the area where he learned the most about his limitations, and how to overcome them. He deeply wanted his players to make those same discoveries about themselves.

Yet, there was this other influence, this opening up to the greater world, good and bad, that often overshadowed the lessons he was trying to instill. Despite being an English teacher, Ben thought of the two influences as the two circles of a Venn Diagram, the intersection illustrating the player's being pulled in two ways. And Ben realized that his influence was only one of many in these boys' lives. In fact, there were probably six or eight circles vying for control of these guys' consciousness, minimizing the likelihood that his influence would be paramount.

Yet, the shouts of exultation from strikes and spares and the razzing that accompanied gutter balls filled the half of Kent's that the team occupied. For an hour or so, the boys played like little children, aiming at the candlepins with absolute determination, rolling the ball accurately and inaccurately like any child trying something that he isn't very skilled at, yet learning from his errors, to improve his roll the next time. Ben watched one of the freshmen, Josh Perkins, a tall boy whom he expected to become a very good player. When Josh came back to his team after rolling a 1 and two gutter balls, Ben could see the sheepishness on Josh's face. He couldn't walk directly back to the seats; he looked down at the floor of the next alley, chagrined by his lack of skill. It was these lessons that Ben found so valuable: how to deal with defeat. If Josh was the player Ben thought he was, then Josh would watch the better bowlers' technique, mimic it, and throw a better ball next time up. But if Josh was eaten up with his discomfort, he would keep his eyes down as others bowled and make no gains in his own technique.

Ben watched Josh sit down, and saw him keep his head down as his teammate grabbed a ball and began his approach to the penalty line. Standing, Ben approached Josh.

"Hey, Josh, you've got a nice delivery. Let's get a few more pins next time. Every pin counts, buddy."

Josh looked up quickly, upon hearing the coach's voice. It was not surprising how much a word from Ben resonated in the ears of the young players.

"Yeah, 'd'you see me? I'm pretty bad."

"Well, that was last time. Next time you'll be good." Ben patted Josh on the shoulder, trying to offer reassurance. Ben knew that he needed to provide more encouragement all the time, but as the years had passed, he had felt that, at times, he would try to build someone up that was no longer interested in being built up. At times Ben felt a player had, instead, moved on to other pursuits, though he still ran up and down the court smoothly and efficiently. It was as if the former player had left a contrail on the court that lasted the entire season, but he was not really there.

Josh looked away from Ben with embarrassment, wondering, no doubt, why Ben had singled him out from the others. He watched his teammates with great intent.

When the first string ended and the pizzas had been delivered, the team moved into a small room where Geoff and Andrew poured drinks for the guys. These were good leaders. They did not ask for any favors from Coach LaMott; in fact, they had learned that it was their duty to clean up the gym after practice and, with a little prodding from Ben, they had also taken on the responsibility of a clean locker room after showers. Ben was very proud of these two young men, boys who had evolved quite distinctly as players, one gaining great ball skills and the other maximizing his strength and conditioning. However, more importantly, they epitomized the way a player and young man should behave on the court and off. Ben knew his team was fortunate to have such leadership.

Ben entered the room and grabbed a full bottle of Sprite. "Hey, guys, thanks for helping set up in here."

"No problem, Coach," replied Geoff. "The kids are having fun. Hey, did you see Jason roll two consecutive strikes?"

Ben said, "I really didn't, but I heard some loud shots from Lane 5. Is that where he was rolling?"

Andrew replied, "Yeah, that was Jason. He got a 112 overall. Did anyone else break a hundred?"

"No, I got all the scores reported to me. Next best was Eric Johnson with a 96. Sophomore. You guys know him?"

"Yeah, sure, skinny little forward?" said Geoff.

"Yeah, that's right. He can rebound for a skinny guy. Gets off the ground. Thanks again for helping out here."

"It's nothing, Coach," said Andrew.

Saturday morning Ben posted the photo of Jason Grutchfield, with the high string of 112 and the high total of 207 on the bulletin board in the locker room. He also posted the names of the winning team: Alex White; Jason Grutchfield; Paul Hackett, a JV; and Bill Carey, a freshman. It was Ben's intention to make the locker room a place where these boys felt comfortable, where they could hang around, shoot the shit. He knew it all depended on the attitude of his leaders and he thought Geoff and Andrew could and would cultivate strong camaraderie within this team. But they could do only so much. It took the effort and interest of all the players to develop a team. He thought back to one of his first teams, a team that went to the state finals, only to lose to a superior team from Lynn. That team had bonded around a sophomore who had loved the game and who had raised the level of play at Casteline to a height never before achieved. That year, as the team won the Commonwealth Conference title and the South Sectional title, this player had started playing the theme to Zorba the Greek on the bus coming home from games, inspiring most of the team to get up and dance in the aisle as the team returned home from another victory. It was that kind of kinship that Ben knew he had to cultivate every year, though many years his ministrations fell short. But he continued to provide the stage for the drama.

Saturday was the team's first scrimmage against Wayland. Ben spent fifteen minutes with the managers, trying to sort out the stats he wanted kept. Janet would keep the clock for the scrimmage, and there would not be a 30 second clock, because there weren't enough hands to handle the extra timepiece.

Ben sent Jason Grutchfield, James Rush, Jonas Boynton, Andrew Monaghan, and Geoff Willis out to start the scrimmage, the same lineup he had offered to Bryan in their pre-season meeting. Nothing that had happened in practice had changed his assessment. He expected Andrew and Geoff to handle the rebounding duties; he expected James and Andrew to be the primary shooters; and he hoped Jason would be able to handle the point against any pressure. That was one of the keys to this team: would Jason need a second person in the backcourt versus pressure defense.

The scrimmage started off evenly, with neither team shooting particularly well. Andrew got a couple baskets off good passes, and Geoff hit Jason with a great outlet pass for an easy layin over the top. But in the half-court set, Casteline struggled to achieve any effective player movement off the ball.

The teams were playing 10 minute periods, time enough for a little fatigue to set in, but short enough for an insightful analysis without any timeouts needed.

But Wayland began pounding the boards halfway through the period, scoring on second shots three consecutive times. Ben called an immediate timeout.

"OK, let's think here," he said to the five seated in front of him, the rest of the team around them. "Why is Wayland winning at this point? Any ideas?" He let his words resonate.

Loyal Geoff Willis knew. "We're not rebounding. We're getting beat on the weakside of the rim."

Ben continued. "Can we figure out why they're getting to the board? Are we not boxing out?"

Jonas offered, "We're getting beat off the dribble, drawing help from our big men, and then their weakside rebounder is not boxed out."

Ben nodded with an exaggerated motion. "I think you're right," he said with mock comprehension. "So, who is responsible for the weak rebounding?" No one volunteered, because the big men didn't want to call out the guards, and it seemed the guards felt it was the big men who should be garnering the rebounds. "Well, I guess it's our guards, who are getting beat. James, Jason, Jonas, you've got to contain these guards. They like to put it to the floor and go by. When you close out, you need to go out under control. I don't want the uncontested jumper, but I also don't want the lane penetration.

"Now let's get some quickness in our feet. One, two, three .. ."

"Tight," the team mumbled.

Ben called them in again. "Let's show some spirit here. One, two, three . . .'

"Tight," the team called with more volume, if not assurance, as they trotted onto the floor.

Ben wondered what it was about some opposing teams that they could sprint on and off the floor, coming to the bench and returning to the court with a sense of urgency. He had always marveled at the propensity of those teams, especially teams that played tenacious defense, to make these sprints to and from the bench with alacrity. Yet, here was his team ambling back onto the court, after his plea and suggestions about better rebounding efficiency.

The rest of the period Casteline remained within hailing distance of Wayland, but the opposition had established its superiority, and maintained it to the end of the period: Wayland 24, Casteline 18. Checking the stats from the manager, Ben saw that Andrew had shot 3 for 7, and James was 2 for 6, not bad, but not enough to establish any control on offense. He also saw that Geoff Willis, for all his effort and team-building qualities, was not a premier rebounder at 6'2". He saw that Casteline could be overwhelmed on the boards. He inserted Nick Mavrikos at the 5 position, hoping to see some fire in the group. He also subbed out all the perimeter players, keeping only Andrew Monaghan on the floor, of the starters.

In the second period, Wayland maintained its control of both ends of the floor. Ben kept trying to insert a different combination, seeking a five that would be fluid at both ends of the floor, but when the team gained some defensive toughness, they lost their ability to score regularly at the other end. Ben was trying to modulate a precise balance

73

that would allow the team to gain control of both ends of the floor at once, but he could not find that fulcrum, that tipping point. One of the sides – offense or defense – always seemed to tip downwards.

In the third period the Panthers had a three on two break, Jason at the point, with Bobbie and Jonas on the wings. The lane was open for a bounce pass to Bobbie, but Jason jumped in the air and tried to make a lookaway pass to Jonas. Wayland's back man read the pass, stepped in, and started a break the other way, a four point swing. Ben called another timeout.

"Jason, you've got a clean 3 on 2. What are you doing going up in the air to make that pass? Haven't we worked on keeping your feet on the ground? Two feet; two hands. Simple basketball. Don't make it harder than it is. Jumping lookaways are OK if you've made fifteen basic plays already. Don't try to do something you can't do. Keep it simple." Ben was trying to keep his voice moderate, but it rose on its own to a pitch that traveled across the gym. "That's all, guys. Nothing else to say here. Let's take care of business. One, two, three.."

"Tight." Not very tightly, but they got the point.

At the end of the scrimmage, Ben pulled the team together in the middle of the floor for a very brief post-scrimmage analysis. Casteline had won one of the ten-minute periods, two were even, and Wayland had won two periods. It was hard to say what Ben had learned. He didn't really know what to say, but he knew that he had to offer some trenchant analysis.

"OK, men, this is the starting point. That Wayland team is a good one, with some very tough players, coming off a very successful football season. They rebounded very well, with good size. We did a great job of not hanging our heads after a tough start. Nice job as the scrimmage wore on, and I think that points to our depth and conditioning.

"We're still trying to find our identity. We run a little. We shoot pretty well, but not consistently. We defend very well some of the time. I'm still looking for that one thing that we can say, 'this is what we do. This is what our team is all about.' I'm still trying to find out what that one thing is.

"It's up to you. Are you going to be a defense-first team? Are you going to be a team that I can say, 'Let it fly' to? Are you going to be a team that gets up and down the court? I really don't know, but today was Step One in finding out.

"Keep your heads up, and each of you, try to figure out how you could have made us more successful.

"Now, get home, spend time with your families, get your homework done, and have a great weekend. One, two, three . . ."

"Tight."

Ten minutes with Bryan, and Ben was ready to head out the door, to get home. He had told Scott that they would go shopping for presents for Willa and Mary this afternoon. Scott and he hadn't said much to each other since Monday night, when he had picked him up at the Streets' house. Scott had said that he and Perry had just gone out for a walk, a long walk. Neither of them had their license, but they had wanted to go to a girl's house a couple of miles away. They had walked to her house and spent five minutes with her in a seemingly pointless conversation. By the time they had returned to the Streets' house, it had become a two-hour trip.

Ben had cautioned Scott about letting his family know where he was.

"But, Dad, I knew you were at practice, and Mom wasn't home when I happened to get a ride to Perry's. You're right, I should have called home and left a message for Mom. We just kind of got excited about going to this girl's house, and we kind of forgot about everything else."

"What's her name?"

"Why? You going to call up and verify?"

Ben looked at Scott, shaking his head. "No, I'm not trying to check up on you. I just want to know who you're trying to see. What is she like?"

"She's kind of different, to be honest. I mean, most of the girls I know are athletic and smart and peppy. This girl's not like that. She's into art and drawing and other things. I don't know. We barely saw her, but it was kind of fun."

Ben remembered when he was a senior, finally finding out that there was a social network in Needham, a network that he had not tapped once for seventeen years, and that, in his last three months of high school, he finally realized existed. Scott was just a little more savvy than Ben had been.

Ben took a chance. "Are you smoking these days?"

Scott stared straight ahead. He held his breath. "I've tried it. I'm not the type to buy cigarettes, but I'll have one sometimes. I know it's stupid, and I don't ever feel like I want one, but I have to admit I've tried it."

Ben knew there was more to the story. "Have you tried anything else?"

Scott continued his stare. "It's around. You know. You're a teacher. I'm not blind and I'm not stupid, so I see other stuff." Scott's answer was noncommittal enough to convey to Ben that he had tried "other stuff," but his answer also let Ben know that he wasn't going to divulge anything specific.

"Well, Mom and I are worried, naturally, about the direction you're going to take. I've seen a lot of kids, guys especially, that head down that path, and it takes them years to come back. I don't want you to get into situations where you can't control the outcome." Ben too was speaking in generalities, but it was all he could offer.

"I know, Dad, you don't have to worry. I'm strong enough to move away from trouble if it's not cool."

Ben loved Scott; he couldn't stand the thought of something tragic happening to his son. "You're doing OK; we can't help but worry. I feel like it's our job. When I talk to Mom again about it, I'll tell her you were just at someone else's house. What's her name?"

Scott still held back. "I don't think that's relevant. We only spent five minutes with her. She's not the issue here. Perry and I just went out for a long walk, and her house came up."

Now frustrated, Ben knew there was more to the story, but Scott was unwilling to volunteer any more information. Trying to keep information flowing between Scott and Willa and himself was not easy, and he didn't want to close any doors.

The shopping trip was as successful as Ben could have hoped. They drove to the Natick Mall, spending twenty-five minutes circling the many parking lots, looking for a space to park. There were thousands of people in the interior of the mall, some ambling to the soft Christmas music piped in, some rushing from door to door, arms full of packages. The Christmas season had always been a bit of a mystery to Ben. He had grown up in a house where he and his family traded a few thoughtful gifts with each other, at some slight expense. Yet, here in Natick a frenzy seemed to have taken hold of the thousands who sought those many gifts that would make for a great holiday for their friends and family, the search impinging on their normal lives like a winch ratcheting tightly. Ben could never share in their urgency, and he felt isolated as a result. He wondered how Scott approached gift-giving.

"Do you have money for your gifts, or do you need some?" Ben asked Scott.

"No, I've been saving up for a long time. I'll make this trip off my own funds, but if I go out again, and you're still offering, I'll probably take you up on the offer. Do you want to stick together, or meet later? Let's meet at some time right here." They were standing underneath a four-sided clock that read 2:45.

Ben liked the idea of separating. He could move at his own tranquil pace, and Scott could be as productive as he needed to be. "Let's meet here at 4:00. OK?"

"That's a good idea. See you then. Do you have your cell phone on? I can call you if there's any change in plans."

Ben reached into his pocket to see if he even had his phone. Taking it out, he saw that it wasn't turned on, as usual. He turned the phone on, checking to see that Scott's number was programmed in. It was.

""Ok, 4:00 right here. See ya."

Ben turned to his right, joining the stream of shoppers that flowed toward the eastern end of the shops. He was swept past Hallmark Cards, Crate and Barrel (he knew kitchen items were not Christmas gift-worthy – too utilitarian), Victoria's Secret (maybe an alluring lingerie set for Willa? No, she would be far less excited by the hint of sexuality than he), Wilson Leather, Abercrombie and Fitch (something fashionable for Mary?), looking down the hallway at Macy's, and he turned toward Macy's, knowing that gifts would show themselves in the deep piles of colorful clothing and bright jewelry. Had Willa said she wanted a necklace this Christmas? He called her on the phone.

The Arc of Intersection

We speak in past tense and talk about the weather
Half broken sentences we try to piece together
I ask about an old friend that we both used to know
You said you heard he took his life about five years ago
We may pass each other on the interstate
We honk and cross over to the other lane
Everybody's going somewhere everybody's inside
Hundreds of cars hundreds of private lives
We are so out of touch yeah

from *Out of Touch* by Lucinda Williams

James

After the Wayland scrimmage, James hopped into Pete's car, knowing Pete had a decision to make. Pete had played sparingly, only at the end, when Coach LaMott spent the last period making sure all fourteen of the players on the team had some extended time on the floor. Pete's performance was adequate: about ten minutes, a couple of shots, a steal, and a couple of rebounds. James had watched his friend carefully, wondering how he would do in his first varsity scrimmage.

"Not a bad start, dude," James offered, as they left the school parking lot.

"Yeah, I can see my role on this team. What the fuck. I didn't really expect much more. Hey, you shot it pretty good your last run." Pete looked across at James, with hope in his eyes.

"Yeah, I did find a groove in the fourth or fifth period. It felt good. All the running we've done got my legs in better shape." James was not pleased, overall, but he did see hope for himself -- and the team. Monaghan had played terrific: all over the floor, running ahead of the pack on some breaks, handling the ball on some others. Andrew was going to have a monster season.

"You up for a little smoke?" Pete asked, real curiosity in his eyes. James shifted uncomfortably in his soft seat.

"I don't know. I think I'm trying to stay straight. Why don't you join me? We can work it out together – maybe a little more Madden Football, maybe a little more late season college football on TV." James was trying to talk himself into a substance-free posture as much as he was offering it to Pete.

"No fuckin way," Pete replied. He whistled disgusted air out of his thinly separated lips. "I'm goin for the Big Lebowski tonight. Wilson is havin a party, and we don't want to miss it. First party since Thanksgiving, and the girls'll be ready."

"I don't know. Take me home, and I'll call you." James felt that he was leaving Pete out on a limb by himself, and he knew that Pete was looking for some company on that limb. Looking out his window at the stone walls that demarcated each house on Pond Street, James noted the spacious lots, the hulking houses, and the lengthy driveways that led to those houses. In a minute it was his driveway, and he realized they had remained silent for the last few minutes, as they each hovered on their own sides of an important decision.

"I'll call you," James said as he slammed the door. Pete looked over his other shoulder, backing the car out.

Inside, James just wanted to sit in his room, close his eyes, and let the moments slip by, with no particular expectations for the evening, no phone calls, just a few hours of thoughtless TV watching, seeing Georgetown playing Louisville, the great talent racing up and down the floor. With his eyes closed, James could hear the squeak of the sneakers as they made hard cuts away from the defense. The announcers' voices rose and fell rhythmically.

"Eleven minutes to play here in the first half, and Louisville leads by two, as Georgetown moves the ball to the left wing, looking for a passing angle into the lane against this aggressive zone defense that Louisville plays."

The other announcer broke in. "Louisville has challenged conventional wisdom with this defense. Most people think of zone defense as being a little passive, defending the middle of the half-court, but putting no pressure on perimeter passing. Rick Pitino has rewritten the book on zones, contesting balls coming out the corner, especially. It's a great idea, and he has the athletes to make it work. Georgetown is laboring to get a good shot, and they have a significant size advantage at nearly every position. Great coaching move by Pitino."

James saw the double-down in the corner clearly, though his eyes were closed. With the clicker in his hand, James turned the audio to the game down to mute, and he listened to any other sounds in his house. His parents were not in. They had both attended the scrimmage, but they had gone on to the mall to shop after the game. Rachel was not home, he didn't think, but then he heard some music coming from her bedroom. She must have been home when he came home, but he didn't notice.

The phone rang, and James did not want to answer it. It was probably Pete, and he just didn't want to make a decision.

"James," his sister shouted. "It's for you!"

James flipped his desk phone to ON. "Yeah?"

James heard the voice of Dan Owings, who had once been James's closest friend, but the two had headed in different directions the past few years. Dan's voice brought James back to their shared middle school experiences, as devoid of purpose as most middle school experiences. But there had been a moment during the summer when they were entering high school, a little more than two years ago, when they had shared something that neither boy would forget.

It had been a hot July day, and James was riding his bike to Dan's house, about a three mile trip. They had agreed to meet at Dan's house, ride to the ice cream shop in the middle of town, and maybe swim at Dalton Pond in the afternoon. As James rounded the corner of Sprindle Street, Dan's street, he saw Dan riding toward him, with a canvas bag over his shoulder. James pulled up alongside Dan and asked, "What's with the bag?"

Dan quietly said, "Just follow me."

James shook his head uncertainly, perplexed with Dan's mysterious reply. There was a note of urgency in Dan's voice, as if he were not in complete control of his movements.

They rode down Sprindle, crossed Lantern Lane, and turned onto Hill Street, another quiet, deserted street. James had been on this street only once, long ago, and he remembered it as a short dead-end. At this moment, Dan turned into a driveway of a beige house, a large, two-story. The mailbox read 8 Hill Street.

Dan rode his bike around the garage, hopping off it once he was behind the garage, not even bothering to look over his shoulder at James, probably knowing that James would question his actions, but that he would still follow along. Without as much as a word, Dan opened the back door of the garage, entering the darkness, leaving the door open for James.

When James did not step off his bike, Dan called, "Well, are you coming in or not?"

James didn't know if Dan knew the family that lived at 8 Hill Street, but he felt nervous. Still in the sunlight at the corner of the garage, he closed his eyes, but the sound of two or three crows made him pick his head up quickly, as he felt the sun's rays heating his head underneath his Sox cap. He looked inside the garage, only to see no sign of Dan. Shrugging his shoulders, James moved to the back of the house, leaned his bike over, let it down, and followed Dan into the garage. Inside the darkness, James saw that the door to the house was open halfway, inviting him to follow Dan into the house. There were no cars in the garage; no sound emanated from the house. James felt he should call for Dan, but he was afraid to make a sound, the moment was so fraught with uncertainty. He looked for Dan in the kitchen, but saw no one.

The house was ghostly dark and quiet. As James silently minced his steps into the adjoining dining room, he still saw no one, not even Dan.

"Dan?" he called. Nothing. At this point James felt he should head out the kitchen, through the garage, and out of the house. He didn't think there was any good reason he and Dan should be in this house, and Dan was offering no explanation at all. In fact, James couldn't even be sure that Dan was still in the house.

Six more steps, and he stood at the bottom of the stairs, looking up to a landing. Was Dan up there? James knew he shouldn't move up the stairs, and after waiting a few seconds, he retraced his steps through the living room and the kitchen, back into the garage and out the back door to his bike. Dan's was still lying on the ground next to the rack where firewood was stored in the winter. Not wanting to emerge alone from behind the house, James waited about six or seven more minutes until Dan came out of the house, the bag still slung over his shoulder, seemingly not weighted down with anything stolen, but James couldn't tell. He waited for Dan to explain the inexplicable situation. But Dan said nothing.

"Hey, Dan, what's going on?" James asked, out of real curiosity. James and Dan had spent the last six years of their lives understanding each other as well as two young boys can expect, constantly challenging each other for physical superiority.

Dan smiled contentedly at James. "I just wanted you to know." He said nothing more.

James did not know what Dan was saying. "Know what?"

Dan smiled again. "I just like to know that I could take anything I wanted, if I wanted to. Money, videogames, photographs, a gun. They've got a little of everything."

James still did not understand. "Do you know these people? What's their name?"

"Cody. They don't lock their house. They have no children. They are both business people, and sometimes they travel on business. When they're both traveling, they lock up the house and they have an alarm system. But when one of them is in town, they don't lock the house or turn on the alarm."

James stared at Dan. It was as if he had never known anything about Dan all those years they had played together. Nothing that Dan said made sense to James. "How do you know all this?"

The two boys still stood over their bikes in the shadow of the garage behind the house at 8 Hill Street, the house owned by the Codys. James did not want to come around to the front of the house until he had the semblance of an understanding of what Dan was doing.

Dan looked at James, as if he were trying to see whether James would understand what he was about to say. He sighed, then said, "I've been watching these people for a few years now. I know their habits. I know their tendencies. I know what they wear, what they like to eat. I could take anything I wanted from them, but I never have."

James continued to stare at Dan, amazed that a friend so close could be so menacing. "Why do you do it?"

Dan didn't answer right away. "It's as if I'm part of their family. I know where they've been on vacation, and what kind of toothpaste they use. I don't really know why, but I get a real thrill from knowing so much about them. I would never do anything to destroy their sanctity."

"Then why did you bring the bag? Were you planning on taking some things?"

Dan didn't even have to think to formulate his answer. "I just bring the bag to test myself. I want to overcome the temptation to take things. I want to know that I could take anything I wanted, but I don't because I respect them too much."

James snorted in disgust. "Fuck you. If you respected them so much, you wouldn't be sneaking into their house and looking around. It's kinda creepy, if you ask me – it's really creepy. I mean, you're standing in their bedroom, sneaking into their bathroom. Sorry, but that's weird."

Dan shrugged with disappointment. "I thought you'd understand. We've been good friends for so long, I thought I could trust you with this. I wanted to share it with someone, and we both know that my parents would not think this is a good idea."

"No shit. I'm just not sure, myself. I mean, what do you get out of all this? The thrill of getting away with it? How the hell did it start?"

Again, Dan did not have to think for an instant. "The first time, I was riding my bike around the neighborhood, as I always do. I kept passing all these houses, and as I rode past, I tried to picture what their lives were like, what TV shows they watched. I just wanted to know them.

"I'd wave to the people who were playing on their front lawn. I always rode around in the evening, when people were getting home for supper.

"But this house, no one ever seemed to come home. If they came home, it was always after dark. Every once in a while, I'll ride over here on the weekend, when people are mowing their lawns, and some people are cooking out in their back yards. But these people never did those things. A lawn service cuts the grass whenever it needs it. There's a grill out back, but it's never been used, not even once. It's like they don't really live here."

At this point, Dan started to falter, realizing how crazy his words sounded. His eyes might have misted over a little. James reached across and put his right hand on Dan's shoulder. "Hey, it's OK. But let's get out of here. I don't want to be found behind these people's house, if you don't mind."

Dan nodded, and seemed willing to follow James out into the sunlight, onto Hill Street, back onto Sprindle, crossing Lantern Lane, and in just four or five minutes they were back in Dan's driveway. James had no idea how long they had been gone, but it seemed like a lifetime.

And so, now, on the Saturday afternoon of the scrimmage against Wayland, James heard Dan's voice. They hadn't talked as much on the phone since that mysterious afternoon when they were thirteen, but it was good to hear Dan's voice.

"How ya doing?" James asked hesitantly.

"Great, really. I was just wondering how you thought the scrimmage went."

James thought for just a second. "Eh, I don't know. I thought we played like crap, really. I know we can do way better. I didn't get loose, and no one but Andrew shot well."

Dan cut in, "Yeah, I never got comfortable out there. I want to do great, but I sucked." Dan sighed, in disappointment.

Considering Dan's scrimmage for a second, James offered, "You got up and down the floor. The shots will go in when we loosen up. LaMott's such a prick we can't get comfortable out there. D'you see the way he ripped into Jason on the break?"

Dan whistled. "Yeah, he let loose on him. I mean, what's up with Coach? He was always our friend, and now he just rips into us for no reason. I mean, it's not like we're trying to fuck up. He just puts too much pressure on us. You made some plays. I think you got a starting job sewed up. I don't know about my spot. Coach loves the new kid, and he played him a lot."

As James and Dan continued to parse the coach's words and actions, James thought about how long it had been since he and Dan had chatted. That summer afternoon had separated them, for all the succeeding years.

"Hey, what are you doing tonight? Wanna come out with me?"

After a few seconds of silence, Dan replied, "Tell you the truth, I have a date."

James did not even know whom Dan was dating. "No shit! Who you taking out? Do I know her?"

"You probably don't know her. She's a sophomore, kind of a crazy kid. She loves to go to dances. I'm learning how to dance with her. We've been going out off and on for about two months, since the day I got my license, in fact."

James shook his head, amazed at his ignorance. "Two months? Where have I been? Haven't I seen you at Grayson's? At Morrison's? You've got a girl friend?"

"Oh, no sweat. I haven't really told anyone. My parents sort of know, but they've never met her."

"What's her name?"

"Joyce Bennett. She's in my journalism class; that's where I met her."

"Joyce Bennett. I know the name. Has she been at any parties?"

"Naah. She's too young. Her mom keeps her on a short leash. She's really nice, though. I've been over to her house a lot of times. In fact, some of our dates is just sitting in her family room watching TV. She loves to watch Dancing With the Stars, and I like to watch it with her. Her mom doesn't really like her to go out with a guy in a car. So we go to get ice cream or to Barnes and Noble to look at books. She finds out about dances at Xaverian, and we go and dance."

At that moment James heard a beep on his cell phone, an incoming call. He chose to ignore it, for the sake of regaining a little familiarity with Dan. "So you're tied up tonight? No partying?"

"Yeah, I'm gonna stay in." Dan paused. "Hey, maybe you should, too." Dan let the idea stand noticeably in their conversation like a stripped October tree.

James heard Dan's exhortation, but he chose to ignore it. "Nah, I'm going to Wilson's. It's Saturday night."

The Arc of Intersection

Ain't it just like the night to play tricks when you're tryin' to be so quiet?
We sit here stranded, though we're all doin' our best to deny it
And Louise holds a handful of rain, temptin' you to defy it
Lights flicker from the opposite loft
In this room the heat pipes just cough
The country music station plays soft
But there's nothing, really nothing to turn off
Just Louise and her lover so entwined
And these visions of Johanna that conquer my mind

In the empty lot where the ladies play blindman's bluff with the key chain
And the all-night girls they whisper of escapades out on the "D" train
We can hear the night watchman click his flashlight
Ask himself if it's him or them that's really insane
Louise, she's all right, she's just near
She's delicate and seems like the mirror
But she just makes it all too concise and too clear
That Johanna's not here
The ghost of 'lectricity howls in the bones of her face
Where these visions of Johanna have now taken my place

Now, little boy lost, he takes himself so seriously
He brags of his misery, he likes to live dangerously
And when bringing her name up
He speaks of a farewell kiss to me
He's sure got a lotta gall to be so useless and all
Muttering small talk at the wall while I'm in the hall
How can I explain?
Oh, it's so hard to get on
And these visions of Johanna, they kept me up past the dawn

from *Visions of Johanna* by Bob Dylan

86

Ben

After three scrimmages, versus Wayland, Newton South, and West Roxbury, Ben was starting to get a sense of the talents and deficiencies of his team.

Indeed, it looked as if Andrew Monaghan was head and shoulders ahead of the rest of the team. Ben would rely heavily on Andrew for scoring and rebounding, as well as helping handle the ball against pressure. Jason Grutchfield looked solid at the point; he still wasn't much of a threat from the 3-point line, but he could penetrate and pass, and he was a solid defender on the other team's best guard. Geoff Willis would set a perfect example of the player who got the most out of the least, and it would be hard to take him off the floor, but Ben really hoped that someone with more skills would challenge Geoff for his inside position.

Beyond that, Ben was unclear. James Rush, of whom Ben expected a great deal, was dependable yet. He was a good shooter and had a good deal of experience, but he hadn't made the strides that Ben had hoped. Archie Stedham, the transfer from Granby, was actually pushing James for time. Jonas Boynton, a senior of whom Ben had expected a lot, was so nervous he was unlikely to provide any significant plays on offense, and he was not a strong defensive player. Ben had started Jonas the first two scrimmages, but Jonas actually looked more comfortable sitting on the bench. But, for now, Jonas would start and things would remain that way until someone definitively outplayed him. Two others who were in the mix at the wing spots were Dan Owings and Alex White.

At Saturday's practice before the opening game, Ben put a challenge to the team, letting them know that he was still very undecided about the starting positions and that this practice would go a long way to determining playing time. Practice that day was heated, as players competed for every inch of floor space, beating their opponent down the floor, boxing out with strong intent, moving the feet to get in front of a driving player. But no one emerged from the competitive practice with any more hold on a playing spot. Though the effort was commendable, the shooting was tentative, and the communication among teammates was poor.

87

At the end of practice, Ben addressed the fatigued team. "You guys really pushed yourselves today. I'm very proud of that fact. You understand the necessity of working hard every minute as we get ready for Natick in our first game. With that effort, we'll compete for every game we engage in, and we'll win our share.

"I'm still looking for a few players to step up as consistent scorers on this team. There were moments when I thought I saw a consistency from someone, but then it would disappear.

"And our biggest problem is defensive communication. We are not talking, we're not calling out 'tight,' we're not calling screens loud enough, and we really don't have a strong sense of team defense.

"Now, I think the reason for this is the fact that I'm putting so much emphasis on deciding who is playing better, that we're putting too much focus on the offense and too little emphasis on the defense.

"When we come in on Monday for our last practice before Natick, let's bring a defensive hunger onto the court with us. We know what we have to do on defense; we just don't seem to have the commitment to making sure it happens.

"Great pre-season. The scrimmages were a great warmup for our schedule. Let's not forget to keep our expectations high. The only group that can stop you from succeeding is the members of this group. In this gym we have the talent to win each game we play. Don't let any negative ideas or thoughts creep in the way. Every day is a new one. Every play is a new one.

"Coach Taft, do you have anything to add?"

Bryan, who had attended two of the three scrimmages, stepped forward. "We have a lot of experience on this team. Our challenge is to assimilate this experience with the new faces that are also needed to make it work. Let's take these first five games, the ones before Christmas, to figure out our strengths and weaknesses. Coach might try different combinations, different defensive looks in different situations, to see what works. Be patient. Don't get hung up about when you're playing or who you're playing with. We're just trying different combinations to see what way works best for us.

"Everyone here will, at one time or another, be a major part of the outcome of a game. Your task is to be ready for that moment or those moments." With that Bryan ceded authority back to Ben, who called for a practice-ending "tight."

As the players drifted off, Ben and Bryan lingered, Ben wishing to hear Bryan's more candid analysis of the team as it was shaping up.

"Bryan, do you see anything we need to be focusing on?"

"Defensive intensity. You were exactly right; there's no defensive unity out there. It's every man for himself. What kind of rotations are you looking for in your man-to-man?"

"We're trying to force the ball baseline, double up outside the block, and slide into passing lanes on the basket side, hoping for a 'tight,' in a tough spot. But we're not quick enough to maintain the pressure on the ball that we need. The big man doubles up or steps up, and the guard is two steps behind. Then the pass goes across the lane, and it's an easy shot."

Bryan moved toward the white board on the wall, drawing a halfcourt graphic, placing players in their spots, to illustrate the concept Ben was developing. "So you get beat on the outside and never catch up. What about a little less pressure on the perimeter players to begin with. A half step of retreat as we close out on the ball?"

Ben gritted his teeth. "I hate to do that. It gives up the perimeter shot, the 3, and it allows easy passing lanes. I want to keep pressure on the ball, but it seems we can't. We do closeout drills, zigzag drills, but we don't seem to be getting better."

Bryan nodded, understanding. "How about a little matchup zone, from time to time? The man nearest the ball can put pressure on the ball, but the rest of the team is in a help position. Mix it up."

Ben liked the idea of a matchup, but with one practice remaining before the first game, he knew it was a concept for another month, or another season. He felt, as usual, underprepared heading into the first game. He had covered all the basics, but he did not feel that the team was efficient at any of the most important elements: defensive toughness, ball movement, rebounding, or shooting poise. Though he did not want another week of tiresome preseason, he would like to be able to hone the skills he had presented. But, time had run out.

"Have a great rest of the weekend," Ben offered to Bryan as they shared their "ppp" (post practice piss, so-named about ten years previously, after countless post-practice conversations leading to one last stop at the urinals before leaving the locker room).

"Yeah, you, too. I'm heading into Boston for some music tonight. Seeing REM at the Banknorth Garden."

"Oh, nice. How many times for you and REM?"

"This will be my . . . sixth? Lisa's never seen them. She's excited. Should be a great time."

"Nice. I've got a neighborhood party, for a little while this evening. Aside from that, I don't have anything but the usual – essays and more essays."

"Agh, you have to make room for yourself, buddy. You can get bogged down this time of the year – teaching, practice, game preparation, travel to the games, planning and correcting. It gets to be too much sometimes. You have to be able to step back and relax, you know?"

Ben nodded his head. "Oh, I know. It seems the weeks fly by, and then it's suddenly Christmas vacation. And we're already five games into our schedule. I want to grab at least three of those games."

Bryan assured Ben, "That seems totally realistic." And with that, Bryan and Ben shut the locker room door and turned into the chill of the December Saturday noontime.

"See you Monday," said Ben, and Bryan nodded.

"Till then," Bryan sang out, and entered his car.

At home, there were two notes, one from Willa and one from Mary. Willa was at the church, working with a group of parishioners who were wrapping presents that they had bought for the homeless and the needy. Ben admired Willa's philanthropic impulses, almost always centered on their church's missions activities. Willa had become a leader in those endeavors, adding to the richness of her life as well as the pace of it. Ben shared her empathy for others, but he felt too tied down by his responsibility to his team to extend himself in another direction. He felt selfish, in his preoccupation, but too invested in the team's success to reduce his involvement.

Mary was shopping with friends, at the Mall, working through her oversized list of friends needing presents.

That left Scott unaccounted for. Ben called up the stairs for him, but, hearing no response, moved to the phone to listen for a message from him. There were three messages, but none from him. Ben sat down in the reclining chair in the family room, took out his set of essays on *Death of a Salesman* from his junior class that he had to correct, after flipping on the college game of the afternoon, Texas vs. Michigan State, in an important early-season matchup between two strong teams. In about thirty minutes, Ben was asleep, seven essays corrected, another on his lap in the warmth of the family room. Michigan State led at the half, 42-38.

A little later Scott came home, entering the kitchen noisily with Alec, a new friend this year. Waking up quickly, Ben heard them raid the salty-cabinet, where the chips, pretzels, nuts, and popcorn resided.

"Chips and salsa," Scott asked his friend.

"Sounds perfect," replied Alec.

Ben called from the family room, "How you guys doing? What'd you do this afternoon?"

Scott called back from the kitchen, "The usual. Over at Wayne's house, hanging out. No big deal."

"Going out tonight?" Ben asked. These days, Ben was trying to track Scott more than in the past, knowing the endless possibilities that lay in Scott's path.

"We don't know yet. Might head to the Mall. Might head to someone's house. Up in the air."

Ben could hear the two talking in low voices in the kitchen, as well as the crunch of the chips they devoured. He wanted to be able to intervene in their conversation, but he knew the moment he entered the kitchen, they would change the course of their dialogue, without even realizing it. It was just an adolescent instinct, one that he had certainly cultivated himself when he was young. Why should adults get involved in the plans and activities of their children? It was enough to keep track of their own lives, to be honest. Ben understood Scott's aloofness, and knew it was a necessary division that widened naturally as the years passed, in order for Scott (and Mary) to separate himself from his parents.

"What's up for supper?" Scott shouted.

Looking at his watch, Ben shook his head. "I don't know. Mom should be home by now, and we're going over to Batschelders for a party at 6:00, I think. Think you could make yourself a grilled cheese?" He didn't know what else to offer. It was usually Willa's intent to have the family eat together in the evening, when schedules allowed, but she was with her church group, later than she expected, and Ben had considered how he would address the upcoming meal, if he were Scott: just eat and move on. He knew Scott was not looking for extended time at the kitchen table with the family.

"Sounds cool. You want one?" It was nice of Scott to ask.

"Yeah, I think I will. We'll eat at Batschelders, but grilled cheese sounds good. Want me to make it?"

"No, I think I can handle it."

Half an hour later, Ben, Scott, and Alec sat together in the kitchen, quickly consuming six slightly burnt grilled cheeses with the accompanying potato chips. Ben wondered where Willa was; it was almost 6:00, the time they were scheduled to go to their neighbors' house. He called Willa's cell phone.

She answered, "Hello?"

91

"Hi, honey. You heading home soon?"

"I'm just getting into my car right now. We had way more gifts than we expected, and there were fewer wrappers than we planned. But we're done, and the project is a success. What time is it? I haven't even looked at my watch since about 3:00."

"Just about six. Do you need time to get ready for the Batschelders?"

"Oh my God, I completely forgot about their party! We're gonna have to go late. What're the kids doing?"

"Scott's in right now, and Mary's at the Mall. I can give her a call to find out her plans. See you when you get home."

After a hasty shower and kitchen cleanup, Willa and Ben walked down the street to their neighbors' house. Willa looked forward to these encounters with their neighbors, embracing the ties that a good set of neighbors developed. Ben felt differently. If he could have planned the evening, they would have gone to a quiet dinner and then a movie, to return home to a quiet house at about 11:00. But he knew that there would be neither a quiet dinner nor a quiet house. Mary and her friends would have invaded the house by the time Willa and Ben got home, much to the gratification of Willa, who overtly encouraged her children to lead their social lives in the comfort of their own home, in part so that Willa and Ben could easily keep track of their activities and their friends. Mary liked the fact that her home was a haven for her friends, a welcome spot where her friends could congregate.

At the party, Ben and Willa stood near each other, Ben moving into the kitchen periodically, to grab a beer for himself, a white wine for Willa. The neighbors were noisy enough to assure themselves that this was a good party, and, in fact, it was. There were conversations going on that hadn't been kindled since the last cookout of the summer, at the Davidsons' house. Ben, as usual, partook of the chitchat as easily as anyone at the party, but he really didn't feel a brotherhood with the other men. He wondered if they felt the same way.

As Ben and Willa walked home, the air offering the wet chill of an impending snow shower, Ben put his arm around Willa's waist. He could feel her hip through the woolen coat, rocking with her stride. He could picture that hip in its nightgown, jutting out in its mature testament to childbirth, her hips wide, the skin between them a creamy reminder of past dalliances, when he would rest his head on that softness, as they became familiar with each other's bodies. That time of exploring each other's wants had been an exciting part of their relationship, as he trained all his passion and sexual interest into this woman with whom he had merged his life. In fact, over the twenty-six years of their marriage, there had been many moments when he understood the concept of complete gratification: emotional gratification, physical gratification, sensory gratification, sexual gratification. He wondered whether spiritual gratification was supposed to accompany these other satiations, but he wasn't much for philosophizing.

"Can you remember walking home from Berensons' at two in the morning, when we were too drunk to drive?" That cold walk had led to an intense twining at his parents' house, on a night when they had the house to themselves.

Willa sighed pleasantly. "Yes. That was a nice night."

"And so is this one. Just like it, it feels." Ben wished for that same intimacy. "You feeling all right?" He was searching for Willa's temperament, trying to determine whether she was as attuned as he.

"Yeah, great. I'm looking forward to seeing Mary's friends at the house. They're such a fun bunch. Aren't you glad that they've chosen our house to spend their nights, rather than somewhere else? It keeps us informed."

Ben, understanding that the evening was headed in a direction that was not part of his intention, agreed, with less ardor. "Yeah, I agree. They're a good bunch of kids. Mary's lucky she found this group to hang out with.

"I mean, I don't think she's lucky, because she has a lot to offer, herself, and she has attracted these good kids, with solid families. I think we're lucky, is what I meant to say."

Willa leaned her head on Ben's shoulder. "Yeah, you're right. We are really lucky."

After spending an hour with Mary's friends in the family room, sharing a slice of pizza, after Willa picked up the kitchen two times, filling the dishwasher and turning it on, after checking on Scott's whereabouts (Perry Street's house, the scene of his independent migration on Monday), Ben asked Willa, "You want me to get Scott at 11:00? I'll be back by 11:30."

"Yeah, that'd be great. I'm really bushed. I think I'll snuggle under the covers and warm myself up so I can warm your feet when you come home."

That sounded nice.

An hour later, when Ben came home with Scott (no noticeable sign of inebriation or even tobacco), Scott slid into Ben and Willa's bedroom to give his mother a goodnight kiss, a ritual the family had concocted to allow them to check his breath, he knew. Willa stirred from her light slumber to speak with Scott briefly as Ben eased himself into the shower. By the time he got to bed, Scott was gone, Willa's breathing had returned to a steady comfort, and Ben lay next to his wife, wondering at the way the evening had turned out. He nudged Willa's hip, hoping to wake her gently, trying to rekindle the intimacy of their walk home.

"You got any energy left?" he inquired delicately, draping his right knee over her right thigh.

Willa turned slightly toward him, her answer a mere humming, noncommittal in nature.

Ben persisted. "Hey, Willa, are you thinking of waking up?"

Keeping her eyes closed, she murmured, "Let's save it for another night. I'm really comfortable right now."

Ben sighed silently, sliding onto his back, his body separated from Willa's. He picked up the Dec. 1 *Sports Illustrated* and started to read about the NBA. He marveled at the way life spun out, and at his incapability of controlling the trajectory of that spin.

In the time of my confession, in the hour of my deepest need
When the pool of tears beneath my feet flood every newborn seed
There's a dyin' voice within me reaching out somewhere,
Toiling in the danger and in the morals of despair.

Don't have the inclination to look back on any mistake,
Like Cain, I now behold this chain of events that I must break.
In the fury of the moment I can see the Master's hand
In every leaf that trembles, in every grain of sand.

Oh, the flowers of indulgence and the weeds of yesteryear,
Like criminals, they have choked the breath of conscience and good cheer.
The sun beats down upon the steps of time to light the way
To ease the pain of idleness and the memory of decay.

I gaze into the doorway of temptation's angry flame
And every time I pass that way I always hear my name.
Then onward in my journey I come to understand
That every hair is numbered like every grain of sand.

I have gone from rags to riches in the sorrow of the night
In the violence of a summer's dream, in the chill of a wintry light,
In the bitter dance of loneliness fading into space,
In the broken mirror of innocence on each forgotten face.

I hear the ancient footsteps like the motion of the sea
Sometimes I turn, there's someone there, other times it's only me.
I am hanging in the balance of the reality of man
Like every sparrow falling, like every grain of sand .

Every Grain of Sand by Bob Dylan

James

James sat back on the couch in John Wilson's living room and let the familiar sounds of the party wash over him. With his hat curved in an arc over his eyes, he listened to the remnants of the Casteline football team shouting over the LSU-Alabama game that purred in the nearby TV room. Loudest of the linebackers was Mark Whiting, who had been named captain of next year's team. From the kitchen he could hear the sibilant pop of the ping pong balls bouncing across the table, intended for a cup that would signal a score in beer-pong. The pitch of the conversation in that room had gradually escalated over the past hour. There was also a murmur from across the family room where he sat, some quiet giggling, as alliances and dalliances were covertly struck.

James had been disappointed that Adrienne was not at the party, but then again, he wasn't surprised. She rarely selected these parties as her form of recreation on a weekend night. Her absence made James feel less comfortable with himself, but from the time he and Pete had slugged down a good portion of the bottle of Jack Daniels in the Audi on the way to the party, James had, quite logically, dismissed the idea of remaining sober for the evening.

"You baked?" asked Pete, suddenly in James's radius. James could hear Pete's excitement. But he kept his eyes closed under the hat.

"Nah, just chillin. Everything cool for you?"

After just a slight hesitation, Pete claimed, "Never better. I'm being pursued by a posse of young ladies. There's no telling where it might lead."

James knew that Pete's stash of pot made him an attractive personality at a party, as long as he still had a bag or two.

"You wanna help me out?" Pete asked.

"Yeah, let's go out back," and with that James stood up, triggering a head rush, he had been sitting for so long. After rotating his head slowly, James followed Pete out of the room, toward the sliders that led fluidly to the back deck, where Pete rolled a joint. After Pete's first deep intake, James reached for the stick, looking forward to the easy wash that would come over him once the smoke hit his lungs. For the next few minutes Pete and James shared their ember, until it burnt their fingers.

It was a little after midnight when Pete, James, and Art Nolan, a senior who was a pot-friend of Pete's, left the deck to walk around the house, seeking Pete's Audi. He had parked it across the street, at the edge of the neighbor's lawn. With the number of cars that spread across the adjoining properties, James was surprised that the police had not made a visit to Wilson's house. Maybe Wilson, being a prominent football player, had some sort of provisional immunity. Pete's car was hemmed in by three or four other cars parked haphazardly across the street. James estimated more than fifty cars up and down the street around Wilson's house. After no small amount of tight steering, Pete managed to get the Audi onto the street, headed away from the party.

The party had been a big one, probably the biggest of the year. James had never gotten involved in the proceedings, though, choosing to remain aloof, even when Meredith crawled up next to him on the couch, her voice soft and intimate. He had been kind to her, drawing the conversation out for maybe an hour, but he had made no move to go anywhere with her, standing up only to refill their cups with beer two or three times. She was a sweet girl, not demanding, not a crybaby. They could sit near each other under a comfortable afghan of silence, and feel less vulnerable in their mutual company. No one could make it through a party in isolation; it was not possible. So they had shared their isolation generously with each other, affording the other a sense of place. But after a while, Meredith had separated herself from James, whether out of complacency or comfort, James didn't know. He had spent most of his time looking at their arms and hands, avoiding eye contact with Meredith almost completely. This was how he liked it: concentrate on the lesser parts, keeping the evening uncomplicated, unwilling to conceive of a bigger awareness that would leave him feeling empty.

After Pete dropped Nolan off in his driveway, he pushed the Audi to a whine in fifth gear: James knew from the sound that they must be traveling more than eighty.

"Coffee?" Pete asked, heading to the strip where the fast food restaurants would be open until 1:00.

"Love some," James replied somnolently. He was in a quiet place, in spite of the engine's noisy, insistent revolutions. A few seconds later the whine of the engine was joined by the higher and louder shrill of a siren. James opened his eyes and twisted his body to look in the side mirror, to see the flashing lights of a police car, gaining on Pete's Audi.

James drew his breath inward. "We got company?"

"I hope not. I hope he's headed for some other sucker," Pete responded, his voice urgently on edge.

As Pete brought his car's speed down to the statutory 35 mph, his downshift smooth and barely discernible, the police car remained locked on the Audi, also slowing, lights continuing to flash. Pete pulled his car toward the strip between street and sidewalk, on Main Street, and James, suddenly alert and anxious, peered at the Casteline police car, trying to will it past Pete's Audi. But the policeman was attendant to Pete's car, like LaMott's eyes on a bad pass.

When both cars had come to a slow stop, Pete fumbled in his pockets, checking for any residue. He reached underneath his seat. "Hey, check under your seat," he ordered James, and James did find the half-finished fifth of Jack Daniels, the source of their initial euphoria earlier in the evening. Since that moment, long replaced by other tastes of a Saturday evening, they had both managed to stay comfortably brain-warm, bathed in that thermal that maintains an elevated mood so gently.

Knowing not to toss the bottle out the door, James shoved it farther under the seat, pulling a slew of papers around it, trying to bury it behind a cloth that lay on the floor. Meanwhile, Pete tried to ease the remaining three cans of Bud Light still hanging in their plastic six-pack holder through the space between their seats onto the floor of the back seat, behind James's seat.

But the policeman was already standing at Pete's window, watching the two of them, surely amazed and amused at their vain attempts to elude detection. He shone the beam of the halogen flashlight across the seat into James's face. Looking across, past Pete, James could see only the policeman's abdomen and belt behind that brightness.

The officer addressed Pete first. "Sir, would you please open your door, and exit the car. Passenger, sir, would you please remain seated?"

Pete glanced at James with a look of horror on his face. Pete had never been apprehended in any stage of his career of self-indulgence, from his first puff of tobacco to the present moment.

And, with that thought, James made the leap to his own situation. He had been insulated from thinking about his own guilt by the alcohol he had absorbed, but suddenly there seemed to be no trace of innocence in his mind, as he followed the arc of this transgression to its end point: a seat in the back of the police car, entrance into the Casteline police station, the look of humiliation and disappointment on his parents' faces when they entered the police station themselves, the combination of anger and sadness in Coach LaMott's voice when he spoke to him on Monday in school. James would have a new relationship with Coach LaMott now, a relationship that would, actually, be a more honest one, now that Coach knew who James really was, not who he hoped he was.

Pete was leaning over the hood of the car, his hands planted on the hood, while the policeman reached through his pockets, coming up with cigarettes, a baggie (probably just about empty), matches, a few slips of paper, his cell phone, a slim cloth wallet, and a straw. James could see the items as the policeman checked them in the headlights, which illuminated the bushes on the side of the road ahead of them.

After just two or three minutes another police car, its lights also flashing, pulled up behind the first police car, to serve as backup. Two policemen emerged from the second car, and one came to James's door. "Sir, would you please step out of the car. Keep your hands away from your body, please. Please remove your hat before you emerge from the car."

James did as he was told, feeling like an actor on a television show. When he got outside the car, the policeman turned him 180 degrees. "Please place your hands on the roof of the car and spread your legs." James complied, while the policeman first patted his coat, reached inside his coat, then patted his thighs outside and inside. This policeman asked James to remove anything that was stored in his pockets; James removed a pack of gum, his wallet, a condom (what a joke that was), his cell, his house key, matches, and a piece of paper on which he had written the number of a girl whose father was looking for some shoveling (James had thought he could make a little money shoveling walks when snowfall arrived).

James could see Pete in the brightness of the headlights, his finger poised in front of his face, trying to place that finger on one ear, then the other, then his nose. The officer then moved the index finger of his right hand slowly across in front of Pete's eyes, checking for the nystagmus that denoted inebriation. After a few more minutes, the officer told Pete, "Would you please accompany me to the back seat of my car," and Pete was led off. James wondered if he, being just the passenger, would face a similar fate.

"Would you please accompany me to the back seat of my car," said the officer in charge of James's examination, in answer to James's question. James moved slowly, wondering whether there was anything in the car that he needed. A pair of gloves that he had worn and removed must be lying on the floor. James didn't say anything.

As James entered the back seat of the police car, he could see the third officer reaching into Pete's Audi, to begin his inspection of the vehicle.

The Arc of Intersection

At the police station the night sergeant asked Pete and James for their parents' phone numbers and made the calls, while the two boys sat stunned in the otherwise empty holding cell. Pete was led away for a few minutes so that a breathalyzer test could be administered. James was not subjected to the same, because he had not been driving.

James had not thought about the inner rooms of the police station in a long time, since he was eleven, when his class had gone on a tour of the police station, as a field trip with a DARE class, but James had no recollection of that tour, which had perhaps allowed for a minute or two inside this very cell.

James did not know what to tell Pete. They had both crossed a line that neither felt he would ever cross. James had the feeling that Pete, as the driver, would face greater disciplinary action, maybe even resulting with a loss of license. James, not having a license yet, did not know what charges might come of the events of the evening, but he knew the repercussions within his family and with his coach would be catastrophic.

"You think there's any way they can let us off?" James asked, wondering at the same time if their conversation was being monitored.

Pete shrugged his shoulders. "You never know. We weren't wise guys to the cops. I didn't get in an accident. No damage to property. I guess I was speeding, but I didn't cross the yellow line once." Pete had learned to float – not carelessly, but in a carefree way – at an early age, and he maintained an insouciant certitude that, to this date, had always protected him.

James shook his head. "I don't see any way out of this," but then he remembered the potential for eavesdropping and stopped talking.

In about fifteen minutes, Pete's parents came to release him, their shouting and bickering muffled by the treacle they directed to the desk sergeant. Pete was being released to the custody of his parents, to be summoned to the county courthouse some time Monday morning, when a magistrate could seat them. As Pete, reabsorbed by his family temporarily, left him, James began to feel his heart quicken, as he anticipated his mother and father's arrival. In about five more minutes, he heard his father's voice in the lobby of the station.

His voice sounded weary. "My name is Arthur Rush. Do you have my son in your custody?"

James listened for his mother's voice, but he heard nothing. He wondered if she had come.

"Yes, Mr. Rush. Your son was a passenger in a vehicle that was operated by a person we suspect was intoxicated while driving. There were drugs and alcohol found in the car."

James could hear sobs from his mother's chest, involuntary and chaste, as she heard the declaration of her son's fall from grace.

"We are prepared to release your son to your custody. We need from you a signature assuring his attendance at a hearing to be conducted some time Monday morning, the time dependent on the magistrate's schedule. Are you prepared to bring him to that hearing?" The voice of the policeman was peremptory, but empathetic, as if the policeman had a son of his own.

James's dad said yes. "Are there any charges being brought against my son?" he asked.

"Yes, sir. Your son is charged with being a minor in possession of alcohol. Whereas your son was not driving, we did not administer a breathalyzer on him. However, there was an open container of alcohol underneath his seat. He will be charged."

James's father sighed. "Thank you, Officer Wentworth. May I see my son?"

"Yes," said the sergeant. James heard the key rattle against the chain, as the policeman came down the hall toward James's cell.

"Time to go home," said the sergeant not unkindly. James thought the sergeant knew how his life had just changed, and he was trying to say that he was just doing his job.

When James emerged into the lobby of the police station, he saw his mother, her shoulders moving up and down with her sobbing, enclosed in his father's arms. His mother was turned away from him. James walked awkwardly toward his parents, peering at his mother's soiled sneakers that she had thrown on to make the trip. His father stared coldly at James, over his mother's shoulder.

"Hey, Dad. I'm really sorry. I never thought this would happen." James's heart heaved, as he tried to bridge the space between his parents and himself. His mother would not turn toward him.

"Let's just go," his father said, turning, his left arm still supporting his mother. "We'll talk about this at home." They left the station, turning on the chill sidewalk to the side lot where their car sat coldly. The first snowflakes of winter spatted insistently across their faces.

At home, in the living room, James sat down in the easy chair when his father told him to, as his parents sat uneasily on the couch, their arms touching, as if they had suddenly become one entity. His mother could not raise her eyes to look at James.

"James, tell us what you did tonight." His father's voice came from somewhere deep in his chest.

James took a deep breath, and recounted the last six hours of his life, from the Jack Daniels in Pete's car, through the hours sitting on the couch at Wilson's, mentioning the proximity of a girl for an hour of that segment of the evening (though he did not offer her name), the trip to the deck to smoke pot (as James told this tale of a son his parents didn't know, he looked at the left knee of his mother and the right knee of his father, sagging against each other), and, finally, the police pull-over. He did not leave out any detail. He did not know what else to do but to say the truth. He was surprised how easy it was to tell the truth of these past hours.

When he was done with his narration, words that were accompanied by no lack of frank tears, he finally looked at his parents, first his father, then his mother. His father looked at him incredulously, knowing how James's life had faltered. His mother raised her head to look at him with surprise, the way she had looked at him when he had mutilated a fork in the garbage disposal when he was five years old.

James felt some connection to his mom. "Mom, I didn't want to hurt you guys. I love you. It's killing me to know how much you're hurt right now. I wish I could take it back, but I can't. I'm sorry." James leaned forward, and touched his mother's knee. His father brushed his hand away.

"An apology won't change things, James. You've chosen to change your life. We won't ever look at you the same, son, and with good reason. What I can't fathom is the lie you've apparently been living the past months or years. Who knows how long you've been doing this? It's like you've been living a lie here under this roof." His father's voice rose in indignation, at having been defrauded by his own son.

"Dad, I know that you're disappointed, and I wish I could go back, but I can't."

His father cut in. "It's not this time I'm talking about right now. It's all the other times you must have done the same thing, but you didn't get caught. How many other times? When did this start?"

James drew back, wondering himself when it started, wondering also, what exactly it was. He had been perfectly honest with his parents to this point, but he didn't know if he could even be honest with himself in recounting the past few years of his life. When exactly had he taken his first drop of alcohol? Was it with Pete in the eighth grade? Or was it on vacation when his father had let him sip his beer at the beach cottage?

"Dad, I can't really answer that question. I don't want to be dishonest about any of this. I think this situation will force me to be more honest with you than I have been for a while, but I can't really say how many times I've done this."

His mother drew up herself to ask, "Well, how many times have you smoked pot? Do you have any idea of that?"

It was a reasonable question, and James tried to think of an accurate answer. "I . . . I . . . would have to say probably twenty times." James saw his mother shrink back in revulsion. "But sometimes just one little hit, sometimes a tiny hit as it's passing by. I'm trying to be honest with you, Mom, but it's not easy.

"I can see that you're scared for me, and I understand. But I'm not a crazy guy. I can't even drive, so I can't get in trouble for any driving infractions. And I do make lots of good decisions, I really do. I mean, I was thinking of not going to Wilson's tonight, I really was, and then I just gave in, because there was nothing else to do. I do think about my actions, but I know I'm weak, sometimes." James trailed off dispiritedly, wishing he could speak clearly about his actions, his decisions, but he really had little idea of the basis for his decisions. He just made decisions and lived with them, and before this day, his plan had worked.

His mom sat exhaustedly in the corner of the couch, her mouth open, as if she had worked a long day and she was depleted of any energy. She tried to muster a response. "Can't you see what a weak person that shows you to be? You take pride in the fact that you almost made a good decision. And that's your evidence that you don't have a problem. I don't know what to say. I can't talk any more. I'm going to bed." With a great effort she raised herself from the deep couch, pushing with her hands on her knees to raise herself to a standing position. Mr. Rush stood with her, trying to support her, but she had moved away from him, alone in her anguish for her son. There was no consolation.

James watched her trudge to the stairs, then push herself up the stairs, his last view of her the back of the left sneaker that she wore in the fertility of the vegetable garden she tended in the spring and summer.

And now it was just James and his father, staring across the room, but not at each other, as if there were other people in the room that attracted their attention. In fact, it was as if there was someone else in the room: the person that James's parents thought he was, that son

103

that had too much respect for his parents to screw up. James stared at an empty chair in the corner of the room, where he used to read his *Sports Illustrated* on Thursdays as soon as it arrived at the house.

Neither son nor father knew how to initiate the conversation. Finally, James's dad, sucking in his breath, said, "There goes your basketball season. Down the tubes. I've seen it before: Coach LaMott doesn't tolerate out-of-line behavior. Last year he buried Billie Watson on the bench after his suspension for smoking. You remember."

James remembered quite well. He assumed Coach LaMott would hold this transgression over James's head for the entire season – rightfully so. But he was disappointed that his father's reaction related only to the basketball team, and not greater issues like what the fuck James was doing with his life.

"Yeah, I know. It's a big hole I'm in right now. I know there'll be a two-week suspension, and then we'll have to see. I can practice with the team the whole time, as long as I'm in school." James's voice dissipated again, as he realized the complete uncertainty of where these two weeks would lead. He hoped he had the wherewithal to re-establish himself within the playing rotation, to regain Coach LaMott's trust. But he also wondered why he had jeopardized his status in this manner. Did he not care enough about basketball to control himself?

He wanted to say some of these things out loud, but he did not have the courage. No one had ever showed him how to be honest in his conversations about his own weaknesses. He always thought of his mother's glib credo: if you don't have anything good to say, then don't say anything at all. Applying that aphorism to himself over the years, he had never been able to express things like self-criticism very well.

His father turned his stare directly at James's eyes. "Of course, you're getting punished by the school, the athletic department, but you'll face penalties here at home, too. When your mom and I can settle down and discuss it, we'll come up with a plan. There are too many kids in this town who mess up like this and their parents just shake their heads and do nothing.

"Think about an appropriate punishment, and your mom and I will do the same."

James nodded, knowing he could not conceive of a punishment that was as monumental as his error. Actually, he did know the answer: being forced to quit the basketball team and to get a job, as his father had done when he was in high school. "Dad, I know this is a major screwup, I know it. I've been waiting for this season and next season since I was eleven. It's like there's two me's, and I can only control one of them."

His father let out an incredulous propulsion of air. Waving his right hand in the air, he said sarcastically, "Oh, the bad you just popped out, but there's still a good you that we can still love? That's crap. Gobble-de-gook. There's only one of you and that person is in a shit hole that stinks, and it's your shit that smells."

James had never heard his dad speak crudely like this. "It sure does. . . . Dad, we can go round and round about this all night long, and if it will do any good, I'll stay up all night, but I'm going to bed, if you think we're not going to get any further now." James watched his father's head sink, his sparse hair and big ears all James could see of his head.

"Might as well, you're right. We're not going to get anywhere tonight. I'm stumped. My final thought: this is a moment you'll have to live with, and it's these moments that define who we are as people. Let's see if you can stand up and grow up from this situation." With that, Mr. Rush stood up, turned from James, and walked to the same stairs his mother had mounted ten minutes before. James wondered if there would be a discussion in their bedroom, but he suspected not.

When his father had disappeared into his bedroom, James wearily stood up and pulled on the same railing his father had clung to, hoping that he would find a way to get to sleep. After his hand left the railing, James moved easily toward his bedroom, pushing the partly open door open, then closing it behind him. Without lighting his desk lamp, James undressed in the dark, leaving his clothes in the corner of the room where he always left them overnight. Donning his BC sweatshirt and sweatpants, he opened his door again, to brush his teeth in the bathroom. After peeing and brushing, James returned to his bedroom and his bed. Only then did he realize that his eyes had been closed since he first hit the stairs.

They say there's wreckage washing up
all along the coast
no-one seems to know too much
or who got hit the most
nothing has been spoken
there's not a lot to see
but something has been broken
that's how it feels to me
we had a harmony
I never meant to spoil
now it's lying in the water
like a slick of oil
the tide is running out to sea
under a darkening sky
the night is falling down on me
and I'm thinking that I should
head on home
been gone too long
leave my roaming
beachcombing

   Beachcombing by Mark Knopfler

Ben

After the church service, Ben came home with the kids, as usual, while Willa stayed longer in her role as childcare supervisor. They used to go to church in one car, but because of Willa's greater involvement, they sometimes took two cars so that Ben would not have to return to St. Andrew's to pick up Willa. In church Ben could feel his normal anticipation of the season. For about the last fifteen years Ben and Willa had been attending St. Andrew's, just about since Mary was born. They had started going in order to get Mary baptized, and their connection had evolved ever since that year. Ben liked the entire service, from hymns to sermon. But he could feel his focus wandering as it always did with the beginning of the season, as he thought of the first game on Tuesday. He sang "Alleluia" (First Sunday of Advent) lustily, but during the sermon and daily prayer, he visualized the first defensive set, when his team would establish their strength in the half-court.

Sunday dinner would come in a couple of hours, at 1:30, after Willa had come home to prepare it. Sunday dinner was a vestige of a culture that had, in general, become outdated, but once or twice Ben had tried unsuccessfully to prepare dinner while Willa finished her work at the church. Will had gently, then emphatically, told Ben that she would provide the Sunday spread when she had time after church. So Ben read the Metrowest News, eager to read the Sunday sports section, to read the league predictions. Turning to page five of the sports, he saw the league preview, with Walpole predictably picked to finish first, and Casteline picked to finish fourth or fifth in their division of the league. Ben shook his head slightly, hurt by the lack of respect afforded his team in recent years, yet admitting to himself that his team no longer warranted the respect it had once deserved. The Panthers had not won the Commonwealth League title in eight years, and there had been one team, the 2003 team, that had gone 5 – 15. Some lean times, no doubt. But Ben was pretty certain that this team had the components and the character to make a run at every team in the league.

"Players to Watch" in the league included Andrew Monaghan and James Rush, and Ben agreed with that assessment. He felt most eager for the season to begin for James, because, though just a junior, his success would signal the renaissance of the Casteline program from its mediocrity. Though James had struggled to achieve consistency in

107

the scrimmages, Ben knew that James's deep commitment to the team would bring him success.

After dinner Ben asked Willa if she wanted to stop up to see his mother with him. She visited Margot at least once during the week, but he wanted to see if she might make the trip with him this day. Not surprisingly, she declined, telling Ben she had loads of work to do in preparation for the Christmas Pageant at St. Andrew's.

"I think I'll head up to see Mom in a minute. You need anything while I'm out?"

"I don't think so. When you get home, let's light a fire and have a nice, cozy evening. I'll make some beef stew – oh, why don't you pick up a couple pounds of beef at Shaw's. You know what we get: a kind of thick, maybe two-inch slab that I can slice into beef chunks.

"Thanks. See you in a while." She stood and embraced Ben warmly, holding the embrace a little longer than usual. Ben's breath changed to feel her warmth against him.

"See you in a little – Hey, kids, you need a ride anywhere? I'm going up to see Nana. Anyone wanna come?" He knew they'd say no, but he had to ask.

"All set, Dad."

"I'm in for the afternoon. Swamped with work."

"OK, see you guys in a while."

In ten minutes he stood at his mother's door, peering in at her as she tried to pull the sleeves of her housedress down over her wrists. As she did this, she looked out the window at the bare trees that filled the view behind the nursing home.

"Hi, Mom. Happy December."

"Oh, what a nice surprise. I thought basketball season had stolen you away. You have a day off. That's nice. Was school called off today?"

"It's Sunday. No practice. I'm checking in on my mom, to get your prediction for the season." For a few years now, Ben had playfully asked for his mother's take on the season before it began. As the season proceeded and ended, it gave them a topic of conversation – even though she had not watched any of Casteline's games in about eight or nine years, when she would visit from Maine and spend a few days with Ben and Willa and the kids.

Margot peered at Ben, a grin of clairvoyance across her face. "Oh, well, you've got a strong player at the heart of the team. He's going to do great. What's his name?"

108

The Arc of Intersection

Sitting on the bed next to Margot's wheelchair, Ben nodded. "Yeah, that's right: Andrew Monaghan. He's going to be a good player. He might be able to play basketball at Bowdoin or Tufts or something. Maybe Wheaton," Ben suggested, knowing that this mention would remind Margot of the gender integration of her alma mater.

"Oh, yes, Wheaton is not the same place it used to be. I don't know why they felt they had to become just like everyone else. Being a women's school made them a little different. Now they're no different." She grimaced in distaste. Margot liked things the way they used to be. "Speaking of co-ed, did you hear about the Pope?"

Ben laughed to himself, trying to follow his mother's segue. "No, what's up with the Pope?"

"Oh, well, I read in the newspaper that he has decided to allow women to serve as cardinals now. If that doesn't sound impractical. What woman would know how to serve the Vatican – why, they don't even know how to serve Communion!" She gave a sibilant sound of disgust. "The thought of it. Women in the Vatican. I don't know. Everyone should go back to the way they were thirty-five years ago. That's when everything made sense."

Ben traced the calendar back thirty-five years, to 1973. It was the end of the Vietnam War, the onset of social engineering, the sexual revolution, the first glimmers of civil rights. In fact, things were changing dramatically in 1972 or '73, not the least change of which was his entry into the whorl that was middle school, with its requisite swear words and homework – and the Big Four, the empty antics of which his mother was fortunately unaware.

"Oh, I don't know if the old days were necessarily the best. But they were good. Any other predictions about the team? Hey, will you come to a game this year? You haven't been to a game in about five years – or more."

Margot rested her hands in her lap. "Oh, I'm too old for those games. I leave the gym in your hands. I do have one more suggestion for you. You have a troubled boy, like that boy that you did so much for from that bad home. You'll need to be very understanding of him, because he doesn't know himself."

Ben nodded. "Yes, I think you can safely say that I'll have a troubled boy. I've had a troubled boy just about every year I've coached. I think it's one of the reasons I coach: to help troubled boys with their troubles."

Margot looked intently at Ben. "This one will give you a run for your money. You better be ready for him."

109

Ben nodded, appreciating his mother's support, knowing that his mother admired his work and felt it was a benevolent way for him to spend his life, even if sports were somewhat childish, and the adults involved in those sports, including her son, were just a little compulsive in their commitment.

Through another twenty minutes of healthy and spirited banter, Ben relaxed, the passing of time punctuated by Margot's staring intermittently at the trees outside, as their trunks and branches changed to charcoal with the movement of the pale sun. The slight snowfall, no more than a couple of inches, spread a smooth carpet beneath the stark trees. Like those cobwebs that she saw hanging from those trees, Margot's days spun out abstractly. James looked out the window, trying to see the impression of pendants hanging from the trees. He wanted to see what she saw, so that he might begin to understand her life. Sometimes, when the branches waved in the wind, he could begin to conceptualize the arc of something hanging. But, the more he thought about it, the more it reminded him of the Beast in *Lord of the Flies*, and he didn't want to think his mother was as troubled as those littluns, seeing the devil embodied in an illusion.

"Mom, I have to go, but I'll check in some time this week." Ben knew that Willa would also check in whenever her schedule allowed, but he didn't want to make any promises on her behalf.

"Oh, Ben, good of you to look in on your old mom. I'll do fine here. Don't make a special effort to see me. I know you're busy with the season on top of your regular schoolwork."

Thinking ahead to the next few weeks, Ben said, "But we have to make Christmas cards for your friends. Some time in the next few weeks, we'll make some pressed-flower cards. I'm pretty sure I have some dried flowers at the house, and we can make some more. I'll bring what I've got, and I'll try to find more." For the past two years, they had worked together to make personalized Christmas cards for Margot's dwindling store of friends and relatives. Her notecards of the same origin had always been impressive in their uniqueness.

"Oh, yes, that'll be fun," Margot replied and reached her face up to Ben's lips to offer a goodbye kiss.

"Bye, Mom, love you," Ben said, as he turned the corner onto the hallway of the second floor.

Monday morning, Ben strode into Casteline High with a bounce in his winter hiking boots. The light snow still covered the yards on the way to school – pretty in its purity. It was first week of the season, one practice to go, and then opening night. Ben checked in at the office, moving on toward his classroom. The principal, Paula Weeks, called him as he passed through the office.

"Ben, you might want to come into my office. There's a matter we have to discuss."

Ben did a double-take. He thought things were going very smoothly in his classes. In fact, his junior classes were really coming together: their work on the recent essays on *Death of a Salesman* were notable for the depth of their thinking, on the most part. He entered Ms. Weeks's office wondering what was going on.

She began right away. "I get a report on my desk every Monday morning about the weekend's activities. There were incidents involving seven students, four of whom are student-athletes. Two of them are yours."

Ben swallowed. He had been so focused on pulling the threads of the team together that he had forgotten about the way it could unravel in an irresponsible instant. He shook his head in astonishment, his eyes wide open. "Who are they?"

Paula sat down. "Peter Semineau and James Rush."

Ben's heart sank. He was glad he was sitting. His breath caught short. "Woah." He shook his head as if such a demurral would negate the validity of Ms. Weeks's information. "What'd they do?"

"Peter was pulled over on a DUI, and James was a passenger in the automobile, where they found open containers of alcohol. The police took them into custody, and their parents picked them up. Saturday night. About 12:00." Paula sat quietly, letting the information sink in. "We'll let Brad know, and he can issue the suspensions. Everything always has to come through the AD, and MIAA has to be informed, too. Brad knows the routine – unfortunately, too well. You know it's two weeks or four games, whichever is greater. What does your schedule look like in the next few weeks?"

Ben knew that Paula did not know his schedule, nor did he expect her to. "We've got four games in the next two weeks, so they'll miss those games." Ben whistled silently to himself as he tried to envision his team without the services of James. Missing a starter, an experienced starter, one of the team's best shooters – would be hard to overcome. These first four games – Natick, Braintree, Wellesley, Waltham – were not the easiest part of the schedule. With a full team, Ben had hoped to go .500 over that stretch; now, he didn't know if they'd win any. He shrugged in apparent acceptance. "Oh, well, it happens. We move on, other kids get to play, and, hopefully, these guys will learn something about being part of a team."

111

"I know you'll make it a lesson for them. I haven't heard from either set of parents. You never know. Sometimes, the parents try to come up with an excuse for their kids – well, you know how that goes. In fact, that's more often the case than not. We'll see. At this time, they'll be suspended for the two weeks. I'll check with you to let you know if anything else develops from this. Thanks. And sorry."

Ben stood up. "Thanks for letting me know right away. It's a kicker, but what can you do? It's not the first time, and it won't be the last."

Ben left the office, his head down, all the bounce that he had brought with him to school that morning gone. He strode reflectively toward the teachers' room, where he found Bryan.

"You hear?" Ben asked him.

"Oh yeah. Just what we needed. Semineau, I can see. He's always been on the edge. But Rush? What's the story? Here's a starter, a veteran varsity player. And Willis is a great leader. You can't blame the tone being set by the seniors. How can a kid be so selfish? And so stupid? If he's gonna drink, he has to know where to do it. In a car isn't the place." Bryan understood the cultural climate at Casteline. There was an implicit license to drink, even though every athlete signed a document stating that he would not do so. So many kids did it, it was hard to stay away. Bryan was younger, closer to the days when he had had to face that same dilemma. He knew.

Ben reasoned, "I don't know. A car is as logical as anywhere else. Wherever they do it, it's illegal. So what difference does it make. I mean, they aren't going to drink in their own houses. In fact, the only ones who are safe are the people who host the parties. They at least don't have to drive anywhere when the party's over."

Bryan nodded at Ben's thoughts. "Well, keep your head up. You've got lots of options. How's Stedham, the new kid, playing? He got a shot at filling that hole?"

Ben thought, as he pulled his messages from his mailbox. He noticed a phone message from Mr. Semineau. No surprise. But none from the Rushes. "I think he could play a big role in these four games. I was going to bring him along slowly, but I just changed my plans." Ben moved off toward his room, as Bryan gave him a supportive tap on his shoulder.

"Hang in there."

"I always do. Keep up your good work – and don't forget the 'responsibility' lecture you give every few weeks. Maybe it'll sink in with the next set of players."

The Arc of Intersection

On his way to his room, Ben thought about the meeting he would have with James and then with Peter. He wanted to treat them the same, even though they occupied different places on the team. Peter was, at this time, a practice player, one who could play hard, but whose skills were not really varsity skills. Ten years ago, Peter would not have made the varsity team, but Ben's recent teams had not been as strong. So Peter's suspension would have little impact on the team. But James's suspension took a real weapon out of the team's hands. James could shoot, handle the ball against pressure, and he understood the concept of team defense as well as anyone on the team, including Andrew Monaghan. It would be impossible to replace James.

But he didn't want to make James feel any guiltier than Peter, because they had both done the same thing: drink during the season. Ben's admonitions, expressed the first day, repeated at the end of each week, had had no effect.

In his room, Ben clicked his computer on, preparing for his first class. Checking his e-mail, he found a message from Mr. Semineau, which read,

Coach LaMott,

I am sure that, by now, you have received the notice from the administration and the police, that Peter and one other player on your team were involved in a drinking situation on Saturday night. I want to assure you that I am completely in agreement about the imposing of penalties on my son, for any proven involvement. However, I do want to let you know that we are contesting this charge because Peter's field sobriety test was conducted in a biased, illegal manner. We are pursuing litigation in this matter. As a result, I would ask that you hold off on any action you might take in regard to Peter, until the legal matter has been resolved.

Thank you for your consideration of my perspective on this matter. I look forward to your response.

James Semineau

Ben was stunned. A parent with a child in obvious violation of the law, yet still cushioning the blow, trying to buy him more time. Ben laughed silently, shaking his head.

At that very moment, an icon blinked, indicating a new message, this one from the Rush family. Ben quickly turned to the Rushes' message.

Dear Mr. LaMott,

We were extremely disappointed to learn of our son James's involvement in a drinking situation on Saturday night. We will discipline him here at home, and we would like to know your disciplinary action as soon as you render it, because we want to know what penalty James will be facing. We know his error in judgment is a disappointment to you and to him, as well as to us. We just want you to know that we are seeking the best path to proceed on with him, so that another event like this does not happen again.

Thank you for all you do for the young men of our school.

Sincerely,

Louise Rush
Arthur Rush

Ben responded to each e-mail, letting both families know that the school's disciplinary action was administered by the athletic department, in response to police involvement of a student-athlete's off-campus behavior that violated the state drug/alcohol/tobacco policy. He told them that the athletic department would be contacting each family about the sanction for their son, and that the customary sanction was two weeks or four games. Ben tried to keep his response as matter-of-fact as possible, keeping his emotions, especially his disappointment, out of the response. He thought he did a fair job of it.

Then Ben turned to the work he had prepared for his first class, one of his freshman classes, studying *Catcher in the Rye*. He wondered how Holden Caulfield, his arms filled with the foils of the fencing team, would have handled the constraints imposed by a twenty-first century athletic policy.

Ah get born, keep warm
Short pants, romance, learn to dance
Get dressed, get blessed
Try to be a success
Please her, please him, buy gifts
Don't steal, don't lift
Twenty years of schoolin'
And they put you on the day shift
Look out kid
They keep it all hid
Better jump down a manhole
Light yourself a candle
Don't wear sandals
Try to avoid the scandals
Don't wanna be a bum
You better chew gum
The pump don't work
'Cause the vandals took the handles

from *Subterranean Homesick Blues* by Bob Dylan

James

James came to school at 1:00, after his 11:00 appointment with a magistrate at the Middlesex County Courthouse. James attested to the amount of alcohol he had consumed, stating when and where he had consumed it. He felt bad at selling out Jackie Wilson, but he didn't think this was the time for prevarication. He tried to represent his actions as accurately as possible. His parents listened intently, trying to discern the patterns their son had fallen into. In fact, Saturday night had been a somewhat typical one for James, unfortunately.

The court found James guilty of being a minor in possession of alcohol and a minor in possession of an open container in a moving vehicle.

Pete met the magistrate at a separate time from James. They hadn't spoken, so James did not know how much Pete would divulge. He faced a more challenging charge: driving while intoxicated, driving with an open container of alcohol in the vehicle. James didn't think he'd be riding to school in James's Audi for a while.

The magistrate issued James a court response stating that he must complete thirty hours of community service, attend a drug and alcohol counseling program, and postpone his test for his license until he was seventeen, which would be August of 2009. If James met all these stipulations, his record would be continued without a finding, and the charges would be expunged, one year from his court date, December 12, 2009. James felt the hearing and the finding were both fair, and he hoped the court's supervision of his behavior would provide a bulwark he could not find in himself.

With just one period and a half to go in school, James joined his Spanish class, trying to slip in with as little fanfare as possible. Such an entrance was impossible. Whenever anyone faced disciplinary action, the student body became mobilized in finding out about and analyzing the student's transgression, and the conjecture about possible punishments always ran the gamut from clemency to expulsion. The whispers stopped when Mr. Linones called for quiet. "Senor Rush, can you join us on page 101?"

James's last period was computer design, where he was still involved in the creation and marketing of a product, his being the sneakers that could elevate a player to new heights. James thought of how grounded he would be for the next two weeks, at least on game days.

The Computer class was astir; they had designated Bill Walker, a friendly, garrulous junior who was a beer-pong expert, to serve as the point man of the probe into James's morning.

"D'you have a hearing?"

"Yeah, community service, no license, and counseling for drugs and alcohol. Nothing very surprising," James replied as he dallied with the keyboard, trying to appear busy.

"D'you hear about Pete?"

"Not yet. We appeared separately. I think he's facing suspended license." James didn't know why he was offering his opinion to an acquaintance with whom he wasn't even close, but he was so angry with the situation into which he had let himself fall that he did not care what he told to whom. He figured he would just state simple facts and let his listener come to whatever conclusion he wanted.

The rest of the class moved on as usual: students working somewhat aimlessly because the due date for the project was the week before Christmas, allowing another week to complete the project.

It was Adrienne that James wanted to see, though he didn't know why. He assumed that she would be unhappy with his weekend choice, and that she would probably move away from him, because he had shown himself to be very different from her. As he climbed the stairs following Computer class, he saw her at her locker. She looked at him, but tactfully looked away, knowing that a conversation would be awkward. But James wanted that conversation.

"Hey," he initiated.

"Hi," Adrienne responded. She wore dark green sweats on her long legs, and a white fleece sweatshirt. Her hair, with its multitude of shades of golden brown, was pulled into an elastic. She looked lustrously divine.

"How's b-ball going for you?" he asked. He did not know whether the subject of his fuck-up was something she wanted to talk about, so he stayed away from it.

"Good. I'm starting to get my rhythm back. In the last scrimmage on Saturday, I got a lot of rebounds, and hit some putbacks. I think I can help on the boards. There's really no one that is a strong rebounder. So I might even be starting." She spoke of her opportunity with confidence, but not with any egotism. It was just a fact. Her team already needed her.

"That's great. I'm glad you're getting back in the swing of it. You'll have fun." At this pronouncement, James knew the discussion

117

was supposed to turn to him, but he wasn't ready for that. "Well, I gotta go. I gotta see a couple teachers to catch up on what I missed this morning," and these words served as his acknowledgment of his hearing. He started to move on.

"If you want to talk, just say the word. I'm a good listener," Adrienne assured him as he turned away. His heart bounced, though he couldn't tell whether it was upwards or downwards.

"Thanks. I might need that soon," James said as he moved away from her awkwardly.

As James neared Room 212, where he would meet with Mr. Olson, his English teacher, to discuss the material he had missed, he saw Coach LaMott moving toward him with a clear purpose. He knew that a meeting was imminent. He turned in to 212, caught up with Mr. Olson, and left in a minute. Coach LaMott waited.

"James, do you have a minute?" the coach asked quietly.

"Sure."

"Let's go to my room. I think it's empty." Coach LaMott led the way, past small huddles of students, many of whom turned toward the pair and then quickly turned away, the direction of their conversation altered with the knowledge of the subject that these two had to address. Not that James was any celebrity in the school, not that at all. It's just that, within the junior and senior classes, the usual Monday topic was the fallout from the weekend parties, and James happened to have attained the lead role in that narrative.

They turned in to Coach LaMott's classroom, with its old-fashioned bulletin board decorated with student writing. James recalled having his essay on the several distinct types of athletes mounted on that wall for a five week stretch last year: the authentic athlete, the hopeful athlete, and the apparent athlete. James had always considered himself the hopeful athlete, hoping to become the authentic one. But he was afraid he had become the apparent athlete, a hypocrite. From that essay Coach LaMott had developed a respect for James's writing after he began to spend more time developing his sub-topics with clarity and specificity. Those were key elements in Mr. LaMott's writing class.

They sat down, each at a student desk.

"Want to tell me about last weekend?" began Coach LaMott.

James kept his head down. He wanted to look Coach LaMott in the eye as he spoke, but he felt too guilty.

"Well, you probably know, I got pulled over as a passenger, and there was alcohol in the car. I was taken to the Casteline police station, where my parents picked me up. This morning I had a hearing at a magistrate's office in Middlesex Courthouse, and I got community service, mandatory counseling, and license restriction until I'm seventeen, this summer." James's cloudy gaze swept across Coach LaMott's face once or twice during his rendering of the evening. He never stayed focused on the coach's face, because he didn't dare, but he tried to read the coach's reaction, with no success.

After a short silence, Coach LaMott cleared his throat. "James, I've faced this dilemma many times in my years here, too many times, to be honest. You're not the first player that's messed up. I'm sorry you made the decisions you made; I'm sorry your life lacks the grounding to resist the incessant pressures that all of you face – and I faced the same pressures, many years ago, and I can't tell you I was completely resistant to those pressures. We all make mistakes. It's just some of them are larger than others. And this is a large one."

James nodded. He looked out the window, watching students heading to their cars, some of them jumping with the freedom that the end of school brings.

Coach LaMott continued. "You know you'll miss the first four games, Natick, Braintree, Wellesley, and Waltham. You'll be able to practice with the team, and you'll sit on the bench in a shirt and tie for those first four games." He paused. "That's the logistics of the suspension." Another pause. "But, more importantly, there's the issue of your commitment to the team. There are a lot of guys here – on this team – that were counting on you for your skills but also for your leadership and your experience. They look to you to see how to be a Panther basketball player.

"You and I go way back," Coach LaMott continued, and with these words, James's eyes filled with tears. He kept his head low, unwilling to show his visceral response. "I had always thought you were one of the good ones, the ones who put the team above the individual. But clearly I was wrong.

"You're going to have to do a lot of proving to your teammates, to Coach Taft, to your parents, and to yourself, to regain the trust that you've lost here. We'll reassess at the end of the two weeks, looking at how you've worked during that time. For the sake of the team, I hope we find someone to replace you who comes in and does a great job, and helps us win all those four games. If that's the case, you'll have to fight hard to get back to your spot." Coach LaMott didn't develop the other scenario: that the team would struggle without James, and he would, by default, work his way back into the rotation somewhat easily, once he was cleared to play. "Do you have anything you want to say? We've got practice in about an hour."

119

James wanted to offer some words that would inspire some hope on the part of his coach, but he had trouble finding those words. "I have to tell you that I'm sorry that I got myself into that situation, and I can promise that it won't happen again. I'm not sure why I do things I know I shouldn't do, but I know they're wrong. I do. If it makes you believe in me a little more, I can tell you, I hope the team does great while I'm sitting, and I hope I have to fight hard to get playing time. That'd make me work harder, and I think I need that." James was trying to be honest with Coach, but he didn't understand himself very well.

"That's good to hear. I'm on your side, James; I want you to succeed. You've made a big mistake, but the mistake is over, in two weeks the punishment will be over, and we'll start fresh at that point. I'm trying to do two things with this team: develop character and win, in that order. If you develop some character through this ordeal, then maybe you'll be stronger for the second half of the season, and we'll get a few wins at that time that we might have missed. I do believe in your ability to change." With that Coach LaMott stood up, to let James know that their meeting was over.

Moving toward the door, James found his eyes closed, but he opened them to look at his Nikes, as they swept across the linoleum of Room 215. Practice at 3:30.

It was a good practice, though James, naturally, played with the second team for every play, in scrimmage time. Alex White took his spot at a wing position, and Archie Stedham got lots of time at the wing, too. They both looked good. James tried to outplay them, but his legs just weren't responsive enough to cut off their driving lanes. He kept fouling because of his slow feet. Coach LaMott bore down on him more than once. "Move your feet, James. Let's get over it." Later he shouted, "James, quit moping. Get down the floor." James didn't realize that the rest of the players were outsprinting him, but it was a fact. He lacked the energy to take the first step. It was almost as if he had lost the anticipation that enables a player to make a successful play.

As the practice proceeded, Dan kept turning heads with his ability to drive past people and his begrudging defensive posture. With fifteen minutes to go in the practice, James saw Coach LaMott take Alex, Archie, and Dan aside to talk with them. When they returned to the floor, Dan took the starting position. James's happiness for his friend tempered his own misery at what he was losing. He had not been part of Coach's little enclave; he wondered whether he ever would be again.

Pete was relegated to third team status in scrimmages, which meant that he didn't enter the court, except for moments when others were spent. Of course, it was the day before a game, the Natick game, so Coach LaMott wasn't running the team very hard. There was a lot of review of Natick, based on last year's returning players, and the game focus for the Panthers against Natick: rebound and take care of the ball.

In the final huddle, Coach LaMott tried to pull the entire team together. "OK, guys, we're going into this Natick game a couple of men down. Normally I think of it as thirteen men working together, but tomorrow it'll be only eleven. But, James and Pete, I don't expect you to be on the bench with your heads down. You've got to be active on the bench, calling out screens for our defense when it's in front of you, calling out shots, giving support to the guys who come out of the game. We're not going to win if you don't give as much of yourselves as you can to the effort. You can't step onto the court, but you can still help us win.

"Starting team will be Jason at the point, Dan at the 2, Jonas at the 3, Andrew at the 4, and Geoff at the 5. No big changes. You all know your roles. Don't try to do anything that we haven't been successful at in practice. Stay within yourselves. Natick is a big rebounding team. Geoff, Mark, Andrew, you've got to concentrate on the defensive boards. Dan, Alex, Jonas, and Archie, you have to keep their wings off the offensive glass. They can kill you if you don't. And then we have to take care of the ball. Jason, keep it simple. We don't need the great play, just the good play." Coach LaMott looked at the floor for most of his pep talk, but he did look at the particular players he was addressing. Then he looked directly at James, and then Pete. "Let's turn this negative into a positive. It's all part of the game. We just have to find a way to win."

Geoff asked Coach LaMott for a minute with the team. When the coaches had turned away, Geoff quietly spoke to the boys in the huddle. "Guys, a few of you have let the team down. That's a hard thing for us to swallow, when we're busting our hump on the floor, and a couple of you won't be available for the game because of your drinking. So we're gonna have to work a lot harder than we thought. To prepare for that we're gonna run an extra ten in a minute right now, just to show our strength. Let's get on the line. I'll call out the start and the finish."

Returning to the group of players, Coach LaMott took out his watch again, to time them. "Set, go," he called, then began his exhortations. "Let's push it, Archie. C'mon Andrew, get to the front of the pack. Let's go, Jason, you're got to be the quickest. Let's go."

James pushed himself to the front of the pack, as well as his legs would allow. He wanted to be first. When he gained on Dan and Bobbie, he thought he could pass them, but they just kicked it a little faster, and James fell back.

On the final sprint, James felt a surge, one he hadn't had all practice, allowing him to finish in the top 4 or 5, a little higher than his usual spot. He felt good that he had tapped a reserve that usually wasn't available to him. After the sprint, and the final team "Tight," James approached Coach LaMott, as Geoff and the managers retrieved the balls and tossed them in the rolling cage they used to store them.

"Coach, can I run an extra ten in a minute?" It was out of James's mouth before he understood the implications of his request: he didn't know whether he would be able to run another ten, after two in the last five minutes.

"I'd love to see it. You want me to time it?"

"No, I'll set it on the clock."

Coach LaMott looked at James with a little pragmatic skepticism. "How about I keep it on my watch. You're not trying to show off here. You're just trying to do what's right." Coach motioned with his head for Bridget to remove the scoreboard keypad.

When James had set up on the line for one last set of sprints, Coach LaMott offered a quiet, "Set, go," and James initiated a full sprint, actually his best start of the day, as he tried to appease his guilt. The pace slowed, and by the sixth leg, a return leg, James's legs felt the heaviest they had felt all day. He had no spring left for his last four sprints, and he lumbered across the finish line heavily, his knees lacking any resilience, his lungs filled with unexpelled air as he labored to finish.

At the wall past the endline, James leaned his head against the cushion, regaining his breathing. Coach LaMott came to him. "That was a great effort. That tells me a lot. Now, if you keep that up, you'll be building something."

Between quick breaths, James asked, "Wha' was my time?" without lifting his forehead off the wall.

"You just missed sixty seconds," Coach LaMott told him kindly. "But that's not the point. You did it, and it's in your reserve now, and you will build off that. That's the way progress happens, slowly." Coach LaMott placed his left arm around James's back, embracing his left shoulder, in a supportive clasp. "Get your shower."

James trudged off toward the locker room, his feet dragging. Geoff Willis stood in the doorway, and as James eased past, Geoff gave him a light tap on the shoulder. "Nice job," he said.

In the locker room James approached Dan, who had been given the starting position in James's place – a big surprise to both Dan and James.

"I thought Alex was gonna start," Dan said quietly to James.

"Yeah, but I guess you just showed better during today's practice. Nice goin."

Dan turned from James toward the shower, his skinny body quickly absorbed in the vapor emanating from the shower room.

When the day is done
Down to the earth then sinks the sun
Along with everything that was lost and won
When the day is done

When the day is up
Hope so much your race will all be run
Then you find you jump the gun
Have to go back where you began
When the day is done

When the night is cold
Some get by but some get old
Just to show that life's not made of gold
When the night is cold

When the bird has flown
You got no one to call your own
You got no place to call your home
When the bird has flown

When the game's been fought
You speed the ball across the court
Lost so much sooner than you would have thought
Now the game's been fought

When the party is through
It seems so very sad for you
Didn't do the things you meant to do
Now there's no time to start anew
Now the party's through

The day is done
Down to earth then sinks the sun
Along with everything that was lost and won
When the day is done

When the Day is Done by Nick Drake

Ben

With four minutes left in the first game against Natick, Ben inserted the transfer, Archie Stedham into the lineup, to try to add another good ball-handler. Alex White had played a strong game, but he had turned the ball over two times in the second half against Natick's three-quarter trap (a defense that had taken the Panthers completely by surprise in the second half). Natick led, at the four-minute-remaining mark, 54 – 49.

On the first press break, Archie set up Geoff Willis with a brilliant cross-court diagonal pass, to cut the lead to three. On Natick's next two possessions, the Panthers fouled, and Natick cashed in on three of four to extend the lead to 57 – 51.

At the two minute mark, Andrew hit a three, only to be answered by a Natick putback (on their third consecutive offensive rebound). Back and forth, hit one, miss one. Casteline was reduced to fouling now, and Natick hit five of seven down the stretch, to end up winning, 63 – 56.

Casteline had played a strong game, never letting Natick break contact with them. Halftime score was a two-point game, and Natick never led by double figures. Casteline had held a brief 24 – 23 lead late in the first half, but the Panthers never had control of the game.

In the huddle at halfcourt after the game, Ben encouraged the team."Strong start, guys. Andrew, great shooting. As a team, we played them even on the boards, but late in the game, they started to take over. I think I saw seven offensive boards for Natick in the last period, and that prevented us from coming back.

"It's tough to win in this gym, but we gave ourselves a chance. Not many teams win in here. Good start. Now we have to get ready for Braintree. We've got Jim Winn scouting, so I'll know about them tonight, and we'll get a plan ready for Friday.

"Keep your heads up. Strong start. Give this effort all year long, and we'll have a great season."

Ben turned from the team, accepting the game stats from Bridget, and turning to the stands to find Willa. She wasn't in her usual spot, next to the railing halfway up the stands at midcourt. He wondered where she had gone. She had been sitting there just before tip-off when he gave her a nod and a smile. He hadn't checked the spot at halftime.

Bryan sidled up next to Ben. "Nice start, Coach. You had 'em on the ropes. At home, with a full team, you've got to like your chances."

"Yeah, but all I can think about is today, and tomorrow. We've got the ball in our hands, and we give ourselves the chance to win, but we didn't win. Bottom line." Ben stared at the floor with disgust. It had been four years since he had won the opening game, and it was getting increasingly difficult to dig out from under a poor start – especially this time, without one of his more experienced players.

In the bus Ben asked Mrs. Nelson, the driver, a veteran of many Panther trips into cold winter nights, if she would keep the interior lights on so that he could check the stats. She understood. Natick had won the boards by five, but, most noticeably, Casteline had turned the ball over 21 times. There was the ball game. Jason Grutchfield had had five turnovers, far too many for a point guard. He had five assists also, but he hadn't taken very good care of the ball. Foul shooting: 11 for 18, not especially good. The team had very little margin for error, and all these stats ratified the fact that they had not played a very well-focused game.

Bryan sat next to Ben, iterating nearly the same points. He wore his blue button-down, open-collared, no tie. Bryan had never found dressing up for games a necessity, though the team always wore a tie to home- and away-games, as a matter of dignity and uniformity. It had been about five years now that the team had chosen to dress up for game days, and Ben had thought it a great idea, though it had had no effect on the results – nor had it served as any sort of moral grounding.

The bus ride home was a sober one, Ben and Bryan grimly seated in the front seat on the right. Geoff Willis took care of the players' attitude with a gentle tongue lashing in response to a few snickers from a couple players who had not played. The managers knew enough to render their impression of the Natick social scene quietly, and the cheerleaders took their cue from the players, coaches, and managers.

Back at Casteline, as the players wandered off quietly, Ben and Bryan entered the small, messy office, shared by the varsity, JV, and freshman boys' basketball coaches, and the ski team coaches, as well as the phys. ed. teachers. On the wall were the President's Fitness regimen and the soccer coach's game results. Ben strolled into the team locker room, where a few of the team members were gathering their books to take home. In this room Ben had mounted the walls with the listings of each of the teams over the past 25 years, every player who graduated listed under his graduation year. There were the strong teams of the early nineties, when he had won the school's only basketball state championship, the equally strong teams in the late nineties. In all there were nine league championships, five sectional titles, and one state championship. This was the twenty-fifth team, a sort of anniversary for Ben.

Geoff and Andrew, two principal seniors, were still sitting on the bench in the locker room, their heads down, as they murmured to each other.

"What do you think, guys? A healthy start?" Ben had learned to keep the conversation neutral, to find out how his players assessed the game. Early in his coaching years, Ben had been much more immediately and overtly critical, but as the years had progressed, he had learned (and been told) that such a lack of diplomacy was ineffective.

Geoff, the captain, spoke first. "No way we should have lost that game. Nothing they did was a surprise. We were ready for them. We just didn't execute."

Ben nodded, but disagreed. "Well, that second half trap press took us by surprise. It's not quite like ours, and we weren't really prepared for it. I'd say we had five turnovers against it in the second half, and that was at the time we were trying to stay even with them. That was big."

Andrew looked up. "Yeah, I had a big one at the start of the fourth period. Tried to dribble up the sideline. I could hear you saying in the time out, don't bring it up the sideline, but it looked like I could get by and cut in. But I didn't."

Ben looked down at Andrew. "Yeah, they make it look like you've got room, but they're really just luring you into their trap. It worked on you; it worked on Jonas; it worked on a lot of people. First game stuff. We'll learn." Ben patted both seniors on a shoulder. "Don't let it eat you up. Keep positive. Braintree is strong, but at least we have them at home. And we'll be more ready for their trap, if they try it." Ben picked up a pair of shorts, left from some long-ago practice. "Let's go. Homework still to be done," Ben said with an ironic smile, knowing that few of the players would have the time or inclination to work on their studies. He knew he'd go home, have a quick supper, spend time with the kids, watch a bit of a college game on TV, and climb into bed, tired and disappointed.

But then he recalled that Willa hadn't been in the stands at the end of the game. He wondered why she had left so quickly. She hadn't said anything about leaving early.

Half an hour later, Ben found a note on the kitchen table, a note from Scott letting Ben and Willa know that he was at Perry's house, studying. Looking at the clock, Ben wondered when and how Scott would be returning home. He called Scott on his cell phone, reading the number off the notepad next to the wall phone.

"Yeah?" Scott answered, the word conveying his sense that Dad was checking up on him.

"What's up? You going to need a ride home?" asked Ben. He fiddled with a pen in his right hand as he spoke.

"Yeah, I guess so. Maybe 9:30? We're finishing up a little project, but we'll be done in a little while. Could you pick me up at 9:30?"

"Sure. You know where Mary is?"

"I saw her at the game, but we didn't talk at the end. She was with her friends. I bet they went to Friendly's." Scott and Mary both had attended the Summit game, a home game vs. Norfolk.

"Who won the game?" Ben asked, just wondering.

"Summit crushed 'em. Probably won by thirty. Santos had 25 and Simms had 20. They looked good." Scott knew the game of basketball very well, having watched dozens of games in his youth.

"Wow." Ben paused. "You know where Mom was going after the game? She came to my game, but she took off right away."

Scott must have shaken his head because there was a silence. "She didn't say anything to me. Maybe she's pickin up Mary."

Ben considered that possibility, then checked off with Scott. "I'll see you at 9:30. You're at Perry's?"

"Yeah, see you then." Scott clicked off, leaving Ben still unsure about Willa. He called Willa's cell, waiting for the full ring, then left a message, "Hey, hon, just wondering what you're doing. Everything OK? Give me a call. I'm picking Scott up at 9:30 at Perry's. I haven't heard anything about Mary; do you know where she is?" After the message, he hung up and looked in the refrigerator for some leftovers, finding the remains of a chicken-noodle casserole from Monday night. Pulling it from the refrigerator, he spooned it onto a blue plate, placing it in the microwave and setting the timer for four minutes.

He sighed, feeling the emptiness of the house, hearing the hum of the microwave as it warmed his dish. Just then the phone rang, and Ben rushed to it, expecting to hear Willa's voice. Instead he heard a man's voice. "Coach LaMott? Peter Grutchfield here, Jason's dad. You got a minute?"

Ben sighed, silently, he hoped. He had had several conversations over the years with Peter Grutchfield, many conversations, in fact, because Mr. Grutchfield had coached these seniors in the youth leagues when they were in sixth, seventh, eighth grade. Peter had been a strong supporter of Ben's when Jason was young, always referring to the Class of '09 as a strong one, and pointing to their record in the youth leagues. Ben knew they had enjoyed some success, but much of it was the result of a persistent and well organized press that Mr. Grutchfield had installed in sixth grade and utilized for three years, with good results. Ben knew, from experience, that such success was not particularly translatable to the high school game, because both their opponents' ball handling abilities and exposure to quality coaching would increase greatly, rendering the press less and less effective as the years went by. But Mr. Grutchfield still harbored a love of those days when Andrew, Jonas, Geoff, Jason and Alex had had their first taste of basketball success.

"Yeah, sure thing. What's up?" Ben asked, as neutrally as he could. When a parent called his house, it usually wasn't to chat about successes.

"Well, Jason came home from the game really disappointed. He felt we should have won that game, and I agree."

"I agree, too. We played well enough to give ourselves a chance. We just didn't take advantage of the opportunities that we had." Ben stopped talking, knowing that Peter Grutchfield had something else on his mind.

"Coach, Peter was disappointed also because of something you said to him."

Ben reached into his memory of the game and of his own responses to the game as it unfolded, to try to distinguish what he might have said to Jason at any point in the game. He had spoken specifically to Jason more than once, about taking care of the ball as a point guard, but that, unfortunately, was nothing new. Ben and Jason had never completely agreed on the role of a point guard. Jason wanted to make the spectacular play, while Ben wanted him to draw double-teams and get the ball to the open teammate. But this game didn't seem any different from any other.

"Is he referring to something specific I said?" Ben asked, wondering where this inquiry was leading.

"Yes, to be specific, late in the third period, you called a time-out and ripped him a new asshole, after he had turned the ball over. I could hear you across the gym. It wasn't pretty."

Ben sat at the kitchen chair, stunned. He didn't know what to say. Should he wonder why Jason himself was not speaking to him? Should he wonder why Peter Grutchfield felt it was his right to call Ben up an hour after the first game, to register his dissatisfaction with his choice of words? But Ben knew that he should not wonder, because when you lose, you open yourself up to painful and public reprobation. "Well, Peter, when the game is on the line, I think we all get a little hot under the collar, and every one of us, including me, might make a mistake. In the case of a player, he might misread a defense. In the case of a coach, he might make the wrong substitution; he might use the wrong words. But it's all magnified when we lose, and forgotten when we win. I know I did raise my voice with Jason and with others as the game moved toward the end." Ben didn't know what else to say. He was trying to keep the conversation general, because he wasn't sure what he had said that had aggrieved the Grutchfield family.

"Oh, it's not just a little mistake. Jason says you've been on his case since the first day of practice, never letting him get settled at the point. This is his senior year, the culmination of all his hard work for seven years. I've watched him develop every step of the way, and, right now, he has absolutely no confidence, and we can thank you for that loss. He never does the right thing. If he shoots, you tell him he should have passed. If he passes, you tell him he missed the better target. If he pushes the ball, you tell him he needs to wait for his targets. He is absolutely confused, and it's got me confused. Is this the way it is for all your players? When they become seniors, you start writing them off and moving on to the next crew, only so you can rip them apart for not living up to your expectations? I already see the new poster child, Archie Stedham, getting long minutes. I guess it won't be long before he's replacing Jason? Huh? Is that the plan?"

All these accusations were a lot for Ben to digest. He didn't know where to start. "Peter, let's let things cool down for a day. How about if Jason and I sit down after school tomorrow, and talk it out between the two of us? If I knew that Jason was having confidence problems, I would certainly handle him differently. But I've never seen Jason lack for confidence. He's always been a leader, setting a fast tempo, bringing the level of the players around him up to his level.

"I do see him struggling so far this year, but that's not uncommon for seniors, when they start to realize that there is no tomorrow, that this is their final season, and they sometimes put extra pressure on themselves to have a memorable senior year. Maybe that's what Jason is dealing with, but I don't know. I do think he and I have to talk about it." Ben stopped theorizing, to let Mr. Grutchfield absorb his ideas.

"Coach, he can't maintain his confidence if you're constantly criticizing him. He says you haven't said a good word to him all year. He has come home more than once and spilled his frustration out for my wife and I."

130

Ben shook his head, in wonderment. "Well, maybe I have to find more opportunities to praise his play, but I find him to be one of the stronger point guards we've had in years. He knows that."

Mr. Grutchfield interrupted, "No, he doesn't. And you've done nothing to lead him to believe that. That's exactly what I'm getting at." His voice had risen in pitch during the conversation, and it was reaching its highest point now.

The phone beeped, signaling an incoming call, but Ben did not care to interrupt the icy tension.

"Let's plan on a meeting after school, Jason and I. If after that conversation, Jason is still confused about what I want for him, then I'd be happy to sit down with you and him, to clear the air. How does that sound?" Ben wanted to bring the conversation to a close, because he knew that Peter's harangue could be endless.

Ben heard Peter exhale. "Well, I guess that's how you handle things, keeping the parents as far away as possible. If you think that would work, then give it a try. But I'm warning you, my wife and I are not happy with the way things are going. This is supposed to be his crowning glory, his senior year. You're making it into a miserable experience."

Ben checked his response, knowing that what he wanted to say would not reduce Peter's anger. "Is Jason home? I'd like to speak with him, if I could."

Peter let out a contemptuous laugh. "I'm sure he doesn't want to speak with you right now. He's still reeling."

Again, Ben checked his temper. "Would you at least ask him if he would like to come to the phone? I'd just like to ask him to meet with me, myself."

Ben could hear Peter put the phone down and call Jason. In a short while, Jason came to the phone, his voice quiet, "Hello?"

"Hello, Jason. This is Coach LaMott. Your dad tells me that you're having a hard time and I might be contributing to that hard time. Can we talk about it right after school tomorrow?"

"Yeah, I guess so. In your room?"

"Yes, that's perfect. Room 215. You know. And, Jason, you didn't have a great game, but you did some solid things today. You are one of the reasons we had a chance to win over a good team like Natick. Don't start thinking about yourself as less than what you are: a very experienced, hard-to-pressure ball-handler that can prevent teams from throwing pressure at us. Keep your head up. I don't think any of us played our best game today, including you. First game. Some tough turnovers. Let's see where we are at the end of the season." Ben knew that a senior puts extraordinary pressure on himself to be the senior leader, and he wanted Jason to see a broader picture, one that included twenty games, not just one. "See you in school. Get back to your homework," Ben concluded.

"OK, Coach." Jason seemed non-committal, unsure that Ben's support was authentic. "Bye."

Ben hung up and stared at the light maple kitchen cabinets, shaking his head. He tried to think of the moment when the balance of power had shifted, from the coach being right to the parent being right. He knew that he would not have had this conversation in the eighties or nineties. It was some time in the new century when somehow he had ceded control to outside interests, but he knew it was gone. It had been so simple when it was just he and a collection of players who inhabited the gym. He could make them into his vision of a team, and it generally worked. Nine times it had worked, nine league championships. But now these players would listen to Bryan and him for two hours, and then go home and listen to dad or mom, usually dad, for another four hours, and the conflict would arise, in many cases. He felt bad for Jason, because he knew that Jason himself could easily work his way into being a singular player, one that could lead Casteline to a great season. But with his father looking over his shoulder, and Jason not having the independence to throw his father off that shoulder, he was twisted in two directions, a recipe for uncertainty. As long as Jason harbored doubts about Ben's coaching, the compact would not work.

Just then Ben recalled that a call had come in during the conversation. He called his voicemail, to hear Jim Winn's voice, his friend who had scouted Braintree. He called Jim and sat at the table, taking notes as Jim recounted Braintree's game. It had been a six-point victory over Milton, last year's league champion. They sounded solid, as Ben had expected. During Jim's report and Ben's spray of questions, the phone beeped again, and Ben told Jim he had to get it, they'd talk again on Wednesday.

"Hello?" Ben asked.

"Hey," Willa said. "I'm sitting at Turner's Garage with Mary. Her car broke down, and I had to get to the car, wait with her for a tow truck, and follow her to Turner's. We're just getting ready to come home. But I have to stop at the church to meet with the hospitality committee. I know I'm really late, but could you pick up Mary at the garage while I catch the end of the meeting at the church?"

"Sure, no problem. What's up with her car?"

"I don't know. It just conked out going up Reddy's hill. I hope it's not a big deal."

"OK, I'll be there in ten minutes. I have to pick Scott up at 9:30 at Streets'. I left you a message, but you must not have checked messages."

"Oh, I got that message. I just didn't have time to call you. Sorry to be dumping this on you, but I gotta get to church."

"It's fine. I'll be there in ten minutes. Maybe I can pick up Scott a little early. Or, if not, Mary and I can get some quality time."

"Thanks. I should be home by ten. How ya doing?"

Ben knew she was wondering how he was taking the loss. "Ah, well, we played well for a lot of the game, just not when we needed to. Can we call it a good loss?" Ben's memory of the game was actually buried underneath Peter Grutchfield's telephone call. He wanted to tell Willa about the call, but this was not the right moment.

"They played hard. They really wanted to win," Willa offered, and Ben knew she was right. Over the years she had displayed a keen sense of the direction the team was heading.

"So nothing to worry about?" he asked.

"No, first game. They really played hard, and they played together."

Ben agreed silently, but he could not accept the discrepancy on the boards in the second half, nor could he accept the turnovers. But it wasn't worth extending the conversation with Willa, who was being supportive and honest in her appraisal.

"Thanks, honey. See you around ten. I've got the kids."

Closing the front door, Ben headed to the Corolla in the driveway, his car for the past nine years, ever since it had been a prized new purchase for Willa. She had since bought a small Subaru wagon, slightly used, but maintaining good four-wheel traction in the winter. Mary's junker was a '96 Civic, with very little life left in it. The mechanics at Turner's had kept it running for the past five months, but it was getting close to that tipping point, when the maintenance cost equaled a monthly payment for a newer car.

The ride to Turner's was a quiet one. Ben kept the music soft, as he mulled Peter Grutchfield's complaints. When Ben was confronted with issues like these, he became defensive of his manner, insisting to himself that he had always done things this way, and that it had worked consistently in the past. Yet, a part of him acknowledged that the times had changed, his administrators had changed, the behaviors of parents had changed, and that he was compelled to alter his approach, too. Quietly, from WERS, Norah Jones added her lament to his, assuring him that there were moments that seemed too hard to take, but that an end always came.

The ghostly trees filed past as Ben slowed at Turner's corner. He could see Mary's Civic beside the closed doors of the two work bays on the left of the building, but he didn't see Mary out front. He pulled up next to the Civic to see if she was sitting inside, with no heat, but the car was dark and empty. Questioning his recollection of Willa's phone conversation, Ben pulled out his cell phone, to see whether there were any messages on it. He had forgotten to turn it on. Turning the phone on, he tried to recall how to check messages that might have come in while the phone was turned off (which was the entire day, apparently).

After successfully maneuvering through the simple menu, he listened to two messages: from Mary, telling him that the mother of one of her friends who had been in the car with her was driving her home, she didn't need a ride, thanks anyway. The second message was from Scott: "Hey, Dad, Wilson's dad is gonna drive me home. I know you're already out, because I tried you at home. I've got a ride. Sorry to make you come out for nothing. See you at home. Bye."

Well, that made two for two: no need for Ben to be out here in the cold, trying to be of service. He was glad his kids were able to fend for themselves, but he had also looked forward to providing some help for them. He backed out of Turner's lot, looking forward to seeing his family at home.

By the time Willa came home, Ben, Mary, and Scott had been sitting at the kitchen table for twenty minutes, discussing the Summit game, the Casteline game, Mary's car (the consensus was to keep it running as long as they could, as long as no monthly bill exceeded $300, an expensive proposition, but, at least, a plan), and Scott's latest foray into meeting the girl of his current interest. With Mary's gentle prodding, Scott revealed a little more about her. His visit to Perry's was another subterfuge for seeing this girl. Her name was Holly Scanwood.

Upon hearing the name, Mary recalled, "I think I've seen her in the photography lab. She's always using the dark room. Does she have long, straight, light-colored hair that's always hanging down in front of her face? Does she wear weird belts?"

"Yeah, that sounds like her. I know she prints a lot of photos. She's really into art and photography. We looked at some folders she's putting together, black and white photos, mostly of still life, an old bicycle leaning against a garage with peeling paint, the bottom of a gasoline pump, with that windshield scraper/cleaner in the little sideways bucket. She seems to catch little scenes that we always see, but that we don't notice."

Ben was impressed. "Sounds as if she has a good eye. Did you spend a lot of time over there?"

Scott furrowed his brow. Then he decided to tell the truth. "Yeah, I was over there for about an hour. I was only at Perry's for a little while after the game. He's not as intrigued by Holly as me."

Ben felt warmed, hearing about Scott's actual life. He knew it wasn't easy for Scott to trust his parents – it wasn't easy for anyone fifteen years old to trust his parents. He knew that his own life was focused a little too much on his efforts at teaching and coaching, and that, as a result, he let his children's lives move in an organic way toward their own passions.

Mary chimed in, "Sounds like you've got the hots for Holly. It's about time. I was wondering when you were gonna start finding out about girls."

"Oh, you should talk, Miss-I-don't-want-to-leave-my-little-circle-of-girlfriends-if-I-can-help-it. Yeah, when was your last date?" Scott responded playfully. It was nice to hear them razzing each other the way friends do. Just then Willa came in the door, her arms laden with two bags of groceries.

"Well, that was quite a night," she said, putting the bags on the counter. She looked at her family, ensconced at the table, leaning toward each other, seeming to feel their shared moment, seeming to feel, consequently, her absence from that moment.

"Hi, hon, how'd the meeting go?" asked Ben.

"Oh, I got there just for the tail end. Naturally, because I wasn't there, I got named the chairperson for the spring plant sale. I don't mind, but I don't know when I'll be able to do everything. Oh well, that's a problem for another day. How's everyone doing?"

"I ended up getting a ride from Cindy's mom, so Dad didn't bring me home," said Mary.

Scott added, "And I got a ride from Wilson, so Dad was basically useless. But thanks anyway, Dad," Scott jeered.

"Well, next time, don't call me, or at least don't call me on my cell, because you know I don't know how to turn it on," Ben responded, in the same playfulness. "What do you say, Mom? I say we swear off these kids, let them fend for themselves for the next five years, or at least until they prove to be inept."

Willa took the bait. "Well, I'm just afraid they'll prove to be inept a little too quickly for my taste. How about we check in with them every few weeks, just to be sure they are making adequate progress, as the NCAA calls it."

The smiles on Mary's and Scott's faces told Ben that it had been a perfect night, even though not much had gone right.

In bed, after the snacks were consumed and the newspaper read cursorily, after Ben had heard Jim's more complete scouting report, Ben and Willa lay against each other, enjoying the contact they provided and received. The weight of Willa's thigh on Ben's was comfortable, assuring. In their mutual fatigue, it was not the time for amorous ardor; rather, it was a time for gentle stability and mutual support. As Willa whispered her entreaties of God, Ben debated telling her about Peter Grutchfield's call. He decided that he didn't want to destroy the mood. The darkness filled the room like a song, or like a prayer, depending on the point of view.

The Arc of Intersection

I can hear the rain come down, I can listen with my heart
I can see with both eyes closed in the dark
Sleep will come in just a while but till it does I choose
To listen to the rain, it's the rhythm of the blues

I walk along these streets of home that once belonged to us
And now baby I walk alone and I am lost
In the sound of my own footsteps on the avenues
I guess I'm only walking to the rhythm of the blues

I don't wanna hear another word spoken, I don't wanna see another tear
shed
I can't seem to fix what's broken, like this record baby in my head

Lonely looks as bad on me as lonely looks on you
And still we keep on moving to the rhythm of the blues

from *Rhythm of the Blues* by Mary Chapin Carpenter

James

Wednesday's practice simmered, competitively and sharply. The team looked especially strong on the break, Jason setting Andrew and Dan up for countless layups. Similarly, if James ran the floor hard, he found he wound up with some pretty easy shots off Bobbie Pitaro's passes, and when Archie Stedham took over the point for the second team, James got even more easy looks.

After forty minutes of hard scrimmaging, Coach LaMott called the team together. "OK, guys, that's a great effort, pushing the ball up and, more importantly, filling the lanes ahead of the ball. Andrew, Dan, James – you're getting easy looks because you're sprinting every time. Jason and Bobbie, you're really pushing the pace, and without any turnovers. Now, let's pick up the defense. It seems we're running downhill on the offensive end, and uphill toward the defensive end." He stopped talking for a few seconds. "Are we really going to get these easy looks, or are we just not giving it much effort at keeping floor balance?" He raised his voice. "Let's not kid ourselves, guys. We're 0 and 1. We have to establish ourselves more on the defensive end. We can't give up this many easy shots and expect to win."

A few seconds later Coach LaMott redirected his focus. "Let's break down and work on our traps; then we can go against the ¾ trap that Braintree uses. Let's carve it up for easy shots, but we're not going to get anything out of it, unless the defense is moving their feet, defending the rim, sprinting to the rim if the ball gets past us."

During the trap drill, James expended as much effort as he could, keeping his feet moving, arms high and active, mirroring the ball when it dropped below the ball handler's waist. He wanted to give the starting group a realistic look. He had tried to stay involved emotionally during the Natick game, as he sat on the bench in his shirt and tie, cheering the Panthers from that seat, banging knuckles with the players who came off the floor. He and Pete sat next to each other; Pete had tried to maintain his focus through the game, also, but he had not come out of his seat very often.

As James jumped up on a trap of Jason once again, he reached in, knocking the ball away, sending the two of them to the floor to recover the loose ball.

"Nice work, James. Jason, protect the ball. If the man moves inside your comfort zone, you have to pivot away from pressure – and,

138

guys, you can't leave him on an island. You have to move back to give him a passing lane."

James attacked Jason again, this time, nicking the ball as it came out of Jason's hands, changing the flight of the ball, allowing Archie to pick off the pass. James knew that Jason favored passing with his left hand predominantly. James was able to gain a little advantage by shading that hand. After the second turnover, Jason let out a yelp of frustration.

James approached Jason, telling him, "Hey, man, I'm playing your left hand; you gotta get the ball to the other hand to make the pass with two hands, so you can alter the pass at the last second."

Looking at James as if he were pissing on his sneakers, Jason jumped away from him, not wanting to hear James's condescending suggestion. "Why don't you worry about your own game, and let me worry about mine?" he uttered disdainfully. James's face reddened, knowing that Jason (and others) resented the fact that James had left the team short-handed for these games, and there was nothing James could do to help during the games.

"Hey, I'm just trying to do what I can to help. Chill out, man."

On the next possession, Jason met the ball, passed it off to Andrew in the middle, and the first team attacked the trap effectively this time, Andrew reversing the ball to Geoff, who ran a simple 2 on 1 for the score.

Coach LaMott congratulated the offense. "That's perfect. Jason, nice job giving it up. I think you're hanging on to the ball too long, allowing the trap to swallow you up, just a little. As soon as the second man commits to you, if you can get it middle, do so, and we've got it beat. Andrew, great job moving the ball to the open side. Just a few more times now."

This time James came at Jason with real quickness, surprising Jason. He almost lost the ball, but, moving it beyond his inside shoulder, he was able to reverse the ball to Dan, who entered the ball down the sideline, and the trap was beat. James noted that Jason had switched the ball to his right hand this time, opening the door to the successful pass. "That's the way to reverse, Jay. Nice job," James murmured, so that Jason could hear, but no one else.

Coach LaMott came over to Jason, putting his arm across his back, around his shoulder, congratulating him on the improved move. James could hear him say, "Don't forget to use both hands equally on the ball. Two feet, two hands on all your passes against pressure." He gave Jason a whack on the far shoulder. The players called it "sharing the love," when Coach gave a player his arm-around-the-shoulder move.

Everyone in the gym had felt it at least once, even Nick, the last player on the squad – especially Nick, in fact, because Coach did his best to keep the end of the bench connected to the team.

Practice ended at 7:30, after two hard hours. The players who had played in the game, and there were nine of them, were dragging by the end. James, catalyzed by his ongoing feeling of guilt, supplemented by his fresh legs, kept running the floor, beating his opponent to the spot consistently. He had never focused on positioning before, thinking more about ball skills and spacing. But today, he was understanding the simplicity of sprinting to the spot, whether it was an eighty foot sprint or a seven foot quick lunge. On defense he was able to deny the cut the entire practice, just with his footwork. He could hear Coach LaMott's words, from the past and at the moment: "Keep your knees bent. First step is the most important."

On one of the last plays of practice, James was running a 2 on 1 with Archie, with Andrew defending. Coming down the left side, James brought the ball to his right side, his inside hand, to get Andrew to commit to the pass, then came behind his back with the dribble to open up his left hand for a layup. Somehow Andrew recovered, pushing off to defend the backboard with his right hand. So James laid the ball down to Archie easily, for a simple layup. He had never gone behind the back in a 2 on 1 before, but the move just came to him easily.

"Nice setup, James. How to pull the defense to you. Good run, Archie," Coach LaMott called. "Just one more basket and we're done."

When the final play had been run, the team lined up at the foul line nearest the training room, to shoot foul shots. "Let's go 9 for 13, guys," Coach LaMott called out. Everyone had to shoot one shot, thirteen players each shooting once. If more than four players missed their shot, then the team would run a 10 in a minute.

Andrew and Geoff hit theirs, but three of the next five players missed, leaving only one miss available. When Pete missed his, the remaining players – James, Archie, Nick, and Dan – all had to hit theirs. James moved back to the back of the line, allowing the other three to shoot first. Shooting last was an honor, and some players were not allowed to assume that role. But last year James had asserted himself as a clutch practice foul shooter (at times) and this year the team had allowed him to assume the cleanup duty at the end of practice. So far he had hit both final shots that he had been called on to hit.

"8 for 12," Coach called out. "Let's finish this up, James. Fifteen feet. Nothing to it."

James dribbled twice, locked his knees down, came up with his knees, his hips, his shoulder, snapped his elbow and wrist and followed through. The ball hung on the back rim and slipped off to the left.

The team groaned around him. Pete yelled, "Thanks a lot, superstar. I thought you were a shooter."

The grumbling team gathered at the baseline, pissed off at having to run another ten full-courts. Coach LaMott came close to the line.

"Hey, do you want to be a team, or do you want to go your own separate ways? Now, I know none of you think James missed that shot on purpose. So is it going to help him for you to complain and push him away? It's times like these that make us a team or deny our identity as a team. When James misses that shot, he needs to hear more than one of you say, 'Next time, James.' He needs to know that you've got his back. If any one of you thinks you're not completely supported by the rest of you, you will play with less authority than you could.

"We've got to know, at all times, that we're in this together. No exceptions. James, get back on that line and take that shot again. Team, if he happens to miss, stay with him. Don't give up on him."

James walked back to the foul line, his twelve teammates looking at him with mixed expressions, some assimilating the coach's words, and encouraging him, a few still with their heads down. James went through the same ritual, in the end snapping his wrist through the shot, achieving that backspin that is so beautiful, the ball arcing upward, then dropping through the net with a nylon whisper, ending practice.

James walked to the baseline, after the team had left the floor, to run his own 10 in a minute. He finished in 58 seconds. Geoff, in the doorway, nodded at him.

James and Pete climbed into Dan's car, for the ride home. Pete had lost his license for a year, and, though the registry had not sent him the paperwork yet, Pete's parents had removed the insurance from his car and clearly let him know that they would not provide taxi service themselves, that Pete had to find a way to get around on his own. Though James and Pete had never ridden in Dan's car perhaps three times in the month and a half that Dan had had his license, Dan offered his ride the day Pete lost his privileges. James admired Dan for that generosity, in the face of their having turned away from him for the past year or two. Some friends were loyal.

Dan's car was a step or two down from Pete's Audi: a Ford Escort, replete with two doors and two manual crank windows. "Nice ride, man," James had said the first time they headed home after practice in Dan's car.

"Gets me where I want to go, man. And if you're hitching, I might pick you up, but then again, my brakes aren't that good, and I might just pass you by," Dan replied, happy to have James and Pete in the car. "Stop for a soda on the way home?"

Pete assented, though James wanted to get home so he could call Adrienne. They hadn't said much to each other since he had seen her in the hallway on Monday. She had been busy in Mr. Tilson's class, and he hadn't felt comfortable approaching her after class. There was still a small aura around him, the remnant of his arrest, as if there were a large inner tube around his middle that prevented people from approaching him. When he walked through the school, the waves parted just a little. He had always pictured people talking about him as he came through the halls, but in his version of those hallways, they were talking about the game-winning shot he had made, or the steal he had made to seal the victory. He had wanted that respectful distance, but this distance was not one born of respect; rather it was born of bewilderment, as they wondered what idiocy would compel a student at Casteline to lose his party privileges by running afoul of the police and, consequently, his parents. James understood their confusion.

Stopping at the Exxon station for quick sodas, they quickly returned to the car, and Dan headed for Pete's house. After dropping him off, they turned to James's house, less than a five-minute ride.

"How ya doin?" Dan asked.

James let out his breath. "It's been rough, really rough. And we've only gone through three days. These two weeks are killin me."

Dan said, in the dark of the quiet streets, "I can see it. You're really quiet, not the same old kid. But I can see why. You're not the same old kid. You've got a burden, and it's heavy."

James agreed silently.

"But you're playing great in practice. I hope Coach keeps his mind open to you coming back and kickin ass. You were awesome in practice today."

James nodded. "Yeah, I felt good today. It's funny, I know what I do in practice has no bearing on how much I'm going to play in the next game, because I know I'm not going to play at all – but it seems to free me up to play better in practice."

Dan agreed. "I know what you mean. And for me, it's just the opposite. I have a real chance to show how much I can contribute right now, because you fucked up, and I can feel it affecting my shot. It's crazy."

The Arc of Intersection

James understood Dan's position absolutely: it was exactly the way he had felt in practice last year, as a sophomore, when he was trying to gain more time from the incumbents at the wing. "Maybe we're discovering something here. If you play like me, thinking that you're not going to play a minute in the game, no matter how well you play, you might get more comfortable." James was trying to convey that calm certainty that he felt in practice this week.

"Nah," Dan countered, as he turned in to James's driveway, "I can't play games with myself while I'm out there. It's too important. I want to do well so bad that I don't get loose."

James reached for Dan's shoulder. "You've got a great shot here. Hey, you played a great game against Natick. What'd you get, nine points? What was the plus-minus for you?" James hadn't looked at the stats on the bulletin board, because he didn't want to see the blank row across from his name.

"I was −2 for the game, 21 minutes. Not bad, but I can't accept anything on the negative side. Just not enough presence on the D yesterday. I wish you were playing. Braintree is good. We've gotta work a lot harder."

James stretched his left arm up to the low ceiling. "Yeah. We'll find a way. I think Coach is right: if we win the boards, we win the game. That was true with Natick and it'll be more true with Braintree. Grab us ten rebounds from your guard spot, and we win."

"Oh, that's easy for you to say. D'you get ten rebounds in any game last year?"

"No, but I didn't start any games last year, either. You're starting right now. Get us ten," James said, raising his voice playfully.

"No prob, buddy," Dan replied, as James slipped out the door.

"Thanks, man. See how much I love you? I gave up my starting position for you."

"Yeah, well, you didn't have to make yourself a nobody just for me, but I do appreciate the opportunity. But come back strong, will you?

"I will. See you tomorrow."

Supper was silent once again, the disappointment and consternation turning his parents' lips into tight, flat slits the thickness of a tissue. Everyone chewed the haddock, rice, and beans thoroughly, with great intent. Rachel stared at James every few minutes, staring a question at him, one he could understand: "What are you doing with your life?" James couldn't even come close to closing his eyes to relieve himself of the tension of the reality.

143

"Do you want another helping of rice?" his mother asked politely.

"No thanks," James said as warmly as his cold body would allow. He ate hurriedly, enjoying nothing. The haddock tasted dry.

Finally, Rachel asked, "Are you practicing with the team?" not knowing, of course.

"Yeah, I get to practice." James wanted to continue the conversation, just to make some noise, but he could think of nothing to say. He looked thankfully at Rachel, who returned his look empathetically. She shrugged her shoulders commiseratively, her eyes trying to probe his.

"Who's playing instead of you?" she asked.

"Dan. It's his big chance. He's playing well. It's going to be hard to get my position back." James looked across the table at Rachel again, feeling his father's hard, silent stare from his right side. Mr. Rush had said nothing for forty-eight hours now. He and his mother had attended the game, humiliated to be sitting among the other parents, whose whispers had halted when they arrived in Natick.

After another stony few minutes, James cleared his plate and glass, rinsed both in the sink, placed them in the dishwasher, and moved toward his room.

"We've taken the phone out of your room, and would you please hand over your cell phone?" his mother said, knowing that he would expect to make some phone calls.

James stopped in his stride. "What for? Because I drank beer last Saturday? I can't use the phone? What am I, eleven? Why don't you make me kneel on uncooked rice on the kitchen floor too?" James shouted. He laughed imperiously, certain his parents were overreacting, knowing that they were passing their embarrassment on to him. He stared directly at his father. "Maybe I could write an apology and put it in the school newspaper. Would that make you feel better?" Reaching into his pocket, he threw the phone in as close to a gentle arc as he could muster to his father. He wanted the phone back in the near future, and he knew that his parents had control of the situation for a while now. He launched himself up the stairs toward his room, seething.

After an hour of homework, toward which he trained his attention diligently, if not rationally, he thought of Adrienne again, knowing that he would not call her, because it was late and because he would not be able to say anything meaningful with his parents eavesdropping. He felt like screaming, but there was no one to listen. After brushing his teeth, he opened his reading book, Fitzgerald's *The*

Great Gatsby, and finished the ninth chapter before shutting his light off and going to sleep.

The Arc of Intersection

Take a little slug of resentment
And an ounce of small regret
Half a cup of wounded pride
It hurts inside and has not faded yet
Add a pinch of passion
And a double shot of booze
When your self-respect is crashin'
You can drink it up, you can cash in
On the blues, on the blues

Ain't it funny how the sunshine
Will never reach my shadow in the shade
Ain't it funny how the colors seem the brightest
Just before they start to fade
If you say that ain't funny
If you say you're not amused
I'll say I ain't surprised, my sense of humor is paralyzed
By the blues, by the blues

from *Shillin' for the Blues* by Chris Smither

Ben

School was a challenge for Ben, after losing the opener. He prepared his classes with his pragmatic detail, detail based on the many years he had continued to teach and alter these same classes. His freshman classes were making progress with *Catcher in the Rye*, preparing themselves for an essay asking them to analyze in what way Holden Caulfield presented a better way of looking at life, even though he seemed to suffer great privation in doing so. Ben's sophomore class was working on a persuasive essay, one in which the writer compels the reader to agree with his premise by presenting what Ben called "inarguable premises." Ben used his own essay on the value of athletics as a model, noting the contribution athletics makes to general health; the value of being able to compete; and the worth of setting, achieving (or failing to achieve), and modifying goals. He wondered whether athletics was as powerful as he had once thought: there seemed to be less of a connection between athletics and success, in Ben's recent experience.

On Thursday Ben collected the essays from his two junior classes, close analysis of poems by James Wright, focusing on the depth of the images, and the novel thoughts that a juxtaposition of images can produce. In studying and teaching poetry, Ben often felt that an understanding was sometimes just out of the reach of the reader, and that the reader's continued analysis might bring him to an understanding impossible, ironically, in the physical world because of its very finiteness. Of course, Ben also rarely voiced these thoughts, so he had a difficult time expressing them to his classes. Yet, his attempts were an exciting challenge.

And so, in short, Ben immersed himself into the other part of his job: teaching. The first game was a loss. His conversation with Jason Grutchfield on Wednesday afternoon had been very satisfactory. Jason had come in right after school, and Jason had started the conversation.

"Hi, Coach. You wanted to see me?" Jason's voice was cool, withholding his emotion.

"Yes, Jason. We need to talk for a few reasons. For one thing, your father called me to tell me that you're having a hard time living with me on the basketball floor. For another thing, you are a very valuable member of our team, one on whom we are placing a lot of trust and high expectations. If you aren't happy or clear about your role, we won't be as good a team." Ben did want Jason to know that there is a burden on seniors that accompanies the status. "What can I do to make things easier for you?"

Jason looked uncertainly at Ben. "I don't know, Coach. I know I need to be a better ball handler, especially against pressure. We didn't – *I* didn't – handle the ball well in the second half against Natick." Jason looked expectantly at Ben, as if he had posed a question with his observations.

Ben stayed quiet for a short while, until he felt that Jason had nothing more to say. "Well, you didn't have your best game, but neither did many other people. It's just that when you're the senior point guard, there is a distinct responsibility that comes with the territory. I'm not sure you know how important your success is to the success of the team. When you stay calm and get the ball to the right teammate, the whole team relaxes. Conversely, when you give the ball up, the whole team tightens up, seeing you, our number one passer, lose his way. It's a big responsibility," Ben cautioned. "I know you have the skills for the job, and I know you want the responsibility of the job. It just requires a little more experience." Ben never wanted to talk this much, but inevitably, he talked to fill the void.

Jason nodded awkwardly, but did not add anything.

Ben persisted. "What do you find challenging out there?"

Jason thought. "I'm having trouble seeing the open man through the double team. I think that's my biggest problem." It was a logical and accurate response.

"You're right. We need to spend more time in practice giving you time against the double. We'll definitely do that today and tomorrow – in addition to working on some rebounding drills."

Jason nodded. "Yeah, we need to get on the boards better," knowing, perhaps, that this was at least one area that was not Jason's domain.

The conversation sputtered along for a few more minutes, when Ben asked, "Is the way I speak to you hard for you to deal with? Would it be better if I offered any criticisms of you quietly, just the two of us?"

Jason thought, considering a reply, then changing it. "I don't want to be treated any different than any other player. If you get after other players, and not me, the other guys won't think it's fair. So, no, you don't have to treat me any differently." Then he added, "In fact, if you treat me differently, it'll hurt my confidence, because I'll think that you think that I can't handle it." Jason nodded to himself, satisfied at his thinking.

"I think you're right, but maybe I can learn from you that everyone needs a little more positive response from me, not just you. But, Jason, as a senior leader, I need you to tell me if I'm mishandling you or, just as importantly, any of your teammates. I've asked the same from Geoff, and I'll ask Andrew for the same. Keep checking on the other players, to see whether they're struggling or not, for any reason.

"I don't pretend to be perfect, or the best coach there ever was. I've had some success and I've had some failure. I just want you to have the best season possible. Does that sound reasonable?"

"Absolutely," Jason responded, with, for the first time, calmness and certainty in his voice.

"And please, if you find that I'm not being consistent, as I coach you and the team, consistent with what I've said, speak to me. I'm counting on you to let me know. I'll try to check in with you every day." As Ben concluded his conversation with Jason, he felt he had hit upon a potentially effective way to avoid further discord between Jason and him.

With no more conversation flowing between them, Jason stood up, a little slowly.

Ben made it clear for Jason that their meeting was over. "Thanks for coming in. I hope we can all live up to our potential, as a coach, and as players. Please, let me know when something's wrong."

After Jason left the room, Ben congratulated himself on not bringing up Jason's dad. He felt it was wrong that Mr. Grutchfield had looked at the team from such a narrow, biased point of view, but, at the same time, Ben knew that Mr. Grutchfield's perspective was often the only one that parents could maintain. Ben also felt it was wrong for Mr. Grutchfield to impose his selfish observations on Ben's handling of the team as a whole. Yet, in a way he was thankful, because Peter had forced Ben to establish a line of communication that might make the team's chances for success better.

Wednesday night Ben and Willa spent some time together, and Ben telling Willa about Mr. Grutchfield's call and Ben's conversation with Jason. Willa was, naturally, angry to the point of hostility.

"What a mean-spirited man. Doesn't he think you care about the players? Does he know how much time and thought you put into every decision you make?" Whenever Ben was challenged by a parent, Willa's deep-seated pride in her husband showed itself. "I can't believe these parents have the gall to confront you with these concerns. Do you remember what you said to Jason?" She asked this just to be sure Ben was not at fault.

149

Once again Ben could not recall exactly what he had said. "I don't really know. I know I've said worse to many other players. I don't know. I must have said something like, 'Jason, keep it simple. We don't need the spectacular play. Who do you think you are?' I know I raised my voice, no doubt about that." Ben wondered whether he had been too forceful, too blunt.

Willa answered his question. "I mean, I saw that Jason was giving the ball away. He's always had that tendency. You've always had to tell him to simplify and not turn it over. This is nothing new." Willa's cheeks reddened with her anger. She tilted her head as she said, "Ben, it's a new day. You have to realize that these parents aren't the parents you were dealing with twenty years ago. Every little thing you say can be magnified and turned against you. You do have to be careful. No 'fuckin pool party' comments in the huddle – especially if the whole crowd can hear you."

They laughed, both recalling one of Ben's more assertive diatribes in the huddle, in the early '80s, when coaches enjoyed more leverage and less scrutiny.

Ben continued Willa's line of thought. "I know. Those days are gone. I haven't sworn in a huddle, out of anger, in probably seven or eight years. I'm changing, and I think it's a change for the better, honest. But I have to let the players know when I'm dissatisfied with them. That's just part of coaching – not a fun part, but a part that has to happen."

They spent another ten minutes considering the changes that time had brought to the coaching profession, changes that had brought several of Ben's coaching friends to a more rapid end of their careers than they had anticipated.

In fact, their conversation about Ben's involvement with his players' parents turned to Ben's curiosity about Willa's church involvement, which had become a considerable part of her life.

And, at this moment, Ben knew that he had become jealous of the part Willa's church activities played in her life. "I don't mean to question your choices, but do you think you have time for all these committees?" Ben asked, inferring that Willa already had enough to fill her life, and that she did not need another significant involvement.

Willa looked at him with more than a little instant resentment. "Do you think I would be doing this if I didn't think it was necessary? Do you think I'm *trying* to drive myself crazy?" She was not comfortable being challenged.

Surprised by Willa's entrenchment, Ben replied, "Honey, I didn't mean anything by it. I'm just trying to make it so you don't have

150

to run around all day, with work, with the kids, with church, with getting supper, with doing the housework, all of that. It just seems overwhelming," Ben said, eyes wide.

"You're right, it is overwhelming. But when I'm at church, setting up an activity, or wrapping presents, I know that I'm doing it for someone else, and it makes me feel very good, very good. I don't always get that feeling from my job – in fact, I rarely get that feeling from my job. I work hard, and they say 'thanks,' but that's it, and I get the feeling they say thanks because they have to so I'll continue to do all they ask." Willa looked frustrated, thinking about her work at Spingold's, assisting the owners in their design of electronic products, as well as managing the production department. It was a busy job, Ben knew.

"And then, I don't always get much satisfaction from my work here at home. The kids are pretty much on their own now, and I worry about every step they take. And when you get wrapped up in the basketball season the way you've always done, it's like you disappear suddenly and come out of hibernation in March, when the days start to get longer. And we don't ever sit down to eat a meal together any more. All those things that we always said were important, sharing our lives with each other – we just don't do them any more." Willa stopped to breathe.

Ben looked at his wife with surprise. He admitted to himself that all that she was saying was accurate, but he also knew that he hadn't noticed these changes himself – probably because, as Willa had said, he was so wrapped up in his teaching and coaching. "Hey, I didn't know this was all happening so . . . so . . ." He didn't know what word to place here. "I'm sorry, hon. You're right. Things have changed – a lot. But things are always going to change. The kids grow up. We have to pay the bills, so you take a job. I understand the reason for the church stuff, I really do. At least there is comfort there." Ben paused. "I just wish there was the same comfort at home."

Willa's shoulders sagged a little. She was lying across the couch, her head on the armrest, her legs across Ben's legs. He was rubbing her feet the way she liked, taking the ache out.

"I don't mean there is no comfort here, I don't mean that at all. That's not fair to say. I just mean that what I do at the church is completely for the benefit of others. And other people appreciate it." She reached for Ben's hand.

Taking her hand, Ben said quietly and rationally, he thought, "Isn't that what you've been doing for twenty years in this house? Are you saying that we don't appreciate it?"

Willa cried out, "No, that's not fair. Don't twist my words. This house has been as comfortable as anywhere I've ever been. I can't wait to get home to this house, day or night. There's something very relaxing about this house, the way we've made it ours, the way we've spent so much of ourselves making it what it is. So don't start trying to make it sound like I don't like our lives."

Ben continued to try to understand. "Then what is it? What do you get from the church that we don't have here?"

"God, I guess. I guess it's something spiritual and sacred. What we have in this family is very personal, and very practical. We do things so we can survive and get along smoothly. But in church, it's not about our physical survival, or our comfort. It's about serving." Willa seemed to come to some understanding with this pronouncement, and Ben could understand what she was saying.

"Well, I just wish I could provide that same comfort. I know I'm not God, but I wish I could give you all a person could give. I guess love was always enough." He looked at Willa, wishing that there were some spirituality that he could draw upon, to give her what she was seeking.

Willa looked at him sympathetically. "Oh, I know you give me everything that you can. And so do the kids. But I get the feeling that there is something more, and I'm just trying to find it."

Ten minutes more on the couch, Ben rubbing Willa's feet comfortingly, steadily, trying to reestablish the exclusivity that had been the cornerstone of their lives together, and then they turned to the staircase that led to their bedroom, toothbrushes and nightwear waiting for them up the stairs.

It was the most they had shared with each other in months.

Practices on Wednesday and Thursday were well played: rebounding was the clear focus, as well as some work on beating the trap that Natick had thrown at them and that Braintree had used (with a slightly different wrinkle) in the past. Jim's report on Braintree indicated that they had shown their trap four times, all after shooting free throws; Coach Dietrick would make the call as they gathered at the foul line. The first team ran the fast break as well as they had all season, the big men getting down the floor very well, to fill the trailer lanes and make themselves available for offensive rebounds. Monaghan continued to shoot flawlessly, and Stedham continued to show strong skills as a guard substitute. The team really had few weaknesses – other than rebounding.

"How you lookin?" asked Bryan after Thursday's practice.

"Solid," Ben answered, as the two walked out of the gym, "but do you have a 6'6" kid you're not showing me? I need a rebounder."

Bryan laughed. "If I had one, I'd gladly give him up, but I got nothing underneath." He thought for a few seconds. "What if you play Monaghan at the 5, and surround him with four guards, make Braintree match up with our speed and small size?"

"I can't sit Geoff. He's too much of a leader. And we sit Geoff and we don't pick up any real talent. Dan is not really accomplishing much, but he allows us to bring Archie off the bench, and give us a little boost."

The two men were heading to the parking lot.

"What about Jonas? Can he give you any toughness or penetration?"

Ben thought for a while. Bryan always had a way of offering a new way to look at things that Ben hadn't considered. "Well, I'm trying to find a role for him. Maybe Jonas could give us a penetrator from the baseline. He could drive and kick, and we'd have lots of shooters spotting up. I don't think we can move to that plan tomorrow, but I'll file it away."

"Want to stop by Willow's for a cold one on the way home?" asked Bryan.

Willa was at church till 9:00, and he was unsure of the kids, but he called them, to find out their schedules. Listening to messages, he found that Mary was at the Summit hockey game, and Scott was at Perry's and needed a ride at 9:00.

"Yeah, I can stop for a while. Sounds good."

Willow's was as steamy as he remembered from two weeks before, and the pleasant chitchat resounded off the walls charmingly. Two men and three women faced the dartboard that was perched on the wall between the two side windows, one of the women tossing a silver, metallic dart knowingly. Sets of tall chairs clustered around six round tables, most inhabited by couples that reached for their beers in tall glasses. The glasses on the table nearest to Ben were still frosted from the freezer, the beer foam rimming the glass.

Bryan moved directly to a table in the back, where Lisa sat with a nearly empty glass of beer. She waved to Bryan, who nodded his head and shrugged off his coat as he approached her table. He gave her a well-directed kiss and sat down next to her, holding his arm out toward Ben, his hand open, to invite him into the empty seat across from them. The scene was cozy and inviting, an easy chair to pull up to a welcoming table.

"How's it goin?" asked Lisa, twirling a strand of her hair in her right hand.

"No complaints," replied Ben. "Just thought I'd see how the other half lives on a weekday night."

Bryan countered, "The other half? What do you mean? D'you think we're a bunch of alcoholics or something?" He laughed.

"Well, I don't see too many people sipping ginger ale, and if they are, they're probably doing so for a reason," laughed Ben. He turned to look over his shoulder at the TV, on which a game played out. It looked like the Celtics, who were hosting Phoenix.

The waitress, bringing a Sam Adams for Bryan, asked Ben, "What can I get you?" in a chirpy voice. She wore a black button-down shirt and an apron over her black pants.

"I'd like a Corona, if you have it. Thank you," Ben replied.

"You want a menu?" the girl asked.

"Yes, please." Turning to Bryan and Lisa, he asked, "You guys going to have something to eat?"

Lisa responded, "Yeah, we'd like to order, thanks," to the waitress, who left to bring menus and Ben's beer.

Lisa looked as vibrant as ever: most of her long hair was pulled up in a knot on the back of her head. She wore a soft gray sweater and a glittery necklace that reflected light in a suffusing arc. She smiled at him as he glanced at her face, eyes dancing. He didn't know what to say. She helped him out.

"Well, Bryan's in his in-season mode: deleting text messages rather than responding, less concentration, doodling offensive plays on napkins. Are you affected in the same way?"

Ben wondered. He didn't really know whether he changed once the season began. "I don't know. What do you think, Bry? Do I change?"

"You change by the day during the season. A win and you're Mr. Happy. A loss and don't come near." Bryan nodded. "Jekyll and Hyde."

"Really? I don't think I'm that volatile. I'll have to ask Willa. She'd know." Ben turned to Lisa. "I hope Bryan's not that moody."

"I'm getting used to it. I know basketball's an important thing for him. Am I right?" she directed this last question to Bryan, as she nudged him in the ribs.

The waitress came back with Ben's beer and took their orders, and in a few minutes they were all eating, Ben enjoying a plate of steak tips marinated in a tangy mushroom sauce.

Midway through the meal, Lisa asked, "Nothing cooking at home?" innocently enough.

"No, Willa is at a church meeting and the kids are scattered. I'm picking up my son Scott at 9:00, but until then, I'm a free agent."

Bryan added, "From what Ben tells me, having a family of teenagers puts you on a carousel that spins pretty fast. I don't know how you handle it," he said to Ben.

Ben looked thoughtfully at Bryan. "It gets pretty crazy sometimes. Sometimes I think about the day, maybe it's Tuesday and we have a game, and then the next time I think about the day – on the calendar, I mean – it's suddenly a Sunday two weeks later, and I don't know what I've done for those two weeks."

"How do you stay connected to your family?" Lisa asked, curious about the direction and the end-point of long-term relationships.

"I don't really know. We fall into routines, I guess. The kids have their cell phones, and we stay connected to them that way. Willa and I?" Ben considered the question. How, in fact, *did* they stay connected? Or, better yet, *did* they stay connected? "I guess we have our rituals. We wash the dishes together after supper, or she lays her legs across my lap on the couch and I rub her feet. She buys me Ring Dings for snacks, even though we both know that they're not good for me or my attempts to avoid getting fat. I clean the bathrooms thoroughly every week, and Willa does a very brief whisk afterwards, bringing it up to code. Little things." Ben was glad Lisa had asked the question, because it made him consider how things did work. " – Oh, here's one: When Willa's feet are cold, when we get into bed, she imploringly places them between my thighs, and I cast my heat into her coldness." He looked at Lisa, wondering whether she would expect such sacrifice from Bryan. "Are you two embarking on a long-term relationship?" he asked to either party.

Bryan looked at Lisa, who returned the look. Bryan said, "Well, it's looking like that right now." He stopped talking, unsure where to go with his response.

Lisa filled in the silence. "All we can ask for is that we're happy today, for now. We'll see where it goes."

Ben couldn't help asking, "How long have you been seeing each other?"

Bryan said, "About six months, I think. We met this summer – well, really, late last spring, at a cookout. I asked her out for the next night, and, naturally, she said no. But I persisted," Bryan added with a proud smile.

Lisa looked softly at Bryan. "I couldn't let him think I had fallen for him on first glance, but I hoped he would call me again. In fact, I made myself available, just happening to haunt the coffee shop he stops at in the morning, so he would see me again."

Bryan looked at her with surprise. "Are you for real? You were stalking me?"

Lisa looked down. "Well, I wouldn't call it stalking, but I made it my business to cross paths with you."

"How come you never told me that? What, I don't find these things out till you tell them to my buddy?" Bryan seemed a little miffed.

Ben interjected, "No big deal, guys. It's the way things work. One person swings the pendulum out there, and the other one notices. It's like elephants swinging their trunks. It's called communication."

"Well, I'd just like to know when I'm being played," Bryan said, looking at Lisa with laughter in his eyes. Their banter was informative, but endearing, too.

After another half hour of gentle and lively chat, Ben stood up from his chair. "Well, I gotta shove. Scott needs a ride." He looked at his watch, which read 9:05. "Ooh, I really gotta go. I'm late." He hurriedly put his coat on, pulled on his gloves and turned toward the door.

Lisa stopped him. "Thanks for stopping in. It's great to have you join us. You're an inspiration: a well-adjusted man in a successful long-term relationship. Maybe we can continue to get pointers from you," she said hopefully. She looked directly at him, as she had done the first time they met.

Bryan added, "Yeah, it's nice to spend a little time with you outside of a gym. Thanks for stopping in," and he clapped Ben on the back.

Leaving a twenty on the table, Ben moved toward the door, Lisa's smile, straightforward and direct, filling his mind. She seemed so open, so honest. He'd have to remember to tell Bryan how lucky he was, to have attracted such a beauty.

Picking up Scott, he observed that his son was even more quiet than usual – not that he talked with his dad much to begin with.

"Everything OK?" Ben asked, trying to open the door.

"Yeah," Scott answered shortly. He didn't offer anything more and he seemed staunch in his silence.

Ben let it lie. He had been glad that Scott had begun to let Ben in on his interest in a girl and he didn't want to close off that dialogue.

156

"Well, if you have anything going on that you need help with, let me know. Please," Ben offered.

"Thanks," Scott answered from the dark of the passenger seat of the Corolla.

At home, Scott went to his room. Mary was due home shortly from the hockey game, and Willa would be home at about the same time from church. Ben opened up his satchel, taking out his book of American poetry, to prepare for Friday's lesson.

'Cause none of us
Can live the perfect life
The kind that we see on nick at night
And sometimes, we all
Just lose sight
Of the pain that will guide us
From dark into the light
We fall down yes, but we get up,
And sometimes we just need
A little bit of love
To help make it
Through another day
Into the night, into the light,
Into a Saturday
So in the morning when I'm waitin'
For the sun to raise
And my head's a little foggy
Like I'm in a haze
I remind myself that
Everything is gonna be okay
I take a breath, slow down and say....
Why must I feel like this today
I'm a soldier but afraid sometimes
To face the things that may
Block the sun from shinin' rays
And fill my life with shades of grey
But still I long to find a way
So today I pray for grace

From *Pray for Grace* by Michael Franti and Spearhead

James

James adjusted his tie before standing up for the *Star Spangled Banner*, played before the opening home game vs. Braintree. Coach LaMott had delivered a temperate but impassioned pre-game talk, imploring the team to make a 32-minute effort on the boards. He did not mention the trap press that Braintree might use, and James suspected he did not do so because he wanted the players involved – Dan, Jason, Bobbie, Archie, and Alex – to approach the game with no undue anxiety. Coach had a habit of not talking about the specific focuses that the team had worked on in practice, the goal of his reticence being that the team was fully prepared for any situation.

Opening tip went to Braintree (6'6" at the post for the Wamps), and they scored on a simple jump shot from the right wing against no pressure from the Panther defense.

Jason pushed the inbounds pass up the left side, looking for Geoff or Andrew over the top, but, not finding them, he settled into a motion offense, passing the ball to Dan and moving off to the right wing to set a pick for Jonas, whose pass went in to Geoff at the high post. A nice high/low pass to Andrew set him up for a simple reverse layup and the game was tied.

For the first period the teams traded baskets (and misses), the result being a 16-15 Casteline lead. In the huddle at the end of the quarter, Coach LaMott spoke quietly. James loved it when Coach spoke quietly: it forced the players to pay attention and it seemed to emanate from confident strength. "Good job on the defensive balance. They don't have an easy basket yet. Let's go with a 3 on the first defensive possession after we score. I'll call it out, but get it in your heads now: 3 on a make. Geoff, you're in the middle. Work on denying the post man. Jason, you're two steps over half court, forcing a high pass.

"Good job on the boards." He turned to Bridget. "How's the rebounding going? What're the numbers?"

Bridget gave the chart over to Coach LaMott, who scanned it quickly. "11-8 Braintree. Not bad, but let's see if we can turn it around 2nd quarter.

"Any questions? Any concerns? Anything got you confused out there?" he asked.

Geoff shook his head. "We're all set, Coach." He addressed the team. "Hey, get a hand up on every shot and call 'shot.' They'll start missing. They can't hit jumpers all night." He clapped his hands, a good leader.

All 13 players stood up. "1,2,3," Coach yelled.

"Tight," the team shouted, with some conviction, and five of them trotted onto the floor to put the ball in play at half court.

With three minutes left in the period, Casteline had taken a 29 - 22 lead, mostly on the strength of their own half-court trap, their "3." Braintree came down in their trap-break, a 2-1-2, and, after reversing the ball before crossing half-court, tried a long diagonal to the opposite corner. Andrew, after suckering the guard into thinking he was guarding the ball-side sideline, took four hard steps across the basket line, and leaped off his left leg (though James knew he should always be leaving off two feet, to guarantee balance and an opportunity to change angle at the last second), trying to intercept the arc of the ball. With his long arms he was able to deflect the ball off its flight to the weakside corner man, the ball bouncing off his shoulder out of bounds, Casteline ball. Braintree took a time-out, their second. The Casteline players streamed to their bench exultantly, shouting, clapping each other on the back, radiant in their success.

"Great job, guys," Coach LaMott yelled over their voices. "Let's just sit here a few seconds and enjoy the moment." He stepped back, his smile enough to let the players know that he was as excited as they. After most of the time-out had expired, he stepped back in. "OK, let's change up. Combination on their two guards. We're running a 6, Jason on Edwards and Dan on Jamieson. What's their numbers?" he asked Bryan.

"Edwards is 22; Jamieson is 30," Coach Taft responded immediately. "Jason, you've got 22; Dan, 30."

They nodded, their excitement evident in the bounce in their step. "TIGHT."

James loved the harmony that had captured the team. They were all in step; they knew their roles perfectly. No one was stepping out of those roles. It was as if they were the template for these offenses and defenses, and Coach LaMott just had to move the marker with his fingers across the white board, and they found the exact spot designed for them. James had felt that same acceptance of the group dynamic many times, and it was inspiring to watch it from the sideline. Of course, a part of him was jealous that he wasn't sharing in the harmony, but he understood the grace of it enough to know that resentment wasn't part of the deal. He even consciously knew that he didn't deserve to be a part of that unity, not until he was due back. But he could see it on the floor.

The run continued until half-time, Casteline holding a 35-25 lead at the half. James sat in the corner of the locker room, intent on the coach from his peripheral position. Coach Taft offered a few distinct and smart observations about the guards' shooting, telling them they could attack a little more, gaining another five feet before they shot, and he reminded them they might use the board on those 'tweeners. Coach LaMott commended the team for their rebounding throughout the half: they had won the boards for the half, 19 – 17, in spite of the fact that Braintree had turned the ball over several times, allowing for no rebound on those possessions. But Andrew and Mark Payne (Geoff's backup) in particular, had hit the offensive board hard, accounting for three or four baskets of their own.

Second half started the same way. Three minutes into the second half Braintree threw their half-court trap at Casteline after a basket. Jason turned the ball over for a layup. Another trap: this time Alex turned the ball over. Coach LaMott signaled time-out.

"OK, guys, here they come. We've been beating them, and it's time they started fighting. This is what we want. We can't let the trap throw us off our game. Jason and Alex, keep your feet on the ground and pass-fake. Get them to jump, and then you have to pivot and find another passing angle to use. When they are in the air, they can't adjust to us, but we have to put them in the air without leaving the ground ourselves.

"Geoff, switch with Andrew. Andrew, come to the high post on offense, and come as far toward half-court as you have to, to make yourself a target. If you're denied, seal him, and guards, reverse the ball and hit him on the backside. Andrew, you're going to get the ball every possession now. Make it happen."

Coach was calm, amidst the uncertainty that had ensued from those two turnovers. He had seen so many successes and disasters over the years, that a couple of turnovers did not rattle him – though his lips were getting drawn just a little tight. James looked at Jason and Dan. As Dan moved onto the court, James told him, "Finish strong if you have a man on the baseline. Don't worry about a charge. Go in hard."

As Jason hopped up, James told him, "See the whole court, buddy. We've got it now." James could see how easy the attack was, from his seat on the bench. But he knew it wasn't as easy with arms in your face and a voice bellowing at you.

The team responded with a solid attack, setting up Mark for a layup against the trap, and it seemed their confidence had been restored.

But halfway through the fourth quarter, Braintree came with a full-court press after a make, and Alex traveled before he got his feet set for his pass. On the next possession, Jason threw a pass down the sideline into one of the giant Cs emblazoned twelve feet up the wall at the end of the gym. After the second turnover, Braintree came down and scored a 3, taking their first lead of the game. From that point on, Braintree continued to attack and Casteline lost its aggressiveness. The final score was Braintree 62, Casteline 58, a very similar score to their first loss to Natick. At center court, in the huddle, James could feel the disappointment in his teammates. Their heads hung and their shoulders slumped. No one wanted to look a teammate in the eye. They had made a great adjustment to the half-court trap, but lost their confidence in the full court at the end, when the game was decided.

Coach LaMott gave a simple speech. "Great job on the boards, today. Mark, you really helped there. Great job.

"Guys, there was a time in the second period where we completely got it together. You guys were completely tuned in, and everything you did was correct and effective. Do you all know what I'm talking about?"

The players who had been on the court nodded. "Yeah," they assented, nodding. James had seen it from the bench himself.

"That's what I'm trying to teach you. The answers are not in Coach Taft or in me. The answers aren't in Pete Semineau or James Rush. The answers aren't in Geoff Willis or Andrew Monaghan or Jason Grutchfield. The answer is in achieving that complete harmony that means you don't have to think out there. You all know what is going to happen before it happens.

"Braintree's press took that knowledge away. We started doubting ourselves for a minute, and we could never get our cohesion back.

"But we got there, for the first time this year. Now you know what we're trying to achieve. Forget about the final score. Forget about any mistakes you might have made. Just think about those three minutes when we had complete control of the game. There was nothing Braintree could do: we were in control of the court. That's our goal." Coach stopped. "1,2,3,"

"Tight."

At home James alternated between two radio stations in his room after another bout of silence in the family room. He was forbidden to go out, though it was Friday night. His i-pod had been confiscated along with his phones, and his computer had been moved to the dining room table. He felt like a first grader, having to ask permission to use the bathroom.

162

In the family room, watching a crime show, his father had made a few derogatory observations about the second half collapse, being careful not to name any particular players as scapegoats in the demise. Uncharacteristically, his mother cheerily noted how well the team had played in the first half. James did not care to discuss the game with them, but he politely responded when called upon. He was starting to feel a truce had evolved between his parents and him, a moratorium that would end, he supposed, when he donned a uniform again.

Tired of fiddling with radio stations, and unwilling to do homework on a Friday night (on general principles, though it might be nice to have no homework for the rest of the weekend), he sighed and turned to the phone on his desk – only to see the empty spot where it used to sit. He rubbed his eyes with the palms of his hands, knowing that he would have to use the phone downstairs if he were to call Adrienne. Staring at the photos of his team and the posters of Michael Jordan and Dwayne Wade that looked down at him, he resolved that this was not a time to show weakness, and opened his door to slide down the banister to the phone in the kitchen. His father sat at the table, marking documents that needed processing the next day at work. He looked tired, but that was not unusual. He didn't always work on Saturdays, but this year had been a hard one, and he had had to increase the amount of work he brought home and work some Saturdays.

James went to the phone and dialed Adrienne's number. His heart was pounding, for two reasons: one, he was going to talk with Adrienne within hearing distance of his father, and, two, he was going to talk with Adrienne.

"Hello," she answered.

"Hello, how you doing?" James asked.

"Pretty well. We won today," Adrienne exclaimed, unable to contain her joy, though she might already know that the boys had lost.

"That's great," James admitted, closing his eyes gratefully. "Was it close?"

They talked about the games for a few minutes, James without much energy, Adrienne with more than enough to compensate. As James wondered whether there was any way he could move the conversation to anything more personal, Adrienne asked, "How're you handling sitting on the bench?" empathy foremost in her voice.

He didn't know how to respond. So he just talked. "It's hard. But I'm seeing things I wouldn't see otherwise. Like there was a play in the second period . . ." and he recounted Andrew's interception of the diagonal pass that had its origin in knowing what was going to happen before it happened, just the way the coach had talked about it after the

163

game. "I may be crazy, but I think I'm understanding the game more because I'm sitting there and I'm not involved." James faced the mirror over the hallway table, his eyes closed. As he talked, he touched the top right corner of the mirror's frame.

Adrienne seemed to understand. "I think I know what you're talking about. In lacrosse sometimes, I move away from the ball because I know who the opponent is going to pass to, not on the next pass, but the next-to-next pass. It's crazy, but I just know. Coach Alberson asks me how I make so many intercepts and I tell her I just know. I guess you can call it anticipation, but that sounds more formal than what I'm doing. I'm just ahead of the play."

James was surprised that Adrienne could already understand what he was seeing for the first time. As a matter of fact, she had been playing sports this way for a while.

"Well, I guess I'm just catching up with you, but I think I'm starting to get it. It's an amazing feeling, huh?"

"Yeah, I don't know if I'd call it a feeling, but it sure helps on the field. Maybe it's an awareness."

After talking about school for a minute or two, Adrienne asked, "Are you staying in this weekend?"

James didn't know what to say. He was leaving his house only for basketball practice on Saturday and refereeing the youth games on Sunday. But maybe she was asking if he was available to see her. He said, "Wait a minute."

He turned to his dad, asking him, while covering the phone against his chest, "Dad, can I go to a friend's house Saturday afternoon? Only for a short while?"

His dad stared at him as if he were crazy. He mouthed the word, "No, N – O, NO."

James thought quickly. "Can someone come over to our house tomorrow afternoon?"

James's father thought for a second, then asked, "Who?"

"A girl named Adrienne Petrulsky," he replied, knowing her name would mean nothing to his dad.

His dad shrugged. "OK."

He returned to the phone. "Adrienne? I'm sorta hanging at the house this weekend. You know. Do you want to come over for a while?"

A moment of hesitation, then, "Well, I don't really know. We've got practice at noon, and then I'm playing in a lacrosse tournament in Hingham the rest of the weekend."

164

James was immediately empty, made only too aware of the heavy air of disappointment that hemmed him in. He was also a little confused. Was she trying to make an effort to see him? "Oh, that's fine. I just thought if you weren't doing anything, we could hang out." He tried to conceal his vulnerable need.

"Maybe some other time," Adrienne offered without much certainty. "Well, I gotta go. I probably won't see you until Monday, but have a great weekend," she offered by way of apology, he thought.

"See you Monday," James replied and hung up, cursing his ineptitude at understanding a girl's intentions.

His dad asked, "No company on Saturday?" knowing the answer.

"No, it didn't work out," James replied, turning to the family room to watch the remainder of the Celtics game.

At Saturday morning practice James's teammates spent half an hour working out the stiffness from Friday night's game; then the scrimmaging became a little more competitive. James, with his fresh legs, continually penetrated past Jonas's defensive efforts. An hour into the practice the groups broke up into cross-court games with the JVs and coaches included in the draft. This Saturday morning scrimmaging, a tradition at Casteline for as long as James had been engaged in the program, was a way of making the game fun: just run up and down, without any formal structure, trying to win. Coach LaMott explained it as trying to recapture the ethos of the 50s and 60s playground, when players who might not know each other formed a team, challenged the winner of the previous game, and stayed on the court as long as they won. In Coach LaMott's version, you called your own fouls, subbed every five points, to allow for equal playing time (a distinction from the playground, where teams were comprised of only five players), and played to fifteen points.

James enjoyed the composition of his team: Andrew; Keith Warren, the freshman coach; Pete; and three JVs, one of whom was a good ball handler. There were times when James and Andrew dominated the defensive end, coming up with the ball and setting up teammates for easy breakaways, and the JV players knew how to release early, knowing that James and Andrew could come up with the ball. Pete, whose legs were as bouncy as James's, of course, ran hard both ways, and contributed to the easy victories. After two games, James's team met up with Geoff's team, the battle of the undefeated teams, for this week's championship. Coach LaMott was on Geoff's team, and before they started the game, Coach yelled out, "On the near court, we've got the battle of the undefeateds. Final game to twenty-one. Switch at eleven points to even out the sun. Good luck, guys."

James liked to battle Coach on these Saturdays. Coach was definitely slower than just about anyone on the court, but he could still shoot, and he knew how to create baskets for his teammates, with backdoor passes, screens away from the ball, and simple movement on his own part. James covered Coach for the beginning of the game. When Coach caught the ball, James came up under his chin, knowing that Coach lacked the speed and the first step to get past him.

"All I got is a lateral move – nice D," Coach told him after passing off and cutting to the rim. James denied the cut easily, and the shot went up from the outside.

When James got the ball, Coach had to lay off him because James could easily get past him with a dribble-drive. James caught and shot; the ball found the net, and James started back to the other end of the court. But as the inbounds pass came in, James reversed his direction, cutting in front of the lazy pass to Coach, knocking it down to the floor for an easy layup. Coach said to him, "Nice pressure," then, to his teammate who had made the soft inbounds pass, in a strident voice, "Let's look at the defense before we pass. Turnovers will kill us."

The game was an easy victory for James's team. Andrew and James were too strong for the other team's defenders. It was nice to be part of a winning team. In fact, no one had been part of such an effort all week, given the outcome of the Natick and Braintree games. Practice ended with a lengthy 15 for 25 at the foul line, Varsity and JVs combined. The team made the standard, avoiding the 10 in a minute that awaited them if they failed to make 15. After the team's "tight," James lined up on the baseline for his own 10. Coach started the clock, and James sprinted home in 58 seconds.

"Nice run, James," Coach congratulated. "Just one more week. Nice job scrimmaging today. You look sharp." Coach clapped him on the back with a little gusto, sharing the love.

"Thanks," James replied, knowing that both of them hated the fact that he was not available for these next two games. Neither one could speak about the continued suspension, but it hung over them like an above-the-court scoreboard, listing the losing scores of the first two games.

Lunch, homework, basketball on TV, a quiet supper with Mom (Dad had to work into the evening and Rachel was at a friend's), then nothing. He wanted to call Adrienne, but he knew she was playing lacrosse. He tried Pete, but he was out with friends. He considered calling Dan, but he didn't want to hear that he was out with his new girlfriend.

Sunday was more of the same. His dad drove him to the gym for his two hours of reffing the sixth graders in their intramural games, picking him up at 4:00. The ride was more silent than usual. He looked forward to Monday, the beginning of the final week of his suspension, after which he would be reinstated to the team.

On the blue side of evenin'
When the darkness takes control
You start lookin' for a reason
To take your lonesome on down the road

'Cause the night is filled with strangers
All you need is one you know
And if she ain't the one you're after
Keep on lookin' on down the road

Though the miles lay long behind you
You have still got miles to go
How's love ever gonna find you
If it ain't here it's down the road

Keep on lookin' on down the road

Down the Road by Steve Earl

Ben

In the cold church pew, Ben and Willa sat close together, sharing a hymnal and prayer book. The church was a little cold. Ben loved to sing hymns loudly, though his voice would never be confused with a choir member's. He just loved the spirit of the music. Willa sang purely and sweetly, obviously carried away by that spirit, though her ardor came more from the divine ideas that lay behind the words than the exhilaration of the melody. After church Willa stayed on for another hour and a quarter, in her role with the children's care, but Ben came back to pick her up at 12:15.

They came home to a warm house, condensation forming on the inside of the window panes, because Mary was fixing dinner for the family, enjoying a rare Sunday off from Dunkin Donuts. She shooed Willa and Ben out of the kitchen into the family room, so she could complete her preparations. Ben loved her ministrations in the kitchen; she had learned well her lessons at Willa's left elbow. He thought he could detect the aroma of chicken piccata, but he wasn't sure. He sat down on the couch, spreading out, to read the Globe, ending up with the sports page. On the final page of the sports page was the Globe's early season analysis of the schoolboy basketball scene, replete with top teams in each division and "Players to Watch." Two players from the Commonwealth League, Lance Previeu from Brookline and Billy Samko from Waltham, were included in their list, no surprise. They had dominated the league last year.

Looking at the listings of top teams, Ben recalled the days when Casteline would be listed in the top teams, when one or two players off his team made the Globe's list of Players to Watch. Those players had gone on to solid college careers at Middlebury, Colby, Princeton, and Providence. It was just three seasons ago when Steve Ramos had been elected league MVP, before he headed off to Union College in Schenectady. Ben wondered whether Andrew Monaghan were of that same caliber. Ben was in contact with five schools about Andrew, small NESCAC schools of the same ilk as Union, and Andrew had the scholastic ability to gain entrance to just about all five of the schools. He would also be applying to another two or three schools where he would not be able to make the recruit list, but where he would be happy without playing basketball. And aside from Andrew, Ben couldn't think of any other players who might make it as a college player. Jason Grutchfield had the skill set, but he lacked the mental fortitude to make the transition to playing in college – though his father certainly would not agree with that assessment. Ben was contacting small college coaches on Jason's behalf, but the colleges where Jason might play ball would not be acceptable to the family – state schools.

He had always thought James Rush would be the same sort of player whom he could assist in the college search, finding the right school academically and athletically, but that was before James had dug a deep hole for himself, a hole from which it was difficult to see the baseline, never mind the basket. The junior year was the year when a player established his credibility with college recruiters, whether the player be Div. 1, 2, or 3. From at least one game in his junior year the player could send a game tape to the colleges he wanted to attract, to show the coach what he could do for 32 minutes. In his junior year he would establish his scoring and rebounding (or assist) averages that would allow the coaches to think there was some consistency to his game. James had given up those opportunities.

Ben was disappointed, very disappointed, and he held James solely accountable for his loss of status. But James was not the first, as he had told him. Once a player decided to forgo the discipline required to maximize his opportunities, it was rare to regain that discipline. The friendships and weekend habits were too ingrained to change. Ben recalled a very promising freshman named Rick Scott who had helped the team win two games with his big shots at the end of games in his freshman year. He had attracted lots of attention when, as a sophomore, he had averaged nearly 20 points a game, hitting over 40% of his threes. But then junior year he had shown no improvement. When he had run the mile before his junior season began, he had labored to a 5:58 (much like James's), on his second try, after failing to finish under 6:00 the first time. During that junior year, Ben spoke to him weekly about trying to maintain his sense of commitment to his future, giving up the temptations that called to him from the social scene that was trying to capture him, and Rick had always told Ben that he was staying away from those temptations. But the court said otherwise. As Bryan always said, "The court doesn't lie."

Rick's senior year was disastrous, for him personally. He missed eight games with mono, and sprained a wrist during the second half of the season, keeping him out of another three games. In all, in his senior year, Rick played eleven games, including playoff games. In his final game, a sectional semi-final loss to Hull, Rick scored five points on 1 for 11 shooting.

Ben felt that he had failed Rick, such a promising young player who lost his way. After Rick graduated, finding no place to play basketball, enrolling at UMass Dartmouth before returning home after a year and a half, Ben began wondering whether the program he had developed was strong enough to motivate the players who were coming along.

But there were players who continued to benefit from the development that Casteline provided, both athletically and academically. Steve Ramos was a great example that the system still worked, if a player stayed within the parameters set out by Coach LaMott. But James Rush, one of those players who had been in the program since fifth grade, had fallen through the cracks. James, for all his extra sprints and support from the bench, would miss the first four games of his junior year, and colleges would put little credence into a 6'1" player who could not avoid getting suspended. No one that Ben had coached had ever played in college after being suspended.

"Dinner is served," Mary called from the dining room. Ben entered, to see a roasting chicken, surrounded by potatoes, carrots, and onions in a warm, steaming gravy. Mary proudly spread out her arms, the meal a gift that she lovingly gave.

"Thanks, Mary," Ben said as he hugged his daughter. Scott sat down hungrily as Willa also stepped forward to hug their daughter. Willa looked absolutely radiant, like an angel.

The games of the second week were both abysmal and triumphant. On Tuesday the team never got off the mark, losing to a mediocre Wellesley squad, 69-54, Casteline's worst effort of the year by far. Wednesday's practice was filled with gloom. Half an hour into practice, Ben bleated a frustrated whistle, calling the team together, to address their attitude.

"OK, guys, enough of the self-pity. We're 0 and 3. That's the facts. We can't change what's happened, so let's stop looking over our shoulder at the past, and start looking ahead at the future. Friday we play a very tough Waltham team, with Billy Samko leading the way. He's averaging over 20 a game, and we can all remember he dropped 31 on us last year. He can shoot, and he's a beast on the boards. Geoff, your responsibility is to get inside his shirt. Mark and Andreas, you will get your turns. If we keep Samko under 20, we win the game. He's an explosive player, but one who struggles to score when he can't get his points off the offensive glass.

"Beyond Waltham: we have to start playing to win, rather than playing not to lose. We've already played our worst game of the year, yesterday's game against Wellesley. I can't think of any part of their team that is superior to ours, but we didn't control one aspect of the

171

game. Therefore, we can conclude that it doesn't matter who is the better team. It's who plays better on a given night. The record says that Waltham is better, but so what? We have proven that that doesn't make a difference.

"So let's pick our heads up, and practice today in preparation for a win on Friday. Jason, control the offense. Geoff and Dan, control the defense. Who is going to be a leader on this team? We're all waiting." In voicing these words, Ben was as honest as he could be. He knew that the team felt it was running out of time, but Ben knew that the season kept providing more time, right up to the last game. He had to get them past the self-doubt that accompanied losing.

And on Friday, at Waltham, the team put together their best performance, for an entire game, winning 66-56, holding Samko to 15 points. When Samko fouled out with four minutes to go, Casteline held a slim two point lead, but without their star, the game was essentially over.

So on December 23rd, after two weeks of games, Casteline stood at 1 – 3, and Pete Semineau and James Rush would be returning to the team.

Saturday, the 24th was a light, early morning practice that included the unofficial reunion game, when as many graduates as Ben could contact and cajole returned to run up and down the court for another day. Ben was looking forward to seeing Steve Ramos among many others, including the five graduated members of last year's team. He expected at least four of them to find their way to the gym.

At 8:30 on Saturday morning Ben and Bryan entered the gym laden with doughnut holes and generic red fruit juice jugs. Both coaches changed in the locker room, quickly, returning to the court to take out the balls and warm up a little themselves, before the team and the alums came. A few snowflakes fell harmlessly outside the windows. Ben and Bryan achieved a comfortable cadence as they shot, loosening their knees, their legs, and their backs as they prepared to catch-and-shoot, catch-and-shoot. Ben liked to take jump shots, especially from the baseline and angled shots off the glass. Bryan was more of a straightaway shooter with limitless range.

Players filtered in gradually, most removing their outer winter clothing to strip down to basketball shirt and shorts, dumping their outerwear against the folded bleachers. The alums all came over to Bryan and Ben to make their little obeisance, testament to the fact that they had enjoyed their years enough to make a return trip early on a Saturday morning. Steve Halter, approaching 35 years of age, had made

172

the trip from the South Shore. Always a great rebounder, he had put on his annual ten pounds from the previous year, making him a very sizable, ever formidable low post player. Pete Nicholas and his brother Brad arrived together, reminding Ben and Bryan of Pete's last game in a Casteline uniform, when the team had overcome a 16 point lead in the second half only to lose at the buzzer to Westport.

At 9:10 Ben blew his whistle, calling the players past and present together. "All right, guys, great to see all of you. Let's get together for one big, slow set of reverse weave, three lines, just to loosen up. Let's shoot to fifty." The players compliantly drifted into three lines, passing and moving away from the pass, to let the weakside wingman come for the next pass. The players from the present team ran it smoothly and quickly; the returning players moved with less assurance, their legs stiffer and their movement less fluid. But after a while all the players moved smoothly, three or four passes, a reverse pivot, a bounce pass and a layup. "31 . . . 32 . ... oops . . . 31." Ben couldn't help but impose his normal restriction: a missed layup was a deduction from the count, as the alums would remember. Ben liked to maintain consistency, and his former players easily regained their familiarity with the routines.

As the players moved toward fifty made-layups, Ben quickly counted the number of players (31 plus two coaches), and set up four teams, to run simultaneous games crosscourt. Eight players on a team, spreading the height and ball-handling across all four teams. Ben put Bryan and himself on the same team, because every once in a while the two of them could recreate the past, with the help of these ghosts from the nineties, and help a team win a set of games, their experience trumping their inability to jump.

Marty Reasoner, an alum from the late nineties, asked Ben, "How's the team looking so far?" Marty was living in the Philadelphia area, and he did not get a chance (or care) to follow the daily progress.

"Slow start, Marty. We won last night, but we got off to a rough start overall. Played two good games and one clunker, but last night might be a catalyst for us. We had two suspensions for the first four games, but those are done, and we'll get stronger now."

"Who was suspended?" asked Marty.

"James Rush, over there at that basket with the blue sweats on," Ben said, pointing to the near left basket, "and Peter Semineau, in black right next to him. Rush will help us a lot when he comes back." Ben didn't feel that he was selling Pete out, because he knew that Marty understood the pecking order on a team, and in ten minutes, he would recognize where the talent lay on this year's team.

"Well, we'll teach them some tricks, Coach," Marty said, bounding toward a bouncing loose ball to hit a putback.

After Marty, there were three or four others who approached Ben to get the lowdown on this year's team, because they either didn't know, or they wondered what was happening to account for the 1 and 3 start. Ben cut the inquisition short by blowing his whistle and beginning the games.

Ben sat out first, along with Dan Owings and Jeff Neville (from the '91 or '92 team), prepared to insert the three of them at the five point mark in the game to fifteen. The ball moved quickly up and down the court. Ben loved to see the older and younger players playing together, joined by an understanding of the rudiments of movement on the court and capable of making the ball join that movement with their skills. At this point in his life Ben almost enjoyed watching this movement as much as generating it himself, because he could take pride in the fact that he had laid the groundwork for this harmonious motion. When a post player sealed and the ball was reversed for a simple backside postup, Ben congratulated the passer and the sealer both, letting them know that he had witnessed the move. When a player doubled down on the post and another player slid across to take away the available kickout pass, Ben applauded the defensive awareness with a laudatory shout. The fact that players who didn't even know each other were performing these maneuvers was fun for Ben to watch, a sign that his coaching could connect the generations like an invisible cobweb, gracing the gym with its arching tendrils.

At five points, Ben, Jeff, and Dan entered the game, and in a few minutes Ben realized once again that he couldn't really keep up with the simple pace of a crosscourt game. Bryan was having no trouble at all; in fact, he was leading the team in scoring and in assists both. But Ben discovered that the full-court pace left him behind regularly, and that he couldn't always sprint back on defense if he went to the offensive glass as much as he should. Ben and Bryan had little chance to make their two-man plays, because the offense was primarily fast break, both ways, as it should be, leaving Ben several steps behind. At the 10-point mark, he excused himself from the game, to let Jason and Harry Romsey, a player from last year's team, back into the game. Breathing just a little heavily, he admitted to himself the fact that he now derived more pleasure out of watching the style of play than in trying to keep up with it.

After six cross-court games to 15, the energy level finally started to wind down. As usual the current players proved to have more stamina than the older players, because they had been running their sprints. The two players who stood out above all the others were Steve Ramos, the junior at Union, and Andrew Monaghan, the leading scorer on this year's team. In about the fourth game, the two scorers were matched up against each other, Ramos beating Monaghan with seductive dribble moves that got Andrew off-balance, and Andrew shooting over Steve and using his shot fake to get by him. It was a great stalemate between the two of them, confirming in Ben's mind the fact that Andrew should get the chance to play in college.

The best players of Ben's 25 years of coaching were too old, too far away, too fatherly to make the day. As the years passed, inevitably, the attraction to this little team in this little gym waned, as it should. Ben hoped that his former players had all cultivated a life for themselves that involved family and stability, precluding a return to Casteline the day before Christmas, but, at the same time, he relished the fact that some of them took the time to make it back. At 11:15, Ben made a last call, shutting the gym down at the conclusion of these last games, seeing Dane, the custodian, waiting in the wings, ready to close down and lock up for Christmas. When Ben had come in he had plunked a 12-pack into the snow in the bed of Dane's truck, thanking him for taking the Christmas Eve shift and for overriding the custodial contract to take it.

One cluster at center court, one "Tight" from voices young and old, and the players drifted off. Hearing the word, strung together with a delightful variance of pitches, made Ben think of the way prayers ended with an "Amen," though he had never made that connection before. The younger players left first, ready to spend a little time with their friends before they settled in with their families for the holiday. The older players hung around longer, trying to catch a few more words with Bryan and Ben. They took a few more shots, shots they hadn't taken in a year, in some cases, their fingers recalling the feel of the leather (that had been replaced by a more durable synthetic leather), their legs reminded of the old ache that echoed from their impassioned strides.

Two or three older players helped Bryan and Ben clean up, tossing the empty boxes and jugs away, sharing a few more moments within the walls that had housed them for four years, most of them sneaking a peek at the banners on the north wall that commemorated their success: '85, '86, '88, '92, '94, '95, '01.

"Catch you next year," said Steve Ramos.

"Hey, Steve, did you get that summer workout regimen you told me about at the Thanksgiving game?" Ben asked.

"No, but I have it saved in my files at school. I'll attach it to you when I get back on campus. I think it really helped."

"How many games have you played?"

"Only five. I'm getting about twenty minutes a game. Probably averaging seven points a game right now. I think I'll get more time as the season goes on. I'm making progress in practice, and I'm starting to contribute defensively a little more. But the best part is that all the guys get along. I don't even care if I don't play a lot because the guys that are playing ahead of me deserve it. I can't argue with the coach's decisions. And it's amazing: when I don't care about playing time, I play a whole lot better."

Ben nodded and clapped Steve on the far shoulder, his embracing gesture of endearment. "Amazing how that works, isn't it? I'm glad you're understanding it. I mean, in high school, you never had to scramble for playing time from the moment you walked on the varsity court. But when you come up against people your own caliber, some people don't like the competition, some people love it, and some people don't even see it as competition, just as a great way to spend a couple hours. It seems you've discovered the last attitude."

"Yeah, and the game comes really easy to me now. Not that I'm dominating at all. Seven points a game is not very impressive. But I don't care about the numbers. They just reflect what I've done; they aren't some goal of their own."

Ben smiled. "I love to see that athletic maturity take root in people. You'll have it for the rest of your life now. Keep having fun. And thanks for coming back"

Steve looked Ben in the eye. "I wouldn't miss it," he said, and he turned to the door.

When it was just Ben and Bryan in the gym, as it often was at the end of a practice or game, Ben turned to his long-time friend. "You heading north for the evening?" Bryan's parents still lived in New Hampshire, and Bryan, since his divorce, usually spent Christmas Eve with his parents, and Christmas Day with his son for the second half of the day.

"I'm heading up this afternoon, but I'm coming back this evening."

"You seeing Taylor tonight?" Ben asked, wondering if plans had changed.

"No, Taylor's tomorrow. With Lisa in the picture, I think she and I'll spend some time together for a little while this evening. Then she goes to her parents' for the night."

"Where's that?"

"Down the Cape. So I'll see her from 7 to 10 or so, then she'll have to leave."

"No chance of going down the Cape with her?" Ben asked hopefully.

"I didn't get the invite. I'm ready, but I have to feel it's right, and if she didn't ask, she's not ready." Bryan shrugged his shoulders.

"And then Christmas with Taylor?"

"Yeah, I've got some nice things for him, but it's not the greatest situation. No Christmas tree – but I've got a little table tree for the season. It spreads a little cheer."

"Hey, bud," Ben said, "have a great Christmas. See you on Wednesday. Have a great few days. Lisa coming back soon?"

"Yeah, she's gotta work on Tuesday, so she'll be back on Monday night. That'll be nice."

"You two heading toward anything permanent?" Ben asked.

Bryan looked at him earnestly, shaking his head reflectively. "I don't know. It's perfect right now. We don't have any complaints at all. But neither one of us seems ready to acknowledge or articulate a commitment. So I don't know. But thanks for asking. One thing I do know is that this" (he motioned to the gym floor) "is permanent," and with that pronouncement, Bryan and Ben gave each other a holiday hug commemorating their two decades of mutual support.

177

It's not that I never been in love before
Just never found a love worth fightin for
Lost my faith in miracles
But now here I go
Believing again

I believe I believe you're the one
I believe I believe you're the one
I been a hard believer
But my heart has come undone
Oh I believe you're the one
Baby

Thought that I'd never take that chance again
Me and lonely were the best of friends
I said goodbye to my loneliness
I went from no to yes with one look at you

I believe I believe you're the one
I believe I believe my time has come
I been a hard believer
But my heart has come undone
Oh I believe you're the one
Oh you're the one

Hard Believer by Tommy Castro

James

In Saturday's workout with the alums, James ran up and down, scoring plenty but feeling a lack of accomplishment. He kept a close eye on Steve Ramos, noting how easy a time he had getting his shot off, what with his authoritative shot fake and his accuracy when he did pull the trigger. In the five or six games the teams played, James's team lost at least four, indolently running back on defense, allowing far too many layups in transition. James pushed himself for the first three games, but, after losing all of them, he lost the intensity that he had brought with him to this first practice after his suspension. In six days, on Thursday the 29th the team would play their next game, his first after regaining his eligibility, at Sharon in a non-league game. He expected to contribute to a win. As he dressed in his street clothes after the last game, after the team "tight," he remembered he had to go directly to Deveny Jeweler's at the Mall to pick up a present that he had selected earlier in the week.

James's imagination had taken hold of him quite unexpectedly on Wednesday evening, while he was shopping for presents for his family. He had gotten mittens and CDs for Rachel, a warm Carhartt thermal shirt for his dad, two pairs of reading glasses and scented candles for his mom. But while he was touring the mall, before his mom's scheduled return time, he had walked into a jewelry shop, looking for something for Adrienne. He hadn't left practice that evening with the intention of buying her a gift, but here he stood, looking down at the necklace counter. He was attracted to a necklace from which hung two sculpted arcs that formed a delicate heart.

James knew that the implications of a heart necklace far exceeded the number of words he and Adrienne had shared with each other, but a heart could just signify that he felt she had a pure heart, that she had a big heart, that she had a strong heart. It didn't have to mean that they were in love with each other. He asked the clerk if he could look at the necklace.

"Of course," the clerk replied, unlocking the table-cabinet with her key, and handing him the necklace. "Actually, it's a simplistic puzzle-heart: the two halves come apart into two separate curves. When it's apart, you click the two meeting points together, and you have a unified piece. The piece can be worn as two separate, abstract curves in space, if you want to wear it that way, because each curve has a welded loop that connects to the chain. It's a unique piece of jewelry. I haven't seen any others like it." She smiled encouragingly at James.

When James held the chain in his right hand, letting the heart dangle into his left palm, he barely felt the heart's weight. After a few seconds, he tried to separate the two arcs, but his fingers weren't nimble enough. "Could you separate the two sides?" he asked the clerk, whose name was Sarah, according to her nametag. She wore steel-framed eyeglasses that showed her dark eyes to an advantage.

"Sure, let me help you with that. Is this for you or someone else?" she inquired.

"For someone else," James assured Sarah. "It does seem really pretty."

"I'd love to get something like this," Sarah said with a broad smile. Using her nail, she edged the heart apart, leaving two modernistic sweeping lines hanging from the chain.. The curves were each less than an inch in length.

"Is it safe to wear it that way?" asked James. "It looks kind of fragile that way, like one of the pieces could get caught on something."

"I don't really know. I think it would have to hang underneath the collar-line if it's worn that way. Here, let me show you." Placing the chain around her neck, she dropped the sculpted pieces against her skin, below the hollow of her throat. The necklace looked very sweet in that territory, like delicate driftwood on an empty beach. James pictured it on Adrienne, underneath one of her buttoned shirts, the dark green one, nestling against her skin.

"I think I'll take it," he said, without letting himself think about the absurdity of the purchase. If he didn't think a Christmas gift was appropriate, he could give it to her at a later date.

"That will be $125.00 and tax," Sarah read off the coded strip of paper that also hung from the chain. James recoiled slightly, never imagining a price that steep. He had only $65.00 left in his wallet.

"Can I pay on any sort of layaway plan?" James asked, not really knowing what was involved in a lay-away plan.

"Well, we really don't do that unless the purchase is over $500.00," Sarah replied. "I can hold the piece for you, wrap it and hold it, if you want to come back another day," she offered.

James nodded. "Will you do that, please? I'll be back on Friday in the afternoon, or Saturday afternoon. Thanks." He asked to see the necklace one more time before he left the counter. "Should I ask for you, or just give my name to anyone?"

"Ask for me, because I'll know where it's stored, but if I'm not in, someone else can get it. Thank you for your purchase. Someone will absolutely love it. She's a very lucky girl." Sarah looked at James approvingly, smiling easily.

"Thank you," James replied, pleased to hear that he had made an attractive selection. After giving Sarah his name so she could write it on the box, he tapped the glass counter with his right hand twice and turned away, nodding to himself.

When Andrew Monaghan offered to drive him to the Mall after Saturday's practice, James readily thanked him, eager to have the necklace in his own hands. At the jeweler's, after waiting for ten minutes in the crowd at the counter, he asked for Sarah as he pulled out his wallet. In another few minutes she glided over to him, recognized him, and turned to pull out a little drawer behind her where the necklace had been stored. "Here you go," she said, again smiling brightly. The small box was wrapped in white paper with thin gold string.

"Thank you," James said, taking the box and handing over the cash. "Are you sure the necklace is in here?" he asked, a little cutely.

"Placed it in there myself," Sarah assured him.

James walked away from the counter, sure of one thing: he could not picture any spot in town where he might comfortably or casually give the present to Adrienne. But he was also sure of something else: no place on earth would be as lustrous as this heart sparkling on her skin.

James called for a ride home after looking somewhat superficially for anything more he could buy for his parents. He did buy an auto seat warmer for his dad, a silly, battery-operated devise that he could turn on by remote from the house before he went outside to start the car. James thought it might be a nice gesture.

At home James circled the phone, hovering in the general vicinity, but not daring to make the call. His parents were paying no attention to him, and Rachel was out, so he didn't have to overcome the risk of being discovered in his silliness by the home team; yet, he just didn't know how to introduce the idea of seeing Adrienne today or, especially, tomorrow. But, finally, James just breathed deeply, dialed her number, and said, "Hi."

"Hi," Adrienne's mother replied.

"Oh, I'm sorry," James sputtered, "is Adrienne there, please?"

"I'm sorry, she's out. Can I take a message?" James realized that Adrienne's mother had no idea who he was, probably because Adrienne had never told her about him, because there was no reason to bring up his name. Maybe she could tell her mother about his suspension? Maybe she could tell her about James's tendency to close his eyes at all times of the day (though, to his knowledge, James did not

181

think Adrienne had any idea he spent much of his life in dark awareness)?

"Yes, thank you, could you tell her that James called? She can call me back if she gets a chance," James added hopefully.

"Of course," Mrs. Petrulsky answered. "James?"

The name meant nothing to Mrs. Petrulsky.

"Yes, James Rush," James replied, just to be sure.

"James Rush. Sure thing. Bye now."

"Bye. Happy Holidays."

The Christmas holiday arrived in the Rush house. James's parents had decorated some time around the first game of the season; piles of presents sat beneath the balsam, which emitted less and less fragrance as it dried in the living room. Rachel kept running down the stairs to place another small package underneath the tree, at times placing a light package in the branches of the tree, so that there would be little, late surprises in the present-opening ritual (though the family knew, from past precedent): presents concealed in the fading green of the tree.

James had extended his money as far as it would go, trying to express his gratitude for the gifts his family had given him over the years, gifts that he had repudiated with his legal entanglement and athletic suspension. The suspension was now officially over, and he hoped that the family's gift-sharing would signal a change in attitude within the family. Rachel had quickly forgiven James, spending time with him in his bedroom or hers, sharing i-tunes tips, searching on-line for gift ideas with James. He had thanked Rachel for her open-mindedness, even as his parents had remained intransigent in their persistent coldness to him.

On Christmas Eve the Rush family always shared one gift, chosen by the giver, making sure everyone had a chance to be a recipient. Rachel chose first, selecting a present for her mother. Mrs. Rush opened the smartly wrapped gift slowly, trying to guess its contents.

"Is it a new pocketbook?" she asked, hefting it to estimate its weight. It was the bulk of a pocketbook.

"No, keep opening," Rachel purred, excited at her selection. Mrs. Rush continued opening the green-clad box only to find a series of individually wrapped gifts inside the box.

"Oooh, you're a sneaky little devil," Mrs. Rush exclaimed, laughing at Rachel. She opened one of the small packages, revealing a pretty glass object hanging from a wiry thread. "It's beautiful. Is it an ornament for the tree?"

Rachel answered, "Not exactly. It's to hang inside the window on the side of the house where the sun shines all day. It creates a rainbow for the house. And there are twelve of them, different shapes, to create different shaped rainbows. A seasonal set of prisms," she announced proudly.

"Ahh, Rachel, it's beautiful. I'll open a few more to see the different shapes." The two that she opened were angled differently, though no one could tell the type of prism that would be generated, because there was no natural source of light at 8:00 p.m. on Christmas Eve. "I'll put one up in my bedroom tonight, so I can see the colors in the morning. Thanks, honey."

Next, James went to the tree and selected a gift for Rachel. It was a pair of jeans from Abercrombie that James had seen some middle school girls wearing, girls who fashioned a more confident stride in the mall. James had a feeling that Rachel would appreciate a pair. He had checked her closet to find her size: 8. When she pulled them out of the tissue paper, her eyes widened. "Hey, James, these are perfect. How did you know?"

"I just had a hunch. You like 'em?"

"Yeah, they're perfect. Thanks." She hugged them to her flat chest dearly.

Next it was Mrs. Rush's turn. She pulled a long item from behind the tree, the apparent shape of a golf club, and gave it to her husband, with a slight embrace to accompany the gift. "Here you are, dear," she said.

Sliding his hand down the shaft (if it was a golf club), he split the paper, to reveal a putter, one with a heavy face, with the name Odyssey across the back of the face. "Oh, wow. That's perfect, sweetheart. Now I'm going to have to find the time to use it this summer."

"Look inside the card, Will," Mrs. Rush told him.

Taking out the card, Mr. Rush found a certificate inside the envelope. He read, "8 rounds of Golf at the Commerce Club in Dedham. Wooh, that's great, Louise. You and I can have a ball," he said, poking light fun at her, because she had never been close to a golf course, except to pick her husband up once or twice. "That's great, Louise, very thoughtful."

James thought the eight rounds of golf were probably very expensive, though he didn't know because, like his mother, he had never hit a golf ball anywhere other than at a driving range, and the prices at the range were ridiculous, he felt.

So it became Mr. Rush's turn to select, and the recipient would be James, because he hadn't received a gift yet. Mr. Rush found a slim envelope leaning against the trunk of the tree halfway up, with James's name written on the back. He handed it to James, without making any eye contact whatsoever. James looked carefully at his dad to try to get a read on the present, obviously some kind of certificate, but he couldn't read anything. Opening the envelope, James saw a check for $1500.00. He didn't, at first know what the money was for, but then, in the lower left corner of the check, he read, "Automobile purchase." James wondered exactly what his father meant. "Hey, Dad, this is great. But do you remember I don't have my license?"

Mr. Rush cleared his throat, still looking away from James, at Mrs. Rush, as a matter of fact. "Your mother and I have always wanted to provide you with some means of transportation when you became old enough to drive. I know your eligibility for your license has been postponed until late summer, but your mother and I want you to know that when you've finished the sanctions from your incident, we want you to have a fresh, clean start. When you do get your license, we want you to look around and buy a used car for this amount, or more, if you use some of what you've saved up. I assume you'll have more money from a summer job by the end of the summer." Mr. Rush finally looked at James. "But we have one condition: you have no problems between now and that date. If you have any more issues with your decision-making, I rip the check up, because you won't be getting your license anyway.

"So, this is our hope, that you have already made your big mistake, and that you won't make the same mistake again – or any other mistake, for that matter." Mr. Rush lowered his head, glancing once again at Mrs. Rush, clearly done with his lecture.

James took a brief moment to compose his response. "Dad and Mom, you know how sorry I am for the giant mess-up. I'm counting on cashing this check in August, when I can take my driving test. I will tell you right now: I will buy that car in August. Thanks to both of you for showing some trust in me. It means a lot." James got out of his chair to give first his mom and then his dad a hug. His mom smelled like vanilla, probably from the cookies she had been baking; his dad smelled of the slightly dirty hair that he always produced from a day of work – he had had to go in for three hours this morning, even on Christmas Eve.

Mrs. Rush, a little teary, said, "We do have a string here that we can pull back, and we don't mean to be unfair, but we don't know yet if we can believe in you." She lowered her face to her lap, embarrassed by her truth.

"I know, Mom. It's only fair. Let's let the next eight months speak for me, OK?" Inside he was humming because he knew he had control of his own destiny.

"Let's have some hot chocolate and cookies," Rachel interjected, bringing her brother's character-debate to a close.

That night, when James got ready for bed, he slipped into Rachel's bedroom for their annual Christmas rumination, which had begun when Rachel was five, and James was assigned the task of calming her down enough to fall asleep on the night before Christmas. In fact, he had read *The Night Before Christmas* every year to her in this situation, and he would not break tradition this year.

"Hey, kid. You ready for our annual reading?" he asked, after knocking and entering. Rachel was listening to tunes and watching photos replace each other on her computer.

"If you have to," she answered, a hint of glee in her voice.

James came in and sat on her bed. She had her long flannel pajamas on, and her blanket was tucked up under her chin. She slid toward the inside edge of the bed to make space for her brother.

James felt comfortable with Rachel, in this place, on this night, because he had grown up providing the same nurturing for seven or eight years now. "You feeling the Christmas spirit?" he asked.

"More than ever," she answered. "I think this Christmas is the best because it comes at a great time. The past two weeks have been a little rough around here."

As James sat on the bed, the only light provided by the images on the computer screen on her desk, he closed his eyes, succumbing to the inevitable conversation they had to have. He tried to picture the photos on the screen as they scrolled in, images of their family swirling on and off the screen; the climb up Mt. Monadnock; Rachel mounted on a horse, when she had attended a 4-H Camp on the Cape; Mom and Dad, cutting the cake at their 20th wedding anniversary last year. He didn't know whether his images matched those of the computer, but he knew they were loaded into their collective memories.

"You've been great, Rachel. I know you can't figure out why I would do such a stupid thing, but all I can say is wait a few years and then, maybe, you'll understand. I go to these parties, and the beer looks great and the beer tastes OK, so I do it. I hope never again."

Rachel sat silently, though James still faced away from her, his eyes closed.

James added, "I know it killed Mom and Dad. They were always so proud of me, and then I kicked them in the gut with this thing. It's not going to be easy to get back to full trust, even if I get the license and the car. I know I lost something. I hope you never lose it, Roachie."

Hearing his term of endearment, Rachel knew she had to say something. "You're right, I don't understand. Just because you get older doesn't mean you have to do crazy stuff. You can still be sensible and have fun doing the simple stuff like hanging out with your friends and talking on the phone. I don't see why beer has to be part of it." He could picture her shrugging her shoulders out of bewilderment.

"You just get older and you see things differently. And it's all around you. You just reach for it. I mean right now, you reach for your i-pod or your cell phone because they're sitting next to you. Well, in a few years, beer or other stuff is sitting right next to you. You just reach for it. And you don't think about it being wrong, because, outside of the stupid DARE program, no one acts like it's wrong. And everyone's having a good time." James stopped, realizing that he was just rationalizing to his little sister. "But the truth is, you know it's wrong, inside of you. You just ignore that voice."

James knew he had destroyed the cozy Christmas Eve atmosphere, but he also knew that he and Rachel had had to have this heart-to-heart, because they had never betrayed each other. He sat silently, eyes still closed, arms hanging down between his legs, his head hanging just a little, until Rachel kicked him from underneath the covers. "Hey Jayboy, are you gonna read to me or what?" James stood, reaching for the book on the lower shelf of Rachel's bookshelf, leaning against the Valentine's Day book and the Halloween book and the Good Night Boston book that she visited infrequently but at least annually. He could feel the raised cover art, Santa and his Reindeer wheeling through the sky in a gentle arc.

Christmas Day the Rushes woke about 8:00 to sit in comfortable chairs, sipping coffee, tea, and hot chocolate, trading presents and pleasantries, but James had already moved past the holiday, to his impending return to the team. Mrs. Rush gushed with a new-found enthusiasm, now that the family had, in their interaction, appeared to return to normal patterns, though James feared she would return to her reticent determination after the holiday spirit wore off.

After the jubilant gift-sharing, as everyone thanked each other and gazed toward the next hour and the next day, James considered a phone call to Adrienne, but reconsidered quickly, having no idea whether Adrienne's family was home or visiting relatives. Instead, he called Pete, to congratulate him also on his revestiture.

"Hey, man, how ya doin?" James asked.

"The usual, a horde of gifts, lots of love and all that stuff," Pete answered cavalierly. He probably had received a raft of gifts.

"Are you ready to return to action?"

"Aaaah, I'm not going to see any action. I go from invisible-ineligible to invisible-not-gonna-play. Not much difference, except I get to wear sweats instead of a tie. I've enjoyed the runs in practice, anyway, and that's not gonna change. How 'bout you, dude? You ready to reclaim the title?"

"Well, I know I'll have to totally outplay Dan and Archie if I want a shot at solid playing time. I don't think it'll happen in one practice. Too bad we aren't practicing Monday, and Tuesday's just optional, so I can't really outplay anyone." Coach LaMott officially gave the team the first two days of vacation off to allow for families that traveled during the holiday season. This year Andreas Pinson was away for the week, meaning he would miss the two vacation games and two more after he returned, but it wasn't James's position, so it wouldn't affect his status; it would just thin the stable of big men available for the next four games.

"Well, I'll be there on Tuesday, bright and early. No sense tying an anchor to my place on the bench," Pete intoned. "Hey, you doin anything tonight? I think there's a get-together at Sue Welch's."

James had heard plenty about the party, but he hadn't considered attending, partly because his parents had not released the reins yet, and partly because he didn't want to return to that scene so soon, if ever. "I don't think I can get out. I'm still quarantined, at least until the New Year." To himself, James had to admit that his parents had not clarified how long his house arrest would continue, but he gave himself this platform, so that Pete couldn't pressure him to come out with him.

"Ah, hell, you can work around that, can't you? I mean, New Year's! You can't sit at home through New Year's! Remember last year?"

James did remember last New Year's Eve, a group of his friends traipsing in the cold, attending one small house party, slugging a couple beers behind the library where they had all met. He had returned home just before midnight, sobered by the cold, though he had felt what was probably a buzz earlier in the evening, but a buzz that was disrupted by chattering teeth. "Yeah, but as I recall, you weren't in the best of shape that night, so I hope you aren't considering a repeat performance," James cautioned.

"I'm a lot smarter. I wouldn't chug beers in the cold anymore. I'll find a warm corner and a warmer girl. That's the way to celebrate the New Year," Pete asserted. "I hope you're right by my side."

"Well, I doubt it. Hey, you want to come over for some football? Got a pro game on at 6."

"I'll check back with you. I might be on the road to my grandmom's in the afternoon. She's visiting my uncle in Acton. And then there's Welch's. Sorry you won't be there. We'll miss you. Maybe Monday we can do something."

After a few more minutes of chat, Pete and James clicked off, and James returned to his ruminations about the team and about Adrienne, though he expected interaction with only one of the two entities in the next few days.

Nine players attended Tuesday's optional practice. Coach LaMott ran a long series of shooting drills, to enable those attending to sharpen their eye. James shot very well, his legs feeling lively and his eye training on the rim clearly. In six-minute shoot James hit for 106, second only to Andrew's 111. James and Pete won two of the three cross-court jumpshot drills that incorporated a bit of running with a dribble. The team broke down to a full-court scrimmage after an hour of layups, shooting, and light zig-zag (Coach LaMott mandating, "Only half-speed on the dribble, guys, just work on your change of directions, but don't try to beat the defender.")

James teamed up with Archie, Bobbie (back-up point guard), Dan, and Coach LaMott. Andrew and Geoff were the major players on the opposing team. James started the game with a nice back-door feed to Dan for a layup. Then he and Archie ran a nice double-team at half-court to force a turnover, generating another layup for his team. James's team won the first game, 11 – 8. Before the game Coach LaMott had laid out the losing team's fate: one down-and-back for each point of losing margin.

The second game was much more competitive. Andrew put down an impressive dunk midway through the game, but Geoff and James did not react; they had seen him do the same somewhat frequently this season. As the game neared its conclusion, score tied 10 – 10, James beat Pete with an inside-out dribble to take the ball to the rim, only to be rejected by Andrew with an impressive block. James felt Andrew's other hand pushing through his shoulder, but, knowing that a foul call would not find any receptive ears, James just chased the play to the other end, a layup for Jason.

As Andrew had blocked the shot, he asked, "Foul?" James just ran.

Down 11 – 10, James penetrated and kicked the ball to Coach LaMott, who was a solid shooter, especially when he had a chance to warm up. Coach stepped into the pass, at the same time, stepping into his shot. His shot was a little flat; Andrew swept the defensive rebound, outletted to Jason, who hit Pete basket-hanging for a layup and the game was over. Coach LaMott grunted an obscenity to himself, coming over to James, to tell him, "Sorry, that was a good pass. I should have made the shot."

James shrugged. "You took a good shot. Nothing more you can do. Next time." As he gave Coach his support, he realized that he was mimicking Coach's very words, perhaps the exact words, Coach LaMott had used to support him over and over for the past three years, since James entered high school.

Coach looked at James to see whether there was any mockery in his voice, but, finding none, gave him a pat on the back. "I'll get the next one." They turned to run the two down-and-backs.

In the last game to fifteen, James's team grabbed a big four point lead early and never relinquished it. The ball movement in the half-court was good; after two or three ball reversals, there was just about always an open shot or good passing angle into the post for an easy bank-shot. Andrew and Jonas moved their feet with more urgency as the game neared its finish, but James's team wound up winning, 15 – 10, leading to five runs for the opposition. Coach LaMott came over to James as the other team ran. "Nice job, James. Nice to have you on our side. Keep up the smooth work; we've missed you and we'll be able to use you."

"Thanks," James said, glad that Coach had noticed. "I can't wait to play in a game."

Coach nodded. "I bet. Tomorrow put your focus on defense. It looks as if your offense is ready. Now you have to make sure you have the defensive rotations, to reunite yourself with the team's scheme. We'll be playing mostly man-to-man, so keep sliding into the lane from the weakside, and, especially, dropping down below the dotted line when the ball goes baseline." Coach blew his whistle to call for twenty foul shots before practice ended.

Calling everyone together, Coach said, "Nice work, guys. That was fun for me. I don't get much chance to run during the season, so that was a bonus for me. Pete and James, welcome back. We've missed you on the floor, and it's going to be nice to have you part of the team the rest of the week.

"See you at noon tomorrow. Be ready for some running, first day back after a long layoff. 1 . . . 2. . . 3. . ."

"Tight."

With five minutes left in the second quarter of the Sharon game, Coach LaMott inserted James into the lineup. Dan had started; with three minutes left in the first quarter, Archie had replaced him in the rotation at the wing, with Jonas Boynton maintaining his spot on the other side of the floor. After one quarter Sharon led 18 – 17, but Casteline was controlling the boards because Sharon was not a big team. Despite the absence of Andreas Pinson, the backup 4 man, the Panthers had a decided edge in rebounding. When James entered the game, the Panthers were tied with Sharon, 32 – 32.

After one sprint down the court, James's legs were instantly fatigued, the result of his excessive expending of energy on the simple 94-foot trip to the defensive end. He tried to keep his arms away from his body, feeling his man (#22) with the backs of his fingers, as he followed the ball into the opposite corner with his eyes. When his man broke off a screen toward the ball, James stepped across his cut, tripping him. The referee's whistle stopped play to assess James's first foul of the season. Already benefiting from the 1-and-1 bonus situation, #22 went to the line and sank one of two, to put Sharon up by one.

On the ensuing in-bounds pass, Sharon ran the three-quarter trap that had bothered Casteline on some occasions in the season, but a reversal through James in the middle brought the ball to Geoff, who fed Mark on a baseline pass, for a layup and a one point lead. The rest of the half passed quickly, James overcoming his initial exhaustion to run the floor smoothly and efficiently. It seemed his extra sprints proved to be beneficial, because he beat his man to a lane on the break twice, leading to one layup for James and one simple pass to Andrew for another layup. By halftime, Casteline held a 4 point lead, and James had a few rebounds and a couple baskets. It felt great to be contributing, though he clearly lacked the confidence to dominate the way he knew he should.

"Nice job building the lead, gentlemen," Coach LaMott told the team at halftime. "You're taking care of the ball and you're rebounding the way you need to. Keep it up and we've got a win here, but don't let up. Schmitt – what's his number, Coach – ?"

Coach Taft to the rescue: "Number 34."

" – and Halsey – "

190

"Number 10."

" – are the real threats. Jason you've got Halsey. Keep it up. When Jason is out, Archie, you might pick him up. At a stoppage of play somewhere near the 4 minute mark of the 3rd, we'll switch to a 6, Jason on Halsey and Dan on Schmitt. We haven't shown them that yet, and we might get a few turnovers if they're not ready. Remember, the other three players in the game at the time: triangle, but match up with them. Don't give anyone a free look at the basket."

Gulps of Gatorade later, the team emerged from the locker room to run through the second half layup lines, most of the boys bouncing to expend the excess energy they were storing up. A second win would be nice, making it two in a row.

Coach LaMott called James over to the sideline with a minute to go before the second half began. "Nice job. Don't try to do too much. Stay within yourself. You're likely to have a hard time feeling in the flow, but you've got too much talent to defer to your teammates all the time. Take what they give you. Remember, the defense is where we set the tone for the game." He clapped James on the backside and sent him back onto the court, as the horn sounded.

With the score 51 – 44 at the end of the 3rd quarter, James was inserted into the lineup, to join Geoff, Andrew, Jason, and Alex. For the next three minutes Casteline controlled the game, exerting good pressure on the ball, trapping occasionally, grabbing every rebound off the defensive board, and moving the ball without any sense of panic on offense. Sharon's defense was just a step too slow to apply pressure to the Panther offense, the result being a series of comfortable shots which propelled Casteline to a 66 – 51 lead with three minutes to go. James felt completely plugged in to the flow of the game, running the lanes, screening and opening up to the ball, stepping up to prevent any Sharon penetrating player from finding an open driving lane. The game seemed easy. When James came out of the game, with Pete replacing him, the score was 69 – 53. The final score was Casteline 75, Sharon 58, Casteline's second win of the year, though this was a non-league game.

For the first time of the year everyone (except Andreas, who was away) played. Having James in the rotation helped the team's depth, it seemed, because when Alex and Dan went back into the game, they were fresher and their shots more sure. The end-of-game huddle at half-court was flowing with smiles and back slaps. Pete even thought it would be a good idea to drop Dan's shorts, though the embarrassment was hidden from the crowd, because Dan was in the middle of the huddle at the time.

191

On the way to the locker room James's parents approached him, his father clasping him in an embrace. "Nice start, James. Great job," he said, looking at James's face to enjoy the happiness set there. His mother stood off to his father's side, smiling, her hand covering her mouth.

"Thanks," James said, unable to contain his pride. It had been a good start, though a delayed one.

Before he entered the locker room, he saw Adrienne, with two friends, standing next to the stands, looking at the players as they walked by. "Hey," she said, raising her head, her hair caught in a woolen cap. "Nice game."

James thought he was seeing a ghost. "Hey, thanks for coming. You saw a good game. I hope there's lots more of those still to come." He wanted to stand and talk, but he wanted to get out of his uniform and shower first. "Are you leaving right now?" he asked, hoping he didn't sound as if he were pleading.

"We'll stick around for a little while. I'll see you when you come out."

After showering and slapping towels and socks at his teammates, James re-entered the gym, partly darkened now. Adrienne, Lucy, and another friend sat at the corner of the bleachers, a crowd of players from each team around them. James wanted the group to dissipate, but he could think of no reason they should, so he joined the crowd.

Adrienne looked at him from the stands. "Sorry I didn't return your call. I wasn't home for a few days, and then we had practice and I went out and . . ." She shrugged. James felt Dan and Pete look at him, just catching on for the first time that James had called her. However, he didn't spend much time looking at their reactions, his eyes drawn to Adrienne's tall posture as she sat on the metal stands, her hands wrapped in blue and white striped mittens, her eyes brilliant green.

"That's OK. I'll call again," James called, tempted to add, "if I have time," for his friends' benefit, but he restrained the impulse. From behind, Pete shoved him in the back.

"Hey, what's the story here, Romeo?" Pete asked, but James wouldn't look at him.

My love she speaks like silence,
Without ideals or violence,
She doesn't have to say she's faithful,
Yet she's true, like ice, like fire.
People carry roses,
Make promises by the hours,
My love she laughs like the flowers,
Valentines can't buy her.

In the dime stores and bus stations,
People talk of situations,
Read books, repeat quotations,
Draw conclusions on the wall.
Some speak of the future,
My love she speaks softly,
She knows there's no success like failure
And that failure's no success at all.

The cloak and dagger dangles,
Madams light the candles.
In ceremonies of the horsemen,
Even the pawn must hold a grudge.
Statues made of match sticks,
Crumble into one another,
My love winks, she does not bother,
She knows too much to argue or to judge.

The bridge at midnight trembles,
The country doctor rambles,
Bankers' nieces seek perfection,
Expecting all the gifts that wise men bring.
The wind howls like a hammer,
The night blows cold and rainy,
My love she's like some raven
At my window with a broken wing.

Love Minus Zero/No Limit by Bob Dylan

Ben

The bus-ride home from Sharon was a comfortable one, Ben and Bryan sitting together in the front seat, diagonally behind Mrs. Nelson, in her hooded jacket. Ben loved to hear the outbursts of exultation that emanated from the team when they had won, the spontaneous reminders that they had joined in something successful, even such a temporary joining. Unconsciously, Ben thought, they enjoyed the moment even more because it was so transitory.

"Everything came together, huh?" Bryan said, tapping Ben on the knee.

"Yeah, it's amazing how things can fall into place with no real reason. I mean we practiced one time, sort of a fitful practice yesterday, and here we are, thinking we can win the state championship. You never know. But that doesn't make it any less fun."

They sat in silence, entertained by the whoops of excitement behind them and the streaky illumination on the wet streets ahead of them.

"What you got on Scituate?" asked Bryan.

"Just a little. They have a really good METCO player, Bello – remember him from the game against Walpole in the tournament when he was a freshman? He's a junior, and he's pretty much the show. Better than Samko, quicker."

"Well, you have some good guard defenders, Dan and Archie, and maybe James can help too."

"Yeah, we do have some depth at the perimeter now. We're just hurting inside, with Andreas gone this week and next week. We could probably apply a little more pressure from the backcourt, but Bello will rip through a press. I don't think we can put any pressure on him, because they have guys that can finish. Tomorrow looks like a tough game for us."

Ben stopped talking about Scituate, partly because he didn't want to take the luster off this win.

As the bus neared the school, Ben stood up to address the team. "Great job tonight, men. You came together against a solid team, and, for the first time, made the opponent look bad. Tomorrow, Scituate won't be as easy to subdue, but if you bring the same strength of will, you can do it. Bus leaves at 4:45; game time is 6:30. Last game of 2008. Let's end the year with a great game. See you at 4:45. Don't forget your ties."

As the managers and players filed past, Ben and Bryan made contact with each player, tapping shoulders, slapping five, making virtual eye contact in the dark bus. Then they picked up the medical kit, the clipboards, and the water bottles.

"I'll take the bottles and the kit," offered Bryan.

"Thanks. I'll see you at 4:45. Thanks for the great day," Ben said. "Lisa back in town?"

"Oh yeah. I'm heading over to Willow's right now. What time is it?"

Ben, looking at his watch, said, "Looks like about 9:00. The night is young."

"You got anything going?" asked Bryan.

"I think the kids are out, but Willa should be getting home soon. She was out with friends at a movie." Ben thought about coming home to an empty house. "Maybe I'll call Willa to see what her schedule is. Maybe I can jump in with you for a burger."

"Yeah, love to have you. For some reason Lisa thinks you're interesting – I guess just a nice reprieve from my dullness. I'm a little jealous, but she's always asking about you, how long you and Willa dated, where you got married. If I didn't know better, I'd think she's got plans for me."

"Maybe she has plans for me!" Ben said, laughing. He called home, checking messages from Scott and Mary, messages letting Ben and Willa know that they were both spending the night at a friend's house. He then called Willa, but got no answer. Thinking Willa would be coming home in the next hour, Ben told Bryan, "I think I should get home now. Willa'll be home soon, and the kids are out."

"Well, I'll tell Lisa that the consummately married man made another considerate gesture for his love-mate, and she'll be even more impressed with you."

"Hey, how'd Christmas go with Taylor? You have a good day?"

"Yeah, in fact it was our best Christmas ever, since the divorce. He's starting to grow up and not need such constant assurances. We played some games that he got – Xbox and stuff. Yeah, it was good. How about yours?"

"A very sweet day: nice presents and a great dinner. Willa does holidays to the max, you know that. I don't think I could spend a more comfortable day. The kids stayed in through the evening, and we got silly, wrestling on the floor for a half an hour at one point. There's something about Christmas, the sameness of it, except the fact that the kids are always getting bigger and older, but this year it seemed that they weren't older at all. I don't know, it was just peaceful, and I guess that's what Christmas is supposed to be about." Ben clapped Bryan on the back. "See you tomorrow at 4:30 or so. Say hi to my girlfriend – I mean, your girlfriend."

"Yeah, say hi to Willa for me. She not coming to the games this week?"

"No, she's working till 5 or 6 this week, no time off for vacation except for the holidays. So she can't run out of the house to go down to Scituate. I don't blame her. She makes the league games and that's great."

"Yeah, I'm just used to seeing her in the stands. See you tomorrow."

At home Ben turned on the TV, sitting in the reclining chair to pull the game stats together, while UConn and Louisville finished a game on TV. Ben was interested in the plus/minus of the game, as usual. The stats revealed Andrew with a +17, Geoff with a +16, Archie and Dan with 12s, and Jonas with a +11 as the most productive, but James with +9 in 11 minutes was impressive in his limited time. He had looked tentative, but his experience from last year had allowed him to settle down and make plays at both ends.

After finishing the stats for the game, Ben turned his thoughts to the next day's game against Scituate, considering a game that looked like a loss. He went over the scouting notes that he had on Scituate, looking for their greatest weakness (or their weakest strength, in this case). Skimming the thin notes he had, Ben determined that Scituate had some weakness inside, though they had immense size, starting two players over 6'5". However, they had been outrebounded in the game that Jim had scouted, mostly because the big men got in foul trouble, and their replacements were both smaller and far less talented. With this in mind, Ben formulated a simple plan to post up Andrew on most possessions, negating his quickness from the outside, but making use of his variety of post moves that could draw fouls from the bigger Scituate players.

At least it was a plan. If Andrew drew a double-team, Geoff could clean up on the weakside board. And James (though he wasn't starting) could also help on the offensive glass, if Scituate doubled the ball.

At about 10:30 Willa came home, energized by her evening out with her friends. She had seen *The Secret Life of Bees* and then enjoyed a cup of coffee and a muffin at the nearby coffee shop in Franklin.

"Hi, hon, how'd you do?" she asked.

"It was our best night of the season. We got control of the game in the second half, and ran away from that point. It was a good night. We won by fifteen or something." He couldn't help but fill up with a little pride that the team had seemed to make a real improvement on this night.

"Wow, congratulations. I'm sorry I missed it, but it was really hectic at work, and I didn't even get to the movies until after it started. I loved the movie, *The Secret Life of Bees*. It was uplifting and I thought it was well-done." Placing her coat in the closet, she sat down across from Ben, her eyes bright, her hands rubbing her arms through her cotton sleeves to warm them.

Ben moved from the chair to the couch, placing his arms around her to share the warmth of his body. She moved easily and familiarly into his embrace, relaxing against his chest, in a movement practiced and practiced many times. Ben closed his eyes, feeling her acquiescence, and she moved her hand down to his stomach, rubbing softly, reaching downward, her indication that all was well on this night, even though she had to wake up early the next morning, even though they rarely shared these moments of intimacy. In a few moments, after no more discussion than, "You want to go upstairs?" they shut off the lights downstairs and climbed the stairs to their bedroom.

The next morning, as Willa dressed for work, and Ben moved into the bathroom to shower, Ben felt as if he needed to talk with Willa, to share with her the odd comfort he had felt at Willow's, the tingle he had felt at thinking he might spend an evening there, out with others, mingling with other men and women who were not in their homes, not settled in their lives as Ben and Willa were. But that was what Ben wanted to discuss: were they settled in their lives? There were times, weeks, in fact, when Ben felt unsettled, when the children were moving on in their own directions, mostly good directions, and Willa and Ben moved in their own directions, too, but not in directions that brought them closer. Ben wanted to ask where Willa's involvement with the church was taking her, and try to determine whether he wanted to go in that direction. There was a lot to discuss, but the night before, there had been a more important matter to settle, and they had settled it raptly.

But that was part of Ben's uncertainty. Their distance had been bridged with their love-making, and at the time, it had been perfect in all its physical and emotional intimacy. But now, in the morning, it was as if they had returned to their roles as mother and father, as they headed off to their respective days, Willa to her job, and Ben to pick up the kids, correct as many essays as the day would allow, then to catch the bus to Scituate.

Returning to the bedroom, Ben began, "Last night was great. I kind of wish it happened more often." He hated the fact that his statement sounded accusatory, but he couldn't think of any other way to introduce a discussion on their relationship.

Willa looked at him with surprise. "I didn't think it required keeping track of. When the time is right, it happens, doesn't it?" She made it sound like an emotionless transaction.

"Yes, I just think there's other ways we can interact, other ways we can get close. I don't know." And he really didn't know.

"Oh, you want to substitute something else for making love? What would that be? Are you not happy with our love-making?" She kept brushing her hair, stroking repeatedly.

Ben sat on the edge of the bed, unable to grasp his next thought. He just wanted to feel closer. "I just want to feel closer," he tried.

Willa looked at him, wide-eyed. "Could we be any closer than we were last night?"

"No, we couldn't. But I want to feel that close all the time, not just when we make love, and not just once a month."

Willa burst out, "Well, then maybe you have to end your marriage to basketball. There's nothing that has put one of us out of this house any more than your affair with basketball. And I've been alongside you just about all the way, to enable us to maintain the closeness that you're talking about. But now that I'm heading in another direction, we don't share quite as much, and we're both feeling that. But I would suggest that, if you want to move closer to me, you need to step away from your obsession with basketball, and see what's been going on in this house for the past twenty years." Willa placed her brush down on her bureau as gently as she could, stood up, and headed out of the room.

"Willa, I don't think that's fair. It's not as if my obsession, if that's what you call it, is any more or less than it has been for, actually, twenty-five years. I know, the dynamic between us has changed, since you've had to get a job, and I've maintained my connection to basketball. So I don't think I've changed one bit. And I know you haven't changed, but the opportunities between us have changed a lot, and I'm starting to feel that change, and it makes me sad to think we can't maintain our closeness. I don't want to be like everyone else, having trouble as we turn middle-aged. I'm not looking for that."

Willa laughed at him, a little incredulity in her voice. "Oh, is that a threat? If we don't change, we'll become like everyone else? What does that mean, splitting up? Are you saying we should get divorced?" Willa had always been good, quite accurate, in fact, at taking his thoughts and projecting them into the future, showing him where they might lead. It scared Ben to hear Willa say the word "divorce," as if it were a specter that neither one could see, but that both of them could feel.

Ben stood, trying to take Willa in his arms, the same arms that had comforted and warmed her the night before. Willa was not at all receptive. "No, Willa, that's not it at all. I just want to talk with you about how we do things, how we interact. I think maybe we need something to replace that connection we had around basketball that has gone away. And I don't fault you for its going away. I know it had to happen. But I think we need – at least, *I* need – something to replace it." Ben was happy with where his words had led him. He thought his words made sense.

Willa continued to pull away from him. "Well, when you can think of something that would work, you let me know. Until then, I'll keep working, raising Scott and Mary, shopping for everyone, putting the meals on the table, and going to church to try to maintain some sense of sanity." She pulled away for good, her eyes filled with tears. "And now, if you don't mind, I'm going to work, when I have absolutely no desire to go to work, because I'm so upset." She walked out the door of their bedroom and started down the stairs.

"Willa, Willa," Ben called after her. "Don't leave with this hanging over us. I don't want you to feel miserable. I feel miserable, but I don't want you to feel that way. Stay for a few minutes and talk about it, will you?"

"Ben, I can't. For one thing I'm late to work. For another thing, I don't know what else to say. We get along. What else is there to discuss?"

"I don't think 'getting along' is enough. Am I crazy?"

Willa looked at him. "Well, you're the one who brought all this up. It wasn't me." She put on her coat in the hallway and opened the door.

"Am I crazy if I want something more between us? Is that crazy?"

As Willa left, she said, "Why do we need something more? Am I not enough for you?"

Ben watched her open the door of the Subaru, her face smeared with tears. He wanted to hug her, to wipe away the tears, but she was backing out the driveway, and then she was gone, as Ben stood at the storm door. The tires of Willa's car left parallel swipes across the wet pavement.

By 9:30, Scott had called to say that he would be home in the early afternoon.

"What's up for this morning?" asked Ben.

"Oh, I don't know. Perry and I are just hangin out. We might go to a friend's."

"Everything go all right last night?" asked Ben, hoping so.

"Oh, yeah. We went over to Mick's to fool around. No party or anything. Just four or five of us deadheads, doing nothing. Nothing to worry about, Dad."

Ben hoped he detected sincerity in Scott's voice.

"See you in the afternoon. Let me know if you need a ride."

"Bye."

Mary sent an e-mail an hour later. She was at work, and she just sent a quick message from the computer at work, saying she'd be home for supper. Ben winced, knowing that he would be gone to Scituate.

With the day clear and empty, Ben settled down at the kitchen table, music set up on the computer, to grade the essays that awaited him. He had two stacks, one from his freshmen, three page essays, two classes worth. The other stack contained the essays from his juniors on an outside American author, the analysis of two books by that author. These were the essays that needed close scrutiny because of the students' tendency to take short cuts: plagiarizing their words from an internet source.

After two solid hours, Ben was finished with the freshman papers, more than thirty essays (he had completed almost half of them earlier in the week). Opening his gradebook, he recorded the grades, closed the book, closed the folder containing the essays, and took a deep breath. It was almost noon. The snowy tree limbs visible out the window reminded Ben of his mother, and he decided to drive up to Fidelity House to see her. On one of his recent visits before Christmas, they had collaborated to make the pressed flower Christmas cards she sent as cards to her closest friends. Ben, for the second year in a row, had worked with her, going through her address book to find the friends and family she wanted to bless with her artwork. It had been a great day, except for one detail. Margot had been signing the cards 'Margot and Dean," Ben's dad's name.

"Mom," he had asked, "don't you think it will be uncomfortable for your friends to be getting a card from 'Margot and Dean'? It might create the wrong impression."

Margot looked at Ben with confusion. "Do you want me to use another name?"

Ben looked at his mother. "I just think it might seem out of line, or something, for them to see the name 'Dean' on the card."

Margot's confusion deepened. "Well, then, what would you like to call yourself?"

Ben thought for a minute, then said simply, "Maybe you could sign the cards with just your name." He shrugged his shoulders slightly and tilted his head to the side.

Neither Margot nor her wheelchair was seated in her room, when Ben arrived. He looked down the hallway toward a few familiar faces. "Have you seen my mom?" he asked a white-haired man who grasped the rail that rimmed the hallway. His shirt was neatly pressed, though his pants were stained and his shoes were untied.

The man stared at Ben, unable to manufacture a response. His eyes filled a little with his effort to assimilate Ben's question.

"That's OK. Have a nice day," Ben offered as he passed the man. Next, Ben looked in the activity room, where he and his mom had created the fifteen Christmas cards they had sent to her friends. A television set, channeled to a cooking show, sent its message through the room, out the door. Margot was not seated in the room.

Turning out of the activity room, Ben swept up the corridor, peeking into any rooms where Margot had found an acquaintance, waving to some of the faces peering out at him, some beaming with welcoming smiles, some muted with uncertainty. One woman smiled and nodded at him, as if she were telling him, "Yes, indeed, I'm still here, and I'm still enjoying myself."

At the nurses' station, Ben asked Bea, the charge nurse, if she had seen his mother.

Bea said, "I think she's in the activity room, isn't she?"

"I already checked in there. It looked empty."

Bea rose from her padded seat behind the desk and came around the counter, to assist Ben. No one wanted to think that a resident could go missing.

At the activity room door, Bea turned to her right to a little alcove in the room. There sat Margot, her wheelchair stuck, her head poking into a floor-to ceiling cabinet filled with paper, puzzles, and children's books. "Now, Margot, you have to turn around here, you know that. Are you stuck?" Bea asked.

Margot tried to turn her head over her shoulder to identify the voice that called her. "Who dat?" she asked in her customary serio-comic voice. A grin played on her lips and her eyes tried to glisten through her cloudy eyeglasses.

"Hi, Mom, I've been looking for you," Ben began, leaning over Bea's shoulder. "Have you been here for long? I checked in this room, but I didn't look over here." Seeing his mother fiddling in this closet made Ben feel as if he had abandoned her. He took her glasses off her face to clean them, replacing them gently.

Margot sat still for a minute. "Oh, I don't know. What time is it?" she asked, as if knowing the time would help her know how long she had had her head in the closet.

"It's about 12:30. Have you had your lunch?" Maybe he could help her clear her plate on this day.

Bea, moving out of the room, said, "No, the lunches are just coming up now. Margot, yours should be just arriving in your room right now. Let's get back to the room and have lunch."

Ben reassured Bea, "I'll get her back. Thanks for locating her."

He wheeled her smoothly back toward her room, adding a couple of personally applied speed bumps just for his mother's amusement. He could hear her chuckle when he did so. And lunch was indeed sitting on the bed-stand at the end of her bed.

Margot invited him to join her. "Can you stay for lunch?"

"Absolutely. Let's roll this bed-stand out into the hallway, so I have room for a chair to sit next to you. OK?" Ben asked.

Margot nodded.

Pulling a chair from Margot's room out into the corridor, Ben sat next to his mother. She took the aluminum cover off the plate, revealing a sandwich that looked like chicken salad. She also had a bowl of melon, a roll encased in plastic, a carton of milk, a cup of tea, and a bowl of cottage cheese, all of which looked as well prepared as a mid-day newscast.

Margot set about adding sugar to her tea, stirring and then setting the spoon down on the saucer daintily. She sipped the tea before she ate anything.

Ben surprised himself by picking up one half of the diagonally-cut chicken salad sandwich and taking a bite, then surprised himself again by asking his mother, "Mom, did you and Dad ever think you weren't going to stay together?"

Margot looked dumbly at Ben, but replied smartly, "Oh, we teetered on the edge more than once. I had to manage the finances while he spent, spent, spent. We didn't ever make it easy on each other." She looked clearly at Ben, knowing what she had said was the truth.

Ben kept wondering. "Did you think you got everything you could have gotten out of the marriage? Do you think it was a great marriage?"

Margot pondered his questions. She looked down the hallway, looking for a younger couple in the shadows, shaking her head, in the end. "No, I think there was more that we could have gotten out of it. I think everyone thinks there's more you can get out of it." She reached for the other half of the chicken salad and slowly brought it to her mouth.

Changing the angle of his chair so that he faced his mother more directly, Ben asked for her counsel again. "What do you think it takes to make the most out of a marriage?" He wondered about his own judgment, seeking this counsel, but he didn't know where else to go.

Margot kept eating, slowly chewing the bread and chicken. She didn't have any response to this last question, the most important one. She did pause before she took another bite.

Ben persisted. "Mom, is there anything that you think a husband or wife needs to do to get the most out of a marriage?" He tried to pinpoint his question to force a response from his mother.

After a quiet sip of tea, Margot tried to formulate an answer. "Oh, well, if you keep your head up and put one foot in front of the other, you'll get the most out of anything you do. Just keep your head up," she said brilliantly, very happy with her reply. She cut a piece of her melon and put it in her mouth, savoring its flavor.

Ben was not surprised to hear his mother make this statement indicating that surviving and maintaining resilience were her suggestions, because he knew that that was her way of coping with all that life had given her. He stopped trying to wrest wisdom from her. "Thanks for the help, Mom. I just thought, with your experience, you might have some words of wisdom. Thanks a lot."

Margot kept eating. "Help yourself, Ben. You're a growing boy. You need to keep up your strength. Have my milk, I won't be drinking it."

They sat comfortably together for the duration of the meal, Ben slipping small portions of the sandwich and melon into his mouth. Margot served the remainder of the tea from the metal teapot into her cup, adding sugar again. After a few minutes of silence, she said suddenly, with clarity, "Your father and I never talked about things that mattered. We talked about money and drinking alcohol and working too many jobs and fixing the car. But we never talked about how to make us happy. We had to figure that out for ourselves, and it kept us apart because we didn't talk about that. We were like the two pendulums in a grandfather clock, passing each other at regular intervals, but never moving along the same direction. But it was a long time ago, and I might not be remembering accurately. I'm just giving you my impressions."

Ben nodded. "I understand. That's important to hear. Thanks."

A few minutes later Ben stood up to leave. "That was a nice lunch. Thanks for having me."

Margot looked up at him. "It was nice to see you. I see Willa more often than I see you, but I know you're busy." In her motherly way, Margot excused Ben's negligence, telling him how much Willa's visits meant. "Don't be a stranger, now."

"Bye, Mom. I love you." Ben patted his mother on the back of her shoulder as he leaned down to kiss her dry face.

After Ben left his mother's room, he said "Hi" to the residents who made eye-contact with him as he strolled down his mother's floor and headed down the stairs to the car. Crossing the parking lot, he looked at the leafless trees that stood outside his mother's window, looking for the lines that would denote cobwebs in his mother's mind, the cobwebs from which she saw monkeys swinging, but he could only envision long pendulums, swinging at cross-purposes, reaching upwards on their heavenward paths, then falling to glide past each other, momentarily aligning only to swing away from each other again. He wondered whether Willa and he would ever coordinate their arcs again.

The Scituate gym held pleasant memories of past tournament games, many of them victories for Casteline. When Ben entered the yellow-lit court, he recognized the A.D. who had hosted those tournament games, as he checked the clock console wiring, setting up for the game. On a vacation night, there would be a slight crowd, maybe seventy-five driving down from Casteline, maybe a few hundred Scituations (Ben chuckled at his cleverness) coming out to watch a solid home team play a mediocre visitor from Casteline. There had been some very competitive games between the two towns over the years; Scituate held a slight advantage overall.

"Hi, how's it going for you?" Ben called to the Athletic Director, whose name he couldn't recall, though they had spoken many times over the years.

"Hi, Ben, good to have you here. We're sitting on a 6:30 starting time – is that what you're expecting?" The man held out his hand to shake Ben's, friendly and familiar.

"Sounds perfect. I just have to duck into the locker room and tape some ankles. We'll come out and shoot for a little while, then come out for game-time at 6:15. Thanks for having us." There was a fraternity of coaches and ADs in the greater Boston area, a cadre of men who made basketball in Eastern Massachusetts an entity around which a lot of interest evolved. There were websites devoted to local basketball teams, especially here on the South Shore. Casteline's region, west of Boston, seemed less insular, more connected to Boston and its suburban sprawl. Scituate, Cohasset, Rockland – here there was local coverage of upcoming games in the local newspapers and internet interest in the relative strength of the area teams. Over the past few years, Ben had visited those sports sites, to glean information about non-league teams that he would play. It reminded him of the hysteria that coaching in Kentucky or Indiana would produce: accepting the adulation for winning and the scrutiny for losing in a very public way.

Ben turned toward the locker room to ready the team for the game. "Got the medical kit in here, Bryan?" he asked as he entered the locker room. Thirty-five minutes later the referee tossed the ball up to start the game.

Scituate grabbed an easy 11 point lead to start the game, cashing in on several Casteline turnovers and converting three fast-break baskets off defensive rebounds and quick outlets. After six short minutes Scituate led 21 – 13, with Andrew Bello accounting for 12 of those points with his speed. Andrew started the game with a couple of buckets, but then went cold, and Ben finally had to replace him in the lineup, he was becoming so timid about shooting. Sliding down to Andrew's seat on the bench, Ben said, "Andrew, don't worry if they're going in or not. If they're good shots, take them. They'll fall. You're our best shooter. If you pass up a shot, we're not improving our chances."

Andrew looked at Coach hopefully, believing in what he was saying. "I'll loosen up." But he looked tight.

Jason Grutchfield pushed the ball into the corner, as Ben looked back at the court, then reversed the ball opposite wing to James, who stepped into a nice shot that missed. Scituate rebound, outlet pass, 2 on 1, layup. Ben called timeout.

"James, great shot. Jason, great reverse pass. Guys, we can't move the ball any better. The shots are just not falling. Hang in there. Try to get some easy points off your defense and work the glass on the offensive end, for two reasons: one, you might get a simple putback. But two, if you work the glass, you'll jam their rebounder, if they do get the ball, and you'll slow down their fast- break. They're getting too many simple fast-breaks.

"Dan, step in for Archie, and take the ball to the rim if you get the chance. If we get their big men in foul trouble, their subs are not strong. Let's go. 1 . . . 2 . . . 3."

The team's "Tight" had no stridency. Ben sometimes would call the team back together for another "Tight," but there didn't seem to be much energy within the team, and he didn't want to underscore their indifference.

With a minute to go in the half, Scituate tried a little zone, leading by twelve, but James, then Dan, then Jason each hit a 3, and two entry passes into the post drew fouls on one of Scituate's 6'5" post men, sending him to the bench with three fouls. All of a sudden Scituate had handed Casteline entry into the game. Half-time score was 38 – 34, Scituate. The locker room held some life, because of the comeback. Geoff, especially, generated some commotion in the locker room, pumping his teammates up, and, surprisingly, James joined him, lending the voice of a junior to the captain's voice of leadership. Between the two of them, they capitalized on the rising spirit of the team, each knowing that a little more confidence and effort would bring them even with the opponent. Andrew hung his head just a little, and on the way back onto the court, Ben spoke to his shooting star.

"Andrew, now we just forget what happened in the first half. It doesn't matter. If you made ten shots, that wouldn't matter either, because now you have the chance to make ten in this half. You've got more talent than your defender. Don't give him more credit than he deserves. It was Jason, James, and Dan that got us back into the game. You've got some teammates that can hit big shots, so don't think you have to score twenty. But if you've got an opening, make them pay." Ben clapped Andrew on the back to send him back into the layup line.

In the second half, the game see-sawed back and forth, Casteline gaining a two point advantage at one point, only to see Scituate sweep that lead away with a burst of their own. With a minute to go, Scituate held a 61 – 59 lead, and Casteline had the ball. Ben held back from calling a time-out; from the time he had started coaching close to thirty years ago, he had tried to instill in his teams the ability to make an important play at the end of the game, a play that evolved from practice, but that relied on players' understanding the essential concepts on which basketball was founded. He called, "Drag-the-line," and motioned with a circle with his hand, as if he were rounding up the cattle in the barnyard. He was calling for a delay game, using up as much of the thirty second clock as he could, then, when the defense came out to pressure in the last few seconds, setting up a back-door bounce pass for a forward on the base-line. The delay worked, and, with six seconds on the clock, Archie penetrated, drawing Andrew's man to step up, and bounced a pass to Andrew, who laid it in, drawing the fifth foul on the big man. The score was tied, and Andrew went to the line to put Casteline in the lead.

From over his shoulder, Ben could feel and hear the small crowd expressing their excitement at the comeback. Bridget and Janet, the managers, gushed their excitement. "Oh my God, did you see that play? That was awesome," Janet exclaimed. Ben called the team over while Scituate huddled around their coach, pending his substitution for his best player.

Ben said as calmly as he could, "Andrew, simple shot here. Guys, make or miss, they have 32 seconds on the clock, so they have to shoot with a few seconds to go. They've lost O'Brien to fouls, so we can help out a little bit off his replacement."

Bryan jumped in. "Want to switch all screens?"

Ben thought for a second. "Switch any screens in the last ten seconds. Until then, stay with your man if you can. We're in a 1, but no fouls." He shouted, "No fouls." He paused. "They'll probably look for an isolation for Bello. If you're covering someone in the corner away from the ball, step into the lane to help stop penetration. Let's make this play. You guys have come back from being nowhere, and now you have the chance to win. Take this game home with you." Ben's voice rose with the joy that this win would produce.

"TIGHT" they all shouted, the managers joining in boldly, swept up by the emotion. Andrew walked to the line, dribbled steadily, and drained the shot, putting Casteline up by one. Scituate took a time-out, though they had just spent thirty seconds in a huddle. In Ben's own time-out, he reiterated all he had said. "Everyone ready?"

The team brought their hands together and jumped up and down. "TIGHT," they shouted, without the 1,2,3 prompting. Ben felt the elevation of the team, the way they stood up for each other, understanding their commitment to each other on the court. There was no uncertainty in any faces.

Scituate inbounded the ball, reversing the ball twice in the back-court to relieve the pressure, the off-guard dribbling to the top of the circle and passing the ball to the wing. Dan nearly stole the pass, deflecting it, but Scituate's star, Bello, regained control and held the ball, letting the clock tick down to less than ten seconds.

As Bello began his dribble, Scituate's next best shooter, Wilson, #41, came off a down-screen on the weakside. Bello reversed his dribble, opening up the cross-court pass, and he hit #41 as he turned to square up. He caught and shot. Ben glanced at the clock as the ball hung in the air. Six seconds left. The ball continued its graceful arc toward the orange hoop, bouncing off the back rim, then the backboard, then through. Ben immediately screamed, "Time-out," and the referee nearby blew his whistle. There were 3 seconds on the clock; Scituate had a 63 – 62 lead.

Ben asked the referee if there should be more time on the clock. After a brief conference, Casteline was awarded another second to make it 4. Ben said, "Just simple press-break. I'm sure they'll press to slow us down. Jason and Archie, you're in the back-court. James and Andrew, you're at half-court. Half-court guys, come hard down the sidelines, to draw your men wide. Jason, step hard toward Archie, to start to set a pick. Then just take off. Geoff, over the top to Jason. If the defense is playing the way we expect it to play, we'll have a layup for Jason."

The team absorbed the play, one they had never run in practice, one that Ben had not utilized in five or six years. The Scituate defense set up just as Ben had expected, except they took the defensive man off the ball and placed him at the opposite foul-line, to ward off any long passes. Ben called another time-out.

"OK, guys, they were one step ahead of us on that one. Back to regular press-break. Geoff, on a 3-count, break to the right to get the ball in to Andrew, if you can't get Archie or Jason on the entry pass. No timeouts left. Geoff, you can't call another time-out. No time for a pass once the ball in inbounded. Whoever gets the pass, two or three dribbles and shoot."

The pass came in to Jason, who was immediately double-teamed. He passed to Archie, who took another dribble and heaved a half-court shot that came up ten feet short as the horn sounded. Scituate had climbed back to win.

Ben noisily expelled the breath he had been unwilling to take as the players dropped to the floor in their disappointment. Bryan clapped him on the back to convey his sympathy. Ben shook his head before he went onto the court to raise the heads of his players.

After the team handshakes, Ben gathered the team to center court, as usual. "Men, that was a tremendous game. You made every play. Scituate is a very good team, and we took them to one point in their own gym. They made a great play at the end, and they made a smart defensive adjustment to stop what would have been a game-winning play on our part. We just didn't have enough time. Another ten seconds and that game was ours. Congratulations on a great, great game. You've made great strides since the beginning of the season. Play that game at Wellesley and we win by twenty." Of course, James hadn't been on the floor at Wellesley, and that made a difference.

One last, disjointed "Tight," and the team stumbled disconsolately to the locker room, Ben's words already lost in their frustration. And Ben joined them in that frustration, knowing that they had played a solid game, but that it wasn't enough. It made him wonder if this team would ever get over the hump to believe in itself. He wondered whether he had the weapons in his own coaching arsenal to allow them to succeed.

The bus ride home was funereal, from the coaches in front, to the player sitting in the last seat. Ben couldn't see who it was, but, thinking of the normal pecking order of seating on the team bus, he suspected that it was Geoff. Bridget quietly handed him the scorebook when he entered the bus. Bryan looked ahead into the empty windshield, knowing in advance that Ben would not be speaking on this ride, even though they had about forty miles to cover. It was the last game of 2008, ending the year with a disappointing loss, one that Ben could not think past.

But as he rode, he thought of Willa, certainly home from work now, cleaning up after a supper with the children. He pictured Scott being picked up by Perry, as they headed out to see what the world of Summit had to offer on this next-to-last day of the year. He saw his daughter, sitting at the hockey game, cheering the Summit team on. He looked down at his long, cashmere coat, the coat he had inherited from his father when he died. He felt for his gloves and, putting them on, clapped his hands together to warm them. After twenty minutes he and Bryan began conversing in a hush, Bryan comforting, Ben suffering. When they stopped talking, Ben felt alone, like the snow-swept granite outcroppings they passed in the dark New England night.

The Arc of Intersection

Take it like a man they said
Take your medicine
Find a golden road and stand
Then I saw exactly what they meant.

Find my homeboys on the dusky road
Who couldn't give a shit about their life
Heed their words of faded brown
Then live it and sing about their strife.

Then bring your song to the river at sunrise
Sing that song 'til the river runs clean
It will happen to you
As it happened to me
Won't you sing that lovely song for me
It's alright mama

Let your children be loud
Watch them run into trouble
So they can figure it out

We spread our seeds far 'cross this land
Hoping they'd fall on good ground.
A vaccination in the sun and rain shine
And take a good long hard look around.

Then bring your song to the river at sunrise
Sing that song 'til the river runs clean
It will happen to you
As it's happened to me
Come clean with me
It's alright mama

Let your children be loud
Watch them run into trouble
'Cause trouble's their medicine
Mama take your medicine.

Golden Road by Martin Sexton

210

James

"Hey, what's up?" James asked Pete, whose call he had just taken in the kitchen.

"You joinin us tonight? We're headin to Boston to cruise First Night. Wanna come?"

James knew he was not going out on New Year's Eve, but he asked Pete anyway, "Who's going with you?"

"We've got a gang of nine, and you'd make ten. Joanne Striker, Ginnie Wakely, and Pam Reiser, to name three who are committed to mayhem. Don't tell me you can pass this up, man. The year only ends once."

"Yeah, well mine ended about three weeks ago. Sounds great; I wish I could go. But I'm inside these here walls, and I'll probably listen to Johnnie Cash."

Pete sighed. "Oh, come on, man, how long can you be expected to pay penance? The world has moved on. My parents are letting me stay out, as long as I call at 2:00 a.m., telling them where I am. If I don't call, I'm in for the next two weeks. Sounds fair to me."

James marveled at Pete's boundlessness. His license was suspended for a year, but he still motored on, undeterred. "Sounds like a good deal for you. I don't think my parents'd go for that deal. I think I'll be forced to call them every hour, even from this living room." James looked at his mother, who was looking over her shoulder at him, an unsympathetic look on her face.

"OK. See you in the New Year then. For He's a Jolly Good Fellow . . ."

"Later," James said, laughing. Pete's invulnerability was infinite.

"What's Pete's deal?" asked James's mother.

James was noncommittal. "He's heading out with friends. Doesn't sound like he's going to go crazy – the way I might, sitting home in this house."

Mrs. Rush sighed, removing her glasses to clean them. "James, you don't really think you should be going out tonight, do you? I mean what kinds of options are there for you with your friends? Is anyone going to sit in a house and drink hot chocolate? No, I think you just have to accept the limitations your father and I placed on you when you revealed your own limitations." She walked into the hallway leading to her bedroom.

James followed her with his eyes. "I'll be OK. I just wish it was eight months from now, and this was all over. Or even twelve hours from now."

He picked up the newspaper, with its slight report on last night's game, the close loss to Scituate. He knew the team had played well, but was mired in some tough luck. Over the two games of his return, he had scored 11 and 8 points, nothing spectacular, but he was starting to get comfortable. He was an integral part of their successful runs; his plus/minus was +11 in the two games, and he knew that Coach LaMott looked at that stat very closely. He had shot 9 for 20, not bad, but he hadn't been to the foul line yet, a result of his timidity with the ball. He was playing conservatively as he got accustomed to his new teammates. The two weeks of pre-season had had no connection to these two games, because the team had evolved without him, developing tendencies that he had tried to keep up with from the bench, but playing on the court provided a different perspective. It was harder to see what was coming when you were engaged in covering a man, or maintaining floor balance. You lost the big picture – though the team on the floor had captured that larger vision in the first half against Braintree, James remembered. They had stayed completely within a mode that they had manufactured for a long stretch in that game, but eventually, in the second half, Braintree's trap had unraveled the team's flow, and the Panthers had lost.

As James lay down on the couch, mindlessly watching the Bowl game from Charlotte, NC, he wondered how a team gained the confidence to play at its peak at all times. Coach LaMott did all he could not to destroy egos when he called the team together. James could hear the restraint in Coach's voice, as he tried to move the team toward that delicate blend of discipline and abandon that was needed to beat an opponent. It took discipline to play within the loose system that Coach conveyed to the team: floor balance, minimal dribbling, triple-threat stance with the ball, hands extended on defense, changing your angle to the ball on every pass or penetration on both offense and defense. These principles had been inculcated in James and most of the team in the many drills they had run since they were ten years old.

But understanding these essential principles was not enough to win. The other teams understood those principles, too, for the most part. Winning – whether it was one possession or an entire game – also demanded the boldness to take the defense on when you had the ball, to create an advantage for the Panthers. When all five players on the floor challenged the defense each time they gained possession of the ball, the defense was overwhelmed at having to both stop the ball and deny the teammates. When the Panthers got their opponents into this double consciousness, they won.

James understood this ironic assimilation of restraint and propulsion. Andrew, too. Geoff understood it, but he lacked the ability to challenge the defense with the ball, because his ball skills were deficient. Jason was a little too much propulsion and too little restraint: he put himself into vulnerable situations, jumping in the air to pass, assuming his teammates would be in a particular spot without feeling how the game had changed on this trip down the floor.

And Dan knew the ratio. Dan had made a nice jump up from JV, and had been part of some solid runs in the first six games, rarely out of position, just about never giving the ball up with a turnover, benefiting, of course, from James's suspension.

James pushed himself up off the couch to call Dan, to see what he was doing for New Year's.

"Is Dan there?" he asked Dan's little brother.

"Yeah," Michael answered sullenly. He was ten and just beginning to lay claim to his awkwardness.

"Yeah," Dan opened. He sounded upbeat.

"Just wonderin what you're doin. I'm sittin here twiddling my thumbs, watching Boise State take down Clemson in a classic."

Dan laughed. "Jeez, wish I was there. Can you tape it for me? I'll catch up on it after I watch the full series of ER from 2007."

"You goin out tonight?" James asked, just curious. He had the kitchen to himself; his mother was still in her room, and his dad had not come in from work yet – another Saturday work day.

"I think I'm goin over to Joyce's house. Her family is having a little family get-together, just hanging out together until midnight; then Joyce and I might get a few minutes of semi-privacy in which we can celebrate the New Year. Home by 1:00, I'd say. Kind of a Prairie Home Companion evening, where everyone's above average, especially me."

James thought it sounded quaint and fun. He wondered whether Adrienne was having a similar engagement. He had tried not to think of her since he had seen her at the Sharon game. He had told her he'd call, but he didn't really have anything to tell her – other than he had bought her a Christmas present that represented an absolute uncertainty.

"Hey, d'you think we got a shot at getting good?"

"I do. I think we almost hit it against Scituate, we just about had the win, except for the last play. And they're good. You're getting back into the feel of the game; Archie's helped – helped a lot. We've got a good set of perimeter players. It hurts not having Andreas for some minutes in the post. It's kind of a waste to use Andrew inside, but we gotta do it sometimes, because Geoff and Mark can't go all day."

James knew Dan was right, but he also thought it didn't matter who played where, in the end. "I think we just need to feel a flow out there. I mean you get it, and Andrew and Archie get it. Geoff is solid. I'm starting to get comfortable. With that five, we should be able to go on solid runs at both ends of the floor. I really think we can beat anyone on the schedule. I know that sounds crazy, but I do think it." James was a little excited, hearing himself so confident.

Dan agreed, with reservation. "Well, we've gotta do it a few times, and then we can believe in ourselves. 2 and 4 doesn't inspire confidence on our part or fear on the part of Walpole or Norwood."

"You're right. It's gotta happen right away. Let's set the tone Monday in practice. Only one practice before Norwood, and you know their half-court zone can be broken with good passes. I'm psyched." James tossed a tennis ball against the wall, short tosses, lightly. When he tried to make the tosses longer, he started fumbling the ball. Finally, he opened his eyes, tossing the ball off the opposite wall, prompting his mother to return to the kitchen with a perplexed expression on her face. "Oh, sorry, Mom," James said, seeing her querulous brow. "Hey, have a great evening. I'll see you Monday," James closed, as he and Dan gave up their conversation.

Mrs. Rush returned to her bedroom, just as his father opened the door from the driveway.

"Hi," Mr. Rush said. He took his coat off and tossed it onto the back of a kitchen chair.

"Hey, Dad. Work OK?" James asked pleasantly.

"Well, it's over. It's over for the year. I can be thankful we need to work OT, to be honest. It's been a pretty good year. Can't complain," he said reflectively. James hadn't accompanied his father to the plant for many months, but he could picture his father's office, a small huddle off the main floor of the small plant.

"You think I could work there this summer?" James asked, not so much because he wanted to, but because he wanted to find some connection to his father.

Mr. Rush stopped pushing his hands through his thinning hair. "Well, I think I could come up with something. It wouldn't pay a lot, but over ten weeks, it'd add up." He looked appreciatively at his son, knowing that he was trying to find a path that had room for two generations.

"We'll keep it in mind," James finished. He added, on another topic, "Hey, Dad, I got the placement for my treatment program. They allowed me to postpone until April – May, as we asked. It's twice a week for six weeks." In a way, James was curious what the program might tell him about himself.

Leaning back, looking at the kitchen light, Mr. Rush said, "Well, I guess that's a nice resolution. Personally, I would like to see it happen sooner rather than later, but it's nice they listened to our plea."

James did not look up at his father, knowing that the plea had been James's and his mother's idea, not Mr. Rush's. The matter of community service was still pending, the court having assigned thirty hours, to be completed within one year's time. James tried to lighten the mood. "Hey, Dad, maybe my work at the office can be my community service! You think they'd buy that?"

His father smiled. "Probably not much chance, though maybe we could get the contract for the signs in the state prisons. That might qualify as community service." Mr. Rush squinted and pushed his cheeks out, tilting his head to the side, and snorted a little, wondering whether his idea was as far-fetched as it sounded. He looked at James, his eyes dancing a little. "How you think the team's doing? That was a tough loss to Scituate." He opened the refrigerator and poured himself a glass of lemonade. "You want some?" he asked James.

"Sure. Thanks. Yeah, it was tough, but I think we've turned the corner. We all know what to do; I'm starting to relax, but I'm not there yet. I hope we can pick off two wins next week. That'd put us to five hundred, and after our start, that wouldn't be bad."

"Yeah, but there's no way LaMott should be playing Jason all those minutes. The kid's a disaster. Put the new kid at the point; time to make a change." James could hear that his father's opinions were derived from the stands, where all the fathers held court, whenever there was a bad play or a loss.

"I don't know. Jason's been there for a long time. He's got the experience. We don't see all the little things he does, because he makes a few mistakes and people just jump on that. I know he gets the ball where it needs to go most of the time."

Mr. Rush flared. "Most of the time isn't enough for a point guard. Hell, you could do a better job at the point, and you've never played there." It seemed Mr. Rush's anger was misdirected, maybe some residual anger from James's suspension.

"Well, the Coach will do what's best for the team, I know that," James assured his father, and he knew that was true. For all Jason's faults, he wouldn't be playing as much as he was if Coach had a

The Arc of Intersection

better option. James felt sorry for his dad, who still bristled at the embarrassment of his son's having to sit out for the first four games. "Anyway, I think we can get it going. It's going to take a lot of hard work, I know that, but I really think we'll be OK."

James's father shrugged. "Well, I guess you've got a feel for it. I just want to be able to enjoy a game the way I did at Sharon. That was fun."

"Yeah, it's nice to win going away, but I don't think that's in the cards. We're going to have to grind it out, and right now, we're not winning the close ones." James tossed the ball in the air a few times, then tossed it to his father across the table. He caught it, and, grinning, tossed it above the light that hung over the kitchen table, the arc almost accurate, but not quite, as it hit the glass globe, knocking it off the suspended pole. They watched it drop heavily, glancing off the table before dropping again to the floor, smashing.

Immediately, Mrs. Rush came from the bedroom, to see what had caused the noise. "What the – " she started, seeing the glass splayed across the kitchen floor.

Mr. Rush held his arm out. "My mistake. We were tossing the ball a little, and I underthrew it. My fault. I'll get it cleaned up."

Mrs. Rush shook her head, amazed. "But we'll have no kitchen light for a few days now. It's New Year's Eve." She couldn't picture entering the New Year with a lightless kitchen.

"We'll make do. I'll pick up a replacement on Monday. Sorry, hon. I was careless." He walked to his wife, his arms out, to end the discussion. James opened the closet door to find the broom and dustpan.

In the darkened kitchen James punched in Adrienne's number. He would receive his cell phone back the next day, the first day of 2009. He sat on the floor, underneath the wall phone, stretched out with his head against the mopboard. As the phone rang, he flipped the guilty tennis ball up and down, with his eyes closed, naturally, gauging the height of the flight of the ball from the force he exerted with this throwing hand. He tried to keep the arc within one dimension, so that the ball would land in his hand, and not out of reach of his fingertips. If he missed the ball with his hand, he tried to catch it on his thighs, trapping it between his legs. It was quite a challenge.

"Hello?" Adrienne's mother answered.

"Hello, is Adrienne there?" James asked. He lost the ball off the side of his thigh; he had to open his eyes to track its roll to the other wall. He crawled after it, then returned to his supine position.

"Yes, just a minute." He could hear her lay the phone down onto a table.

In just a few seconds Adrienne said, "Hello?" She didn't know who it was.

"Hi," James said, hoping she would recognize his voice. When she hesitated, he added, "It's James."

"Hey, how you doing? I saw you lost a heartbreaker. 'D'you have a chance to win?"

"Well, yeah, I guess, but the last shot we had was a half-court heave. But we played really great. I think we could get good soon, even though time is passing us by." He tossed the ball blindly up in the air, trying to anticipate its downward flight, grasping at just the right instant. "How's your team doin?"

"We had just one game, and we won it. We're three and two."

"We're two and four." James didn't want the conversation to be stuck on basketball, but he didn't know where to go. He held the ball for a second as he pictured Adrienne, leaning back on her couch, her long legs up in the air against the wall, her heels pushing against the white wall. Her head lay off the cushion of the couch, her ponytail hanging down almost to the floor. Her white T-shirt fell away from her sweatpants, showing the tautness of her mature, athletic body. "You heading out tonight?" he asked finally.

"Yeah, I'm going out to eat with five of my friends. We're going to the Grill in Wayland. We have reservations." She sounded proud of her plan. "I think we're sitting down at 9:00. We made the reservations about a month ago. I'm psyched."

James said, "Sounds like a great time. Who's going?"

"Oh, you know, Lucy, Michelle Saples, Diane Webster, Stacy Hart, and her little sister Minny. Do you know Stacy?"

James didn't. Nor did he know her little sister Minny. "I don't think so. You getting dressed up, a big deal?" He pictured her in a navy blue dress, knee length, fitted to her athletic body, curvy and clinging.

"Yeah, I'm wearing a dress. And we're all wearing heels." She was gleeful.

"You all wanta stop over at my house and I'll take a picture of you, like the Prom or something?" He did not know where that idea had come from, but it just sprang out. "I mean, no obligation or anything, but you could stop over here for a cocktail." He hoped she heard the irony of his mentioning a cocktail.

"Well, I don't think we're the cocktail types, but I think Lucy might be psyched to show off the look. Yeah, I'll check with Luce to see. We'd be over about 8:00. Might be a plan."

217

James felt his spontaneous suggestion had been ratified. He was sure his parents would not object if five girls stopped at the house for a visit. He didn't know whether the girls would expect alcohol or not. He spoke more quietly, the ball hopping up and down on his hand. "Seriously, would you be looking for booze, or not?"

Adrienne assured him, "No, not at all. We're not boozers, even on New Year's Eve. That's why we're going out: most everyone else is going to parties in town or in to First Night in Boston, after picking up vodka at the packy. I'm not going that way." She squared her shoulders on the couch, pulling her head back onto the cushion, focusing her stare at a spot on the ceiling (James figured). Her long feet pointed to the ceiling.

"Well, I admire you for your resolve," James told her. "You're making an intelligent decision." He marveled at the irony of offering his blessing to her plan.

"Thanks, I think so, too, though I don't know it's much of a decision. It's just what we want to do. There's not really much of a choice."

"Hey, let me ask you, if I could go out, could I come out with you guys?"

Adrienne didn't even hesitate. "Of course. It'd be a blast, having you. We could all preen in front of you and flirt with you and compete for your attention. You wanta come with us? I'm sure we could change the reservation."

James considered the idea. He knew he was marooned to the house for the night, but maybe, just to accompany five very responsible girls? He'd ask.

"If you're serious, I'll call you back. I have to check with my mom and dad. You see if you can change the reservation. I'll call you in a few."

James hung up and went into the living room, where his mother was sitting alone, writing something in a spiral notebook. "What're you doing, Mom?" he asked.

She sighed. "Oh, just writing some hopes for the New Year. I always write some predictions." She looked tired, as usual.

"Do any of the predictions involve me?" he asked quietly.

"Maybe," she replied, looking down.

He just blurted it out. "Hey, Mom, I know I'm supposed to stay in tonight, but can I go out to eat with five girls who asked me to join them at the Grill in Wayland at 9:00?" He let the question hang in the air like the tennis ball, hanging over his hand.

His mother looked at him, surprise opening her eyes wider. "You know the agreement. Nothing until the New Year. You have just one day to go. Why do you have to give in to temptation now, when you're so close to your goal?"

"I know. I could stay in easily. It's not like I'm going out with my buddies to hang out. This is something completely new. It'd be like being adults. I'd get dressed up with a tie."

"James, don't you understand, we're trying to instill patience and discipline in you. You obviously have been lacking both virtues. And here you go, unable to meet the challenge of a time limit. Don't you see how weak that makes you look?"

He understood his mother's argument, very well. However, his need to see Adrienne somewhere other than at the close of math class drove him to challenge his mother. "I've got the discipline, Mom. And now it's time to move on. If I wait another day, it's not gonna change who I am or, more importantly, who I've become. I know inside myself that I've changed. I know it may not be apparent to you, but I know. And anyway, this time limit is your imposition, not mine. I don't feel any responsibility toward it." James knew he was becoming too belligerent. "But I'd like to talk about this possibility like two adults."

His mother looked at him. "Let me talk it over with your father. He's pretty firm about this. We discussed that New Year's Eve was out of bounds for certain for you. I don't think he'll change his mind."

"You want me to go ask?" James said.

"No, I think I'd better approach him." She was making herself sound like James's ally, and James knew that wasn't the case. She left the living room to visit Mr. Rush in the workshop in the basement. A minute later, an exasperated Mr. Rush marched up the stairs.

"What's going on?" he challenged James. His peremptory tone brought out the fight in James.

"I want to go out with a few girls who are getting dressed up and going out to dinner at a nice restaurant at 9:00 tonight. I know it's New Year's Eve, but it's a completely responsible thing to do. No one's drinking. We'll be home before midnight." James didn't know if this would prove to be true, but he had to make the case.

James's father exhaled. "No, no, NO. This is exactly what I'm talking about. The reason you're in trouble is that you do not have any self-discipline. We agreed – you, your mother, and I agreed – that until New Year's Day, you were in the house. Why would I let you go out on New Year's Eve, when there is the most drinking going on of any day in the whole calendar? Are you crazy?"

219

Without thinking, James moved toward his father. "No, I think you are. You think keeping me locked up in this house will straighten me out, and that's where you're wrong. I've done all the right things for two weeks now. And I'm going out tonight, with five girls none of whom drink, and I'm going to have a nice dinner. Believe me, it beats sitting here in this house, watching you and Mom pretend to be having fun."

Mr. Rush met James's challenge. "Well, you can kiss your car goodbye if you go out. I'd like to think that having a long-term goal is important to you, but I can see that you are just like everyone else your age: you need instant gratification, everything right now. You're pathetic." He turned away from James in disgust.

James felt his shame. "Dad, I get it. You think I'm weak. That's exactly why I need to go out, to prove to myself and to you that I'm not weak, that I can behave responsibly. Staying in this house is not going to help me mature in any way, other than to let my resentment grow." James started to turn away from his father, turning toward his room.

His mother looked at both of them, knowing that the argument was unresolved. She didn't have the courage to re-initiate the conversation, but she looked at her husband imploringly. He responded with an explosion.

"If you go out, that's the result: no car." He motioned with his right hand as if he were wiping out an agreement, or wiping the dust off a dirty table.

"That's fine with me. I don't need a car to show that I'm growing up. And," he took a deep breath before his last declaration, "you can't buy me off with that offer of a car. I can't be bought." He had never stood up to his dad with such vitriol, but his ego had strengthened as it had been squashed the past three weeks.

His father walked to the mantle, where the envelope with James's check sat. He opened the envelope and pulled the check for $1500.00 out. He ripped it into two pieces, then four, then eight. He crumpled them and carried them to a wastebasket that sat next to the easy chair. He didn't say a word.

James responded, "You told me that if I made good decisions, I'd get that check. You did not tell me that I had to obey every one of your stupid edicts. I am making a good decision to go out with these people for a simple dinner. So I am not breaking any covenant. In fact, you are breaking the covenant by withdrawing the offer even though I have done nothing to discredit you or this family." James strode out of the room, certain in his rectitude. But, then, aren't all the self-righteous certain of their rectitude?

When James and the elegant ladies entered the Grill, the hallway leading into the dining room was filled with customers waiting for their tables. In the vestibule, James took off his BC hat, blowing on his hands to warm them from the short walk across the parking lot. Lucy, who had driven her family's Highlander, to provide room for the six of them, pocketed the keys in her skinny purse, which she snapped closed and then grasped demurely as she approached the dais where two young ladies made an attempt at maintaining order in the holiday crowd.

"I'll check on the reservation," Lucy said, the leader of her crew. James and the others found a wall to lean against, awaiting word on their table. Twenty minutes early, they knew they had a wait ahead. James looked down at his tie.

"Is this knot all right?" he asked the general bevy.

Stacy came to him, her hands grasping the knot tenderly. "I think I can make it respectable," she said. After she had reclaimed James's knot, she sauntered indolently toward the ladies' room. "See you guys in a minute," she threw over her bare shoulder.

"Let's people-speculate," Michelle said brightly, an activity with great potential, James thought. He loved to speculate about people. He had spent the last five years of his life invading people's lives with his imagination.

Diane pointed to a pair of couples in their early thirties that sat adjacent to each other on a bench. The women talked animatedly across the man seated between. The brown-haired woman nodded with interest as the woman with lighter hair spoke. James could make out bits of her conversation. " . . . at the dealership . . . neither of us could follow him . . . I finally . . ."

Michelle mused, "The guys work in the financial business. Look at the power ties." Indeed, one wore a bold reflective blue tie and the other a wool yellow tie that bulged at the neck.

Diane added, "Two kids for the woman in red and black, three for her friend."

Everyone seemed to have an opinion – except Adrienne, though she looked curiously at the couple under scrutiny and at many of the other people huddled in the vestibule. In another minute, Lucy returned to her friends. "We've got a thirty minute wait. Are we people-speculating?" She knew the routine well, apparently. "Have you seen any angry people yet? They're the most fun." She pulled

Stacy's sister Minnie over to her and pointed to a couple engaged in a heated exchange. "They're thinking that they shouldn't wait to be seated at this restaurant, but the girl knows that they won't have any better luck anywhere else, unless they go to a place that's dead, and then they won't have any fun. It's a conundrum, really." She spoke knowingly, well versed in other-analysis.

After an amusing and lively span of speculation, their table was ready. The girls made sure that James and Adrienne were seated next to each other. As Adrienne sat down, James couldn't help but stare at her silver dress, so shiny, expensive-looking. She looked extravagant. It was as if they were being seated at a Hollywood engagement.

"You all look really beautiful," he observed, looking especially at Adrienne, but being sure to include all the girls in his survey.

"Well, we had to get dressed up for our date with you," replied Lucy, taking the lead in their appreciation of his comment. "It's not often that we get to spend time with a jock star. We usually hang with more studious types, but we welcome the breath of fresh air, even though we have to dumb it down a little." She smiled directly at James, her eyes flaring. In fact, all the girls took turns taking stabs at flirting with him – all except, of course, Adrienne, who maintained a calm sense of tranquility, as she always did, refraining from partaking of the heightened energy that New Year's Eve produced. And, of course, Minnie, just stared openly at James, unable to conceal her patent gawking at him. James turned to his left, looking over his shoulder, stealing glances at Adrienne, wondering whether she were doing the same with him, never meeting her eyes. She just seemed to soak in all the frivolity, loving the company of her friends, of whom he was a peripheral and, probably, transient member.

Some time between the main course and dessert, Adrienne took a short bathroom break. Lucy took the opportunity to address James directly. "Well, are you going to make a move on her or what? She's pretty excited that you're here, and you seem to be ignoring her."

James was surprised. "Well, she sure knows how to hold her cards close to her chest – no pun intended. I would think she doesn't know I'm here for all the attention she's giving me."

Stacy said, "No, you're just misreading her. She's flattered that you would like to join us; she's always thought you were somewhat mysterious, and she wants to know more, I think. Don't be a stranger to her. She'll think you're not having fun."

It was good advice, and when Adrienne returned, James did pay more attention to her, asking about her team and her involvement with the team, commenting on his hopes for his team, and taking the opportunity to look at her face, which held all the illuminated promise of the New Year.

"I love New Year's Eve," she said softly, her eyes pouring into his gently. "There's so much at stake." Her voice thrilled with that promise that he felt.

"What do you mean, at stake?" James tried to draw her out. Her friends sat quietly, waiting for Adrienne to explain herself. They were hoping she could postulate the reason for their own excitement.

"Well, I think the New Year represents the opportunity to re-make yourself. You know how it takes a few days to acclimate yourself to writing the new year-date on your papers in school? Well, that's because the old year is so embedded in you that you have to re-calibrate, before you can start thinking in terms of the new year.

"And, potentially, it's the same with yourself. Each one of us is also changing, just like one year changing into another year. We are changing from one person into another person – and it's not just every year, but it's every day, every minute. Look at cars: they get retooled every year, just slightly, but if you look at two models of the same car ten years apart, they might look entirely different. Same with us. And we don't have to wait for designers and manufacturers to change us. We change every minute. I'm not the same person I was when I walked into this restaurant. I'm older. Some of my cells have sloughed off, and I've generated new ones to replace them. Even the cells that make up our body are constantly dying and being replaced by newly formed cells." Adrienne's face glowed with her news. "It sounds pretty profound, I know, but it's what I feel all the time – especially as we make the turn into a new year."

When Adrienne stopped talking, the table sat quietly, knowing that their rejoinders would be puny next to her pronouncement. Finally, James spoke. "I think I've felt what you're talking about a couple times. If we see things that way, we can feel more comfortable going in new directions, because every minute is the origin of the next minute." He didn't know where these profundities came from, but they made temporary sense to him.

Adrienne nodded. "Yeah, I think you've got it." Lucy nodded too.

Stacy's sister Minnie, all twelve years of her, said, "Meanwhile, are you going to finish that ice cream pie?" to her sister. Stacy shoved her plate across the table cloth, so Minnie could finish up her dessert. The evening shone brightly.

As Lucy dropped James off at his house, at about 11:15, James, emboldened by the promise Adrienne had noted in the air, asked Adrienne if she wanted to come in. No one was home. Rachel was spending her New Year's Eve with an overnight at her friend Ari's house. James's mom and dad were at a house party at the Kendalls', and they would be coming home about 1:00, if past precedent were any indication.

"How can I get home?" Adrienne asked.

James thought. "Maybe I can call Pete or Dan. They could give you a ride."

Adrienne thought. "I don't think so. No telling what they've been doing, and I don't want to wreck their New Year's Eve." They sat awkwardly in the back seat of Lucy's warm SUV.

"I'll come pick you up after midnight," Lucy offered. "I'll take everyone home, hang at Michelle's until midnight, watch the ball drop, and come back. No sweat."

Adrienne's face maintained its preternatural calm. "That sounds great," and she pushed James out the door. "See you about 12:15."

James walked stiffly across the icy front yard. Here was a seminal moment for him: an hour with Adrienne Petrulsky, on New Year's Eve.

Inside, when he had taken her coat, he asked, "Do you want something to drink? I've got whatever you want," leaving the door open for her.

"How about soda?" she replied simply.

They settled on the couch in the family room, glasses of Sprite on the table next to them. James had trouble breathing; he certainly couldn't talk easily. She looked at him, the sound of the New Year's celebration on TV in the background. She smiled, the light and shadows of the TV screen sliding across her face. He moved toward her and pressed his lips against hers. She responded, moving her left hand onto and behind his shoulder, drawing him to her. They stayed engaged in this kiss for at least one commercial, eyes closed, hands pulling, legs rearranging themselves to provide a better angle for their bodies to fit together. James opened his mouth, and Adrienne did the same, allowing for timid exploration with their tongues. James's heart pulled upwards toward the kiss. He felt the softness of her skin as he rubbed her cheek, her neck, her shoulder. Her shiny dress slid easily off that shoulder, leaving a dainty bra strap.

Nothing that James did met with any resistance on Adrienne's part. She was as comfortable with these expressions as he was

224

confused. He wanted to protect her from his own desires, because she didn't seem to be at all defensive, as the few girls he had spent time with in his admittedly inexperienced past had been. Her acceptance of him amazed him. When he moved his hand down to the softness of her breast, her kiss quickened, as she pulled him toward her with her mouth. It wasn't long before he reached down to pull her dress upwards, giving him more access to her body.

Adrienne gently placed her hands on his, drawing his palms back to her shoulders, leaving her dress a symbolic gate through which they wouldn't pass. James could read her purpose, and he immediately changed the path of his probing, wanting to satisfy whatever she wanted, unwilling to disturb the connection that was pulling them toward each other. "Let's keep it simple," Adrienne whispered with as much promise as James had ever heard, and James nodded.

"I'm sorry. I didn't know what you wanted," he replied, still pulling her toward him, still kissing her cheek, still moving against her with his body.

"It all gets so complicated," she said, rubbing her teeth across his chin. "If we want to have any chance at being together, we have to keep it so simple." Her voice arced with its urgency, like an electrical transformation. He understood.

When they separated, and James reached for a sip of soda, first offering Adrienne a sip of hers, he was surprised to see that they had passed into the New Year. Turning on the table lamp, he saw the clock on the wall read 12:25. Adrienne, seeing the time, pushed herself up from the couch, pulling her dress down, adjusting it around her shoulders. The wrinkles resisted her ministrations.

"I think I might have a ride outside." She moved to the window. "Yep, little Lucy is sitting out in the cold, by herself." She rushed to the kitchen to pull on her coat.

James walked Adrienne out to Lucy's car. Lucy rolled down the passenger window. "Sorry to break up the party, but it's time to get home."

Adrienne pulled the door open. "Thanks, Luce. I love you."

James closed the door quietly behind Adrienne, then, sticking his head in the window, kissed Adrienne on the mouth that she offered him. "Thanks, Lucy. I owe you one, too."

Lucy giggled. "Aah, what are friends for? We do what we have to do to make this world a better place." She shifted into drive.

James watched the car ease onto the road smoothly. He turned to enter his empty house, noting the intensity of the stars as they shed light across his icy, snow-scattered front yard. He pushed open the door and entered his house, chilled by the cold air of New Year's Eve, but thrilled with the fact that, as one year had passed into another, he had changed.

Bridge just south of town
They've been working on it for years now
Just about finish up 'fore it occurs to anyone
They built that damn thing just about a foot off the ground
Way way higher than the road around
So if you happen down that highway, 'specially at night
Hit the bridge at fifty-five
Feel like you might just take flight
And every time the crossing comes as a surprise
See me flying

I've found quiet in this room
Down by where the trains run
I've learned to hear the rumble, long before it comes
And the things I'm working on
Are invisible to everyone
Something 'bout an empty hip or the angle of the sun
Every time the crossing comes as a surprise
See me flying

Maybe these stitches in my throat
Have just about dissolved
Like the sad moan of the drunkard
walking home from the bar
I hear the thin song of the fire house
when they sound the alarm
I hear the church bells on Sunday... ringing out

Used to be a town of dirt and horses
Now it's all liquor and cars
There's still a whole lot of nothing
up between those stars
Take the dog out for a walk
On the Episcopal church lawn
My God we're still tryin' to find a way
To get ourselves beyond
And every time the crossing comes as a surprise
See me flying

The Crossing by Meg Hutchinson

The Arc of Intersection

Ben

On the first teaching day of the new year, Ben entered his third period freshman class, ready to distribute copies of the short story anthology that they would spend the next two months absorbing. He called their attention to one of his favorite stories, "Where Are You Going, Where Have You Been?," a Joyce Carol Oates story about the seductive attraction of danger.

Ben started the discussion. "Have any of you done something you know you shouldn't do?"

No one responded. The class lay inert, still recovering from the shock of school, so soon after a yawning vacation. Ben moved to the stack of lined paper that sat in back of the room. "Let's take five minutes to recall, in writing, the most dangerous thing you have ever done – not something that is socially accepted, like bungie-jumping, but something that our society tells us not to do. Think of Romeo, in *Romeo and Juliet*, attending the ball at the Capulets', after being told that there was to be no contact between the families. Think of Gene and Finny jumping off the tree in *A Separate Peace*."

Ben gave the class three or four minutes to fill their pages. "Let's fill the front of the paper. Go on to the back if you're in the middle of an idea. Don't edit yourselves. Don't be afraid of saying something that suggests you could get in trouble. We'll read these anonymously." Ben thought for a few seconds. "But don't write anything that I'd have to go to the police with – like attempted murder or anything." He gave a little snort at his attempted humor.

After another three minutes, Ben collected the pages, some of them partly filled in, many of them nearly blank. "Let me take a minute to look through these, to see what ideas we can discuss." He spent the next few minutes picking out the best of the submissions, as the class began to chat quietly, acclimating themselves once again to the straitjacket known as a classroom. He made an easy decision.

"Here's the best that I received," he offered, and began to read a story of three boys breaking into a convenience store by jimmying a back window, then racing away when their actions triggered an alarm from within the building. As he read, the class members looked curiously at each other, trying to ascertain the writer and perpetrator.

When Ben had finished, one of the boys near the bulletin board, Peter Milton, shouted, "No way. That's made-up. Someone's just trying to sound tough." Many class members agreed.

The Arc of Intersection

Quieting the insurrection, Ben asserted, "Now, Peter, you make a very valid point, but it doesn't really matter whether this event really occurred or not. You see, the stories we tell each other are always some combination of what has happened and the way our imagination works to process that action. Fiction is always a fabrication of reality, a fabrication that we hope reflects the truth. So let's not spend our energy determining whether our author is telling us something that actually happened. The point is, he or she wants us to think that this happened."

The class was quieted with Ben's explanation.

"Now, let's try to figure out why three boys would try to break into a convenience store. I'm going to hand the paper back, and I'd like you to write on the back three reasons, if you can think of three, that might prompt people to break into a store. Please be as specific as you can."

After more writing, Ben asked, "Any ideas?"

The most dutiful student in the room, Marty Chaplin, replied, "The obvious answer is that the kids are poor, and they want to get something they can't afford. But I have another reason: they want to prove to each other that they are willing to do anything, no matter the consequences." Marty stopped talking, pleased that he had gotten the attention of the class.

"Great idea. Any others?"

"I think it's just wanting people to think you're a little crazy, that no one can tell you what to do," said a thoughtful girl, Mary. "You know, wanting to prove that no one can tell you what to do," she repeated.

Ben said, "Yeah, that's a good extension of what Marty said. Any completely different ideas?" Ben looked directly at his students, first one, then another, trying to coerce an answer from each – with no luck. "Well, let me collect the papers, and maybe I'll find another unique idea in here somewhere."

Perusing the slight lists on the back of the sheets, Ben paused on one that he thought would lead to interesting discussion. "They broke in because they have everything, but they don't want to admit that they're privileged, so they wanted to take a walk on the wild side." Ben read the response to the class, interested himself in the identity of the author. "What do you think? Do we do things sometimes just to prove that we don't have the conveniences that we do have? Ironically?" The class murmured, following his idea slightly. "Let's look at that phrase, Take a Walk on the Wild Side. Has anyone heard that expression before?"

One girl who had heard the Lou Reed song mentioned that she had heard the song and remembered the title. Ben saw Paul look at her, making Ben think that Paul might have been the author. "Why would people walk on the wild side? What are they looking for?"

"Excitement," more than one student yelled.

"Sex," one bold boy called, trying to be bad.

Ben halted the discussion. "Did you hear Mark's word? Sex? Now I'm not going to start talking about sex, but do you see how we are drawn or driven to step across some imaginary line? Maybe a few of you were thinking of sex or drugs or drinking or smoking, but only one person dared to shout it out. Mark was doing exactly what those boys were doing in breaking into that store: he was declaring that he thinks the rules are pedestrian, that they're made by people who are old and outdated and out of touch. And, by and large, that's true. Our legislators are pretty old, pretty establishment. And it's young people, people like you that keep our society vibrant with your instinct to rebel against the rules we impose. That's a normal attribute of any culture. Mark, thanks for shouting out that word."

Ben turned the focus of the discussion to Oates's opening paragraphs, noting the way Connie showed herself to be one way in front of her parents and another way when she left the house. After collectively looking at the incident at the drive-in restaurant that serves as the initiating moment for the main character to see the face of danger, Ben asked the class to finish the story on their own, and they read silently to finish the period. Ben felt satisfied that he had led them into the story and, more importantly, the idea of the lure of danger.

The rest of the day unspooled for Ben in a familiar fashion. Lunch was a good chance to catch up with his friends, most of whom he hadn't seen for a week and a half. In his junior classes he handed out a collection of poems he had assembled, their final focus before mid-year exams. He tried to summon the same energy that he had found when he introduced the Oates story, but he missed the mark with his juniors. In any event, he had gotten his classes off to a purposeful, if not meaningful, start to the new year; after school he sat down with Bryan to try to find a direction for his team.

Bryan began, "The game with Scituate was a beauty: you were one point away from a great win. I'm not saying that having Andreas would have made the difference, but if you're looking for one point, having your back-up big man makes a difference."

"That's a good point, but I don't want to look back. I want to look forward, at Norwood and Dedham. What is our focus in these next two games?"

Bryan did not hesitate. "Getting James back into the flow. Let's face it: he's your second best player, after Andrew. He's starting to get back in the mix, but you have to give him extended minutes. It'll mean cutting back on Dan and Alex and Archie's time, but that's the facts." Bryan started to outline an offensive play on the half-court chart that lay on the desk between them, showing how James could capitalize on coming off the down screen, but neither of the others could.

Considering Bryan's postulate, Ben offered a qualifier. "I just think I'm hesitant to put a lot of trust in James, after he screwed up once. I'm not sure he won't leave us hanging again, and if he does, he's gone for the year. At least I know I can count on Dan and Archie."

Bryan countered, "You're right: Dan and Archie are dependable. But dependable won't give you your best team. You have to play the best team available. Right now James is part of your best team." Bryan drew up an out-of-bounds play that got the ball to James (if Andrew was double-teamed), again showing a situation that called for James.

"I know you're right. And I don't want to be punitive – he's served his suspension, and he's run extra sprints, and he hasn't said a word that suggests that he feels unfairly treated. I think he does understand how he let his teammates down. But I just don't know if he will stay straight."

"You have to give him the chance to succeed," Bryan finished, as they picked up their scraps of paper and headed to the gym for practice.

After stretching and warm-ups, Ben announced his new starting lineup, inserting James into one of the wing spots, dropping Dan onto the reserve squad. "Dan, you've been a great starter for us," he assured. "I just think it's time for James to get back in the starting lineup. I expect you to be just as productive off the bench as you've been in the starting lineup. Your minutes may stay the same, who knows?" Ben turned from Dan to the team as a whole. "I hope we can all stay focused on the overall goal of giving ourselves the best chance to win. Great job versus a very strong team in Scituate and a great individual player in Bello. Dan and Archie, you did a great job defending him. With that kind of effort and focus, we'll have a great week against Norwood and Dedham.

"Let's get into 11-man drill. Plus one for a basket; no more than two passes in the front-court; minus one for a turnover. Let's go. Push the ball with your weak hand," Ben announced, ending the discussion, getting the boys back to what they loved: playing with the ball.

For the first practice after New Year's Eve and Day, the team moved somewhat briskly. This was always a difficult practice. Ben knew that more than a few of these players had violated the drug, tobacco, and alcohol policy that prevailed in the state – he didn't know for a fact, but he knew from knowing the nature of the adolescents he supervised. They had all signed letters provided by the athletic office that said they would refrain from all such activity, but they also were adolescents, with the propensities that came with that age. He assumed that those who had chosen to drink or smoke had done so in a circumspect manner. Believing this, Ben felt complicit himself, because he did not in any way probe or investigate their behavior away from the school. He just hoped that they were smart about their habits.

When Pete and Jason began to lag behind their teams in pushing the ball up the court, Ben reminded them, "Let's go, guys. There was no activity that occurred this past weekend that would compromise our conditioning. We're in just as good shape as we were last week, right? If we look fatigued, we're going to have to spend more time on our conditioning. Let's go."

Both players picked up the pace, knowing that he would impose mid-practice sprints if they didn't.

James looked sharp. He bounced into his catch, squaring his shoulders with good footwork, maintaining balance as he pushed his shot out. He shot well; he hadn't looked this good from the 3-point line all year.

Ben introduced a variation on the zone offense, anticipating a flat 1-3-1 zone from Norwood, no traps, but sagging toward the baseline, allowing for undefended wing shots. If James and Andrew could hit from opposite wings, Casteline would have an easy time scoring.

Practice ended with team foul shots, trying to hit 9 out of 13 foul shots to prevent the 10 in a minute sprint. After hitting 6 of 10, three players, Jason, Geoff, and James had to hit their shots. Jason missed his. "All right, let's get on the line. Next time, Jason." Jason slowly crept to the baseline, angry at himself for forcing the sprint. "Remember, it's not just the guy who misses. Others missed along the way. Don't put any resentment on one guy. We're all working together. Let's fly through this sprint to show we've gotten the vacation legs out of our system. Bridget, set . . . go!" The clock started its countdown from 1:00.

232

In the last two sprints, there were four players coming up short: Jason, Pete, Andreas, and Mark. "Let's pick it up, men. Five . .. four . .. three . ." When the buzzer rang, all four were short of the line, disappointing both themselves and Ben.

"All right, thirty seconds rest, then back on the line for a 6 in 36. We've got this, come on."

Everyone made the mark but Jason. "All right, everyone together here for a TIGHT." When the team had gathered around him, Ben said, "New year, guys. Let's start fresh and strong. You have the information on Norwood. They'll give away the outside shot. We have to be ready to take that shot, and go by, if they are closing out out of control. We're not in the best of shape right now, but I understand. We'll get there. The main thing is to make your teammates better with your work rate. We'll show them tomorrow. 1 . . . 2. . . .3 . . . "

"Tight."

"Jason, just hang in here for a minute. 4 in 24 when you're ready." Ben knew that Jason would bridle at the extra sprint, but he could not let one player slip under the radar. Ben also considered what Jason would say at home to his dad, but he knew that consistency across the team was essential.

"Set . ..go!" Ben called. Jason glided smoothly up and down the court twice, finishing in 23 seconds.

As Jason hunched over, his hands on his knees, Ben approached him. "Jason, I hope you're not doing anything to jeopardize your strength and conditioning for this team. We're counting on you to direct this team, and if you're not on the court or not in the best shape, you can't dominate your opponent the way you need to." He looked at Jason, who did not look up. They were nearly alone in the gym, though the girls' team was starting to enter from the door to their locker room.

"I know. I'm working at it. It's hard coming back after the vacation week. I'll get back in shape." He still did not look up.

Ben probed a little. "Everything all right?"

Jason did not respond. Then he said, "Yeah, everything's fine."

Ben knew it wasn't. "If there's anything you need to talk about, let me know. You can talk to me, or Geoff, or Coach Taft. I don't want anything to hang over your head, because if you're having some kind of trouble, you can't have fun on the court. I'm not just worried about winning. I want you to get the most out of this year and this team. If you're bothered by something, you can't get the most out of yourself. This is your senior year. Last chance. Make the most of it."

Jason looked at the net hanging near him. "That's what I'm trying to do. But my dad keeps expecting more. He's upset that we're not winning." He switched his weight uncomfortably from one tired leg to the other.

Ben put his hand around Jason's shoulder, trying to reassure him, trying to bring him into the Coach's circle. He spoke quietly. "You can't play for someone else. You have to play for your own enjoyment and for the joy of being with other guys who love to play. It never works if you're trying to please someone else. Believe me, I've seen it over and over." He crouched just slightly, to try to look at Jason's eyes.

Jason nodded.

"Is that all that's bothering you?"

Jason nodded again.

"Well, again, if there's anything more, please speak up. You are our engine. Without you, we don't run. But, more importantly, you need to have fun. Whatever gets in the way of that fun has to be dealt with."

Jason turned toward the locker room. "Thanks, Coach."

As Jason entered the locker room, Ben determined that he needed a check-up talk with his captain, Geoff.

In the locker room Ben and Bryan spoke for a minute, Ben noting his concerns about the team's commitment level. Bryan agreed. "Yeah, I think you've got some people to keep an eye on. I'm not sold on a few of the guys." Neither coach wanted to name any particular players, but Ben had to mention Jason. "He was really slow today. No bounce. Ran out of gas pretty quickly. Had to run extra sprints at the end because he couldn't do the 10 in a minute. It's not like him."

"You talk to him?"

"Yeah, he said his father is leaning on him, but that's all he said. If you get a chance tomorrow, check him out, OK?"

"Sounds good. I'll bump into him."

Ben changed the subject. "You going to Willow's?"

Bryan was surprised that Ben brought the subject up. "Yeah. You coming?"

Ben nodded. "I think I'll have a quick beer on the way home," he said as they headed out the door to their cars.

At Willow's Ben just asked for a ginger ale, not really wanting a beer, but finding the warm bar pleasant. Lisa grinned at him. "Too much to drink on New Year's Eve?" she joshed.

234

Ben said, "No, in fact, it was a pretty quiet night. We went over to our neighbors', munching snacks and playing some cards. They taught us a game we didn't know. Pretty uneventful."

Bryan chimed in. "What can you do? Suburban parties for middle-aged people are either too crazy or too boring. No in between. I'm assuming yours didn't get crazy."

"No, not exactly. The highlight was some out-of-wedlock kissing at the stroke of midnight. I have to admit I did observe one kiss that lingered longer than it should have, but I may be imagining that." He recalled that languorous embrace of Peter's and Sharon's, wondering if it represented anything more than a mutual loss of propriety.

As Ben and Bryan emptied the bowl of nuts on the bar table, Ben noticed a sign next to the doorway leading to the kitchen: "Bartender needed. Part-time. One or two nights a week." He thought about the idea: one night here at Willow's, wiping off the counter, pouring beer out of the tap, tilting the glass to reduce the head. He wondered whether the job required any training.

When Ben stood up to leave, he motioned to the sign, to gain Bryan's attention. "I'm going to check out the job opportunity."

Bryan looked at Ben with surprise. "Are you kidding? Do you have the time? That sounds crazy."

Ben nodded. "I know. But one night a week wouldn't hurt. I'm sure I'd get the dead night, and I'd take home about eleven dollars in tips, but it'd be a start. Maybe I'd like it and I could work more in the off-season. I like this place."

Lisa offered, "I'd give you big tips," and added a generous smile.

"I bet you would, but I couldn't take them. I want to earn them. I don't want sympathy tips."

He approached the bartender. "Who do I talk to about the job? Do you know if it requires any experience?"

"Hi, Pete Amoroso here. What I know about the job is this: they're looking for someone Monday nights, tonight. Our fill-in girl moved, and we're stuck. She used to take Monday nights and other nights when she could or when we needed her. The new girl or guy would start on Mondays, when it's kind of slow."

"Is there an application to fill out?"

Pete brought Ben into the kitchen. "Here, fill this out, and we'll get back to you later in the week. Do you have any experience?"

"No. I'd have a hard time mixing drinks at first. No bartending school, and I don't order anything very elaborate myself. I'd have to defer to you for anything complex."

235

Pete shrugged. "That's OK. We don't get much beyond Jack and Coke, and I think you look like you could handle that." Pete had an easy way of talking that made Willow world look and sound simple. He moved back through the doorway to the bar, moving down to the far end to refill four glasses.

Ben filled out the application, leaving it next to the cash register, waiting for Pete to return. "I left it right over there. My phone number is on the app. Give me a call."

"OK. It's not me that makes the call. I'm just the bartender. Larry Olson will call you later on. See you later," he said, lifting the dishwasher cover to grab the clean, hot glasses.

Waving goodbye to Bryan and Lisa, Ben walked to his car, to pick up Mary, who needed a ride home from her late afternoon shift at Dunkin Donuts. Her car was almost fixed, a transmission repair that had been estimated at $700.

Mary was sitting at the counter, waiting, sipping a hot chocolate. "Hi, honey, how was work?" Ben said, when she emerged from the glass-enclosed building.

"Not bad. There was some dead time around 3:30, but the last hour or two were good."

"You get much in tips?"

"No tips. Company policy. Some of the kids take some, but I don't."

Ben had forgotten their discussion of the matter of tips.

Ben eased the Corolla out onto Summer St. "I might take a job at a bar in Natick. Willow's."

Mary looked up at her dad. "Why?"

Ben stumbled a little. "Well, we're a little tight on money right now. Your car is going to cost a lot, and my car isn't anything great. I don't get my coaching check until the end of February. I don't know whether I'll keep pursuing it, but I filled out an application."

Pulling her bookbag off her shoulder, Mary said, "Do you even know anything about Willow's? How did you even find out about the job? Have you been looking for a job?" She screwed her face up in skepticism.

"Not really. I went over there with Bryan, and I saw a sign. It just rang a bell. It seems like a nice place. I might be able to make some decent money."

Mary shook her head. "Bars are for drunks, Dad. How could you work there and still teach? I don't get it." She looked straight ahead, embarrassed.

236

Ben didn't know how to appease her. "Well, it might not happen. But I'm checking it out. It'd probably be just one night a week."

"What about practice? Are you going to go right to a bar from practice? What if the players find out? What'll they say? A coach isn't supposed to work in a bar."

Ben silently agreed. "Well, we'll see. I haven't even talked about it with Mom yet, so we'll see."

At home, Scott was finishing up his macaroni and cheese, clearing his plate off the table onto the counter.

"Hi, hon. How was work today?" Ben asked.

Willa looked at him. "Not bad. Mary, did you have any supper?"

"No, not really. DD doesn't really have any dinner food. I'll have some mac and cheese. It looks good."

Ben agreed. "Yeah, it looks really good." He stood near Willa. "I stopped at Willow's with Bryan after practice. I had an hour to kill before I picked up Mary. I heard from Scottie Turner about Mary's car. He estimated about $700.00. He sounded like it would be a good idea, because the body is good and the mileage is still on the low side."

Willa nodded, unaffected. Since their lash-out, she had been superficially polite to Ben, offering nothing. He wanted to tell her about his job idea, but he felt she would object in the same way, with the same rational objections, as Mary had objected. Willa's objections would make sense to Ben. So he did not tell her.

Before Tuesday's game with Norwood, Ben spoke with Geoff in the locker room during the JV game. Geoff was, as usual, frank.

"Well, Coach, I think we're right where we were before the season. We've got some who follow the rules, and some who don't. Probably a fifty-fifty split."

"Does it matter about the names? Anyone I should talk to specifically?"

Geoff thought for a while. "I don't know. I think you know as well as I do. Actually, I think James has cleaned his act up. I don't hear about him at the parties any more. Dan either. It's just Pete. Andreas and Jason are hanging out a little. Even Andrew is hanging out a lot now, but I don't see it affecting him. Archie, well . . ." They both knew that Archie was not likely to indulge. Geoff looked comfortable offering the names, as if he were some sort of liaison with Coach LaMott. Captains have their roles.

237

"Thanks, Geoff. I was wondering about Jason. He had a slow day yesterday. I think he needs direction. Keep working on him, OK?"

Geoff stood up. "I'm trying. Jason is a tough one. He has a world of talent, but he plays too much for himself."

Ben disagreed. "Actually, I think he's trying to spread the ball around. He's just under the gun with his father. Whatever he does is never enough. We've got to get him to relax and get into the moment, just enjoy his senior year with you guys.

"Anyway, thanks for sharing your thoughts. Let's have a great game. You're doing all you can, and I appreciate it, Geoff. Keep it up." Ben banged Geoff on the back of the shoulder.

Geoff returned to the court to watch the JV game.

Seven minutes into the varsity game, Ben subbed Dan and Archie for James and Jason. Neither one had made a basket. Norwood led 12 – 7. Shaking Jason's hand as he came off, Ben said, "Tough start, but you'll get comfortable. Keep pushing the ball and looking for the wings ahead of you. Don't drop your hands on defense. We're looking for a couple deflections to get us going. Be ready."

To James, he said, "Well, your first start isn't going to set any scoring records, but at least it's behind you. Keep your eye on the game now. When you get back in, you're ready to explode." Turning his attention back to the court, he said to Bryan, "Check out James; make sure he's not hanging his head, OK?"

Bryan assented, moving down the chairs to speak with James.

With an eleven point lead early in the second period, Norwood began holding the ball with their strong ball-handling guards, drawing Dan, Archie, and Alex out to pressure, then exploding past them to get into the middle of the lane. On one penetration, their best guard, Wilson, took the ball at Andrew, who tried to draw a charge. Wilson, a football player in the fall, crashed into Andrew, sending him sprawling backward. The call was a charge, but Andrew did not get up. He lay on his right side, writhing. The referee motioned Ben out to the court.

Ben trotted to Andrew's spot in the lane, to kneel next to him. "You OK? You look like you're in pain." Andrew's teeth were gritted.

"I think I got a twist in my left knee. I felt it tear when he hit me." Andrew grunted loudly. "I hope it's nothing big." His eyes teared as he admitted his concern.

Ben reassured him. "Nothing that can't be fixed. You'll be all right. Don't worry about anything but getting yourself over to the bench now." The Norwood trainer helped Andrew to his feet, and he made his way to the trainer's room, dragging his left leg. Ben put James in for Andrew, creating a small lineup around Geoff in the post.

238

"Play the 4, but pull your man away from the hoop. Let's give ourselves a lane for driving the middle. You're gonna have to cover a big guy, but just deny him and spin to box out. Let's go. We've got it." Ben could not keep himself from talking in these positive terms, even while he tried to imagine facing Norwood and a succession of opponents without his leading scorer and rebounder, Andrew Monaghan.

In the second half the Panthers reduced the Norwood lead to 3 at least five times, but they could never hit the shot that would bring them closer. James did not come off the court once in the second half, finally becoming comfortable, playing a variety of positions, ending up with 18 points. Jason also played a strong second half, with five assists and two steals, a good floor game. But Norwood held on to win, 57 – 50, Casteline's fifth loss of the year. Andrew sat on the bench for the second half, his knee wrapped in ice. He would go to the hospital after the game for an x-ray. The knee was swollen considerably. He would not be playing for a while.

In the post-game huddle, Ben tried to salve the wound left by the two losses: the game and their best player. "Solid second half, guys. James and Geoff, good rebounding. Archie, Jason, Alex, Dan, great defense on the perimeter in the second half. You just dug too big a hole for yourselves. No way we can afford to spot Norwood a double-digit lead. They're too good. Everyone in this league is too good. We've got to come out with the intention of winning two halves, not just one.

He looked at Andrew, leaning over on a pair of crutches, keeping weight off the injured left leg. "Andrew, we're all thinking of you. Get yourself checked out, and call me at home when you know. We're all going to have to do more to fill this hole, for however long it lasts. It's part of the game. Andrew, get your hand in here at the bottom. Let's make contact with him; we've got to each add a little bit to our game to fill in for him. One . . . Two . . . Three."

"TIGHT," the team shouted, looking past their defeat at the prospect of overcoming Andrew's loss. The prospect overwhelmed them, but they did not know it yet.

The Arc of Intersection

Wake me up when it's over,
Wake me up when it's done,
When he's gone away and taken everything,
Wake me up.

Wake me up when the skies are clearing,
When the water is still,
'cause I will not watch the ships sail away so
Please say you will.

If it were any other day,
This wouldn't get the best of me.

But today I'm not so strong,
So lay me down with a sad song,
And when it stops then you know I've been
Gone too long.

But don't shake me awake,
Don't bend me or I will break,
Come find me somewhere between my dreams,
With the sun on my face.

I will still feel it later on,
But for now I'd rather be asleep.

Wake Me When It's Over by Norah Jones

James

When James got home, he called Andrew's cell, trying to find out about his injury. His mother answered Andrew's phone. "Hello?"

"Hello, is Andrew there? This is James Rush. I'm wondering how he's doing."

"Hi, James. This is Andrew's mother. We're at the hospital, waiting for the results of the x-ray. His knee swelled up a lot more. It looks pretty bad."

James wanted to reassure Andrew's mother, but there was little he could say. He fiddled with the cord that connected his alarm clock to the wall outlet. "Well, tell him that we're all pulling for him. Can you tell him to give me a call when he gets any more definite word?"

"Sure thing. Thanks for calling. He might not call if it gets too late, but you'll probably see him in school in the morning. Thanks again for calling. . . . Oh, here he comes. Maybe he's got some news." James could hear Mrs. Monaghan's mouth move away from the phone. "Honey, did they tell you anything more?"

James could hear them talking, but he could not hear any specifics. Then he could hear Mrs. Monaghan say, "Oh, James is on the phone. You can tell him what the doctor said."

"Hey," Andrew said.

"Hey, how's it going?" James offered. He felt for the corner of the bureau next to his bed. He could feel a very thin patina of dust on the wooden surface.

"Uh, not much going on here. The doctor said it looks like a partially torn ACL, might need surgery at some point. I asked him if I could play without surgery; he said probably not, but maybe. Probably have to rest it a month or so. We'll go day-to-day." Andrew sounded very tired, probably from trying to keep his disappointment in check.

"Can you rehab it without surgery? Make it stronger?" James asked, moving his right hand to the cotton rectangle that sat under the lamp in the middle of the bureau top.

"Don't know yet. I have an appointment with the doctor on Friday, MRI on Thursday. Then he'll know more. It kinda sucks."

"No kidding. You're playin great, and the rest of us are just tryin to keep up. Shit, I get back into the lineup, and you check out. What a bummer." He pulled slightly on the cloth, feeling the weight of the lamp.

Andrew agreed. James could see his head nodding, from his voice. "We'll just have to do the best with what we have. I guarantee I'll be back on the floor in less than a month, unless he says I need surgery right away. I can probably play with a wrap and get back. We'll see."

It was the right time for James to say, "Hey, Andrew, I'm really sorry I fucked up. Your injury was in the line of duty. I was just being a wise guy. I feel so bad for you, because you're doing everything you can do to make us good, and then you get knocked down. It's not really fair; I should have been injured, not you."

Andrew disagreed. "No way. We all find our way, at different rates and levels. You're making a great comeback now. Don't lose your focus. I'll join you, but I'm leaving the scoring in your hands until I do."

James was gratified to hear Andrew offer his blessing to him. He didn't know he had earned Andrew's confidence, and, in fact, he thought he had thrown it away when he was suspended. "Thanks, Andrew. I'll try to step it up. You've got big shoes to fill."

"Well, I gotta go. See you in school. Get ready for Dedham. We gotta win that one."

James felt the wooden base of the lamp. He traced the lamp up through its bronze middle, his wrist banging into the shade. "We've got it covered. We're going on a streak, starting Friday."

"Good to hear. See you at practice. Thanks for calling."

James had heard three slight electronic breaks in their conversation, indicating other inquiries of Andrew, and he knew that Andrew would answer all the other teammates and friends who were calling, in his patient and thoughtful manner.

As soon as he hung up with Andrew, James called Adrienne, needing to hear her voice. They had seen each other in school, though James had not found the courage to seek any intimacy with her in school. He remembered Lucy's exhortation at dinner on New Year's Eve, and he remembered far better the kiss that had launched him into the New Year. It was not easy to dissociate himself from his past behaviors with girls: generally ignoring them in public, letting them come to him if and when they chose to at more unrestrained social gatherings (parties). Even though Adrienne had spoken of the human ability to remake oneself every moment, James had difficulty putting her notion into practice. But he called her, for the first time since New Year's.

"Hello, Adrienne?" He called Adrienne's house phone because he still did not know her cell phone. It was the only person he might call on a house phone.

"No, this is her mother. May I ask who's calling?" Though her words were measured, they were distinctly pleasant, as if she were hoping for a particular answer to her question.

"Yes, Mrs. Petrulsky, could you tell her it's James Rush?" He included the last name this time, having a little fun with Adrienne's mother, who, he hoped, would find humor in his self-mockery.

"Oh, James *Rush*. Yes, I think she would be glad to talk with you. Just a minute, James."

When Adrienne came on the phone, with a rush in her voice, James found he could not keep up with her, she had so much to say. The girls' team had won their game, and Adrienne had scored twenty points for the first time in her brief career. She had spent New Year's Day playing lacrosse, making some fantastic errors, but somehow winning every game she played. She had missed all of James's calls; had he left a message?

James paused before he answered. "Well, I didn't really know whether you wanted me to call. You said to take it slow. I figured I'd wait and see where it went on its own, without trying to force anything."

Adrienne's voice rose suddenly. "James, I'm not asking for an engagement ring, just some words to say that New Year's Eve meant something. It's not as if I kiss just anyone, you know." James had never heard such emotion in her voice.

Taken aback at Adrienne's stridency, trying to fabricate a reasonable explanation for his silence, James said, "I'm not very good at relationships – though I'm not suggesting that's where we are. I've just never been able to gauge properly the level of depth a girl wants." James began tossing his pillow into the air with his feet, feeling the pillow landing on his expectant feet, catching it and balancing it, not letting it fall to the bedding on which he lay.

"Well, don't you want something?" she asked curiously.

With another toss, "Well, yeah, I want to spend time with you. I just don't want to encroach on your life. It seems so busy and perfect and productive. I don't want to mess it up."

Adrienne reassured him, "I don't think caring about someone is messy. In fact, it fills the heart, don't you think?"

"No doubt. I do care about you." He thought of the heart that lay in his bureau. He also thought, at the same time, about Andrew's injury, about which he told Adrienne, and their conversation turned to more general issues, like the team, James's opportunity for success, and then school, where James thought, in this new year, he might give more effort. As their conversation proceeded, Adrienne's tone returned to its normal calm – James wondered whether he had imagined the provocation in her voice when he first called.

"Hey, do you have to work hard for your grades?" James asked naively. Adrienne's wisdom seemed so intuitive, he wondered whether she had a preternatural awareness, or whether she had come to it through great intellectual effort and curiosity.

"I don't really know. Everything just seems connected to me. I study because I have questions inside me; as a result, I learn what I study. But I've always been kind of smart, not to brag, but I've always gotten good grades and never had to kill myself. It's just kind of fun."

James wondered, "I'm just trying to figure out what we're doing in the same class. I drift along, get my Bs and Cs, without really learning anything, and you stay focused and expound on things that no one even considers. It's like you're just playing with the system."

She replied, "Maybe I am. I'm a dabbler. I love to try things, to explore them. That's why I joined basketball this year. I wanted to experience something new, to challenge myself."

James cut her off. "And you're scoring twenty points now. Heck, I've been playing non-stop for eight years, and I can't even score twenty points." He was actually a little resentful, knowing that Adrienne's success came so easily.

Adrienne ended the conversation. "I don't want to talk about it. I'm not competing with you or anyone. I'm just trying to make the things I get involved in successful.

"I gotta go. I'm going to do my homework, even though it's 10:30. See you tomorrow?"

He hoped she was asking for more than a casual walk-by. "Yeah. I'll see you outside your homeroom after homeroom period." His suggestion resounded with the slight timber he gave it, denoting a change in their public relationship, one that he welcomed, but in which he had no experience: demonstrating his care.

"OK, see you there. Thanks for calling, James."

In school James was happy to display a lively, though not new, interest in Adrienne. When he wasn't with her, he was envisioning where she was sitting and with whom she was talking. He already knew her schedule from his previous, unrequited focus on her; now, he walked with her on some of those migrations from one class to the next. As they walked down the hall side-by-side, so clearly side-by-side, he pulled aside from time to time to converse with his friends and she noted hers, their old connections, in fact, separating them from looking at each other. James stopped frequently, to push Pete, or to make fun of Meredith's little brother. He fell behind Adrienne passing down the stairs when he had to put his arm around Jason, to pull him from his mock submission to Nicole Rossetti. He realized that he was immersed in a deeply developed world of his male friends, mostly from the basketball team, that punctuated his journey through the hall with quips and simple wrestling moves that defined who he was in a physical way.

Meanwhile, when he was able to measure Adrienne's progress through the corridors and down the stairs, he noted that her contact with friends was full of hugs and lingering hand-clasps, her long hair, unrestrained today, resting luxuriantly on her back, at times sweeping through the air when she twirled to see someone on the other side of the hall, her eyes glittering with interest, her steps accelerating to acknowledge her friend.

James's view of Adrienne was abruptly truncated when Adrienne, at the door to her Physics class, said, "I can't believe what a tight bunch you guys are. I never saw the interaction among you. You have to make a power move every time you pass another member of the throng. It's like a male ritual. I am impressed." She gave him a little shove, to try to be part of the fraternity, and disappeared into Rm. 118, already looking ahead to the possibilities that Physics offered her. James moved hastily to his Chemistry class, with less enthusiasm.

In the next few days, James followed this new pattern around the school. He now had two directions to follow: Adrienne's and his own. At times Adrienne surprised him by coming to a doorway out of which he was emerging, to accompany him to his next class. One time she came to meet him as he was returning from lunch, only to ask him what he had drunk with his lunch, and then she was off to her own lunch, apparently to follow his libationary suggestion. And then there were many passing periods when they did not answer the silent call they were feeling, a call to re-pattern their routes, to restructure their lives, and in these comfortable interludes they sank back into their customary trajectories, a more pedestrian trajectory, but a familiar one.

Practice without Andrew felt like a car with bearings that needed to be replaced. Thursday, Coach set the lineup for Dedham: Geoff, James, Dan, Jason, and Alex White, a very short team that Coach hoped would bring some quickness onto the court. They practiced that way for about fifteen minutes at the end of practice; they did not beat the second team.

After foul shots and sprints, Coach gathered the team around him. "All right, men, we have a real challenge ahead of us. Andreas is not available until next week; Andrew is out indefinitely. We've suddenly become a small team. But that doesn't mean we aren't a good team. We need to draw the defense out to us with good shooting and real shot fakes. We also need to work the weakside boards with quickness. I want the weakside wing to go to the boards on every shot, unless it proves to put too much pressure on our defensive balance. Dan, Alex, Jonas, Bobbie, Archie, Pete – whoever is on the weakside, I want the offensive rebound. Let's get eight offensive boards from our wings.

"If the shot goes up from the middle of the court, the deepest wing becomes a rebounder. The other wing has to get back with Jason."

The players looked at each other, wondering whether to believe in Coach's plan. The logic seemed flawed: because the team was smaller, they would send more men to the offensive glass. Well, at least it was a plan.

"We'll also press run-and-jump. Remember, no double-team until they've put the ball down for two dribbles. Then jump up and rotate on the circle toward the ball. Weakside defender drop back to protect the basket. Our press will work if we are constantly sprinting from behind, coming from behind to turn the 2-on-1 into a 2-on-2. We might even get a few steals pursuing.

"We've got quickness at four positions. Let's utilize it."

On Friday night the game started off auspiciously: after losing the opening tap and giving up a layup, the Panthers came down and scored on a pretty back-door feed from James to Dan, drawing a foul on Dedham's big man, ending in a 3-point play. As James helped Dan up from the floor, it felt that they had spent all of the last few years together, rather than separated.

On the ensuing in-bounds, Jason stepped into the dribbling lane, picking up a charge, returning the ball to the Panthers. James gave Jason a whack on the backside, seeing the Coach's ideas starting to take shape.

In the next three minutes, Casteline gained a 12 – 5 lead, secured mostly from pressure on the ball in the back-court and the front-court. Every starter scored a basket in that run, Jason scoring two on breakaways. Dedham took a time-out at the 3:23 mark of the first quarter, and the Panthers came into their huddle with the enthusiasm of a playoff team. Andrew met them at the sideline. "Way to go, guys.

That was awesome. Exactly what we needed. You're playing your asses off."

James approached Andrew. "Just tryin to fill the gap." He turned to the players coming off the floor. "Great job. Let's keep the pressure on."

High-fives and whoops of delight sent the five back onto the floor. James couldn't remember if Coach LaMott had said anything, but assuredly he had.

The rest of the half was more of the same: Casteline pressing when they scored, and turning some of that pressure into Dedham turnovers. When Dedham set up in their half-court offense, they scored easily. But when Casteline was on offense, they picked up four offensive rebounds for six put-back points. James hit a 3 with a few seconds remaining in the half, to put Casteline up 31 – 21 at half-time.

The locker room was jubilant. Coach LaMott cautioned them against overconfidence in the second half. "We've still got a half to play. Dedham has not even started to play good basketball yet. If they keep possession of the ball and keep us off the offensive glass, we're in for a tough finish. Let's get that lead up higher to start the second half. Let's run double screen down for James coming off the baseline. James, if you have some good looks, take the shot. Deepest wing follow the shot to the boards and let's see what we can get."

Archie started the second half instead of Dan, but the change didn't affect the flow at all. Defensively, they all covered for each other, despite giving up inches at every position. James was covering a 6'3" banger who didn't shoot well from the perimeter. James played him to drive every time, and he hit only one of four shooting over him. James, well practiced in boxing out, kept his opponent off the boards on every shot. With seven minutes left to play, Casteline had increased the lead to 56 – 39, and Dedham was barely hanging on.

One minute into the fourth quarter, Jason picked up his fourth foul, trying to draw a charge, but getting called for a block. With Alex taking the point, there was a noticeable drop off in pushing the ball on the break, but Alex took care of the ball, setting up the Casteline offense, often for a jumper for James or Archie, who both continued to shoot well. With three minutes to play, Casteline holding a 22 point lead, Coach pulled all the starters except for Jason, whom he had just inserted, and Geoff, the only real rebounder on the team. James came off the floor feeling that he was wearing the sneakers he had designed in computer skills class, the dunking shoes.

"Who-o-o-o!" he gushed to Dan. They had played off each other with uncanny awareness. Many of James's baskets were either feeds from Dan or putbacks from Dan's shots that attracted help.

"What'd you get, 25?" asked Dan.

James didn't know. "I have no idea, but I know it felt good. It was like there was something telling me where to go and how fast or slow to go there. My man didn't have a clue!"

They sat on the bench, drinking sips of water from their tiny paper cups, watching the Panthers finish off their victory. The final score was 71 – 58, an easy win practically from the start.

In the mid-court huddle, Coach LaMott noted three things, at least that was what he started to say. But James couldn't hear anything past, "Great job on the offensive glass. We had eleven offensive rebounds, eight from our wings." After that pronouncement, James turned to Dan and wrapped his arms around his friend.

"That was a fuckin pounding," he yelled in Dan's ear. Dan nodded, his face spread wide with an ineluctable grin that came from his gut. James felt that he had the same grin on his face.

The moderate Friday night crowd filed out, glancing over their shoulders at the team as they stood together in their transitory omnipotence.

Coach ended his talk with his "1 . . . 2. . . . 3" and the team found some unison in their "Tight." The locker room was a buzz of expectation.

Pete, who had played the last four minutes and scored a basket, waited in Dan's car as James sauntered out the locker room door. The night was a windy one, the temperature feeling like low single digits. James had his BC hat on his head, to try to keep his wet hair from freezing.

"What's up, my man?" asked Pete, sharing in the glow of the win, as James eased into the back seat of the cramped and messy Escort.

"We kicked ass," James shouted, full of his own sense of power.

Dan, ready to pull out of the parking lot, said, "That was what we've been waiting for. That was a ball game." He reached over and punched Pete and reached back to trade knuckles with James. "You guys headed to Pete's?"

Pete looked at him. "We are gonna celebrate, my man. You joining us?" Pete looked back at James. "Are you goin out or what?"

James stared at Pete. He didn't know what to say. He shouted an intemperate, "Fuckin A!" and pounded on the seat

Dan looked back at James. "Well, where should I drop you two assholes off?" James could see a look of doubt on Dan's face, and, for an instant, James shared in Dan's caution, but he was too energized to call things off right now.

"Let's head over to Jamie Shore's house. There's a belated New Year's party going on." Avoiding Dan's continued gaze by looking out the window, James lay back in the cloth seat, his head languishing on the headrest. James knew that he had told Adrienne that he would call her after their games, but he still didn't know her cell number. He decided he'd call her house from Shore's when he got there, and he lay back, his eyes closed, feeling the car slide into and out of the ice patches in the parking lot, as Dan pulled out.

This is it
It's time for you to go to the wire
You will hit
Cuz you got the burnin' desire
It's your time (Time)
You got the horn so why don't you blow it
You are fine (Fine)
You're filthy cute and baby you know it

Cream
Get on top
Cream
You will cop
Cream
Don't you stop
Cream
Sh-boogie bop

You're so good
Baby there ain't nobody better (Ain't nobody better)
So you should
Never, ever go by the letter (Never ever)
You're so cool (Cool)
Everything you do is success
Make the rules (Rules)
Then break them all coz you are the best

Yes you are

Cream
Get on top
Cream
You will cop
Cream
Don't you stop
Cream
Sh-boogie bop

Cream by Prince

Ben

When Ben got home after the Dedham game, he felt jubilant, but sorry that Willa had not shared in the accomplishment. In the old days, Willa – and the kids, too – would attend the game, shout their encouragement for the Panthers, and join in Ben's after-game mood. Willa had initiated dozens of post-game analyses. And she had a very shrewd eye. She had known when a player was not giving his best effort; she had seen when a player would fail to acknowledge a teammate out of resentment. Ben felt undermanned without Willa's observations.

No one home, Ben flipped on the Celtics, who were in the midst of a slight slump, after a stellar start to their season. Leon Powe was shooting foul shots; there were six minutes left in their game vs. the Nets. The notes on the kitchen table had Mary at the hockey game and Scott "out." Willa had left a note saying that she was visiting Margot and then hustling to the church for a youth musical concert.

The past week had been dispassionate: Willa had been a responsible wife, making supper whenever two or more of them gathered, folding the laundry, ironing her blouses for work. Ben had done all he could to share the domestic duties, cleaning up after supper as he usually did, making sure the children had rides when they needed them, throwing laundry into the washer or dryer as needed. He tried to keep the bathrooms spotless. As he sat in the reclining chair, he looked around him, trying to see discern any way he could anticipate a need and contribute. He got up and checked the dryer, finding a load of underwear and jeans that had been dried; he folded them and put them away. Hanging up two shirts in Mary's closet, he took a look at her wardrobe, in its entirety, one end of the closet to the other. He wondered what she was wearing at the hockey game, in the end accepting the fact that he did not know what Mary tended to wear when she went out. Around the house she wore sweatshirts and jeans, but he couldn't picture her at the game. She would not be wearing her DD uniform, he knew.

In Scott's room he spent a little more time, checking out the artifacts on his desk: the Swiss army knife (what for?), a receipt for a CD he had bought (Radiohead: was Scott a Radiohead fan, or was it for Holly?), DVD cases lacking the DVD, and more than one roll of duct tape. Ben tried to imagine what this detritus added up to, coming to no conclusion whatsoever. He didn't think there were the elements here for a pipe bomb or crystal meth, but he wasn't even sure of that.

In fact, he had little idea about his two children. He wanted to believe that they were headed in a productive direction, but he couldn't tell. Willa and he tried to use their report cards as indicators of their tractability, and, in general, they had remained steady in their grades: nothing below a B- (except Mary's C in Spanish 2 when she had missed three weeks of school with mono).

Ben shook his head as he returned to his reclining chair in the living room, the Celtics having expanded their lead over New Jersey to eleven. He wanted to convince himself that he had a handle on the kids, but he knew that they were independent people, with lives that were consumed with establishing their own track in the firmament. Ben just wondered whether he was being negligent in not knowing what that arc was.

Spreading the stats from Bridget, Nancy, and Janet, he started compiling the game stats. It was great to see James Rush emerging as a leader, especially since Andrew was missing from the lineup. Checking the book quickly, he saw that James had scored 24 points, though he had taken only (he checked Bridget's shot chart) 13 shots. 9 for 13 from the floor, including two 3s, and 4 for 4 from the line. This was the kind of game Ben had expected from James from the beginning of the season, but James's indiscretion had postponed his success for more than a month. But at least he was reaching that level now. The other wing players had also played well, especially Dan, who had handled his demotion out of the starting lineup maturely. Dan was a solid kid, unwilling to give in to the normal petty resentments that bothered many players about playing time and coaches' criticism. Dan had displayed an unusual equanimity all season long, more than just any other player on the team except Geoff.

When the stats were completed, entered into the computer on the excel program he had designed years ago, and sent to the school for posting on-line at school, Ben shut off the light, sitting in the darkness, staring at the screen. The Celtics game was over. The light from the kitchen illuminated a triangle in the family room faintly. He felt like a character in a Ray Carver story: alone, staring at the TV. The only thing he was missing was the glass of whiskey.

But it was just a few minutes before Scott came in the door, with three of his friends. "Hey, Dad, how'd you do?" he asked. "What's with the lights?" Scott turned on the table lamp next to the doorway.

"We had a great game – beat Dedham by 20," Ben exclaimed, rising from the chair. "You have a good night?"

Scott looked at his friends. "Well . . ."

They laughed and laughed, trading jabs with each other.

Scott's friend Marty said, "Yeah, we had a blast. It was awesome," generating another blast of laughter.

"Anything you can share with me?" asked Ben, intrigued.

Scott glanced at a tall boy with goofy hair. Ben did not remember his name. "Think we can trust him?"

The goof shrugged his shoulders, not knowing.

"I think it's OK," said Scott, sitting down on the couch. His friends found a seat.

"We started off going to Hammy's house," and when Scott looked at his goof-haired friend Ben recalled his name, "where we just hacked around for an hour or so. Then Keith Fromland called to see if we wanted to help him."

Scott's friends started chuckling. Ben became a little worried.

"Keith was trying to get a car into a friend's backyard." Scott stopped.

Ben furrowed his brow. "And . . .?"

Scott held his breath a little longer. "Well, we had to take a fence down to get it in there." He started belly laughing at the thought of the fence-dismantling. His friends joined him, hooting as they sprawled across the arms of their chairs, recalling their efforts. "There were about ten of us. We had to lean one of the fence posts way over, but after we took the eight foot section out, we got the car in and replaced the section and tilted the fence post back to normal."

Marty added, "We had to do a little shoveling, of course, but they needed the roadside cleared just a little."

Hammy added, "We were thinking of putting the car in the pool, but we didn't think we'd be able to get it out, so we didn't." He broke off into hilarious giggles.

Ben tried to think of a mature response. He was having a hard time. "Whose car?" he asked, giggling himself just a little at his question.

"Georgia Quinlan's. She's like Murph's girlfriend," saying this as if it explained the escapade.

Ben still probed, free of judgment. "And was it at Jerry Murphy's house where you planted the car?"

"Of course. That's the joke. He spends practically his whole entire life at her house. And they were at her house at the time. We put her car in his backyard as a symbol of their everlasting love," Scott said, unable to stop laughing.

At that moment, Mary rushed in from the driveway, with her friend Suzanne. "Hey, did you guys hear? Georgia Quinlan's car is stuck in Jerry Murphy's backyard!" Her eyes were lit up with excitement.

Suzanne added, "The police are searching for clues. It's like a helicopter lifted the car into the backyard, because there's a big fence all around the yard. It's like King Kong lifted the car into the yard."

Scott tried to keep his glee restrained. "You're kidding! What the hell is that all about?" His friends took their cue from Scott, keeping their mouths closed.

Ben kept his silence, but he did raise the question, "Who would do something like that?" just to antagonize Scott to a response.

"Maybe Georgia's moving in with the Murphys," Scott offered, and his friends exploded.

Mary looked carefully at her brother. "Hey, do you guys know anything about this?" She looked from Scott to Hammy to Marty to Alex, who had been quiet throughout Scott's tale.

Scott teased his sister. "How would we know anything about it? Do we own a helicopter? Do we know King Kong?"

The living room was aswirl with accusations, denials, probing questions, and innocent looks. In a minute the large group moved to the kitchen to raid the cabinets and refrigerator. Ben watched them trail after each other, very comfortable, very familiar. He was glad they were in his home, safe and warm for the moment, making their attempts to understand what it meant to be a young adult. For an evening he understood Willa's preference to have their home filled with adolescent antics.

By the time Willa got home, half an hour later, the group had moved on to other topics. As she took her coat off and hung it up in the hall closet, Willa gushed about the talent and energy of the youth concert at the church. "Ben, you should have seen the Marx kids, playing piano and guitar. They were absolutely amazing. I've never seen anything like it, from kids so young. I mean they're only twelve and fifteen, I think. And Burl Chestney, you should have seen him on flute. It was amazing." Willa's eyes lit up the same way Mary's had as she told what she had learned about the Quinlan car.

Scott came into the room. "Well, then you're going to be even more amazed when you hear about Georgia Quinlan's car," he said, as he launched into a detailed account of the car-heist, failing to mention, of course, the identity of the perpetrators.

Willa couldn't help but laugh at Scott's story. He was a gifted story-teller. "And do you know who accomplished this engineering feat?" asked Willa.

Scott looked quickly, but covertly at Ben. Ben nodded very slightly. "It was us and about six other guys. I got a call from the mastermind, and we all met at Quinlan's house. Once we pushed the car away from Quinlan's it was easy. We just pushed the car with Hammy's; it's only about a half a mile. Then we had to do some snow-shoveling, but that was just good exercise. Finally we tackled the fence, but, with a lot of people contributing, that was no problem, either."

Willa's smile had diminished with each of Scott's words. "Scott, do you think that was a smart thing to do?" she questioned. "I mean, someone's going to have to take that fence apart. Has anyone called the police?"

No one knew.

"We're going back in the morning. The Murphys aren't home till Monday. We'll approach it as a community service project, just helping out a friend in need, Georgia." Scott jammed his hands into the front pockets of his still-wet jeans.

Ben said, "I'm glad you have a plan to rectify the situation. What if the police are involved tomorrow? Are you still going to move the car back?"

Scott shrugged. "We'll have to play it by ear. If the police are involved, they'll call a tow truck and haul it out of there. And then the Murphys will be called, and it'll probably become a crime scene, with yellow tape and fingerprinting." Scott stopped his projection at that point, understanding at last his potential liability.

"Do you think what you did is illegal?" asked Willa

"Illegal? Probably. Wrong? I don't think so. People have to be able to take a joke. We'll take care of everything tomorrow." He turned to his friends, trying to signal the end of the conversation. In a minute they had moved downstairs to the TV room, where they commenced a game of Grand Auto Theft on the computer.

In their bedroom Willa and Ben got ready for bed, Willa brushing her teeth and donning her nightgown, Ben following her into the bathroom to brush his teeth also.

"Do you think Scott's a bad kid?" asked Ben.

Willa measured her response. "No, I just think he's a follower. He didn't dream this escapade up, but he jumped on the bandwagon with all of his unchecked energy and enthusiasm. I don't know, what if they thought it would be a good idea to turn the electricity off at the Cumberland Farms on Rt. 116? It would seem to be the same harmless prank, but involving a commercial entity would definitely be a crime." Willa flicked on the reading light on her bedside table.

"I have to say, I think it's a creative idea, and I think it's a victimless crime, as long as the car gets back unscratched and the fence is not weakened. It shows some ingenuity," Ben said.

"But it's not Scott's ingenuity. It's someone else's. And what do you think are the odds that the car gets back unscathed? What about the fence? Do you think it's stronger than before they took it apart? I just wonder if it's Scott's insecurity showing itself again. Remember when he was having trouble at recess in grade school? He didn't play with the kids, and he hung back from involving himself in the organized games. Remember what he told us?"

Though he couldn't remember, Ben said, "Sort of. I forget. What'd he say?"

"Oh, he told us he felt isolated from the boys in his grade. He told us that story about walking home and having rocks thrown at him by the bigger boys. He said he never walked out of the house without looking down the sidewalk both ways, to make sure the way was clear. I have never forgotten that image: he felt there was something or someone out to get him, waiting for him around every corner."

Ben did not recollect Scott's intimations to his parents. He wondered whether he had even been with Willa when Scott had shared his anxiety.

"When did he outgrow that feeling, do you think?" Ben asked.

"I don't know if he ever has. I think he still looks over his shoulder. That's why his relationship with Holly is so important. It seems that he's found someone that makes him feel complete, maybe for the first time in his life. He talks about her all the time. She's a great kid – so polite and so creative."

Ben was startled to hear that Willa knew so much about Scott's girlfriend, thinking that Scott had been breaking new ground in confiding in his dad. "Yeah, I'm glad she's right for him. It's funny, it makes me trust him a little more to know that he is grounded by his relationship with her." He hastened to add, "Not that I didn't trust Scott all the way. But, you know, as they get older, their capacity for trouble increases."

Willa agreed. "Oh, I know. And we've had some pretty good talks about his lack of motivation. He knows how we feel: if he's doing his best, he doesn't have to worry about us giving him a hard time. But, you know, it's hard for a kid." Willa's empathy was evident. She shook her head.

"Yeah, it is." Since they were talking openly, Ben shifted the conversation to the discord that hovered over Willa and him. "But then, it seems just as hard when you're all grown up, too," he said gently.

256

Willa looked at him, understanding. "Yes, it is. I guess we never get completely settled. But we get so busy, we don't have a chance to alter our course, it seems. We just set out in a direction, and then we land in a place that's a little unfamiliar to us. I know I feel it sometimes when I come home, and the family has shifted just a little in the time I've been gone. I feel left out, as if the shift took place *because* I was gone, not just while I was gone."

Willa's words were right. In fact, his conversation with Willa had revealed to Ben the depth of the shift in his family every time he set out the door, the changes in Willa and his two children becoming more and more pronounced. In that vein, he desired to know more about Holly, Scott's girlfriend, if that was the right nomenclature. "Like Scott's budding romance with Holly?"

Willa nodded. "Yes, exactly. I mean, when did he suddenly become a devoted boyfriend? And when did he gain an appreciation for photography?"

Ben thought he knew. "Maybe when he looked into Holly's eyes directly and she didn't look away. There's something about looking directly into someone's eyes that bridges that gap between people. And I think it generates some bit of electricity that you can feel when it happens. Remember it happening to us for the first time?" Ben pictured being alone with Willa in her parents' living room, his arm around her, and she, for the first time, knowing what he wanted, and asking, with her eyes, if he could be trusted. The gaze was deep, focused and unfocused at the same time. He could still feel the way her steady eyes made his heart feel.

Willa looked at the ceiling, responding to Ben's first thought – about Scott. "Yes, that might have been the moment. You're right."

Ben still wanted to learn more about Holly. "When did you meet Holly? Did she come over?"

"No, I picked them up at Friendly's one afternoon, and they were so cute. He offered to carry her books; he opened the car door for her. I didn't even know he had been paying attention to the way gentlemen behave, but I guess he was. We spent half an hour in the car, talking, before she got out at her house. She's not the cutest thing in the world, but she's got a great laugh." Willa laughed herself, recalling.

Ben envied Willa. She knew so much. In another minute their conversation diminished to slightly uttered thoughts, then to unspoken thoughts, then the feelings tied to long-held emotions, then a brush of recollection of the event that triggered those emotions, then sleep.

At church on Sunday Ben spent the latter part of the service admiring the architecture of St. Andrew's from his seat in a middle pew with Willa. It was a small church, with a capacity of about three hundred. The side walls were built of stone, each wall reaching upward to fill a regal archway. Ben looked at the stone and mortar of the arch nearest him, wondering how such a span was bridged during construction. He knew the topmost stone was called the keystone, so named because it provided the connection between the two curvilinear sets of stones that led to it, and when it fit into that slot between the rising arcs, it secured and stabilized the archway. But he wondered how the builders supported the rising arches before they were connected. Probably with temporary trusses that were removed when the arch was complete. Ben had always loved the soft curve of the arch as it reached upward, only to be borne gently back to the ground.

During the recessional hymn, *Almighty Fortress*, Ben sang lustily, loving the strength in the words; Willa sang clearly. Ben looked at Willa, who stood next to him holding the left side of the hymnal as he lifted the right side. Willa shifted her gaze from the words on the page to Ben's eyes, making contact for an instant before she returned to the page for her cue to the words. Ben changed his tune to attempt harmony, finding the harmonic note as each note of the melody presented itself, achieving an animated blend in most cases, a harsh dissonance occasionally. Willa nudged him with her right knee, an attempt to get him to desist, but he marched onward, exulting in the sound rising to the pinnacle of the church.

After church Ben took the car home.

"I'll be back in an hour," he said to Willa. Ben had joined her the second year she had stayed for childcare, and had taught in the Sunday school for a year, but his interest had waned as the year strode on, until, at the end of the year, he gained no joy and perceived none in his students either. All the excitement and privilege he felt in the school classroom was missing in the wooden-floored St. Andrews' classrooms, so he stopped, happy that he had tried to meet the church's needs, but happier that he could return home after church and read the Sunday Globe with a cup of hot chocolate. He still wished he could feel Willa's fervor, but he had to admit that his passion derived from a different source.

"See you then," she replied, giving him a slight squeeze on the outside of his shoulder.

"You want coffee when I come back?"

"No, I'll get some now when I go downstairs. See you at 12:00," she said, and headed downstairs, her coat over her right arm, her legs fetching beneath the dark green dress swinging on her body. Ben watched her head descend until she was gone.

On the way home Ben stopped at Dunkin Donuts, to give Mary a hard time as she worked the drive-in window. He ordered a large hot chocolate, then changed his order twice, to try to confuse her, but she knew immediately who it was. "That's enough, Dad. I'll get the hot chocolate and would you please move up to the window?" she admonished. He knew she was smiling at his foolishness.

"Hi, Honey, how's it going?" he asked at the window.

"Great. I got a $5.00 tip from one customer. At the window we can keep tips as long as we don't make a big deal out of it. Another one hundred of those customers and I can pay for my car." She laughed, handing Ben his hot chocolate.

"I hope you can find something better to spend $500.00 on, if those generous customers decide to patronize this fine establishment." He gave her a ten dollar bill. "Keep the change, please."

At home Scott lay on the floor, trying to draw a cartoon based on a Batman comic book that he had spread in front of him. Holly's flair for arts had fostered a renewal of his interest in drawing that he had had as a young boy, but that had disappeared because of a lack of exercise.

"Did you take the car back?" Ben asked Scott.

"Yeah, about twelve of us showed up. It was even easier than getting it in there. The fence came apart more easily, and the path was already shoveled. Took about an hour and a half, I'd say. It was just about as much fun as stowing it in there.

"We saw Georgia. After she looked at the car to make sure it was OK, she laughed with us, saying that she wished she could have been part of the hijacking. As far as I know, the police were never called. Georgia didn't even know it was gone until the morning, and then she figured someone had shorted it or stolen her keys and had an extra key made. Then Jerry called her in the morning to let her know that her car was in his backyard." Scott laughed once again, still amused at his wondrous prank.

Ben joined him. "That was a good move. The only problem with a move like that is you think you have to exceed it on your next show of cleverness, and it can get pretty tough to top what you've done before."

Scott nodded, but his attention had jumped back to his drawing, which was an attempt to replicate the flight of a motley beast, as it spanned a dark sky.

Tuesday's game with Milton loomed over the team like a cold sun in January, emitting strong light, but little heat. Milton, with their 7 and 1 record, was led by a pair of 6'4" forwards that each averaged fifteen plus. They ran a very structured flex against man-to-man, and they had ripped Casteline to shreds with that offense twice last season. Ben worked zone defense at practice Monday, as well as a triangle-and-two, with James and Dan on the forwards, leaving Geoff at the base of the inverted triangle in the lane. Douglas and Bain, Milton's two forwards, got most of their points on the baseline and from the block, so the defense had the look of a 2-3, with James and Dan covering the baseline. Ben hoped it would be enough disguise to check Milton's offensive flow.

After school on Tuesday Ben went to the gym to watch the freshman game that started at 3:30. He took his usual position at the scorer's table, running the game-clock, because it was hard for Keith, the freshman coach, to find someone to perform the duty. There were parents who had run the clock when their sons were playing in the youth leagues, but their abilities were a little compromised by the fact that they spent their time counting the minutes of their sons' playing time, comparing them to the minutes that their friends' sons were garnering. The clock was ticking, from these parents' perspectives, to establishing a rung on the varsity roster in two years, and the number of minutes and points were Exhibit A in their advocacy for their sons.

And so they had trouble concentrating on turning the clock on and off and adding a score for either team. Consequently, they remained in the stands, trying not to make eye contact with their sons across the floor as they sat on the bench.

The freshman team was 3 and 3, having lost their last two games in the last minutes. Ben loved to watch these games, projecting the best players into a varsity uniform, impressed less by a basket than by an assist, and far less by a steal than by a charge. At freshman practice every other week, Ben stopped in to reinforce the principles that Keith was instituting: basic skills, movement without the ball, and movement in response to the ball on defense. He looked for the boys who met his gaze as he talked, who sat up straight and followed the path of his minuscule discourse.

With two and a half minutes left in the freshman game, the Panthers held a 41 – 35 lead. A skinny, tiny guard for Milton then hit a 3 and stole the inbounds pass for a layup, to cut the lead to one, with 2:14 left. Keith called timeout, his last – Ben signaled that fact to Keith.

The Arc of Intersection

The Panthers came out in their normal press-break alignment, moving the ball through the middle to a 3-on-2. Justin Rebose fed to his left side a bounce-pass that hit Paul Robinson in stride, but he missed the layup. Milton's tall post player grabbed the rebound, pushing the ball up court for a good shot.

The last two minutes were back and forth, Casteline finally winning by two, but the outcome was less important to Ben than the play of Justin Rebose, who, in the last quarter, engineered five plays in the middle of press-break, setting up five baskets, of which Casteline converted two. Rebose also jumped up into a surprise double-team that forced a Milton turnover with less than a minute left.

After the game, Ben joined the freshman team in their locker room, waiting for Coach Warren to finish his post-game analysis before interjecting, "Great finish, guys. That was a good team you beat. Justin, you did a great job handling the ball in the middle of the floor. You made five great plays down the stretch, and that's hard to do late in the game. Nice work. Great job overall, gentlemen." Ben waved his hand, an acknowledgement of their effort, his gesture reminding him of the minister's benediction at the end of the church service. He tried to look at each player, though some hung their heads in spite of the win. Ben knew that Justin was not a starter on this team, but his improvement was at the top of Keith's list of accomplishments for this team.

As the varsity team gathered in the locker room, Ben watched the beginning of the fourth quarter of the JV game. When he left the floor, the Milton JVs held a comfortable 56 – 39 lead over Casteline. In the locker room he reviewed the information about Milton.

"Bain. #20. Douglas. #51. When we're in a 2, Dan, you've got Bain. James, you've got Douglas. We'll start in a normal 2-3. We'll switch to the Triangle on a call from the bench. It's a '6,' our combination defense. If we're in the 6, and we sub for James or Dan, the replacement, Archie, Alex, Jonas, you've got to know and find Bain or Douglas early.

"Let's take the great work we did with Dedham and keep it going. Forget about the score. Just play the way you know how to play.

"Don't expect a big crowd. This is a Tuesday, mid-January. No one's paying much attention to us. But, in the same vein, Milton won't be expecting much, either. Bring complete attention to what you're doing, and maybe Milton will be looking past us.

"Let's get ready." Ben looked at his players, seeing they indeed had the calm anticipation that was a prelude to a strong performance.

261

The Panthers' defense stymied Milton's attack for much of the first half, allowing Casteline to carry a 30 – 28 lead into the locker room at half-time. Geoff Willis led the team with 8 points and 5 rebounds, and James Rush was playing outstanding defense on Dan Bain, holding him to 5 points.

As Milton came out in the second half, their veteran coach, Peter Burns, made a very effective adjustment, constantly crossing his two big forwards under the basket, scraping Rush and Owings off, forcing them to switch (or not switch), involving Geoff Willis in the mayhem, eventually freeing up their non-descript center for four early baskets in the third quarter. As the teams entered the fourth quarter, Milton had wrested a 47 - 44 lead from Casteline. The Panthers needed to make some baskets, because their defense was not going to stop Milton as they had in the first half.

Ben called for a couple top screens for James, and he scored on one of them and fed for a couple foul shots for Andreas on another play. An unexpected 3 from Dan Owings gave the Panthers another lead, but Milton regained the lead with two foul shots. With 1:45 left, Casteline took the lead again on a 3-point play by Jason, fouling out Milton's point guard, Jermayne Withers, on the drive. Ben called for a 1-3-1, a defense Casteline hadn't used all day, to try to get Milton out of any comfort they might have established against the combination defense. When the ball was reversed to Dan Bain in the corner, James and Alex double-teamed him to the baseline, forcing a weak pass that Geoff Willis picked off, to give the Panthers the ball with a two point lead, 1:21 on the clock.

Jason ran the delay for twenty seconds, passing to Archie and then Dan and then reverse-pivoting to get the ball back. With eight on the shot clock, Geoff and James ran a double down for Archie, who came off the screen, took the pass from Jason, and drained a two-pointer to give Casteline a four point lead with 54 seconds left.

Five out of six foul shot later, it was over., Casteline coming away with a 65 – 62 victory over a strong – and shocked – Milton team.

In the mid-court huddle, Ben quieted the exultant team. "Hell of a win, tonight, guys. You played within yourselves and made big plays at crunch time. That was a great screen, James and Alex. Perfect execution. And Archie, welcome to Casteline. That wasn't exactly the game-winner, but without that shot, we wouldn't have held the momentum.

"Great night, guys. Andrew, get in the middle here. We're just trying to give our best effort, and now we know two things: one, without our best effort and our best player, we have little chance; and, two, with our best effort, we can accomplish a lot. Tonight is a great example of that."

Andrew began the call: "One . . . two . . . three – "

"TIGHT!" the team shouted, and the fans remaining in the gym, mostly parents, shouted and applauded, sharing in the victory.

The ride home was euphoric. Ben stopped with Bryan at Willow's for a quick beer, just one, but it had been a long time since they had defeated a strong team.

"Great job, Ben," Bryan cried, clapping him on the back as they entered the dusky tavern. As they took their coats off, Lisa approached them with a wide smile.

"Well, I can see that someone is feeling good about tonight," and she looked at Ben.

Bryan deferred to his friend. "Yeah, at least someone can feel good about the night." He patted Ben on the shoulder, deferentially.

"Not a great night for you?" Lisa asked Bryan.

"Not exactly. We shot about 20 percent. But that's OK. I'm just trying to develop the next set of stars. The wins and losses don't measure our progress." Bryan gave Lisa a tight squeeze.

When the couple had pulled apart, Lisa made a motion to give Ben a hug, too. In his blissful state, he accepted her embrace, hugging her, smelling her clean freshness.

Just then the bartender came over to the little group. "Hey, are you Ben LaMott?"

"Yes," Ben replied.

"You're on the schedule for Monday night next week. Larry told me to call you, but since you're here, I'm just telling you. Can you come in for a night of training before Monday, just shadowing me?"

Ben grinned more widely. "No problem. What's a good night for you?" Then he thought: practice Wednesday evening, game Friday evening, training on Saturday night probably wouldn't be a great idea. "How's Thursday night?"

The bartender replied, "Actually, that's my night off. Any other possibility?"

"What about Sunday night? Probably a slow night, but that might make it good for training."

"Sounds good. You need a comfortable pair of shoes – sneakers are a good idea. If you can get a mixology book and look it over so you know the basics, that'd be good too. Collared shirt, like a golf shirt is good. Probably come in at 5:30, because we close at 10:00 on Sundays. That way you get a good four hours."

"Is the Monday shift with you? And, I'm sorry, but what's your name, again?"

"Sorry, Pete Amoroso. Yeah, Monday you're Number Two with me. I'll tip you off on Sunday about what it entails. Pretty basic, to be honest.

"I've gotta go take care of business. See you on Sunday," Pete said as he slid along the counter, removing empty glasses and collecting two bar bills and credit cards.

When Pete had left, Lisa looked at Ben. "Excuse me, but can you give me discounts?" She laughed easily.

"Maybe after a few years. But at first I'm gonna play it straight. Maybe I can strengthen your drinks a little, I don't know."

Bryan eyed Ben. "Congratulations. A new career."

After one quick beer – and a new job offering – Ben continued home, still lifted by the team's win. As a coach he still reveled in the absolute pleasure of a victory, taking as much affirmation out of it as he had always taken about a win when he was a player. The years since he competed as a player, nearly thirty now, hadn't reduced the thrill of winning. There was something about planning and preparing, and then expending more ounces of effort than a player knew he had, in order to secure a victory – not much exceeded it. Sex? Well, yes, sex did indeed give him that same release. But he had had much more success at gaining victories than he had at seducing girls when he was young, so he had learned to exact a commitment from himself to bring his team to a winning position every time he walked onto the court. As a coach he had maintained that expectation stringently, even though he no longer could expend that energy.

The sky emitted a few random snowflakes, which drifted through the streetlights as he passed them, then disappeared against the darkness of the night sky on the country road leading to his house. The car moved smoothly over the wet road, never sliding, but responding to his touch as if the wheels were lubricated. He turned into his driveway, anxious to see Willa, his companion through all those years between then, when he was becoming a coach, a father, and a husband, and now, when he was not sure what he had become.

264

I waited 'til I saw the sun
I don't know why I didn't come
I left you by the house of fun
I don't know why I didn't come
I don't know why I didn't come

When I saw the break of day
I wished that I could fly away
Instead of kneeling in the sand
Catching teardrops in my hand

My heart is drenched in wine
But you'll be on my mind
Forever

Out across the endless sea
I would die in ecstacy
But I'll be a bag of bones
Driving down the road alone

My heart is drenched in wine
But you'll be on my mind
Forever

Something has to make you run
I don't know why I didn't come
I feel as empty as a drum
I don't know why I didn't come
I don't know why I didn't come
I don't know why I didn't come

Don't Know Why by Norah Jones

265

James

For once, James could brag a little about the Panthers' victory, but he was unwilling to call Adrienne, because of the mess of the previous weekend.

James and Pete had indeed gone to Shore's Friday night, both boys feeling elated and elevated, willing to take the route this party would lead to. James had felt a slight pull to avoid the pong games in the kitchen, but after a half hour of chitchat in the living room, he strode into the kitchen, to refill his cup of beer and to challenge the reigning champions of beer-pong. One half hour and four beers later, Ben and Pete retired to the playroom in the basement, to watch the second half of the national championship game between Florida and Oklahoma.

"I got Florida," said James, looking at the 7-7 halftime score.

"You got it, bro," Pete replied. "Five bucks."

They joined the primarily football team crowd, woofing and cheering whenever there was the slightest change in momentum from one team to the other. By the time the fourth quarter was about to begin, James was slopping his beer as he returned from refilling it, crossing over the prone bodies of the fans gathered on the floor of the playroom.

Returning from one refill, James ran into Adrienne's friend Diane, who was seated in the dining room, playing poker with a mixed group of people, including Fanny Peavey, a football friend of James's.

When Diane caught James's eye, she stood up from her chair and pointed her finger at James. "Hey, what's up, buddy?" she said as if they were long-lost friends.

James approached her. "Nothin much. Just celebrating a win over Dedham." Though he knew the answer, he asked, "Is Adrienne here?"

Diane shook her head. "No, but she's picking me up in a while and I'm going to see her tomorrow too; we're in a lacrosse tournament Saturday and Sunday at Tabor Academy. You want to come and see it?" she asked hopefully.

James scrunched his mouth as if he were considering the idea. At the same time, trying to grasp Diane's arm, he lurched over the small, rectangular throw rug that separated him from Diane, throwing a portion of his beer onto the corner cabinet, leaving beer dripping down the upper panels of glass onto the lower cabinet, a trail of beer running to the floor down the polished wood.

"Oops," James said lightly.

"You need some help?" Diane asked, turning into the kitchen for paper towels.

James nodded to no one. Diane returned, with a wad of towels, working on the glass panels first, working her way down to the hardwood floor, on which beer was dripping into a puddle. James stood dumbly, watching Diane clean up after him.

Diane looked up. "How you getting home?"

James shrugged. "I think I have a few friends that can help me out. I haven't thought that far ahead yet," and he hadn't.

"Do you want a ride with me? Lucy and Adrienne are coming to pick me up in about ten minutes, at about 11:30."

James turned from Diane. "There's one quarter left in the Florida-Oklahoma game. Do you think you could wait till that's over?"

Diane looked at James. "Uh, sorry. The train's leaving in ten minutes. I have to win a few more hands in poker, then I'm good to go. If you're coming with us, I'll meet you at the front door in ten. I'm not coming down to the football-ugga-ugga room. I don't think women are allowed."

James considered Diane's observation, and indeed admitted that it was an all-male crowd watching the game, surprisingly, because there were some die-hard female football fans at Casteline and at this party. He wondered whether women had been officially excluded.

"Yeah, I'll see you there if the game goes quick. I doubt it." James turned down the stairs.

In about forty minutes, after Florida executed a perfect late-game drive to capture the national championship, the football fans flooded up the stairs, all to refill their empty cups, only to find that the keg was empty and party was winding down. Surprisingly, Pete had left the room midway through the third period, heading upstairs. Pete owed him five bucks.

Knowing he had missed Diane, James gravitated toward Fanny, who lived somewhere near James. "Hey, Fan, any chance I could hook a ride with you?"

As Fanny turned to answer, James saw over his shoulder Adrienne, standing next to the hat rack in the Shores' living room. James didn't hear Fanny's response. He walked to Adrienne, who looked at him questioningly.

"Hey, Aide, how's it going?" he asked.

"I'm doing fine. How're you doing?" she asked hopefully.

"Not bad. Not bad at all. Is Diane still here?" He was still hopeful that he could catch a ride home with her.

"Uh-uh. She had to go home. I had her leave me here when she said you were here. What are you doing?"

James shrugged his shoulders. "Just havin a little party. It's national championship day. Gotta celebrate with the boys, you know?"

Adrienne shook her head. "I really don't know. All I know is you're on the basketball team, and you're lucky the cops stayed away from this party. Are you looking to end your season right now?" She huddled in her coat, looking surprisingly weak.

"Ehh, I'm just havin a mellow night, and I'm ready to go home. Are you heading home?"

"I really don't know how I'm getting home, but I think I'll make sure you get home. How are you going to get past your parents? What's the official drinking policy in the Rush house right now? Are they good with having a mellow night?"

James paused. For the first time this evening, he considered entering his house to face his parents. He stopped breathing for a few seconds. "I don't really know the answer to that question. We've kinda stopped talking to each other ever since I blew them off on New Year's Eve." He shifted onto his back foot and leaned back, as his friends streamed out the front door of Shore's house. Jamie Shore and some of his best friends were starting the cleanup, green trashbags in their hands, carrying the partially emptied cans and cups to the sink in the kitchen, draining them. James could see in the dining room where he had spilled his beer onto the corner cabinet, the wood case still marked by the trail of his beer.

Adrienne regained her composure. "Well, first things first. Let's get a ride out of here. Is there someone you can tap to give us rides?" She crossed the threshold of the door, looking across the front yard at the stragglers, one group huddled around a joint, another hunched over a clear bottle of what looked like tequila.

James saw Pete at the edge of the street. "Hey, Pete, man. D'you gotta a ride?"

Pete waved his arm, indicating it was all squared away. James pointed to Pete, and he and Adrienne moved off across the squeaky patches of snow that littered the Shores' front yard. James brushed Adrienne's arm as he slipped on a mound of snow. She felt solid.

After fifteen minutes of hair-raising flight across the roads of Casteline, James asked the driver, Rob Preston, to pull over so he could get sick. When Rob didn't hear him, James tried to roll down the window, but he was too late. He puked down the inside of Rob's door. He tried to wipe it up with his sleeve, but it was too much liquid. It reminded him of the beer dripping down Shore's dark-wooded cabinet. His eyes teared as he tried to get rid of all the bad taste in him. He could feel Adrienne's thigh next to his left leg, but he couldn't look up at her for several reasons.

"Hey, sorry, man. I blew it here," he muttered at Rob.

Rob, still careening down the road, now slowing to turn onto James's street, said, "No worry. Goes with the territory. That's why my parents let me have my own car, so I don't fuck theirs up. I'll get it in the morning."

At James's house, he opened the door, looking back in at Adrienne. She uneasily looked at him, a question in her eyes, her hair tucked inside her green wool hat, her boots encasing the legs of her jeans.

"Aide, come on in with me. I don't want you riding in this car any more." He reached for her arm, and she came outside, not reluctantly.

Rob hurtled off, with Pete and one other partier inertly lying on the back seat.

"Thanks," James shouted as Rob retreated down the road.

James looked at Adrienne. "Well, this may be the moment of truth. Let's go in and see who's up. If my parents are sleeping, I'm good to go. I can walk you home. I'd say I'd use my dad's truck, but I don't think that'd be the best idea right now. I'd offer the truck up to you, but I don't want you to get on the bad side of them, so . .."

James led Adrienne to the side steps of his house, turning the handle of the storm door as quietly as he could, then the doorknob of the door. Shit. It was locked. He reached into his pocket, looking for a key that he knew he didn't have. "Looks like we get to walk a few miles," he determined, shrugging his shoulders and holding his hands up in an air of resignation, as if he had just forgotten to sharpen his pencil before a test.

Adrienne clapped her hands together. "I'm just going to call my mom on my cell. It'd be an hour before we get to my house walking, and I don't want her to worry all that time." She looked at her wrist. "It's 12:40 now. Too late for walking, but thanks for the offer." She pulled out her phone, and called home. After a short minute, she clicked off and said, "Let's wait at the corner; I told her I'd be waiting at that corner. She should be about five or ten minutes. She has to get dressed." There did not seem to be any resentment in Adrienne's words – just resolution.

James walked with her to the corner, his bare hands stuffed into the pockets of his hooded Carhartt, wondering what he could say to try to rectify the night. Nothing came to mind.

At the corner, he tried to make icy snow into snowballs, to throw at the street sign, but the remnant snow was too hardened into icy fragments to allow for any sculpting. He threw chunks of snow anyway, to distract himself. Adrienne made a few tosses too, once grazing the signpole, a puff of snow splitting from her missile. After another minute James changed the game, to one of trying to land an icy snow missile in the iced birdbath that sat in corner of the Restons' yard, about twenty feet from Adrienne and James. James tried underhand lobs, overhand tosses and even shotput style projections. An arc too high and he had no control over distance; an arc too low and he had little chance of getting the snow over the rim of the stone sculpture. With his eleventh throw, a graceful shotput arc, he landed a snow shot in the birdbath. Adrienne clapped her mittens together wordlessly and twirled around, just as the lights from her mother's car began their probe down the street, searching for the corner to James's street. When Adrienne jumped into the street and hopped clownishly from one foot to the other, waving her arms crazily, her mother pulled over slowly, easing to a stop beside Adrienne and James.

James opened the door for Adrienne. "Hi, Mrs. Petrulsky. I'm very sorry for the late hour. It's my fault." James didn't know how to tell Mrs. Petrulsky why Adrienne was with him. But Adrienne filled in the void.

"We were just out walking, and it got really late. We were enjoying the stars. I thought of making snow angels, but I knew the snow was too frozen, but it would have been a perfect night to make angels in people's front yards, don't you think?"

Mrs. Petrulsky nodded, her eyes, half-shut. "Let's get going, dear. We can talk in the morning. James, how do you put up with all the energy coming out of this girl? I tell you, I stopped being able to match it when she turned thirteen. Good luck to you, if you try to keep up with her."

When Adrienne was safely settled and buckled in the front seat, James started to close the door. "Thank you, again, Mrs. Petrulsky, and Adrienne, thank you for a great night." He closed the door and turned toward his house, completely dark, except for the light next to the locked back door. James's head was just starting to clear.

The side door was still locked. James tried the garage door, not expecting it to be open, but it rose quietly; James expected the door to the house to be locked, but there was a key underneath the steps leading to the entranceway. Bending in the dark, James felt for the key, and, finding it, let himself into the house. He let out a relieved breath.

Inside there was just as much silence as outdoors and in the garage. Hyper-alert, James removed his sneakers and tiptoed up the stairs to his bedroom, noting the closed door to his parents' bedroom. He shook his head at his apparent fortune. The morning would present a series of questions from his mom, but his dad would be out the door before he got up for practice.

After brushing his teeth, James slid into his bed, his head clearing.

In the morning, James had showered as soon as he was awake, hopping down the stairs to greet his mother, who was looking in the shelves for items she needed to buy at the grocery store.

"Did you have a good night?" she inquired.

James felt like a hooked fish, uncertain of the strength of the fishing line holding the hook.

"It was OK. I hung with Pete, and then we ran into Diane and Adrienne." So far no untruths.

"Where did you go?"

"Jamie Shore's." The shorter the answer the better.

"We tried to wait up for you, but we gave up at midnight. What time'd you come home?"

" 'Bout 12:30. I was walking around with Adrienne for a while. Her mother finally picked her up at about 12:30. We were just talkin and hangin around." Ever since New Year's Eve, there had been a silent truce between James and his parents, ever since his father had ripped up his check for the car. James didn't know whether he was still following the same rules as before New Year's or the rules before his arrest, but the less discussion about it the better. His mother was not really confrontational, and James could count on her to let it slide too, if nothing was clearly wrong. His dad had barely spoken to James in the New Year, apparently thinking James not worth the time.

At Saturday morning practice, the usual Saturday scrimmages, James drew Archie, Coach Taft, two JVs, and Andreas, who would be back next week after missing four games, a powerful rebounder and inside post defender. Before they started playing, they loosened up with full court weave, 3 on 2, 2 on 1 crosscourt, and paired up for jumpers on the run. Coach LaMott was in a very positive mood, congratulating just about every varsity player for his contribution in the Dedham game.

"Great job last night, James," Coach said to James, who lumbered past the coach, trying to catch his breath. He hoped he would not have to leave the court to throw up. He had awakened with an intense headache, which he had tried to assuage with three Advils. So far they weren't helping. His legs felt as if they were the granite pedestals of the Restons' birdbath. He was thirsty.

"Thanks, Coach," he puffed, as he moved past, trying to maintain his lane without narrowing it.

When the warmup drills ended, the teams took the court. Coach LaMott came over to James to speak with him, before the games began. "James, you hit a homerun last night: defensively, moving without the ball, shooting. You looked really composed and natural, just the way you should look in your second year of varsity. I'm really proud of your progress. I guess you took on the challenge of your suspension seriously. I'm very happy for you."

Coach LaMott's words resounded in James's abdomen like a hand slapping on a hollow drum. He could feel his gut tighten in response. It was hard to look Coach in the eye. Staring at Coach LaMott's sneaker laces, James responded, "Thanks, Coach. It was a great game. I did feel more in the flow than any other game this year or last."

Coach pulled away from James to address several other players individually before he blew his whistle to start the games. James looked at the wall of the gym opposite the championship banners and breathed deeply.

His team split their first two games, then took on Coach LaMott's undefeated team, with Jason, Pete, Geoff, and some younger players. Coach LaMott hit two early jumpers, which was about all he could do at his age, but he then threw two three-quarter court passes leading to layups. James kept finding himself chasing the play, unable to fill a lane on his team's fastbreak, and completely incapable of getting down the floor in front of Coach's team's fastbreak. Final score: Coach's team 15, James's team 6. A pitiful showing.

Two sets of ten foulshots (James hit 14 for 20) and then shooting fouls to try to avoid running. There were 24 players shooting; Coach set 17 as the dividing number to avoid running 10 in a minute. Far end shot 8 for 12; James's end shot a weak 6 for 12 and they stood on the line.

"Anyone over 6'0" on the line now," Coach shouted, displeased with the numbers. He had just won the Saturday morning

272

championship game, but he expected better than 14 for 24. "Set the clock, Bridget."

On the sixth turn, James felt his legs give out. From that point on, he couldn't sprint – all he could summon was a leg-churning that made him look as if he were running through two feet of water. And he still felt as if he had those heavy sweatpants on. He was just beginning the last leg when the buzzer sounded. There were two others caught short. Coach stared directly at James, his eyebrows raised, his head leaning forward.

"Other group, on the line," he continued, turning from James to the greater group. Overall there were seven players short on the 10 in a minute. Coach lined them up for an abbreviated 6-in-36, but James didn't think he had enough recovery time to make that shorter distance.

He tried not to sprint at first, trying to keep something in reserve for the last two sprints, but he fell short again, along with two JVs. Even Pete finished ahead of him, finishing in under 36.

He finished the final, ignominious 4-in-24, along with both JVs, and Coach called everyone together. "Great win, last night, Varsity. It was smooth and involved many different players. To win without Andrew is a great accomplishment. We have a challenge ahead of us on Tuesday, as we take on Milton. They're one of the best on our schedule. We won't be able to beat them without a solid game from all of you. Congratulations on making progress, and I hope you're making the necessary sacrifices off the court, to make our season as successful as possible. Tonight's a Saturday night, chance to watch the hockey team play, a chance to catch up with your friends. Let's not abuse the freedom that a Saturday night represents.

"Have a great weekend, guys, and I'll see you on Monday, for our preparation for Milton." Coach LaMott seemed to hover near James for a few seconds, as if he wanted to speak with him, but he then moved on, and James headed into the locker room, his stomach more settled, though his legs were as heavy as the first day of practice. He knew he owed himself an extra 10 in a minute, but he also knew what the result would look like.

In the afternoon James tried Adrienne on the phone, but, as her number rang, he remembered that Diane had told him she would be away at a lacrosse tournament, at Tabor Academy in Mattapoisett. James wanted to ask her sister Adrienne's cell phone number, but he also thought he should know it already, so he didn't ask. He did call Lucy, to try to get ahold of Adrienne's cell number, but Lucy was also out.

273

James needed to tell someone of his perfidy. He was starting to feel better physically, but he was disgusted with himself. He called Dan, out of the blue, hoping that his old friend was home.

"Hey, dude, what's up?" he asked.

"Not much. Just chillin," Dan replied, noncommittally. James could feel that Dan was not interested in investing himself in James's dilemma, but James needed him.

"You doin anything this after?" he invited.

"Nothin much. I might head over to Joyce's for a little while. You wanna get together?"

James felt relieved to hear Dan's goodness. "Yeah, you want to go out to get a pizza?"

No hesitation. "See you in five," and Dan hung up.

As they pulled into the lot of Walpole's House of Pizza, James finally took the risk: "I fucked up last night."

"Yeah, I kind of got that impression. Kind of ironic, wouldn't you say? You have a big game against Dedham, and then you crash?"

"No shit. It's like once I got back to the full status of being a major part of the team, I thought I could go out and feel good about it."

"I mean, I don't think you're an alcoholic, but you have to think as if you are, because you don't seem to be able to just dabble a little, you know?"

James wondered, "Hey, how do you avoid it? I mean, you don't seem to be attracted to the crazy stuff anymore."

Dan thought for a few seconds. "I think I know myself; I've thought about drinking a lot, and I've seen how it fucks people up. My mom would never admit it, but she drinks every day, and there are things she can't do or won't do, because she has to have her wine or whatever she drinks. I mean she never drives the car after about 4:30 every day. She just about shuts down before supper every day. I can't tell if she's drunk or depressed, but I can't see any difference." Dan dropped into silence, considering the subject at more length.

James said, "I didn't know. That's tough."

"There's a lot we don't know about each other. . . . Remember when I took you to that house when we were kids? That house I was haunting?"

James remembered every detail as if they had ridden their bikes to that house a few hours ago. He nodded, opening his eyes, noting that Dan was staring straight ahead at the windshield, then said, "Yeah, I'll never forget it." James didn't want to mention that it had been just two and a half years ago, not "when they were kids."

"I kept it up for another six or eight months, something like that. I probably visited another five times. Finally, I realized that I was risking my future to fill this crazy impulse. But the times I went over there, and there were many, I came to understand that we all have thousands of stories inside us that other people don't know. I felt I was peeling away layers of this family's life, and every time I visited, I learned something new, but I also realized that I'd never know them completely, partly because they were always changing, and I couldn't keep up with them. And more importantly, I didn't really know them. I mean I have never talked to them in my whole life. I was deluding myself into thinking that I knew them inside-out."

James nodded, understanding completely. "But maybe we can understand ourselves," he murmured.

Dan considered James's assertion, then countered, "I don't know how much we can know ourselves, but I do know that we can get to know someone else pretty well, and we can keep up with the changes in that person if we are attentive to them. That's what I think I'm accomplishing with Joyce. And maybe we're getting there, you and me."

A few seconds later, they hopped out of Dan's Escort and scooted into House of Pizza. Inside, their talk turned to more mundane matters, like the Oklahoma-Florida game and the Dedham game; they talked with their mouths full of pizza.

When Dan was about to drop James off at his house, James said, "Hey, I know I've been stupid, but at least there's one thing that it has produced." He looked at Dan respectfully.

"What's that?" Dan asked innocently.

"At least it's gotten us together a little. I kind of like the simplicity of an Escort."

"Oh, I definitely could afford much more, but I like the stripped down life."

Dan looked up at James, who stood next to the open passenger door. "Hey, stay cool tonight, huh?"

James nodded. "I think I got it," he said, as sure of himself as he could be, given the past twenty-four hours.

After a silent supper with his mom and dad, James called Adrienne again. This time she was home from her tournament, but she was about to go out with her friends to the hockey game. James called to his mom to see if she would drive him to the game.

"Sorry, hon, but your dad and I are leaving for the movies. We're late already. Can't you get a ride from one of your friends?"

275

James shook his head, though he had tried no one. He didn't want to have to call his friends and beg for a ride. "I'll see if I can get a ride now. You guys go ahead."

His dad spoke to him quietly. "You'd better be in by 10:30. Last night was way too late."

"Yeah, sorry. I lost track of time." James was tempted to add that he was sorry that he had caused them any worry, but he stopped short of the hypocrisy. "Don't worry. If I go out, I'll be home early."

His father followed his mother out the door, shutting it firmly. James tried Alex and Bobby for a ride to the game, but they had already left. He knew Dan was at a dance with Joyce at a teen-age club in Franklin. He shrugged his shoulders and walked out of the house to hitchhike to the rink across town.

But he had gotten no further than the woods at the end of the street when he started throwing snow, gradually throwing it more and more angrily at the trees he passed. Last night with Adrienne, they had thrown so gently and softly, trying to hit their target with a little pluff of snow. Now James threw with anger, as if he were trying to wound the tree trunk with an icy rage.

He started adding momentum to his throws with an epithet timed to each release: "Idiot." "Shithead." "Asshole." "Shithead." After a few more throws, he changed from nouns to adjectives: "Weak." "Pathetic." "Soft." "Shameful."

As he continued to use up the icy detritus in the gutter and on the edge of the curb, his voice became a little more strident, until gradually, he realized that he was not moving down the street at all, but standing about fifteen feet from a wide tree trunk, assaulting it with all the disappointment and bitterness he could expel. He didn't feel any better, but after another minute of assault, he finally felt weakened and a little chilly. He turned around and headed back to his house, eyes closed, trying to trace the curve of the curb, his balance compromised by the ice at the edge of the road. He could feel the driveways as they slid by, until he turned into his own.

Sunday was a day of studying, catching up on his reading. When he got back from refereeing the youth games at 1:00 and 2:00, he watched the Patriots put away the Jets in the penultimate regular season game. As the Patriots' game was winding down, Rachel asked him, "Hey, did you come home late Friday night?" She looked scared.

James nodded. "Yeah." He looked over his shoulder, to make sure his parents weren't nearby. "I got hung up with some of my friends watching the Florida game. Then I saw Adrienne and we hung out for a little while."

"James, you don't have to lie to me. I saw you Saturday morning. You didn't look too good. Did you mess up again?"

James couldn't look at Rachel. He felt like crying. It was easier to close his eyes, even as he continued talking with his sister.

"James, don't close your eyes with me. You can't just make me go away. I'm your sister. I hope we're still talking like this fifty years from now. Tell me what happened."

James wondered where his sister's maturity came from. He wondered if he would want to cry at age 66 the way he wanted to cry now. "I got wasted." He couldn't say any more and he didn't need to. Rachel stared at him with a mixture of pity and love. He was lying on the couch, tossing the pillows up into the air and trying to catch them with his feet.

"I'm sorry," she said, and those kind words finally prompted James's tears. He cried silently into his hands, rubbing his wet face, trying to hide from his sister's love.

"Did Mom and Dad find out?" she asked quite logically.

"No, I don't think so. I just did it, and now I have to live with it. Coach doesn't know, but I sucked at practice yesterday, and Coach was giving the 'let's keep straight' lecture, looking at me. I don't think I can stay straight. I think I'm fucked up." He rarely used his locker room language with Rachel, but he was just blurting out his thoughts, and they came out simply.

"Is there anything I can do to help? Do you want me to go places with you or something?"

It was a pathetic idea, but it showed how much Rachel cared about him.

"No, I don't think there's anything anyone can do. I think I like this girl Adrienne and even she can't keep me straight. It's like I have to declare my independence from anyone and everyone's rules and controls over me – no matter the cost. I get a good thing going, a nice, pure direction, then I have to take a sharp left, so that people can't pigeonhole me. I don't know." He stopped for a half minute, but Rachel did not intervene. "But then I think again from another angle, and I say, it was just one really stupid night out of twenty-five, and I've been good every other night. So I let it slip one night."

He could tell Rachel wasn't buying his second perspective. "James, I think you need help. If you feel you can't control yourself, don't you think you need help?"

"Rache, you don't understand. When you get older, you'll have this feeling, this feeling that you need to assert yourself in some way that people aren't forcing you into, some path for yourself that you are completely responsible for. It may not look pretty to the other people – it might look self-destructive – but at least it'll be your path. You need to go in a direction that is yours, no one else's, just yours – like your own star moving across the sky."

Rachel nodded, "I understand, I think I do. But the route you take doesn't have to be self-destructive."

"I know," James replied. "And I don't want you to worry about me. I'll be OK, I really will."

Mr. Rush entered the room at that moment, and Rachel hopped out of his recliner, joining James on the couch.

"Pats are winning going away," Rachel told her dad.

James thought about the path he had suggested to Rachel, wondering where his curve ended up.

And then there was Tuesday's game against Milton. James had not expected much, what with his desultory Monday practice and the strength of Milton's forwards. James did like Coach LaMott's defensive plan, to triangle-and-two Bain and Douglas, disguising it as a 2-3. That defensive stratagem accounted for the tight first half, which gave Casteline a chance to grab hold of the game in the end.

What was best about the game was the cohesiveness of the team. James didn't know who accounted for all the points, but he knew that he himself had a lousy shooting night, something like 4 for 13. He did hit a few foul shots late, but, in general, he had a mediocre game offensively. And so did many of his teammates. But they scored now and then off their defense; they scored off a few offensive rebounds. They didn't turn the ball over very much against Milton's stifling man-to-man defense that customarily forced fifteen or more turnovers in the frontcourt. Jason took very good care of the ball, and everyone moved the ball away from pressure.

When the team was moving and sharing the ball so well, the game became very easy. Best of all, James had been able to forget about his personal failure on the weekend in the strain to make the victory happen. It was a real joy to feed Dan on the break late in the third quarter, fulfilling a vague dream the two had shared for a long time. The play was so basic, James felt like Coach LaMott feeding Coach Taft on a Saturday, drawing and dishing, the rudiments.

When there were only twelve seconds left in the game, and Casteline held a five point lead, James trotted over to Dan to give him a congratulatory hug. He was singing inside, the way he felt when he recalled the kiss he and Adrienne had shared, as if he had a soul and it was bursting, or as if he and Dan each had a soul and they were somehow joining their insubstantiality. And after James crushed Dan with a tight hug, Geoff came over to him and lifted him off the ground, making the win official, sealed with the captain's respect.

He only wished he could gush about the game to Adrienne, but too much had happened in the last few days. She wouldn't be able to understand how James could swing so naively from guilt-ridden to proud, from hopeless to elated, based on the outcome of a basketball game. James couldn't understand it either, but he knew that it was true.

Wednesday in English James received an essay assignment, asking him to trace the evolution of the character James Gatz into the newly made Jay Gatsby. James knew the story – impoverished youth who sees opulence in the form of a yacht and invents himself to fulfill his dreams – but Mr. Olson was clear that the students in the room had to demonstrate logically the mental processes that lead to Gatz's self-reinvention. The subject was fascinating to James – he kept his eyes open long enough to take down six page references the class suggested as key passages explaining the changes in Gatz's mental state. The subject of reinvention reminded James of Adrienne's New Year's Eve expostulation on the newness of every moment.

Wednesday night practice was awful, the product of a team coming off a big win over a superior opponent, a team playing without its best player, a team coming to practice at 5:30 at night, after wasting the afternoon accomplishing nothing, and a team that felt they were better than their next opponent, Newton North. To add one more element to the players' disinterest: next Tuesday they were playing Walpole, their annual rival, their Thanksgiving rival. Coach LaMott called the team together after just fifteen minutes of practice on Wednesday.

"OK, guys, I can see that you are not interested in working on skills or in learning about Newton North's offensive sets. I'll say one more time: congratulations on a big win over Milton.

"That's the last time I'm going to congratulate you for that win. Now I am looking to assess your progress in today's practice and your progress in absorbing what Newton North's going to do as a team.

"Geoff, can you help me out here. It seems I'm not getting through."

Geoff moved away from the team, turned, and addressed them. "A win is a win. A loss is a loss. And then we have to move on. I can't sit here and tell you that you're going to lose to North, but with this effort, we wouldn't beat the JVs right now. Let's take five laps, slow to fast, and get our minds back into the idea of getting better. Let's go." Geoff took off slowly, the first two laps always at the pace of slug, trying to store and generate momentum for the final laps.

James trotted slowly, thinking about his 3-point shot that extended Casteline's lead in the third quarter the night before, from a spot about twenty feet from where James was striding right now. He thought also about the hugs he had shared with Dan and Geoff just before the game ended. And he thought of one more hug, after the team huddle, a hug with Pete, a hug of exultation, but also of relief: that the two of them had not fucked up the karma of the team with their self-indulgence.

The rest of practice was more focused, after Coach's exhortation, and in response to further exhortations. Coach knew the tempo of a team, how it responded to wins and losses, and he had the poultice for whatever was hurting the team, especially when it was complacency.

Friday after Geometry James caught up with Adrienne as she scooted out of the room with Lucy.

"Hey, Aide, do you have a minute?" he asked.

Adrienne was hoisting her bookbag over her right shoulder, the black strap falling over the orange sweater, as she turned to address James. "Oh, hey, I didn't see you. What's up?" She acted as if she didn't have time for James.

"I don't know what's up. It seems you're in a big hurry these days. Are you pissed off at me?"

Adrienne shrugged, looking up at the spot where the two walls met the ceiling. "Not at all. I've just been super busy. We had lacrosse last weekend, I've got lots of homework this week, we have a big game with Newton North today, and I'm really hungry and I want to eat my snack. Do you want to come down to the caf and hang out?" She was not accusatory at all in the way she spoke to James, but he knew she had not been anywhere near him during the past week.

They walked together toward the caf, the way they had been walking in the halls before James's Friday night, nudging friends, making over-the-shoulder comments to those they couldn't prod. Finally, they were in the cafeteria, Adrienne with a few minutes of free time, James expected in Chemistry.

Wanting to ask Adrienne if their relationship had changed, James tried to summon the courage to broach the subject. All he could come up with was, "So you're not pissed." It wasn't much of a conversation-opener, not at all. She just shook her head and started talking animatedly about her friends and her team's game with Milton (an easy victory over a weak team). There was nothing to indicate that Adrienne was bothered by anything that had happened.

James finally cut in. "Well, I have to go to class, but I was just wondering why we weren't finding each other in the morning the way we used to. You've been pretty scarce."

Adrienne looked frankly at James. "I've been in all my usual places. Maybe it's because you had your head down for two solid days before the Milton game, and you couldn't see anything other than people's boots." Adrienne's eyes shone brilliantly, a gray/green in the bright light that suffused the cafeteria. "I'm always ready for company."

And it was that simple. He had never met anyone so capable of starting each day with a clear perspective, so incapable of harboring resentment or even annoyance. James wanted to squeeze Adrienne the way he had squeezed Dan at the conclusion of Tuesday's game, but he didn't think it was the time or the place for such a gesture. So he pulled Adrienne toward him to allow for a demure embrace, which she shared. He said, "I gotta run, but I'm glad we talked. I'll call you after the game."

"I've heard that before," she smiled and sat down again to eat her peach.

How many dreams
you've chased
Across sand and sky and gravel
Looking for one safe place

Will you make a smoother landing
When you break your fall from grace
Into the arms of understanding
Looking for one safe place

Life is trial by fire
And love's the sweetest taste
And I pray it lifts us higher
To one safe place

How many roads we've traveled
How many dreams we've chased
Across sand and sky and gravel
Looking for one safe place

One Safe Place by Marc Cohn

Ben

As Ben picked up Willa after church on Sunday, he told her of his interest in working at Willow's, knowing he was expected for training that night.

"Hey, hon, I've got a job opportunity that I'm going to pursue, to see if I like it." He left the off-hand remark lie out there like a puffy cloud in an open sky.

Willa turned to him, her eyes querulous. "What on earth are you talking about? What job?" She unbuttoned the top two buttons of her wool coat, as if she had suddenly become hot.

"Well, I've been at Willow's a few times with Bryan, as you know, and there was an ad for a bartender one night a week. I thought I'd give it a try. I've always liked the warm, homey atmosphere there. A few extra dollars would be nice." He glanced over his right shoulder as he turned toward Mary's Dunkin Donuts, to say hi.

Willa shook her head. "Are you serious? What are you going to bring home, forty dollars? For a night out? I don't understand what you're trying to do here."

Ben shrugged his shoulders. "I guess I'm just trying to diversify. Who knows? Maybe it'll be a retirement job down the road. No harm giving it a try, is there?"

They turned into the drive-through of the Dunkin Donuts. "Uh, hello, could I please have a plate of steak and eggs?" Ben asked, expecting a giggle from his listener.

"Uh, we don't have that on our menu," a friendly but unfamiliar female voice replied. "Can I help you with something on our menu?"

"Oops! I'm sorry. I thought Mary LaMott was working the window. This is her dad. We'll have two coffees, one regular, one black with sugar. Thanks."

At the window, Mary handed them their coffees, and Ben exchanged them for a ten dollar bill. "Keep the change, please, from the FIVE," Ben said, for the benefit of the surveillance cameras that recorded all transactions (who reviewed those tapes? he wondered). "Thanks, honey. We'll see you at home at 3."

"Hey, Dad, Geoff Willis came by. I didn't know he ever came to Summit. He was with a couple of guys I didn't know. We talked

283

about the game for a minute. He said you guys played OK, but not good enough to win."

"Yeah, it was a close one, but didn't end up in the win column. Thanks for the report. I'll continue to use you as my spy. Do you mind working at the local package stores and infiltrating the drug dealers' scene, just to give me a complete picture?"

"No problem. I'm friends with all of them already. I'll just have to wear a wire more often."

"Bye, hon. See you later."

Willa called, "Call if you have any plans. See you for supper," across Ben, as he started to pull away.

The conversation with Mary had interrupted Ben and Willa's discussion of Ben's plans. As Willa opened the lids of the two coffees, handing the black one to Ben, Ben resumed his explanation. "I'm just training tonight, with one of the experienced bartenders. Tomorrow night I'll take my first shift, with the same guy. Hours are 5 to 10:30 tonight, 6:30 to 1:00 on Monday." Thinking about the long hours on Monday, Ben thought about the absurdity of his new venture, yet he still looked forward to the opportunity.

"Well, I think it's great for you to be pursuing something that seems to interest you, but I just wonder about the people that hang at a bar all the time. I mean, aren't they a bunch of drunks? I know you don't have any problem with alcohol, and you and I are lucky in that regard, but it just seems the whole ethos of the place is skewed." A disgusted look captured her face.

"Actually, when I've stopped over with Bryan, it's seemed kind of homey and embracing. I'm hoping that's the atmosphere. If it's a dive, with people slurring their words and becoming belligerent, I won't do it. I'm not looking for aggravation; it's more I'm looking for something gratifying."

Willa sipped her coffee quietly, contemplating another comment, but she refrained. She sighed instead. Ben understood.

With Scott at Holly's for the early afternoon, Ben and Willa entered the house, Ben eager to relax a little before he worked on the essays he needed to correct. On TV the Patriots were playing their final regular season game, as Willa read the Globe with moderate interest and Ben entered the game stats from the Newton North game into his spreadsheet program, cumulating season's totals as he entered game stats. Dan Owings and Archie Stedham had led the team with 15 points apiece, providing a strong perimeter game, but the Panthers had accomplished nothing inside, shut down primarily by North's 6'7" big man, who had blocked six shots and shut down any inside game. Geoff Willis had totaled 3 points. Final score: Newton North 57, Casteline 51. James Rush had had an abysmal game: 2 for 12 for 7 points, with 3 turnovers. Ben had kept James on the bench down the stretch, he was so unproductive. James's ineffectiveness perplexed Ben: just a week ago, James had struck for 24 points, and he had contributed to the big win over Milton. But he was out of it on Friday.

From the couch, Willa asked, over her glasses, "Do you want some lunch? We've got chicken salad, or there's pastrami in the frig."

Ben nodded. "Either one. I think the chicken salad sounds great. Got any chips?"

Willa rose and headed into the kitchen. Ben reached over to his backpack, removing his folder of essays from his sophomores. With the Pats' game on in the background, he turned to the first essay, covering the heading so he didn't know the identity of the writer, in his attempt at objectivity. Over the years he had saved a good collection of student essays, which he used as models for the students he was teaching presently. He always hoped, and offered that hope to his students, that one of the essays he was correcting would be interesting enough to add to his long-term store.

When Willa came back in with the sandwich, he made room in his lap for the plate. She seemed to be hovering near him. It reminded him of their earlier years of marriage, when they spent much of their time together. On a Sunday afternoon, they would often return to the bedroom for unhurried and unfettered lovemaking. In fact, he would be willing to set aside these essays for just such a return to form.

Looking at Willa, as he finished a bite of her sandwich, he asked, "Do you want me to put these essays aside for a little while?" She gave him a sympathetic look, as if she acknowledged his patience.

"You know I'd love to, but we don't know when Scott will be home, honey. Maybe it can wait a little while? Hold that thought, OK?" She smiled at him, the memory of the coquette brushing her face.

Ben persisted. "Well, you know we don't have to make love on the kitchen table. We can lock the door and still enjoy each other's company."

Willa looked at him, indecision on her face. "It sounds great; but I don't know. Can't it wait?"

Ben couldn't help but let out an expulsion of air. "Of course it can wait. It can wait until the summer." He hated to lose his patience so easily, hated to be so readily hurt by Willa's indifference, but he couldn't help it. He sighed deeply and turned back to his folder. He didn't want to look at Willa, for fear that she would see the way his jaw muscles were clenched.

Ben's first night at Willow's proved to be as interesting as Ben had hoped, busy but manageable. Pete Amoroso proved to be a kind teacher, patient and very skilled at both mixing drinks and making his customers feel well attended.

"First priority: the customer feels at home. Whatever it takes. The game on TV has to be loud enough to draw attention, but not too loud to disrupt conversations. The drinks have to be next to their hand, but not as if we are pushing liquor down their throat. It's like every customer is a date, and your job is to make her feel special and wanted. The hard part is to have twenty separate dates at the same time. Quite a juggling act. Of course, if they're happy, they don't even notice you spending time with other dates, because they're talking with friends or watching the replay on the TV.

"Do you think you can treat her right?" Pete asked metaphorically.

Ben had always had an easy time chatting with people, strangers or friends both, as long as he was in a good mood himself, which was usually the case. On this night, he worked extra hard to establish a line of communication with anyone who looked as if he wanted one.

"Second priority: keep the bar neat looking. One glass per customer. Keep the nut bowls filled. Clean up the slop, get it below bar level. The lower back counter can be a mess, but the bar is ready for a photo op. They want to feel they're in a place where someone is taking care of them. Looks go a long way. And for the new customer coming in the door, there's a welcome spot at the bar for them."

It all made sense to Ben. As the night wore on, Pete spent more and more time cleaning up, stocking, and preparing orders for the next week, allowing Ben to work out front.

There were also seven tables away from the bar, the tables where Ben, Bryan, and Lisa had spent a few evenings. When he had the bar customers all set up, Ben went out to the small tables, with tall stools for two, in most cases, and attended to their orders. After attending to the bar for another round, he moved out to the far table, to take the order of a couple that had been sitting for five minutes.

As Ben approached, the man, in his early thirties, casually dressed, said loudly, "Oh, you serve drinks here too? I thought it was just a place to watch a game. Well, honey, what do you know? They might take our order!"

Ben smiled graciously. "Sorry for the delay. What can I do for you? What would you like?"

The man continued in his contempt for the serving person who happened to be in front of him. "Well, you might start with a menu." The man's date took his rudeness in stride.

Ben turned back to the bar. "No problem. Be right back." He knew there were angry people in Natick, but he had hoped they wouldn't find the need to drink at Willow's. But, of course, angry people often found the need to drink. As he turned the corner to the back of the bar, Pete moved toward him.

"I'll keep an eye on you with that couple. I'm sure you can handle them, and you have to learn to put up with the assholes. But I've got your back if you need me." He kept his head down as he spoke, stacking glasses in the dishwasher.

Bringing the menus back, Ben asked, "Do you want to start with something from the bar or from the kitchen?" in a voice that tried to show that he was establishing a clean slate.

"Well, do you think we'd come here for the food?"

Ben almost laughed out loud. "Well, believe it or not, I've eaten here without the aid of an alcoholic haze. The food's very high end bar food, to be honest. Can I make a suggestion?" Ben loved the challenge this man represented.

"Are you suggesting that I'm an alcoholic? Hey, bartender," the man exclaimed, seeking Pete's attention. "Your new guy here said I'm an alcoholic." Now belligerence was creeping into his voice, as if he were hoping the confrontation would escalate.

Pete yelled back, "Let's keep it simple, Ronnie. Either make an order or get out. I know it's just Sunday night, but we still have to be civil here. Maybe you're in an unservable condition?"

Ronnie shouted back, "No, you know I don't drink anywhere but here. So in fact I'm stone cold sober. It's just that you have hired an idiot. I hope you know that."

Ben stood to the side, since Pete and Ronnie had a history that needed reviewing at the moment.

Pete responded, "That's OK, Ronnie. Just don't let the door slam on your way out. Ben, we've got some customers here at the bar that need your attention. Ronnie, maybe we'll see you tomorrow night. Good night." Even from forty feet away, Ben could see that Pete was inflexible in his assessment of Ronnie's condition. Ben didn't know whether to add a "Sorry, sir," but he did not want to undermine Pete's authority, so he abandoned the vituperative man and returned to the comfort of the bar, where he refilled glasses and tallied up two bar bills.

287

It seemed his tips were a little larger than he expected from these two customers, one woman and one man, each single, the result, no doubt, of their sympathy for him in his dealings with Ronnie and his date.

After the couple left, Ronnie spewing his rant, his date walking just as haughtily, apparently seeing things from Ronnie's point of view, Ben had time to visit the other outlying tables, taking a few food orders, replenishing drinks as often as he could. Though it was a very slow Sunday night, he never had a moment to rest. He ignored his customers for two short trips to the bathroom.

The pace was steady, and Pete interacted with Ben as often as he needed to, serving some customers when Ben was overwhelmed, backing off when Ben had things under control. "The guys at the crook of the bar: they don't need any more," Pete said, his face turned toward the kitchen. "If they ask for another round, tell 'em we're a responsible tavern. Be nice but be firm." Pete moved into the kitchen, checking for any more food orders to bring out.

Ben kept an eye on the group of five that hovered around the Keno sheets, watching the screen for winning number loudly. They were boisterous but kind-hearted. When Ben turned down their final request for beers, they gave him a little guff, but backed off without any rancor. They kept betting every five minutes as they finished their last beers.

At the 10:00 closing, Pete came out to show Ben the final cleanup, wiping everything down, as the final fifteen patrons filed out, most of them shouting "G'night" over their shoulders to Pete. He waved silently, growling a response. He was a gruff man; it seemed he had spent many, many years in the business, his big hands and slow, his rocking gait perfectly suited to his tasks. They were cleaned up by 10:45. Pete emptied the tip jar, counting out $104.00 and handing it to Ben.

"Oh no, I'm the apprentice. I'm not going to steal your tips. I'm here to make your life easier, not poorer. It's all yours." He held his arms out determinedly. Pete tried to push the bills into Ben's pocket, but he backed away. "Honest. I can't take it. It's your money. I couldn't work here if I needed to depend on your good heart. When I work a real shift, I can take my share, but not tonight." He knew he couldn't earn Pete's respect if he took the money.

They gave each other a bump on the shoulder as they met the outside air when they finally left. "See you tomorrow night," Pete said. "When can you get here?"

"I'm practicing till 5:30. I can get here by 6, but let's make it 6:15, just so you don't have to start looking for me."

288

He hopped into his Corolla, the sound of classical music greeting him when he turned on the car, activating the radio.

Walpole had been the Panthers' primary rival ever since Ben began his time at Casteline; in fact, the two teams had played many bitterly fought games well before Ben began his coaching career. The two teams had always played on a Friday night, marking the halfway mark of the season and the finale. This year the half-way game happened to fall on a Tuesday, but, for Ben, it still held more weight than any other game. In Ben's first fifteen or so years, he had had Walpole's number, winning seven league titles to Walpole's two, and beating the Walpole Rebels' about two-thirds of the time. However, the balance of power had shifted in the past ten years, Walpole winning four recent league titles to Ben's one, and winning about that same two-thirds of the games. Walpole's success – and Casteline's mediocrity – was the greatest source of Ben's frustration in coaching. He had always taken great pride in defeating the school's rival; the graduates who came back to see him always asked about the Walpole game, as a litmus test of the Panthers' strength. Recently, he felt that Walpole had found a better way of developing players than he did, and he took the difference personally.

So, Tuesday's game with Walpole was a benchmark for him. Facing them without Andrew Monaghan was daunting. They featured a great shooter, Peter Kennedy; a talented ball-handler, Rob Evans; and two solid rebounders. Ben saw their defense as their weakness. He would try to exploit it by having his perimeter players put the ball on the floor. It would come down to the Panthers' ability to hit jump shots off the dribble.

For a Tuesday night, the Walpole gym was pretty full, probably four hundred fans, including the Rebel Gang, a band of young, primarily male, supporters who were not afraid to shout their objections to the referee or their criticisms of their opposing individual players. The warm-up music made for a perfect setting, loud and tingling. When the music stopped for the Star Spangled Banner, Ben stared through the flag as he did in every gym, considering not the blood shed for this nation's freedom, but rather, the effort shed in preparation for this game. His eyes moving quickly horizontally, he counted the stars, finding fifty, then counted them again diagonally, coming to the same count. After the Anthem, his final pre-game words were forceful and direct: "Beat them to every loose ball, on the floor and on the boards. Make them wish they hadn't let us into this gym tonight." There was something about this rivalry that reminded Ben of what combat must be like.

For the first four minutes, the Panthers dominated in every facet, taking a 14 – 2 lead. Andreas Pinson, who had missed four games, two on vacation and two more for missing those games, had played a growing role in the games against Milton and North. Ben started him to provide Geoff with assistance holding off Walpole's two rugged rebounders, and the move seemed just right: Andreas had three early hoops and four rebounds. Jason was circumspect with the ball on the break, feeding for two easy baskets and pulling the ball out wisely when he had nothing. No turnovers.

After Walpole's time-out, they crept back; the quarter score was 17 – 13. By halftime the game had become what it should: tight as a collar on an old shirt. 34 – 33 Walpole.

Ben's halftime speech in the locker room was impassioned, more than normal, the product of the tension he felt playing this Walpole team that had taken what had once been his: local supremacy. His players felt it too. Most of them traveled the short distance to Walpole to eat their pizza and fast food. They bought their cell phones in Walpole, their ice cream; they got their haircuts there. They understood Ben's emotion.

Geoff stood up. "Look, guys. This is my last time in this gym. We've played here about eight times, going back to youth basketball. Have we won one?" There was no response. That was a No. "I'm not going home with another loss in this gym. We need to get that in our heads. Jason, Alex, Jonas – don't get up off these benches if you don't plan on winning." His voice became more and more strained as he fought back the emotion of the moment. Andrew stood up proudly. "I'm with you, Geoff," though he was clad in jacket and tie.

And Geoff's passion gave the team the same lift that Ben's had at the start; Casteline took a 55 – 45 lead at the end of three. Archie and Dan played great off the bench, and Geoff and Andreas continued to dominate their Walpole counterparts.

As expected, the Rebels made a strong comeback, knocking the lead down to three with under a minute to go. Bryan looked at Ben to see whether a time-out was coming, but Ben, as usual, kept the team on the floor, forcing them to find a way to win – or lose. Jason expertly ran the clock down with two precise passes to beat double-teams. With 31 seconds left, James took a bounce pass from Jason and put up a balanced 18 footer, a shot he had to take, with the shot clock near 0. The ball hit front rim, bounced high and came down in the hands of one of the Rebel rebounders, who outletted to Evans, who pushed it to set up Kennedy for a good look at the 3-point line. He hit it with 18 seconds to go, tying the game.

Now the gym could expect a time-out – but Ben did not relent. As the Walpole players relaxed, one of them even heading toward the bench. Geoff took the ball out, threw it in to Jason, who could see James and Archie running the wings. Andreas stood in the middle of the court, a target if Jason needed one. But when Jason put the ball on the floor, Andreas moved to the sideline, a trailer on Archie's side. Archie and James ran below the foul line, then crossed underneath the rim, as Andreas filled the right lane as a trailer, with an open lane as the wings ran to the 3 point line after their baseline cross. Jason pulled the ball left, looking at James, who drew defensive attention. Andreas came through toward the rim, expecting a pass from Jason, but Jason cannily held on for another two seconds, allowing Andreas to pull the last defender through with him. With five seconds to go, Jason hit Geoff, the second trailer, who had a clear slot to the rim. All Walpole's defenders could do was foul him, and they did. He went to the line with two seconds on the clock.

Geoff hit the first, then missed the second intentionally, allowing Walpole to gather the rebound as the final horn sounded. The Rebel Gang was silent; the Casteline stands were pandemonic, claiming their first win at Walpole in four years. Geoff and his seniors had claimed their first victory at Walpole in their lives.

In the middle circle, Ben shouted some words that might make sense and might not; the important thing was the hands together, the "1 . . . 2. . . .3" "TIGHT."

The Arc of Intersection

I once loved a woman, better than I ever seen
I once loved a woman, better than I ever seen
Treat me like I was a king and she was a doggone queen

from *Statesboro Blues* by Blind Willie McTell

James

The win over Walpole was the greatest game in which James had ever been involved – better than the win over Milton, though Milton was a better opponent. It's just that Walpole was the nemesis, the perpetual reason that Casteline never succeeded. It was always Walpole that got the local newspaper coverage, Walpole players who had special features written about them. Just before Christmas, Wally Post, the long-time sports feature writer of the Metrowest News, had written a laudatory story on Peter Kennedy and Rob Evans, Walpole's dynamic pair of seniors who each were completing successful careers. As James read the article, he couldn't help but feel envious of their local fame.

But with two smartly directed foul shots, Geoff had temporarily halted Walpole's claim of superiority. Wednesday morning's newspaper featured a photo of Jason dribbling up the left side of the court, in front of the Casteline bench (Pete visible in the midst), trailed by Rob Evans. The article, which was the primary local story, told of a team full of passion and opportunism, a team generating its own chances to score, despite its lesser record. A game like this one confirmed James's long-held desire to play basketball for Casteline High School and Coach LaMott.

Wednesday was a review day for exams, which began on Thursday and continued until Monday. The review in Mr. Tilson's room was lively: Mr. Tilson had constructed a lesson plan that forced each student to go to the board to demonstrate one principle that had been introduced during the semester. James was seventh to go to the board; his topic was the proportion between an increase in the radius and an increase in the area of a circle. He knew his stuff.

But first, James had the pleasure of listening to six of his classmates reviewing other principles: vertical angles, perpendicular bisector, exterior angles, area of a trapezoid. As his classmates were called to the board, he knew their identity because Mr. Tilson called their name, but he tried to picture their graphic demonstration (silent because the markers the students used slid so easily on the whiteboard – Mr. Tilson, in his old school way, still used the chalk on the green board) on the board as they spoke haltingly on their subject.

Lucy's topic was determining the length of diagonal bisectors in a regular cube. When she had arrived at the board, Lucy said, as she drew, "Here's the cube . . . wait a minute, that's too long . . . Here's the cube. Now here's the midpoint of this line. Here's the midpoint of that line. Can you see how there's a line that lies along the bottom of the cube? Let me draw that line, that diagonal on the bottom surface.

"Wait a minute, let's call each line one inch long."

Mr. Tilson intervened, "One inch? What about two units, for each line, because we're going to be bisecting that length to one unit."

"OK, that's right, two units. We use two because it's so easy to divide in two. Now you can see that this diagonal must be . . . let's see . . . (James could picture her diagram clearly; the diagonal on the bottom plane would be radical 2) . . ." Lucy halted in her progress, perhaps needing a calculator. At that point James stopped listening, choosing, instead, to try to pick up on Pete's daily attempt to impress the young lady seated in front of him, Kate Sloan. Since the first week of school, Pete had continued to entertain her, but he had had to increase his animation considerably since he lost his license and the concomitant Audi that had served as an effective bargaining chip. James couldn't hear Pete's distinct words, but he could hear the saccharine patter he devised, a rhythm not unlike the hiphop lyrics they both enjoyed. James could hear a few muffled giggles, signs that Pete's charm was finding fallow soil.

"Mr. Rush, are you prepared to show us the proportional increasing of radius and area?"

James's eyes snapped open underneath his BC hat, as he strode up to the board, passing Adrienne en route. He turned at the board, resetting his cap so his classmates could see his eyes, then proceeded to demonstrate the principle, using a tripling factor, showing that the ensuing larger area would be nine times the initial one. He then quickly used three other pairings, to show that the increase in area would be the square of the increasing constant. James actually enjoyed the responsibility of instructing his peers. "So the thing to remember is this: if radius is increased (or diminished) by a certain factor, the area is increased (or diminished) by the square (or square root) of that factor. It only makes sense because of the exponent of 2 that is affixed to the 'r' in the basic formula." When James was finished, he looked at Adrienne, who had a grin on her face, acknowledging the fact that James had surprised the class with his acumen.

Adrienne was assigned the task of showing that an angle bisector at the vertex of an isosceles triangle would be a perpendicular bisector of the base. James suspended his visual boycott to watch her walk to the board, maize skirt swaying sensually as it brushed the tops of her long black boots – very fashionable, it seemed. Her hair was held up on her head by a pencil stuck in as a clip – James had no idea about the physics of that hair arrangement, but it showed her strong neck nicely as she took the seven steps boardward, skirting Mr. Tilson's desk with a hand just brushing its corner to redirect her stride. All in all Adrienne's trip to the board seemed like a languid ballet, even though she was just taking a few steps in a Geometry class.

Adrienne's explanation worked its way smoothly from drawing to analysis to conjecture to conclusion, just the way a math or science teacher would like it. When she returned to her seat, she mouthed to James, "OK?" as she grinned broadly.

Each class held a review session on Wednesday; then it was studying time at home. No practice until Friday afternoon; no game on Friday because of the school's focus on exams. James had become used to the opportunity that this exam period afforded him to catch up on the ideas that had been explored in each subject area. The only area where he felt unprepared was in US History, where he had hundreds of names and dates to acquire and correlate. His natural intelligence would help only so much with Mrs. Tallent, his history teacher.

James stood up from his desk at home at about 9:00 Wednesday night, after studying for a few hours in the afternoon and again in the evening. He felt prepared for Chemistry and Spanish, his two exams on Thursday. Stretching his tired back, he walked into the family room and called Adrienne, to see how she was doing with her studying.

"Hello?" she answered.

"Hey, can I ask you something? What's your cell number?"

"447-866-9291."

"Wait a minute, wait a minute. I need to put that in my cell phone. Can you say it again slowly?"

After Adrienne did so, James sat down on the couch, his feet up on the coffee table. His dad watched the Bruins with the sound turned down low. "Are you all set for tomorrow?" he asked.

"Yeah, I've got it covered. I spend a little time each weekend from Christmas on going over my notes, so it's just review right now. I'm OK. If I don't get A's, I'm OK with that – hey, you guys kicked Walpole's butt, huh? What was it like in the gym?"

James lay back even more on the couch. "Oh, it was just the way you'd picture it: final shot goes in and the gym is silent. Geoff hit the foul shot that won it, off a great feed from Jason. It was textbook."

He could hear a level of awe in Adrienne's voice as he pushed the phone against his left cheek. "Must have been chilling. I get that

295

feeling in state level games in lacrosse. Everything matters, and you just do the right thing – not even a second thought." Adrienne paused to let her empathetic response sink in. "So, are you back on line?"

James shook his head silently, making his lips a thin line, like the crack that he knew reached across the ceiling of the family room (he opened his eyes to confirm his visual memory). "Not exactly. I'm contributing, but I'm not even close to leading the way. I'm definitely a step behind right now. I can't connect it logically to that Friday night, but it's definitely been since then. It's as if there's a God watching, and He's not letting me catch a break."

Adrienne disagreed. "It's not a God watching. It's you. You have to feel you deserve the success. As long as you keep the image of your failure in your mind, you're doomed – even if it's a moral failure – *especially* if it's a moral failure. I mean I'm a religious person, but I don't think God would bother to affect the shooting accuracy of one immature teenager. He's got famines and wars and epidemics to address. No, you just won't let yourself off the hook. And you have good reason not to: you completely failed yourself. You failed your parents; you failed your team. You shouldn't feel the self-assurance you felt just a couple weeks ago. But you have to start building it up again. You have to enjoy the game."

James nodded. "Yeah, you're right. Remember when I was sitting on the sideline at the beginning of the year, and I could see the plays so easily, and I felt I was learning so much? Now, I can't get back to that same objectivity. I'm too worried about returning to form."

"I know exactly what you mean. If you try to accomplish something personal and specific, you won't do it. You have to just get into the flow and let your instincts come back to you. But let me make one little suggestion: if you mess up again, you might not be able to overcome that one. There's only so much distress one ego can overcome."

James nodded again. "Yeah, I can feel that. It serves as a little reminder to stay straight. Speaking of which, what are you doing Friday night?" A game-less Friday night seemed like a perfect time to take Adrienne out, maybe give her the Christmas present he had bought her.

"I haven't thought that far ahead, but if you're asking me out, I'm up for it. But I'm not going to a party, let's rule that out right now."

James rubbed his head against the cushions of the couch. "I'll come up with a plan. Of course you're gonna have to provide some Wranglin transportation, but, if you can't, I think Dan might be able to help."

Adrienne cut in, "The Wrangler is temporarily out of commission. There's something wrong with the electrical system, I think. We're getting it looked at next week. But my mom's car might work."

"Great. So Friday night's on, right?"

"Yep."

"I'll see you after exams tomorrow. Good luck."

The conversation over, James leaped up the stairs three at a time (there were only six to the upper level of the split-level in which the Rushes lives), stumbling onto the carpeted stairs when he landed short by the length of his arch. But he was leaning forward so much, he just propelled himself to the top with just the slightest hesitation.

He even spent another half hour grinding Chem. formulas into his head.

After exams on Friday, James joined his teammates in the gym at 4:15 for their first practice since Walpole. They were spirited and talkative, having missed each other for two days. The routine of being with each other six days a week generated a closeness that was slightly dispelled at exam break.

Coach LaMott called them together after a lengthy warmup. "All right, guys, let's see whether that win over Walpole was real. At this point we have five wins and six losses. But let's look at a very bright picture: we have two wins over our three toughest opponents, Milton, Braintree, and Walpole. That speaks to our ability to rise to the occasion and just play the game the way it needs to be played. I'm very proud of our effort in all our games. Let's build on it. We have three practices to get our timing back, to prepare ourselves for the second half of the season, and to get on a roll that can carry us into the post-season.

"It's been a little while since we played tournament ball. This team should expect a post-season, even though Andrew will probably not be ready for it. But let's plan for his return, OK? Let's get to the post-season, then add an all-league player to our lineup, OK?" Coach raised his voice with this last question, and the team responded emphatically, led by Geoff: "Come on, it's in our hands!" James felt the emotion, but he couldn't voice it.

James pushed himself through the conditioning drills, trying to regain the life he had felt in his legs in early January, when he was rejoining the starting lineup. In three on three cross court, James, Andreas, and Archie dominated two other teams, winning each game by a wide margin. Archie seemed to have endless energy, always

297

pressuring his man defensively, ready to change defense-to-offense in an instant, ending up with easy layups as a result.

With about half an hour left in practice, Coach set up an offense-defense 5 on 5, first team on defense. He called Jason, Dan, Archie, Geoff, and Mark out on the first team defense. He didn't say anything to James, but he put him with the second team offense. James kept his head down after he heard the lineups, unwilling to make eye contact with Dan or Pete, who would be raising their eyebrows questioningly. James played as hard as he could, wanting to prove Coach wrong, but knowing that if he tried to play to impress him, he would reduce his productivity. He remembered his conversation with Adrienne, stressing the need to get into the flow. It didn't really matter who his teammates were; he just needed to let his instincts loose.

Of course, James was covering either Dan or Archie, one of whom had supplanted him in the lineup – Archie, probably. This knowledge gave him just a little more quickness than usual on defense, and he found himself taking away the outside shot of either one, without letting him by on the drive. Dan, especially, he could give a little cushion to, because his shot was a little suspect.

Eight-minute scrimmage, full court, switching defenses, no substitutions. A great conditioner, and real game situation. Score on the board: 53 – 49 2nd team ahead, at the start of the Bridget-manned clock. James ran the floor relentlessly, looking for easy baskets ahead of the defense, but Alex White, his point guard, didn't have Jason's court vision, so James didn't get any easy looks there. In the half-court he looked for good screens from Andreas, with and without the ball, and, using this assistance shrewdly and repeatedly, he was able to get some open looks. And James kept down-screening for Mark, looking for another down screen from Alex. With this movement, James was getting the ball at the top of the key, able to reverse it to Jonas for an easy entry to the post.

After a lot of frustration at making sound plays, but not getting any reward for it, there were 17 seconds left, the first team leading 62 – 60. Coach was calling fouls, but all fouls were non-shooting fouls, team just taking the ball out-of-bounds with a stopped clock. The first team had the ball, and the 2nd team had to make a defensive play to get the ball back. James and Alex doubled Jason, who easily beat the trap to get the ball to Dan, who drove the lane, feeding off to Geoff, who had an easy look – until Andreas came over to block the shot, the ball dropping into Bobbie's hands, who pivoted up-court, seeing Alex in the front-court unguarded. A quick pass off the dribble and the game was tied, with four seconds left. Archie called a quick timeout, and the first team had the ball underneath its own basket.

Coach shouted, "Good time-out, Archie. Get the ball in – no huddle. Let's see what you got."

Geoff took the ball out, looking for Jason at the near foul line. Mark went to halfcourt, but both Dan and Archie tried to set a screen for Jason, bringing their defensive men into the backcourt, filling up the space. At about a four-count, Geoff threw a bounce-pass to a spot that Dan was cutting back to, but Bobbie was in the passing lane, knocking it off Dan's leg. 2nd team's ball, two seconds to go. Andreas took the ball out as Bobbie and Alex set a double for James – but he backcut the screen, taking Andreas's lob pass and making a bankshot for the win. He ran to Andreas, slapping hands with him. "YEAH," they shouted in that low, guttural voice that accompanies male victory.

Three scrimmages later, James's exuberance had collapsed in fatigue, but through all four scrimmages James played to his ability, clearly leading whatever team he was on to a competitive level. The games were fun. He gained in his defensive smarts covering Dan and Archie, because they moved so easily and effortlessly without the ball, like Rip Hamilton or Ray Allen. James wore down in the last scrimmage, but so did all the players. After the first scrimmage, Coach mixed the lineups up, bringing James to play with the starters sometimes, having Jason play with the second team too. But James remembered Coach's initial lineup, and took it as a fact.

After practice, Coach pulled James aside. "I think I'm going to go with this lineup for a little while. You've lost some of that spurt you had when you came back from your suspension, and both Dan and Archie are playing lights out. It'd be great to have you coming off the bench, ready to attack with fresh legs. You OK with it?"

James looked at Coach LaMott's whistle. "Absolutely. I think it's the right move. I'll make a difference." He believed exactly what he said.

"That's great. I'm glad you're mature enough to handle it. I'm just trying to get the best out of every player. I think both Archie and Dan deserve to start, and I'm going to give it a chance. Great practice today. See you tomorrow."

James said, "See you tomorrow, Coach," thankful for Coach's directness.

"Oh, and one last thing: no more screwing around for you. OK?" Coach looked at James with a challenge on his face, as if he was asking for a one-on-one with him.

James walked back toward Coach LaMott, answering his challenge. "You got it. I understand."

As James walked away, a spring still in his step, he silently thanked Coach LaMott for looking out for him.

Unable to locate a ride to the T stop in Newton, James sheepishly had to call Adrienne at suppertime on Friday, to ask her for a ride.

Adrienne said, "Sorry, my lame mom needs her car. But I have a friend – you might know her – Lucy?"

Lucy's contribution to New Year's Eve had earned her a beloved place in James's incipient romantic world. "I think she might work, if she doesn't mind. Doesn't she have a life of her own?"

"Oh, her life is very full, don't worry. But she's just a great friend, too."

"I'll see if Dan can help on the other end, coming home. What time?"

"Six-thirty?"

"How about six?"

"Great."

James walked his left hand up the wall to the ceiling as he hung up the phone, trying to anticipate the exact moment when his index finger would touch the rough texture of the ceiling. He missed the intersecting moment by about two inches, maybe less.

Lucy and Adrienne picked James up in Lucy's family's BMW X-5, spacious and luxurious. James slid into the back seat, feeling like a little boy heading to the ice cream stand with his parents.

Lucy asked, "And where are you two crazy kids headed this evening?" in a decidedly maternal voice.

James coyly answered, "Well, let's just see how the evening evolves, OK, Mom?" Adrienne looked as radiant as he had ever seen her, as she looked over her shoulder at him.

The ride in on the T brought them to Copley, where James indicated they should disembark. He led Adrienne up to the street level, where they walked a short distance in the balmy late-January darkness to a coffee shop he had visited a couple times. "Just to get us started, have you eaten dinner?"

Shaking her head, Adrienne preceded James into the small diner, where they ordered the simplest of meals. James stared at Adrienne in her long white sleeved shirt and deep green woolen jumper, the color reflected in her soft eyes. She looked like a college girl, the kind he would see on the side streets around Harvard when he and Pete checked out the Harvard Square scene. The long argyle socks seemed almost too collegiate.

After fish and chips, James squired Adrienne to a coffee house in the South End, where he had read there would be a local act playing. He had never heard of the name, Antje Duvekot, but she sounded entertaining, and she did not let him down. Her voice was a little haunting, melodious with a tinge of melancholy. As she ached with her words, James felt his breath shorten; when he looked at Adrienne, she glowed with the same emotion. During a brief intermission, during which Adrienne went to the back of the small room to pour two cups of tea, James brought out his gift, the necklace, placing it on the table where they sat. When Adrienne returned to the table, placing the cups of tea down, she looked at the wrapped box.

"What's this?" she inquired, surprised.

"Just something I thought you'd like."

Opening it eagerly, Adrienne took the necklace out of the box, admiring it, then placed it in front of her neck, dangling the two gold curving figures in front of her. "I think it's beautiful. Such soft curves."

James proudly said, "It's two parts of a heart. When you attach them, they form a heart." Looking more closely, Adrienne found the tiny clasps and merged the two pieces into a unified figure. "Wow, that's even more beautiful. I'm blown away. That is really nice of you. I love it. Thank you." She stood to lean toward James to give him a kiss on the mouth. He held on to the kiss as long as he could.

"You're welcome. When I saw it, I thought of you." He wanted to ask what the heart might mean to Adrienne, but he refrained.

As she sat down, Adrienne held onto James's hand, and they took sips of tea and held hands for the second act of Antje Duvekot. One of her last songs told the sad story of a modern-day Judas Iscariot, who sat in the back of the bus and developed a resentment that resulted in a school shooting. James had actually heard the song on the radio a few times, though he never noted the singer's name. "That's a great song," he murmured to Adrienne when it finished, sadly.

Adrienne sighed. "There's a lot of sadness, isn't there? I've been reading this book by a guy named Russell Banks, *Continental Drift*. Just a sad world that many people try to survive in." As she looked into James's eyes, his heart pounded.

He wanted to hold her, but he settled for squeezing her hand tightly, a tiny offering compared to the emotion he was feeling. "I have to say: I'm not feeling any of that sadness right now. This song, this place, you – there's all beauty here right now."

Ms. Duvekot began her final song at that moment, muffling Adrienne's response. The acoustic guitar was amped so that James could hear her fingers as they slid on the metal strings, bringing an unintended back rhythm to her song. James could not concentrate on her words, the wholeness of the place filling him like a balloon. He stared at Adrienne, taking in her rapt profile; after a minute, she turned and returned his gaze, eye to eye contact, pulling them together bravely. James had never felt such attraction. The heart lay between the crisp collars of her white shirt, centered between the two thin bones that rose from her chest, the thin cord climbing around her soft neck, only to disappear underneath the hair that lay softly against her back. James stood awkwardly to kiss her, his back bent, his hands on the table almost knocking it over in its imbalance.

James had arranged for Dan to pick them up at Woodland Station at 11:00; he called Dan as they boarded the train in Boston. Dan assured James he would meet them in twenty minutes. At the Woodland stop, when James and Adrienne got off the train, hand in hand, Dan's Escort sat, exhaust streaming out the tailpipe, Joyce lying back in the passenger seat, the light from the pole illuminating her striped pants, leaving her upper body and face in a shadow. She reached to open her door. Dan called over her, "Well, here's the happy couple, swinging arms and holding hands as they walk. I take it you had a good evening?"

As Joyce leaned far forward and pulled the seat with her, Adrienne squeezed into the back seat and James followed. "Thanks for picking us up, Mom and Dad. I don't suppose you want to go make out in a dark cul-de-sac, do you? Oh, that's right, you've already had kids. You probably want to get home to watch the weather channel."

Dan replied, "Well, you know there's a storm-watch out over New England. Your mother and I have been to the market to stock up on beef stew and low-fat milk. So we do have to get home, to make sure the milk doesn't spoil. Otherwise, we'd definitely be getting naked pretty soon." James giggled to himself, still holding Adrienne's hand.

Joyce, on cue, started to unzip her coat and remove her sweater. "Not now, honey," Dan said. "Oh, by the way, have you met? James, this is your mother. Joyce, this is your son, James. He's a little out of control, but we're trying to get a handle on him."

James introduced Adrienne to Joyce. Adrienne had seen Dan plenty in the past few weeks around school.

"Are you guys headed to one house or the other?"

James looked at Adrienne. "Let's go to Adrienne's. I'll get a ride home from there." She nodded, one earring reflecting the lights from a passing car, the heart tucked underneath her coat.

At Adrienne's house, at the door of the Escort, James thanked his long-time friend. "Sorry to get you so far out of the way. I'll return the favor when we're on Social Security, and you've lost your night vision. See you for practice tomorrow."

They entered Adrienne's living room through the front door; Adrienne's little sister Ginnie was watching a movie with a couple friends. They were dressed comfortably in pj's, most of them wrapped in sleeping bags. Ginnie whispered boisterously, "Shhh. It's a scary movie!" Adrienne jumped onto the couch, landing with her shoulders on Ginnie's legs. She squealed. "Hey, cut it out!" Someone hit the clicker to stop the movie while sisters wrestled and everyone else watched jealously, including James.

"Hey, why don't you go to the kitchen, where you won't bother us," Ginnie asked playfully.

"No problem. I know when I'm not wanted. Enjoy the show," Adrienne said, rising from the couch, Ginnie's limp body in her arms.

"Hey, put me down."

"Oh, is that you? I thought it was just a blanket. Put some meat on those bones," Adrienne exclaimed, dropping Ginnie lightly back onto the couch as she and James moved on into the kitchen.

Adrienne opened the refrigerator door. "Do you want something to eat?"

James nodded. "What's available?"

"We've got cold cuts, leftover pizza, I could cook some eggs. What do you want?"

They settled on cold pizza, heading into the family room, where Adrienne's mother sat sleepily, a book on the arm of her overstuffed chair. "Oh, here you kids are! Did you have a good night?" Her eyes gradually came alive to challenge the lucidity of Adrienne's.

James nodded respectfully. "I'd vote yes, but I'm going to leave it up to your daughter to cast the swing vote." He looked expectantly at Adrienne.

"Well, Mom, do you see anything different about me?" She swung her arms around her, twirling as she had done that late night in the road as her mother approached the two of them near James's house.

"Well, you have a big smile on your face, but that's not new. And you have knee-high argyle socks on, that's something new."

303

Adrienne leaned over her mother, to let the necklace dangle over her face.

"Oh, well, you have a new necklace." Mrs. Petrulsky reached for the piece of gold, stilling it to see it was a heart. "Oh, how lovely. Is it a gift?"

"James gave it to me." She looked at him, her eyes shining with excitement.

"That's really nice, James," Mrs. Petrulsky said. "Very thoughtful." She rose out of her chair. "Well, I guess I'll just get along to bed, now that you two are home."

James looked at Adrienne, holding his hand up slightly. "Uh, don't forget that I'm gonna need a ride home. I'm still a youngster, no license."

Adrienne said to her mom, "May I use your car to take James home?"

"Oh, sure, sweetheart. You know where the key is. No pulling off into dark lanes, though," she teased.

"Maybe we'll hang here for a little while."

"Sure, honey. Just call upstairs when you're leaving, so I'll know when you're gone. You'll be back in about twenty minutes then?" She retreated to her room graciously, leaving her daughter and James alone.

She wasn't more than eight steps up the stairs, and James and Adrienne were spilling across the coffee table toward each other, James pulling Adrienne to him, Adrienne searching for his mouth with hers. Their teeth glanced off the others'. James could hardly breathe. His arms felt heavy, they held so much. Adrienne curled her left arm around him, her hand pulling his spine into the tightening circle of her embrace. She whimpered just a little. James's right knee slid across the table toward Adrienne.

After several minutes of this desperate pulling and grasping, sliding into a chair, Adrienne straddling his legs, James pulled his face back, nearly breathless. "What a feeling. I can't believe I can feel this good. Is it amazing for you?"

Adrienne nodded, her eyes looking into his eagerly. "I don't think I've ever felt this way."

When they pulled apart, they could hear the music from Ginnie's horror movie from the other room. But then they would grasp at each other again, Adrienne's hair swirling around James's head as she pushed herself forward. All James could hear was the blood rushing in his ears.

We've been married all these years
We know each other deeply
And oh my dear oh my dear
You still make me sleepy
The children they are nearly grown
Oh and ain't they turned out sweetly
They're out tonight and we're alone
Oh, babe, you make me sleepy
I know your stories, you know mine
Oh but tell that one to me
Bout that walk in the wet woods
And the red wine
Oh, babe, it makes me sleepy

Lullabye by Greg Brown

Ben

After Saturday's practice – the customary breakdown into teams for cross-court games – Ben cozied up to the essays remaining from the exam he had given on Thursday. He had 45 essays to correct, the multiple choice sections of the exam having already been completed. He also had 20 writing portfolios to read. He knew he'd finish this weekend, but he also knew he wouldn't be socializing much.

"I'm going to the church to help plan for the reception to next weekend's wedding. Do you remember we have the Morgans' wedding next Saturday?" Ben did not recollect the date of the wedding. He did know that Tom Morgan, a long-time member of the parish, was getting remarried to a younger woman he had met after his divorce. Ben and Tom had coached a couple seasons of church basketball together when their sons were nine. Tom was getting married in a small ceremony at the church, reception to follow, also at the church – low-budget but high-spiritual octane, Tom remembered now.

"Yeah, I sorta remember. How many people at the reception, do you know?"

"His fiancée says about sixty. We're planning for seventy-five, just in case some parishioners come unannounced. I'm going to stop at your mom's on the way home. I know you're stuck with your essays for some long hours. How about I bring home a pizza in the late afternoon? We can eat it when you want to take a break." Willa was considerate. "I hope you get your work done today, so tomorrow isn't too crazy for you."

"Speaking of remembering: do you remember we have a team brunch at the Grutchfields' tomorrow? I won't be going to church. I've got to put in my appearance with my adoring fans – Peter Grutchfield, especially. At least Jason had an awesome game on Tuesday. Peter won't have any ammunition for me."

Willa thrust her chin out just a little. "Oh, I'm glad I won't be at the Grutchfields'. I wouldn't guarantee to keep my mouth shut. What a hateful man." Willa was as loyal as ever. "Well, maybe we can build up some good vibes, as we enter the second half of the season. You never know. We've had some teams catch their stride at midpoint and get on a roll. I'll enjoy being with the players, at least. And some of the parents are great people – the Rushes, for instance. They've got their hands full, but they don't let James get away with anything. They supported the school and me on the suspension completely." James reached for his blue pen to try to make inroads on the next essay.

Willa started out the door. "I'll see you for pizza when I'm done. Anything you want me to get for your mom? I'm going to buy some hard candy for her; she loves those little candies from CVS."

Ben knew; he just never remembered to buy it. "Thanks, honey. See you when you get home. I'll try to be close to done. And I'll try to be awake," he added, with a grin.

"Oh, I'll be surprised if you don't take a nap for at least part of the afternoon. I know how exhausted you are after a Saturday practice." She came back into the room, leaned over him, and gave him a kiss. He reached upward from his chair to give her an off-handed caress, his hand wandering aimfully.

"See ya. I love you," he said, and she left.

The afternoon was a balancing act between the essays Ben had to assess and the basketball games on TV. Ben achieved a healthy attitude between the two: an essay had to be completed every three minutes or so, during which time he would tune in to the essay, and after which he could turn to the game for a lazy minute. In this zig-zag way he could be focused enough to give the essays their due without driving himself into absolute boredom. Looking forward, extrapolating his pace over the afternoon, he deduced he would finish about 5:30, leaving the portfolios for Sunday afternoon – not a bad compromise. Since the Patriots were gone from the playoffs, his interest in the pro playoffs was diminished.

A couple of phone calls interrupted Ben's pace, one call from Scott letting Ben know he wouldn't be home for supper.

When Willa came home, she was full of energy, almost a Christmas kind of cheer. She opened the large box of pizza on the coffee table. "Beer?" she asked him.

"Sure. Sounds good." He pushed his essays aside, after counting the remaining essays: six. "I made good progress. How was Mom?"

"She was really good," Willa said, bringing two Coronas into the family room and placing them on coasters on the coffee table. She went back to the kitchen for two plates. "We talked about your Aunt Jean and Uncle Ben for a long time. I'd forgotten you were named for him. What was he like? I only met him once or twice before he died."

Ben thought back to trips to Uncle Ben's house in Pennsylvania, his farm and the flies in the kitchen. "We took a trip to his farm every other year. He was my mom's favorite brother. I think she

307

tried to get me to think as agriculturally as he did, but I just never got the cultivating bug. She liked her small garden, and she'd try to get me to take an interest in planting vegetables, but I always thought it was easier to go to the store and buy lettuce. My Uncle Ben had a whole farm with produce and animals that he slaughtered. I'm sure I was a disappointment to her from that perspective. I thought the garden was just a place to lose a ball in."

Willa scrunched next to Ben. "Well, we talked about you, too. She doesn't overwhelm her listener with good vibes, but you're her star. She just loves it when you walk in the door. She tells me you stay for hours," she said, laughing.

Ben laughed too. "Well, that's nice. I'm glad she can't read the clock very accurately."

The pizza was tasty; Willa's hand brushing his felt good, familiar. Such an easy time to sit here and chat, pizza box open in front of them the way it was almost thirty years ago in their apartment on a Saturday afternoon, Alabama-LSU on TV, snow blowing outside, plans for a movie in the evening possibly short-circuited by a passion that rose like the wind across a November football field.

Standing to get paper towels from the kitchen, Ben said, "Great pizza. Thanks."

"Paper towels right here," Willa said, knowing where he was going, holding up the towels she had brought with the pizza fifteen minutes before.

"Thanks," Ben murmured, looking at Willa, her face shining with its own benevolence. How could he harbor resentment for a woman who gave so much, in so many ways, to so many people? As he chewed the pizza, he tried to recall the last time he had thanked Willa just for being her. It had been a long time, and he didn't know how to say it, but he thought he'd give it a try. "You're remarkable, you know that? So much time for everyone around you. It's amazing."

Willa looked up uncomfortably. "It's just what I do. To be honest, there's never enough time for anyone. I can always think of ten more things I should be doing. Right now, I should be making plans for my parents' fiftieth wedding anniversary party. I've got to call Louise to get her thinking about it with me. We have to start planning."

Ben nodded, reminded of her parents' long marriage. "That will be fun. Mid-August?"

"The 9th, but we'll go to the Saturday after, something like the 11th. I haven't really looked at a calendar yet."

They retreated into silence, Willa commenting on the game intermittently, comfortably, gradually gathering herself on the couch, pulling into a gentle retreat, her hair falling over her face as she dropped into sleep, comfortable as a ballad, in her quietude.

At the Grutchfields' on Sunday Ben stood with his back to the kitchen counter, Mrs. Grutchfield lifting quiches out of the oven, her granite island filled with fruit, bread, French toast, racks of bacon, pitchers of orange and cranberry juice. Three coffee urns kept pace with consumption. Around Ben stood Mr. Willis, Mr. Grutchfield and Mr. Monaghan, all sipping coffee, three fathers who had worked along the way with the boys when they were young. The kitchen cabinets shone with the dark red of cherry, wine glasses standing on their heads in the glass-front panels.

"What a game," Mr. Willis said, his face full of pride. "No way that Walpole team should have lost the game. You just made the plays."

Ben nodded. "It was a little miracle, I'll admit." He cut his French toast with his fork on his paper plate, his orange juice on the granite counter that he was resting against.

"Let's just hope we can get some momentum going," Mr. Grutchfield added, his face suffused with the roseate tint of hypertension. "We've just been moving along in fits and starts, no continuity. One good game, one bad game, no consistency. We can't put two games together. Just no consistency." Ben wondered whether he could say the same thing again in more synonymous words.

Mr. Monaghan broke in, as if to rescue Ben. "Well, it'd be a different season if Andrew hadn't gotten hurt." He hastened to add, "I mean, I'm not saying Andrew is so great he'd be the difference in every game, but he has a lot of experience and he's got some height. We're getting hurt on the boards in a lot of games."

Ben nodded and was about to respond when Mr. Grutchfield broke in, "Well, I would love to see what we could do with a full team – I mean, first it was James getting suspended, then it was Andrew getting injured. We've just about never had the full lineup together for one game. Remember back in eighth grade, when we took the Suburban title?" Peter had a way of bringing the seniors' eighth grade title in the district suburban league into every conversation he had with Ben. Ben knew his agenda, and he would not take the bait. He said nothing, somewhat rudely.

Mr. Willis stepped into the awkward void of words, resting his coffee cup on the kitchen table behind him. "Yeah, that was a good developmental league. We got our feet wet playing some pretty good teams, Cambridge, Newton, Lexington. We played in the Division I league, and we hung in there. And then in the playoffs, we just caught fire. I'd say that's our M.O. this year, right, Coach?"

Ben leaned his head over his right shoulder. "Well, I'd love that scenario, but to be honest, I agree with Peter – no consistency. We beat Walpole and Milton and we lose to Wellesley and Dedham. I'm sure it's frustrating to the players, the parents, and I know it's frustrating to the coaches. But I hope we can gain some momentum over the second half of the season." Ben wished he were in the other room, with the players, sharing their relaxation between semesters. He could see the yawning living room, with the stonework of the fireplace reaching above the ceiling line.

Peter Grutchfield turned to Mr. Monaghan. "Any chance of Andrew returning sometime in the second half of the season or the playoffs?"

Ben had not heard any definitive word on Andrew's knee since his MRI, which had indeed revealed a partial tear of his ACL and the meniscus of the left knee. The doctors had said he had to rest for at least a month; at that time (early February) he would be reevaluated. Andrew was still a great presence at practice, always there early, his knee in an immobilizer. Every day, with one of the girls, he would sit in a chair and shoot fifty shots at the side hoop, working on his shot form. He also did five sets of twenty pushups every day. There were players who used their injuries to withdraw from the competition of the daily practice, but Andrew immersed himself into those frays, asking to coach one of the teams in scrimmage situations. He had the making of a coach if he chose to pursue that avenue, though very few of Ben's players ever went into teaching or coaching. He knew why: not lucrative enough.

Mr. Monaghan replied, "We're waiting for a doctor's evaluation on Feb. 10th. There's a slim chance he might play some time after that. But he can't do any rehab until after that date. And he might just go into surgery at that time, too. They had to let the joint settle down. It was really swollen."

Peter Grutchfeld looked at Mr. Monaghan shaking his head in disappointment. "That was a hell of a tough break. Thank God, knock on wood," he tapped the cabinet underneath the granite counter, "Jason has had no injuries. He's been healthy as a pig in shit. He just has to pick it up. He finally had a game against Walpole. I've been waiting for that kind of a game from him for two years."

Mr. Willis assured Peter, "He was immense. We don't even come close in that game without Jason. He's a great point guard."

"Nah, he's got a lot to learn. He's just starting to reach his potential. It's taken him a long time to learn the position. There's no way he should be struggling the way he has struggled this year. He's had a private trainer to work on his conditioning, he has a shooting tutor to work with him on Sundays over at the Y in Newton. He's got no excuse. He just doesn't take advantage of his skills."

Mr. Willis asked, "Weren't you a guard in college?" just as Peter wanted.

"Yes, I played at Williams. We had some great teams – went to the ECAC finals three times in my career." His smile was practiced and self-interested. "Kids today don't know how easy they have it."

With these words of Peter Grutchfield's Ben officially stopped listening. He had heard it far too many times, from far too many officious dads – and, in fact, Ben agreed with Peter's assessment of the modern-day high school athlete, but he would never offer it as any factor in the debate over how good a certain player might become. It was still a boy, a ball, a basket, and a vision. Yes, the vision often became impaired, but it was Ben's job to help these players restore their vision along the way – and, more importantly, to merge the weakened vision of his individual players into a strong collective vision. Yes, he had grand ambitions for his players; but, somehow, his idealistic thoughts disappeared in the vanity of Mr. Grutchfield's vision.

Just then, Mr. Grutchfield's voice rose, bringing Ben back to the kitchen. He wondered where the mothers were mingling, though he had seen Mrs. Grutchfield striding in and out of the kitchen several times, giving orders to the young serving girls who were moving through the company, offering plates of pastries and trays of coffee.

Ben looked at Mr. Willis, who backed away cautiously. Peter Grutchfield continued. "Coach, you did it again. You yanked Jason after he turned the ball over. I think we've talked about this. You can't develop any confidence in your players if you strip them of their self-esteem every time you make a substitution."

Ben shook his head slightly, as if he were emerging from a swim on the pond when he was young, shedding the beads of water that clung to his hair. "I'm not sure I follow you, Pete," he said, trying to remain friendly. He could see Mr. Monaghan moving behind him, whether to shield himself from Mr. Grutchfield's assault, or to lend his support, Ben didn't know.

Mr. Grutchfield's voice rose to another tier. "I'm talking about the way you eviscerate every one of your players before they finish their careers, taking good boys and making them hate each other, with all the in-fighting you make them do. And then, every time a player makes a mistake, you make sure he won't ever get past that mistake by taking him out and giving him that phony handshake of yours. It's disgusting."

Mr. Grutchfield's face was within a foot of Ben's. Ben could smell the remains of cigarette smoke on Peter's breath.

Ben would not back away. He spoke in an even voice, trying to maintain his poise. "Mr. Grutchfield, I'm sure you believe in your view of my coaching. But I'm not sure you have any ratification for those views. I'm sorry you feel this way. And I'm sure you can see that it's time for me to leave. Thank you for hosting this brunch. I know the boys appreciate it." After staring at Peter for a few more seconds, silently, his chin thrust out, assuring Peter that he would stand his ground, Ben moved away, looking for Mrs. Grutchfield to thank her for her hospitality. He found her standing with several other mothers in the four-season room off the family room, huddled, it seemed, shielding themselves from the volatility that had filled the kitchen.

"Thank you, Mrs. Grutchfield, for having the team. They love getting together, and it helps team chemistry a lot. I can see you've really put yourself out in planning and hosting us. Thank you very much. I have to be going."

Mrs. Grutchfield looked at Ben with a pause in her face, visible in her half-opened mouth. An ornamental, yellow apron covered her shirt and jeans. When she regained her breath, she said, "Thanks, Coach, for all your efforts. The boys are enjoying the season. It's what they've looked forward to for half their lives." She reached out to brush Ben's arm with her hand. "It's not always smooth, but it sure is exciting. Thanks again."

Ben looked directly at Mrs. Grutchfield, to see the depth of her sincerity. She looked directly back at him, almost pleading with him for forebearance.

With one more practice before the home game against Natick, Ben tried to shore up the confidence of the team, looking for smoothness in scrimmages and comfort in the shots that his perimeter players put up. Archie and Dan took a lot of jumpers in Monday's team scrimmage, making some and missing some. Ben called the team together for a minute. "Hey, guys, we're putting a lot of pressure on ourselves to make outside jumpers all day. Let's try to get into an attacking mode, so we can penetrate and pass, giving ourselves some easy looks off the glass. OK? Jumpers only if there is no driving lane. OK?"

The team assented. They were poised for a strong game, expecting to capitalize on their Walpole victory. When they returned to the court, they showed a greater willingness to drive the ball to the rim, forcing the defensive big men to slide off their men to pick up the penetration.

As the practice concluded, Ben called the team together again. "We're ready. No more to do. Nice job attacking the rim. That's exactly what we're looking for. Let's review.

"We're starting Jason, Geoff, Archie, Dan, and Andreas. Geoff and Andreas, you've got your hands full taking the boards from Natick. Archie and Dan, you've got to get to the defensive glass, to hold Natick to one shot. But then we have to sprint on the break, to make them pay for sending three to the offensive glass. That's where you will be most important, Jason. You're going to make fifty important decisions tomorrow night, triggering the break or slowing it down to set up. Just think Walpole, Jason, Walpole. You were the master of the break last Tuesday. No sweat, Jason. No sweat." Ben looked Jason in the eye, raising his arm to embrace Jason's shoulder, his right hand landing on Jason's right shoulder, pulling him toward Ben. "Let's get together here, guys, One . . . Two . . . Three . . ."

The team, gathered around Ben and Jason tightly, shouted a "Tight" that stayed in Ben's ear for a while, much longer than the voice of Peter Grutchfield had echoed the day before.

Monday night at Willow's was busier than Ben's opening night. The outside tables were sprinkled with customers. Of course, Bryan and Lisa sat at a round table in the corner, watching the Villanova take on Syracuse.

"Hey, how ya doin?" Bryan asked, as Ben migrated to their table, taking orders and replenishing drinks.

"Great. I think we're ready for Natick. It was a solid practice and we've had three solid practices now, in preparation. I just hope we can pull this one off. It'd be nice to get back to .500."

Lisa smiled supportively. "Bryan tells me you're coaching your ass off. I've seen parts of your games. Your team is playing very disciplined basketball. I'm impressed." She held Bryan's hand lightly.

"Thanks. We're just inches away, I think, from being something really good. I just have a hard time getting those last inches." He wiped the table, placed new coasters on their table and centered their replacement beers on the coasters. He wondered whether he looked as if he knew what he was doing.

Bryan let him know. "You're on the ball, here, big guy. We don't even finish our beers and you've got another round coming. I've never had such service." He nodded.

"That's nice. Wish I could join you, but it's kinda fun on this side of the bar. The time passes really quickly." He turned back to the

313

bar. Lisa reached out and touched his shoulder, patting him like a mother would her son.

After Ben finished his rounds of the outside tables, he returned to his place behind the bar, where he was beginning to feel comfortable. At the left end of the bar sat a woman who was demurely sipping her second white wine, absent-mindedly watching the basketball game. She seemed isolated, turned away from the young man on her right who drummed his tattooed hands on the counter. Ben was trying to develop the patter that marks a good bartender and a good folksinger: the ability to fill the gaps to make the venue a place that felt like home.

"How's the wine going down?" he asked, noting the vacuity of his question.

The patron looked at him with misery in her eyes. "Too smoothly." She didn't proceed, killing the conversation, but she didn't lower her head either.

Ben wiped the counter in front of her, where she had tried to finish an appetizer of fried calamari. "Are you a steady customer here? I'm sure you know I'm the new guy. Let me know how I'm doing, OK?"

"I'll be kind in my analysis. I don't have much room for criticism, I can assure you. All my cynicism is directed in another direction. You'll have a free pass." The woman gave a slight, wry smile. She was maybe a bit older than Ben, mid-fifties, her hair thick and curly, her mouth down-turned gloomily, her chin softly retreating to her neck. She had been a beauty, for sure, though her despondency obscured the echo of that attractiveness.

"I appreciate that," he said. Ben nodded, turning away. He didn't know how much to involve himself in her sadness, but he made a note to keep checking on her.

Pete bumped Ben in the back to remind him that the dishwasher cycle had been finished for at least fifteen minutes, meaning the dirty dishes were piling up on and behind the counter. "Keep up with the flow, my man," he said kindly, as he began emptying the dishwasher himself, the steam rising from the burnished glasses and squeaky plates.

"Sorry, Pete, I'm trying to learn to fly around here, but I get grounded with conversations at times." He looked at Pete for guidance.

"You'll figure it out. You're right: you have to offer yourself to your customers first, but you can't let the shit work get ahead of you either. It's like those Venn diagrams that we studied in ninth grade math: the secret to success is in letting those two circles overlap as much as possible, so you can work while you're providing therapy.

Remember, the real therapy comes from the alcohol, not from your wisdom."

Ben was sorry to hear Pete minimizing his effect on the patrons, because he was drawn to the job for the same reasons he was drawn to teaching and coaching: he wanted to help people find solutions in their lives, solutions derived from mastery of something in which they were involved. He did not want to think that their solution was in the glass that he poured for them.

"Maybe so, but I don't want them to think they could find that same therapy somewhere else, right?"

Pete nodded, admitting that Ben had a good point.

At closing time, the woman with the curly hair still sat despondently at the end of the bar. Bryan and Lisa had left by 9:30 and the succeeding three and a half hours had gone by as slowly as the changing of the seasons. As customers had left, few people had replaced them, leaving the tavern with only five customers in the end. Pete was working in back, having closed up one of the two registers, working on tallying up the final count. Ben made one last sweep of the room, collecting all the trash and empties off the last tables. The woman remained at her post.

"Everything all right?" he asked her. She had not had a drink after 11:30, at which time she had finished her third glass of wine.

"As good as it gets," she replied, shrugging. She looked ready to cry.

"We're closing up in a few minutes, I'm sure you know. Can I get you a glass of water?"

She looked at him with an attempt at nobility. "No, thank you, but you've been very kind to me, and I appreciate it. Maybe I'll see you again." There was an air of mystery surrounding her pronouncement, as if she might look forward to his attention some other day.

Thinking it inappropriate to tell her his minimal schedule, Ben said, "I'll keep an eye out for you, too," remembering inwardly a joke with that punch-line he had heard when he was about fifteen. He looked at the woman to assure her he had enjoyed their dialogue.

The pre-game music suffused the mostly empty gym tinnily as the Panthers warmed up for their Natick game. Pockets of fans took their customary stations in the home section, and a sporadic stream of parents took their positions in the visitors' section.

Bryan stood next to Ben, recalling the first Natick game. "They just wore us down on the boards, didn't they?" he remembered.

315

"Yeah, and we had Andrew in that game. But I think we can break on them, because they go to the offensive glass so hard. I'm looking for a big game from Jason, pushing the ball up the court and making good decisions. But you're right: we've gotta rebound."

The game began with a flurry of turnovers, both teams playing tight. Natick was 7 – 5 on the season, looking to add to their wins, moving toward a post-season berth. The Panthers needed every win possible, at 5 – 6. After a few minutes the Panthers calmed down, taking care of the ball. As Dan took a couple foul shots, Ben called for a half-court trap, to try to take advantage of the Natick guards' jitters.

After Dan's successful foul shots, Jason took the point in the 3-2 trap, with Dan and Archie on the wings. The Natick guard tried to beat Dan down the sideline, but Dan turned him back to the double-team with Jason, and the guard traveled. Ben felt good, having stolen a possession from his opponent. He called for another trap after Geoff put in a follow-up basket for an 11 – 7 lead. This one worked also, leading to a layup for Jason, forcing a Natick time-out with three minutes left in the first quarter.

"Nice trap, guys. James, get in there for Archie. Let's keep fresh legs on the court. No trap this time. Let's just play some good half-court man-to-man. Jason, don't let this kid penetrate on you. Jump at him, then jump away. Keep him thinking you're pressuring him, but your first priority is to contain him. If he picks up his dribble, jump and 'Tight' him, of course. Great start. We're on a roll. Let's keep it up."

But the momentum withered and turned Natick's way, as they pounded the boards, putting in three second-chance baskets. At the quarter the Panthers held a slim 19 – 18 lead.

The second quarter served Natick well, as they continued their assault on the glass. They didn't do anything very skilled; they just muscled their way to the boards.

As the Panthers came off the floor, Ben asked Bridget for the rebounding totals.

"Natick 24 and we've got 11," she said sheepishly, knowing these numbers would prompt a grimace from Ben.

"Thanks, Bridget. It's not your fault. Do you want to put a uniform on and rebound for us?"

316

I can't stop myself from calling
Calling out your name
I can't stop myself from falling
Falling back again
In the mornin'
Baby in the afternoon
Dark like the shady corners
Inside a violin
Hot like to burn my lips
I know I can't win
In the mornin'
Baby in the afternoon
I tried to quit you
But I'm too weak
Wakin' up without you
I can hardly speak at all

In The Morning by Norah Jones

James

At half-time the locker room was silent, except for the drip of the faucet across from the second urinal. James kept his head down, displeased with his first half: 4 points and 1 rebound.

"Well, guys, it all comes down to rebounding. We can't do anything about our height, but we can do something about our position, our willingness to go after the ball, our desire to grab the ball, and just our need to compete. Every game in this second half of the season is going to be a war, and I'm sorry, but it seems like not many of you are willing to fight. That was just a sorry exhibition." Coach LaMott was rarely this bluntly disappointed, but he had good reason.

Geoff Willis spoke up. "Coach, you're right. I'm not calling out anyone in particular, and I'm the worst offender. I'm not doing my job at all. I'm looking to get down the floor, and we don't even have the ball in our possession. Mark, Andreas, Dmitri, we have to commit to taking over the boards. If we don't, it's going to be a bad night." Geoff walked to his fellow post men, striking them on the shoulder to rev them up. They responded in kind, jostling Geoff with their own bristling dissatisfaction.

Growls of "Let's get 'em" and "Don't hold back" seemed appropriate, but, to James, these utterances sounded hollow and predictable. Too many times he had sat in this locker room, surrounded by and contributing to disappointment that then took the form of noise. He didn't think noise was the answer. But he didn't know what the answer was. Maybe it was certainty.

As they took the floor for the second half warmups, James prepared himself for his role coming off the bench. He drove the ball to the rim as hard as he could to try to generate a little excitement in himself, an energy level that he would try to sustain as he sat on the bench, following the play end-to-end, envisioning his role on the court if he were there. His first half had been a fucking waste. He had done nothing to help the team; in fact, his plus-minus was probably about -8.

Midway through the third, with Natick leading 51 – 44, Coach LaMott called for James, Mark, and Bobbie to go in. Coach called for a 41 on defense, a 1-2-2 zone that might help on the defensive glass. James was playing a wing, but he knew he had to come down to the baseline to help with the rebounding. On his first defensive possession, a shot went up from the other side of the floor, putting James and the weakside baseline player from Natick in prime position for the weakside rebound. James dug his hip into the Natick player, slapping his right elbow on the boy's chest, to prevent his entry into the lane. The referee whistled a foul on James. He heard Coach shout, "That's OK, James. Good work. Keep it up."

By the end of the third quarter Natick had crept out to a bigger 58 – 48 lead. James was battling; he had grabbed four defensive rebounds, but the Panthers couldn't put the ball in the basket at the other end. James had made a couple shots and missed one.

"Gut check time," Coach LaMott said calmly. "Archie, you've got to go in at the point and give Jason a little rest. He's exhausted. Look for that ¾ trap they threw at us last game. I know it's going to come. Reverse before half-court and then hit middle. James, you've got the middle of the X. Attack from that spot when you get the ball. Guys, keep up the effort on the glass. We were pretty even with them on the boards for the third period. Bridget, what've you got?"

"11 – 10 us," she called, ready.

"That's great. That's all I can ask. Keep it up, break their trap, and let's get this game."

In the first three minutes of the fourth quarter, Casteline chopped the Natick lead to 3, with their precise attack of the trap that Coach LaMott had anticipated. James fed off for two baskets and scored two himself. When Jason came back into the game for Dan, the Panthers were poised for a come-from-behind win. The home crowd had swelled slightly as the game wore on, and they were caught up in their vocal, rising support. If the gym were an auditory aquarium, the water level would be halfway up the wall. James could feel that depth of support, though he never snuck a peek into the stands, unwilling to break his connection with the game that he held in his focus.

After three more possessions, the Panthers were trailing by only one, Geoff starting to intimidate his taller Natick counterparts with his manic attack of the ball as it came off the defensive rim. He was able to outlet the ball to Jason for two easy fast-breaks. Natick no longer scored on easy putbacks. James could feel the uncertainty of the cuts of the Natick players, as they began to doubt themselves. "Just a couple more stops," James shouted to Jason and Geoff. "We've almost got them. They're almost broken!" He believed himself.

After another Natick miss (they must have been shooting under 25% for the half), James outfought #41 for the rebound, looked for Jason at the outlet, but, missing him, looked over the top as he dribbled toward the sideline, buying time and freeing himself from the ball pressure. Seeing Dan curling in from the left wing, he tossed him a three-quarter court pass for the layin that gave Casteline a one point lead, with under a minute to go. It was Casteline's first lead of the second half.

No time-out. Maybe Natick had used them all up and was hording one last time-out for the last seconds. James thought it would be too late.

Coach called for a 1, full court man-to-man. James was matched up on a slow forward that couldn't handle the ball. He knew he could rove off his man, to provide a little double-team if the ball were being pushed up toward him. Jason pushed his man left sideline, looking for a trap, but James was too far back to help him. The Natick guard slowed his dribble down, in the forecourt, with 40 seconds to go, 18 on the shot clock. Jason kept jumping at the guard, and, finally, Jason committed to ball pressure, forcing the man to pick up his dribble. "TIGHT!" he shouted just as James did the same, jumping in front of his man to cut off passing lane. All the Panthers closed down the angles, forcing Natick to call their last time-out.

"Twenty-one seconds, guys. They have no time-outs. We have two if you need them."

"You want a 2, Coach?" asked Dan.

"Uh, let's jump to a 3, trap twice, and cover the inside passes. Only give them the cross-court corner, let's see if they can see it."

The Panthers came out looking like a man-to-man matchup, but when the referee handed the ball to the Natick inbounder, they slid to their 1-3-1, trying to entice a pass into the sideline-halfcourt corner. Natick obliged, Dan and Jason leaping into the double-team, Geoff and Mark overplaying and James retreating to the weakside elbow looking for anything over the top. The desperation pass came to the baseline man that James had kept in his range. He jumped to deflect the pass, but the Natick player went up over him to tip the ball to himself. When he came down, he had an easy look at the backboard. Leaning in, James having flown past, he put up a 10 foot bank shot for the win. It fell out, and Geoff hustled down for the rebound, snaring it with his two strong hands, protecting the ball from the foul that was planted on his arms immediately. There were ten seconds left, and he would go to the line for 1 and 1.

Coach LaMott called for a 2, make or miss, picking up at halfcourt. "No fouls," Coach Taft added adamantly. "No fouls." He moved his arms like a baseball umpire signaling a safe call at home plate.

Geoff made his first, missed his second, leaving a possibility for Natick, down two. They put up a three at the buzzer that glanced off the backboard and rim, but fell away, and the Panthers had their sixth win of the year, an exhausting effort. James could feel his heart rise in triumph even as his legs gave out on him and he sank to the floor.

As James, Dan, and Pete closed up their lockers, the victory secure in their memory and ego, Coach LaMott strode toward them, his voice brimming with pride. "That's the way to gut it out, guys. If you work hard enough, you'll get your reward. James, we're lucky that guy missed the banker, because he was right there. But you had worked on him for ten solid minutes; he was tired. He missed an easy look, but you were responsible for his fatigue. That's where we win games, putting fatigue in the bodies of our opponents. Great job, Dan. You have made so much progress." Coach LaMott could have doled out accolades for another hour, as his eyes moved with satisfaction from player to player in the locker room. James could see what drove Coach LaMott to keep coming back year after year: it was the possibility for a game like this one, in which it wasn't skill or technique or talent that made the difference; rather, it was believing in what you were doing.

"Coach, when I flew past him, he should have just taken a dribble and scored. He had a layup."

Coach agreed. "You're right. But he was tired. He had nothing left. He put it all out to beat you to the ball, and he had nothing left." Coach clapped James on the shoulder in his trademark embrace, signifying the closeness between them, pulling James into a two-armed embrace. "Great job," he murmured, overcome with the moment.

James left the locker room thinking he understood what Coach LaMott was looking for better than he ever had. Everything that Coach taught in practice was part of a design that would work, if everyone understood it clearly enough. He thought back to his half-time observation that the noise in the locker room sounded hollow. He tried to remember what he had concluded the team needed. He couldn't recall his conclusion, but he knew with certainty that they had achieved it in that last quarter.

Wednesday in Geometry class James found the need to leave class midway to go to the bathroom, taking a route that forced him to walk past Adrienne, who sat in front of him concentrating on the blackboard on which Mr. Tilson was working. As he came up behind her, he could see the gold chain of her new necklace because her hair was pulled up and piled on top of her head. She was writing careful notes on Mr. Tilson's analysis of tangents to a circle, meeting in just a point, of course. Mr. Tilson was explaining that the tangential object might be a point, a line, a three-dimensional figure, or an entire plane.

Adrienne's orderly notes reflected her rational interest in his ideas. James brushed her left shoulder with his hand as he passed. He would look for the heart on his return to the classroom.

After walking down the steps to the front window of the school, and meandering along that corridor as if he were waiting for someone to pick him up, he returned to Mr. Tilson's room, passing Coach LaMott's classroom, where he saw Coach sitting on the front of his desk, engaging the class of sophomores (he recognized a few JV basketball players) in a discussion. On the board were the words, "Samsara" and "Nirvana," recalling for James his reading of *Siddhartha* with Coach, a book that helped James understand some of the ideas that Coach espoused: reaching a point at which there were no choices, just right behavior. James wasn't there yet; but it seemed that Adrienne had achieved that inner peace. He wished she would share her equanimity with him, somehow.

Returning to Mr. Tilson's classroom, as he turned down Adrienne's row, he looked for the heart, lying casually on her soft black sweatshirt. It looked very slight, an unremarkable sliver of gold. Moving his glance upward, James saw Adrienne's rapt face, her attention still directed to Mr. Tilson, though she did give a quick glance to James, accompanied by an instant smile. She nudged his leg as he passed.

Back in his seat, James tuned in to Mr. Tilson's remarks, still centering on the concept of two figures finding one or several, at most, points of intersection. He could hear Adrienne's voice complementing Mr. Tilson's offering. "But what if you intersect a sphere with a plane? Wouldn't that create a circle?"

James nodded in his reverie. He wondered whether Adrienne had raised her hand or just interjected her remark spontaneously. He wanted to open his eyes, but he could feel the curve of his hat low on his forehead, comfortingly.

"Well, Adrienne, you raise a great point. When are dealing with three-dimensional figures, in both cases, the intersection will be more than a point or series of points. The intersection will be a two dimensional figure in its own right. For instance, what if two circles intersect, class?"

James could hear nothing, though he had expected Adrienne to continue her dialogue with Mr. Tilson. Finally, a voice from front right, Ben Hecker's, probably, answered, "It would look like two arcs, wouldn't it?"

James pictured Ben's figure, then thought of the merging of his life's with Adrienne's, wondering about the figure of their intersection.

322

For an irreverent moment, he thought of their intersection in its sexual form, but, after giggling silently, he moved his mind back onto a theoretical plane (did the theoretical plane and the real plane intersect? In what form?). He thought of the heart that lay on Adrienne's chest as their intersection; the bell rang.

James accompanied Adrienne halfway to her Spanish class, then turned off toward the Science Wing for Chemistry class.

Wednesday's practice was a ball-buster. Coach always followed a big win with a hard practice, just to keep the egos in check. James acquitted himself proudly, knowing what Coach was after, while some of the other guys complained to each other. But James still couldn't assert any mastery over Archie or Dan. They kept answering his successes with great shots of their own. It was the big men who started to lose their composure, the fighting on the boards leading to a series of well-placed elbows and shoulders, and, eventually, forearms.

Coach blew his whistle, signaling the team to gather around him. "All right, guys, let's keep our cool here. I like the intensity, but don't let it get personal. You can bet Braintree is working at least this hard. Heck, they're not 10-3 because they just shoot it straight. They work hard up and down the floor. We've got to have that same 94 foot intensity." Coach had seen big guys getting tired and ornery before. He didn't want to quell that fervor, just to direct it in a productive direction.

The next defensive possession, James boxed Archie out more physically than he normally did, to see what Archie's reaction would be. Archie tapped him on the hip as they ran up the floor, signaling his appreciation of James's effort. At the other end, he returned James's effort, sending James off the court, underneath the basket. James smiled to himself, glad to see the kid's heart was strong. For the next few possessions, they traded solid boxouts, taking a few extra steps in each case, to try to get the other player to submit, but, in the end, there was no victor, just two tired competitors.

On the ride home Dan said, "Hey, you and Archie really got into it, huh?"

"Yeah, I just wanted to see what he has. He's got a lot. I really respect that kid. He doesn't say 'boo,' but he lets his game talk for him. He's made us a lot better, and he's let us overcome Andrew's injury. He's really good. We're gonna have a great set of wingmen next year, you, Archie, and I. Maybe Archie can take over the point." James spent far too much time looking ahead to his senior year, as all athletes did, considering the day when they would reach their fulfillment as a scholastic athlete. James fully knew that such projection was really just a way of rationalizing present difficulties, but he couldn't help doing it anyway.

"Yeah, we're starting to show some cohesiveness on the court. And I think it all comes from pushing ourselves up and down, the same repetitive drills over and over, believing in the system. Archie came in believing right away."

"Yeah, he's blended in great," James agreed.

James could hear Dan start to say something, but then stop. He wondered whether Dan was holding back about something. James took the lead and asked, "Anything goin on with you?"

The two had had many nights together since Pete had found a faster ride home with Jonas Boynton, a senior who had gradually lost his playing time with the return of James and the emergence of Archie. The two old friends had gotten comfortable sitting with each other, falling back into their pre-adolescent familiarity, no need to talk, but ready at any time.

Dan started again. "My mom's really sick. I don't know if it's the result of all the alcohol or if she's been sick for a long time. We don't really talk about it, but she's getting weak."

James opened his eyes and looked at Dan. He reached across the small space of the Escort to tap Dan on the shoulder. "I'm sorry, man." He wished he could offer more consolation, but he didn't have the right words. Dan looked ahead as he drove. In the silence James found an opening. "Is there anything I can do to help?"

"I don't think so. Joyce is coming over to the house some afternoons to help out. My mom can't really get supper ready. My dad's job is such long hours, my mom is home alone a lot of the time. Joyce is really helping."

James remembered his conversation with Dan on the afternoon they had pizza. Dan had remarked how much he had learned about the Codys, through his invasion of their home, and the way it represented how much we want to enter into the lives of someone else. James was starting to understand. "Hey, would it be OK if we stop by your house before you take me home? If it's OK with your mom, I'd like to see her, just to say hi."

Dan hesitated. "I think she'd really like it, but I'm afraid she'd think it was a pity-visit, some indication that she's dying or something. I don't know.'

James assured Dan, "Yeah, I understand completely. I don't want her to feel worse, but I used to spend some long hours in your yard, throwing the ball, squirting the hose, sucking down twinkies."

James did have a fond remembrance of the Owings' house, warm and simple: Mr. Owings coming home after one of his cross-country long-hauls (he was a truck driver), embracing Mrs. Owings with a long hug, James and Dan wrestling in the living room.

Dan turned toward his house. "Oh, hell, I think it'd be great for my mom to have you in the house again. It's been at least a year or two."

A few minutes later, they entered the Owings' darkened kitchen, a light suffusing the stovetop with a penumbral glow.

"Hey, Mom?" Dan called into the hallway. "James is here with me. We just stopped for a snack. I'm driving him home from practice."

Joyce Bennett walked into the kitchen, her gray fleece pulled up to her chin in the cold house.

"Hi," she said easily.

"Hi," James replied. "How is Mrs. Owings?"

Joyce said, "She's doing great, actually. She seems stronger this week. She has a doctor's appointment tomorrow that'll tell us a lot." Dan noted Joyce's "us," including herself in Dan's family in a proud way.

Dan called, "Mom? Dan wants to say hi. Do you want to come into the kitchen, or should we come down to see you?"

A faint voice came from down the hall. "I think I'd like to come out to the kitchen, if James will forgive me for appearing in company in my robe." In a minute she appeared in the doorway to the kitchen, tying the belt to her pastel robe, leaning against the doorjamb. She looked decrepit, but her eyes were bright. "I don't think I've laid eyes on you in a year. What have you been doing with yourself?"

"Well, you know I've been trying to get my position back from your son on the team, but he just keeps playing too well. I thought we were good friends, but he hasn't been very friendly when it comes to giving me a chance in basketball."

"You know you were always the one who was ahead of him. Maybe he's just a late bloomer. I don't know. I do follow the team, though I haven't been able to get to the games. Maybe I'll make the playoffs. You boys'd better make the playoffs. Those games are always so much fun."

James could see the life in Mrs. Owings's eyes spread a bit to her cheeks and her mouth, as she pushed into a smile, recollecting past tournament games she and Dan and her husband had attended. James had accompanied them to several of those games.

325

Mrs. Owings sat down in a hard-backed kitchen chair. "I've just got a few health issues to take care of, as you might know. When I can put them behind me, I'll be back to my normal self." She looked at James for his assurance.

After a few more minutes of reminiscing, and half a bag of cookies from the cabinet next to the refrigerator, where they had always resided, Dan said, "Mom, I gotta take James home. Joyce'll stay with you till I get home. When's Dad getting home?"

Mrs. Owings thought, but couldn't recollect his schedule. "I don't know, Dan. I think his route is written on the calendar on the desk in the family room. You know. Check it out for me, would you?"

Snapping a lamp on in the family room, Dan called, "He's on a haul to DC today, left at 5:00 a.m. Should be back at 10:00 tonight, with a trip to Detroit tomorrow, back on Saturday." James had never realized how busy Mr. Owings' schedule kept him.

Returning to the room, Dan said, "Joyce, I'll get supper going when I get home. Please don't think about it," but Joyce looked at him to indicate that supper would be well on its way when he returned.

"Just don't get lost getting home. How about 7:30?"

In the car, as Dan pulled out of the driveway, he said, "My mom looked great. Better than she's looked all week."

James asked, "Has she been diagnosed with anything?"

"Yeah, it's high blood pressure and something like myocarditis, but it's really bad. She might need bypass surgery. They don't know yet. She has a really hard time eating. You could probably see, she's lost about forty pounds."

James said, "Thanks for bringing me over to your house. I'm glad the cookies are in the same place as always. Maybe I'll stop by for cookies, just haunt the house a little the way you haunted Codys', on the way home from practice – Oh, that's right, I don't have my license. You're my ride. Well, maybe we can stop by a lot, to see your mom and to sugar-load a little after practice."

Dan didn't reply, but when James opened his eyes and turned to Dan, he could see that he was nodding, his face illuminated by the headlights of an oncoming car.

Four minutes into Friday's game against Braintree, the Wamps had raced out to a 15 – 3 lead. The Panthers were being limited to one well-defensed shot per possession; it was clear that Braintree was one of the elite teams in the league, and Casteline was second tier. By halftime the lead was twenty. Braintree was pushing the ball down the floor effortlessly, as if the game were a simple practice and each Casteline were some kind of traffic cone that the Wamps just dribbled around.

James kept his head down in the locker room, awaiting a tongue-lashing from Coach LaMott, who, after a silent thirty seconds, offered these words: "Guys, sometimes, it's just their night. It just might not be our night. I know that happens sometimes. But if there is such a thing as 'their night,' then maybe it was just 'their first half,' and not their entire game." His voice rose in hope. "And maybe the second half is ours. Let's not go out there conceding anything. I do not want to see anyone hanging his head." He let his words sink in; James lifted his head after Coach's silence sank in.

Coach Taft added, "They can't keep shooting as well for an entire game. Janet, what's Braintree shooting?"

"18 for 29," Janet called, "61%."

James shook his head. He had been covering Bryan Edwards, Braintree's explosive guard, for the entire second period, and he had not stopped him once. Edwards had missed some shots, but not because of James's defense. He heard Coach talking about the second half, but he couldn't get past the embarrassment of the first half. His head dropped again, his eyes closing around his image of Edwards blowing past him.

Coach's voice connected to his thoughts, like a fishing line snapping out of the spinner. "We were embarrassed in that first half. No one in this room can feel proud of those 16 minutes of basketball. And if we let those emotions linger, we'll be just as bad in the second half." He stopped talking for so long that James lifted his head and opened his eyes, to see whether Coach had left the room. "But if we go out with the same preparation that we entered the game with, we'll be able to knock this lead down and make it a game."

James kept his head up, hearing the Coach's advice. He never did this, but he looked at Dan, to see how he was responding to the first half and to Coach's words. Dan was staring intently at Coach, sitting on the front of the bench, seemingly ready to jump up when called on.

After a few more minutes of encouragement and a simple adjustment (three quarter man-to-man, trying to pressure the ball with one trap at half-court), the team rose and gathered for a "Tight." James joined in the effort to bolster their confidence.

But the second half was more of the same. James entered the game with Braintree leading, 63 – 40, and when he came out with three minutes to go, the lead was 81 – 49. Nothing had worked all day long. Final score: 84 – 58, Braintree, the worst thumping of the year by far. In fact, with the exception of Wellesley, in the most desultory performance of the year, the Panthers had been within 10 in every loss to this point in the season. But they were never in this one.

After the game, on the ride home, James sat with Dan, who quietly reviewed some of the worst plays of the game. "What about when Jamieson brought it down and dunked on Geoff?"

James countered, "Not as bad as when I threw one cross-court for a steal and layup. We were crap." James leaned back, his head planted against the tall bus seat, his knees high on the seat in front of them.

"Yeah, you got that right. But we're 6 and 7, still got a shot at tournament. Let's see what we can do from here on out. It starts at practice tomorrow. Let's see how we respond. Saturday practice – old school scrimmaging."

James nodded silently, frozen by his disappointment.

The bus moved quickly down the highway, bearing its disconsolate load of athletes homeward.

Dan asked, "You goin home?"

James thought for a split second. "Yeah, I should. Joyce at your house?"

"Yeah. Dad's away till tomorrow. I'll drop you off at your house."

"How's your mom?"

"Same. She saw the doctor today. He's ordered a couple tests of her heart – I forget the names, but it might let them know what's going on. I heard something about congestive heart failure, and that sounds bad." Dan was speaking very softly.

James gazed through his eyelids, noticing the illuminating streetlights. He wanted to offer Dan his encouragement, but he didn't know how. Finally, he said, "Hang in there. Sounds as if she might make a big recovery, once the doctors make the diagnosis. That'd be nice." He looked at Dan as he pulled into James's driveway. "Thanks for the ride and the company. Sorry I sucked so much in the game."

Dan extended his arm to push James on the shoulder. "Don't take it so personally. We all sucked. You just contributed to the suck, like a good team member. Tomorrow we're gonna kick ass in practice." He pushed James again to shove him out the door.

"Thanks again, bud," James said as he slammed the Escort's light door.

In his house James threw his gym bag into the laundry room, followed it in, and took his uniform and sweats out of the bag, tossing them into the washing machine, after emptying the machine into the dryer, after emptying the dryer onto the floor. He kicked his father's work clothes, rugged, and his sister's underwear, delicate, toward the sink.

In the family room he punched Adrienne's cell number, assuming that she was home also from her home game.

"Hello?" she called. "Hey," she said, after realizing that it was his cell number.

"Hey," James replied, with an effort. He didn't really want to talk, but he needed to talk to someone. He knew the party at Reynold's was heading into its stronger hours, and if he were with Pete, he could be watching the Celtics on a big screen TV in their living room, the sound of cans being built into pyramids and cascading to the floor coming from the garage through the kitchen. He could picture the layout of Reynold's, room enough for three or four separate groups to find their own niche.

"You home?" Adrienne asked.

"Yeah, how'd you do?"

Adrienne gushed. "We won! We scored 21 points in the fourth quarter to beat them by six. I heard you guys got rocked," she said, the excitement draining from her voice sympathetically.

"Yeah, it was a nightmare. But it's over and I'm home." He sounded hollow.

"That's good. As a matter of fact, I'm out with a few lacrosse friends. We're heading over to the Dairy Queen on Union Ave in Framingham, for some ice cream. Do you want us to swing by to pick you up?"

James raised his feet up the wall over the couch, his head scraping the floor as he lay upside-down on the couch. "Who're you with?"

"Oh, you don't know any of them. They're kids from Needham, Wellesley, and Acton. They don't play a winter sport, and they came to my game, so we could go out afterwards. We can pick you up no sweat."

James wanted to see Adrienne, but not with a bunch of girls. He shook his head. "No, I'll just hang here. My mom and dad will be home soon, and I'll just watch the C's. Have fun." He tried to sound happy for her, but he didn't have the energy.

"Aw, come on. We'll pick you up in a few, OK?" She sounded excited.

James shut her off. "No, don't. I don't want to have any fun. It was too embarrassing tonight. I would just be hangin my head."

"That's why you have to come out. Come on. We'll be there in five."

James sighed, bringing his feet over his head, his hips still leaning against the edge of the cushion of the couch. "Whatever," he murmured. "See you in a few."

Before Adrienne and her friends could reach the house, James's dad and mom came home, entering the kitchen where James sat morosely, his hat pulled over his eyes, an orange Fanta on the table in front of him.

"Well, that was one to forget," his dad offered.

"No kiddin. We might as well have been a JV team."

"Well, you don't have to play them again," his mother said to encourage him. "Coach have anything good to say?"

James thought. He looked at his mother. "Not really. He wondered if something was going on to distract us. Nothin I know of, but maybe there's some bad chemistry between some of the guys. All I know was I was pathetic."

Adrienne's friends honked from the driveway. James could hear a door slam, telling him that Adrienne was heading to the kitchen door.

"Hey, I think I'm going out with Adrienne and a friend. I won't be late. We're just going out for an ice cream."

James mother nodded. "That's a good idea. Just forget about it."

James could see his father turn his head away to suppress his displeasure at James's willingness to forget about his performance. He said nothing.

James met Adrienne at the door just as she was starting to knock. "Hey, let's go," he said as he exited the house, following her white ski parka to the Lexus that sat in the driveway.

Inside the car, Adrienne made introductions. "Kath, Lainie, Mitch, Weezie, this is James. James, these are my lax buds." He could see them vaguely in the darkness of the SUV; they all looked tall, their hair pulled back in elegant ponytails, shoulders as wide as Adrienne's. The car smelled as fragrant as fresh flowers.

After an hour of driving – to Dairy Queen in Framingham, through Natick, down a dark road in Wayland, heading nowhere, it seemed – Adrienne asked James, "Do you want to roll with us?"

He heard Adrienne's friends giggle. He didn't know exactly what Adrienne was referring to by "rolling."

"I don't really know what you're talking about, but I don't expect it's anything crazy, so why not?"

Adrienne cuddled into the crook of James's right arm, her thigh pressed against his. "Just watch."

Adrienne took out a tin of Altoids. Inside, mixed in with the white discs, were green tablets, shiny like Advil. "It's E. We're gonna go to Michelle's house and take some Ecstasy." She looked at James expectantly.

James could feel his head pull away from Adrienne's. His thoughts started to whirl, as he tried to reconcile the girl he had assumed her to be with this new person. She looked just as wholesome; her voice sounded just as assured. It was just as exhilarating to sit next to her. He could see the heart against her neck, reflecting the lights as they passed by.

He knew he had to respond. The girls all awaited his answer. "I'm in," he said, and Kathy accelerated toward Michelle's house. A green tab slid down everyone's throat before they turned onto Michelle's street in Wayland.

After fifteen minutes in Michelle's living room, meeting new people, boys and girls both, the lights subdued, though he could still see faces and feel the embrace of these new people, James began to submit to the bass of the CD that was playing emphatically in the den. He found himself dancing with a short, athletic girl whose short blond hair rose and fell rhythmically with the smooth movement of her hips, and they spun around each other as if they were Mr. and Mrs. Rush at an oldies night at the town hall. He didn't know her name, but it didn't seem to matter. Another girl replaced the short girl; James hoped she was as good a dancer, because it seemed James could dance better with these girls than with anyone he had ever danced with. This new girl bounced a lot as she danced; James enjoyed watching her bounce and he imitated her, finding a rhythm and a reserve of energy he hadn't tapped into since mid-season. It was a B-52s song, something about the mall. James thought the song rocked. The bouncing girl swung her arms gracefully, reminding James of the way people had danced at Woodstock. There was an abandon that this girl accepted, an offering of herself to the music, and James felt swept along.

At times James sat down on the bench that sat in front of the couch – probably a coffee table. He watched the swirl around him, as people came together earnestly, their faces filled with their emotion for each other, their embraces lasting more than a few excited breaths, their arms encircling each other, their feet playing alongside each other's in some amazing harmony, their heads tuned to the music that emerged cleanly from the   speakers, bodies pulsing, the beat like some Rio Carnival leviathan, grabbing people, coupling them, hands lingering on elbows, pulling bodies together, cheek nestling for a span of notes against cheek, then a voluptuous separation, voluptuous in the promise of a rejoining, another long and lingering embrace – until, eventually, the embrace became more of a nestling, or maybe a nesting, as the faces separated, and the heads pitched back, but the hips never lost their purchase, and bellies and groins stayed locked together.

And then James was swept into their midst, his breathing in concert with the drumbeat, which always seemed to be accelerating, so his legs moved faster and faster, his hands finding ways to hold these girls in ways he had only imagined, though everyone was still fully clothed, and he moved smoothly, dampness filling his shirt and shorts, the den like a greenhouse, breeding a conjoining of these sinewy limbs, as they twisted and extended their shoots, arching over other compliant limbs, a dense-pack of lushness, their fruit almost too heavy to hold now, so they began to bestow this ripeness upon each other in generous offerings, the juice sweet, running down James's dry throat, the beat continuing outside and inside, cotton becoming lace becoming mist becoming just an ideal, no longer anything tangible, just the electrical impulse that is the miraculous essence of every atom, no weight, just a particle of light or energy or electricity, all those particles joining to form an organic body, that rose from its own birth, rising, sweeping, in arcs of familiarity and comfort, in swaths of light that caught James's breath short just for sheer, pendulous excitement.

Adrienne appeared and disappeared in the dance, and James would start after her, to try to join his aura with hers, but she would be gone, and he would find himself dancing with someone else, someone with long hair pulled back into a ponytail, her fingernails lightly stroking his back, then digging in just enough to control his migration, her mouth nearing his, lips searching, hair twirling, wrapping itself around his shoulders at one end of the twirl, at the other end, their fingertips lying so lightly, like a butterfly's wings, opening and closing, but never separating, then their bodies coming back together in a spasm of craving that had suddenly emerged from their movement, a craving that seemed so natural and ineluctable that neither one could resist it as they continued their search for perfection, in perfect harmony, in absolute surrender to the music that controlled them.

Hours later James blinked his way to the kitchen, to check the clock on the stove, to see that it was 2:10. He returned to the den, where the music continued, though its denizens were starting to lose their appetite, or had been sated in their appetite. James could only recount the last five hours vaguely, as if he had been underwater, viewing these roiling, shadowy people and his own involvement with them with some kind of out-of-focus lens. He took deep breaths to try to restore himself to a reality that said he needed to get home. He was probably 12 miles from his house, and he knew only one person at the party, Adrienne. He started asking for her.

Finally, in one of the bedrooms, he found her, dreamily draped with two other figures on the bed, a candelabra of light spinning on the ceiling. He saw a stereopticon in the hands of the other girl. James hated to put a chill on their reverie, but he had to go home. "Adrienne," he whispered. "Adrienne," he whispered more loudly. Her head rose off the pillow.

"Yeah?" she asked sympathetically.

"What's your time frame here?" He didn't want to seem immature, but he had to try to find a way out of this maze that his evening had become.

"I hadn't even thought about it. What about you?" He could see her starting to reconnoiter, seeing his anxiety.

"I hate to admit it, but I gotta get home some time soon. My folks are pretty much lookin the other way, because they've basically written me off, but I don't want to completely blow it all in one night. What do you say we get out of here in ten minutes?"

Adrienne rose from the bed and pulled James into the hallway. "Actually, we thought we'd spend the night. No way we could drive right now. My mom knows I'm staying out."

"Well, I didn't clear that with my folks. I gotta get home. Can you find someone to drive me?"

"I'll see." After gliding down the hall for a minute, Adrienne returned. "We're gonna wake up Michelle's brother, who's been asleep for a couple hours. He didn't party at all. He's 22 or something. He's gonna take a couple kids home. I'm gonna stay. OK?" She leaned on James, her right leg bent around and behind his legs at the knee.

"Yeah, I'd love to stay, but I know it would not turn out cool."

In a few minutes Michelle's brother met James at the door, where he, another boy, and three girls all gathered to return to their quiet and (hopefully) dark homes.

At 2:50 James entered his house. His mother was sitting up at the kitchen table, her gray bathrobe pulled up to cover her neck, a cup of tea in front of her, no steam rising from the cup. James's eyes opened wide before he dropped his head.

His mother seemed resigned. "Where have you and the girls been?" she asked.

James looked at his mother. "We got ice cream; then we went over to a friend of hers in Wayland. No drinking. No smoking. We did a lot of talking, a lot of listening to music. To be honest, it was a little crazy, but I kept my head. No alcohol at all." He felt more guilt than he had felt the night he had been apprehended by the police, lying to his mother about the night, trying to make himself feel better by letting her think he had resisted temptation this evening, when his perfidy had been more extreme than ever before.

"You know your father and I worry about you every time you leave this house, especially since you were caught drinking. It's not fair for you to put us through this. We deserve better." Her voice was broken, splintered by his self-absorption.

James did all he could to bolster her. "Mom, I know it's impossible for you to watch me grow up and go out, and, believe me, it's hard for me too. I think I'm getting control over it, and then my stupidity breaks out again. But I do love you and Dad, and I will keep trying to do the right thing." He felt the truth of his words pierce the depth of his concealment, causing him to join his mother in her tears. He could not contain his misery. "I'll keep trying. And thanks for caring for me." He put his arms around his mother's shoulders, bending over her, his head coming to rest next to hers, as she sobbed.

"Kathy, I'm lost," I said
Though I knew she was sleeping
"I'm empty and aching
And I don't know why"

from *America* by Paul Simon

Ben

As Ben headed out of the house for a short, one hour practice (because the wedding at the church began at 11), Scott opened the refrigerator door, awake early, though he did not look alert.

Ben paused at the door. "What'd you do last night?"

"We went to the Summit game against Draper. We won a close one, three or four points, I guess." He poured orange juice into a tall glass and scratched his belly underneath his sweatshirt. Ben stayed silent, knowing Scott would be compelled to fill in the blank about the rest of the evening. "Holly didn't go to the game, but I got a ride to her house, and her mom gave me a ride home later." He left the time that he came home vague.

"Did you see your sister when she came home?" Mary was already at work, but he thought she had come home late last night.

"No, I didn't see if she was home or not." Scott was a good brother, not selling his sister out. Ben understood.

On his way to practice, Ben stopped at Mary's Dunkin Donuts, to grab the munchkins for the team and to see Mary.

He pulled up to the drive-through, hoping that Mary was working. "Fifty donut holes and a cup of hot chocolate?" he ordered.

Mary's voice answered politely, "That will be $7.28; please drive right up to the window. . . . And a Happy Saturday to you, Dad," she added, having recognized his voice.

At the window he gave Mary a ten dollar bill. "Keep the change. Hi, honey. What time'd you start this morning?"

"Six. It was an early wakeup call. I was out with Janey, and we went over to see some guys in Wayland. It was a late night, I'll admit, and the guys were kind of crazy. I'll fill you in later. But my alarm worked just fine." Mary's face lit up with the promise of a weekend. "I'm off at one o'clock, and the rest of the day is mine."

"Well, your mom and I will be at the wedding at the church. It starts at 11:00. The reception's at the church, too. I'd guess we'll be home around 5 or 6, maybe a little later. Have a relaxing afternoon."

Ben left practice in Bryan's hands, after running two full-court dribbling drills and setting the teams up for the Saturday practice. He had not even changed into his sweats, keeping his jeans and flannel shirt on. Before he left, after the first set of games, he pulled the team together.

336

"Last night was a disaster, any way you look at it. It shows how horribly we can play. I think there was one other game, the Wellesley game, that was as abominable, another game that set the standard for how poorly we can play. But last night lowered the bar considerably. I'm just glad we don't have a brunch planned for this weekend, because I don't think any of us wants to be reminded about that Braintree game. It's over. Done. I can't even remember it myself right now." He paused.

"Anyway, all I want to talk about is Monday's game with Wellesley. Remember, next week is our three-game week. We'll have a one-hour practice, varsity only, at 7:00 tomorrow night, shooting and reviewing Wellesley. Use today as a day to get the bad thoughts out of your system.

"Dan, Geoff, and Jason, you were on the mark in our first scrimmage today. You ran the floor and talked constantly on defense. Nice work. The rest of you have to get up to that speed. No carryover from last night.

"I have a wedding at 11:00, and I am out the door in one minute. Coach Taft, play hard, have fun, and give me a full report on the second half of practice tomorrow night at 7.

"See you guys. One 'Tight,' and I'm gone." The team gathered awkwardly, the JV team granting the inner circle to the varsity, the players exchanging places, the younger players not knowing how to give voice to their desire to be part of the whole. "One . . two . . . three."

The team issued an attempt at redemption with their "tight," and James strode to the door.

Seated halfway to the front on the right side of the church, pulled toward the middle, naturally, to have a good view of the matrimonial rites, Ben and Willa sat very close to one another. The second marriage of a friend seemed to bring out the fierceness of one's marital commitment, if Ben was any judge. Willa sat next to the aisle, but she spent little time admiring the bride, out of deference to Tom's first wife, Alice, from whom he had been divorced for about two years. Tom's children, two boys, stood in the first row, in front of Ben and Willa, near the aisle on the right side. Ben was drawn to the simple beauty of Devin, Tom's new wife, a woman who looked as if she played a lot of tennis and golf, her hair short and blond, her shoulders not broad, but raised with strength from her collarbone, her bare arms toned and tanned – even in January – a waistline narrower than the bouquet she had handed to her sister, the matron of honor. As Ben sat at Willa's side, he turned to look at her, his wife, her brown eyes, her fashionable, miniaturized glasses, her settling figure well-hidden in a tailored black dress. Willa's shoes were black, pointy and uncomfortable – he knew from past evenings with her in those shoes. Ben knew the comparison was unfair and that a 51-year old woman couldn't compete, in physical attractiveness, with a thirty-something woman who had obviously lived in luxury.

"I feel bad for Alice," Ben offered, thinking of her on this day that excluded her.

"I've felt bad for her for three years," Willa replied, referring to those rumors that had swept the church about Tom's infidelities, not necessarily with Devin, but with more than one other woman, while his marriage with Alice collapsed.

"Yeah, she is a nice woman. I just can't see what he would see in someone else." As Ben tried to fathom the temerity and urgency it would take to act on an impulse to step outside his marriage, he looked, as usual, at the stone arches that vaulted the church, arches comprised of two majestic, leaning lines of stone, mutually supportive of each other, secure in their interdependence. He loved to trace those lines, seeing them disappear into each other at the pinnacle of the arch. He wondered how arches came to be icons of religious edifices, especially Catholic churches, though this one happened to be Episcopalian. Being a teacher, he was usually surrounded by utilitarian architecture, and his church was perhaps the sole structure that stirred awe in him. He looked across at the corresponding arch on the other side of the church; he could not see the peak, just the grand stones that supported the arch and the church itself.

"Don't you love the stone arches in here?" he asked Willa.

She looked upward for a moment, reporting, "They're nice, yeah." She seemed unimpressed, though he could understand her indifference. He himself rarely noticed architecture. And they never talked about it because they never observed it.

In fifteen minutes the short ceremony was completed, Reverend Harris keeping his homily abbreviated, another nod to Alice, Ben thought. Tom was an ardent church-goer; consequently, he wanted his second marriage to carry the sacral weight of his first. Ben didn't know Devin's background, other than the fact that she came from Wellesley and she had one young child of her own, who sat with his grandparents on the other side of the church in the first pew.

In the Parish Hall the six-piece band played dance music, swing, blues, country two-steps. Ben found himself sitting at the circular table where he and Willa had eaten the tasteful dinner prepared by the support group within the church, of which Willa was a member. He sat because he lacked comfort in his dance movement. Willa and he did dance occasionally; he led her familiarly in the slow dances. When the band played Louie Armstrong's *What a Wonderful World*, Ben felt his heart well up at the promise of the song, a song and a promise to which he and Willa had capitulated at their own wedding. The guitar lead-in to *We Are Family* inspired Ben to follow Willa onto the cleared section in front of the band-stage again, this time to kick his limbs out without restraint. The band was very good. Tom's newly created family clustered purposefully in a circle, the three children intermingling hesitantly, Tom's oldest obviously wishing he were elsewhere.

But, in general, Ben sat, his friends stopping by occasionally to see if he wanted any more punch. Ben watched Willa dance with her cool rhythm, her hair flying as she twirled to a downbeat, her feet (shoes abandoned) prancing smartly. She had always been able to lose herself in dance; she had taken four years of dance lessons when she was a kid.

Willa and Peter Harrison, a long-time church member whom Ben knew casually, had fun dancing the swing to the band's faster numbers. Peter had the handle, moving and turning Willa, providing a great lead, reining Willa in just when she showed signs of floating away, then tossing her away again, only to open his arms again to welcome her back. Ben was jealous of Peter's ease on the floor, an ease Ben didn't possess. Ben turned his attention to the band, hearing the saxophone especially, though the lead guitar challenged the horns consistently.

When Tom and Devin stopped by Ben's table, he was the only one seated, everyone else up on the floor dancing. Devin looked happy, her son in tow. Tom said, "Ben, glad you could make it. We're so appreciative of all Willa did to make this day happen. The hall looks beautiful. And the food was great, didn't you think?"

Ben nodded, standing, shaking Tom's hand and giving Devin an embrace that included a kiss on the cheek. She said, "Tom says you and he coached together a few years back. That must have been fun. I love his boys. They're good kids." She stepped back to look at Ben with a frankness that made him feel welcome in their new marriage. As he smiled at her, he was startled by her beauty. Her dress shimmered, but no more than her face.

"You look beautiful," he said to her boldly, then, turning to Tom, said, "And you look pretty good for an old man." He quickly wished he had not said these two phrases together because they made note of the age difference between Tom and Devin, and he wanted to note their happiness, not the disparity of their ages. "You both look radiant," he said, more to the point.

339

"Thanks," they replied, almost in concert, and they moved on. Tom gave Ben a clap on the back as he left.

Ben moved on to a table where a few friends had gathered. Willa remained on the dance floor, Peter Harrison still in control. Ben loved how she moved as a dancer. Normally, as he was escorting her, he did not have the opportunity to appreciate the way she flowed on the floor – he could feel it, when he danced with her, but he couldn't see it. And when they danced, he was always trying to take the lead, but unable to consummate the role. It always seemed to be a tug of war, as he led Willa and she tried to respond. But, leaning on a metal folding chair, he could see the lightness in her feet, the way she could make the motion of her body into a perfect circle, and the joy that she exuded in dance. She was like a bird that took flight in the middle of a song, landing lightly, then taking off again. Ben didn't know if he had felt so attracted to her in a long time. Her face shone with its secret knowledge of her assurance as she stepped so delicately, one arm tethered to Peter's hand, the other pointing to some invisible place where this grace would lead her. It was beautiful to watch.

Four songs later, Willa finally tired; she moved toward the table where she and Ben had been sitting, but, seeing him near the windows, she came to him, her shoulders bunched in excitement. "Isn't the band unbelievable?"

"Yeah, they're probably the best this hall has ever heard. You're having a good time, huh?" She looked resplendent. Her face shone with a youthfulness culled from her dance. Her hands flew up to her hair to arrange it neatly. "You look beautiful."

She turned away slightly, deflecting the compliment. " I just can't get enough of the band. That's exactly the music I learned to dance to when I was a young girl, taking dance lessons. For some reason my instructor loved swing music, and I learned to move to that sound. And Peter is a heck of a dancer, too. That helps." She didn't seem to notice how her last remark cast its shadow on Ben, she was so dreamy.

During the next song, Blood Sweat and Tears' *Spinning Wheel*, Tom and Devin made their exit, and then the party was over, the seventy or so friends gathering their shoes, jackets, and purses, heading to the double door of the Parish Hall.

"Ben, I've got to clean up here for an hour or so. Do you want to come back and pick me up, or should I get a ride home?" Willa still beamed.

Ben, still envisioning Willa dancing languorously, hadn't thought about clean-up, thinking instead of a close, intimate snack, the two of them, maybe a Margherita flatbread at Giovanni's in Framingham, two glasses of Pinot Noir, and some meaningful handholding under the tablecloth . "I'll stay and help. No problem. Just lead the way."

Heading off to the closet, where the tables and chairs would be stacked, Willa said, "Oh, that's all right. I know we have enough people. You can go home. I'll catch a ride in about an hour. You're not on the functions committee, I am." After opening the doors to the closet, she approached one of the tables, collecting silverware and removing the centerpiece. "Do you want to take this home with you?" She held the flower arrangement out to him.

Shrugging his shoulders, Ben gathered that he was not in the ranks of the service people, and he closed, "I'll be back in an hour? Is that good? Maybe I'll check on my mom. I haven't seen her in a while."

"That's a great idea. Just grab a little supper with her, OK?" She laughed at the joke, knowing that Ben scrunched his face unpleasantly thinking about Fidelity House's food. "I'll see you around 5:30?"

Ben headed toward the doors. "5:30."

At Fidelity House Margot's room was empty; Ben walked down B corridor to C corridor, thinking she might be visiting her friend who made wooden figures. When she wasn't there, he returned to her wing, and, seeing most of the residents eating their suppers in their beds, the hospital table extended over the bed, Ben wondered where Margot might be. Her food tray was not on her bedside table, nor was her pocketbook tucked in her closet when he looked there.

At the desk, when he inquired about his mother, the nurse said, "I think she might be eating downstairs tonight. There's entertainment this evening, a sort of cocktail hour leading into supper. A man playing piano, and I hear he's really good."

Downstairs Ben followed the music to the large dining hall that was usually empty, but on this occasion, there were perhaps fifty or sixty people sitting at small tables draped in linen, rapt by the romantic music emanating from the piano. Margot motioned for Ben to join her at her table.

"Looks like you've got a nice performer here," Ben offered.

"Yes, he's quite good. He actually makes me feel young, with these songs he's playing." His present piece was a Gershwin tune that Ben knew slightly.

341

Some couples were dancing; in fact, one elderly man was dancing with his spouse with a fervor that surprised and pleased Ben. Sitting in the chair she offered him, he thought he would be polite. "Mom, do you want to dance?"

"Oh, I don't think that's necessary," she replied, dismissing the idea as if it were something that called up bad memories.

"Oh, I know it's not necessary – but maybe it would feel nice. I don't think we've danced since my wedding, and that was a few years ago."

Considering Ben's time table for a moment, Margot agreed, "I bet you're right. But that doesn't mean an old lady has to get up and make a fool out of herself. I'm in a wheelchair, remember?"

"Oh, I'll support you, don't worry. Let's just give it a try. Next song." He let the suggestion hang out there, and when Margot did not reject this latest request, he knew she would like to try.

At the beginning of the next song, another melodious song from his mother's youth, Ben stood and held out his hand. He reached over to pull his mother from her chair, leading her gently between tables, his hand under her elbow for each slow step. When they got to the space in front of the piano, Ben moved his right hand behind Margot's back, trying to find some part of her that he could support while they danced. She stood stiffly, as he extended his left hand and her right, and they began to sway cautiously. He couldn't help but laugh to himself, thinking what they must look like.

One dance and they returned to their table, slowly. Margot had finished her supper; she offered her untouched peaches to Ben, and he spooned them into his mouth.

"Ben, if you don't mind, when this is over, I'm going to have to ask you to leave. There's a gentleman who escorted me down to the dining hall, and he will take me back to my room. I don't want him to think that I have found another escort. I feel a little silly, but I guess it's a kind of date."

Ben laughed, his eyes wide. "Are you kidding me? You're on a date? Then why isn't he sitting at your table?"

Margot had the answer. "Oh, when you came, he had just stepped out to use the facilities. Here he is now. Phil, I would like you to meet my son, Ben. Ben, this is Phil." Phil moved in a sprightly way, belying the height of the waistband of his pants.

"Howdy, youngster. How's it going?" He sounded a little like someone from an old Western, his accent traceable to Wyoming or Utah.

"Very well, sir. I see you have my mother safely in your custody. I don't want to interfere," and at that moment, the piano player ended his concert, and people started to gather themselves to leave.

Margot finished her expulsion of Ben. "Thanks for stopping by, Ben. You saw a wonderful show. He plays just about every month. Phil and I have seen more than one of them together now."

Phil looked at Ben as if he might not have joined her for any previous concerts, but Ben did not know whether Phil or Margot were more inaccurate in their memories.

"Bye, Mom. I'll see you later."

Back at Parish Hall, earlier than he had expected, Ben opened the door from the parking lot, wondering how much of the cleanup remained. The hall was bare, except for the band's instruments, lying in cases on the floor, as the bandleader wrapped up mike cords on the stage. The sizable speakers sat on dollies, waiting to be transported to the van that sat in the lot.

When Ben opened the door to the kitchen, which was surprisingly dark, illuminated by just one light over the sink, a couple quickly separated from each other's embrace at that sink, where dishes sat on the counter waiting to be dried. Ben was stunned to see that he was looking at Willa and Peter, facing away from the door, looking out the dark window, their faces reflected in that window looking out on darkness. Willa's head was down. Ben didn't know whether to leave quietly, or to announce his arrival noisily. He did neither as he approached the double sink. "Looks like you still have a lot of work to do," he mused, unable to address what he had witnessed.

Willa could not respond. Peter, bolder, filled the deadness in the air. "If you want to pick up a dish towel, we'll be done quickly. Thanks." He only half turned, giving Ben an inquisitive glance, trying to determine what Ben had seen. Willa still faced the window. She still had her shoes off.

Ben picked up a towel and, after five minutes of silent labor, the job was done. Peter wiped the sink down, Willa put the last of the dishes in the large wooden cabinets, and Ben snapped the wet dish towels. "Is there a washing machine here?" he asked.

Willa said, her voice catching, "Yes, I'll take them. Thanks." She walked to him, her hand out, her eyes averted. When he handed her the five or six wet towels, he could feel her hand, and he wanted to hold it, to feel the familiar fingers, their length and strength always impressing him.

343

In the car Ben turned on the lights, and pulled the Subaru in a circle, heading to the exit of the parking lot. He did not know what to say, but he knew that if Willa did not say anything soon, he would ask her what was going on. He felt as if he were standing on an icy sheet that hung suspended over a deep lake, and that these first words would crack the ice in a way that might not be remediable.

Willa looked ahead at the road, just as she had looked down at the sink and out the window in the kitchen of the church.

"Can I ask what I witnessed when I came in the door?" he kept his voice quiet.

"You saw two people who were very tired, giving each other some support." Willa's response lacked depth.

"Willa, I don't think I have to tell you that that answer is not even close to an explanation of what was going on. I guess I have to rephrase the question: of what *is* going on. I would like to hear you explain what *is* going on." Ben waited.

Willa sat huddled in her seatbelt, all the grace of her dance dissipated like a suntan dispelled by the freeze of winter. She could not respond.

"I don't want to sound accusatory, but I would like the courtesy of an honest explanation," Ben continued.

Willa remained silent, clinging to that shred of decency that might accompany a non-explanation. Ben could hear her crying to herself, trying not to let it out. But it was inevitable.

Ben suggested, "Shall we go somewhere? The kids are home. I don't want to see them, and I don't want to just pick this up later, either. How about we go to Willow's? There's a nice dark corner there where we can talk about this."

His suggestion drew Willa out of the corner in which she was hiding. "I don't want to go to your new home-away-from-home," she spat out nastily. "No thanks. Meet all your new friends? Spare me," she added hatefully.

Ben sighed deeply. He wanted to stop at the side of the road and just yell it out, but he wanted there to be some civility to their confrontation, because there was going to be a confrontation, he knew that. He steered the Subaru carefully, because, despite the four wheel drive, the roads were icy, getting slicker as the nighttime cold came on.

After ten minutes of aimless, silent driving, Ben pulled out his cell phone, to call home. "Hey, Scott, is Mary home?"

"Not yet. I think she's going to the hockey game. 'R'you coming home now?" he inquired.

"No, we're gonna grab a bite to eat before we get home. Maybe Wallace's, we're not sure. You OK?"

"Dad, I think I can handle myself. Hammy's picking me up in about twenty minutes. I'll call Mary and tell her to call you when she knows her plans. Have fun. Can I talk to Mom?"

"Sure." Ben handed the phone to Willa.

"Hello?" she asked with all the bravado she could muster. "Yeah, sure. . .. OK. . . . I'll see you around midnight? . . . Thereabouts, hmmm. . . . OK. See you later. I love you." Her voice broke as she said the last. She handed the phone back to Ben without looking at him. He snapped it closed and placed it in the pocket of his overcoat.

"Ben, are we going to just drive around all night?" Willa asked after a few more minutes of movement.

Ben did not know how to respond. He could not think of anyplace that would be available for a conversation that might be quiet and might be explosive. Then he thought again. "How about the church? Would there be anyone there?" He knew she had a key to the side door.

Willa did not reply, consenting.

In the church Ben followed Willa's lead, as she opened the door from the Parish Hall into the church itself. She sat in a pew and immediately knelt down and began to pray. In the darkness Ben could not see her lips moving. He gave her a few moments to affirm her relationship with God.

"Anything you can share with me?" he asked after her continued silence.

In just a brief moment, she said, "I'm trying to sort it all out in my own mind. I'm asking God for help in understanding what's going on, because I don't know."

It was a start. "Please talk to me. You have lots of time to talk to God. But I need to be clued in. God already knows what's going on, every detail, what you're thinking, what Peter's thinking, how many times you've been together, what you've done together, how you feel about him, how you feel about me, how Peter feels about you, and I think that's pretty obvious." Ben could hardly stop himself, his voice turning down all those avenues that his mind had tracked in the last half hour.

Willa still held on to her silence, causing Ben's voice to rise. "Willa, I don't think you are offering me the slightest courtesy here. We are married. We share things with each other, even if they are hard to talk about. When I've had doubts about coaching, I've let you know.

345

When I've felt you are screening me out, I've tried to let you know. When you've felt overwhelmed, you've shared your frustration with me. This is a time for talking."

Willa began crying again. "Ben, I didn't know where to turn. You have just been putting up a bigger and bigger wall as the years have gone by. First it's basketball, then it's school, then it's running summer school, then it's making your camp bigger and more successful. I've tried to talk to you about it, but you are always too busy moving off in another important direction. It never ends. And it never includes me. And now, you've added bartending to your resume," she concluded somewhat facetiously, her bitterness still evident.

"So I just started putting my faith in God, and he opened the doors of the church to me. I've found great comfort in that church, more comfort than I find in our house, more comfort by far."

Ben had resisted the impulse to interrupt her when she said she found "comfort" in the church. Now he felt there was an opening. He said icily, "How can you tell me you're getting advice from God when you've gotten support from the arms of another man? How can God be telling you to do that? I don't get it. It's you who are in another man's arms." His anger was hard to control, but he sighed again and waited for her answer.

"Ben, you won't understand this, but Peter listens to me. He provides support when I am just filled with anguish. You know we've been having problems; I know we've been having problems. Peter is patient, never demanding anything of me, nothing at all. He's just there for me, and I know he'll make me feel better." Ben looked at Willa, and her gaze seemed transfixed on the cross at the front of the church. The emergency light at the doorway across the church gave a slight glow to the sanctuary, now that Ben had become accustomed to the light.

"How many times have the two of you been together?"

Ben knew from the hesitation in Willa's voice that she was not revealing the intricacy of their relationship. "Only at church, I swear. We are on the same committees, and we will spend time together afterwards, I'll admit. That's when I confide in him." Willa told this as if their conferences were what a good marriage needed. Maybe she was right. Ben didn't know. But it didn't feel right.

"There just seems to be something wrong when you have to confide in someone outside our marriage in order to survive our marriage. There is either something essentially wrong with the marriage, and I don't disagree with that, or there is something essentially wrong with your relationship with Peter. I think it's both. And I don't want to hear you say that it's all innocent. I think your God knows it's not." He hated to bring God into their torment, but He had been keeping vigil for a long time, Ben knew.

Willa protested. "It is innocent, I swear. We have never done anything that could be considered a betrayal of this marriage. If you want, we can have a meeting with Peter, to make sure you believe me."

Ben almost laughed at Willa's attempt at an alibi: to confirm her innocence by asking her co-conspirator about their innocence. "Willa, I'm sorry, but I would like to think I can trust you more than I can trust Peter Harrison. I don't even want to bring him into this discussion at this point. This is a matter between you and me."

"But that's just it: I haven't felt you've provided me a real audience for a long time, and Peter has. So he has to be a part of the discussion."

Ben could not believe that he was becoming the source of Willa's displeasure, in a mind-boggling piece of rationalization. "I'm sorry, honey, I'm just not buying it. How can you honestly blame me for your wandering eyes or hands or mind, or whatever it is that you're not able to control. I'm not buying it, not one piece of it. That's just bullshit." Ben knew that, when he launched into invective, he lost credibility with Willa, but he could not help it.

Willa cringed, the way she would have cringed when Scott dropped an action figure in the sanctuary during church twelve years ago. "Ben, I knew you would start swearing, and I can honestly say I understand." A quick expulsion of disbelief exploded out of Ben's lips upon hearing her condescension. He could not help himself. "I'll sit here as long as I have to, to try to make you understand what Peter offers me: someone who has time for me and who will listen. That's all. That's all. How many times can I say it? How many different ways can I say it?" Willa believed what she was telling Ben. But Ben didn't. IIc had seen them. They were embracing in a way that does not happen the first time two friends embrace. There was a history in that embrace.

"It doesn't seem we're going to get past our different versions of what happened tonight," Ben surmised. "Let's go home. I can't pretend it didn't happen, and I'm glad I saw the two of you, so I know that it's happening, but it sounds as if it'll take a long time for us to agree on what happened. Maybe we'll never agree. I hope not, because that sounds like an awful marriage." He left this awful pronouncement hanging in the air as he rose, recalling for the first time in a while that they were sitting in the church, where his thoughts were usually so comforted and eased – just the way Willa said hers were with Peter. He could not see the stone arch in the obscurity of the church, but he knew it was there, just as solid as it had been about eight hours ago, during Tom and Devin's wedding.

The next few days passed in a slow dance of solitude. On Sunday Ben and Willa went to church, sitting close to each other, speaking in monosyllables, sharing the hymnal, each praying silently. When Ben stopped at Dunkin Donuts to see Mary at the drive-through, he had a hard time initiating his amusing prattle with her, but he managed to muster some humor, drawing a girlish giggle from her before he drove up to get his hot chocolate with five helpings of whipped cream, as he had insisted.

When he picked Willa up after Sunday child-care, an hour later, she looked warm coming out of the Parish Hall, walking carefully on the icy parking lot, bundled up with a scarf and a woolen hat pulled down over her hair. As Ben drove home, they concentrated on the cold conditions outside the Subaru.

Sunday night's practice, just one hour long, the only Sunday practice of the year, swiftly passed, drills taking up most of the hour. He had few words about Wellesley, other than to remind the team that they had laid a fifteen point loss on the Panthers. They had few weapons and fewer victories, two, putting them in last place in the conference. "If we put out a sustained effort for four quarters, they will wilt," Ben assured the team, his words lacking their customary resonance. When they gave a desultory "tight," at the end of practice, Ben stopped their retreat into the locker room.

"Gentlemen, please come back here." They came back, ready to be chastened. "I don't think you have the proper frame of mind approaching this team. Half an effort will not get it done. If today's practice is any indication, we're in for a disappointing evening tomorrow night. Now let's get together and try to make this team into something that we can be proud of. Every minute we are together, we have to understand that this will all be over in a month or less – it's up to you how long this season will continue. If any of you doesn't have the desire to be here, then please just step out of the circle right now." Ben looked at each of his players, trying to generate an urgency that he didn't really feel himself. He knew he was hoping for the players that he knew he could rely on – Geoff, Archie, Dan – to provide him with a connection he needed.

In a minute, they came together for a boisterous shout, leaving the gym filled with the echo of their youthful noise.

Monday proved to be a busy day in school, as Ben spent his free period working with one of his freshman dissidents, Paul, who needed help in revising an essay he had barely begun.

"What are you trying to say here, Paul?" Ben asked, as they sat at a round table in the media center.

Paul looked at his hand-written first page. "I think I'm trying to say what the poem is about."

Ben nodded. "And what is the poem about?"

"It's using a lot of figurative language to get his point across."

Ben nodded again, extending his patience patiently. "And what is his point?" Paul had chosen the Langston Hughes poem *Mother To Son*, with its admonition, "Life for me ain't been no crystal stair."

Paul hesitated.

"Is Hughes saying that life is easy and full of joy?"

Paul continued to hesitate. "Not really."

Ben and Paul continued to hover around the expression of an idea for another ten minutes, Ben refusing to give Paul what he wanted: for Ben to tell Paul what to say. In the end Paul had advanced to the notion that the persona was not happy with "his" life because it had been hard. Ben had not even gotten to discuss the idea that she was telling her son to continue in his own pursuits because she was continuing to pursue her own ambitions despite her tribulations.

The game with Wellesley came and went without Ben's even raising his voice. The Panthers won, 61 – 51, everyone getting a chance to play, since Casteline held a seventeen point lead at halftime, and extended it through the third. Willa did not come to the game, but she had been to only three or four games so far in the season, her obligations with work and church taking an increasing portion of her time. The team was delighted with their victory, evening their record at 7 and 7, making the possibility of a post-season appearance more likely. After the game Ben had to leave quickly, because he was working at Willow's, having told Pete that he would be late because of the game. By the time he got to Willow's, it was 8:45. He removed his jacket and put on his bartender's apron, nodding to the customers who were set up at the bar, including the sad woman with the curly hair who took the first seat and sipped her white wine.

The sink was overfilled with glasses and plates, but Ben caught up with a fervent pace, to make amends for his tardiness. Pete commented more than once that Ben didn't have to do everything at once. "Don't have a coronary, for Christ's sake. Just be smooth." Pete seemed to have an effective bartending demeanor: keep moving and everything will get done.

Bryan and Lisa had boneless wings and drafts. "Everything OK?" Bryan asked him as he brought their second glasses.

Ben knew his head had been down most of the game and here at the bar too. "Yeah, it's just a busy day, you know?"

Bryan looked at him skeptically. Lisa said, "Nice game tonight, huh?" She had not been there, but Bryan had filled her in on their common successes that evening.

"Yeah. Bryan's team is looking solid. As usual, they're making a second half run, solid defense and the offense is catching up. And we played OK, but, to be honest, Wellesley didn't put up much of a fight."

Setting his glass down, Bryan interjected, "But at this time of the year, some teams are still putting out the effort and some are not. And yours put out the effort."

"You're right. Sometimes that's all it takes." Ben said, pulling back, their empty glasses in his hand, moving back to the bar, where the woman watched him as he passed. He didn't have the time to chat tonight.

But two hours later, when some of the tavern had cleared out, she still sat on her stool, her shoulders slumping further. She had slowed down in her intake, but she had not stopped drinking her wine.

"You ready to head out into the chill?" he asked, by way of telling her he had the time to chat now, finally.

"Just about. It's been a long night." She looked dissatisfied.

"Anything that can be fixed?" Ben asked.

"No, thanks. Unless you are an attorney as well as a bartender and a coach."

Ben was surprised to learn that she knew he was a coach.

"I'll admit that I lack a knowledge of the court system, and I can say I'm glad that I am ignorant in that arena."

She smiled ironically. "Well, unfortunately, I'm too well versed in that venue"

Ben asked lightly, "Oh? I hope it's not for a major felony," opening the door for further conversation.

"Well, I guess you wouldn't call a divorce a felony, but it sure felt like a crime every time we started shouting at each other, and he told me I was not at all the person he thought I was when we got married."

Ben found a need to empty the dishwasher the instant his guest began talking about her marital difficulties. He did not want to follow that line of inquiry in any direction that might lead to his own burden.

But before he closed the tavern up, he brought a cup of coffee to the woman, who had taken an interest in Jay Leno after he had moved away suddenly. "I thought you might want this before you headed out into cold," he said kindly.

She looked at him appreciatively, holding out her right hand. "Laura Ruben," she said, and he shook her extended hand.

"Ben LaMott," he said, smiling.

"I know. I've been a fan of local sports for a long time. You've been coaching a long time, and quite successfully, I know. I live in Natick, and I've always been amazed how you could squeeze so many wins out of such average teams." The woman made Ben recall those years, not too long ago, when Casteline was considered a tough out, able to claw its way to a win, sometimes with the help of the coach's inventive use of defensive and offensive schemes.

"Well, those days are in the past, that's for sure. We're just scratching out a win here and there, now."

"Well, just last Tuesday, you stole one from Natick."

He wondered how she knew, but she answered his question. "I was there. My boys played for Natick a few years ago – actually, a long time ago – and I still get to some of the home games. I took a little trip to see the game at your place. Nice job." She smiled, knowing how much the game had meant to Ben. But that was before Tom's wedding.

When Laura Ruben rose to leave, Ben felt wrong to look at her, but he couldn't help it. At the coat rack, she slid her coat off the hanger, calling over her shoulder, "Good night. Thanks."

After an hour of cleanup, as Ben was leaving, Pete asked him, "Any chance of you working Thursday? It's a more lively night. You got a game?"

"Actually, no, we have an early practice. I could get down here by 6:00."

"No need, but if you can come in at 7 or 7:30, till closing, I'd appreciate it. You could get some real tips."

"I'm happy to help. I'm having fun. And I want to see what it's like when it gets really busy."

Wednesday's game at Waltham was a Billy Samko show: he dropped 43 points on the Panthers, who had done a good job on him in their first meeting. But he was now realizing his great potential, always evident, but underutilized. In this game he looked like the Division I player he was, having signed a commitment to Northeastern as a 6'6" swing man, able to shoot the 3 and dunk in traffic, too. He hardly missed a shot against the Panthers, and Ben couldn't find a man who

351

could guard him. Waltham held Casteline at arm's length the whole way, winning 71 – 58.

On the ride home Bryan kept quiet, though Ben was not as destroyed by the loss as usual. It was odd to approach a basketball game without the usual emotional attachment; as a result, he was less elated by Monday's victory and, similarly, less dismayed by this defeat. Maybe it was the way to survive: expect less and reduce the disappointment.

But after fifteen minutes of gloomy silence, the team behind them on the bus subdued by the knowledge that Billy Samko had shown them what a real basketball player was, Bryan could not remain excluded. "Ben, what's up?"

Ben sighed, weighing the prospects of revealing to Bryan his doubts and suspicions about Willa. He didn't know how he could tell him just a little part of the story. He finally gave way to his trust in Bryan. "Willa and I are going through a tough time."

"What's it all about? Anything you can talk about?"

Ben looked ahead into the darkness of the empty lane in front of the bus. "I think she's seeing someone else."

Bryan recoiled. "Wow. No way I'd suspect that." He waited for Ben to continue.

"I think it's someone from church, where she's been spending all her time the last year or two. There's a chance that nothing's going on, and that's what she's claiming, but I just saw something between the two of them, and I don't like the feeling I'm getting. It blows my mind."

Bryan agreed.

"I mean, I'm not the best catch in the country, but I'm faithful, I work hard, and I keep the lines of communication open with the kids. And I still want us to have a meaningful relationship – more than anything.

"So – my mind has been on other things."

"Understandable. I remember when I was moving toward my divorce, I had weeks that went by and I didn't know if I was coming or going. There were some days I ended up at Smokey's house or Matt's house, and I had no idea how long I'd been there. And I admit I had a few more beers in those days, just to fill the void."

The bus was turning off the highway, onto the two-lane road that led to the high school. Ben opened up again, "What sucks is to think that you're not the one any more." He thought about that possibility, an idea he had not contemplated until he expressed it.

"I know what you mean. But I did find, a long time later, that there's still hope, that you can be the one again, maybe with someone else, but at least it's not forever."

Ben did not want to think about someone else. He could only admit to one love for himself, and he would also admit that maybe he had taken that love for granted.

When the bus got to the high school, Ben and Bryan stood in their seat, giving nods and encouragement to the team as they filed past Ben clapping hands on his players' shoulders and tapping knuckles with them. "See you at practice tomorrow . . . Good work . . . We'll get Norwood." Ben wondered whether his words sounded as empty as they felt.

And you know the light is fading all too soon
You're just two umbrellas one late afternoon
You don't know the next thing you will say
This is your favorite kind of day
It has no walls, the beauty of the rain
is how it falls, how it falls, how it falls

And there's nothing wrong, but there is something more
And sometimes you wonder what you love her for
She says you've known her deepest fears
Cause she's shown you a box of stained-glass tears
It can't be all, the truth about the rain
is how it falls, how it falls, how it falls

But when she gave you more to find
You let her think she'd lost her mind
and that's all on you
Feeling helpless if she asked for help
or scared you'd have to change yourself

And you can't deny this room will keep you warm
You can look out of your window at the storm
But you watch the phone and hope it rings
You'll take her any way she sings,
or how she calls, the beauty of the rain
is how it falls, how it falls, how it falls
How it falls, how it falls, how it falls

The Beauty of the Rain by Dar Williams

James

There were many reasons to be disappointed with the game versus Waltham, but the biggest disappointment was the fact that it seemed Coach LaMott had quit on the team. During and after the win over Wellesley, Coach had not been very emotional, but James figured that he was just placing the burden of responsibility on the team, where it should be. After the Panthers had beaten Wellesley, James expected a tough workout in preparation for Waltham, but Tuesday's practice was just routine drills, a plan to keep Samko from scoring in the paint, and a lot of work on shooting, on the expectation that there would be few driving lanes, with Samko defending the basket. But the thirteen point loss to Waltham had left Coach LaMott speechless and reactionless.

James had played a lot in each game, playing alongside Jason, Dan, and Archie, with Geoff at the post, in the small lineup that had been successful the past two weeks. He had scored 10 and 11, but played uninspired ball, much like Coach's coaching.

At the beginning of Thursday's practice, as the team broke up to scrimmage full court, James called both scrimmage teams together. Coach LaMott was near the clock, placing six minutes and a specific score on the scoreboard.

"Hey, guys, we've done nothing this week. We beat a weak Wellesley team and we got smoked by a great player in Billy Samko. Practice so far is crap. We have no life; we have no spirit. It's as if we have no expectations. I don't know about you, but I'm not gonna fuckin let this season slip by us like last year's did. We gotta start goin all out right now. If we don't, we can kiss the Norwood game goodbye; we can kiss the season goodbye.

"Andrew has been coming to every practice, shooting in a chair, dribbling an hour each day, yelling for us to keep going hard. Why? So he can join us for at least one more game at the end. We owe it to him give him that chance. Let's go." He spoke loudly at first, but then he realized that his words carried all the import that he needed, and that he did not need even to raise his voice.

"Let's go. On three. One . . . two . . . three. . ."

"TIGHT!"

The scrimmage was what James was looking for. The first team flew down the floor, controlling the boards, allowing James's team only one shot, and then sprinting down the floor ahead of the second team. The first team came from 8 down to win by 5, in a six minute span.

James ripped into his scrimmage-mates. "That's all you got? You're gonna let the first team crush you like that? What, are you happy being second team? You're satisfied to be on the bench?

"Well, I'm not."

When Coach came over to alter the teams, James asked, still bristling with combativeness, "Coach, can we roll it back one time with the same teams? I think we've got more than we showed."

Coach's eyes gleamed a little. "I think we can manage that. Bridget, set the clock up the same way, OK?"

The second scrimmage was a fight. James's team led by 5 with three to go, gave up a three pointer to Archie, then turned the ball over to set up a tying shot from the first team. But Jonas and Andreas bullied the ball out of Geoff's hands for a tough defensive rebound, sending Bobbie down the floor on a breakaway, turning the momentum back to the second team. In the end they held on, winning by one. James outplayed both Archie and Dan, defending them as he had not been able to do all season.

Slapping hands, the second team shouted to each other, "That's it! Oh yeah! What starting team?" It was vindication for the week of bland somnambulance that had been the team's output up until that point in the week.

After practice James called Adrienne, knowing she was done with her practice too. He had felt peculiar with her this week, after Friday night's Wayland activities. In school she had been the same unruffled, bright girl, unchanged in her persistent pursuit of engagement in the classroom. He had not talked about the Ecstasy in which they had indulged. He wondered whether it was a regular habit of hers, or whether Friday had been an anomaly.

She answered, "Is this the Billy Samko fan club?" She was a good needler, major league, definitely. She and her lacrosse buddies must be merciless, James thought.

"Yeah, I'm heading over to Waltham's practice right now. Do you want to come?"

"Do you mean, do you want my mother to drive you?" She wouldn't let him up for air.

"No, I want that lacrosse friend of yours to drive me, except I'm afraid of what she might put in my coffee." This was James's way of turning the conversation to last Friday night.

Adrienne had no quick rejoinder. After a second she said, "I'm afraid there is a very limited supply of that additive, and it's not available right now," trying to dismiss James's inquiry.

But, feet in the air, butt on the edge of the cushion of the couch, head on the rug, James persisted. "Can we talk about that for a minute?"

"Yeah, sure."

"Is that something you do a lot? Because I've never done anything like that, and I'm not sure I'll do it again. But I just want to know what's your connection to it."

Adrienne's voice lacked its customary strength. "We do it once in a while, these lacrosse kids I play with. Some of them are really into it. I thought it would be fun to do it with you."

"Well, that's what I don't really understand: we weren't really together. I was never alone, but I just about didn't ever see you. What's that all about?"

Adrienne knew. "I know when I take E, I just latch onto the person who is close to me, and we really get into it." She paused. "To be honest, I was a little afraid to find you, because I kind of knew where it would lead us, and I wasn't ready for that." James had never heard Adrienne express anything like fear.

James's hat pushed into his forehead. "I wouldn't mind that at all." He hoped he sounded sure of himself.

"Well, we'll probably have another chance some time. But not soon." She changed the subject consciously. "You gonna beat Norwood?"

"I think so. We had a strong practice. You guys in good shape?" Adrienne was becoming a leader on her team, keying an impenetrable defense, sprinting the wing for easy layins. She had scored 20 twice in the past two weeks.

"Yeah, I think so. This will be our 10th win, qualifying us for the tournament. I think we're improving. I'm glad I went out. The kids are great, and I'm staying in shape better than I expected. It's a tough game, really tough. I just get by on athletic talent; I'm no basketball player." She talked as if she knew her limitations, but, in fact, she had none.

"Well, I'll see you tomorrow. Quiz in Geometry?"

"Yeah, on solid tangents. You all set?"

"Yep," James nodded, crushing the crown of his head on the floor at the point of tangency.

James entered the Norwood game with two minutes to go in Period One, with Norwood holding a $7 - 5$ lead in a game that had no direction or passion. There had been more turnovers than field goals, by James's count. Grabbing a defensive rebound, he outletted the ball to Jason, who tossed to Archie for an easy layup. On the next defensive possession, Geoff stepped in for a charge; the Panthers converted that turnover into a 3 for James from the left corner.

For the rest of the half, the Panthers found a comfortable, spirited groove, anticipating Norwood's shots, getting a hand up in the face, boxing out fervently, running the break smoothly, and scoring on most of their possessions. At half-time Casteline led, 33 – 27, a nice turnaround.

"Great job, James, coming in and lighting a fire under us. We need that catalyst, and James, you did the job. Gentlemen, this is what we're looking for from all of you. It's there if you're willing to put yourselves on the line. James isn't better than all of you. He is just playing as if he is, and that's all that matters. He's got Norwood convinced." Coach came over and gave James one of his arm-around-the-shoulder clasps, sharing the love. "Keep it up," Coach murmured, cheekbone to cheekbone. James felt his heart swell, with Coach's laudatory words.

With three minutes to go Norwood put on a surge, tying the game with less than a minute left. James knew Coach would not call a time-out, forcing the Panthers to set up a play on their own. Jason held the ball for most of the shot clock, making a quick pass-and-return-pass with Archie to avoid a five-second count. With six on the clock, Jason penetrated and kicked to James, who had a good look at an eighteen footer. But he faked past the defender, drove to the basket, and put up a tough glass shot, knocking down the help-man as he released.

The referee blew his whistle, and put his hand behind his head, indicating a player control foul on James, his fifth. It was Norwood ball with 32 seconds left, and James headed to the bench.

"Great game," Coach exclaimed as James moved behind the bench for the water bucket. Bobbie Pitaro went into the game.

With 8 seconds left Norwood put up a runner that missed, but Mark Payne was whistled for his fifth foul; Norwood's #22 made both his shots, leaving Casteline 8 seconds to tie or hit a 3 to win it.

Coach took time-out, leaving the team with two. "Jason, come off a double from Archie and Mark. Going right to left, if you can. Dan, you're setting up on the right wing. After the double, Archie, you're left wing, nice and wide so you don't crowd Jason. Mark, you've got to get to the glass on a shot, for a put-back. Geoff, you've got a time-out if you need it. Follow the play. Jason, if you've got no options, you've got Geoff for a trail play. Geoff, take the 3 if there's no time. Let's have some fun." Coach made it sound like a purposeful plan.

The inbounds came to Jason, who immediately got trapped. He kept his feet, throwing through the double to Archie, who pushed the ball middle, laying it off for Dan at the right wing. He put up a shot that arched too high, missing the rim long, but caroming off the glass, ripping through the net, giving Casteline the win.

The sparse Casteline crowd jumped in the air, already having been standing for the last play. Dan came to the middle huddle, his smile telling everyone of his joy. Coach clasped him in a bear hug that James could feel standing alongside. It was these hugs that James and Dan had watched when they were young: Steve Ramos hitting the winning shot, Coach running to him on the court to hand out his tribute. Now it was Dan's turn. James was next to hug him. "Way to go, buddy. That was a game-winner!"

"Yeah, off the glass," Dan chuckled, but he smiled just as broadly as if he had intended the shot.

"Final score, that's all that counts," James shouted in his ear.

Saturday Adrienne was headed to Connecticut for one of her lacrosse tournaments. She and her friends would stay over in a hotel outside Norwich. The tournament was held at Coast Guard Academy, gathering eight strong teams from the Northeast, three games guaranteed, an additional semi- and final game for the four teams with the best record. The girls' basketball team had won on Friday at home, guaranteeing them a tournament bid, their record 10 – 6 now. Adrienne had scored her usual 16, with 11 rebounds.

On the phone James and Dan talked for a few minutes about his mother, but Dan didn't think it would be a night for James to visit: his father was assisting his mother with supper and a bath. James stayed home, watching the end of the Celtics game as they lost to the Rockets. Kevin Garnett keyed a final surge on defense, but, in the end, Yao Ming was too tall, scoring 10 points in the last two minutes to seal the game. When the Celtics had finished, James flipped to the DVR, so that he could retrieve an episode of *Friday Night Lights*, his favorite and only TV show. As James settled into his father's recliner, he thought about his parents, their worries about him. Sitting in this chair of his father's, James felt stifled, no doubt, but maybe restraint was the first step toward independence. His mom and dad had been visiting his grandmother in Beverly all day. He had expected them home by now.

Rachel came in and out of the family room, a phone on her ear at all times. She laughed and replied quickly and wittily to her friends' comments. When one phone call ended, another was already in progress from an interrupting call. James could see his sister preparing for her high school social network, her excitement with and commitment to her friends developing.

When there was a momentary pause in her telephone dialogues, James said, "Hey, Rache, I notice that you're pretty close with your friends, even though you're not with them. That's pretty cool."

Rachel pranced in front of James, blocking out the TV. "Yeah, I do have a social life, even though Mom and Dad think I'm too young to be out on my own. But at least I have friends. What happened to yours?" She laughed, jumping on the couch, hugging her flannel nightgown over her bare feet.

"They're just a little too wild for me. I choose to live a more sedate life. I'm trying to set a good example for my little sister. Do you know her?"

She giggled. "Yeah, I think she's in her room studying right now. If I get a minute between phone calls, I'll let her know how positive a role model you are."

As they talked, Rachel had to ignore three incoming calls; finally, after punching James in the shoulder, she broke away, back to her circle of friends, jabbering away once again.

James fell asleep as soon as *FNL* was done, James's favorite character, Tim Riggins looking out over the open reaches of Texas in the last image. When he woke up, he went into his parents' room to say good-night. They had come home after their visit and not disturbed James in his sleep. When he entered the room, they were sharing a bowl of ice cream, watching the TV that sat on top of an old walnut chiffonier.

Welcoming James into the room, his mom said, "Nice game last night. I'm still remembering the thrill. That was a great shot by Dan. He deserved it." She was happy for the boy for whom she had spread peanut butter and fluff when they were nine.

"Yeah, he's worked hard. He earned it."

He gave his mom a hug and bumped knuckles with his dad.

James fell asleep after a few minutes of restlessness. He slept soundly, expect for one anxious moment, when he saw Adrienne slipping the heart he had given her down her throat.

Monday after school James and Adrienne sat in the library, waiting for his practice. She would practice at 5:30, after his team was finished.

"How'd the tournament go?" James asked.

"We won. It was a great final: we were down one with four minutes to go. We scored twice inside a minute, then one more just to

360

be sure. We won all five games we played. It was awesome, maybe our best tournament of the season."

"Did you score some goals?"

"Yeah, I got my share. There are a lot of good players on this team."

"Oh, so you don't get the chance to dominate like in the high school season? OK, how many goals did you get in the five games? Five?"

Adrienne looked down.

"More?"

Adrienne looked at him but silently, shrugging.

"Come on. How can I be jealous? I don't even play lacrosse? How many? Tell me the truth."

"Twenty-one."

James laughed. "Unbelievable. You're playing with the best players in New England, and you score 21 goals. Do you know how good you are?" James shook his head in amazement. He had known she was good, but she was better than he had imagined.

"I'm getting a clearer picture from these games. But I'm playing with really good players who can beat their girl and set me up for some easy scores."

James nodded, then leaned back in his chair. "Any extracurricular activities?"

Adrienne looked at him with a quickly annoyed look. "What are you, my younger brother? I can take care of myself, don't worry. If you don't trust me, I can manage on my own, thank you." She stood.

James did not relent. "I just want to know how much you do. It was a one-time thing for me, but I'm just curious about you."

"Well, you'll have to remain curious. I'm not going to report to you every time I'm out with my buddies. It's not like I'm a junky. I invited you last weekend, and I'll invite you again. And maybe next time, we'll just be having ice cream floats and lime rickeys. You don't have to be my guardian."

The word 'guardian' made James consider Adrienne's father, a man he had never met. "Does your dad live with you?"

Adrienne's face changed from piqued to blanched. "Why do you want to know?"

James shrugged. "I just never see him and I've never heard you talk about him. Your mom seems great." He left that compliment in the air as a prelude to a conversation about her dad.

"Let's just say he's not as great." Adrienne stopped talking. She lowered her head, unable to keep her gaze straight ahead on the present moment and place. Finally, she stood up. "You want to go for a walk?"

James stood with her. He felt as if she were inviting him into the closet of her bedroom, and he followed, eagerly, elated that she would share her life with him so.

They walked past the trophy case in front of the gym, with their reminders of past boys' basketball championships and recent girls' lacrosse championships. They mounted the stairs and entered into Mr. Tilson's Geometry classroom, which was empty. On the board was a rough sketch of planes intersecting a sphere, creating circles. They sat down in chairs, facing each other, their legs turned toward each other's. James looked at Adrienne expectantly. She looked at the wall behind him, her face clouded.

"My dad struggled with lots of things. He loved my mother a lot, almost too intensely, she tells me. He was almost obsessive about her, and that led to trouble. He didn't want her to work, but he couldn't keep his jobs longer than two years at a time. He'd be out of work for a year or so, maybe collecting unemployment, and then he'd get another job."

"What'd he do for work?" He reached across to touch her elbow.

"Something like advertising. One of those things that a company needs, and then they have to cut something and that's what they cut."

"So is he working now?"

"I don't know. He moved out about four years ago. He and my mom were fighting all the time. I think he got mad and towered over her sometimes, I don't know for sure. But I know she cried all the time, and she had to go to work, but he tried to stop her, but she went anyway. One time he locked her car and took the keys away. She tried to reach in his pocket to get them, and he pushed her. I saw that one. It was scary."

James reached across with his other hand. As James touched her arm, their knees squared and knocked into each other's. Awkwardly, standing from his chair, James hunched forward, reaching his hands underneath Adrienne's arms. He lowered his head silently to her shoulder. She did not cry.

"I'm sorry. I can't believe it. Did he drink?"

"No, I don't think so. He's not a bad man. He just couldn't let my mother go out and do things. He was really controlling. He wouldn't let her use a checkbook or a credit card. He had to take care of everything. It wasn't healthy for my mom, but he still loved her, you know?" Adrienne revealed the conundrum that was her father in a way that allowed James to see him clearly, asking him to solve the puzzle for her. He couldn't.

"Sounds like an unstable house. Have you seen him since he left?"

"Just on the phone. He calls, and sometimes he's crying. He wants to be with us, but he knows it's bad for my mom. You see? It's because he loves her so much, you know? I think he's doing OK."

"Does he send money? Is he supporting your mother and you and Ginnie?"

"I don't really know. I know we don't have a lot of money, and I know my mom talks about moving to a smaller house in a town with lower taxes. But she always gets it done staying here in Casteline. I think he sends her a check every month, but I don't know. I know she's learned to write her own checks, and I've still never seen a credit card in my mother's hand. She's a pretty amazing lady." Finally, Adrienne's eyes teared over, in appreciation of her mother's sacrifice. "It's like she's giving her life to Ginnie and me. I can't believe what a gift she's giving. I think of my life like the embryo that my father's egg entered, altering the genes, initiating the growth of the egg, but then withdrawing. My mother then has to bring that egg to maturity, with her watchful care and attention." Adrienne laughed momentarily. "It's like I'm a duckling."

James brushed back the hair hanging next to her cheek. "I had no idea. Thanks for letting me know." He wanted to ask her about the Ecstasy in this new context, but he knew that, in Adrienne's mind, there was no connection between the two elements, and it would end their intimate conversation.

James reached and clasped the heart that hung from the soft skin of Adrienne's neck. He kissed it. "I'll try not to control you. I think you're doing pretty darn well as a person who is reaching her independence. Does your dad know how well you're doing?"

She sniffed. "Yeah, he's very proud. I can hear his voice get choked up when I tell him about what I'm doing. I think he wishes he were here. Sometimes I think he's at the perimeter of a lacrosse field, but I just can't see him. But I'd know if he were here, because my mother would get all tensed up, I know." Her voice evinced the hope that her father was present, from time to time, to share in her successes.

Adrienne tried to stand up, though James was, in essence, leaning on her, clasping her in his arms. He understood her need for freedom. She stood up. She said, "Time for your practice, I think. I'll go out the front. You've got to run." She leaned in to him as he stood, almost using him as a support, but then regaining her balance, moving to the doorway with her customary, self-assured grace.

James got his Geometry quiz back on Tuesday; he scored a 93, missing one calculation that involved cubing a square root. He forgot that the exponent would be simply 3/2. He was pleased. After class, when he showed the quiz score to Adrienne, she looked happy for him.

"What'd you get?" he asked.

She said, "I did well."

When he reached into her notebook to search for the quiz, she held his hand away, boxing it out cleanly. After she relented, he found the quiz neatly catalogued in the "quizzes" section; she had received a 105%, answering the extra credit problem that James always found impossible to understand. "How do you know that stuff?"

She shrugged. "It doesn't seem hard, to be honest. But I do study every night. It's not like it's luck or anything." He knew she was right.

Tuesday's game against Dedham looked like a very likely win for the Panthers; they had won by thirteen the first time, and everyone was playing better. James had gotten mid-20s in the first game, his best shooting game by far. He checked Coach's stats on the locker room wall after every game, to see whether his average had crawled into double digits yet, and he was finally averaging 10 ppg – very unimpressive, especially compared to what James had expected of himself for his junior year. But Dan was playing far better than James had anticipated, and Archie was contributing a lot. The three wing players were averaging 28 points among them, which showed how spread out the scoring was. The leading scorer, by average, was Andrew, at 17, but he had played only seven games. The leading scorer, by total points, was actually Geoff Willis, who had scored 131 points, an average of just over 8 points a game.

On the bus to the game, James listened to his most recent warmup mix on his i-pod, a blend of year-old hip hop – Talib Kweli and Timbaland – and newly found old school R & B – Al Green, Aretha Franklin, and Gladys Knight. He felt a tap on his shoulder from Dan, with whom he was sitting. He looked past Dan to see a Middlesex Bank sign slide past the bus. "What's up?" he asked Dan.

"I think my mother has to be hospitalized. She's going to need surgery, maybe this week. My dad is taking the rest of the week off, and maybe next week, too. So I know it's pretty serious. I think they're going to do something with her heart, but I don't really know for sure.

She's pretty vague about it, and my dad doesn't like to talk about it at all."

James stopped Dan's monologue. "I want to help you some way I can. Is Joyce at your house right now?"

"Yeah, I feel real bad that she's gotten sucked into this whole thing. I can't believe she still thinks it's cool to hang out with me. I mean she's spending more time with my mother than with me. Not a great deal for Joyce. I owe her a lot." Dan stared at the back of the seat in front of him. Because the seats were tall, they had a little privacy for their conversation.

"You've got a lot to think about. Can I stop over to the house, after the game? Would she like to see me again?"

Dan shook his head. "I mean she really liked seeing you last week, but she's not getting out of bed any more. She's trying to eat some food in bed, but she's having trouble keeping food down." Dan swallowed.

"And we have to try to play Dedham." James laughed in derision. "Did you think about telling Coach and staying with your mom? I think he'd understand."

"Oh, I'm sure he'd understand, but my mom would not let me stay home. She knows how much playing basketball for Casteline means to me. You know. We've been getting ready for these two seasons all our lives. My mom completely goes along with that. She got really upset when I suggested that I stay home – she started having trouble breathing. So my dad was home and Joyce was there, so I left. My mom was crying and my dad was crying and I was crying. It was pretty tough. But I know I've gotta play this game. We'll see about Friday."

In another minute James could see the long wooden sign for Dedham High School that rose off the ground at the corner, as they turned into the driveway alongside the school. The ride was over.

"Thanks for letting me know. I'll keep her in my mind. I'd pray for her, but I'm not sure I believe in prayer."

As James rose out of his seat, Dan answered, "I'm starting to think about God myself."

James wondered whether it would help.

During the JV game James asked Coach LaMott if he could have a word with him. They moved to an empty spot in the stands, a few rows behind the JV bench.

"What's up, James? Everything all right?"

"Well, sort of. It's about Dan. His mother is having surgery this week for diabetes. I don't know all the details, but she was having trouble breathing when Dan left this afternoon. I just thought you should know. He's having a hard time with it, and I don't blame him." James wondered whether Coach LaMott would try to send Dan home.

"James, thanks for telling me. I had absolutely no idea. He's been so solid all year. I'd never know something like this is going on. He's a pretty special kid." James winced hearing Coach commend Dan so effusively; he wondered what Coach would say about him.

"Well, maybe you can check with him tomorrow, to see what's happening." James moved away, glad he had let Coach LaMott know. Coach would know how to approach the issue.

Before the game began, Coach addressed the team about Dan's mother. Coach stood in the doorway, surrounded by the door frame. "Guys, I've learned from Dan and his friend James that Dan's mother is very ill, probably needs to be hospitalized today or tomorrow. I want you all to know this as you take the court tonight. I'm not looking for anything dramatic or anything. I just want you to understand what's going through Dan's mind tonight. He assured me that his mother would not let him consider missing the game, and I value her judgment, but if you would all add one level of care to your attitude tonight, it would be great. Dan's a pretty quiet kid, and he might be a little quieter than usual, so let's give him our best effort tonight, because I'm sure his heart is aching to do the same for his mother." Coach stopped speaking, his hands spread apart like a pastor blessing his congregation. There was no noise in the room other than Coach's words and a vent ticking erratically.

James had never felt such a transcendent, group determination as he felt that night. No one failed to call out a pick; everyone boxed out. If Jason overcommitted in his ball-pressure, Dan or James stepped up on the ball handler before he could develop a driving lane to the basket. On offense the guards came off the big men's picks with a sense of urgency and dispatch. When James set a pick, he made sure he scraped the defender off cleanly. He was called for a moving screen once, and so were Geoff and Mark. But those three offensive fouls were a small price to pay for the sixty great screens they set on the day. The final score was 67 – 52. James felt bittersweet with the victory. On the one hand, they had played their strongest game of the year; on the other hand, it had done nothing to help out Mrs. Owings.

Coach tried to make sense of the game afterwards, in the huddle. "That was a great team effort, gentlemen. You gave yourselves to the greater good for the entire 32 minutes. That's the way a sport has to be played, if you are to have any chance of doing your best. I'm sure we were able to accomplish this great interaction mainly because we were feeling empathetic for Dan and his family. Unfortunately, our win does nothing to resolve her medical issues.

"But I hope she will feel how much we worked in her behalf, and if the medical community which is going to deal with her illness works just as hard, with the same perspicacity, Mrs. Owings will be able to see Dan play before this season is over.

"Congratulations on caring about your teammate so much. You made me feel proud to be your coach." He ended his comments by dropping his head as if he were praying for a moment. Then he called for a Tight; the response was as unified as the effort during the game.

Dan called his father's cell phone after the game, as they moved through the lobby to the bus. James stayed far enough away to give Dan his privacy.

In a minute he reported to James, "She's in the hospital. She might have had a slight heart attack. They're giving her tests now. She might need two stents to support the arteries in the heart."

James gave Dan a hug. "We'll stop by to see your dad on the way home, OK? Can I stop in?"

Coach LaMott came up alongside Dan. "Any word?"

Dan repeated what he had told James.

"That sounds like a good step. Sounds as if they might have a plan for her treatment. Tell me how you're doing with this. If you need to take a day or a week or the rest of the season off, tell me. I understand completely. She's your mother. You need to take care of each other." Coach opened the door leading to the sidewalk. There was still a little warmth in the air; maybe winter was nearing the end of its tyranny.

At the hospital James followed Dan to the elevator that took them to the fourth floor. James sat in a chair in the hallway as Dan pushed open the door to Room 422A. He could hear Dan's father's voice, and Joyce's, but not his mother's. After a few minutes Dan came back out with his father.

"You guys won going away, huh?" his father said, batting James on the arm. He wore a faded yellow sweatshirt and gray work pants, unbelted, James could see, when he turned away. His work boots were worn.

"Yeah, we played a great game, Mr. Owings. How's Mrs. Owings?"

"Well, she's gonna take a little while in here, I think. They found a weakness in the coronary arteries. She's waiting to get her operation scheduled in the OR. Some time this week, it looks like. You want to come in? She'd love to see you."

James hesitated, mostly because Dan did not look as if he thought it was a good idea. Mr. Owings insisted. "She's always loved you. She still talks about the days when you two were stealing cookies and pushing each other off the hill behind our house. Come in, come in. She's gonna be fine."

Inside the room Mrs. Owings lay on her back, an oxygen tube in her nose. She looked pale. IV bags were draped on an aluminum tree, dispensing their nutrients to Mrs. Owings through two tubes that merged near her right forearm. Her eyes were closed. Across the room another patient watched a silent TV screen, a wire bringing sound to her ear.

"Mom? Mom?" Dan spoke quietly. "James is here to visit."

Mrs. Owings stirred, half opening her eyes. A brief smile softened her lips. "Oh, James, how nice of you to stop in. I'm sorry I'm such a mess. But I think I'll be OK in a few days."

Just then the door opened again, and in walked Coach LaMott, with a plant in a terra cotta pot in his hand.

"Hi, Mr. Owings. Hi, Mrs. Owings. You doing all right? I hear you're on the road to recovery." He spoke a little loudly. James felt bad for the roommate. Mrs. Owings became more lively with Coach LaMott in the room; she tried to sit up straighter, though she slumped badly to her left side, where her arm was not anchored by the IV tube.

"Great to see you, Coach. Thank you so much for dropping in. I'm going to be all right, you can bet on that." After these words, her smile disappeared, as fatigue or pain gained hold of her.

"Well, I don't want to stay long, but I want this plant to flower just as you're going to flower in a few days, after you have some minor surgery." It was a revelation to see Coach LaMott taking control of the hospital room, just as surely as he controlled a time-out in a game. James could understand the way some families regarded the Coach with veneration. It didn't surprise him.

The team was now one win away from playing in the postseason, an unspoken goal every season. Playing in the competitive Commonwealth Conference, the Panthers played in a Division 3 tournament, unlike most of the teams in their league, who played in Division 2 or 1. If the team could survive the bumps of the league, they were well prepared for the tournament, though there were traditionally strong teams in the tournament also, Chatham, Avon, Cohasset, Westport, and Hull, to name a few. But James was excited to have the opportunity to play in March; they just had to win one more game.

But that one win would be a challenge. They faced Milton, Brookline (for the first time), and Walpole, all three teams gathered at the top of their conferences. Brookline held first place in the other division of the league, and Milton and Walpole were battling it out for first in Casteline's league.

The two practices leading to the Milton game were spent redesigning the strategy to slow down Brad Douglas and Marcus Bain, Milton's two powerful forwards who averaged 34 between them. The Panthers had done a great job holding them down in the first game, but the Milton coaching staff would be more prepared for Coach LaMott's wrinkles this time. He would have to come up with another wrinkle.

The strategy would be to double down on both big men when they had the ball inside the foul line. The problem with that strategy was that Milton ran the flex offense, which brought both men out to the elbow. The Panthers couldn't double from underneath, and both men could beat the defender easily with a dribble to a simple 8 footer. Strategy #2 was to play a disguised 2-3, the system that had gained them a victory in the first game.

School slowed appreciably as James approached this seminal game. Last year the team had lost their last two games, scuttling their opportunity to play in the state tournament. James had not played as significant a role a year ago, but he felt culpable nonetheless. This time he wanted to help bring the team over that same hurdle.

So, every class crawled, as he waited for practice. On Thursday Mr. Tilson's Geometry class spent most of the period discussing the way a line in space has no orientation unless it is seen from the perspective of a particular plane. James opened his eyes three times in the class: to open his book to the night's homework assignment so he could get a head start on the work; to see what Adrienne was doing, though she held to form by taking notes studiously; and to toss a pen at Pete, to try to maintain some connection to his old friend from whom he had separated in the past two months.

Pete wrote a note with the pen James had tossed at him, throwing the note with pen attached back onto James's desk. Hearing the scurry of the paper as it slid onto his desk, James opened his eyes again, to read, "Hey, dude, what's happening?" James shrugged his shoulders, unable to respond. Too much to tell.

In Chemistry double lab that same day, James and his lab partner, Emily Willets, tried to find the temperature at which the solubility of compounds in different liquids is affected. Emily and James's task was to measure the effect of decreasing and increasing temperature on the solubility of a carbon compound in hydrogen peroxide.

James never wanted to be viewed as a dumb jock, accurately or not. First of all, he was not much of a jock, and secondly, he considered himself fairly intelligent. He and Emily had equitably shared their responsibilities in their labs over the year: Emily took the lead in performing the experiments while James recorded her ministrations with accuracy and brevity. At times they switched responsibilities, enjoying the change. The challenge for James was keeping his eyes open to observe accurately Emily's experimentation. He much preferred it when she made the readings herself and called them out to James, in which case he could rest his eyes between readings.

On this day, James followed Emily's minute alterations, recording every temperature change and weight measurement attentively. After half an hour James had three pages of data. It was as if the clock had nearly stopped. At the bell signaling the end of the first period of the double period lab, he raised his hand to ask Mrs. Prefontaine whether there was any correlation between reduced temperature and the stoppage of time. She laughed, noting that there was a distinct correlation between speed and time, as Mr. Einstein had theorized, and maybe James was just moving very quickly. James chuckled, continuing to move his pencil as quickly as he could, to keep up with Emily, who continued in their experimentation, altering the conditions to produce varied results.

The correlation between this Chemistry experiment and the game Friday night was simple: measurement of the effect of heat on breakdowns. James loved a hot gym, because it forced the players to dig into their conditioned bodies to find the energy to make one play more than their opponent, the way the Natick game had ended, James flying past the passing lane, his opponent lacking the energy to put the ball on the floor to hit the last second shot.

However, James knew of one variable that played a significant part in the equation: his personal conditioning. He knew that he had been in better shape a year ago, before he had developed the weekend habits he had tried to quell during this season. This weakness would, in the end, hurt him.

"Did you get the last calculation?" asked Emily, and, turning back, he opened his eyes to the table to read the thermometer.

English, lunch, and Spanish, to wrap things up, then an afternoon waiting for late practice. As Adrienne turned into the girls' locker room to change for her practice, James caught up with her.

"Did you hear about Dan's mother?"

She nodded. "Yeah, that sounds really tough. I can't imagine seeing my mother in the hospital having a hard time breathing. I'd lose it."

"I think Dan's having a hard time, too. I'm doing what I can to give him help, but there's really nothing I can do." James looked at Adrienne as if she could give him a solution. She pulled him to her, laying his head on her shoulder, as a mother would comfort a child. He felt her compassion in the way her shoulders and breasts and hips and thighs met with his in an ingenuous way, offering him all of her. He sighed and relaxed.

Friday night, one week left to the season, one game to win, the stands buzzing with anticipation partway through the JV game, the varsity players made their exit into the locker room to change for the game. The rituals that make a sport give comfort. The time before the game was now finite: four minutes left in the 3rd quarter of the junior varsity game. Fourth quarter to follow, then warmups, and the referee would toss the ball in the air.

Dan was at the hospital, his mother having had surgery at 10:00 a.m. James had stopped in to see Dan at the hospital at around 3, with Andrew and Geoff. Dan said his mother's surgery went perfectly, and she should be coming home on Sunday. He looked relieved but still distraught.

"Hey, remember the Codys?" he said to James, as he pulled him aside.

James wondered how the Codys could be occupying Dan's thoughts as his mother lay recovering from heart surgery. "Yeah?"

"While my mother was having her surgery, I realized that by going over there I was looking for something real to happen to me, something that would decide who I am. I must have felt no connection to the people around me. Well, now I know that my mother is the one who gave herself to allow me to have a chance. And my dad too. We've been sitting together a lot lately, and we don't talk much, but I can see how tired he is, driving all week, one end of the country and back, to pay for the roof over our heads." Dan stopped, his breath short from his revelation. "It might not sound like much, but I think I appreciate them now, and nothing more real has ever happened to me than her surgery."

James could understand. "I see what you mean. Even this game tonight, biggest game of the year, by far, it's not as important as your mother taking her next breath."

Dan grabbed him. "That's it exactly! You know." He shook his head in wonderment. "I didn't think it would make any sense to you. But you get it." He stopped, then grinned. "But that doesn't mean that you don't bust balls tonight."

James felt something in his gut release, something that made his eyes water as he looked over Dan's shoulder at Andrew and Geoff, standing at the window, hands in pockets, looking at their teammates.

Douglas and Bain put a hurt on Andreas and James the entire first half. With Dan and Andrew out of the lineup, James had returned to the starting five, drawing the assignment of marking Marcus Bain, when they were in a man-to-man, while Andreas tried to control Brad Douglas. At halftime, Bain had 15 and Douglas 16, accounting for 31 points of Milton's 41. Casteline stayed in the game by driving the lane, getting Milton in foul trouble, hitting 12 of 15 at the line, to stay within recovery distance, 41 – 32.

Geoff picked up his fourth foul halfway through the third quarter, bringing Nick into the game, when Mark got tired. The only way Casteline could keep up with Milton was to push the ball and fan for threes on the break, and then continue penetrating in the half-court set, to try to push Milton into greater foul trouble. The strategy worked, mainly because Jason was having a spectacular game, flying up the court, ball under control, making the right reads, dishing off when it was right, taking the ball to the hole when there was an opening.

In the end, there was just too much Douglas and Bain. In the last four minutes the Panthers had to resort to fouling Milton's best, who had the ball in their hands in their stall game, passing over the top with little resistance offered. The two stars hit 9 for 11 at the foul line down the stretch, resulting in a final score of 74 – 65 Milton. Jason had had a solid game, his best, something like 18 points and 11 assists. James could remember only one turnover for Jason the entire game. James had played a good game, taking the shots that came his way, driving and drawing fouls when there was a lane, maybe 20 points, he wasn't sure; both Bain and Douglas had scored more than 25.

The huddle was subdued as the quieted crowd filed out of the gym. "That was a tremendous game. You have exceeded my expectations for much of this season, and this game adds to that accomplishment. Congratulations. And now we turn our attention to Dan's mother, who came through surgery very well, I was told before the game. If you get a chance, stop in to see her on Saturday afternoon after practice. She loves her son and she loves this game of basketball. It's been a very difficult week for Dan. He would love to see you, and maybe he'll be able to relax a little now that the surgery is behind her.

"Have a great night, see you tomorrow morning. Don't forget, you're a member of a great team. Act accordingly."

James was surprised that Coach was still cautioning the team about their behavior on the weekend. He felt he had lived through three seasons of vicissitudes, but that he was now able to understand the responsibility that a team placed on its members. He assumed that his teammates had made the same realization – though he had to admit that he himself still harbored the same suspicions.

My life stretches out before me
Full of every size word
Little bright ones
Fat, dull, sharp, long words
Round and straight words
Words that approach from the side, from below
Words that go straight at you
Silent words, slippery ones
Ones that work from the inside out

And then those other ones, that strike like lightning
Words you've known your whole life
That you use for the first time.

Words by Meg Hutchinson

Ben

After the game Ben went to the hospital to see Mrs. Owings. He was not allowed into her room because she had just returned from post-op, but he spoke with Dan and his dad, discovering that the stents had been inserted with no resistance, and that she had immediately felt relief in her breathing. Ben gave Dan a hug as he left the 4th floor hallway, taking the stairs down to the first floor, a nod to the exercise he wished were a part of his life.

From the hospital he headed to Willow's for a beer and wings, delaying his return home to a house that felt cold to him, as he considered it. Having worked the extra shift the previous Thursday and his regular shift on Monday, he felt comfortable at Willow's now, feeling he could walk behind the bar to say hi to Pete, if he wanted.

Standing at a table in the corner, he noted how busy Friday nights were, and hoped he would start to get shifts like these when the season ended. He could not help but glance at the end of the bar near the post, to see if his needy patron, Laura Ruben, was there. He could picture her looking at the TV, her hair framing her sad face, the level of white wine in her glass slowly but steadily descending. Ben did not know whether to feel good or bad when he saw her, seated on the barstool, her left arm leaning on the bar, her face turned to the game on TV.

He felt awkward seeing her from this side of the bar, but he approached her nevertheless, not wanting to appear unfriendly, if she had seen him.

"Hi, Laura," he called, as he came on her from behind. When she saw him, her face gained some inner light. "Oh, you're here by yourself," she said in a confused voice.

"Yeah, my wife is home. I'm just coming home from a game. Not a win this time. I think the team needs you for support." The gentle byplay felt natural.

"Well, sorry, I just don't know your schedule. Can you give me a schedule next Monday night? That way I can bring my good luck charm to you. What's the record overall?"

"Nine and nine. Two tough games coming up, with Brookline and Walpole. We're hoping for one win, and then we'll play in the post-season. But they won't be easy." Ben stood just behind her swivel stool on her left side; she turned to face him.

375

Laura looked hopeful. "Well, I think I can find time in my schedule to make it to one of those games. How about Friday night? Is that a home game against Walpole?"

"Yes. It should be a fun game to watch, a lot like the Natick game that you saw. It would be great to see you there."

A bartender he did not know came to the slice of bar that he was commanding, swiping it clean with his towel. "Get you a beer?" he asked amiably. Ben waved to Pete over the man's shoulder.

"Yes, a Corona and a plate of wings. Do you want something?" he asked Laura. She screwed up her face, contemplating another wine. "Yes, I'll have another Chablis, thank you."

Ben began to watch the TV screen, an NBA game from the West Coast. Pete moved out of the kitchen to shake Ben's hand. "You wanna get behind the bar? We can always use a veteran hand."

Ben leaned back. "I think I'm good, thanks." He leaned over the bar, to whisper. "What's this bartender's name?"

"Bob. Bob Hill. He's a Friday night specialist. He's good." Pete moved out to the outlying tables, to help Bob out.

Laura brought their conversation back to life. "Well, if I come to your game, I'll be coming alone. It's just me and my shadow these days. At least there is a little comfort here most nights. Pete is a nice man, and you've taken the time to listen, too." Her hope lingered on her face. "I'm starting to enjoy the company of a few of the other patrons. We can enjoy the Bruins together and the Celtics. It beats sitting home alone." Her voice sounded a little nasal.

Ben hated to hear the emptiness in her. "I'm sure you can find a soul mate, if that's what you're looking for; you just have to keep your eyes open. Don't give up on people. There are lots of nice ones around – maybe not all at Willow's, but just try different situations. What about going to a dance, ballroom dancing? There are lots of singles there, I bet. Maybe there are even singles dance lessons type of thing." He added his hope to hers. There was a momentary instinct to hold her, to support her, but he resisted.

"I'll keep my head up. I appreciate your concern. May I ask you a question?"

"Sure."

"Are you happily married?"

Ben had to look away from Laura for a moment. "That's a good question. If you had asked me that question one week ago, I would have said definitely, 'yes.' Right now I'm not so sure. I'm trying to figure that out." He looked at Laura again, seeing the eyes that had once looked forward to the day and even more eagerly to the events of an evening. Her eyes were bigger than he had remembered them. Dark eyes. Long eyelashes that slumped just a little.

"I do not want to be someone that becomes involved in someone else's marriage, but if that marriage goes south, maybe I'll see you at a dance some evening." She tipped her head toward Ben's shoulder to feign the proximity that dancing would give them. She smiled at the thought.

Ben nodded, flattered to think that he might appear attractive to someone, in a way that felt like dating. "I'm sure my wife and I will work it out. But I want you to go to those dances, thinking that maybe I'll show up. Then you'll find the man who is right for you. Sound like a plan?"

She nodded and leaned closer and gave him a kiss on the cheek.

Ben backed away, though the whisper of her lips on his cheek felt seductive. "I'd like to maintain that patron-service provider relationship, if you don't mind." He was still playing and enjoying the interplay, but he felt she had crossed some line that made him wonder whether he would dare cross that same line.

Ben's wings came out from the kitchen, and Ben turned his attention to their sweet, hot taste. He offered the plate to Laura.

She was delighted to share in the tasty chicken. They ate indelicately, their fingers requiring more napkins than the bartender had provided. After a few more wings, napkins, and quiet minutes, Ben's Corona gone, Ben thought he should get home. "Well, it has been a real pleasure to see you on this side of the bar. I'm really glad I stopped in."

"Me too. Thanks for saying hi," she replied.

"And don't forget to get out to those dances, where you can show your best stuff. Good night. It's been great to talk with you." Ben could not deny the current that their conversation had lit in him.

"It's been my pleasure," Laura agreed, her cheeks sanguine from initiating that current.

"Probably see you on Monday?"

"I think so. Good luck next week." She patted his shoulder the way Ben might pat a freshman's.

Leaving a twenty on the counter, Ben turned to leave, trying to dismiss the possibilities that he felt were being presented to him. Outside the door, in the cold, Ben turned his thoughts again to the team's prospects in the next week. Andrew had spoken to Ben on Wednesday, telling him that his knee was being evaluated on Monday and that he hoped he would receive clearance to play later in the week. Of course, he would have no conditioning or timing, and his knee would

377

feel unstable, having been immobilized for over a month, but the prospect of having Andrew for even four minute stretches gave Ben a little more assurance that they could find a way to win.

On the way home Ben called Mary, to see what she was doing. The kids had become attuned to the friction between Willa and him, and they were staying closer to home, afraid, he guessed, that if they strayed too far away, one of their parents would not be there when they returned. They were close to the truth. Mary was coming home after the Summit basketball game, another win for them. She would bring some pizza home with her, she said, if he wanted any.

Willa had still not answered his essential inquiry about her relationship with Peter Harrison. She had had one meeting at the church on Tuesday night, and she had gotten home before he returned from his game. On Wednesday night they were sitting in the living room together, Ben with a folder of papers to correct on his lap, Willa glancing at a CSI on TV as she pulled laundry out of the basket, separating and folding. Both kids were out. Ben had said, "Can we get any more clarity about you and Peter Harrison? It seems it was never resolved."

Willa looked at him with a challenging stare. "I've told you all there is to say. I'll say it again. We are on two committees together, which brings us together twice a week, usually. I have had some issues with our marriage for some time now, and I've found comfort in his listening. I haven't been bashing you; I've just spoken of my own sadness. I feel there is an emptiness at the heart of our marriage, and I don't know how to fill it." Her words brought out a gentleness in her that belied the anger that framed all of her contact with Ben.

Ben could not stop himself from attacking Willa, "And confiding in some predatory church-goer fills that emptiness?"

He had more to say, but Willa cut him off – "Let's look at this moment, OK? This is as intimate as you and I get: you accusing and me trying to explain. Meanwhile I'm tired from work, I just finished making supper – which you cleaned up after, thank you – and now I'm doing three loads of wash, while you correct papers and think about your game on Friday. The kids are who knows where, and I have a musical social to make final plans for on the 18th. Would you call this a heavenly marriage?"

Ben didn't disagree. "No, but I'd like to think that we're in this challenging situation together. I have the crazy notion that if we confide in each other, it'll lead to a closer relationship that will show itself in more affection and intimacy."

"Is that why you chose to take on another job? That was the straw that broke the camel's back, to be honest with you. I just don't get it: you need another two evenings out every week? Don't you see how fragile things are at home? Yet you choose to be away more?"

Ben nodded, as he brought the recliner down to its level-seated position. "I understand your criticism there. And maybe I'm just unconsciously combating all those meetings you go to, saying I can make a new set of interests for myself too. I can tell you it's pleasurable to just serve and clean and tally up. I love the simplicity of it. And there's an artificial family feeling at Willow's that, I'm sure, fills a need in the lives of some of the patrons." Ben tried not to think of Laura Ruben and the need she offered him.

Willa stood, laundry basket in hand, headed for the bedrooms to put clothes away. "But isn't that ironic? You leave a house in disarray, thinking that you're providing some kind of home for a bunch of strangers. I just can't see it. And maybe you can claim that I'm doing the same thing with my church involvement, but at least that arose out of our connection to the church. I don't see any real connection to a bar, at least I hope there is no substantive connection." With that final probe, she left the room, her steps muffled on the carpeted stairs.

And so he came home on Friday night, after a game in which his team had played nobly. Scott and Marty were playing Madden NFL in the playroom; Mary was sitting at the kitchen table with her friend Marissa; they were almost finished consuming a large pepper and mushroom pizza. Ben sat down and helped them out.

"You guys have a good evening?" he asked.

Mary was a little subdued. She still had her coat on, though the kitchen was pretty warm. "Yeah, nothing special. The game was cool. We were out for a while before we grabbed the pizza. How come you're so late?" She did not sound accusatory, just curious.

"The mother of a player on the team had surgery today. I stopped by the hospital to see the family, and then I stopped at Willow's for a beer and some wings." He could see the curiosity alter to concern.

"I thought you just worked at Willow's. Are you hanging out there now?"

Ben shrugged. "Not really. I just wanted to relax a little. I guess that's what an alcoholic would say, but I didn't think one beer would indicate a problem." He could sense the tension in the house. Mary's eyes contained a question that she did not know how to phrase. "Let's just do a little relaxing here, OK? The two of you think you can beat me in three-handed cribbage?"

Mary smiled slowly, batting Marissa on the arm, "Oh, he thinks he's so good. Let's show him real talent."

Willa was not in evidence in the house, but Ben did not want to ask Mary where she was, for fear of her answer.

Just about eleven thirty, Ben, after subduing his daughter and her friend in the card game, mounted the stairs. Willa lay in bed, asleep, with the light off. Ben cleared his pockets onto the bureau quietly, went back out to the bathroom, brushing his teeth, changed into his nightshirt, and slid into the bed, trying not to wake his wife.

Saturday night Ben and Willa sat silently in the living room, Celtics moving soundlessly across the screen. Willa read a Joyce Carol Oates book from the library, *The Falls*; the two of them offered nothing to each other.

Ben fell asleep late in the game, after the Celtics replaced Pierce and Garnett with House and Scalabrine, the Celtics having the game well in hand over the Nuggets. The game had started at 10:00; it was after twelve.

Scott and his friend Marty rushed into the house, their eyes bright, their voices full of news. "Hey, Dad, did you hear about the accident? It was a Casteline kid driving, but I guess he ran from the scene. A couple kids got hurt. They're at the hospital, I guess. Did you know about it?"

Ben was immediately concerned. Of course he had no idea the accident had occurred, and he wondered who was involved. He thought about calling Geoff, to see if he had heard anything, but it was too late. Then he thought about the Casteline police. He called, but they told him that the information was confidential. Ben had expected their non-committal response.

Willa moved quite naturally to be near Scott, protectively, as Ben tried to track down the accident. Entering the kitchen, she snapped on the light and opened the cabinets, to pull down the boxed popcorn, and placed one package of popcorn in the microwave.

After trying to find out more, Ben said to Scott, "Thanks for letting me know. I wish I could find out more. Is there any way you guys can find out anything for me?"

Scott said, "I can check some blogs. I know a few kids from Casteline." He went to the computer to scan blogs and checked his phone for any texts. His friends knew that his dad coached at Casteline and that he might want to know about an accident involving students there.

"Here's something. It says there was an accident on Bridge St, a single car accident. I don't know how reliable the information is, because it's just a kid's twitter. Says two people hurt, taken to the hospital. The driver is unidentified."

Willa, reentering the living room from the kitchen with a ceramic bowl of popcorn in one hand, came behind Scott to put her other hand on his shoulder. "It's such a tough time to be a teenager, isn't it?" she said sympathetically. Scott looked over his shoulder at his mom, feeling her concern. Willa called Mary's cell phone to see where she was, and, after a quick conversation, came back to the room, satisfied.

"She's at Lynn's, spending the night. Not out on the road." She looked relieved. "And you," she said to Marty, "you take my son's life in your hands when you go out of this house. Can I trust you?" There was a trace of concern in her voice.

"Mom, Marty's a great driver, very conservative. You don't have to worry about me. Mary, on the other hand, . . ." he said, laughing.

"Scott, that's not funny," she said. "I hope she's even more conservative. I know she drives very responsibly when I'm in the car."

"Of course!" Scott joked. He was not fazed by the accident. There were always accidents, accidents involving teenagers. It was nothing new.

After another half hour of fruitless inquiry, Ben said, "Well, I'm beat. I'm heading to bed. Marty, drive safely on the way home. Scott, see you in the morning."

In bed he waited for Willa, to see if she needed comfort in her concern for her children – knowing that he needed far more comfort than his son at the moment.

Sunday morning the newspaper had no report of the accident. Ben called Bryan to find out if he had heard anything, but he knew nothing more than Ben.

"What about Mr. Willis? Why don't you try him? Father of the captain. I bet Geoff knows the details."

"Good idea."

Mr. Willis said there was some uncertainty about the accident. Three people had been injured, a junior girl and boy and a senior boy. What was up in the air is that the driver had left the scene of the accident. And then he said, "It was Jason Grutchfield's car, the Escalade."

Ben drew in air suddenly, the pencil in his hand writing the word Jason on the pad of paper and placing a rectangular block around the name. "Was he driving?"

"No one knows. And Coach, one of the injured people was Pete Semineau. He's in the hospital, maybe a broken leg."

Ben shook his head. "Thanks, Bob. I'll check at the hospital."

"No problem. Sorry to have to give you this news. It's always a fear in all our hearts, you know that."

Ben knew that Mr. Willis could not help but feel thankful that Geoff was not involved. No parent could keep his child away from these dangers completely.

"It's a tough time to be raising kids, that's for sure. Thanks again."

Ben moved quickly into the bedroom. "Willa, you're going to have to do church alone this morning. I'm going to the hospital to see Pete Semineau. He broke his leg in the accident last night." After putting on a shirt and sweater, he sat down next to Willa on the bed. "Will you give me a little prayer at church, to help me understand us?" He leaned to give her a kiss on the mouth, which she accepted, though neither of them knew what the kiss meant.

At the hospital's patient information desk, Ben learned Pete's room number, 221W. As he neared the room, he heard the sound of James Rush's voice, saying, "I have to bail soon, because Adrienne is waiting, but you're looking pretty good for an invalid. Hang in there." Ben came around the corner, to see Pete lying in bed, his leg uncasted, encased in a compression splint; James, his hooded coat on; and Pete's mother, whom Ben did not know. He introduced himself, "Hi, Mrs. Semineau? Ben LaMott, Pete's coach."

She looked at him appreciatively. "Oh, of course. So nice of you to stop by. He's doing pretty well considering." She smiled nervously.

Pete filled the awkward gap. "Hi, Coach. Guess I'm not starting Tuesday night?"

"Well, I'll have to hear the doctor's report before I rule you out. Let's just say it depends on Monday's practice, OK?" He clasped the hand Pete offered him, leaning over to pull him up a little bit from the bed, as he leaned down.

James said again, "Hey, bud, see you later. I'll call you," and he headed for the door.

"Great to see you, James," Ben said.

"You too, Coach," James said, ducking out of the room.

"So, anything else the doctor had to look at?" Ben asked Pete.

"Some scrapes on my side, my neck is really sore. I racked up my fingers," he said, showing his left hand, gauzed.

"You were pretty lucky, it seems." Ben did not want to discuss the accident or the driver, because he knew Pete would have a hard time revealing any information to him. He did not know how much his mother knew. "Well, I hope to see you in school Monday, but, if not, I know where to find you. Mrs. Semineau, take care of your son, please. We need him on the court." He wondered how hollow those words would sound to Mrs. Semineau, as he left the room, headed to Mrs. Owings's room, where he would find Dan and his dad.

Monday in school Jason was on the absent list. Ben had learned the identity of the girl who was injured, Rose Beach, and the other passenger, Art Goldstein. Ben tracked Geoff down in the library after third period.

"Any idea what's going on with Jason?"

Geoff looked at Coach LaMott frankly. "I think he's being charged by the police for leaving the scene. He ran home because he was only about half a mile from the house when he crashed. He left Pete and Rose and Art there at the scene. I don't know whether he called the police when he got home. I hope so." Geoff looked uneasy, but hopeful. He and Jason had played together for eight years, on the teams that Mr. Grutchfield had helped coach. "I called him, but they've turned the machine on for all calls."

"I agree with you: I bet he called the police when he got home. He's a good kid, you know that." Ben wondered about the involvement of alcohol in the accident, but there would be nothing official about that until the police investigation was completed.

"Coach, I hope he wasn't drinking," Geoff said, hope bursting his voice apart.

"I bet he wasn't. He hasn't had a problem this year." Ben stopped. "Has he?"

Geoff looked down. "He was one that I kept worrying about. Never in trouble, but not always in the right place. The party was at his house. He had taken a couple kids home and he was coming back. His parents weren't home. They were up in New Hampshire at their ski house. They came home in the middle of the night." His hope was waning the more he spoke.

"Not a great recipe for success, is it?" Ben said. "But that's not to say he was drinking. I mean he offered to drive some people home. How drunk could he be to do that?"

Geoff said nothing by way of an answer.

Practice was sullen. Andrew was at the hospital for his orthopedic evaluation. Ben laughed to himself, thinking how much the hospital had become a part of his life recently. Dan was at practice, his mother having been released in the middle of the day. Dan said that his father was taking the week off to care for Mrs. Owings. Pete was facing surgery, and Jason was MIA.

"Gentlemen, we've been sent a challenge by the basketball gods, or the adolescent gods, or the medical gods, or whatever gods you want to believe has the power to create chaos. Pete is going to have his leg set, Dan's mother has been released and is recovering at home, and Jason's situation is being sorted out. And Andrew is checking out the knee, but I don't expect anything to come of that.

"In the midst of all this uproar, we have to prepare for Brookline, a team that is scoring 84 points a game, and who has a player, Lance Previeu, who is averaging 28 himself. He's probably going to prep school, but UConn is recruiting him. He's a horse. So . . . we've got our work cut out for us. We just have to dismiss all the distractions, and do our best. Dan, it's great to have you back, and we're really happy that your mom is doing great." The team interrupted him to applaud Dan to show him their support.

The plan was to put Archie Stedham at the point, with Bobbie Pitaro backing him up. Archie lacked Jason's quickness and experience, but he was stable and he would not allow himself to give the ball away carelessly. It was amazing how much Ben had come to rely on Archie, a boy whom he had never met three months ago. He had been a real gift.

"We'll have to rely on the half-court a little more than in the past, because Archie is not as much of a speed merchant as Jason. We'll take the break if it's there, but, Archie, don't push it more than your comfort level. Dan and James, be ready to peel back in case they put good pressure on Archie, OK?"

The Panthers executed the half-court offense as if Archie had spent the season playing point. Ben could see this lineup as next year's setup on the perimeter, a very good and experienced core of players. But there was work to be done first: Brookline.

That night at Willow's was the first time his new job as a bartender felt uncomfortable. He enjoyed serving Bryan and Lisa, finding numerous reasons to wander out to their table, another draft, clearing the table, offering them the Monday night special, barbecued ribs. But he did not know what to say to Laura, who sat in her usual place at the bar. She sat a little straighter in her bar chair. She smiled more readily; she drank less wine. Ben wondered whether Pete would chide him for reducing profits by way of reducing her alcohol intake.

"Nice to see you," he said cordially.

She smiled and nodded. She seemed to be holding a secret in her, one that she wanted Ben to discover. When he brought another glass of Chablis over to her, she shook her head and covered the glass she was sipping, to indicate that she was not keeping her normal pace. Every time he looked at her she smiled, almost shyly, as if they were at a high school dance and he was approaching her to ask her for a dance.

After more than an hour of this stilted ballet, Ben could not help telling Laura, "Laura, I am not feeling comfortable tonight. It seems something changed when we talked on Friday, and I'm not sure what."

Laura spoke quietly. "I know what. We made a connection. And it made me feel good. But I do not want you to misinterpret what happened. I gave you a kiss of appreciation for your care. I am not looking for anything to evolve out of that evening, as I am sure you are not, also. You are married, and I am single. There's nothing in that equation that would bring us together." She spoke certainly, as if she were trying to convince herself of the veracity of her words.

Ben appreciated her clarity. "Thank you. I was a little concerned that I had given you the wrong impression too. But thank you for clearing the air. I feel a lot better."

As the evening came to an end, Laura rose earlier than usual, leaving a modest tip. "See you Friday night," she called softly, as she turned away from the bar.

He nodded, hoping that it would be worth the five dollar ticket.

The game at Brookline was always a tough one. Brookline was a city school, with chain nets on the outdoor courts, with city players. Their court was long and narrow, making the timing and spacing of the visitor's fast break just a little off-center. And then there was Lance Previeu, the most talented player in the league, better than Billy Samko at Waltham.

Brookline began the game with a zone press following their field goals, a press that the Panthers handled but did not punish for layups because they attacked it smartly, but conservatively. At the end of the first quarter, Brookline had a 17 – 14 lead. The Panthers' backcourt junior triumvirate had all 14 points. Geoff and Mark could not get a clean shot off inside.

When Ben brought Bobbie and Alex and Andreas in from the bench, Brookline stepped up the pressure, forcing Ben to come back with his starters before they were really rested. Halftime score was 41 – 32 Brookline. Previeu had 17 at the half.

"Guys, we're hanging in there. But you can see, that's just not going to be enough. We've got to catch fire somehow – defensive intensity or better preparation before we shoot so we can make a run on offense. I hate to say it, but this season is starting to come to its own inevitable conclusion. You seniors, Geoff, Mark, Bobbie, Alex, Jonas, you've got to play with just a little more urgency. There's no time left. All that we've learned, you've got to put it out on the floor in the next sixteen minutes." Ben could find nothing else to say. He felt he was making the same exhortations he had been making at the end of the last five seasons. He did not want to admit to himself that the same story was playing itself out again.

Geoff, his solid captain, stood up. "Guys, I have thought about this season for a long time. It's my last season in a Panther uniform, and, like you, I always looked forward to fame and glory in this uniform. When you go out there right now, I want you to do everything you can do to bring honor to this uniform." He pointed to the 30 on his chest. "I want people to remember #30 as a warrior." He remained standing, gathering his teammates around him. "One . . . two . . . three." The team gave him a unified answer.

The Panthers cut into the lead gradually. Dan regained his shooting touch and made a 2 and a 3. Archie reversed the ball as if he had played point all his life, though he couldn't get past his man from the point, unable to create an angle. James played as if he would die if he lost, the level of his play rising as they approached the end of the game. He kept deflecting passes intended for Previeu in the post, destroying Brookline's timing, giving his teammates time to double down and prevent Previeu from pivoting toward the rim. With two minutes to go Brookline held just a four point lead, 66 – 62. On their next possession Archie fouled their point guard, who made one of two at the line. But James made a drive, collected a foul, and finished the 3 point play to cut the lead to 67 – 65, with 1:06 to go.

After a time-out, Brookline got the ball down low to Previeu, and Geoff was forced to foul him as he shot. Fortunately, Geoff was strong enough to prevent an easy layin as he gave the hit. Previeu hit both his foul shots, making it a two possession game.

Archie split the zone press, attacking aggressively as the clock wound down. He hit Dan on the baseline, who put up a shot that rimmed out; Andreas grabbed the rebound and kicked it back out to

James, who hit a 3, making it 69 – 68, Brookline. There were 22 seconds left. Casteline had to foul.

James fouled Samson, a wing player who had had a good game, who had hit 4 of 4 at the line in the game. But the Panthers could not be picky at this point. Samson hit one of two, making it a two-point margin.

Last possession, twelve seconds to go. Archie split the double again, but this time Pringold, Brookline's quick guard, picked his pocket, taking the ball the other way for a layup that sealed it. Brookline 72 – 68. A heroic game, but a loss. Ben could not help but think of their chances if Andrew and Jason had played. But he could not blame the loss on their absence. The team had had the ball with a chance to win, but they had not won.

They had one game to go, needing a win to qualify for the tournament.

Wednesday in class, just two more days until February vacation, Ben was working with his juniors on a portion in *The Great Gatsby*. He loved this section, almost as much as he loved the final page. At the beginning of the period, he asked Tom Mannix, a bright hockey player, to read the paragraph on p. 110 about Gatsby "sucking on the pap of life." Tom read loudly, emphasizing appropriately that the moment Gatsby "forever wed his unutterable visions to her perishable breath, his mind would never romp again like the mind of God."

"Great job, Tom. Mandy, what does Fitzgerald mean here? What is Gatsby doing here?"

Mandy was a good thinker, though not a risk-taker. Ben was trying to put her on the spot.

She remained silent, trying to parse the prose. "I think Gatsby is giving something up here, for the sake of gaining something more important."

Ben nodded, elated. "Exactly. Great job, Mandy." He wrote her analysis clearly on the board. "Chad, what is Gatsby giving up?"

Chad, a leader in the school plays, very dramatic, made a loud sigh, as if he were about to say something profound (which was a possibility). "Gatsby is giving up his independence, committing himself to Daisy Buchanan."

Ben nodded enthusiastically. "Yes, that's right. Is there anything else he is giving up? Hmmm? Peter? Amy J?"

Amy noticed. "He's connecting his visions for himself to her 'perishable breath,' which means that he's losing his sense of immortality because he thinks gaining her is more important."

Ben became more excited. "Awesome. You guys are pretty smart. It's as if you're connecting to some truth that F. Scott Fitzgerald laid out and that you're discovering. Do you see how, in a way, you're transcending time?"

A few heads nodded slowly. "Why is God mentioned? How was Gatsby at all like God?"

Tom came back into the arc of thinking. "He was feeling like God because, he had said before, 'he sprang from his own Platonic conception of himself.' It's as if he had created himself the way God creates life."

Ben applauded. "Wow. You guys are pretty remarkable. When the literature is good, the response is great. Can we take a minute to talk about a little philosophy that I've devised as a way of thinking about our lives?"

Tom and Peter and Amy and several of the other students looked at him expectantly, as if they indeed wanted to hear him put forth his concept. The rest of the class remained respectfully silent.

"Here it is. I may not say it very eloquently, but if you don't understand, ask questions. If you care.

"I think life has little worth, unless we have things that we think are important – like, for Gatsby, Daisy became important. The things that might gain meaning in a person's life are things like basketball" – the class laughed at this example, knowing his perpetual connection to the sport – "playing the piano, family, friends, religion, God. Do you see how these things might become a focus to our lives, and give us real direction? We'll spend lots and lots of time, or lots and lots of money, if it brings us closer to this ideal or concept. We'll spend lots of money that we would never think of spending on something of less value to us, and you know we aren't talking about monetary value here, but personal value." Ben paused, collecting his thoughts. He sat on an empty desk in the front row.

"I call these things we believe in 'fictions', because they don't have any intrinsic value; they have value only if we attribute value to them. I think love or marriage is the best example." He paused again, looking at the flag in the corner of the room, but pondering for an instant the status of his own marriage, the fiction into which he and Willa had poured almost thirty years of their lives. "A lot of people spend a lot of time trying to find love, falling in love, spending time with people we love. But, if you think about it, what is love? What is it, really?" He looked for an answer.

Julie suggested, "It's a feeling of closeness we feel with another person."

"That's good. But we can feel really close with some people without thinking we love them. What about people who work with each other for long hours? We might develop great trust in those people, but we don't necessarily love them.

"What I'm trying to say is that love has great moment and value in our lives, if we believe it does. Same for marriage. Same for a sport. Same for academic excellence. But many other people don't see the same value in these aspects of life; therefore, they don't really have absolute value, just relative value because of the way we see things.

"I think Gatsby represents the person who has a vision for himself, a vision of wealth, no doubt. And then he sacrifices that vision for a vision that he thinks is more sacred: Daisy. And you're right, Amy, it is her perishability that makes his sacrifice so profound. Because when we commit to something mortal, we consign ourselves to a tragic fate because everything tangible withers and dies." Ben stopped talking, noting that the silence in the room had life. He began again. "Nothing with material substance lasts. It is only our dreams that can last." Ben was winding down, only hoping that something of his wonder had been transferred to his students.

"And one last fiction that I believe in, and I think we saw its value here in the last fifteen minutes, is fiction itself. Books like *Gatsby* and *Huck Finn* and *Catcher in the Rye* and *Native Son* have the capacity to force us to think in ways we wouldn't otherwise think. It's true for me, that's for sure. I would never think about or talk about these ideas unless the authors brought them to my attention. I'd suggest the same is true for you. So, to wrap it up, think about the fictions that you give credibility to with your own passions. And understand that committing to those fictions is, in a way, setting yourself up for failure, because, in the end, you will move on out of this world, and you will be forced to leave that passion – or fiction – behind. But, here's the greatest thing: even though you're going to encounter failure, you'll be most alive when you strive to consummate that commitment to whatever you believe in.

"That's all folks. Enough philosophizing. I'm amazed you've remained conscious through all those words. Keep them in mind, but, please, live fully."

Ben sat, swinging his legs in front of him, trying to find better words, but knowing that he'd done the best he could.

Amy J said, "I get it," and Ben smiled at her and nodded.

Andrew gained clearance from his orthopedic doctor to practice on Wednesday and play vs. Walpole on Friday. At practice he showed

389

no signs of limping, though his conditioning was very poor. He shot well in drills, but in the full court workout, he did not make a shot, because his balance and stamina were so compromised.

"That's OK, Andrew. Today's the first week of tryouts. Tomorrow is the second week. Friday is the first game of the season. You'll be ready. Walpole is looking for revenge, but we're ready."

Jason had been out of school all week. Ben heard that he had left the scene because he was drunk while he was driving. He had run home to avoid the field sobriety test, abandoning his friends in the car. Ben knew Jason would probably need an attorney, and he wanted to call the family to suggest Peter Kearns, a player on the team in the 80s who had gone on to become a successful defense attorney, taking on many controversial cases. Ben did not condone what Jason had done, but he wanted him to have the best chance for acquittal, or, at least, for a bright future.

After practice Ben called the Grutchfield house, and, the answering machine intervening, as it probably had for the past four days, Ben left Peter Kearns's name, number, and background. He wished Jason and the family a safe journey through the trials to come.

On Thursday Ben's freshman class presented their poetry projects to each other. They had to read three poems apiece, two that they had written and one that they had read and liked. There were some beautiful poems, usually read inaudibly with painful diffidence. Ben had to ask most of the readers to speak up, as he sat in the back seat in the room.

Julie Pendergast read a poem about a girl swinging on a swing, hurling herself into the air "with the hope of conception." Ben stopped her in her reading. "Julie, that's a wonderful word, 'conception,' in all its meanings. Wow. Class, I don't know if Julie spent any time choosing that word, but it conveys lots of ideas. She may have just stumbled on that word, but because she was giving herself completely to the task of writing the poem, the right word found its way onto the page. You were giving yourself completely, weren't you, Julie," he joked, to make her laugh.

"Oh, yeah, completely," she said, understanding. She finished the poem and read her second, another poem punctuated by precise diction.

John Noyes delivered a long poem about violence, then wrapped it up with the line, "And some people lose their voice because it has been cut out of them by the sword of violence."

Ben called the class's attention once again to the word chosen: the "sword." "Of course it is another reference to the violence that dominates the poem. And there is the hint of slicing someone's vocal cords, a horrible concept. But isn't he really talking about our inability to talk about the atrocities that we witness, rendering us silent?" Ben was excited to hear poetry so alive.

Then Paul, Ben's cynical non-student took his place in front of the room. "I wrote a poem about hate. First of all I want to read a poem, it's a song, really, written by Antje Duvekot. It's called 'Judas.'" And he read a wondrous, fearsome song about a boy who sat in the back of the bus, whose father was a drunk, and who, in the end, brought a gun to school and opened fire.

Paul turned awkwardly to his own poems. His first poem was fairly short, but powerful:

> A child born of hate
> Learns the language of grudge
> And excuse and resentment
> He speaks with his hands
> And his slouch and his indifference
> He carves his initials in the bathroom stall
> With his swear words
> And his refusal to perform
> And the hair that covers his eyes
> And he muffles his fear
> With his apathy
> And his crude laugh
> And his rage.

The class sat silently, looking down at their desks. Ben stood up from his seat in the back of the room. "That was amazing. Paul, I don't know if you know a person like this one that you're writing about, but that doesn't matter. Because you've made us think you know him."

Ben stopped the class. "Paul, I know you have another poem, but I just want the class to end with that poem in our heads. Everyone, please hand in your poetry projects in five minutes. Until then you can look at each other's, read each other's, or do nothing." Ben slapped his desk with his hand, to gain the students' attention again. "One more time, may I introduce to you Paul Desillets."

Finally, the game with Walpole arrived. The school had slouched its way to the February vacation. Many students were absent this last Friday because their parents had taken the last day or two of the week preceding vacation to gain a better price for flights to the South, where the sun shone brightly and the sand felt warm under their feet. There was no holiday for everyone to prepare for, like Thanksgiving or Christmas, unless Presidents' Day had become something more than a chance to sell cars. Ben passed the last classes spinning word games with the students, trying to get them to play with the words that they uttered every day without thinking.

As the stands filled in for the Walpole game, Ben sat next to Bryan, who was coaching his last JV game of the year. Though Ben would not see it, because his team would be on the floor warming up, he knew that Bryan would collect the uniforms of the players as they came off the floor, and he would take a few minutes to find a frame for their season. Once again, Bryan had found a way to make the junior varsity experience something that fed the flame that varsity meant to these kids. The freshman team had lost a 54 – 42 game, a little lackluster, but a close game throughout. At halftime of Bryan's game, the Panthers led 23 – 21, both teams jittering in front of the rapidly filling stands, more fans constantly emerging from the doorway to the gym.

By the second half of the JV game, the stands were nearly full. The Walpole varsity was playing for a chance at the league title; Casteline was playing for a tournament berth. There was a well-woven narrative between these two teams, a history that both Bryan and Ben knew, a history that the players on both teams could sense in the presence of past players in the crowd. Most gratifying were the elder parents who came for this game, knowing history would be perpetuated this night. Ben could see Mr. James, Mr. and Mrs. Mark, Mrs. Marble, even Mrs. Cookson and her father who must be in his 90s now.

Bryan continued to change defenses, keeping Walpole off-stride, keeping the Casteline team close. With five minutes to go, Ben headed to the locker room, tapping Bryan on the shoulder.

In the locker room Ben wrote the names of Walpole's five starters on the white board. The Casteline players knew the Walpole players well, having played them five or six times since they had entered high school, but also having played them in summer league and summer camp and travel teams when they were in sixth and seventh and eighth grade. There were no secrets between the two teams.

Ben could feel his heart swelling, not with pride, but with adrenaline and emotion. Maybe it was pride, pride in knowing that this evening was one of the fine fictions of all their lives at the moment, filled with intent and purpose. "Men, you're never ready for a game like this. On the one hand, it means so much: last regular season game for seniors, last home game, possibly the last game as a team, a continuation of a legendary rivalry, stands are full, mothers getting their flowers, last game against Walpole. There's a lot going on.

"But I want to change your perspective a little. Let's just think of this as just a backyard game of horse, simple bragging rights. Winner gets first dibs on the water in the hose. Keep it simple, in your mind. We know how to attack Walpole's defenses. We know how to change our defenses and how to apply different pressure from different looks. By February 17th we don't have to think about how to do something. We just have to play. Let's enjoy this moment, a moment we're probably all going to remember the rest of our lives. Those of you who play football, Mark, Dmitri, you know what I'm talking about. Just be in the moment, completely. Don't think about winning or making the tournament or the shot you missed a minute ago or the great rebound you got two minutes ago. Be in the moment. Get in perfect stride with the flow of this game. You will play your best if you do that.

"Think of this game as a beautiful shot heading toward the basket, arcing beautifully, perfectly released. This game is going to happen, just like that ball is going to go up, reach its peak, and then come down perfectly in the basket. Do you see what I mean? There is no doubt this game will come to a wonderful conclusion. There is no doubt that ball will fall through the net and make that beautiful sound: SWISH. The ball is already out of your hands. You just have to follow its natural flight into the basket. Be smooth."

Bryan came in from the smaller locker room, the uniforms collected, the season having been summed up meaningfully as only Bryan could do. He was jazzed up from his team's exciting comeback win, a perfect way to end their junior varsity season and a better way to send the varsity out onto the floor against Walpole.

As the team warmed up, Ben felt humbled by the noise and the crowd; he always marveled at the way a game could command such attention, even in high school. He thought of the fictions he had spoken of in his junior lit class: this game was one of those fictions to which a tumescent crowd of people gave life. Ben felt fortunate to be at the center of it once again. He saw Dan Owings's father in the stands, but not his mother. He saw Willa, with Mary and Scott, the kids shouting with the cheerleaders as they had done seven and eight years ago, expecting to be Panthers when they grew up. When he looked at Willa for an extended period of time, she looked at him with the open simplicity that had drawn them close thirty years ago. He had seen that same glance across the court twenty-five years ago, before Mary and

393

Scott were born, when these twenty-five years were ahead of them and they saw nothing intruding on their dreams for each other. He felt sad to think of the passing of those twenty-five years and the conflicts and selfishness that had buried many of those dreams.

The night before, he had turned down Pete's call to work another Thursday, hoping that he and Willa might clear the air, somehow. After an expeditious supper, Mary out at the library, Scott tolerating the company of his silent parents, Ben asked Willa if she would come in the bedroom with him. She was uncomfortable with this break in their routine, but their routine had become stultifying.

In the bedroom Ben asked Willa to sit on the bed with him. He had closed the door on the way in.

"What are you trying to do here?" Willa said suspiciously.

"I promise to keep my clothes on," Ben said, spinning some humor into his mystery.

"The first button that gets unbuttoned, and I'm out of here," Willa said lightly.

"No, I just want you to consider one thing, and I want to consider another. Follow me out, OK?"

Willa shrugged.

"I am seeing your moment with Peter Harrison was just that: a moment, with no underlying relationship, no history, just a hug between two considerate people." He stopped talking.

Willa looked at him expectantly, waiting for him to come forward with his irony.

"And that's all. I'm seeing that explanation without rancor or prejudice."

Willa nodded. "That's great. That's exactly what it is."

Ben nodded too. "Perfect. Now I'd like you to see that same embrace from another perspective: as a symbol of commitment and intimacy between two people who have been moving toward each other in an emotional and physical way for a long time, who have a shared history now, just like a married couple, a history the details of which only these two know, these two, two people who are looking for a relationship, one of whom is single and lonely, the other of whom is unhappy in her marriage.

"This embrace looks innocent, seen from one angle, but carries deep import to the two people, an import that her husband has been searching for for a long time." Ben could go on and on, but he wanted to try to present a fair counterbalance to his other picture.

Willa looked at Ben with a trace of resentment. "That's not fair. You let me think you see it my way, then you give your biased version, embellished with your own loneliness." She sat on the bed, her head leaning back on the pillow, one foot on the bed, one on the floor.

"But I just want you to see my way of thinking. I am admitting that I understand your way of thinking, and that's a hard admission for me. I understand that that might be the answer. But I need you to understand that my vision might be the answer too." Ben looked at her, pleading with her.

Willa nodded. "I understand. I just can't get past my own perspective, but I see what you're saying."

Ben leaned over her and kissed her on the shoulder where Peter Harrison had been leaning his head.

And so, on Friday night, Willa and Ben sent their conflicting perspectives across the gym floor toward each other, sensing their own long history, a history built of expectations and disappointment and joy and fatigue, a history that had the gravity to overcome their long and vitriolic fight, but a gravity that could tether their future from rising with promise.

At Willa's knees, in the row below her, was Ben's mother, coming to her first game of the year, her first game in more than eight years. She looked blankly at the court; she could see Ben if Willa pointed him out across the gym floor, but she lost contact with him just as quickly. Yet there was a smile on her face for having been brought to this place of excitement, a place that confused her delightfully. She might be seeing her monkeys hanging from their vines, but she might be seeing the ball coursing its flight into the basket.

Ben, breaking his usual habit, probed the crowd for more familiar faces. He saw Steve Ramos, all the way back from Union; he must have a game in the Boston area for which his team had come in early. He also saw Brad Newman and Pete Cushing from other recent teams. His friends from western Massachusetts, Tim and Katie Agida and Jack and Rhoda Kennedy had taken a Friday night drive, getting off work early to make the 7:00 starting time. Casteline's retired principal, Bob Merusi, sat with his long-time assistant who still worked at the high school. The superintendent was crowded into the lower part of the student section, enjoying the volume the excited students offered. Brad Lane, the AD, stood facing the crowd, his ears attuned to any off-color chants, his finger ready to point at the offender. Laura Ruben sat near mid-court, dressed in a white jacket, looking as if she had a son playing, her eyes watching the balls as they lifted easily toward the rim, finding that parabolic arc that fed the basket rhythmically. She caught Ben's eye as he looked across, giving a self-conscious wave of the fingers of her left hand that lay on her purse.

When it was time for the Star-Spangled Banner, Ben was overcome with the emotion that always accompanied the acknowledgment of the flag, not because he was patriotic, but because the National Anthem connected all those athletic events he had made a central part of his life. He always wondered if anyone else cared as much as he did about the outcome of the ensuing game, whether he was a high school player himself, a second-year coach, or a twenty-five-year coach. He held out the possibility that he indeed did have a greater vested interest in the game that was about to be played, and that greater vestment would translate into better performance.

He took a deep breath, turning back to the court.

Ben took the microphone to introduce the seniors, who then gave a rose that he had provided them to their mothers. Ben felt the void resulting from the absence of the Grutchfield family. He acknowledged Jason for his contributions, knowing how deeply he missed this day.

Ben's friend Jack Carson, who kept the clock, took the mike from him to announce the starting lineups. "For Walpole, starting at guard, #21, a junior, Larry McGill. At forward . . ." The final two players announced were the captains, Peter Kennedy and Rob Evans.

When Jack said, "And now, starting for the Panthers . . .," he paused for effect; the crowd rose and roared on cue. The starting lineup would be five seniors, in honor of their constancy and commitment: Bobbie Pitaro, Jonas Boynton, Alex White, Geoff Willis, and Andrew Monaghan. Mark Payne, the only senior on the bench, would be an early substitution and a valuable contributor if the Panthers were to win. When Jack announced, "And returning for the first time in five weeks for the Panthers," the crowd's excitement drowned out Andrew's name. This night was a passionate homecoming for him.

After Geoff, the captain, had been announced, Ben shook Bryan's hand and trotted down to Walpole's coach, Steve Brennan, to shake his hand. Steve took his hand and tried to crush it, but Ben was one instant quicker.

It seemed as if the game would never start, there was so much formality to get through, but finally Mike McCarthy, a veteran official who might be a few years past his prime, tossed the ball in the air to start the game. All was as it should be: everything came down to this one game. The ball arced beautifully, hanging in the air at its apogee, then falling toward the two hands that reached for it.

Andrew showed that he was ready to play by winning the tap, flicking the ball to Bobbie, who tossed to the weakside corner for a Jonas 3. He missed, but it was a great way to begin the game. Walpole ran a staggered screen for Peter Kennedy, who knocked in a simple jumper for a 2-0 lead. Walpole sank back to a sagging man-to-man, putting slight pressure on the ball, but nothing oppressive or impressive. At the point Bobbie had no difficulty getting the team into their half-court set, drawing the defense away with two ball reversals, before punching it inside for Geoff, who missed a six-footer, but Andrew cleaned up the weakside board for a 2 – 2 tie.

The seniors' intensity wore down after three or four minutes, and Walpole began to assert themselves, taking a 12 – 7 lead, before Ben inserted Archie, James, Dan, and Mark Payne into the lineup, keeping Geoff in the game. Andrew had had trouble negotiating the full court after his initial surge; it was clear he would be good for only two or three minutes at a time. But the junior trio on the perimeter began breaking down Walpole's defense, drawing a first foul on Kennedy and a first and second on their supreme point guard, Rob Evans. Casteline closed the gap to a one-point differential at the first break, 18 – 17 Walpole.

"Great start, guys. What a great atmosphere. You are perfectly prepared for this game. I can see the resolve in your eyes, but, more importantly, in your feet. You are one step ahead of Walpole on most of their cuts and drives. But you need a quicker first step in the full court. They've beaten you down for two clean, uncontested layups. Evans is a hell of a point guard. You have to respect that. And Kennedy can finish. Once he gets an angle on the glass, he's untouchable.

"Andrew, back in for Geoff, just three minutes. I know you can't run the floor the way you know how, but we'll try to slow it down a little with you in there. Archie, pull out if you don't have something easy on the break." Ben loved the level of noise that he had to overcome to get his instructions across. The gym was trembling with the expectations that so many people had brought with them. No one maintained a middling stance in this game. It was us or them.

She's got everything she needs,
She's an artist, she don't look back.
She's got everything she needs,
She's an artist, she don't look back.
She can take the dark out of the nighttime
And paint the daytime black.

You will start out standing
Proud to steal her anything she sees.
You will start out standing
Proud to steal her anything she sees.
But you will wind up peeking through her keyhole
Down upon your knees.

She never stumbles,
She's got no place to fall.
She never stumbles,
She's got no place to fall.
She's nobody's child,
The Law can't touch her at all.

She wears an Egyptian ring
That sparkles before she speaks.
She wears an Egyptian ring
That sparkles before she speaks.
She's a hypnotist collector,
You are a walking antique.

Bow down to her on Sunday,
Salute her when her birthday comes.
Bow down to her on Sunday,
Salute her when her birthday comes.
For Halloween give her a trumpet
And for Christmas, buy her a drum

She Belongs To Me by Bob Dylan

James

Going out to start the second quarter, James was fatigued. He had played only four and a half minutes, but the intensity of the game – as it always was with Walpole – left him gassed. But he did not want to let Coach know, so he drank a lot of water and tried to restore his breathing to a normal pace.

The Rebels scored easily twice to start the second period, pushing the lead to 22 – 17. Archie moved the ball in to Andreas at the high post on the next possession; he touched it on a backdoor pass to Dan cutting on the baseline for a layup. They had never run the play before, but the rules of movement that Coach had always preached dictated that Dan make that cut on the entry pass, leading to the bucket. At the other end Peter Kennedy ran from one corner to the other wing, then reversed himself to cut off a baseline double pick for an open 3; James could not keep up with him. Kennedy was a master at moving without the ball. Basket was good.

The Panthers kept close, but could not close the gap. At half-time Walpole led 38 – 30. Rob Evans, Walpole's point guard, had three fouls, but no one else on either team was in any foul trouble.

Coach spoke calmly to the team. "Solid first half. You can see Kennedy's talent. When he's coming off that baseline screen, let's switch out onto him off the high man on the double. But the wing that's chasing him has to continue to chase Kennedy down. When James is back in position, on balance, the big man retreats to the post defense. For a second, one guy will have to cover two at the block. Understand?"

A couple of the players nodded.

"Let's also run some 3 at them. We didn't show it in the first half. We should get a couple indecisive attacks from them even if we don't get any steals. We're gonna need to change the momentum in this half; they never got rattled in that first half, and that's our fault. We need to mix it up a little, change defenses more, apply a little more pressure from time to time.

"Geoff, Andrew, see anything out there?"

Geoff deferred to Andrew, who replied, "I just think we need to set much better screens for our shooters. And I'm sorry I'm not shooting well, but I'll get it going in the second half." Andrew had shot maybe 2 for 7.

Geoff added, "We gotta kick their ass on the boards. We're not going after the ball with any passion. Gotta get 30 rebounds this half."

He shouted, "One half to go, Seniors. Play like it's the end. It is the end." James could feel the hardness of that truth for the seniors.

On the way out onto the court, James caught his father's eye; he was sitting near the entryway from the locker room. Mr. Rush nodded at James, sharing in his effort, revealing his hope. James returned the nod and clapped his hands loudly. "Let's go," he shouted.

When James had come home after practice Thursday night, his dad had proposed a project that needed James's assistance: replacing a supporting column underneath the main beam of the house, stretching across the basement ceiling, supporting the joists that spanned the house. These projects had always been a way for James's dad to teach James the skills that he considered essential to becoming a self-sufficient man. In the past the two had replaced a bulkhead, added a dormer to Rachel's room, re-insulated the attic for better heat retention, installed a drop-down ladder to the attic – those home improvements that owning a home mandated. Mr. Rush gave little direction during these home fix-its; he just asked for James's help and needed it at times.

In the cellar the project was already laid out. "Here's the replacement column, an adjustable metal column. We need to cut a piece out of the wooden plate, so we can run the column from the slab to the beam, perfectly plumb." Mr. Rush picked up his sawzall. "Do you want to make the cut?"

As enthusiastically as he could, James said, "Hey, Dad. Can you give me a minute? I'm still in my school clothes. I'm gonna change and I'll see you down here in five, OK?"

Mr. Rush agreed, though he could not put the saw down.

As he changed into jeans and a Duke sweatshirt, James realized that his dad had not included James in his home projects for the past two months, ever since his incident with the police. This project was a sign of reconciliation on the part of his father, and James knew he needed to be receptive and alert.

Once again down cellar, James said, "OK, let me make the cut." He looked at the heavy pencil lines his father had drawn. "If we are fat on one side, which side, inside or outside?"

"Inside. I've left a half inch clearance on the plate. We can squeeze it a little."

James made the cut, and the two men continued, adjusting the column to an inch less than the required height, 77 ½", placed the column into its slot, dropped a plumb line to establish perpendicularity, toe-nailed the upper plate, set the column, and expanded it to full height. They worked for about an hour, with little conversation, like two

400

tradesmen, one licensed, one an apprentice. James enjoyed the physical labor and the precision. Without his father's guidance, he would never be this exact, but he knew that his father was right in being so accurate in his measurements and his execution.

When they were done, they had to reinforce the existing lally column, by grinding it down, and applying body filler. They would sand and paint another day. When the grinding was done, Mr. Rush asked, "Do you want to apply the filler?"

"Sure. Whatever goes wrong, I can just sand it away."

His father smiled. "That sounds like a perfect way to approach it. We're never perfect the first time through, but in most cases we can fix it to be perfectly functional."

After their basement repair was done, tools put away in their bins and chests, they went upstairs to the kitchen where James's mother was sitting at the table, an expectant look on her face. "Well, did you save the house?" she asked brightly.

James said, "I think it's safe for another week or two, at least. But there's still more work to be done."

His father smiled, comfortable in their temporary solidarity. James could see him reach out to put an arm around him, like Coach LaMott's "sharing the love," but he withheld the gesture, not ready for that intimacy yet. Instead, he said, "I think we got the job done, and done right."

Supper sat in tin foil on the stove. It was almost 8:00.

His father sat in one of the kitchen chairs, extending his hand to offer James a seat across from him. "James, let's talk about this season."

James did not know if he was ready to talk openly with his father about the season or, more importantly, about his life away from the house over the past two months, but he was interested in hearing what thoughts his father had been harboring in these months of indifferent silence.

James sat down in the empty kitchen chair. He looked expectantly at his father, glancing furtively at his mother to try to read her face. She too was looking for direction.

"I think you know how your mother and I were let down by your getting involved with alcohol and the police. We tried to provide you with direction with the offer of a car when you were done with your penalty, but you threw that check right in our faces. I don't know when I've ever been angrier than when I ripped up that check for the car.

"Since that day, for two months, there's been a kind of silence in this house: we haven't restrained you, and you haven't toed the line the way you did as a sophomore. Can we agree on that?"

James replied slowly. "That's right." The less he said, the better.

Mrs. Rush now spoke, betraying her subordinate role. "Can you tell us how you've done in these seven weeks? Have you drunk? Have you done things we should know about? Have you been in any more trouble?" She implored him to tell the truth, as if he were in second grade, telling her his escapades on the way home from school. James remembered their nearly silent meeting in the kitchen at 2:40 a.m. just a few weeks ago.

James breathed deeply. He let his voice take over. "I'll be honest with you because I think that's the best way to show you that I respect you. I have not been a complete angel since my suspension. But I have tried to make every decision with you and Dad and Rachel and basketball in mind. I have stayed away from trouble many times. I am still trying to figure out how to be a sixteen year old kid. There are some moments when I do something immature or unwise, I'll admit. But I'm getting way better." James stopped his nervous chatter, his attempt to be revelatory without being self-incriminating. In James's mind the primary fulcrum that made this discussion difficult was understanding whether his parents wanted honesty from him or obedience. He was trying to argue that honesty was more important.

Mr. Rush pushed back from the table, angry. "Well, I guess that's your way of telling us that you still don't have any regard for the principles that we espouse. I was hoping that we had reached a place where you would understand our perspective and honor it." He looked disgusted with James.

Mrs. Rush stepped in. "Arthur, you don't have to demand all or nothing. There are no absolutes in growing up. You know that." She spoke with more assurance than James had recalled hearing in her. "James, can you tell us with all your heart that you've done nothing to make us disappointed in you since the New Year began?"

James looked directly at his mother, then his father. "I have found myself in a difficult situation two or three times. I have worked my way out of those situations in each case. Right now, I know I am far stronger than I have ever been in my life. I know what's out there, and I know the repercussions if and when I fail to meet your expectations." He paused, then said, "And, I might add, my expectations for myself are as high as yours for me."

Mrs. Rush nodded. "That's what we were hoping." She looked at James's dad, hoping that Mr. Rush could acknowledge the importance of James's last assertion.

Just then Rachel came downstairs from her room. "Aren't we having any supper tonight?" she asked from the living room, unaware that something else was simmering in the kitchen.

Mr. Rush would not let the discussion end here. "Rachel, honey, we're just finishing up an important discussion. Can you give us five minutes?"

Rachel poked her head in the door, staring at James to see how guilty he looked. He looked at her as innocently and honestly as an infant. She smiled and turned on the TV in the living room. James felt good with her in the next room.

Mr. Rush brought the discussion back to James. He finally used the same first person plural that Mrs. Rush had used. "We do see you trying. And we hate to see your relationship with us turn to anger and resentment." Mr. Rush looked up to the ceiling. "I will admit that I have not been very receptive to discussing this with you – " he stopped, thinking, " – partly because I was not ready to hear from you some of the admissions you'd have to make." Mr. Rush stood from his chair, looking at Mrs. Rush. "But now I realize that the boy that I thought I was raising is gone." He said this without anger, just resignation. "And I suppose every parent has to come to the realization that he can only do so much, then his son has to make his own way." He paused again. "We just hope your way – even if it's not our way – is a safe way." His voice became almost gentle as he said the last.

James was warmed by his dad's vulnerability. "I've made some poor choices; I know that. And I accept the fact that I will not be getting my license until August, while Dan is already driving now. I am old enough to pay the price when I mess up. And I messed up. What I am telling you is this: I will mess up less and less now, because I know there is too much at stake. I'll be taking the drug and alcohol course in the spring, and I hope that will give me some guide points, too." He tried to tell them he was ready for the independence that he was being offered. "I think I am learning to set and reach my own standards. And I would like to hear you tell me how you think I'm doing in both directions, good and bad, proud and disappointed." He nodded his head at his own declaration.

Mrs. Rush's face brightened in agreement. "Oh, I know that that's what's more important, in the long run. It's just so hard to let you decide for yourself what you're going to do."

Mr. Rush joined in her admission. "I have a hard time letting go of the controls." He let it go at that. James reached for his father's hand, feeling the restrained strength, trying to answer it.

His father ended the discussion. "And now, you've got something else to focus on: tomorrow night's game. I wanted to clear the air before that game, not for you, but for me. I haven't had a lot of fun this season because we haven't been able to share this season at all. I'd like, for this final game, to think we're fighting this fight together."

James rose from his chair and stood behind his father, his hands on his father's shoulders. "Any supper? I've got a lot of homework to do," he said.

Facing an 8 point deficit, James knew there was little room for error in the second half. Walpole was a 14 – 5 team, but one of those losses had been to Casteline, at Walpole, without Andrew Monaghan in the lineup. This game was very winnable.

The starting lineup for the second half was Geoff, Andrew, James, Dan, and Archie, the best five (in Jason's absence). Andrew was good for only three or four minutes at a time, but the Panthers had to take advantage of his skill when he was on the floor.

James pulled Archie aside as they walked onto the court. "Archie, let's keep running down screens for Andrew while he's in there. He can catch and shoot."

And for the first six possessions, James and Dan set a series of screens for Andrew that freed him up. He made five of six, two of them 3s. When Andrew came off the court with 4:11 to go in the third, the lead was down to three, 45 – 42. Andrew had scored 12 straight.

Without Andrew the Panthers had to spread it out, running their Drive and Dish, Calipari-ball. Coach had been slipping the drive and dish into most every practice since the exam break, and now, with Andrew on the bench, it was as well-aimed as a dart. Dan, Archie, and James took turns attacking Walpole's defense, finding a seam, kicking to the adjacent teammate, who then reversed the ball to the third player, who had an open look against Walpole's defense, which had sagged to the penetration. It was as if they were playing 3 on 3, ignoring Geoff and Mark in the post area, but twice they tossed into Mark, who finished with a post-up. At the end of three the Panthers closed the gap to one point, 53 – 52.

At the defensive end James was having a hard time stopping Peter Kennedy, who was coming off screens better than Andrew at the other end. Peter was 6'2", with a little reach over James. Following Coach LaMott's half-time instruction, Andrew, Mark, or Geoff was switching out to cover Kennedy, but Kennedy was too quick for them. He would just take a one-dribble jumper or penetrate and pass. And Evans was getting into the lane if there was too much attention given to Kennedy without the ball. Walpole's big guys could all finish strong if they got the ball down low.

The season was down to one quarter: if they won, James would be playing in his first tournament game ever. He thought of the many tournament games he and Dan had traveled to, in Avon, at Xaverian in Westwood, at TD Banknorth, in Brockton, Braintree, Norwell, Durfee. They had gone with Dan's or James's father, sometimes the four of them, watching the Panthers make crucial free throws, one time seeing Dave Rowean make two blocks to end a great game with Cohasset, seeing Steve Ramos hit a jumper with 3 seconds on the clock to defeat Cathedral three years ago. He also thought about his conversation with Adrienne Thursday night, after he had found support in his parents.

He had called her soon after supper, though, to be honest, he had wanted to spend some time studying for Mr. Tilson's quiz, a Friday-before-vacation quiz that would not be hard because he wanted to reward those students who were not heading south for vacation, the quiz on shifted conic sections.

"Hey, Aide, what's up," he opened, still suffused with the joy of his reconciliation with his parents.

"Well, you're feeling pretty chipper. Are you just anticipating the outcome of the game?" She was upbeat, but not like James.

"No, but I feel really good about it. And I feel really good about me and the p's. We just had a great conversation, and I think I detected a little trust coming my way." He had taken his usual position on his bed, lying on his back, his feet stretching toward the ceiling, his back this evening on the mattress, buoyed by pillows, trying to scrape his socks on the rough pattern of the ceiling. He wanted to push himself into a head-stand, but he lacked the coordination. As he talked, he grunted with his effort.

"No way. That's great. I'm so happy for you. Was it an easy conversation?"

He strained, his weight pressed onto his shoulders. He had turned his phone to speaker, because he had to spread his hands out for balance. He shouted, "Actually, it was. I think we all told the truth."

Adrienne, doubt in her voice, said, "I can barely hear you. Are you holding the phone far away from your mouth? And you didn't tell *everything*, did you? That'd be really impressive."

405

Lowering his feet to relax for an instant, James said, "Not everything, but I made many blanket confessions, admissions of going off track and learning to avoid the repeat." James made a lunge with his feet, trying to swing them along the ceiling in a wild arc that left him overturned. He reached for the phone, pressing it to his mouth. "I told them I needed their feedback whether it was good or bad. I think that's what's been missing – along with good decisions on my part." He lay on the bed, gathering strength and coordination for another assault on the ceiling.

"That sounds promising. If you can reach that accord and keep it, you'll all be much happier. And you're right: you still have to make good decisions." He could hear a little uncertainty creep into her voice when she talked about good decisions.

"Anyway, I'm feeling great. Studying for Tilson's quiz next. Hey, how do you remember the formula for the asymptotes for a hyperbola?"

Adrienne explained the derivation and the formula clearly. James could picture the lines that the curves neared.

"And how about the shift in cones? How do you remember whether to slide the focus left or right?"

"Just remember that you are subtracting the distance from the central focus, so subtracting a positive integer would move things to the right, or upward, and adding an integer is really subtracting a negative integer, moving things left, or downward." It all sounded so simple, coming from her mouth.

"One last thing," James added. "Are you gonna see me play basketball any more this year?"

"Well, you have to do your part to make that happen. I know I'm playing in the post-season. And I know you'll be coming to see me play. What I don't know is whether you'll be playing in the post-season. I'd really like to come cheer for the Panthers' boys' basketball in the tournament. I'm talking to the one person I know who can make that happen. Let's get it done, OK?" The support in her voice was as strong as the column he had installed in his basement earlier in the evening.

"I will deliver a victory to you as a belated Valentine's Day present." They had exchanged cards in school, but not much of a kiss. "And then I'd like to share a real Valentine's Day kiss, if you're prepared for one."

"Well, if it's contraception that you think I'll need, then I don't want that kiss, but I could use a passionate kiss, I'll admit. Wait for me after the game?"

"Yeah, I'll be there, but you'll have to wait until the fans clear out."

To start the fourth quarter Walpole went on a run to open up a 60 – 54 lead. Coach turned the defense to a 3, to try to force some off-rhythm shots from the Rebels. James didn't think Kennedy knew what off-balance meant. He kept drilling his jumper, now from the corner. With less than five minutes to go, Andrew on the bench to recover enough for a final push over the last three minutes, Coach inserted Mark, Geoff, and Andreas to throw some height on the court. In the backcourt were James and Dan, Archie catching a blow for a couple minutes. They played a 2-2-1 on scores, James and Dan up front. Andreas and Mark showed good anticipation at their sideline trapping and weakside pinching in the middle, picking off two passes, taking one charge, and finally getting Walpole out of their rhythm. The defense took the ball out of Rob Evans's hands, putting pressure on Kennedy and their other wing, Andy Bedosian, to make plays far from the basket. When Andrew and Archie came back into the game, for Dan and Geoff, the game was tied, 63 – 63. There were two and a half minutes left.

James penetrated and kicked to Archie for a three that he missed, but Andreas followed up with a putback for a 65 – 63 lead. Kennedy hit two free throws, answered by James's two at the line: 67 – 65. The Panthers stayed in their 3, but they were not forcing turnovers any more. They just had to scramble to prevent clean looks. James jumped to put pressure on Evans's shot, but he made it anyway to tie the game. At the other end, James and Andreas set a down screen for Andrew, who came off it to drop in another jumper, allowing Casteline to regain the lead. The Rebels answered easily, a drive by Kennedy and a dish-off for a 3 point play after their big man made the foul shot. The Rebels had regained the lead, 70 – 69. On the foul shot, Archie reentered the game. There were 21 seconds left.

James knew there would be no time-out coming. Walpole came with a 1-2-2 trap of their own, trying to force a turnover from the Panthers, but with three ball-handlers on the floor, they got the ball middle to James who attacked the bottom of the zone, 3 on 2, Geoff on his left and Andrew on his right. But as James pulled into his jump-stop at the foul line, Peter Kennedy swiped at the ball from behind, knocking it free of James's grasp. The ball bounced toward Walpole's big man, Dan Howell, who leaped for the loose ball just as James made the same move. The resulting jump ball gave the ball to Casteline underneath the Walpole basket. There were 7 seconds left.

Here, Coach took his second time-out of the game. "James, you've got the ball out of bounds. We'll run our 3 under the basket, but they'll probably play zone until the ball comes in. So, James, look for Archie over the top. Archie, we'll set a double for James coming in from out-of-bounds. Archie, you've got your own drive, a pass to James, or hit one of the big men rolling. Dan, after your cut, get to the right baseline and be ready to attack when you get it.

Coach knelt to lower himself underneath the huddle, looking up, whispering, "This is what we play for. Enjoy the moment."

James looked for Geoff and Andrew rolling off their screens, but Walpole had indeed played zone, forcing the pass to the perimeter. James faked the long pass to Archie over the top, then leaned far to his left, to improve the angle of his pass to Dan, but a defender got his hand on the pass anyway. Dan closed to the ball, getting there just as Evans reached back for the bouncing ball. Dan outfought Evans for the ball on the floor, pulling it to his right side, raising his head, to see whether Andrew was setting a screen for James coming in from out-of-bounds. But James had already come off that screen, and was well covered. Dan squared up, trying to get a shoulder past Evans; James fanned to the top of the circle, showing his hands, ready to fend off Kennedy if a pass came his way.

But Dan found a way to get a foot past Evans, taking two dribbles and then getting a shot off, a glass shot, as he leaned in on the right baseline. The ball came off the rim, but here came Geoff Willis to find the ball just off the rim, meeting the ball as it moved away from the rim, tapping it with his left hand back to the rim, the ball hovering on the nearside of the rim before falling through the rim for the game-winner. James looked at the clock: Home 71 Visitor 70 Time 0:00.

James could not believe it. He jumped, tears filling his eyes and leaking off his eyelashes onto his cheeks. His teammates disappeared beneath the crowd that swept onto the court. He landed awkwardly, stumbling on the court where he had felt so graceful for the past hour. He searched for Dan and Geoff, finding them in an embrace with Andrew, whose face showed no hint of the pain he had endured during the game.

Feeling a tap on his shoulder, James turned to find Rachel hopping up and down, her feet flipping up like a string puppet's nearly to her butt, her face gleeful. She jumped into his arms. Looking up into the stands James saw his mother and father beaming down at him, his mother's eyes watery, his father's fists still raised and clenched, his mouth clenched too in some restrained form of jubilation. James carried Rachel in his arms to the frenzy that surrounded Geoff and Andrew, the heroes of the finish, swinging her around him, her arms locked around his neck, his arms reaching past her to his teammates, squeezing her in their midst, her laughing face conveying the rapture of being caught up in the eye of this storm. James did not want to put her down, as he banged shoulders with his teammates.

It took another minute for the chaos to die down, but then James remembered they had to line up for the handshake with the players from Walpole, who had played so well that it took a singular effort from the Panthers to win. Midway through the line, James shook Peter Kennedy's hand. "Great game, man. You're an awesome player," he said to his opponent.

"Congratulations," he said. "I could see you playing with your backs to the wall. You got it done. Good luck in the tournament."

"Same to you. You'll do well. Win it," James offered.

When James peeled out of the hand-shake line he looked up at the rafters, their rectilinear beams of light steel. His skin was so hot and his body so dehydrated, he felt he was having some kind of visionary experience. As he continued to look upwards, the beams seemed to bend into the arches of a cathedral, like the campus chapel at Duke, a tall, Medieval vault, reaching upward as it created space for the rich panoply inside. Though he heard the exultation around him, he felt transported, until he finally realized that his eyes were indeed closed, he was so rapt in the moment of completion. It was then he felt strong arms gently take him into their radius and a warm, soft cheek nuzzle against his. It was Adrienne, returned from her game at Walpole. He did not need to hear her voice.

My favorite plum
hangs so far from me
See how it sleeps
and hear how it calls to me
See how the flesh
presses the skin,
It must be bursting
with secrets within,
I've seen the rest, yes
and that is the one for me

See how it shines
it will be so sweet
I've been so dry
it would make my heart complete
See how it lays
languid and slow
Never noticing
me here below
I've seen the best, yes
and that is the one for me

Maybe a girl will take it
Maybe a boy will steal it
Maybe a shake of the bough
will wake it and make it fall

My favorite plum
lies in wait for me
I'll be right here
longing endlessly
You'll say that I'm
foolish to trust
But it will be mine
and I know that it must
cause I've had the rest, yes
and that is the one for me
I've seen the best, yes
and that is the one for me

My Favorite Plum by Suzanne Vega

Ben

After shaking Steve Brennan's hand for the second time in less than two hours, this handshake less competitive, more a concession on Steve's part, Ben turned to gather the team for their center-court huddle. Dozens of people clutched the boys who had accomplished the improbable. He made his way to the C in the center circle, hand in the air, calling the team. "Let's get together, guys," he shouted. It took another minute, but when Geoff and Andrew were able to move out of their parents' embraces, they extracted their teammates from the clutches of adulation, bringing the team together in the middle.

"Not much to say, guys. The game said it all," Ben shouted, his clammy hands weighing down other hands. "There is something about being a player at Casteline that we can tap into when we are working collectively. Andrew, that was an amazing game for you." The team overwhelmed Ben's voice with their shouts and "Whoo . . . whoo . . . whoo."

"Seniors, congratulations on a great regular season. Now we get to see what a post-season is all about.

"Nothing till Wednesday. College visits, family time, trip to the mountains if you ski. See you Wednesday. We'll scrimmage Friday, tournament should start Tuesday after vacation." Ben stopped talking for a second, to try to feel the power of their success. "Just stay together for another few seconds. Can you feel what we accomplished tonight? Can you feel it?"

Andrew's and James's acknowledgment led the team into another community shout, followed by Ben's "One . . . two . . ." The team could not wait for "Three."

There were so many people to see: Steve and other past players; Katy, Tim, Jack and Rhoda; Scott and Mary; his former principal; current teachers who had gotten swept up in the team's drama; even Walpole parents and former players who pressed toward Ben, feeling the import of the win. As the crowd around Ben thinned, he looked into the stands at Willa and his mother, who sat watching the swirl on the court.

Willa understood completely Ben's sense of accomplishment. As he approached her, she said, "Hey," just "hey," the word connoting so much that they had shared this year and twenty-four others, but declaring so little about the future.

411

Ben stepped up into the stands, sitting next to Willa, hugging her with the energy that was starting to dissipate, finally. He slipped down to his mother's row and gave her a slighter hug. "Hi, Mom, thanks for coming. You saw a great game, didn't you?"

"Oh, yes. There were balls flying all over the place. I don't know how you keep track of it all. It's like a circus out there."

Ben nodded. "You're right. It's pretty crazy. But that's why we practice. It looks crazy to you, but it's all part of a bigger plan, really." He smiled at her. Turning to Willa, he said, "The kids enjoy the game?"

Willa nodded. "It was like they were five and six years old. They cheered with the cheerleaders, stood up and tried to distract Walpole's foul shooters. They had a ball. It was like ten years ago, really." She smiled widely.

"Well, ten years ago we were kicking everyone's butt. I really had a handle on things then." He looked at Willa. "Now, it's not as easy. But when it works, it feels that much better." He pushed himself up to Willa's face and crushed his lips into hers, holding her head to his with his right hand. She returned his pressure.

Willa left in a minute, to take Margot back to Fidelity House; before she left, Ben asked her, "Hey, Tim and Katie and Jack and Rhoda are heading over to Willow's for a drink and snacks. See you there?"

Willa nodded as she ushered Margot toward the exit.

Of the people remaining in the stands, Laura Ruben was most noticeable, sitting by herself, a smile playing across her face, her eyes watching the parade of victory move gradually into the locker room. Her white jacket lay next to her, a victim of the heat that the gym had generated. Her black sweater and yellow pants were neatly pressed, one leg draped over the other at the knee. A small purse sat on the bench next to her. Ben approached her, still suffused with satisfaction. "Well, you're two for two now. You're gonna have to find out where we're playing in eleven days, and bring your good luck charm to the game. It'll be an away game. I hope you're ready to travel."

She understood his self-satisfaction. "I would not want to deprive you of the motivation I provide. That would not be fair to your great players. Let me know when and where." She extended her hand. "Congratulations. You deserve it."

He stood in front of her, accepting her hand.

After jubilantly calling the score and game details in to the newspapers, Ben joined his friends at Willow's, where they could rehash the game, recount the vicissitudes of the season, and share a few beers. Willa had already gotten Margot to her room at Fidelity House and arrived at Willow's herself. When Ben entered the bar, he saw the group seated at three of the round tall tables pulled together. At one end Bryan and Lisa huddled together like two college freshmen planning a night-long tryst in an empty dorm room. Bryan gave Ben a rich hug. "That was a good one."

Tim made a few observations about the game, having been a long-time coach himself. "Hey, Archie Stedham has really helped, huh?"

"Yeah, he's solid. What a find."

"Yeah, I knew him at Granby. He was promising. Out west, he was making a name for himself. He even came to our summer camp for a few summers, and he was the greatest player to work with – so appreciative."

"Yeah, he's still that way. It's great how easily he made the transition to a new team." Archie proved the point that a player who can play has a currency that has value in any team situation. It proved a point that Ben had always believed: that a sport is a language of its own, with its own distinctive cadences and communication.

Rhoda and Katy kibitzed with Willa easily, catching up on the events in their children's lives. Jack respectfully sat back a little, sipping his draft beer, interjecting observations, asking questions to keep the group connected.

After an hour, near ten o'clock, Tim said, "Well, we've gotta get going. We have a long drive ahead of us." His old friends lived an hour and a half away, near Springfield.

Ben stood, "Hey, thanks for coming. It was great to see you, and I think you helped bring the energy level to what we needed to win. I really appreciate the effort." He shook Tim and Jack's hands, kissing Rhoda and Katie on their cheeks. Willa joined him in thanking them and wishing them a safe trip home. Rhoda was on her cell phone, trying to get the UMass score from one of her sons.

In another minute Ben thought he and Willa should get going. "Hey, Lisa, can you keep this guy occupied until next Wednesday, when we practice again?"

Lisa smirked. "I'll do my best. But he's a little slow in the learning department. I have to keep going over the basics again and again." She rolled her eyes.

Bryan laughed. "I'm starting to get the idea, though. It just takes practice." He put his arm around Lisa and gave her a lingering kiss.

413

Ben looked away awkwardly, and just then, he saw Laura Ruben in her white jacket, seated in her usual place at the bar, her back to him.

"Well, let's get going. I'll see if I can get a bill from this lousy bar. Just can't get good service at a place like this." He walked to the bar, looking for Pete. As he passed Laura, he said, "Hope you're still feeling uplifted."

She looked at him, her cheeks a little rouged from Chablis. "Hey, congrats again. I see you brought your victory party to Willow's. You deserve it. Keep it up." She looked at him, wondering.

"Yeah, I guess I'm starting to think of this place as my home away from home. It was a nice place to get together with friends. Four of the people were friends from the western part of the state, old friends who still stay connected. They still love sports." He moved behind the bar, looking for the check for their table.

"That's nice," Laura replied.

"Well, see you on Monday, probably. Get home safely," he offered.

Laura nodded and turned away from him to take in the sports news on TV.

Saturday was the music social at the church. Willa left at 3:30 to begin the set up of microphones on the stage in the Parish Hall at the church.

"I'll see you around 7:15," Ben said as she was heading out the door. "Are you going to be backstage for the show, or should I save a seat for you?"

"I'll be backstage for the first act. Hold a seat, because I should be done soon after the intermission." Her words were indistinct with the wind that shook the house. A late-winter storm watch had been posted; the air felt laden with snow, as Ben stood at the door, watching Willa duck into the Subaru.

Ben pushed back in the recliner, an empty afternoon ahead of him, a slate of college basketball that would stretch into the early evening. Louisville was playing Georgetown at 3:00, and Duke was playing Virginia at 3:30. Ben settled in, a coke at his side, to watch John Thompson III challenge Rick Pitino's Cardinals, who were 21 – 2. Ben had no essays to correct, and no books to read for upcoming classes. Scott was looking for a job (much to Ben's surprise) and Mary was shopping at the mall, or, really, traversing the mall, because she never came home having bought anything in her trips there. At halftime of the Duke game, with Duke ahead by twelve, Ben started to sleep, fitfully. When he let his eyes close, he kept seeing Willa and Peter Harrison working together on the Social, opening closet doors, Willa supporting Peter's leg to secure him as he stood unsteadily on a chair to run a mike cord along the linear archway of the proscenium. Ben wondered whether his curiosity and suspicion would be alleviated if he went to the church.

Finally, after failing to settle in for the games on TV, Ben put on his coat, opened the door to the cold outdoors, and turned the key in his Corolla, with the pretext of a trip to the hardware store to buy sandpaper and urethane for the bedroom refurbishing he was planning for the vacation week. He had already bought the paint, rollers, and roller pans. After his stop at the store, he headed over to St. Andrew's, despite his best intentions not to. He pulled into the parking lot, sprinkled with fewer than a dozen snow-laden vehicles, and parked his Corolla near the Parish Hall main door, close to Willa's Subaru. As he passed her car, he kicked the frozen slush from beneath the wheel wells, wetting his boot.

Inside, the room was not yet warm. The deacons had just turned the heat on; it was just after 5:00. The folding chairs were laid out in two sections, with an aisle cut down the middle, the chairs angled slightly to allow for better sight lines to the center of the stage. Bob McKinstry, one of the deacons, and a woman Ben didn't know, were carrying an 8' table to the rear of the hall, where Ben stood. Bob welcomed Ben. "Well, couldn't stay away, huh? We can always use another hand."

Ben shook his head. "Oh no, I'm not here to work; I just popped in to see Willa."

"Well, she's around. But I haven't seen her for a while. I don't know where you'd find her." Bob and his partner put the table down and turned away from Ben.

"But if you need help, I can stay for a while. Just point me in the right direction. I'll do anything you need."

Bob laughed. "Oh no, we're all set, really. Thanks for the offer. Ben, do you know Marie Lombardi?"

"No. Hi, Marie. Ben LaMott. You've probably been working with Willa, my wife?"

Marie nodded. "She's such a great help in everything we do here. I don't know if I've ever seen anyone give so much to the church. The rest of us stay out of trouble just trying to keep up with her. I don't know where she disappeared to. She's been setting the stage up, and I think she's all done. I think she was working with Peter Harrison."

Ben nodded. "Probably. If you see her, tell her I stopped in, OK?"

"OK. See you at the show?"

"I'll be back."

Ben could do nothing but leave the hall and return to his car, none of his suspicions allayed. He did spend a couple minutes trying to determine if Peter Harrison's car was in the parking lot, actually walking by each car to see if he could identify Peter's gear, but as people started to arrive in the lot, he abandoned his prying. He felt a little like Sorcerer, of *In the Lake of the Woods*, skulking and spying on his lover. Though he wanted their relationship to return to some normalcy, he had to agree with Willa's assessment that their marriage had been riding in shallow water for a long time.

At 7:30, seated in the fourth row, Ben watched Joan Fleury sing a show tune, accompanied by a piano accompanist. She sang sweetly, her eyes squeezing shut on her prolonged syllables. The piano gave her a strong bulwark of support.

Over the next half hour, the acts varied from a slightly awkward dance ensemble to an a cappella trio to a rock number featuring four members of the senior youth group trying in vain to harmonize. The crowd supportively applauded all the performers, extending their applause especially for young Laurie Westbrook, whose brother had died a year ago, who sang a soft melody of hope and faith.

At the intermission Ben wandered to the back of the hall to grab a cup of tea and a program. He chatted with Mary and Paul Donnelly and the Snows; he knew many of the attendees. Paul Snow asked him, "So, what is Willa's song all about?"

Ben looked quickly at Paul, to see if he was pulling Ben's leg. Seeing that Paul's face was sincerely curious, Ben looked quickly in the program to see that Willa LaMott would be singing a song entitled *Ghost in This House*, accompanied by Peter Harrison. Ben's voice stumbled. "Uh, I don't really know. It's a surprise."

Paul laughed, thinking that Ben was joking.

When Willa and Peter came on the stage, Willa dressed in a flowered dress that fell from her shoulders to her ankles, Ben froze in his position in his metal chair, his left foot hooked behind the chair leg. Willa moved to the mike as Peter sat at the piano, trilling the keys to find his place on the scale. Willa introduced her song: "This is a song by Alison Krauss, a bluegrass singer who has branched into contemporary singing. It's a song of loss and loneliness." Her voice

416

sounded resonant. Ben had never heard Willa's voice through a microphone. It was strong.

The song was the lament of a woman whose relationship with her spouse or lover had dissipated, leaving her nearly lifeless. Willa captured the desolation of her abandonment convincingly. Ben watched his wife cradle the mike as if it were a baby that she was comforting, or an emotion the depth of which she was giving a voice. Peter, in her train, played very simply and slightly; he was obviously a very skilled pianist, but he was careful to stay in the background, his light and harmonic notes highlighting Willa's voice adeptly.

As Willa floated through the song, she seemed to become saddened by her loneliness; at times her body swayed subtly, as if in despair, leaving her leaning forward, her balance compromised. But as her physical certitude faltered, her voice gained control of the emotion, leaving her beautiful in her vulnerability. When she finished, the applause was instantaneous and extended. Clapping loudly, Emma and Ted Williams turned in their seats to look at Ben admiringly, as if he had assisted Willa in her preparation. On stage Willa bowed demurely and Peter Harrison stood at the piano bench and held out his arm to Willa, channeling all the acclaim to her. She bowed slightly again, her eyes filled with light and joy. She looked at Ben and gave the specter of a smile, just a hint, a remnant, as it were, of their happiness.

After her performance, Willa did not join Ben in the seat he had saved for her, but Ben understood: her entrance into the audience would be a distraction to whatever performer was about to begin, and she did not want to take any attention away from the remaining performers. When the show was over, Ben stood at his seat, accepting the congratulations of his friends, who, like Ben, had never before witnessed Willa's talent.

Finally, as the hall was emptying, Willa came from the hallway beside the stage. "I think I'm off the hook tonight. We've got a cleanup committee and they pushed me out the door to go home." Willa walked toward Ben, the flowered dress now partly covered by her winter coat. She looked tall.

Ben slid his way down the row of chairs to meet her at the side of the hall. He reached out to Willa and held her silently, squeezing her to him, feeling her give herself to his clutch. When they separated slightly, he whispered, "That was amazing. You are a wonder."

She could not help but give him a smile greater than she had been able to offer on stage, and then she pulled him back into the same embrace. It had been months since they had shared such an attraction to each other. He did not know what this closeness meant, but he was glad that it was not disturbed by words. It felt warm to be in the circle of her arms.

Sunday snow covered New England, more than a foot falling on Summit and the surrounding towns.

Monday morning, as Willa prepared for work and Ben came out of the shower, she mentioned to Ben, "You know, today's Scott's birthday. We're planning a dinner around 6:30, OK?"

Ben's heart spun for a second: he often forgot his children's birthdays, but Willa always came through with a timely reminder.

"Do you have a present?" Willa continued.

"No, not yet. But I happen to have the luxury of having a day off! I'll square things away. Thanks for the gentle reminder." Ben thought of one more complication: he had told Peter at Willow's that he could work a double shift today because he was off from school, 3:00 to midnight. He'd have to call Pete and ask for a few hours off.

Sunday had gone well. After Ben had shoveled the driveway out, he and Willa had gone to church, and Ben had returned at 12:00 to pick Willa up. On the way home he had wondered aloud about the import of Willa's song, the desolation and loneliness that it conveyed.

"Well, I've loved the sound of that song for a long while. I can't honestly tell you why – maybe it resonates somehow with me, I don't know. And I didn't know whether I could perform it in front of an audience, but Peter encouraged me to do it, and he's a great pianist, so I gave it a try. It was good?"

Ben said, as he had said on Saturday night, "It was amazing." He paused. "Have you and Peter been working on it for a while?"

"Quite a while, as you can imagine. I never worked on it at home, because I wasn't sure I would actually do it, but we'd get together – at church and at his house." She said the last detail in a flat, casual tone, as if it were of no importance that she had been at his house.

"Were you there before the show? I stopped by the church to say hi and you weren't there."

Willa did not hesitate. "Yeah, we were working out the last second jitters. We hadn't gotten through the whole piece ever before that night. So we ran through it twice at his house."

Ben wanted to check on times, but her explanation was plausible, and he didn't want to continue to challenge her, after their embrace the previous night. When they had emerged from the church, it was as if they were a couple of adolescents coming out of the movie theater, the vapor from their mouths merging into a moist cloud that trailed them as they huddled together approaching Willa's Subaru. Ben

418

opened the passenger door to Willa's car and ushered her in, a gentleman wooing his damsel. "See you at home," he said, heading to his own car. She waited for him to start his car before she left the lot.

Monday morning, pulling his socks on his cold feet, Ben said, "One thing I have to work out: I'm supposed to work a double at Willow's. When I go in at 3, I'll tell Peter that I have to have 6 – 8 off for the birthday party."

Drawing a scarf around her neck, Willa said, "You're working on Scott's birthday? What are you thinking? Oh – don't answer – I know: you're not thinking. I know." She looked in the mirror, adjusting her scarf and smoothing her skirt across her abdomen. "We'll see you at 6:15." And she was off.

Ben did not feel any more irresponsible than he had always been, as if that was any consolation.

When Scott awoke at 10:15, Ben approached him at the kitchen table spooning his Frosted Flakes.

"You wanna go out to lunch? I'd like to take you to lunch and stop by Dick's to see if you need anything. Sound OK?"

"Yeah, sure. What time you thinking?"

"Oh, how about 12? We could shop first, then catch lunch on the way home."

Scott looked at the clock. "Sounds perfect. Marty and Ham are comin over at 2:00. We're gonna go into Boston on the T."

Ben winced. "I think Mom's planning a supper for you, with all of us. Did you forget?"

"Oh yeah. I forgot. What do you think about if I miss dinner? Not a good idea?"

Ben shook his head. "Uhhh, no, Mom is expecting a birthday dinner. Cake and all, I'd say. Maybe you need to save Boston until the evening, after dinner."

Scott nodded, washing his bowl, and opening the refrigerator to take out some eggs.

"You sure you need that? We're having lunch in less than a couple hours."

Scott looked shocked. "So what? I still need a full breakfast. And I'll ask for a full lunch, as long as you're paying."

At Bugaboo Creek Scott ordered steak tips and Ben ordered the soup of the day. At Dick's, Scott had revealed to Ben that he wanted a pair of flip flops, and Ben had fulfilled Scott's request, in addition to buying him a new lightweight jacket and a carrying bag for his baseball bat. With the gifts in the car, unwrapped, Ben felt prepared for Scott's birthday dinner. He called Willa at work to see if he could help with the cake, but she was planning to pick it up on the way home from work. "Maybe a gallon of ice cream? Buttercrunch?" she suggested.

As Ben stirred his soup, a cheddar and broccoli, Scott cut his tips down to a gargantuan size and chewed them, taking heaps out of his baked potato too. The asparagus received less attention. Scott suspended his enthusiastic address to his food to say, "Hey, Dad, are you and Mom going to get a divorce?"

Ben stopped stirring, staring at the pale cheesy soup. He did not know how to answer Scott. "You can see we're having a rough time. I don't know what it is exactly. But you can be sure: we are not getting a divorce," he said, using the same words that all parents in discord use to assure their children, the words that precede nearly every divorce. "I'm sorry you're feeling it, too. I don't want you to feel uncomfortable or vulnerable, but I guess it's unavoidable."

Scott looked down carefully at his plate. "Everything was always so solid and predictable. But now you and Mom hardly spend any time together, and you've picked up the extra work, and Mom spends lots of time at church. It just feels awkward at home. It's like you're ignoring us." He cut his meat with less fervor.

"I don't know what to tell you. I know we haven't even talked about getting a divorce, because we're nowhere close to that stage. And I think we're starting to understand each other better.

"Do you want the four of us to have a conversation about it?" Ben had no idea how such an event could transpire, but if Scott and Rachel wanted information about their parents, it seemed they were entitled to that information.

"I don't think so. That sounds pretty ugly, if you two can't even get it straight between the two of you. But I would like it if you and Mom talk to me about it now and then, to keep me in the loop about what's going on."

Ben reached across the table to assure Scott. "I'll definitely do that. Have you talked to Mom yet?"

Scott shook his head. "I didn't know how to bring it up. I don't even know how I brought it up with you, but it just came out."

After swallowing a grainy spoonful of the soup, Ben said, "Well, I'm glad you asked. I don't think it's going anywhere, but I'll let you know. Maybe it'll help, to be able to talk to you and Mary." The waiter hovered over them, wondering how the meal was going, since there were only two other tables occupied. "Have you and Mary talked about it?"

"Yeah, lots. She's not as curious about finding out – maybe because she doesn't want to know the answer." Scott looked over Ben's shoulder.

"I'll make sure I talk to Mary, too." Ben looked over Scott's shoulder, too, his eye drawn to the high arches in the vaulted ceiling in this faux lodge setting. He tried to see how the wood had been pieced together. He had heard about the way a carpenter bends wood: using steam and braces to turn the wood just a few inches at a time, adding to the curve over a period of days, until the desired radius is met. He marveled at the ways building materials could be reshaped to make for beautiful and elaborate structures. The interior of this Bugaboo was filled with bent wood forming impressive vaults, though they were not nearly as impressive as those vaulted stone ceilings at Duke he and Willa had seen.

As they finished their meal, their talk turned to Ben's team's chances in the tournament and to Scott's plans for the week, which included a trip to a museum in Worcester with Holly.

"Do you see you and Holly continuing together? Is it going well?"

"Yeah, we take it day to day, but I know we like to be together. She's a great kid. I never thought I'd find someone who trusted me the way she does."

Ben knew exactly what Scott was talking about. "Yeah, trust is an amazing thing. When you feel it, it just brings the two of you close together. It's like a magnetism, the opposite poles sticking together, not letting anything come between you." He could remember that feeling with Willa before they were married, when they were just starting to date, and he could tell her his craziest ideas and she would nod and tell him hers.

Scott stood up. "Yeah, sometimes I think she knows me better than I know myself."

"Get used to it. There's not much a woman doesn't know about a man. And the more you can reveal yourself to her, the closer you'll become."

On the way home they stopped at Dunkin Donuts, to see whether Mary was working, but she was not at the window. Ben knew she had told him her plans, but he did not remember them. Calling her, he discovered (as he immediately remembered) she was helping her friend Marissa move her clothes from one bedroom to another in her house. Her mother having just remarried, Marissa was moving to a bedroom farther down the hallway from her mother, giving both of them more privacy. Now Ben remembered the conversation clearly.

421

Supper was boisterous for a while, Scott jubilant about his sixteen years, Mary happy for her little brother, who was starting to show slight signs of maturity, and Ben happy they were sitting together at the table. After Willa doused the lights and carried the cake into the room as if it were a tray of well-balanced tall cocktails, a formal presentation, they sang Happy Birthday and Scott, making his wish, blew out the sixteen candles.

He opened Ben's jacket first, then a gift from Mary, a set of mix CDs and two new games for his Xbox. Willa's gift looked like a book. Tearing the wrapping paper off, Scott found a set of framed portraits, one each of Willa and Ben, age eighteen.

"Those are your dad's and my graduation pictures. They aren't the ones that made the yearbook. They're other prints that each of us like. Remember when we shared those photos together?" Willa asked Ben.

Ben could pinpoint the place and time of day. It was in Willa's apartment; they had started talking about moving in together. Willa had gone through five boxes of stuff she had taken from her house (that her mother had asked her to remove). The sun shone brightly across the prints as Ben had looked at them, covered with a slight film, thin glimpses of the high school girl she had been before he knew her. He had selected one portrait of her, with a slight smile, her chin raised expectantly, as if she had just heard her voice called out some distance away and she was waiting for another call, her eyes softly seeking the attention the voice promised.

A few days later, Ben had brought his set of portraits from high school to Willa's apartment, and they had decided that the print that showed his wide, toothy smile captured his spirit the best. That sharing of photos helped them feel they had known each other even before they met.

"Thanks, Mom. I've never seen these pictures. You guys look great. I think I remember the graduation pictures. These are different."

"Yes," Willa said. "Daddy and I always thought these showed our nature better than the ones that everyone else helped us pick for the yearbook. They're our secret sides revealed."

After Scott opened the other presents, the jubilation died down to a strained whisper, Mary pulling the ribbons through her fingers and Ben cleaning up the dishes and putting them into the dishwasher. Willa talked about the responsibilities that Scott was facing: driving a car, getting ready for his college applications, continuing to share valuable time with Holly. "You're very lucky. You've found someone you can share your life with. That's a real gift – maybe better than any of the gifts that we've given you today."

Scott agreed.

Ben hurried into Willow's, feeling he had let Pete down by leaving him with just one tender. Pete was out in the room, wiping down a table as he took the order.

Ben gave him a nudge as he passed by.

"Slow down, no big deal," Pete assured him.

The night was actually not a busy one. Once Pete returned to his customary haunt, moving invisibly between the bar and the back room, restocking, bringing food from the kitchen to the bar, ringing people out, Ben took over the outside tables. Bryan and Lisa were not there, having taken a little vacation up north, skiing for a couple days. But there were familiar faces, familiar orders.

Of course, Laura sat at the corner, nursing a Chablis, an empty plate in front of her when Ben first attended to her. "Here, let me clear that plate, for you," he said.

She smiled at him. "Are you still flying high from the game?"

He thought for a second. "No, not really. A lot of water over the dam since the game. But it's nice to have that one in my memory bank."

Laura initiated a conversation with him two or three more times, and, as time went by, Ben became more comfortable resting in front of her place, collaborating in the conversation. As the evening approached its end, Laura said, "Do you want me to wait until you've cleaned up? I can wait outside or come back, if you want."

Ben looked at her, all his senses heightened, thrilled to be called. He hesitated, and in that hesitation, revealed his unhappiness. He took a deep breath. "No, I don't think so. I'll go home and be with my family." His voice lacked conviction.

When Ben arrived home, Willa was asleep, but Ben, unwilling to go through another night of uncertainty, woke her insistently. She looked at him querulously.

"We need to talk – again. I'm still not sure I trust you, and I hate this feeling. I'm walking around thinking shitty thoughts about you and Peter Harrison."

Willa opened her eyes wider. "I am not going into this tonight. You seem to want some confession out of me for a transgression that never happened. I'm sorry. I can't give you that. If you can't stand being with me, then I'll sleep down on the couch. But I'm getting up at 6:30 tomorrow morning and I need to go to sleep."

Ben wanted to shake Willa, to force from her mouth that confession she was denying, even if she didn't want to offer it. But he kept his hands at his side, the voice inside him screaming. He said, "I guess that's it, then. Time at Peter's house with him, no one around, no witnesses. I guess you have me over a barrel. You don't have to sleep on the couch. I'm going down there myself." He opened his drawer to pick out his nightshirt, wanting to slam the drawer shut, but not wanting to wake the children, who were probably awake anyway, trying to ignore their parents as they had been doing for a month – or maybe a year.

The Arc of Intersection

I'm just a whisper of smoke
I'm all that's left of two hearts on fire
That once burned out of control
You took my body and soul
I'm just a ghost in this house

from *Ghost in This House* by Hugh Prestwood

James

Monday morning Andrew gave James a ride to Adrienne's house. She had talked about the two of them doing some conditioning together, running telephone poles, she called it. James felt stranded again, both his parents having left for work when he woke up. Feeling the need to tend to Adrienne's invitation, he called Andrew, who he knew was going out himself to physical therapy. Andrew did not hesitate to give him a ride, and they talked easily and fondly of the memorable game against Walpole.

At Adrienne's house James knocked on the door, the sun sparkling off the snow. He proprietarily saw that he would have to widen the walkway and driveway. It was a breathtakingly beautiful morning, a foot and more of snow having come down on Sunday, but the snow not yet sullied. Adrienne came to the door dressed in light sweats, purplish.

"You want to come in, or do you just want to start the workout now?" she asked.

"How about I leave my jacket in your house, and then we can start running."

He ducked past Adrienne at the doorway, depositing his jacket on the arm of the chair underneath the bay window. James had been at Adrienne's house briefly on Friday night, after the game, an exultant stop in his mindless parade around town after the win. Dan had driven Joyce, James, and Adrienne to each of their houses, just to share their exuberance. Dan's mother had risen from her chair to embrace Dan and James, as if they were soldiers returned from the Middle East. Joyce's parents weren't awake, but Joyce and Dan commandeered two bags of cheetos at her house along with a 2 liter bottle of ginger ale. James's father stood when the group entered his house, his arms out, welcoming James in a comfortable and shoulder-wrenching embrace. James's mother stood to the side, her eyes teary. At Adrienne's house Ginnie jumped up and down, still exhilarated by the end of the game. Mrs. Petrulsky offered cookies to the group, which they gobbled. They had dropped in to a few other houses, but he couldn't recall whose. He and Adrienne had removed themselves from the back seat at each house, but their attention was focused more on their moments in the car, tumbling into the seat, eagerly finding each other again and again.

In front of the house Adrienne outlined their workout. She said she ran a series of sprints, running the distance between one telephone pole and another, then walking one, then running two, walking one, running three, walking one, until she reached five poles. Then she came home, reversing the regimen. "In all, it's about a mile and a quarter of sprints, with recovery time built in. I've been doing it for three years now, and I've gotten a lot faster. We don't have to keep a clock on it, since we'll be keeping each other honest."

James liked the challenge she was offering. The street looked a little treacherous, the plow having brought the snow on the street down to a slippery slick. "You think the street's OK for sprinting? I don't want you to fall and jeopardize your scholarship."

"Actually, the slipperiness is good for us, because it'll force us to stay balanced, working on the core muscles as we sprint. It won't be easy, but it'll be more effective that way." Bending at the waist, she stretched languidly, her hands behind her legs, her head almost poking between her knees. James stretched as best he knew how. When Adrienne placed her legs apart and brought her head to the side, over her right knee, she looked like a duck, its neck arched as it probed underwater to clean its feathers.

"The distance between poles is just about 200 feet, down my whole street. So we'll be running from 200 feet to 1000 feet. I just give it my all every time, all out sprint if I can. You ready?"

"Yeah. Let's let 'er rip."

Adrienne called, "Go," and she was off like a gust of wind, her hair tied in a knot on top of her head, her muscular shoulders leaning forward, her hands driving her pace, her gait steady and fleet. James strained to keep up with her, tried to pass her, and found it impossible. Yet, in pushing to pass, he forced her to reach into her lungs for more reserve. At the first pole, they decelerated to a walk. Adrienne, her breathing easily maintaining its normal rate, commented, "That was awesome. I never can push myself like that. This is perfect."

James breathed deeply. He knew his thighs would be burning before they turned back toward her house.

On the long segment, five poles, Adrienne started up in an easier pace, and James achieved a gap of about twenty feet between them before Adrienne accelerated over the last 200 feet, passing James in the end. He could not respond. He felt his feet slipping as he tried to dig into the hard, snowy plane that covered the road. He did not want to fall.

On the return each segment became a battle of performance, Adrienne gliding easily and, seemingly effortlessly, James straining noisily, usually able to hold her off. But over the last two sections, shorter and therefore inducing a quicker sprint step, Adrienne just motored ahead of him, shimmering in front of him as his feet landed heavily on the street. When they were done, Adrienne said, "James, that was great. I've never pushed myself so hard on this workout. We should do this more often."

James huddled over his breath. "Easy for you to say. But I agree: this is great for both of us. You're an amazing athlete." He could see Adrienne laboring to breathe also, but she stretched upward as she tried to rid herself of the carbon dioxide that cut their breathing short.

Inside the house Adrienne said casually, "I'm going to take a shower. You can take one if you want. I know you don't have any clothes to change into. But it's OK if you want to shower after me. We can find something for you to wear."

"I'll probably wait till I get home. Is your car fixed?"

"Yeah. It was some sort of switch, not a big deal," she said, pulling her sweatshirt off as she entered the bathroom.

He sat down on the couch, flicking the TV on, to ESPN. After catching up on the NBA, he retrained his attention on Adrienne. He could see the door to the bathroom open just slightly, the steam from her shower seeping out. After a few long moments, moments in which the sounds of ESPN faded out, he pictured her in the shower, tall and strong, the water bouncing off her as she poured liquid soap onto her shoulders and breasts, rubbing it across her smooth skin, rinsing the soap off, cleaning the salty residue of the sprint from her body, replacing it with her berry-scent. She took her hair out of the knot and soaped it too, standing under the shower, her eyes closed, her hands kneading her thick hair, rubbing the soap from her scalp, the soap trailing down her body as she rinsed her hair under the hot shower water. She soaped her arms, her legs, the breath-taking place between her legs, then let the shower rinse the soap away, always leaving her skin pink and fragrant.

James felt uneasy thinking of Adrienne this way, but he had never been so close to a fantasy that might become a reality.

When she was done with her shower, James pictured her putting on a light robe that was just a suggestion of clothing, whispering of what she concealed. She would move out of the bathroom quietly, the robe reaching halfway down her thighs, clinging to her as she came from the bathroom to him on the couch, her face radiant, her eyes lustrous as she brought to him the news of her renewal, her skin still a little wet, her breasts hardly concealed by the light cloth of the robe, James reaching out to her and Adrienne willfully giving herself to him.

At that point James had a more difficult time seeing how their amorousness would unfold. He could see she was offering herself to him and he knew he wanted to accept that offering. He just had no idea how to do that. He had never shared the gift of another person's body – though he had had the opportunity at several parties. But he continued to see Adrienne and him, entwined on the couch, as her robe opened, and, unceremoniously, he got himself out of his own clothes, so the two of them were no more than an idea apart, the weight of their bodies pressing against each other in a perfectly mutual gift, one that he had been hoping to share for a long time.

As his reverie dissipated, James opened his eyes to try to give life to his vision, to close the gap between his vision and the truth that swept across the floor just a room away. The bathroom door was open now, and in an instant Adrienne came out of her bedroom, dressed in jeans and a Northwestern sweatshirt. Her hair was still wet, curling around her face. She wore his heart necklace. Her feet were clad in flipflops.

"Hey, what's with Northwestern?" he asked, hesitant to address straight-on the passion he had imagined.

"I'm going out there for a visit in April. They're national champions two times, and they get some of their players from Massachusetts. I was at a camp on their campus last summer."

James looked admiringly at her. "Pretty impressive. Anywhere else you're being recruited?"

"Yeah, Maryland and Duke. I'm going to visit all three over April vacation. And BC is going to offer a scholarship too." She said it all so matter-of-factly, as if these opportunities existed for everyone.

"I guess you're a real talent," James said. "I never saw you play before, but I hope I get to see you this spring."

Looking at her watch, Adrienne said, "I'd better take you home now. I've got a term paper due in two weeks and I have to do some research. My computer is OK, but the library's computers are so much faster, and it's so quiet there." Adrienne looked as if she had lost interest in James since she took her shower. Maybe she had expected him to follow her into the shower. After all, she had left the door open.

James was losing ground. "What do you think about spending some time here alone for a little while? I don't have to get home at any certain time, and you can always do research a little later, can't you? Is Ginnie gone for a while?" He was trying to sound as if he was lightly kidding her, with a serious base – the way kids talked to each other at parties.

Adrienne was not about to reflect his banter. "No, I really have to get to the library. I'm not even thinking about you and me in my bedroom, if that's what's you're picturing. Sorry." She was coldly blunt.

He had lost his opportunity. Feeling a little desperate, hoping she might warm to his desperation, he said, "Last chance. When you and I were on E, you said you didn't dare come near me. Well, we're not on E, but here's the chance."

Adrienne looked at him sadly. She took a step back from him, her mouth pursing itself into a circle. "James, to be honest, when I was done with my shower, I came out in just a towel, to see you, to see where things might lead. You were lying on the couch, your eyes closed, this weird look on your face. I stood near you for a minute, waiting for you to notice me, my hair practically dripping on you, but you never returned to this world. You were off in la-la land. It didn't seem you were sleeping, but you were definitely gonzo. It was kind of weird. I tiptoed out of the room, got dressed and came back. You had returned to this world. What were you thinking about?" She pulled the heart back and forth on her necklace, eventually swinging it around so that it faced behind her, tucked underneath her wet hair.

James could not bring himself to tell her about the narrative he had concocted, his version of their love that was so deeply isolated in him he could not give it the voice of reality. She turned away from his silence to get her car keys.

Practice on Wednesday brought the team together for the first time since their emotional victory over Walpole. At Coach LaMott's direction, the team devoted the first thirty minutes to running, with the ball, without the ball, defensive slides, fast breaking, anything to reinforce to the players that they had lost the conditioning that had built up over the previous month, from having taken five days off. James's calves felt almost bruised from Monday's workout with Adrienne.

James had heard from Andrew that Jason would not be returning to the team. He still faced criminal charges for leaving the scene of the accident, and circumstantial evidence led to the conclusion that he had been consuming alcohol. The school's stance on his case was that he would not be reinstated until the charges had been settled, one way or the other. Mr. Grutchfield was appealing the decision with the school committee, who would meet on Monday after vacation to adjudicate the case.

In the meantime, it seemed that Archie Stedham had taken over the point, with Dan and James on the wings. Andrew had trouble running the floor still; he was scheduled for surgery to repair a torn meniscus in late March. Until then he had been cleared to play as much or as little as his knee allowed. Geoff, proudly reminding anyone that might have forgotten, "Did you know I tipped in the winning basket against Walpole?" ran the floor the best, lifted by his Friday success. Everyone was there except Pete, who had gone to Saint Maarten with his family for the week, and Jason.

Friday the Panthers scrimmaged Westborough, a 14 - 6 team from Central Massachusetts. James's legs still felt tender. Over the second half of the scrimmage he started to regain his wind and his fluidity, getting his legs ready before he caught the ball, preparing himself to shoot before the defense could step up. He hit four of five perimeter shots in the last two periods. Archie struggled a little at the point because Westborough's point guard was quick as a mosquito, hands reaching in while he maintained perfect balance. Overall, the scrimmage reminded the team that they were deeply flawed, a conclusion that Coach LaMott had hoped they would come to.

"All right, guys, that was a great re-introduction to the game of basketball," Coach intoned in the post-scrimmage huddle. "We got some of the rust off. We're starting to step into our shots. We're not going to put in anything new at this point of the season. We just have to believe in what we're doing." He stopped speaking, gathering his thoughts. "But more importantly, we have to believe in each other. There have been a lot – a LOT – of variables in our team this year, people in and out of the lineup, injuries, problems. But you ignored all that stuff for seven seconds last Friday night, and for that reason, we're here practicing this week, something we haven't done in two years. Congratulations.

"Just to let you know: a tournament game is just the same as a regular season game. The only difference is that there will be more people in the stands, and, after that first win, more people at each succeeding game. To the fans, the games seem to become more momentous with every game. But to us, every game is the same. If you start getting caught up in the hype, you will lose your ability to replicate all the things we've worked on all year."

Understanding Coach's words, James still felt more keyed up than he usually did for a game that would not occur for another five days. Then Coach calmed him.

"You've already reached your goal. If we win another game – or four – that's gravy. You don't have to do one more thing this season – other than to enjoy every moment you're on the court with your teammates." He stepped away, making eye contact with each of them, helping them to feel their shared closeness. "Friday night you made yourselves a team. One . . two . . . ."

In the locker room Geoff called the team together; the coach was in his changing room with Coach Taft, who would be with the varsity the rest of the way, since his season was over. Geoff said, "OK, men, we've done something that hasn't been done here in three years: making the tournament. Let's not screw it up by doing anything crazy over the next three weeks. It's so hard to get everything to come together for a win, and so easy to throw it all away for the sake of a beer or a joint. I know there are lots of parties and opportunities just driving around, now that most of us have our licenses – James, sorry you're not one of us – and I know you all think you can do it just a little, that no one will catch you, and no one will know. But let's just make a little sacrifice for a few weeks, until this chance is behind us, OK?" Geoff put his hands in the middle of his teammates and they encircled him, as he asked for a "Tight." Though the conviction in their voices was slightly hollow, James could feel Geoff's words linger long afterward.

James had regained his conditioning by the end of Saturday's practice: ten in a minute felt good. He had called Adrienne on Thursday, after the scrimmage, to see if she wanted to run another set of poles, but Ginnie said she had gone to a lacrosse tournament in New Jersey for the weekend. James wondered how Ms. Johnson, the girls' coach, was handling her loss of practice time, or if she had cleared it with the coach before she came out for the team. Knowing Adrienne, she had probably worked it all out before she joined the team, just to avoid any problems.

On Saturday night, there was a big party at Graysons', the place where James had eluded the police. Meredith Dawson, the girl with whom he had spent a meaningful solitude, called him out of the blue to see whether he was going. He was tempted, knowing that Adrienne was away. But then he thought of Dan and his sister, Rachel, and Geoff Willis, who was trying to herd the team members as if he were Snow White and they were his little Eleven Dwarfs. He decided to see what Rachel was doing.

"Hey, Rache, you wanna do something together?" he asked her, as he pushed open her bedroom door. Talking on the phone, she held one index finger up to ask for a few seconds. She was talking softly.

James stood at the door for more than a minute before he retreated to his room, to wait for her to finish the call. In a few more minutes, she came to see him.

"So who was that, you new boy friend?" he asked.

Rachel hesitated. "Maybe," she said softly.

James's eyes opened. "Woah!" he replied, shocked at her answer. "Are you ready for love?"

She smirked. "Oh, Mr. Experienced. What do you know about love?"

James shrugged his shoulders, turning toward the wall as he lay on his bed. "I might know more than you think. The ups. The downs. The turnarounds. If you want to ask me for advice, I'm available."

Rachel laughed. "I'll be sure to text you if I'm in any difficult circumstances. No problem. Actually, David and I want to go to the movies and maybe you could drive us – oh, I forgot, you don't have your license either. Maybe we could all get a ride from Mom." She continued laughing.

James turned over to face her. "Very funny. But I'm serious, if you want a chaperone for your movie trip, I'm willing to volunteer." He was serious.

Rachel snorted. "I'm sure David wouldn't mind you coming along with us, because he thinks you're the coolest dude in Casteline. But I don't think I would appreciate your hanging around with us; I'm sure you'd make life miserable for me – unless, of course, you've suddenly matured." She retreated from the room, the discussion over as far as she was concerned.

"Well, just a thought. I'll be home listening to *Prairie Home Companion*, if you need me." He turned back to the wall.

Saturday night passed so slowly for James, he thought it was a Spanish class.

On Sunday the pairings for the tournament were published in the Globe. Casteline would play at South Bridgewater on Tuesday night. The Panthers were the 19th seed, facing the 14th seed, a 12 – 8 team. James and Dan talked about the matchup on the phone. There was another light snowstorm during the day; James went outside to clear the driveway as the snow continued to fall, uncovering the area where he and Pete had shot that Sunday three months ago, the day before the first day of practice. James scraped the foul line down to bare asphalt, retrieved the dead ball from the garage, and shot fifty foul shots, making 38. The last two shots represented the end of the East Bridgewater game, Casteline trailing by one, James on the line for a one-and-one. He missed the first, ending Casteline's season. But as he had shot that miss, a little puff of snow rained down from the netting, giving James a reprieve, because the snow represented an opponent moving early at the foul line, giving James another shot at the line. This time he made the first, made the second, and Casteline was headed for a quarterfinal game on Thursday.

Sunday night James called Adrienne to see how her tournament had gone.

"We came in sixth out of fifteen teams – not our best weekend. The competition was unbelievable. I think I saw ten or twelve girls that have been recruited to play at Northwestern and Princeton and Syracuse. For some reason we didn't play well."

"D'you play well?"

"I played all right. It wasn't the best for me either." James had never heard her talk about not making the grade. He was surprised.

"I saw you guys are playing home on Wednesday night. I think I'll be able to go. Quincy? You know anything about them?" He sat at his desk, his legs on the wall over his desk, his back arched. He wondered why he made himself into a contortionist when he talked to Adrienne on the phone.

"Yeah, they're OK. Big and slow, Ms. Johnson says. I talked to her on the way home from New Jersey. And we practiced late this afternoon." James wondered whether Coach Johnson had scheduled this late practice for Adrienne's benefit. "We had a great scrimmage against Wayland. We're getting better."

"Hey, how do you handle missing time with the basketball team for your lacrosse tournaments? Does Coach Johnson get mad?"

Adrienne sounded surprised. "No, I gave her the dates before I went out. I got them sanctioned in advance through the athletic department. Most of my lax teammates have the same deal. There's a form we have to fill out, so missing practice is acceptable by MIAA. I feel a little guilty – OK, I feel a lot guilty – missing practice, but I'm getting in shape and I'm staying athletic. I think it's OK with the other kids. They treat me nice anyway."

"Sure, you can get them fifty rebounds and score thirty points. No shit they treat you nice." There was a slight note of jealousy in James's voice; he wondered whether Adrienne could hear it.

She chose to ignore it. "I'm just glad I can do both." She changed the subject. ""D'you have a good weekend?"

James told her of the excitement that had filled his weekend, from Friday's trip to get pizza with Dan, to Saturday morning's muffin, ending with Sunday's college game on TV, BC at Florida State, followed by the beginning of a fishing show.

Adrienne laughed easily. "Well, I guess you were so busy, you didn't even realize I was gone."

James knew he had kept listening for the house phone to ring all day Saturday and Sunday, his eyes closed, and he had felt the laconic presence of his cell phone in the pocket of his jeans.

I dreamed you were standing
On the edge of the world
And I thought I heard you call out
With one foot on the rock
And one on a cloud
Was it just the wind that I heard
Close your eyes
This world won't stop spinning you know
Close your eyes
Why don't you just let go
Thousands of people searchin' out there
Most of em lookin' for love
But nothing is something
That there's plenty of
In time we'll all get our share
When I was a child
And they put me to bed
They always took care that I prayed
But the part that goes, if I should
Die fore I wake
Echoed all night in my head

Close Your Eyes by Steve Earl

Ben

The first day back to school after a vacation is like getting back on a bicycle, pushing that left-side pedal hard enough so that you can get your right leg over the seat and settle yourself in for a long ride once again. If the teacher does not push hard enough, the bike will falter and tumble to the road, taking the rider with it. Ben's first push was delayed as he passed the office on the Monday after February vacation: Paula Weeks called him into her office to discuss the Jason Grutchfield issue.

"The school committee is meeting tonight to deliberate on the matter," she said. "The hearing will not be held for a few weeks, but our position, at this point, is that he cannot represent the school as long as charges are pending against him."

Ben nodded. "I respect the school's position completely. However, if the school committee gets pressured to allow him to play, and their counsel advises that he be allowed to play until the hearing, I also feel I have to give him that opportunity."

Paula agreed.

"So," Ben continued, "where does that leave us for practice today?"

Paula let out a puff of air. "Your call, Coach. I will support you either way."

Not surprisingly, an email awaited Ben at the computer in his room: an email from Peter Grutchfield, outlining just what the principal had told him, demanding that Jason be allowed to practice today, in the event of an overturn in the school's stance. Ben sent a reply to Mr. Grutchfield's email.

Dear Mr. Grutchfield,

Thank you for your email. I know the past two weeks have been very difficult for your family, and for Jason in particular. I will abide by the school committee's decision, which I assume they will reach tonight. Jason's status being uncertain until that point, he will be allowed to practice with the team in our preparation for the state tournament. I will speak to Jason myself during the day, to be sure that he knows that. I hope for the best in the resolution of this case.

Ben LaMott

In his classes, Ben welcomed his students back with as many humorous remarks as he could foster, noting the sun-splashed hue of many of his students, the beaded cornrows of the girls who had

437

journeyed to the Caribbean. He tried to make a case for staying at home by running a little contest: a reward for the student who had traveled the least distance from home for nine days. In one of his classes the winner had journeyed only to the McDonald's in Natick, a four-mile trip. Ben gave this home-bound student a Milky Way left over from his Halloween stash. It felt as if it still had some cushion to it. After a few minutes of reacquaintance, he opened his short story book and asked his freshman students to follow his lead, as they haltingly entered the fictional world of *Paul's Case*.

Ben's junior class was harder to acclimate to the world of academics: it took fifteen minutes to get their right legs over the bike seat, but, after downshifting the gear several times, Ben managed to get the bike moving haltingly down the street toward Ethan Frome's cold house in Starkfield. Passing out the reading schedule, Ben said, "I know it's hard to adjust from a slow and luxurious vacation to the demands of school, but let's look at it this way: at least you've had some time off. Ethan Frome never had any time off. He had to live in these New England winters without a break, and we'll see why." Ben, at the age of fifty-one, could now identify with the reticent New Englander who had lived his life chained to his community, with no chance of escape. But Ben could also understand how only his best students would be able to unearth the layers of obligation that prevented Ethan from ever achieving anything personally gratifying. Ethan Frome "never got away," he was so rooted to the girl who, ironically, provided him a momentary glimpse of freedom.

Ben himself was feeling especially closed in, given his vacation week at home. When he had chosen to sleep on the couch in the living room on Monday night, he had plotted a new course in his relationship with Willa. Of course, when Mary woke up to go to DD on Tuesday morning and found Ben on the couch, she had whispered, "Is everything all right?"

Ben had reassured her that he had merely had trouble sleeping and that there was nothing to worry about, passing it off lightly. "Not a spat, don't worry." But it was more than a spat; it was a grave uncertainty.

On Tuesday evening, after an awkwardly played cribbage game and a period of reading, as the Celtics found a way to lose to the Pistons on TV, Ben did not feel like perpetuating the chasm between himself and Willa by sleeping alone again; he and Willa prepared for bed at the same time and Ben joined Willa underneath the blankets just before 11:00.

Willa tried to curtail her sarcasm, but it emerged anyway. "Well, I guess your principles were compromised for just one night?"

Ben felt provoked, but he did not have the energy or the resources to accept the challenge. "I guess I'm just getting tired of the fight. Is there any end in sight?"

"I don't know. You're the one who keeps insisting that we have an issue to resolve. I am not having trouble sleeping at night," she lied, the righteousness of her voice resonant.

Ben tried to conciliate. "Well, maybe we can find a way to help each other sleep. Let's give it a try." Through all the vicissitudes, Ben had never lost the urgent nerve that had served as the catalyst to their lovemaking – foolishly, he still persisted.

Willa's turning away from him on the bed told him that the best they could hope for was collateral warmth.

The stalemate continued the rest of the week.

On Thursday, after the Westborough scrimmage, in which the Panthers had showed great impatience in looking for a good shot opportunity, Ben stopped by Fidelity House to take his mother out to lunch at Laurel's in Walpole where she had developed a taste for the strawberry parfait. He had tried calling his mom on Wednesday at supper time, thinking she would be near her bedside stand where the phone sat, but she had never answered, not an unusual occurrence. Margot had had increasing difficulty using the phone over the past months. Unable to reach her by phone, Ben had stopped in Wednesday evening to ask his mother whether she would like to have lunch the next day at Laurel's. She said she would have to rearrange her schedule completely, but she would be ready at 12:30, for a very late lunch.

Thursday Ben wheeled her chair to the elevator and out to the Corolla, helping her shift from the chair to the seat. It was becoming hard for Margot to take even one or two steps on her own now. The slippery snow in the driveway challenged her stability further. But grasping Ben's left hand and using the door as another support, she took her seat and sighed loudly. Ben collapsed the wheelchair and dropped it into the trunk.

On the ride to Walpole, Margot spoke of the dangling monkeys again; Ben nodded, saying, "Well, I guess as the weather gets warmer, they'll be out a lot more." It was indeed a warm day for February, almost sixty degrees. Margot had not needed her woolen gloves on this day.

"I think I've come to understand what the monkeys mean," Margot told Ben.

"What do you think?" Ben asked. "I didn't know they represented anything, but it's nice if they do."

Margot looked ahead at the windshield. "I think they are the times I wish you would visit me."

There was silence in the car. Ben felt his heart flail. He knew he had to respond to his mother. He just didn't know how to answer her revelation.

Margot filled in the silence. "I look out the window, looking for you to be driving in the driveway. But when I don't see you, I see other things. Every time you don't drive in, another monkey swings from the branches. They have fun up there. They pull their ropes and kick their legs and go higher and higher. They make these little cheep-cheep noises, like chickens." Margot stopped talking, perhaps realizing how irrational she sounded.

Ben was starting to find a way to answer his mother. "So when I don't drive in to see you, another monkey starts swinging? I guess there must be hundreds of monkeys up there, swinging. Do you think if I do visit you, there is one less monkey?"

Margot thought for a while. "I bet that's true. I bet there is one less monkey today. I didn't actually see them today, because I was so busy getting ready for you. So I don't really know. But it's nice to be with you now, so let's forget about the monkeys, OK?" She smiled, a recollection of another time stirring in her memory.

For the rest of the lunch, and the ensuing drive into the snow-drenched, forested climes of Walpole and Norfolk and Wrentham, Ben kept talking to Margot, unable, or unwilling, to run out of things to talk about. He asked her about her years as an au pair in Florida, a time he knew a little about and found an interesting part of his mother's life before she had a family. Her details about those days were vague and possibly inaccurate, but it was good to hear her talking about her life with such clarity – even if it was fabricated. She talked about her years as a young mother in the military life, as Ben's dad fought in World War II. Ben talked about his children's lives, lives that were taking shape. He talked about Willa, her love of the church.

"That's a good thing," Margot said. "I know the church means a lot to you, too," she added almost hopefully.

Ben thought about his involvement with St. Andrew's. "I love church. But I don't use it as the basis of my social life, the way Willa does. She's there three or four times a week." He tried not to sound resentful.

But Margot knew. "And you're not at school with your basketball six times a week?"

Ben nodded. "You're right. You're right." He wondered how a woman whose mental capacities were diminishing so severely could have such insight.

The sun glanced brightly off the hood of the Corolla as Ben turned into the driveway of Fidelity House, his mother now sleeping lightly, warm in her yellow wool sweater. When Ben opened her door to help her into her wheelchair, she startled to see him. Once they had returned to her room, they agreed it had been a wonderful afternoon.

On the way home Ben still marveled at the insightful illumination his mother had given him. He felt heart-broken knowing he had failed her so continuously, since she had moved into Fidelity House, a nursing home less than five miles from his house. And she was right. She had been provided a room in an institution and frequent visits from his family, but he had withheld his own care, always immersed in his own concerns. His mother's brave statement recalled in Ben other glimpses that had left him heart-broken: seeing Willa bent over, sitting in a rocking chair, trying to repair a hem on a pair of pants, the light inadequate; Mary leaning away from the kitchen table, her head flopping back in an exhaustion that a seventeen year-old should not come to; Mary Oliver, a timid freshman student who spent a minute gathering her pencils and pens at the end of each class, her head down, hair covering her face, to avoid any social contact with Ben even as Ben tried to engage her in a conversation that she would never join; Laura Ruben, sitting at her place at Willow's, hoping for one more connection in her life, her face eagerly searching his for an admission; and he saw himself, sitting in his reclining chair, alone, trying to stay alert as he corrected essays, Willa at the church planning an activity, Scott and Mary rushing to their next destination, but Ben still isolated in his chair.

Passing the grade school where Mary and Scott had started school, Ben saw a lonely tetherball, the pole planted in the ground desolately, the ball hugging the pole, absent the glee and shouts that give it life and meaning. Ben pulled over to a stop, staring at the isolated pole, as the sun sank. He felt the emptiness of the playground, centered in that skinny iron rod casting no shadow on a darkening playground, a pole around which the ball should be flying in a rushing arc, just like his mother's monkeys.

Sunday night the LaMotts had had a family dinner attended by the entire family, an unusual occurrence. Ben had offered to make a chicken recipe that he had managed to master despite his culinary ineptitude. He had cooked baked potatoes and heated cut corn in a pot.

When they sat down together, Willa lowered her head in a silent prayer, a practice she had been following for more than three years. Ben wanted to add to her silent prayer. He said aloud, "God, thank you for bringing us together this night. We pray that we can enjoy and share your gifts, the greatest of which are the loving people seated at this table. Amen." He didn't know where his prayer came from, but he meant it. Mary looked at him, then at Willa, seeking an answer to an unspoken question. Willa looked at Ben directly for a long moment.

The supper was relaxing – slow and fulfilling. Scott, whom he had asked to make a dessert, had baked brownies in the afternoon, and he topped them with ice cream. Though the meal seemed to demonstrate the wholeness of the family, Ben knew otherwise. As the supper ended, Ben tried to keep the family together. "You guys looking forward to being back in school?" Ben asked.

"Oh yeah. I'll finally have some homework. It was a rough week last week," Scott replied. Mary, who had moved away from the table into the living room, was on the phone, lying on the couch, connected peripherally with the family. In another minute the kitchen was empty except for Ben, who was filling the dishwasher. Willa had moved into the study to write and send out an email for the church women's annual retreat, a weekend at a house in Maine at the house of a parishioner. Willa had never attended, but Ben thought she might choose to go this year.

Practice for South Bridgewater on Monday was appropriately intense. Ben had to hold the players back, reminding them to save it for the game tomorrow night. The rebounding was especially combative, Andreas and Mark pushing Geoff and Andrew for position at both ends of the court. Andrew was unstable on his left leg when his opponent pushed for rebounding position, though he was getting better at recovering his stride up and down the floor. Needing to protect Andrew's knee, Ben kept him out of half of the scrimmaging, though he did need the time on the court to regain his shooting touch when he was tired. Jason, playing with the second unit completely, showed flashes of his talent, but he was two weeks away from any conditioning and clearly distracted by all the consternation about his case. He interacted with the team as best he could, but it was awkward.

When Ben blew his whistle to end the scrimmage, he told the team, "You have the perfect approach to this game, guys. I can see that you will not let anything or anyone get past you without a challenge, and that is exactly what you will need to win these tournament games.

Andreas and Mark, if you can bottle this need to dominate, you will give us a huge lift off the bench, and our depth will wear them down.

"South Bridgewater is a team with two very talented players," he reminded them, "a shooter, Ben Spriggs, about 6'2", and a point guard, Mason Warrick, about 5"11". They score 40 between them, and Warrick attacks on every play. They don't have great size inside and they don't have great post players. It'll be our overall team defense against their two talented seniors."

After practice Ben spoke to Archie, James, Dan, and Bobbie Pitaro, who would share the defensive responsibility for containing Spriggs and Warrick. "James, you've got Spriggs to start with. Archie, you've got Warrick. Archie, don't waste any energy trying to steal the ball. He will show it to you and pull it away, to try to get past you. And he's good. You're not going to come up with the steal. He's better than Evans from Walpole. I know you do a good job staying home; make sure you keep him between your shoulders.

"James, you've got the shooter. He will take probably 25 shots, some of them are way past the 3 point line. He puts it on the floor pretty well, so don't leave your feet when you try to close out on him. You're not as tall as he is, so you're not going to block his shot. He gets off the ground on his release. Just keep your hand in his face, work your butt off to get around the screens. It's like covering Kennedy for Walpole. In fact, this team is a little like Walpole, but not as good, to be honest. But we're playing at their home court, and their crowd will be loud and aggressive."

Ben's report had come from Art Gibson, a friend who coached at Avon, and who had scouted S. Bridgewater twice, thinking they would meet in the tourney. In fact Avon and Casteline would meet each other if they both won their first round games. Ben and Art had met five or six times in the tournaments over the years; they had each won two or three games in that rivalry. It was nice of Art to help him out. They looked forward to another meeting between the two schools, sort of a long-standing post-season tradition that had recently been truncated because of Casteline's inability to make the tournament. Avon had qualified fifteen consecutive seasons.

From practice Ben had to rush to Willow's, maybe his last night of tripleheader duties: teaching, coaching, and bartending. He enjoyed his involvement with Pete and Larry a lot. It had not taken long to understand the rhythm of the bar and to understand the balance between service and conversation. As he walked into the tavern, he quickly surveyed the status of the patrons, including, of course, Laura.

"How's it going?" he asked.

"Doing fine," she answered in a soft voice. As the weeks had slid by, she had taken on a beauty that had at first been distilled in alcohol. "Do you have your tournament schedule yet?"

Ben nodded. "Yep, we've got a game in South Bridgewater tomorrow night. If we win, we'll play later in the week, somewhere far away, I'd guess. It could be Avon, I know that." He was excited to be able to tell her of the post-season plans, as he had been excited after church when Paul Snow and Mary Donnelly and a few others had asked him who he would be facing in the tournament. Many of the churchgoers of Summit were basketball fans, and Ben stood a little taller, looked for after-church chitchat a little more when his team was on a winning streak.

Willow's was more crowded than on past Monday nights, even though it was a slack sports night on TV. There were several new groups of people that Ben had never seen, young people whose ID Ben had to screen. It was as if a new generation of patrons had found out about the place, making Ben feel like an old veteran, the same way he felt at school and on the court.

As the night neared its end, Laura stood. "Well, maybe I'll see you at TD Banknorth," she said brightly, knowing it was the site of the state semi-finals.

"I certainly hope so," Ben said, clearing her place. "I want to tell you, it was fun seeing you in the gym the other night. Now, I want to ask, are you going dancing other nights?"

Laura, sliding her left arm into the sleeve of her coat, said, "Not yet, but I'm still hopeful I can find a dance partner down the road." She looked at Ben with a coy smile on her face. He looked away as if he shouldn't know what she was talking about.

"I'm sure you will."

The drive down to South Bridgewater reminded Ben and Bryan of dozens of trips to the southeastern reaches of Massachusetts, trips to Harwich, New Bedford, Fall River, a scouting trip to Fairhaven with Willa – emblematic of the connections that tournament games fostered. It was as if the state were connected by a nexus that became tighter and tighter as the tournament progressed, until finally there were only two teams left, tethered by their success through the draw, representing two regions that would vie for state supremacy. Ben knew he had entered those other tournaments with a far stronger roster, but, as usual, he expected this team to succeed like the others.

As the team changed into their uniforms in the visitors' locker room, Ben wrapped two ankles, Bobbie Pitaro's and Jonas Boynton's.

444

He also made sure Andrew's brace was properly padded. The rest of the players, after they were dressed, filtered out to the gym to get used to the rims and to feel the bounce of the floor. Pete Semineau was in street clothes, having missed the vacation practices for a family trip. Jason Grutchfield had been cleared, at the school committee meeting, to play with the team, until the legal resolution of his case was reached. Jason changed and ran out onto the floor, with as much energy as he could muster.

On the court, as the team members rehearsed their shots and worked on their dribbling, Ben approached Jason. "Hey, Jase, I'm very sorry about what's been going on for you. I get the feeling it's been a really hard time for you."

Jason kept his head down. "Yeah, it has." He started to continue talking, but he stopped.

Putting his arm around Jason's back to grasp his left shoulder, Ben said, "It's great to see you back, but you're probably not gonna see any action tonight. You've missed a lot. We've gotten into a sort of rhythm, with the Walpole game and the scrimmage. Maybe, if we go far, and you get back into the groove, there will be an opportunity for you."

"I understand, Coach. No problem. It's just great to be here."

"I bet. It's great to have you here. Give us all the support you can, OK?"

At 6:35 Ben called the team back into the locker room, to go over the matchups once again.

"James, you've got Spriggs. Number . . .?"

"32, Coach," Bryan said, reading off the notes Ben had typed up.

"And Archie, you've got Warrick, #11. We'll play a lot of 2, but we'll definitely use a 6 on these two guys. Any subs, please go onto the floor knowing our defense. If you're not sure, ask before you go out, so you know. If we're in the 6, be sure you know where you are in the triangle.

"In about two minutes, we'll head out onto the floor for a game of basketball. It's no different than what we did in early December, except we know each other a lot better and we have been through a very tough season that has prepared us perfectly for this game. We will not play anyone of the caliber of Brookline, Waltham, Braintree, or even Walpole in this tournament. South Bridgewater is a very solid team, but we have become just as good.

"Now, let's pull ourselves together here . . ." Ben paused so the team could gather around the hand he extended in the middle of the room. He could feel an electricity connecting the players, born partly out of nervousness and partly out of energy. "Same as always, One, Two . . ."

"Tight."

With fourteen seconds left in the first period South Bridgewater held a 20 – 11 lead. The Panthers were shooting poorly and S. Bridgewater was ripping up the 6, having seen plenty of triangle and 2s, apparently. Spriggs had hit three 3s over James and his replacement, Alex, as he came off a series of double picks, sometimes three in each clock possession. It was impossible to keep him from getting the ball. On the last possession of the period, Geoff put up an awkward bankshot that didn't even hit the rim.

"OK, now the nervousness is gone – well, maybe Geoff's shot shows it's not gone completely – but let's settle down. We have to be more directed on offense. Archie, let's work on setting up Andrew on the curl a little. I know they're zone, but let's run our motion anyway. Andrew, keep looking for screens to rub off of, as you come out from the baseline. If they press you on the shot, look for Geoff or Mark underneath. And, guys, we should be PUNISHING them on the boards. We're just about . . .?"

Bridget interjected, "South Bridgewater 11, Casteline 8."

Ben shook his head in disappointment. "All that energy in practice yesterday, and today, nothing. Nothing." He let his words hang in the middle of the huddle.

"You know you have way more to offer each other. Don't let yourselves down."

In the second period Geoff went after the ball so hard he knocked the South Bridgewater center off the court, drawing a foul. As he ran past the bench on the next fast break, Ben shouted to him, "Twenty more times."

On the next stoppage of play, Ben called James over. "You tired?"

"No."

"Then let's sprint the floor. Nothing to hold back for now. This is it."

When Archie turned down a shot, Ben replaced him with Bobbie for a couple of possessions.

"Archie, you gonna shoot when you're open?" he asked his transfer from Granby.

Archie looked down.

446

"You can't let them give you anything. You're a great shooter, Archie. And if you happen to miss, Geoff and Andrew are all over the boards now."

When Andrew came off, limping, Ben told him, "Give it all you got. We can't ask for what you don't have, but I know there's more in that tank. Dig down."

Andrew sat down with a grimace.

By halftime the lead had been cut to four. Dan was penetrating the zone with some success. James made two layups on the break in the last two minutes. Andrew hustled for a putback for the last basket of the half.

As the Panthers struggled to gain control of the game in the third quarter, Ben continued to maintain contact with the players on the floor during dead balls. He used his bench liberally, knowing that South Bridgewater only went six deep and the Panther depth would pay off in the final quarter. When any of his players' confidence flagged, Ben tried to find a word that would allow the player to regain his focus. It was easy with Dan and Geoff, because they never wavered in their supposition that the team would win. But the confidence of the rest waxed and waned so quickly, Ben felt he had to sustain it constantly, as if he were the tetherball pole that he had passed on his way home from Fidelity House – as if he were that pole and his players were strung to him, sailing out into the air, like his mother's monkeys, flying out in confidence but then returning to the center pole dispiritedly, following the laws of simple physics. He laughed softly to himself, at the thought of his mother's hallucinations appearing in this hot gym.

Pushing the ball diagonally through the middle of the court on the fastbreak, Archie cut off the defensive pursuit, setting up an easy layin for James with three minutes to go. After that easy bucket, the Panthers pulled away, winning by nine points in the end. The team shot 8 for 11 at the line down the stretch, when South Bridgewater fouled to try to cut into the lead. Final score was 73 – 64.

Ben was pleased that the huddle in the middle of the court was less exuberant than the one that had followed the Walpole win, because it meant that the team had greater aspirations than just one win in the post-season. "Solid win, gentlemen. You took their early shot, and then you gained control of yourselves, your emotions, and the game. You are a very solid team. And I emphasize the word 'team,' because there is no one in this huddle that can do it all himself. Andrew, maybe if you were playing on two legs, you'd have that capacity. But on one leg, you're just like the rest of us: you need us as much as we need you. It's a perfect balance. It's beautiful to watch, even if we don't shoot as well as we'd like or spread the floor the way we should. But, it's beautiful. In fact, it's perfect." He meant it. He knew the team was flawed: they lacked the potency that characterized a championship team. But they were a team.

On the bus coming back from South Bridgewater, Ben asked Bryan, "What should we do with Jason?"

In the dark of the late February night, Bryan said, "If he's ready, he's good to go. You can't punish him when the school says he can play."

Ben didn't respond. Then, "I just want to do what's right."

"I know," Bryan said.

The bus turned from Rt. 495 onto Rt. 95 heading east.

The Arc of Intersection

Hey baby tell me what we're gonna do
It's getting crazy and I need some help from you
We were so connected that you were a part of me
Now I feel an emptiness right to the heart of me

But you pretend and I pretend
That everything is fine
And though we should be at an end
It's so hard admittin'
When it's quittin' time

Hey baby I'm running out of things to say
Please don't hate me this feeling just won't go away
Now we're spending all our time caught in a fantasy
Just trying to keep in mind the way it used to be

But you pretend and I pretend
That everything is fine
And though we should be at an end
It's so hard admittin'
When it's quittin' time

But you pretend and I pretend
That everything is fine
And though we should be at an end
It's so hard admittin'
When it's quittin' time

Quittin Time by Robb Royer and Roger Linn

James

When James came out of South Bridgewater's tiny locker room after the game, he saw a few Casteline fans still hanging around, including his family. He joined them for a congratulatory hug, picking Rachel off the floor with the strength of his self-satisfaction.

At the corner of the stands stood a large group of girls: it was the Casteline girls' basketball team, on a road trip to support the boys. In their midst stood Adrienne, nearly the tallest of the girls. Clearly the most stunning. She wore her white ski parka over black sweats. Her hair lay on the hood of the parka, a little unkempt and uncharacteristically curly.

"Hey," he said, sidling over to the group.

"Great game," several of the girls said. "You coming to our game tomorrow night?"

"Sure thing. You guys made quite a trip down here. Thanks." He looked at Adrienne in particular. "Thanks for the effort. It helped."

Twirling around, her arms extended, Adrienne said, "You guys played a great second half. Nice game, hot shot." She had spun away from her teammates.

Together, they walked away from the small gathering. James said quietly, "Are you ready for your game?"

Looking up at the scoreboard, Adrienne nodded. "You guys are one game ahead of us now. We have to catch up. We had a weak practice today, but I know we can roll tomorrow night." James couldn't see whether she had the necklace on – if she did, it was underneath the sweatshirt. He stood uncertainly. "Well, I'll see you in school. Thanks for coming."

It felt as if they hardly knew each other.

Just before the girls' tipoff against Quincy, James entered the Casteline gym with Dan. On the ride over to school Dan had told him that his mother was recovering slowly. He was hoping that she could go to a game in the next week, if the team continued to win. His father was back on the road. The boys seated themselves across from the Casteline bench. They had not sat in these seats since they were JVs, two years ago, in James's case. It felt odd to see the game from this side of the floor.

Adrienne easily won the tip from a taller Quincy girl, batting the ball to Susan Sparks, who gathered it in, to allow Marcy Stanton time to get over the time line so that Casteline could set up their offense.

450

Three passes later, Adrienne hit Susan on a back-cut for a layup for a 2 – 0 lead.

By the end of Quarter One, Casteline had a 14 – 7 lead, and they continued to pull away the rest of the half. Adrienne ran the floor so gracefully, it was as if she needed only three strides from rim to rim. Of course, she ran wide, her lead arm up. She made four fast-break baskets, easy layins, and she had gotten the defensive rebound on two of those occasions. She always had a smile on her face; she talked constantly to her teammates, letting them know how to move on defense, alerting them to picks that came from behind, patting Susan and the other perimeter shooters on the back when they missed a shot.

The game was sloppy at times, but when Adrienne took the ball to the rim, there was no one that could stay with her. With a big lead, Coach Johnson took her out with five minutes to go. James figured she had scored more than twenty, and, more importantly, she might have had an equal number of rebounds – against two girls who stood over 6'2". Adrienne just jumped over them.

"Wow," he said, when she emerged from the locker room, her hair a mess of hay. "You've got game." He could smell the berry of the shampoo.

Adrienne giggled a little. "We're getting pretty good. Coach Johnson knows how to wring the most out of everybody. Did you see Mary Ellen's 3?"

James remembered a three from someone he didn't know, late in the game. "Was it in the fourth quarter?"

"Yeah. Mary Ellen couldn't shoot a layup at the beginning of the season. Now she'll take a 3 in a tournament game and make it. It's an impressive improvement."

"You playing again on Saturday?"

"I think so."

"Probably no lacrosse tournament this weekend then." He laughed slightly.

"To tell you the truth, there's a big tournament at Yale, but I won't be going. I might join them for the Sunday games, I don't know." She stood a little impatiently, long shiny black boots up to her knees.

James felt the way he had felt when he had first called Adrienne: he didn't know what to talk about.

James turned to Dan. "Well, we're on the way home. Got a little homework. It's a school night, you know."

Adrienne gave him a little shove on the shoulder. "I bet your light's out before mine."

451

"I don't know about that. I've got to get going on my literature essay. I'm looking for quotes tonight. You're not the only one who's studious, you know," he said, trying to bring the levity back into their conversation.

She failed to match him. "See you tomorrow, in Geometry," she said as she pulled away from him. "See you, Dan. Thanks for coming."

Booting the computer on his desk, James pulled off the shelf above the computer the books he had been using for his research paper: Fitzgerald's *The Great Gatsby*, which he had read with Mr. Olson's class, and *Tender is the Night*, James's outside book. In trying to find a theme that connected the two books, which would serve as the subject to be explored in his essay, James kept returning to the ending of *Gatsby*, the line that said, "So we beat on, boats against the current, borne back ceaselessly into the past." James could see Fitzgerald's idea here, an idea of hope, but a hope that caused his characters to move backward in time, to try to recover some lost opportunity or lost joy that the years had erased. Yet, James felt Fitzgerald admiring these people for their attempts to rise above the tide that they faced. It was one of the most compelling ideas James had ever seen in literature, stronger even than the feeling of self-denial he had considered when he had read *Siddhartha* in Mr. LaMott's class a year ago, stronger because it made reference to the essential sadness that accompanies anyone's dreams. James could think of his own dreams, swept away so easily in his immaturity, as he rode in Pete's Audi, heading to a Casteline party. When he took Fitzgerald's perspective, looking down on the two boys in the speeding car, he could almost see the arc of his dream falling with each increasing RPM of the Audi. He did not know what to do with this information that he was gathering, but he felt its truth. And so he started his essay about lost dreams in F. Scott Fitzgerald's fiction.

Coach LaMott had never prepared a more thorough scouting report than the one he presented to the team at Thursday's practice detailing Avon's strengths and weaknesses. Avon was the three seed with a record of 19 – 2 after an easy 85 – 44 win in their first tournament game. Coach had details on six players, but primarily on three: David Amato, 5'8", averaging 29ppg; Gene Dominee, 6'3, 250, averaging 12 and 14; and Herbert Wilson, averaging 19. Avon scored over 80 points a game.

"We'll double Amato whenever he comes off a ball screen. Dan, you've got him in the opening matchups. It's usually a forward that screens Amato, not Dominee. He stays near the basket and cleans up on the offensive glass. Geoff and Mark, you'll stay with Dominee. No need to help off him at all, even if someone has a driving lane. They can toss the ball high when they get help, and he can just about dunk it on the lob. So nothing gained by leaving him. He'll wear you down, but we have two strong bodies to try to wear him down. Wilson is the x-factor. He goes under the radar, but he still gets 19. He's scrappy and versatile, and he never runs out of gas. James, you've got him. He will kill you if you let him get away from you without the ball.

"So, where does that leave us? We can help only off the other two players, Simon and Branwell. You see their size on the sheet here.

"They're only six deep. The big three play just about the entire game. They're used to blowing people out. If we can keep them engaged for 32 minutes, they might get into a situation they're not used to: having to make key foul shots down the stretch, for instance. On the other hand, we've been in tight games all season long. We know how to execute in late-game situations."

In half-court and full-court scrimmages, Jason played the point with the second unit, but, now that he had three practices under his belt, he was regaining the fluidity and conditioning that he had lost. In three or four situations, he displayed his talent for splitting two defenders and setting a teammate up for an open look. James knew that the Panthers would need that ability.

As they shot foul shots, James asked Geoff, "Hey, d'you think Jason's gonna play tomorrow night?" He had not gotten into the game vs. South Bridgewater for even a second.

"I don't know. I'll ask Coach."

Andrew had regained a little strength in his left leg. He was able to elevate on his jumper more than he could when he had just come back. He was wearing a neoprene sleeve over his left knee, but nothing else to protect him. James asked, "How's the knee?" of him at the next break.

"It's not getting any better, but I'm more mobile on it than I was two weeks ago. I don't have to come off the floor to rest it as much. But Avon's a bunch of rabbits. I'll have a hard time keeping up. You're gonna have to sprint back on defense a lot. We can't give em a lot of open looks. They rely on those layups from their speed."

In the last half hour of practice, Coach ran five different end-game situations, sometimes with Archie in the lineup, sometimes with Jason in the lineup. He did not add anything new; he just forced the team to employ the shot-clock control dictated by time-and-score.

James hit 5 of 5 foul shots during the scrimmages. Jason hit a big 3 to force OT in another scenario.

When the horn sounded to end the fifth late-game scrimmage, Coach called the team together at the center circle, as usual. James could feel the excitement arising from their proximity. This was their team. The next time they gathered on a court, they would be facing a speedy and highly successful Avon team – just like the games James and Dan and their fathers had viewed when they were younger. Back then he had wondered what it felt like to be on the floor, wearing a Panther jersey, trying to stay alive in the tournament. It was too bad that Pete would be unable to wear a jersey, but aside from that fact, the team was as strong as it had been all season.

Standing in their midst, Coach LaMott reminded the team, "First of all, I want to clarify an issue that you may be wondering about: Jason's status. Jason," Coach said, turning to face Jason squarely, "welcome back. I don't know exactly what's going on off the court, and neither of us knows what's going to happen in your case in the future. But, for now, you've made a strong statement on this court that you want to and are able to help us with our goal to win any games remaining on our schedule. You won't start, but we are very fortunate to have you back with us. I hope you can concentrate on playing basketball while you're on the court. You've been dealing with a lot of stuff around you recently. I hope that basketball can provide you with some relief from that swirl."

Jason nodded and looked down.

Coach continued, "What a great opportunity we have tomorrow night. No one gives us a chance. We will shock them. We will take from them their confidence. How? We will not give them an inch of the floor for 32 minutes. If they want to get a rebound, they'll have to come through us. If they want a driving lane, they'll have to drive through us. If they want to set a screen, they'll feel us fighting through. In every element of the game of basketball, we will be there first. If we do that, they will not have their way, as they usually do. We will have our way.

"One . .. two . . ."

"TIGHT."

Friday after Geometry Adrienne asked James if they could meet after lunch in the hallway in front of the cafeteria. James, keyed up for the game since he had awakened, said, "Sure," not even wondering why she would want to meet with him.

In the hallway after lunch, Adrienne held out the necklace with the heart. James's heart dropped. "James, I feel really bad about saying this, but I don't think I deserve this necklace. I am not the girl you think I am, and I can't take this symbol of your affection." It seemed she had rehearsed the words, but she conveyed them as ingenuously as she did everything in her life.

James's arms trembled. "Oh, Adrienne, the necklace does not have anything to do with you being deserving. It's just a way for me to tell you I think you're special. And you have to admit: you're special."

Small pockets of people dribbled out of the cafeteria. Their voices were low, like James's and Adrienne's, who moved down the corridor toward the exit door. Adrienne wore her game jersey over a yellow sweatshirt.

"You know that's not true. You've seen me fuck up. I'm not perfect, and I think that's one of the reasons I have to give it back to you: the heart is too true for me. I'm not that true." Once again she extended the necklace toward James's left hand.

"The necklace doesn't say you're perfect. It says you're special – and you know that's true."

"Then it's like an award, an MVP award? I'm special and I'm getting this trophy?"

James knew that wasn't it, but he could not find another way to explain why she needed to keep the necklace. Then he said, "And it's because I love you, too." As soon as he said it, he knew it didn't matter.

"I know. But that's what makes the necklace wrong. I don't think I love you the same way." She stopped talking, not knowing how to explain herself. She still held out the necklace. It hung from her hand, the heart wrapped inside her fist. She pushed it toward James.

He did not want to open his hand. But he knew that the romance that the heart represented was gone, for whatever reason. His mind went back immediately to the Monday of vacation, in Adrienne's living room, when she came out of her bedroom, admitting that she had been ready to offer herself to him. "Then why did you come out of the shower to me last week?"

Adrienne looked at him with her eyes full. "I thought something was there that wasn't. I'm sorry." She dropped the necklace toward his hand and pulled away, walking toward the stairs that led to her locker. He watched her disappear up the stairs, the necklace tangled around the fingers of his left hand, the weightless heart swinging idly underneath his hand.

455

At home James listened to his most recent favorite songs on his computer, songs he had downloaded in the splendor of thinking he and Adrienne shared a view of life: more of the Antje Duvekot, whom they had seen in Boston, where he had given her the necklace -- James could not move past her songs. As Ms. Duvekot's plaintive voice traced and retraced her laments, the necklace hung from a shelf bracket, the separated halves of the heart lying against each other like two unclaimed apostrophes. Every few minutes James pushed the chain softly, giving it a swinging motion reminding him of the Walters Grade School, where he had tried to swing himself to the height of the swing set's horizontal bar, loving the feeling in his stomach.

He also thought about the speedy Herbert Wilson, #23. As the apostrophes would come to rest, James would send them off, as if he were heading onto the floor for the second quarter, looking for #23, so he could station himself nearby.

When the team emerged onto the floor at Avon, the clock just starting to tick down from 15:00, James took his place in the rebound line, as Geoff laid the first warmup layup in the basket. He peeked at the crowd that already filled Avon's tiny gym. There were stands on both sides of the gym, but only five rows. People were queued up near the entrance to the gym, looking for seats that were not available. James did not look again, but he could not help but think again of the tournament games he and Dan and his dad had traveled to, where they had to squeeze into a tiny space in the crowd. He felt he had finally arrived as a Casteline basketball player.

The Star-Spangled Banner was sung by a student from Avon, just a few notes that strayed from the original, but her heart was in it. The crowd roared. Coach LaMott's eyes shone brightly.

"All right, guys, the stage is set. As I said before Walpole, just think of this as a fun game of horse, winner gets first dibs on the drinking fountain. I also tried to have you think of a shot that is arching toward the basket, smoothly released, perfect in its flight. That flight is the product of your hard work all this season, the 10-in-a-minutes, the defensive slide drill, the zigzag drill, the shooting drills. It's also the result of your ability to take a hit and keep on going: Andrew's injury, James's and Pete's suspension, Jason's time missed, Andreas's time missed. All the nagging injuries that have slowed every one of you down. You've taken those hits and continued to improve. Somehow. It's a miracle – but any success is a miracle, given the odds against success. So the ball is arcing toward the rim. We've already shot the ball. Now we just have to watch it go in the basket."

Coach's words were eloquent, but James wanted something more tangible – like the feel of the ball on his fingertips.

"No more philosophizing. It's time to go to work. You know how to do it. Let's win this one for each other." Coach's voice started to falter, with the emotion.

"TIGHT!"

The first four minutes were exhausting: Avon swept down the court in a tsunami of speed, setting up easy layups for Wilson and Amato. Dominee swept the defensive board easily and tossed half-court outlet passes to initiate the break. Dominee even sprinted the floor at times, providing a second trailer to the break, though he could not shoot the jumper when the ball was reversed to him. Dan missed his first few shots; James was reluctant to shoot, because he didn't feel fluid yet. But there was a small window between tightness and exhaustion, and James passed through that window quickly, leaving the floor with two minutes left in the first period, Avon leading 15 – 10. James had not scored.

Coach LaMott shook his hand as he came off the court. "You a little tight?" he asked.

James nodded.

"Just pretend you're sitting in my English class, and I'm talking about Vasudeva in *Siddhartha*. You'll start relaxing."

James reentered the game to start the second quarter, along with Jason, Andrew, Archie, and Geoff. It was a lineup that had been productive before Andrew hurt his knee.

James took a charge on Wilson as he tried to beat him baseline, Wilson's first indication that he was frustrated. When Wilson left the floor because it was his second foul, James started shading toward Amato's penetration, his arms spread so that Amato couldn't see passing lanes, but keeping him out of the lane.

Coming off a great screen from Geoff, James hit a jumper and, two possessions later, he hit a 3 on a kickout pass from Andrew. He felt no fatigue, only exhilaration. The game was slowing down, from his perspective. He was one step ahead of his man on the break, leading to some easy shooting opportunities for him and his teammates. Time after time, he produced a basket for the Panthers, as a result of running the floor and beating his man, Wilson's sub. Avon called timeout to slow the Panthers' run, Wilson coming back onto the floor. But he couldn't guard James with any conviction because he didn't want to pick up his third foul. Jason kept getting the ball to James in a place where he could make something happen. By halftime the Panthers had assumed a 40 – 39 lead. James had scored five or six baskets in the

457

second quarter. Archie had three fouls and Dan and Jason had two, almost all incurred in trying to stop Amato, who probably had twenty points. He had hit at least ten foul shots.

Coach's half-time was short and to the point. "Great job taking on the pace of the game. This team flies, and we're doing a great job playing at their pace. If we don't have the easy look over the top, Archie and Jason, settle it down and use clock. They don't like to play 30 seconds of defense. We'll get them to commit more fouls if we are more patient. Archie, let's call Providence, to bring James off the double screen on the block. If they go back to the zone, we have to attack inside-out. No jacking up quick 3s without one post touch, OK?"

James heard Coach's words, but he didn't need to: he already knew what Coach was going to say before he said it. There was nothing Coach could tell him that he didn't already know.

When James took the floor for the second half, he felt the presence of the crowd, hunkering down in their seats momentarily, but ready to leap to their feet in support of their team. The seven cheerleaders were drawing a steady response from the Casteline section of the stands. James had felt the involvement of the spectators in the ebb and flow of the game, just as he had felt it from the stands five years before. These fans were tied to the outcome like a thermometer reacting to sudden rises and drops in the temperature. And the temperature in the gym was oppressive, just the way James loved it. Coach LaMott always tried to get the custodians to raise the heat in the gym to assist the players in their conditioning work. This gym felt perfect.

The flow of the game was constant throughout the third quarter. Until Andrew had to go off to get his rest for his knee, the Panthers punished Avon with their half-court execution. Avon went to a zone for four possessions, but, first Dan, then James hit jumpers off ball reversal, and then Dan kicked it in to Geoff, who hit Andreas on a back-cut from the foul line for a five point lead. Avon had to get out of the zone.

Amato continued to pile up the points, but James, by not leaving Wilson to help, kept Wilson's shot opportunities to a minimum. Wilson wasn't very good at generating his own shot; rather, he came alive off the penetration of Amato, if James left him. So he didn't leave him.

To start the fourth quarter, Jason took the floor, with Dan, Andrew, Andreas, and Mark. Three of these players had not been starters when the season began, and the two starters on the floor were now limited in their ability because of time away from the court and injury. But Coach thought they were the right matchup at the moment, and James, Geoff, and Archie needed a blow. Amato elevated his game the way great players do, taking the ball to the hoop mercilessly, pounding the ball past his defender, splitting the help, rarely passing off, but getting fouled frequently. By the time James returned to the game, with 5:50 to go, Avon had cut the lead to three. Dan had four fouls and Jason had three. After three more rapid trips up and down the floor, James felt tired for the first time all day. He knew he had a lot more strength; he just had to call on it. Jason threw a pass into the post that got knocked out of bounds, and then Andrew threw away the in-bounds pass. Coach took a time-out.

"Less than five minutes to go. We have three time-outs if we need them. These five minutes are what you've been preparing for since you were nine years old. Gentlemen, get yourself in a mindset where you do not feel fatigue, and there is no such thing as frustration or indecision. If you can get there, this game will be easy." James remembered Mr. LaMott making the same observations when he was teaching *Siddhartha* a year ago, talking about that ability to dissolve one's needs to nothing and thereby achieve nirvana.

The Panthers beat Avon's press, but not smoothly. Avon set up a man-to-man in the half-court. Jason and James ran clock down to eight on the shot clock, then ran a post-up for Andrew. Dominee blocked the shot. Avon raced down the court, Amato passing off to Simon to cut the lead to one. Avon set up its 2-2-1 again, but this time the ball was reversed then pushed middle to James, who spun before Amato could back-tap, attacking Dominee, then feeding Dan for a layup that pushed the lead back to three. The teams traded baskets on the next two possessions. Amato and Jason got into a pushing match on a loose ball; Coach took Jason out, replacing him with Archie, who remained calm in any circumstance. But Amato drew Archie's fifth foul right away, bringing Jason back into the game.

"Totally cool, now, right, Jason?"

Jason nodded, completely tuned in. "I know what it's all about. I've got him."

"We don't need anything heroic, just team ball."

"I know."

James felt good about the conversation, as Amato hit both free throws.

On the in-bounds pass, Jason attacked the 2-2-1, but as he approached the double-team, he left the ground, looking for James in the middle. Avon's weakside forward slid into the passing lane, and, though James tried to step in front of him, Branwell picked off the pass, turning it into an easy basket for Wilson. Avon had a one-point lead. There were forty seconds left.

This time Jason reversed the ball to Dan, who looked middle, but James was denied. Dan pushed the ball toward a double-team, jump-stopping away from the sideline, reversing to Jason who had dropped, who hit James in the middle after looking sideline. They just beat the 10-second clock by an eyelash. James attacked, but Avon retreated desperately. James had to push the ball sideline. He looked for Andrew coming off Geoff's pick. He threw the ball into the lane, for Andrew, who was doubled. Andrew kicked out to James, who had repositioned himself. He caught, stepping into the catch, and shot a jumper. It went in off the glass to give the Panthers the lead back.

Casteline set up in a 2; there were 20 seconds left. Amato pounded the ball, with Jason trying to maintain his position. All the Panthers knew that Amato would attack with five or six seconds left. James was covering Wilson, who had not had a productive game. When Amato broke past Jason, James stepped up as if he were stepping in for the charge. He had to hope that Andrew would step out to take the pass away from Wilson.

When Amato picked up his dribble just inside the foul line, James dropped to the post behind him, figuring that Andrew had jumped out on Wilson, leaving Branwell alone in the post. Amato jumped, started to dump the ball to Branwell, but, seeing James's hand in the passing lane, had to double-clutch into his own shot, somehow still smoothly. It arced upward, hit the glass, and fell through the hoop. James called time-out before it was through the net. There were three seconds left, Avon holding onto a one-point lead.

Coach came onto the floor. "Great defense, guys. He made an incredible shot. Andrew, you have the ball out, as usual. We need to set back picks for Geoff and Dan. Take off over the top. Andrew, if you're going to throw to one of those guys, you have to throw to the outside shoulder. If one of you catches it, immediate time-out. If Andrew passes to James or Jason, you can take two dribbles, and then you have to shoot. Let's do it."

The crowd cleared a space for Andrew to take the ball out on the baseline. James and Jason set the back picks for Geoff and Dan. Avon switched automatically. James and Jason came hard toward the ball, but they were denied. But on the switch, Dan peeled back for the ball at mid-court. Moving to his right, Andrew hit Dan, who pivoted, took two dribbles and put up a 25-foot shot. It rose beautifully, with backspin. Dan's hand followed through. He landed squarely on two feet, shoulder-width apart. It was a perfect shot.

But it didn't go in. Avon won 73 – 72.

James stood just outside of the key, watching the Avon players storm the court to pile onto David Amato, who had hit the winning shot. James felt nothing – no jealousy, no fatigue, no disappointment, no anger – nothing. He relaxed as he stood, looking at Andrew, who knelt to the floor sobbing, his high school career over. Jason stood near half-court, his face covered with a patina of rage, as if he wanted to swing his fist at the closest Avon player. Geoff walked over to Andrew and tried to lift him from the floor. James watched all these interactions without moving.

Coach LaMott strode onto the floor, heading straight for Andrew, to help Geoff lift him. Coach Taft sidled up to Jason, his arms out to clasp him in an embrace. The gathering of people around James was comforting: he could see people reaching out to assist others, offering a shoulder and comforting arms to those in need, like paramedics at a crash site. Still, James did not feel the absence of comfort, though he stood alone. He knew he had played the best game of his life, in the face of one of the best players he had ever faced. Though Amato lacked the height of Brookline's Previeu or Waltham's Samko, he could completely dominate a game. He had taken James's most intuitive defensive adjustment and trumped it.

When Coach LaMott made his way over to James, he said just that. "James," he shouted over the glee that filled Avon's gym, "you made a heckuva play at the end. He was just one idea ahead of you. Nothin you can do. You played it perfectly. He just had the ball in his hands. Congratulations. You know the game." Coach LaMott gave James a long and tight hug that conveyed all the joy of the game as well as the heartache of the loss. James returned the grip. Then he felt tired.

After the team lineup for handshakes, Coach LaMott called the team together one last time to try to find meaning in their effort. He spoke for a couple minutes, but James heard very little of what he said. James was staring, without focus, at the orange championship banners on the walls of the Avon gym, knowing the effort and the knowledge required to claim them. He understood. The buzz in the gym continued for a long while, gradually dissipating. James's parents came and gave him consolatory hugs. His dad told him he was very, very proud of him, and his mom could not speak she was crying so much. Rachel clung to him wordlessly, all her hopes for him unfairly reduced, but that's what sports do: they make us see the players as successes when they win and disappointments when they lose. Rachel could not help it.

James approached Dan near the bench, as he collected his warmup sweats that he would turn in on Monday.

"Helluva game," he murmured to Dan.

"Yeah, we had em. I thought we played pretty fuckin good down the stretch." He shook his head in disbelief.

James put his arms around Dan. "Nothin more we could do. Congratulations on a helluva season and a helluva game." He couldn't let go of his friend.

Over Dan's shoulder James could see the girls' team, standing with their heads down, knowing how the boys felt, unwilling to flaunt their still-alive status. James knew the girls would win on Saturday – they would probably win another game or two, because they were good, they were big, and Adrienne was a thoroughbred, like Previeu and Samko. She had what it takes, and he didn't begrudge her for it. He walked to the girls' conclave, approaching Adrienne. The other girls cleared away.

"Hey," he said.

"Hey," she said. She looked him in the eyes. "Wow." She paused, reaching for his hands. "You've got game," and she left it at that.

"Thanks. See you around. Good luck in your game," he said, knowing he wouldn't be there.

Adrienne took a deep breath, wondering, just maybe, whether she had made the right decision. She exhaled, turning away from James. He grabbed his sweats and headed for the locker room.

The Arc of Intersection

I found myself outside
Walking in the dark and staring at the sky
I'll never understand how my life unfolds
But fate just is, fate does not console

Then they pulled me to the side
They put their arms around me and led me inside
They told me I was not the only one in pain
But they console, they do not explain

Faster than I can spin
The world turns and changes again
Sweeter still, till the end
I still want it all again

And there beside me in letters ten feet tall
The words of God were scrawled on the wall
But I was not oblivious, I chose to ignore
For words explain, words do not restore

Faster than I can spin
The world turns and changes again
Sweeter still, till the end
I still want it all again
Faster than I can spin
The world turns and changes again
Sweeter still, till the end
I still want it all again

And I could wait until
I regained my balance and made the world stand still
But I would wait forever for my will to be that strong
And as I waited, the rest of my life would be gone

Faster than I can spin
The world turns and changes again
Sweeter still, till the end
I still want it all again
Faster than I can spin
The world turns and changes again
Sweeter still, till the end

Faster by Mieka Pauley

463

Ben

In the locker room Ben tried to console his players, while trying to contain his own grief. The end of a season was, for a coach, like a child moving out of the house, and, though Ben had not experienced that loss yet, he was starting to feel the sadness in the midst of the great opportunity to which a child's maturity led. Similarly, he felt the sudden distance that now separated him from his seniors: Andrew, Jason, Geoff, Bobbie, Alex, Jonas, and Mark. He spoke to each of them individually, letting them know that their efforts had made it a season he would never forget.

"You were one of my best," he said to Geoff quietly, his mouth next to Geoff's ear. "Being a captain is a very difficult thing. You did it with ease. You never let down; you never gave up. You always believed in the players' chance to redeem themselves and to join the team's common goal." Ben released Geoff from his tight hug and looked at him. "And you had the tip-in against Walpole that made this a special season. " Ben could not keep his voice quiet when he said the last.

Andrew lay on a bench behind a set of lockers, staring up at the crumbling ceiling above him. Ben crouched next to his most talented player. "You were robbed this year, but you found out something new about yourself: you are a fighter. You could have just rested the knee. You knew it wouldn't allow you to play the way you know how. But you chose to do what you could to help us. Thanks. Walpole will never forget your game against them."

Andrew nodded, unable to talk.

Visiting with his seniors and talking with all the players gave Ben a value in the destitute locker room. Each team member needed some encouragement, because for each of them, a dream was over. Ben had to admit that he felt the dissolution of that dream nearly as much as they, but providing a shoulder to his team members helped him out. He would sit alone when he got home, trying to understand how he had fallen short, so that he could make that adjustment for next year.

As Ben kept revolving around the room, tapping one player on the shoulder, sitting next to another for a word, he started to come to grips with another grief that he was holding in: his mother had been taken to the hospital in the late afternoon.

On the bus ride to Avon, Ben's cell phone had rung, an unusual occurrence. It was Willa, with the news that Margot had been taken to the hospital, dehydrated and somewhat non-responsive. Willa had been called at work when there was no answer at the house. Ben wondered if he had received a call on his cell phone that he had not heard.

"I'll go over to the hospital. She needs someone beside her. I don't mind," Willa had said easily.

Ben sat in the bus seat, Bryan next to him trying not to listen. The school bus, driven by Mrs. Nelson, was cruising down Rt. 95 south, soon to take the exit for Rt. 24 toward Brockton. Ben felt the throb in his pulse that said he should return to Summit as soon as he arrived at Avon, finding a ride with a sympathetic Castelinian who had driven to the game.

"I'll get a ride home. I'll see you at the hospital."

"Don't be crazy. There's nothing you can do. There's nothing I can do. She just needs company. She and I have spent many hours together talking about you. Don't worry. Nothing'll change. We won't say anything unkind – or at least nothing new."

Ben could hear her attempt at light-heartedness and he thanked her for it. "I don't want it to fall on you. It's my responsibility."

Willa hushed him. "It's not falling on me. I want to do this. It's not a burden at all. I think the kids are coming down to your game. I'm not sure. If not, maybe Scott or Mary will drop by."

Ben shook his head, knowing what he should do, but listening to Willa talk him out of it.

"Well, I'll call you when I get to Avon, to see if you've gotten to see my mom yet."

At Avon, Ben asked Bryan to tape the ankles as he checked with Willa. Responding to his call, Willa said, "I'm sitting with her in the ER. She's got an IV drip and she's talking pretty easily. Sometimes she drops off to sleep, but she's doing fine. You know how she avoids drinking fluids because she thinks she'll have to urinate more often. She must have gone past a healthy point with her intake."

Ben did know of his mother's propensity to deny herself liquids. "Did she fall? Was she unconscious?"

"I don't know. I met her at the hospital. There's no one from Fidelity House here with her. She was brought by ambulance with EMTs. They say her blood pressure and her heart are good. I think she'll just get rehydrated and she'll be fine. Don't worry. Are you at Avon?"

"Yeah. We're doing the shoot-around. Warmups will start in six or seven minutes."

"Go take care of the team. You have to give your A game."

Ben closed his eyes. "Thanks, Willa. I can't believe you're there and I'm here."

Willa did not reply for a second, letting Ben's statement resonate. She tried not to sound accusatory. "Isn't that the way we do things?" She said it gently.

Ben turned back to the locker room. "You're right," he said quietly. "See you. I'll call you after the game. Thanks, honey."

During the game he had forgotten about his mother and his wife, as if they inhabited another universe for the hour and a half of the game. Now, the game receding into the past like a boat bobbing on the out-going tide, he stepped into the hallway outside the locker room to call Willa's cell again. "How's it going?"

"She's stable. She might be here a while. Her blood has been sent to the lab. She's coherent sometimes, and then she drifts off. But you know she was that way sometimes in her bed at Fidelity House. She's pretty strong. Come here when you get home."

"I'll see you there. You want me to pick up any food on the way?"

"Yeah, maybe a sub from Famous – we could share one. Hey, did you win?"

Ben breathed deeply, trying to rid himself of a teary voice. He sighed. "No, we lost by a point at the end. It was incredible. We played great. Avon was just too good." He raised his fist to hit the locker that he faced in the dark hallway. He lowered the hand. "It hurts."

"I know. That's why you need to get here."

On the bus Ben told Bryan about his mother. Bryan clasped Ben's shoulder. "I'm sorry. Tell me anything I can do to help, OK?"

"I'm OK. Willa's there with her. And I didn't see my kids at the game, so they must have stayed with her too." Knowing his children had shared their concern with his mother did not make Ben feel any better.

At the school Ben and Bryan shook the hand of each player as he trudged off the bus. The ride had been a quiet one, subdued, of course, but as the bus neared Casteline High School, Ben could hear the boys starting to reflect a little about the season and the joy they had provided each other.

At the hospital Ben found Willa and his mother in the ER. "Have Scott or Mary been here?"

"Yes, they were both here. They left just a few minutes ago. They came separately."

Looking at his mother in the bed, Ben said to her, "Hey, Mom. How's it going?"

She stirred, her eyes closed. She reached out her hand for his. He took it in his two hands, pulling her hand toward him. Around their draped enclosure in the ER, nurses and EMTs from other ambulances called out numbers and data to each other, bringing care to the needy that came to this place.

Ben visited his mother for a few hours on Saturday and again on Sunday. Margot showed slight improvement. The blood work showed her to be anemic; her circulatory system had almost shut down. Though her blood pressure had been strong on the way to the hospital, it had diminished. She needed both glucose and red blood, administered intravenously.

After church on Sunday, when Ben returned to pick up Willa, he looked for Reverend Harris, who was just finishing up his Bible study class. Stephen Harris was a kindly man, always intent on sharing God's word with anyone who cared to listen. Ben had gotten to know him when the two men played on the St. Andrew's basketball team in a church league. Stephen – or Steve, as he wanted to be called on the court – was a good rebounder and a diligent defender. He was probably a little older than Ben.

"Hi, Reverend. You got a minute?"

"Yes, Ben. Anything I can do for you? How are doing after your tough game with Avon."

They stood in the oak-floored hallway next to the kitchen where Willa had shared that intimate moment with Peter Harrison.

"Oh, I'm getting over it, slowly. It's always a rough end to the season, win or lose. You know that."

Reverend Harris nodded.

"But, I'm actually wondering whether you could help me out with a few issues that have been bothering me."

"I'd be glad to. When's a good time for you?"

Ben thought. "What's Tuesday afternoon like for you?"

"Maybe 3:30?"

"Sounds good. See you then."

"Anything I can do for you until then?" Reverend Harris held out his open hand.

"No, but I'm looking forward to Tuesday. See you then."

When he returned to the car, Willa was already out of the day-care, sitting in the passenger seat. "What's up?"

Getting into the car, Ben said, "I was just saying hi inside. How was day-care?"

"Great. The kids are so sweet."

"Anything coming up on the church calendar?"

"Just the women's retreat, the third weekend in March."

"You planning to go?"

Willa looked at him. "I don't know. I've never thought it was all that useful to get away with a bunch of women. But the idea of communing with our prayerful thoughts is more appealing to me, this year. Maybe because I'm getting older. I don't know. I've got a few days to decide. What do you think?"

Turning into their driveway, Ben said, "If it would make you feel good, you should do it. The kids are fine; I'll keep them under control somehow. I want you to be happy," he wanted to add 'with me,' but it wasn't the time.

Stephen Harris's office was spartan. On his desk there were pictures of his wife June and their two daughters. Stephen offered Ben a chair that faced a small round table and took a chair adjacent to Ben's.

"Nice to see you, Ben. It's been a long time since we played together on that team."

"Yeah, a long time. That was fun. I'm not so sure it would be as fun these days."

Stephen shifted his weight. "The body is not quite as willing."

Ben muted his response, noting the irony of the Reverend's word, given the subject matter he wanted to discuss with the Reverend. "Did Willa tell you my mother's been hospitalized?"

"Yes, she did. I hope for the best. We included her in our prayers on Sunday."

Ben remembered.

They talked about Ben's guilt at not being with his mother on the day she was hospitalized and on the many, many other occasions he had driven past the street that would lead to Fidelity House.

"Ben, you do what your heart says is right. Your mother knows how much you love her. And she's doubly blessed to have Willa in her family."

Ben became more animated. "That's part of the problem, Reverend. Willa just sets a standard that I can't honor." He stopped talking, knowing he had cursed her in his praise.

"Ben, Willa and I talk a lot. She knows she is far from a saint, though she does have remarkable care-giving skills. She's very good at healing and at facilitating. She has a way that makes people feel better. I've felt it many times."

Ben could not keep himself from saying, "Well, then why is she making me feel so lousy?"

They looked at each other. "That's why you're here, isn't it?" Reverend Harris said.

Ben nodded, looking down at his hands that lay in his lap.

After more than an hour of finger-pointing and soul-searching, Ben took a deep breath. "I didn't know I would be able to tell you all this, but it just came out. I don't know what to do, and telling you hasn't given me any insight, I'll have to admit."

"Well, God is always waiting for us, whenever we're ready. He casts a circle of light into our lives, and when we're ready, we step into it." Reverend Harris looked very human, in spite of his spiritual words.

Ben wondered at the simplicity of the Reverend's spiritual concept. God's grace was available at any moment. It was an amazing idea, one that Ben had heard many times before, but had never needed to know personally.

"Thanks, Stephen. I don't know where to go from here, but I feel better for having spoken to someone. A little less alone, maybe."

"You've never been alone. In fact, Willa has been praying that you would find this way to resolve your issues. I can't tell you about my conversations with her, but she has been hoping that you might speak with me. The power of prayer is amazing."

Ben had to agree, if that was what Willa had been praying for.

"Maybe we might meet again, and then the three of us could sit down. Does that sound like a plan?"

Ben felt a little hope. "I'd love that. I just want an answer."

"We'll find an answer. God will provide."

Ben wished he could believe the way the Reverend believed.

Back at school Ben found the players gradually emerging from their desolation. He went out of his way to maintain contact with his seniors, who would be graduating in three months. They finally relaxed, as they severed their emotional attachment to the team that had been the object of their passion for the past three months. The juniors were more upbeat, looking ahead already to their senior year, and Ben talked easily with them, as he also sought out the members of Bryan's team who

469

would move on to the varsity next year. It was a healing process that happened naturally, given enough time.

Suite Bergamasque, Third Movement (Claire De Lune) By Claude Debussy

Epilogue

Shortly after the Panthers were knocked out of the tournament, Margot returned to Fidelity House, her health greatly improved. Ben picked her up at the hospital, a balloon attached to her wheelchair. Margot smiled wryly at the festivity that celebrated her return to the nursing home. When Ben brought her to her room, they found a new wooden figure propped on her window sill, next to the duck she had already adopted. This was an elegant pussycat, its tail curled gracefully underneath its body. It was signed "Phil."

Picking up the cat, Ben said, "What a nice man."

His mother nodded. Then she squinted her eyes, looking out the window. She asked him, "Any monkeys out there?"

He laughed quietly. "I don't see any. Keep me informed, please. Bye. I love you."

"Mmmm," she replied.

James turned in to Mr. Olson his thesis paper on Fitzgerald's attraction to the lure of the past, the way it provided some unavoidable direction, creating a circular approach to life, pushing forward only to try to recover some lost innocence that the past holds. Briefly, James wondered what essence in his past would produce that control over him, but he knew it was Adrienne.

Ben and Willa went to Reverend Harris's counseling sessions, finding his words a stimulus to their own. The subject of Peter Harrison came up frequently; Willa admitted that they had served a supportive purpose to each other, but never elaborated beyond that admission. Ben did not feel combative enough to challenge her in Reverend Harris's study. In a month, Reverend Harris recommended a marriage counselor, and they agreed it would be a good idea.

James felt Adrienne's loss profoundly. When the girls' team went to the sectional finals, playing Duxbury at UMass Boston, James and Dan traveled to the game in Dorchester, joining a crowd of adoring spectators, many of them emblazoned with Panther face paint. Adrienne scored 28 in a tough loss. She flowed so effortlessly on the court, it was as if she were a college player returning for the alumnae game. And she was really a lacrosse player. James could not take his eyes off her the entire game. Dan saw James's fixation, but he didn't say anything.

472

The Arc of Intersection

Pete ran with a crowd that included Jonas and a few other seniors, checking in during Geometry with James irregularly. He had moved his seat nearer the door.

Some time in the early spring, Mr. Tilson brought out his wooden compass again, but this time as just a prop. "Instead of intersecting a line with a line, today I want to talk about intersecting a multi-dimensional figure with a figure that has fewer dimensions. Let's say we are intersecting a six-dimensional figure with a three-dimensional one. Now I can't draw these figures, because we are limited to three dimensions in our graphic capability, but we need to use our imagination. What does that intersection take the form of?"

After an intellectual stasis, Felicity offered an insight. "If we think of an infinite number of three-dimensional figures, like spheres, extending infinitely in all directions, do we create a four-dimensional figure?"

"Nice thought, Felicity," Mr. Tilson confirmed. "That's a great way to think beyond three dimensions. If we add the variable of time, actually, then these figures do gain another dimension by which we can measure them. Anyone else?"

James raised his hand, looking at Mr. Tilson. "Doesn't the smaller figure lay its mark on the larger figure, no matter how many dimensions between them? Like, a one-dimensional figure like a line, will still be a line in its intersection of a three dimensional figure, right?" Adrienne bent down, as if to tie her shoe, looking back at James, her eyebrows raised, her eyes wide open.

Mr. Tilson nodded.

Adrienne took up the conversation. "I think it's significant that the smaller figure actually leaves its impression on the larger figure, like a shooting star across the sky."

"That's right, Adrienne. And, conversely, the greater figure cannot leave a mark on the lesser figure because the lesser figure has no way of absorbing it."

Adrienne said, "But isn't the intersection the point? If there is no intersection, there is no consciousness, right?" James looked at Adrienne from behind her, hoping for the illumination that comes only after sacrificing one's own perspective, trying to see things from her perspective, the concept Mr. LaMott had taught him, looking outward rather than inward, finding one's own self in the greater universe.

Ben kept up his gig at Willow's through the spring. Laura Ruben continued to make her appeal to Ben, and he continued to pay attention to all the patrons of Willow's, including Laura. He tried to tell

473

himself that she was no one special, just a customer, but when he found himself talking to her about the prospects of next year's team, the way he had always shared his future with Willa, he knew he was, in fact, being no more faithful to his marriage than Willa had been in sharing her unhappiness with Peter Harrison.

James entered his court-mandated drug and alcohol counseling program, joining a group of men and woman, young and old, all of whom had a story that seemed to reveal a much more hardened user than James. But over time James came to understand that everyone in the room felt the other people were the hard-core users – just another form of self-deception.

With his tips, Ben bought Willa a bracelet with musical notes dangling from it, an acknowledgment of the love she held for music and dance, though she had precious few opportunities to profess that love. On the women's retreat, she had composed a song that she performed at an impromptu show in the hour before they returned from the Cape. Her friends had found her performance the highlight of the weekend.

Ben asked her to perform the song at home.

"I don't have an accompanist. Missy Sinclair played for me."

Ben tilted his head. "Can't you just sing it for me a cappella?"

Willa gave him the words. It was a song that followed the roads we travel in life, the paths that cross each other – so random but so determinate in their intersection. The final line read, "We bless each other with our presence and add to a story that has no end."

At school the pages turned and the students' hands rose and fell. The boots that brought mud into the corridors were replaced by light sneakers and sandals that still held onto grains of sand from the previous summer. Paul continued to recline in his apathy, even after his poetry reading, using his "language of grudge" all too often. James Rush and Dan Owings were elected captains of the 2009 – 10 basketball team. Students' essays came in, most of them on time, and Ben added his annotations to their slight ideas, knowing that these little puffs of thought would grow and grow until they became something like a habit or a principle that would give them the tiniest bit of direction in their forays into the swirling chaos that we call life.

One evening in April, Ben met with Dan and James to lay plans for the 2009 – 10 season. As daylight diminished outside, they met in the gym, right in the center circle, seated on three chairs that Ben had set out, the painted C underneath their sneakers. The emergency lights were the only illumination in the gym, casting a yellow glow over the little group in the otherwise obscure gym. The three of them discussed the AAU teams that players had joined and laid the initial plans for the summer league team. James and Dan heard Coach's words and tried to add their own, but they kept looking down at the central C, where Andreas would be jumping center in less than a year – their year. In this meeting and in subsequent meetings, all three felt comfort, knowing they had shared a tumultuous season together, and, now that they had shared that rehearsal, they would bring vitality and value to the next season. They knew this fiction above all else.

9188064R0

Made in the USA
Charleston, SC
18 August 2011